**Just beyond the red ruin of the nun was a single
clear footprint in the blood and ordure,**

which was already brown and sticky in the moist, cool air. Some of the
blood had begun to leech into the pine floor boards, smooth from years of
bare feet walking them. The leeched blood blurred the edge of the print,
but the outline was clear—it was the size of a warhorse's hoof or bigger,
with three toes.

The captain heard his huntsman come up and dismount outside. He
didn't turn, absorbed in the parallel exercises of withholding the need to
vomit and committing the scene to memory. There was a second, smudged
print further into the room, where the creature had pivoted its weight to
pass under the low arch to the main room beyond. It had dug a furrow in
the pine with its talons. And a matching furrow in the base board that ran
up into the wattle and plaster. A dew claw.

"Why'd this one die here when the rest died in the garden?" he asked.

Gelfred stepped carefully past the body. Like most gentlemen, he carried a short staff—really just a stick shod in silver, like a mountebank's
wand. Or a wizard's. He used it first to point and then to pry something
shiny out of the floorboards.

"Very good," said the captain.

"She died for them," Gelfred said. A silver cross set with pearls dangled
from his stick. "She tried to stop it. She gave the others time to escape."

"If only it had worked."

BY MILES CAMERON

The Traitor Son Cycle
The Red Knight

MILES CAMERON

www.orbitbooks.net

Orbit
Hachette Book Group
237 Park Avenue, New York, NY 10017
HachetteBookGroup.com

First U.S. Edition: January 2013
First published in Great Britain in 2012 by Gollancz, an imprint of the Orion Publishing Group
Orion House, 5 Upper St Martin's Lane, London WC2H 9EA
An Hachette UK Company

Orbit is an imprint of Hachette Book Group, Inc. The Orbit name and logo are trademarks of Little, Brown Book Group Limited.

The Hachette Speakers Bureau provides a wide range of authors for speaking events. To find out more, go to www.hachettespeakersbureau.com or call (866) 376-6591.

The publisher is not responsible for websites (or their content) that are not owned by the publisher.

Library of Congress Control Number: 2012951500
ISBN: 978-0-316-21228-1

10 9 8 7 6 5 4 3 2 1

RRC-C

Printed in the United States of America

To my sister-in-law, Nancy Watt

Chapter One

Albinkirk—Ser John Crayford

The Captain of Albinkirk forced himself to stop staring out his narrow, glazed window and do some work.

He was jealous. Jealous of a boy a third of his age, commanding a pretty company of lances. Riding about. While he sat in a town so safe it was dull, growing old.

Don't be a fool, he told himself. *All those deeds of arms make wonderful stories, but the doing is cold, wet and terrifying. Remember?*

He sighed. His hands remembered everything—the blows, the nights on the ground, the freezing cold, the gauntlets that didn't quite fit. His hands pained him all the time, awake or asleep.

The Captain of Albinkirk, Ser John Crayford, had not started his life as a gentleman. It was a rank he'd achieved through pure talent.

For violence.

And as a reward, he sat in this rich town with a garrison a third the size that it was supposed to be on paper. A garrison of hirelings who bossed the weak, abused the women, and took money from the tradesmen. A garrison that had too much cash, because the posting came with the right to invest in fur caravans from the north. Albinkirk furs were the marvel of ten countries. All you had to do to get them was ride north or west into the Wild. And then come back alive.

The captain had a window that looked north-west.

He tore his eyes away from it. Again.

And put pen to paper. Carefully, laboriously, he wrote:

My Lord,
A Company of Adventure—well ordered, and bearing a pass signed by
the constable—passed the bridge yesterday morning; near to forty lances,
each lance composed of a knight, a squire, a valet and an archer. They
were very well armed and armoured in the latest Eastern manner—steel
everywhere. Their captain was polite but reserved; very young, refused to
give his name; styled himself The Red Knight. His banner displayed three
lacs d'amour in gold on a field sable. He declared that they were, for the
most part, your Grace's subjects, lately come from the wars in Galle. As
his pass was good, I saw no reason to keep him.

Ser John snorted, remembering the scene. No one had thought to warn him
that a small army was coming his way from the east. He'd been summoned
to the gate early in the morning. Dressed in a stained cote of fustian and
old hose, he'd tried to face down the cocky young pup in his glorious scarlet
and gold, mounted on a war horse the size of a barn. He hadn't enough real
soldiers to arrest any of them. The damned boy had *Great Noble* written all
over him, and the Captain of Albinkirk thanked God that the whelp had
paid the toll with good grace and had good paper, as any incident between
them would have gone badly. For him.

He realised he was looking at the mountains. He tore his eyes away.
Again.

He also had a letter from the Abbess at Lissen Carak. She had sent to
me last autumn for fifty good men, and I had to refuse her—your Grace
knows I am short enough of men as it is. I suppose she has offered her
contract to sell-swords in the absence of local men.
I am, as your Grace is aware, almost one hundred men under strength;
I have but four proper men-at-arms, and many of my archers are not all
they should be. I respectfully request that your Grace either replace me,
or provide the necessary funds to increase the garrison to its proper place.
I am your Grace's humblest and most respectful servant,
John Crayford

The Master of the Guild of Furriers had invited him to dinner. Ser John
leaned back and decided to call it a day, leaving the letter lying on his desk.

Lissen Carak—The Red Knight

"Sweet Jesu," Michael called from the other side of the wall. It was as high
as a man's shoulder, created by generations of peasants hauling stones out
of fields. Built against the wall was a two-storey stone house with outbuild-
ings—a rich manor farm. Michael stood in the yard, peering through the

house's shattered main door. "Sweet Jesu," the squire said again. "They're all dead, Captain."

His war horse gave the captain the height to see over the wall to where his men were rolling the bodies over, stripping them of valuables as they sought for survivors. Their new employer would not approve, but the captain thought the looting might help her understand what she was choosing to employ. In his experience, it was usually best that the prospective employer understand what he—or she—was buying. From the first.

The captain's squire vaulted over the stone wall that separated the walled garden from the road and took a rag from Toby, the captain's page. Sticky mud, from the endless spring rain, covered his thigh-high buckled boots. He produced a rag from his purse to cover his agitation and began to clean his boots. Michael was fussy and dressed for fashion. His scarlet company surcoat was embroidered with gold stars; the heavy wool worth more than an archer's armour. He was well born and could afford it, so it was his business.

It was the captain's business that the lad's hands were shaking.

"When you feel ready to present yourself," the captain said lightly, but Michael froze at his words, then made himself finish his task with the rag before tossing it back to Toby.

"Apologies, m'lord," he said with a quick glance over his shoulder. "It was something out of the Wild, lord. Stake my soul on it."

"Not much of a stake," the captain said, holding Michael's eye. He winked, as much to amuse the onlookers of his household as to steady his squire, who was pale enough to write on. Then he looked around.

The rain was light—just enough to weigh down the captain's heavy scarlet cloak without soaking it through. Beyond the walled steading stretched fields of dark, newly planted earth, as shining and black in the rain as the captain's horse. The upper fields toward the hills were rich with new greenery and dotted with sheep. Good earth and fertile soil promised rich crops, as far as the eye could see on both sides of the river. This land was tamed, covered in a neat geometric pattern of hedgerows and high stone walls separating tilled plots, or neatly scattered sheep and cattle, with the river to ship them down to the cities in the south. Crops and animals whose riches had paid for the fortress nunnery—Lissen Carak—that capped the high ridge to the south, visible from here as a crenelated line of pale stone. Grey, grey, grey from the sky to the ground. Pale grey, dark grey, black.

Beyond the sheep, to the north, rose the Adnacrags—two hundred leagues of dense mountains that lowered over the fields, their tops lost in the clouds.

The captain laughed at his own thoughts.

The dozen soldiers nearest him looked; every head turned, each wearing matching expressions of fear.

The captain rubbed the pointed beard at his chin, shaking off the water. "Jacques?" he asked his valet.

The older man sat quietly on a war horse. He was better armed than most of the valets; wearing his scarlet surcote with long, hanging sleeves over an Eastern breastplate, and with a fine sword four feet long to the tip. He, too, combed the water out of his pointed beard while he thought.

"M'lord?" he asked.

"How did the Wild make it here?" The captain asked. Even with a gloved hand keeping the water from his eyes, he couldn't *see* the edge of the Wild—there wasn't a stand of trees large enough to hide a deer within a mile. Two miles. Far off to the north, many leagues beyond the rainy horizon and the mountains, was the Wall. Past the Wall was the Wild. True, the Wall was breached in many places and the Wild ran right down into the country. The Adnacrags had never been cleared. But here—

Here, wealth and power held the Wild at bay. *Should have held the Wild at bay.*

"The usual way," Jacques said quietly. "Some fool must have invited them in."

The captain chuckled. "Well," he said, giving his valet a crooked smile, "I don't suppose they'd call us if they didn't have a problem. And we need the work."

"It ripped them apart," Michael said.

He was new to the trade and well-born, but the captain appreciated how quickly he had recovered his poise. At the same time, Michael needed to learn.

"Apart," Michael repeated, licking his lips. His eyes were elsewhere. "It *ate* her. Them."

Mostly recovered, the captain thought to himself. He nodded to his squire and gave his destrier, Grendel, a little rein so he backed a few steps and turned. The big horse could smell blood and something else he didn't like. He didn't like most things, even at the best of times, but this was spooking him and the captain could feel his mount's tension. Given that Grendel wore a chamfron over his face with a spike a foot long, the horse's annoyance could quickly translate into mayhem.

He motioned to Toby, who was now sitting well to the side and away from the isolated steading-house and eating, which is what Toby tended to do whenever left to himself. The captain turned to face his standard bearer and his two marshals where they sat their own fidgeting horses in the rain, waiting for his commands.

"I'll leave Sauce and Bad Tom. They'll stay on their guard until we send them a relief," he said. The discovery of the killings in the steading had interrupted their muddy trek to the fortress. They'd been riding since the second hour after midnight, after a cold camp and equally cold supper. No one looked happy.

4

"Go and get me the master of the hunt," he added, turning back to his squire. When he was answered only with silence, he looked around. "Michael?" he asked quietly.

"M'lord?" The young man was looking at the door to the steading. It was oak, bound in iron, and it had been broken in two places, the iron hinges inside the door had bent where they'd been forced off their pins. Trios of parallel grooves had ripped along the grain of the wood—in one spot, the talons had ripped through a decorative iron whorl, a clean cut.

"Do you need a minute, lad?" the captain asked. Jacques had seen to his own mount and was now standing at Grendel's big head, eyeing the spike warily.

"No—no, m'lord." His squire was still stunned, staring at the door and what lay beyond it.

"Then don't stand on ceremony, I beg." The captain dismounted, thinking that he had used the term lad quite naturally. Despite the fact that he and Michael were less than five years apart.

"M'lord?" Michael asked, unclear what he'd just been told to do.

"Move your arse, boy. Get me the huntsman. Now." The captain handed his horse to the valet. Jacques was not really a valet. He was really the captain's man and, as such, he had his own servant—Toby. A recent addition. A scrawny thing with large eyes and quick hands, completely enveloped in his red wool cote, which was many sizes too big.

Toby took the horse and gazed at his captain with hero-worship, a big winter apple forgotten in his hand.

The captain liked a little hero-worship. "He's spooked. Don't give him any free rein or there'll be trouble," the captain said gruffly. He paused. "You might give him your apple core though," he said, and the boy smiled.

The captain went into the steading by the splintered door. Closer up, he could see that the darker brown was not a finish. It was blood.

Behind him, his destrier gave a snort that sounded remarkably like human derision—though whether it was for the page or his master was impossible to tell.

The woman just inside the threshold had been a nun before she was ripped open from neck to cervix. Her long, dark hair, unbound from the confines of her wimple, framed the horror of her missing face. She lay in a broad pool of her own blood that ran down into the gaps between the boards. There were tooth marks on her skull—the skin just forward of one ear had been shredded, as if something had gnawed at her face for some time, flensing it from the bone. One arm had been ripped clear of her body, the skin and muscle neatly eaten away so that only shreds remained, bones and tendons still hanging together...and then it had been replaced by the corpse. The white hand with the silver IHS ring and the cross was untouched.

The captain looked at her for a long time.

Just beyond the red ruin of the nun was a single clear footprint in the blood and ordure, which was already brown and sticky in the moist, cool air. Some of the blood had begun to leech into the pine floor boards, smooth from years of bare feet walking them. The leeched blood blurred the edge of the print, but the outline was clear—it was the size of a war horse's hoof or bigger, with three toes.

The captain heard his huntsman come up and dismount outside. He didn't turn, absorbed in the parallel exercises of withholding the need to vomit and committing the scene to memory. There was a second, smudged print further into the room, where the creature had pivoted its weight to pass under the low arch to the main room beyond. It had dug a furrow in the pine with its talons. And a matching furrow in the base board that ran up into the wattle and plaster. A dew claw.

"Why'd this one die here when the rest died in the garden?" he asked.

Gelfred stepped carefully past the body. Like most gentlemen, he carried a short staff—really just a stick shod in silver, like a mountebank's wand. Or a wizard's. He used it first to point and then to pry something shiny out of the floorboards.

"Very good," said the captain.

"She died for them," Gelfred said. A silver cross set with pearls dangled from his stick. "She tried to stop it. She gave the others time to escape."

"If only it had worked," said the captain. He pointed at the prints.

Gelfred crouched by the nearer print, laid his stick along it, and made a clucking sound with his tongue.

"Well, well," he said. His nonchalance was a little too studied. And his face was pale.

The captain couldn't blame the man. In a brief lifetime replete with dead bodies, the captain had seldom seen one so horrible. Part of his conscious mind wandered off a little, wondering if her femininity, the beauty of her hair, contributed to the utter horror of her destruction. Was it like desecration? A deliberate sacrilege?

And another, harder part of his mind walked a different path. The monster had placed that arm *just so*. The tooth marks that framed the bloody sockets that had been her eyes. He could imagine, far too well.

It had been done to leave terror. It was almost *artistic*.

He tasted salt in his mouth and turned away. "Don't act tough on my account, Gelfred," he said. He spat on the floor, trying to get rid of the taste before he made a spectacle of himself.

"Never seen worse, and that's a fact," Gelfred said. He took a long, slow breath. "God shouldn't allow this!" he said bitterly.

"Gelfred," the captain said, with a bitter smile. "God doesn't give a fuck."

Their eyes met. Gelfred looked away. "I will know what there is to know," he said, looking grim. He didn't like the captain's blasphemy—his face said as much. Especially not when he was about to work with God's power.

Gelfred touched his stick to the middle of the print, and there was a moment of *change*, as if their eyes had adjusted to a new light source, or stronger sunlight.

"Pater noster qui es in caelus," Gelfred intoned in plainchant.

The captain left him to it.

In the garden, Ser Thomas's squire and half a dozen archers had stripped the bodies of valuables—and collected all the body parts strewn across the enclosure, reassembled as far as possible, and laid them out, wrapped in cloaks. The two men were almost green, and the smell of vomit almost covered the smell of blood and ordure. A third archer was wiping his hands on a linen shirt.

Ser Thomas—Bad Tom to every man in the company—was six foot six inches of dark hair, heavy brow and bad attitude. He had a temper and was always the wrong man to cross. He was watching his men attentively, an amulet out and in his hand. He turned at the rattle of the captain's hardened steel sabatons on the stone path and gave him a sketchy salute. "Reckon the young 'uns earned their pay today, Captain."

Since they weren't paid unless they had a contract, it wasn't saying much.

The captain merely grunted. There were six corpses in the garden.

Bad Tom raised an eyebrow and passed something to him.

The captain looked at it, and pursed his lips. Tucked the chain into the purse at his waist, and slapped Bad Tom on his paulder-clad shoulder. "Stay here and stay awake," he said. "You can have Sauce and Gelding, too."

Bad Tom shrugged. He licked his lips. "Me an' Sauce don't always see eye to eye."

The captain smiled inwardly to see this giant of a man—feared throughout the company—admit that he and a woman didn't "see eye to eye."

She came over the wall to join them.

Sauce had won her name as a whore, giving too much lip to customers. She was tall, and in the rain her red hair was toned to dark brown. Freckles gave her an innocence that was a lie. She had made herself a name. That said all that needed to be said.

"Tom fucked it up already?" she asked.

Tom glared.

The captain took a breath. "Play nicely, children. I need my best on guard here, frosty and awake."

"It won't come back," she said.

The captain shook his head. "Stay awake anyway. Just for me."

Bad Tom smiled and blew a kiss at Sauce. "Just for *you*," he said.

Her hand went to her riding sword and with a flick it was in her hand.

The captain cleared his throat.

"He treats me like a whore. I *am not*." She held the sword steady at his face, and Bad Tom didn't move.

"Say you are sorry, Tom." The captain sounded as if it was all a jest.

"Didn't say one bad thing. Not one! Just a tease!" Tom said. Spittle flew from his lips.

"You meant to cause harm. She took it as harm. You know the rules, Tom." The captain's voice had changed, now. He spoke so softly that Tom had to lean forward to hear him.

"Sorry," Tom muttered like a schoolboy. "Bitch."

Sauce smiled. The tip of her riding sword pressed into the man's thick forehead just over an eye.

"Fuck you!" Tom growled.

The captain leaned forward. "Neither one of you wants this. It's clear you are both *posturing*. Climb down or take the consequences. Tom, Sauce wants to be treated as your peer. Sauce, Tom is top beast and you put his back up at every opportunity. If you want to be part of this company then you have to accept your place in it."

He raised his gloved hand. "On the count of three, you will both back away, Sauce will sheathe her weapon, Tom will bow to her and apologise, and Sauce will return his apology. Or you can both collect your kit, walk away and kill each other. But not as my people. Understand? Three. Two. One."

Sauce stepped back, saluted with her blade and sheathed it. Without looking or fumbling.

Tom let a moment go by. Pure insolence. But then something happened in his face, and he bowed—a good bow, so that his right knee touched the mud. "Humbly crave your pardon," he said in a loud, clear voice.

Sauce smiled. It wasn't a pretty smile, but it did transform her face, despite the missing teeth in the middle. "And I yours, ser knight," she replied. "I regret my...attitude."

She obviously shocked Tom. In the big man's world of dominance and submission, she was beyond him. The captain could read him like a book. And he thought *Sauce deserves something for that. She's a good man.*

Gelfred appeared at his elbow. Had probably been waiting for the drama to end.

The captain felt the wrongness of it before he saw what his huntsman carried. Like a housewife returning from pilgrimage and smelling something dead under her floor—it was like that, only stronger and wronger.

"I rolled her over. This was in her back," Gelfred said. He had the thing wrapped in his rosary.

The captain swallowed bile, again. *I love this job,* he reminded himself.

To the eye, it looked like a stick—two fingers thick at the butt, sharpened to a needlepoint now clotted with blood and dark. Thorns sprouted from the whole haft, but it was fletched. An arrow. Or rather, an obscene parody of an arrow, whittled from...

"Witch Bane," Gelfred said.

The captain made himself take it without flinching. There were some secrets he would pay the price to preserve. He flashed on the last Witch-Bane arrow he'd seen—and pushed past it.

He held it a moment. "So?" he said, with epic unconcern.

"She was shot in the back—with the Witch Bane—while she was alive." Gelfred's eyes narrowed. "And then the monster ripped her face off."

The captain nodded and handed his huntsman the shaft. The moment it left his hand he felt lighter, and the places where the thorns had pricked his chamois gloves felt like rashes of poison ivy on his thumb and fingers—if poison ivy caused an itchy numbness, a leaden pollution.

"Interesting," the captain said.

Sauce was watching him.

Damn women and their superior powers of observation, he thought.

Her smile forced him to smile in return. The squires and valets in the garden began to breathe again and the captain was sure they'd stay awake, now. Given that there was a murderer on the loose who had monster-allies in the Wild.

He got back to his horse. Jehannes, his marshal, came up on his bridle hand side and cleared his throat. "That woman's trouble," he said.

"Tom's trouble too," the captain replied.

"No other company would have had her." Jehannes spat.

The captain looked at his marshal. "Now Jehannes," he said. "Be serious. Who would have Tom? He's killed more of his own comrades than Judas Iscariot."

Jehannes looked away. "I don't trust her," he said.

The captain nodded. "I know. Let's get moving." He considered vaulting into the saddle and decided that he was too tired and the show would be wasted on Jehannes, anyway. "You dislike her because she's a woman," he said, and put his left foot into the stirrup.

Grendel was tall enough that he had to bend his left knee as far as the articulation in his leg harness would allow. The horse snorted again. Toby held onto the reins.

He leaped up, his right leg powering him into the saddle, pushing his six feet of height and fifty pounds of mail and plate. Got his knee over the high ridge of the war-saddle and was in his seat.

"Yes," Jehannes said, and backed his horse into his place in the column.

The captain saw Michael watching Jehannes go. The younger man turned and raised an eyebrow at the captain.

"Something to say, young Michael?" the captain asked.

"What was the stick? M'lord?" Michael was different from the rest—well born. Almost an apprentice, instead of a hireling. As the captain's squire, he had special privileges. He could ask questions, and all the rest of the company would sit very still and listen to the answer.

The captain looked at him for a moment. Considering. He shrugged—no mean feat in plate armour.

"Witch Bane," he said. "A Witch-Bane *arrow*. The nun had *power*." He made a face. "Until someone shot the Witch Bane into her back."

"A nun?" Michael asked. "A nun who could work *power*?" He paused. "Who shot her? By Jesu, m'lord, you mean the Wild has *allies*?"

"All in a day's work, lad. It's all in a day's work." His visual memory, too well trained, ran through the items like the rooms in his memory palace—the splintered door, the faceless corpse, the arm, the Witch-Bane arrow. He examined the path from the garden door to the front door.

"Wait on me," he said.

He walked Grendel around the farmyard, following the stone wall to the garden. He stood in his stirrups to peer over the wall, and aligned the open garden door with the splintered front door. He looked over his shoulder several times.

"Wilful!" he called.

His archer appeared. "What now?" he muttered.

The captain pointed at the two doors. "How far away could you stand and still put an arrow into someone at the *front* door."

"What, shooting through the house?" asked Wilful Murder.

The captain nodded.

Wilful shook his head. "Not that far," he admitted. "Any loft at all and the shaft strikes the door jamb." He caught a louse on his collar and killed it between his nails. His eyes met the captain's. "He'd have to be close."

The captain nodded. "Gelfred?" he called.

The huntsman was outside the front door, casting with his wand over a large reptilian print in the road. "M'lord?"

"See if you and Wilful can find any tracks out the back. Wilful will show you where a bowman might have stood."

"It's always fucking me—get Long Paw to do it," Wilful muttered.

The captain's mild glance rested for a moment on his archer and the man cringed.

The captain turned his horse and sighed. "Catch us up as soon as you have the tracks," he said. He waved at Jehannes. "Let's go to the fortress and meet the lady Abbess." He touched his spurs ever so lightly to Grendel's sides, and the stallion snorted and deigned to move forward into the rain.

The rest of the ride along the banks of the Cohocton was uneventful, and the company halted by the fortified bridge overshadowed by the rock-girt ridge and the grey walls of the fortress convent atop it, high above them. Linen tents rose like dirty white flowers from the muddy field, and the officer's pavilions came off the wagons. Teams of archers dug cook pits and latrines, and valets and the many camp followers—craftsmen and sutlers, runaway serfs, prostitutes, servants, and free men and women desperate to gain a place—assembled the heavy wooden hoardings that served the camp as temporary walls and towers. The drovers, an essential part of any company, filled the gaps with the heavy wagons. Horse lines were staked out. Guards were set.

The Abbess's door ward had pointedly refused to allow the mercenaries through her gate. The mercenaries had expected nothing else, and even now hardened professionals were gauging the height of the walls and the likelihood of climbing them. Two veteran archers—Kanny, the barracks room lawyer of the company, and Scrant, who never stopped eating—stood by the camp's newly-constructed wooden gate and speculated on the likelihood of getting some in the nun's dormitory.

It made the captain smile as he rode by, collecting their salutes, on the steep gravel road that led up the ridge from the fortified town at the base, up along the switchbacks and finally up through the fortress gate-house into the courtyard beyond. Behind him, his banner bearer, marshals and six of his best lances dismounted to a quiet command and stood by their horses. His squire held his high-crested bassinet, and his valet bore his sword of war. It was an impressive show and it made good advertising—ideal, as he could see heads at every window and door that opened into the courtyard.

A tall nun in a slate-grey habit—the captain suppressed his reflexive flash on the corpse in the doorway of the steading—reached to take the reins of his horse. A second nun beckoned with her hand. Neither spoke.

The captain was pleased to see Michael dismount elegantly despite the rain, and take Grendel's head, without physically pushing the nun out of the way.

He smiled at the nuns and followed them across the courtyard towards the most ornate door, heavy with scroll-worked iron hinges and elaborate wooden panels. To the north, a dormitory building rose beyond a trio of low sheds that probably served as workshops—smithy, dye house and carding house, or so his nose told him. To the south stood a chapel—far too fragile and beautiful for this martial setting—and next to it, by cosmic irony, a long, low, slate-roofed stable.

Between the chapel's carved oak doors stood a man. He had a black habit with a silk rope around the waist, was tall and thin to the point of caricature, and his hands were covered in old scars.

The captain didn't like his eyes, which were blue and flat. The man was nervous, and wouldn't meet his eye—and he was clearly angry.

Flicking his eyes away from the priest, the captain reviewed the riches of the abbey with the eye of a money-lender sizing up a potential client. The abbey's income was shown in the cobbled courtyard, the neat flint and granite of the stables with a decorative stripe of glazed brick, the copper on the roof and the lead gutters gushing water into a cistern. The courtyard was thirty paces across—as big as that of any castle he'd lived in as a boy. The walls rose sheer—the outer curtain at his back, the central monastery before him, with towers at each corner, all wet stone and wet lead, rain slicked cobbles; the priest's faded black cassock, and the nun's undyed surcoat.

All shades of grey, he thought to himself, and smiled as he climbed the steps to the massive monastery door, which was opened by another silent nun. She led him down the hall—a great hall lit by stained glass windows high in the walls. The Abbess was enthroned like a queen in a great chair on a dais at the north end of the hall, in a gown whose grey had just enough colour to appear a pale, pale lavender in the multi-faceted light. She had the look of a woman who had once been very beautiful indeed—even in middle age her beauty was right there, resting in more than her face. Her wimple and the high collar of her gown revealed little enough of her. But her bearing was more than noble, or haughty. Her bearing was command-ing, confident in a way that only the great of the land were confident. The captain noted that her nuns obeyed her with an eagerness born of either fear or the pleasure of service.

The captain wondered which it was.

"You took long enough to reach us," she said, by way of greeting. Then she snapped her fingers and beckoned at a pair of servants to bring a tray. "We are servants of God here—don't you think you might have managed to strip your armour before you came to my hall?" the Abbess asked. She glanced around, caught a novice's eye, raised an eyebrow. "Fetch the captain a stool," she said. "Not a covered one. A solid one."

"I wear armour every day," the captain said. "It comes with my pro-fession." The great hall was as big as the courtyard outside, with high windows of stained glass set near the roof, and massive wooden beams so old that age and soot had turned them black. The walls were whitewashed over fine plaster, and held niches containing images of saints and two rich books—clearly on display to overawe visitors. Their voices echoed in the room, which was colder than the wet courtyard outside. There was no fire in the central hearth.

The Abbess's people brought her wine, and she sipped it as they placed a small table at the captain's elbow. He was three feet beneath her. "Perhaps your armour is unnecessary in a nunnery?" she asked.

He raised an eyebrow. "I see a fortress," he said. "It happens that there are nuns in it."

She nodded. "If I chose to order you taken by my men, would your armour save you?" she asked.

The novice who brought his stool was pretty and she was careful of him, moving with the deliberation of a swordsman or a dancer. He turned his head to catch her eye and felt the tug of her power, saw that she was not merely pretty. She set the heavy stool down against the back of his knees. Quite deliberately, the captain touched her arm gently and caused her to turn to him. He turned to face her, putting his back to the Abbess.

"Thank you," he said, looking her in the eye with a calculated smile. She was tall and young and graceful, with wide-set almond-shaped eyes and a long nose. Not pretty; she was arresting.

She blushed. The flush travelled like fire down her neck and into her heavy wool gown.

He turned back to the Abbess, his goal accomplished. Wondering why the Abbess had placed such a deserable novice within his reach, unless she meant to. "If I chose to storm your abbey, would your piety save you?" he asked.

She blazed with anger. "How dare you turn your back on me?" she asked. "And leave the room, Amicia. The captain has bitten you with his eyes."

He was smiling. He thought her anger feigned.

She met his eyes and narrowed her own—and then folded her hands together, almost as if she intended to pray.

"Honestly, Captain, I have prayed and prayed over what to do here. Bringing you to fight the Wild is like buying a wolf to shepherd sheep." She looked him in the eye. "I know what you are," she said.

"Do you really?" he asked. "All the better, lady Abbess. Shall we to business, then? Now the pleasantries are done?"

"But what shall I call you?" she asked. "You are a well-born man, for all your snide airs. My chamberlain—"

"Didn't have a nice name for me, did he, my lady Abbess?" He nodded. "You may call me Captain. It is all the name I need." He nodded graciously. "I do not like the name your chamberlain used. Bourc. I call myself the Red Knight."

"Many men are called bourc," she said. "To be born out of wedlock is—"

"To be cursed by God before you are born. Eh, lady Abbess?" He tried to stop the anger that rose on his cheeks like a blush. "So very fair. So *just*."

She scowled at him for a moment, annoyed with him the way older people are often annoyed with the young, when the young posture too much.

He understood her in a glance.

"Too dark? Should I add a touch of heroism?" he asked with a certain air.

She eyed him. "If you wrap yourself in darkness," she said, "you risk merely appearing dull. But you have the wit to know it. There's hope for you, boy, if you know that. Now to business. I'm not rich—"

"I have never met anyone who would admit being rich," he agreed. "Or to getting enough sleep."

"More wine for the captain," snapped the Abbess to the sister who had guarded the door. "But I can pay you. We are afflicted by something from the Wild. It has destroyed two of my farms this year, and one last year. At first—at first, we all hoped that they were isolated incidents." She met his eye squarely. "It is not possible to believe that any more."

"Three farms this year," said the captain. He fished in his purse, hesitated over the chain with the leaf amulet, then fetched forth a cross inlaid with pearls instead.

13

"Oh, by the wounds of Christ!" swore the Abbess. "Oh, Blessed Virgin protect and cherish her. Sister Hawisia! Is she—"

"She is dead," the captain said. "And six more corpses in the garden. Your good sister died trying to protect them."

"Her faith was very strong," the Abbess said. She was dry eyed, but her voice trembled. "You needn't mock her."

The captain frowned. "I never mock courage, lady Abbess. To face such a thing without weapons—"

"Her faith was a weapon against evil, Captain." The Abbess leaned forward.

"Strong enough to stop a creature from the Wild? No, it was not," said the captain quietly. "I won't comment on evil."

The Abbess stood sharply. "You are some sort of atheist, are you, Captain?"

The captain frowned again. "There is nothing productive for us in theological debate, my lady Abbess. Your lands have attracted a malignant entity—an enemy of Man. They seldom hunt alone, especially not this far from the Wild. You wish me to rid you of them. I can. And I will. In exchange, you will pay me. That is all that matters between us."

The Abbess sat again, her movements violent, angry. The captain sensed that she was off balance—that the death of the nun had struck her personally. She was, after all, the commander of a company of nuns.

"I am not convinced that engaging you is the right decision," she said.

The captain nodded. "It may not be, lady Abbess. But you sent for me, and I am here." Without intending to, he had lowered his voice, and spoke softly.

"Is that a threat?" she asked.

Instead of answering, the captain reached into his purse again and withdrew the broken chain holding a small leaf made of green enamel on bronze.

The Abbess recoiled as if from a snake.

"My men found this," he said.

The Abbess turned her head away.

"You have a traitor," he said. And rose. "Sister Hawisia had an arrow in her back. While she faced something terrible, something very, very terrible." He nodded. "I will go to walk the walls. You need time to think if you want us. Or not."

"You will poison us," she said. "You and your kind do not bring peace."

He nodded. "We bring you no peace, but a company of swords, my lady." He grinned at his own misquote of scripture. "We don't make the violence. We merely deal with it as it comes to us."

"The devil can quote scripture," she said.

"No doubt he had his hand in writing it," the captain shot back.

She bit back a counter—he watched her face change as she decided not to rise to his provocation. And he felt a vague twinge of remorse for goading her, an ache like the pain in his wrist from making too many practice cuts the day before. And, like the pain in his wrist, he was unaccustomed to remorse.

"I could say it is a little late to think of peace now." He sneered briefly and then put his sneer away. "My men are here, and they haven't had a good meal or a paid job in some weeks. I offer this, not as a threat, but as a useful piece of data as you reason through the puzzle. I also think that the creature you have to deal with is far worse than you have imagined. In fact, I'll go so far as to say it's far worse than I had imagined. It is big, powerful, and angry, and very intelligent. And more likely two than one."

She winced.

"Allow me a few minutes to think," she said.

He nodded, bowed, set his riding sword at his waist, and walked back into the courtyard.

His men stood like statues, their scarlet surcoats livid against their grey surroundings. The horses fretted—but only a little—and the men less.

"Be easy," he said.

They all took breath together. Stretched arms tired from bearing armour, or hips bruised from mail and cuirass.

Michael was the boldest. "Are we in?" he asked.

The captain didn't meet his eye because he'd noticed an open window across the courtyard, and seen the face framed in it. "Not yet, my honey. We are not in yet." He blew a kiss at the window.

The face vanished.

Ser Milus, his primus pilus and standard bearer, grunted. "Bad for business," he said. And then, as an afterthought, "m'lord."

The captain flicked him a glance and looked back to the dormitory windows.

"There's more virgins watching us right now," Michael opined, "Then have parted their legs for me in all my life."

Jehannes, the senior marshal, nodded seriously. "Does that mean one, young Michael? Or two?"

Guillaume Longsword, the junior marshal, barked his odd laugh, like the seals of the northern bays. "The second one said she was a virgin," he mock-whined. "At least, that's what she told me!"

Coming through the visor of his helmet, his voice took on an ethereal quality that hung in the air for a moment. Men do not look on horror and forget it. They merely put it away. Memories of the steading were still too close to the surface, and the junior marshal's voice had summoned them, somehow.

No one laughed. Or rather, most of them laughed, and all of it was forced.

The captain shrugged. "I have chosen to give our prospective employer some time to consider her situation," he said.

Milus barked a laugh. "Stewing in her juice to raise the price, is that it?" he asked. He nodded at the door of the chapel. "Yon has no liking for us."

The priest continued to stand in his doorway.

"Think he's a dimwit? Or is he the pimp?" Ser Milus asked. And stared at the priest. "Be my guest, cully. Stare all ye like."

The soldiers chuckled, and the priest went into the chapel.

Michael flinched at the cruelty in the standard bearer's tone, then stepped forward. "What is your will, m'lord?"

"Oh," the captain said, "I'm off hunting." He stepped away quickly, with a wry smile, walked a few steps toward the smithy, concentrated . . . and vanished.

Michael looked confused. "Where is he?" he asked.

Milus shrugged, shifting the weight of his hauberk. "How does he do that?" he asked Jehannes.

Twenty paces away, the captain walked into the dormitory wing as if it was his right to do so. Michael leaned as if to call out but Jehannes put his gauntleted hand over Michael's mouth.

"There goes our contract," Hugo said. His dark eyes crossed with the standard bearer's, and he shrugged, despite the weight of the maille on his shoulders. "I told you he was too young."

Jehannes eased his hand off the squire's face. "He has his little ways, the Bourc." He gave the other men a minute shake of his head. "Let him be. If he lands us this contract—"

Hugo snorted, and looked up at the window.

The captain reached into the palace in his head.

A vaulted room, twelve sided, with high, arched, stained glass windows, each one bearing a different image set at even intervals between columns of aged marble that supported a groined roof. Under each window was a sign of the zodiac, painted in brilliant blue on gold leaf, and then a band of beaten bronze as wide as a man's arm, and finally, at eye level, a series of niches between the columns, each holding a statue; eleven statues of white marble, and one iron-bound door under the sign of Ares.

In the exact centre of the room stood a twelfth statue—Prudentia, his childhood tutor. Despite her solid white marble skin, she smiled warmly as he approached her.

"Clementia, Pisces, Eustachios," he said in the palace of his memory, and his tutor's veined white hands moved to point at one sign and then another.

And the room moved.

The windows rotated silently above the signs of the zodiac, and the statues below the band of bronze rotated in the opposite direction until his three chosen signs were aligned opposite to the iron-bound door. And he smiled at Prudentia, walked across the tiles of the twelve-sided room and unlatched the door.

He opened it on a verdant garden of rich summer green—the dream memory of the perfect summer day. It was not always thus, on the far side of the door. A rich breeze blew in. It was not always this strong, his green power, and he deflected some with the power of his will, batting it into a ball and shoving it like a handful of summer leaves into a hempen bag he imagined into being and hung from Prudentia's outstretched arm. Against a rainy day. The insistent green breeze stirred through his hair and then reached the aligned signs on the opposite wall and—

He moved away from the horses without urgency, secure in the knowledge that Michael would be distracted as he moved—and so would the watcher in the window.

The captain's favourite phantasms depended on misdirection more than aethereal force. He preferred to add to their efficacy with physical efficiency—he walked quietly, and didn't allow his cloak to flap.

At the door to the dormitory he reached into his memory palace and *leaned into the vaulted room. "Same again, Pru," he said.*

Again the sigils moved as the marble statue pointed to the signs, already aligned above the door. He opened it again, allowed the green breeze to power his working, and let the door close.

He walked into the dormitory building. There were a dozen nuns, all big, capable women, sitting in the good light of the clerestory windows, and most of them were sewing.

He walked past them without a swirl of his scarlet cloak, his whole will focused on his belief that *his presence there was perfectly normal* and started up the stairs. No heads turned, but one older nun stopped peering at her embroidery and glanced at the stairwell, raised an eyebrow, and then went back to her work. He heard a murmur from behind him.

Not entirely fooled then, he thought. *Who are these women?*

His sabatons made too much noise and he had to walk carefully, because power—at least, the sort of power he liked to wield—was of limited use. The stairs wound their way up and up, turning as tightly as they would in any other fortress, to foul his sword arm if he was an attacker.

Which I am, of a sort, he thought. The gallery was immediately above the hall. Even on a day this grey, it was full of light. Three grey-clad novices leaned on the casemates of the windows, watching the men in the yard. Giggling.

At the edge of his power, he was surprised to find traces of *their* power.

He stepped into the gallery, and his sabaton made a distinct metallic scratch against the wooden floor—a clarion sound in a world of barefoot women. He didn't try to strain credulity by *willing* himself to seem normal, here.

The three heads snapped around. Two of the girls turned and ran. The third novice hesitated for a fatal moment—looking. Wondering.

He had her hand. "Amicia?" he said into her eyes, and then put his mouth over hers. Put an armoured leg inside her thighs and trapped her—turned her over his thigh as easily as throwing a child in a wrestling match, and she was in his arms. He rested his back plate against the ledge of the cloister and held her. Gently. Firmly.

She wriggled, catching her falling sleeve against the flange that protected his elbow. But her eyes were locked on his—and huge. She opened her lips. More there than simple fear or refusal. He licked her teeth. Ran a finger under her chin.

Her mouth opened under his—delicious.

He kissed her, or perhaps she kissed him. It was not brief. She relaxed into him—itself a pleasing warmth, even through the hardened steel of his arm harness and breastplate.

Kisses end.

"Don't take the vows," he said. "You do not belong here." He meant to sound teasing, but even in his own head his voice dripped with unintended mockery.

He stood straight and set her on the ground, to show that he was no rapist. She blushed red from her chin to her forehead, again. Even the backs of her hands were red. She cast her eyes down, and then shifted her weight—he watched such things. She leaned forward—

And slammed a hand into his right ear. Taking him completely by surprise. He reeled, his back hit the wall with a metallic *thud*, and he caught himself—

—and turned to chase her down.

But she wasn't running. She stood her ground. "How dare you judge me?" she said.

He rubbed his ear. "You mistake me," he said. "I meant no hard judgment. You wanted to be kissed. It is in your eyes."

As a line, it had certainly worked before. In this case, he felt it to be true. Despite the sharp pain in his ear.

She pursed her lips—full, very lovely lips. "We are all of us sinners, messire. I struggle with my body every day. That gives you no right to it."

There was a secret smile to the corner of her mouth—really, no smile at all, but something—

She turned and walked away down the gallery, leaving him alone.

He descended the stairs, rubbing his ear, wondering how much of the exchange had been witnessed by his men. Reputations can take months to build and be lost in a few heartbeats and his was too new to weather a loss of respect. But he calculated that the grey sky and the angle of the gallery windows should have protected him.

"That was quick," said Michael, admiringly, as he emerged. The captain was careful not to do anything as gross as tuck his braes into his hose. Because, had he taken her right there against the cloister wall, he would still have re-dressed meticulously before emerging.

Why didn't I? He asked himself. *She was willing enough.*

She liked me.

She hit me very hard.

He smiled at Michael. "It took as long as it took," he said. As he spoke, the heavy iron-bound door opened and a mature nun beckoned to the captain.

"The devil himself watches over you," Hugo muttered.

The captain shook his head. "The devil doesn't give a fuck, either," he said, and went to deal with the Abbess.

He knew as soon he crossed the threshold that she'd elected to take them on. If she'd decided *not* to take them on, he wouldn't have seen him again. Murder in the courtyard might have been closer to the mark.

Except that all the soldiers she had couldn't kill the eight of them in the courtyard. And she knew it. If she had eight good men, she'd never have sent for him to begin with.

It was like Euclidean geometry. And the captain could never understand why other people couldn't see all the angles.

He rubbed at the stinging in his ear, bowed deeply to the Abbess, and mustered up a smile.

She nodded. "I have to take you as you are," she said. "So I will use a long spoon. Tell me your rates?"

He nodded. "May I sit?" he asked. When she extended a reasonably gracious hand, he picked up the horn wine cup that had obviously been placed for him. "I drink to your eyes, *ma belle*."

She held his gaze with her own and smiled. "Flatterer."

"Yes," he said, taking a sip of wine and continuing to meet her stare over the rim like a proper courtier. "Yes, but no."

"My beauty is long gone, with the years," she said.

"Your body remembers your beauty so well that I can still see it," he said.

She nodded. "That was a beautiful compliment," she admitted. Then she laughed. "Who boxed your ear?" she asked.

He stiffened. "It is an old—"

"Nonsense! I educate children. I know a boxed ear when I see one." She narrowed her eyes. "A nun."

"I do not kiss and tell," he said.

"You are not as bad as you would have me believe, messire," she replied.

They gazed at each other for a few breaths.

"Sixteen double leopards a month for every lance. I have thirty-one lances today—you may muster them and count them yourself. Each lance consists of at least a knight, his squire, and a valet; usually a pair of archers. All mounted, all with horses to feed. Double pay for my corporals. Forty pounds a month for my officers—there are three—and a hundred pounds for me. Each month." He smiled lazily. "My men are very well disciplined. And worth every farthing."

"And if you kill my monster tonight?" she asked.

"Then you have a bargain, lady Abbess—only one month's pay." He sipped his wine.

"How do you tally these months?" she asked.

"Ah! There's none sharper than you, even in the streets of Harndon, lady. Full months by the lunar calendar." He smiled. "So the next one starts in just two weeks. The Merry month of May."

"Jesu, Lord of the Heavens and Saviour of Man. You are not cheap." She shook her head.

"My people are very, very good at this. We have worked on the Continent for many years, and now we are back in Alba. Where you need us. You needed us a year ago. I may be a hard man, lady, but let us agree that no more Sister Hawisias need die? Yes?" He leaned forward to seal the deal, the wine cup between his hands, and suddenly the weight of his armour made him tired and his back hurt.

"I'm sure Satan is charming if you get to know him," she said quietly. "And I'm sure that if you aren't paid, your interest in the Sister Hawisia's of this world will vanish like snow in strong sunshine." She gave him a thin-lipped smile. "Unless you can kiss them—and even then, I doubt you stay with them long. Or they with you."

He frowned.

"For every steading damaged by your men, I will deduct the price of a lance," she said. "For every man of mine injured in a brawl, for every woman who complains to me of your men, the price of a corporal. If a single one of my sisters is injured—or violated—by your Satan's spawn, even so much as a lewd hand laid to her or an unseemly comment made, I will deduct *your* fee. Do you agree? Since," she said with icy contempt, "Your men are so well disciplined?"

She really does like me, he thought. *Despite all.* He was more used to people who disliked him. And he wondered if she would give him Amicia. She'd certainly put the beautiful novice where he could see her. How calculating was the old witch? She seemed the type who would try to lure him with more than coin—but he'd already pricked her with his comment about Sister Hawisia.

"What's the traitor worth?" he asked.

She shook her head. "I do not believe in your traitor," she said, pointing on the enamel leaf on a wooden platter by her side. "You carry this foul thing with you to trick fools. And I am not a fool."

He shrugged. "My lady, you are allowing your dislike for my kind to cloud your judgment. Consider: what could make me to lie to you about such a thing? How many people should have been at that steading?" he asked.

She met his eye—she had no trouble with that, which pleased him. "There should have been seven confreres to work the fields," she allowed.

"We found your good sister and six other corpses," the captain countered.

"It is all straightforward enough, lady Abbess." He sipped more wine. "One is missing when none could have escaped. None." He paused. "Some of your sheep have grown teeth. And no longer wish to be part of your flock." He had a sudden thought. "What was Sister Hawisia doing there? She was a nun of the convent, not a labourer?"

She took a sharp breath. "Very well. If you can prove there is a traitor—or traitors—there will be reward. You must trust that I will be fair."

"Then you must understand: my men will behave badly—it is months since they were paid, and longer since they've been anywhere they might spend what they don't have. The writ of my discipline does not run to stopping tavern brawls or lewd remarks." He tried to look serious, though his heart was all but singing with the joy of work and gold to pay the company. "You must trust that I will do my best to keep them to order."

"Perhaps you'll have to lead by example?" she said. "Or get the task done quickly and move on to greener pastures?" she asked sweetly. "I understand the whores are quite comely south of the river. In the Albin."

He thought of the value of this contract—she hadn't quibbled at his inflated prices.

"I'll decide which seems more attractive when I've seen the colour of your money," he said.

"Money?" she asked.

"Payment due a month in advance, lady Abbess. We *never* fight for free."

Lorica—A Golden Bear

The bear was huge. All of the people in the market said so.

The bear sat in its chains, legs fully extended like an exhausted dancer, head down. It had leg manacles, one on each leg, and the chains had been wrought cunningly so that the manacles were connected by running links that limited the beast's movement.

Both of its hind paws were matted with blood—the manacles were also lined in small spikes.

"See the bear! See the bear!"

The bear keeper was a big man, fat as a lord, with legs like tree trunks and arms like hams. His two boys were small and fast and looked as if they might have a second profession in crime.

"A golden bear of the Wild! Today only!" he bellowed, and his boys roamed through the market, shouting "Come and see the bear! The golden bear!"

The market was full, as market can only be at the first breath of spring when every farmer and petty-merchant has been cooped up in a croft or a town house all winter. Every goodwife had new-made baskets to sell. Careful farmers had sound winter apples and carefully hoarded grain on offer. There were new linens—shirts and caps. A knife grinder did a brisk trade, and a dozen other tradesmen and women shouted their wares—fresh oysters from the coast, lambs for sale, tanned leather.

There were close on five hundred people in the market, and more coming in every hour.

A taproom boy from the inn rolled two small casks up, one at a time, placed a pair of boards across them and started serving cider and ale. He set up under the old oak that marked the centre of the market field, a stone's throw from the bear master.

Men began to drink.

A wagoner brought his little daughter to see the bear. It was female, with two cubs. They were beautiful, with their gold-tipped blond fur, but their mother smelled of rot and dung. Her eyes were wild, and when his daughter touched one of the cubs the fearsome thing opened its jaws, and his daughter started at the wicked profusion of teeth. The growing crowd froze and then people shrank back.

The bear raised a paw, stretching the chains—

She stood her ground. "Poor bear!" she said to her father.

The bear's paw was well short of touching the girl. And the pain of moving against the spiked manacles overcame the bear's anger. It fell back on all fours, and then sat again, looking almost human in its despair.

"Shh!" he said. "Hush, child. It's a creature of the Wild. A servant of the enemy." Truth to tell, his voice lacked conviction.

"The cubs are wonderful." The daughter got down on her haunches.

They had ropes on them, but no more.

A priest—a very worldly priest in expensive blue wool, wearing a magnificent and heavy dagger—leaned down. He put his fist before one of the cubs' muzzles and the little bear bit him. He didn't snatch his hand back. He turned to the girl. "The Wild is often beautiful, daughter. But that beauty is Satan's snare for the unwary. Look at him. Look at him!"

The little cub was straining at his rope to bite the priest again. As he rose smoothly to his feet and kicked the cub, he turned to the bear master.

"It is very like heresy, keeping a creature of the Wild for money," he said.

"For which I have a licence from the Bishop of Lorica!" sputtered the bear master.

"The bishop of Lorica would sell a licence to Satan to keep a brothel," said the priest with a hand on the dagger in his belt.

The wagoner took hold of his daughter but she wriggled free. "Pater, the bear is in pain," she said.

"Yes," he said. He was a thoughtful man. But his eyes were on the priest. And the priest's eyes were on him.

"Is it right for us to hurt any creature?" his daughter asked. "Didn't God make the Wild, just as he made us?"

The priest smiled and it was as terrible as the bear's teeth. "Your daughter has some very interesting notions," he said. "I wonder where she gets them?"

"I don't want any trouble," the wagoner said. "She's just a child."

The priest stepped closer, but just then the bear master, eager to get a show, began to shout. He had quite a crowd—at least a hundred people, and there were more wandering up every minute. There were half a dozen of the earl's soldiers as well, their jupons open in the early heat, flirting with the farmers' daughters. They pushed in eagerly, hoping to see blood.

The wagoner pulled his daughter back, and let the soldiers pass between him and the priest.

The bear master kicked the bear and pulled on the chain. One of his boys began to play a quick, staccato tune on a tin whistle.

The crowd began to chant, "Dance! Dance! Dance, bear, dance!"

The bear just sat. When the bear master's tugging on the chains caused her pain, she raised her head and roared her defiance.

The crowd shuffled back, muttering in disappointment, except for the priest.

One of the soldiers shook his head. "This is crap," he said. "Let's put some dogs on it."

The idea was instantly popular with his mates, but not at all with the bear master. "That's my bear," he insisted.

"Let me see your pass for the fair," said the sergeant. "Give it here."

The man looked at the ground, silenced, for all his size. "Which I ain't got one."

"Then I can take your bear, mate. I can take your bear and your boys." The sergeant smiled. "I ain't a cruel man," he said, his tone indicating that this statement was untrue. "We'll put some dogs on your bear, fair as fair. You'll collect the silver. We'll have some betting."

"This is a gold bear," said the bear master. He was going pale under his red, wine-fed nose. "A gold bear!"

"You mean you spent some silver on putting a bit of gilt on her fur," said another soldier. "Pretty for the crowd."

The bear master shrugged. "Bring your dogs," he said.

It turned out that many of the men in the crowd had dogs they fancied against a bear.

The wagoner slipped back another step, but the priest grabbed his arm. "You stay right here," he said. "And your little witch of a daughter."

The man's grip was like steel, and the light in his eyes was fanatical. The wagoner allowed himself, reluctantly, to be pulled back into the circle around the bear.

Dogs were being brought. There were mastiffs—great dogs the size of small ponies—and big hounds, and some mongrels that had replaced size with sheer ferocity. Some of the dogs sat quietly while others growled relentlessly at the bear.

The bear raised its head and growled too—once.

All the dogs backed away a step.

Men began to place bets.

The bear master and his boys worked the crowd. If he was hesitant to see his bear in a fight, he wasn't hesitant about accepting the sheer quantity of silver suddenly crossing his palm. Even the smallest farmer would wager on a bear baiting. And when the bear was a creature of the Wild—

Well it was almost a religious duty to bet against it.

The odds against the bear went up and up.

So did the number of dogs, and they were becoming unmaneageable as the pack grew. Thirty angry dogs can hate each other as thoroughly as they hate a bear.

The priest stepped out of the ring. "Look at this creature of Evil!" he said. "The very embodiment of the enemy. Look at its fangs and teeth, designed by the Unmaker to kill men. And look at these dogs men have bred—animals reduced to lawful obedience by patient generations of men. No one dog can bring down this monster alone, but does anyone doubt that many of them can? And is this lesson lost on any man here? The bear—look at it—is mighty. But man is more puissant by far."

The bear didn't raise its head.

The priest kicked it.

It stared at the ground.

"It won't even fight!" said one of the guards.

"I want my money back!" shouted a wheelwright.

The priest smiled his terrible smile. He grabbed the rope around one of the little cubs, hauled the creature into the air by the scruff of the neck, and tossed it in among the dogs.

The bear leaped to its feet.

The priest laughed. "Now it will fight," it said.

The bear strained against its manacles as the mastiffs ripped the screaming cub to shreds. It sounded like a human child, terrified and afraid, and then it was gone—savaged and eaten by a dozen mongrels. Eaten alive.

The wagoner had his hands over his daughter's eyes.

The priest whirled on him, eyes afire. "Show her!" he shrieked. "Show her what happens when evil is defeated!" He took a step towards the wagoner—

And the bear moved. She moved faster than a man would have thought possible.

She had his head in one paw and his dagger in the other before his body, pumping blood across the crowd, hit the dirt. Then she whirled—suddenly nothing but teeth and claws—and sank the heavy steel dagger into the ground *through* the links of her chain.

The links popped.

A woman screamed.

She killed as many of them as she could catch, until her claws were glutted with blood, and her limbs ached. They screamed, and hampered each other, and her paws struck them hard like rams in a siege, and every man and woman she touched, she killed.

If she could have she would have killed every human in the world. Her cub was dead. *Her cub was dead.*

She killed and killed, but they ran in all directions.

When she couldn't catch any more, she went back and tore at their corpses—found a few still alive and made sure they died in fear.

Her cub was dead.

She had no time to mourn. Before they could bring their powerful bows and their deadly, steel-clad soldiers, she picked up her remaining cub, ignored the pain and the fatigue and all the fear and panic she felt to be so deep in the tame horror of human lands, and fled. Behind her, in the town, alarm bells rang.

She ran.

Lorica—Ser Mark Wishart

Only one knight came, and his squire. They rode up to the gates at a gallop, summoned from their Commandery, to find the gates closed, the towers manned, and men with crossbows on the walls.

"A creature of the Wild!" shouted the panicked men on the wall before they refused to open the gates for him—even though they'd summoned him. Even though he was the Prior of the Order of Saint Thomas. A paladin, no less.

The knight rode slowly around the town until he came to the market field.

He dismounted. His squire watched the fields as if a horde of boglins might appear at any moment.

The knight opened his visor, and walked slowly across the field. There were a few corpses at the edge, by the dry ditch that marked the legal edge of the field. The bodies lay thicker as he grew closer to the Market Oak. Thicker and thicker. He could hear the flies. Smell the opened bowels, warm in the sun.

It smelled like a battlefield.

He knelt for a moment, and prayed. He was, after all, a priest, as well as a knight. Then he rose slowly and walked back to his squire, spurs catching awkwardly on the clothes of the dead.

"What—what was it?" asked his squire. The boy was green.

"I don't know," said the knight. He took off his helmet and handed it to his squire.

Then he walked back into the field of death.

He made a quick count. Breathed as shallowly as he could.

The dogs were mostly in one place. He drew his sword, four feet of mirror-polished steel, and used it as a pry-bar to roll the corpse of a man with legs like tree trunks and arms like hams off the pile of dogs.

He knelt and took off a gauntlet, and picked up what looked like a scrap of wool.

Let out a breath.

He held out his sword, and called on God for aid, and gathered the divine golden power, and then made a small working.

"Fools," he said aloud.

His working showed him where the priest had died, too. He found the man's head, but left it where it lay. Found his dagger, and placed a *phantasm* on it.

"You arrogant idiot," he said to the head.

He pulled the wagoner's body off the mangled corpse of his daughter. Turned aside and threw up, and then knelt and prayed. And wept.

And finally, stumbled to his feet and walked back to where his squire waited, the worry plain on his face.

"It was a golden bear," he said.

"Good Christ!" said the squire. "Here? Three hundred leagues from the wall?"

"Don't blaspheme, lad. They brought it here captive. They baited it with dogs. It had cubs, and they threw one to the dogs." He shrugged.

His squire crossed himself.

"I need you to ride to Harndon and report to the king," the knight said. "I'll track the bear."

The squire nodded. "I can be in the city by nightfall, my lord."

"I know. Go now. It's one bear, and men brought it here. I'll stem these fools' panic—although I ought to leave them to wallow in it. Tell the king that the Bishop of Jarsay is short a vicar. His headless corpse is over there. Knowing the man, I have to assume this was his fault, and the kindest thing I can say is that he got what he deserved."

His squire paled. "Surely, my lord, now it is you who blaspheme."

Ser Mark spat. He could still taste his own vomit. He took a flask of wine from the leather bag behind his saddle and drank off a third of it.

"How long have you been my squire?" he asked.

The young man smiled. "Two years, my lord."

"How often have we faced the Wild together?" he asked.

The young man raised his eyebrows. "A dozen times."

"How many times has the Wild attacked men out of pure evil?" the knight asked. "If a man prods a hornet's nest with a pitchfork and gets stung, does that make the hornets evil?"

His squire sighed. "It's not what they teach in the schools," he said.

The knight took another pull at his flask of wine. The shaking in his hands was stopping. "It's a mother, and she still has a cub. There's the track. I'll follow her."

"A golden bear?" the squire asked. "Alone?"

"I didn't say I'd fight her in the lists, lad. I'll follow her. You tell the king." The man leaped into his saddle with an acrobatic skill which was one of the many things that made his squire look at him with hero-worship. "I'll send a phantasm to the Commandery if I've time and power. Now go."

"Yes, my lord." The squire turned his horse and was off, straight to a gallop as he'd been taught by the Order.

Ser Mark leaned down from his tall horse and looked at the tracks, and then laid a hand on his war horse's neck. "No need to hurry, Bess," he said.

He followed the track easily. The golden bear had made for the nearest woods, as any creature of the Wild would. He didn't bother to follow the spoor exactly, but merely trotted along, checking the ground from time to time. He was too warm in full harness, but the alarm had caught him in the tiltyard, fully armed.

The wine sang in his veins. He wanted to drain the rest of it.

The dead child—

The scraps of the dead cub—

His own knight—when he was learning his catechism and serving his caravans as a squire—had always said *War kills the innocent first.*

Where the stubble of last year's wheat ran up into a tangle of weeds, he saw the hole the bear had made in the hedge. He pulled up.

He didn't have a lance, and a lance was the best way to face a bear.

He drew his war sword, but he didn't push Bess though the gap in the hedge.

He rode along the lane, entered the field carefully through the gate, and rode back along the hedge at a canter.

Tracks.

But no bear.

He felt a little foolish to have drawn his sword, but he didn't feel any inclination to put it away. The fresh tracks were less than an hour old, and the bear's paw print was the size of a pewter plate from the Commandery's kitchens.

Suddenly, there was crashing in the woods to his left.

He tightened the reins, and turned his horse. She was beautifully trained, pivoting on her front feet to keep her head pointed at the threat.

Then he backed her, step by step.

Crash.

Rustle.

He saw a flash of movement, turned his head and saw a jay leap into the air, flicked his eyes back—

Nothing.

"Blessed Virgin, stand with me," he said aloud. Then he rose an inch in his war saddle and just *touched* his spurs to Bess's sides, and she walked forward.

He turned her head and started to ride around the wood. It couldn't be that big.

Rustle.

Rustle.

Crack.

Crash.

It was *right there.*

He gave the horse more spur, and they accelerated to a canter. The great horse made the earth shake.

Near Lorica—A Golden Bear

She was being hunted. She could smell the horse, hear its shod hooves moving on the spring earth, and she could *feel* its pride and its faith in the killer on its back.

After months of degradation and slavery, torture and humiliation she would happily have turned and fought the steel-clad war man. Glory for her if she defeated him, and a better death than she had imagined in a long time. But her cub mewed at her. The cub—it was all for the cub. She had been captured because they could not run and she would not leave them, and she had endured for them.

She only had one left.

She was the smaller of the two, and the gold of her fur was brighter, and she was on the edge of exhaustion, suffering from dehydration and panic. She had lost the power of speech and could only mew like a dumb animal. Her mother feared she might have lost it for life.

But she had to try. The very blood in her veins cried out that she had to try to save her young.

She picked the cub up in her teeth the way a cat carried a kitten, and ran again, ignoring the pain in her paws.

Lorica—Ser Mark Wishart

The knight cantered around the western edge of the woods and saw the river stretching away in a broad curve. He saw the shambling golden creature in the late sunlight, gleaming like a heraldic beast on a city shield. The bear was running flat out. And so very beautiful, Wild. Feral.

"Oh, Bess," he said. For a moment he considered just letting the bear go. But that was not what he had vowed.

His charger's ears pricked forward. He raised his sword, Bess rumbled into a gallop and he slammed his visor closed.

Bess was faster than the bear. Not much faster, but the great female was hampered by her cub and he could see that her rear paws were mangled and bloody.

He began to run her down as the ground started to slope down towards the broad river. It was wide here, near the sea, and it smelled of brine at the turn of the tide. He set himself in his saddle and raised his sword—

Suddenly, the bear released her cub to tumble deep into some low bushes, and turned like a great cat pouncing—going from prey to predator in the beat of a human heart.

She rose on her haunches as he struck at her—and she was faster than any creature he'd ever faced. She swung with all her weight in one great claw-raking blow, striking at his horse, even as his blow cut through the meat of her right forepaw and into her chest—cut deep.

Bess was already dead beneath him.

He went backwards over his high crupper, as he'd been taught to. He hit hard, rolled, and came to his feet. He'd lost his sword—and lost sight of the bear. He found the dagger at his waist and drew it even as he whirled. Too slow.

She hit him. The blow caught him in the side, and threw him off his feet, but his breastplate held the blow and the claws didn't rake him. By luck he rolled over his sword, and got to his feet with it in his fist. Something in his right leg was badly injured—maybe broken.

The bear was bleeding.

The cub mewed.

The mother looked at the cub. Looked at him. Then she ran, picked the cub up in her mouth and ran for the river. He watched until she was gone—she jumped into the icy water and swam rapidly away.

He stood with his shoulders slumped, until his breathing began to steady. Then he walked to his dead horse, found his unbroken flask, and drank all the rest of the contents.

He said a prayer for a horse he had loved.

And he waited to be found.

West of Lissen Carak—Thorn

A two hundred leagues north-west, Thorn sat under a great holm-oak that had endured a millennium. The tree rose, both high and round, and its progeny filled the gap between the hills closing down from the north and the ever deeper Cohocton River to the south.

Thorn sat cross-legged on the ground. He no longer resembled the man he had once been; he was almost as tall as a barn, when he stood up to his full height, and his skin, where it showed through layers of moss and leather, seemed to be of smooth grey stone. A staff—the product of a single, straight ash tree riven by lightning in its twentieth year—lay across his lap. His gnarled fingers, as long as the tines of a hay fork, made eldritch sigils of pale green fire as he reached out into the Wild for his coven of spies.

He found the youngest and most aggressive of the Qwethnethogs; the strong people of the deep Wild that men called daemons. *Tunxis.* Young, angry, and easy to manipulate.

He exerted his will, and Tunxis came. He was careful about the manner of his summons; Tunxis had more powerful relatives who would resent Thorn using the younger daemon for his own ends.

Tunxis emerged from the oaks to the east at a run, his long, heavily muscled legs beautiful at the fullness of his stride, his body leaning far forward, balanced by the heavy armoured tail that characterized his kind. His chest looked deceptively human, if an unlikely shade of blue-green, and his arms and shoulders were also very man-like. His face had an angelic beauty—large, deep eyes slanted slightly, open and innocent, with a ridge of bone between them that rose into the elegant helmet crest that differentiated the male and female among them. His beak was polished to a mirror-brightness and inlaid with lapis lazuli and gold to mark his social rank, and he wore a sword that few mere human men could even lift.

He was angry—but Tunxis was at the age when young males are always angry.

"Why do you summon me?" he shrieked.

Thorn nodded. "Because I need you," he answered.

Tunxis clacked his beak in contempt. "Perhaps I do not need you. Or your games."

"It was my games that allowed you to kill the witch." Thorn didn't smile. He had lost the ability to, but he smiled inwardly, because Tunxis was so young.

The beak clacked again. "She was nothing." Clacked again, in deep satisfaction. "*You* wanted her dead. And she was too young. You offered me a banquet and gave me a scrap. A *nothing.*"

Thorn handled his staff. "She is certainly nothing now." His *friend* had asked for the death. Layers of treason. Layers of favours asked, and owed. The Wild. His attention threatened to slip away from the daemon. It had probably been a mistake to let Tunxis kill in the valley.

"My cousin says there are armed men riding in the valley. In *our valley.*" Tunxis slurred the words, as all his people did when moved by great emotion.

Thorn leaned forward, suddenly very interested. "Mogan saw them?" he asked.

"Smelled them. Watched them. Counted their horses." Tunxis moved his eyebrows the way daemons did. It was like a smile, but it caused the beak to close—something like the satisfaction of a good meal.

Thorn had had many years in which to study the daemons. They were his closest allies, his not-trusted lieutenants. "How many?" Thorn asked patiently.

"Many," Tunxis said, already bored. "I will find them and kill them."

"You will *not*." Thorn leaned forward and slowly, carefully, rose to his feet, his heavy head brushing against the middling branches of the ancient oak. "Where has she found soldiers?" he asked out loud. One of the hazards of living alone in the Wild was that you voiced things aloud. He was growing used to talking to himself aloud. It didn't trouble him as it had at first.

"They came from the east," Tunxis said. "I will hunt them and kill them."

Thorn sighed. "No. You will find them and watch them. You will watch them from afar. We will learn their strengths and weaknesses. Chances are they will pass away south over the bridge, or join the lady as a garrison. It is no concern of ours."

"No concern of *yours*, Turncoat. Our land. Our valley. Our hills. Our fortress. Our power. Because you are weak—" Tunxis's beak made three distinct clacks.

Thorn rolled his hand over, long thin fingers flashing, and the daemon fell flat on the ground as if all his sinews had been cut.

Thorn's voice became the hiss of a serpent.

"I am *weak*? The soldiers are *many*? They came from the *east*? You are a fool and a child, Tunxis. I could rip your soul from your body and eat it, and you couldn't lift a claw to stop me. Even now you cannot move, cannot summon power. You are like a hatchling in the rushing water as the salmon comes to take him. Yes? And you tell me 'many' like a lord throwing crumbs to peasants. Many?" he leaned down over the prone daemon and thrust his heavy staff into the creature's stomach. "*How many exactly, you little fool?*"

"I don't know," Tunxis managed.

"From the east, the south-east? From Harndon and the king? From over the mountains? Do you know?" he hissed.

"No," Tunxis said, cringing.

"Tunxis, I like to be polite. To act like—" He sought for a concept that could link him to the alien intelligence. "To act like we are allies. Who share common goals."

"You treat us like servants! We serve no master!" spat the daemon. "We are not like your *men*, who lie and lie and say these pretty things. We are Qwethnethogs!"

Thorn pushed his staff deeper into the young daemon's gut. "Sometimes I tire of the Wild and the endless struggle. *I am trying to help you and your people reclaim your valley. Your goal is my goal.* So I am not going to eat you. However tempting that might be just now." He withdrew the staff.

"My cousin says I should never trust you. That whatever body you wear, you are just another man." Tunxis sat up, rolled to his feet with a pure and fluid grace.

"Whatever I am, without me you have no chance against the forces of the Rock. You will *never* reclaim your place."

"Men are weak," Tunxis spat.

"Men have defeated your kind again and again. They burn the woods. They cut the trees. They build farms and bridges and they raise armies and your kind *lose*." He realised that he was trying to negotiate with a child. "Tunxis," he said, laying hold of the young creature's essence. "Do my bidding. Go, and watch the men, and come back and tell me."

But Tunxis had a power of his own, and Thorn watched much of his compulsion roll off the creature. And when he let go his hold, the daemon turned and sprinted for the trees.

And only then did Thorn recall that he'd summoned the boy for another reason entirely, and that made him feel tired and old. But he exerted himself again, summoning one of the Abnethog this time, that men called wyverns.

The Abnethog were more biddable. Less fractious. Just as aggressive. But lacking a direct ability to manipulate the power, they tended to avoid open conflict with the magi.

Sidhi landed neatly in the clearing in front of the holm oak, although the aerial gymnastics required taxed his skills.

"I come," he said.

Thorn nodded. "I thank you. I need you to look in the lower valley to the east," he said. "There are men there, now. Armed men. Possibly very dangerous."

"What man is dangerous to me?" asked the wyvern. Indeed, Sidhi stood eye to eye with Thorn, and when he unfolded his wings their span was extraordinary. Even Thorn felt a twinge of real fear when the Abnethog were angry.

Thorn nodded. "They have bows. And other weapons that could hurt you badly."

Sidhi made a noise in his throat. "Then why should I do this thing?" he asked.

"I made the eyes of your brood clear when they clouded over in the winter. I gave you the rock-that-warms for your mate's nest." Thorn made a motion intended to convey that he would continue to heal sick wyverns.

Sidhi unfolded his wings. "I was going to hunt," he said. "I am hungry. And being summoned by you is like being called a dog." The wings spread farther and farther. "But it may be that I will choose to hunt to the east, and it may be that I will see your enemies."

"Your enemies as well," Thorn said wearily. *Why are they all so childish?*

The wyvern threw back its head, and screamed, and the wings beat—a moment of chaos, and it was in the air, the trees all around it shedding

32

leaves in the storm of air. A night of hard rain wouldn't have ripped so many leaves from the trees.

And then Thorn reached out with his power—gently, hesitantly, a little like a man rising from bed on a dark night to find his way down unfamiliar stairs. He reached out to the east—farther, and a little farther, until he found what he always found.

Her. The lady on the Rock.

He probed the walls like a man running his tongue over a bad tooth. She was there, enshrined in her power. And with her was something else entirely. He couldn't read it—the fortress carried its own power, its own ancient sigils which worked against him.

He sighed. It was raining. He sat in the rain, and tried to enjoy the rise of spring around him.

Tunxis killed the nun, and now the lady has more soldiers. He had set something in motion, and he wasn't sure why.

And he wondered if he had made a mistake.

Chapter Two

Harndon Palace—The Queen

Desiderata lay on the couch of her solar chewing new cherries and savouring the change in the air. Because—*at last*—spring had come. Her favourite season. After Lent would come Easter and then Whitsunday, and the season of picnics, of frolics by the river, or eating fresh fruit, wearing flowers, walking barefoot...

...and tournaments.

She sighed at the thought of tournaments. Behind her, Diota, her nurse, made a face. She could see the old woman's disapproval in the mirror.

"What? Now you frown if I sigh?" she asked.

Diota straightened her back, putting a fist into it like a pregnant woman. Her free hand fingered the rich paternoster at her neck. "You sound like a whore pleasing a customer, mistress—if you'll pardon the crudity of an old woman—"

"*Who's known you all these years,*" the Queen completed the sentence. Indeed, she'd had Diota since she was weaned. "Do I? And what do you know about the sounds whores make, nurse?"

"Now, my lady!" Diota came forward, waggling a finger. Coming around the screen, she stopped as if she'd hit an invisible barrier. "Oh! By the Sweet Lord—put some clothes on, girl! You'll catch your death! It's not spring yet, morsel!"

The Queen laughed. She was naked in the new sunlight, her tawny skin flecked with the imperfections of the glass in her solar's window, lying on the pale brown profusion of her hair. She *drew* something from the sunlight falling on her skin—something that made her glow from within.

Desiderata rose and stood at the mirror—the longest mirror in the Demesne, made just for her, so that she could examine herself from the high arches of her feet, up her long legs, past her hips and thighs and the deep recess of her navel to her breasts, her upright shoulders, her long and tapered neck, deep cut chin, a mouth made for kissing, long nose and wide grey eyes with lashes so long that sometimes she could lick them.

She frowned. "Have you seen the new lady in waiting? Emmota?" she said.

Her nurse chuckled alongside her. "She's a child."

"A fine figure. Her waist is thin as a rail." The Queen looked at herself with careful scrutiny.

Diota smacked her hip. "Get dressed, you hussy!" she laughed. "You're looking for compliments. She's nothing to you, Miss. A child. No breasts." She laughed. "Every man says you are the beauty of the world," she added.

The Queen continued to look in the mirror. "I am. But for how long?" She put her hands up over her head, arching her back as her chest rose.

Her nurse slapped her playfully. "Do you want the king to find you thus?"

Desiderata smiled at her woman. "I could say yes. I want him to find me *just* like this," she said. And then, her voice coloured with power, she said, "Or I could say I am as much myself, and as much the Queen, naked, as I am clothed."

Her nurse took a step away.

"But I won't say any such thing. Bring me something nice. The brown wool gown that goes with my hair. And my golden belt."

"Yes, my lady." Diota nodded and frowned. "Shall I send some of your ladies to dress you?"

The Queen smiled and stretched, her eyes still on the mirror. "Send me my ladies," she said, and subsided back onto the couch in the solar.

Lissen Carak—The Red Knight

At Ser Hugo's insistence, the master archers had set up butts in the fields along the river.

Men grumbled, because they'd been ordered to curry their horses before turning in, and then, before the horses were cared for, they were ordered to shoot. They had ridden hard, for many long days, and there wasn't a man or woman without dark circles under their eyes.

Bent, the eldest, an easterner, and Wilful Murder, fresh back from failing to find a murderer's tracks with the huntsman, ordered the younger men to unload the butts, stuffed with old cloth or woven from straw, from the wagons.

"Which it isn't my turn," whined Kanny. "An' why are you always picking on us?" His words might have appeared braver, if he hadn't waited until Bent was far away before saying them.

Geslin was the youngest man in the company, just fourteen, with a thin frame that suggested he'd never got much food as a boy, climbed one of the tall wagons and silently seized a target and tossed it down to Gadgee, an odd looking man with a swarthy face and foreign features.

Gadgee caught the target with a grunt, and started toward the distant field. "Shut up and do some work," he said.

Kanny spat. And moved very slowly towards a wagon that didn't have any targets in it. "I'll just look—"

Bad Tom's archer, Cuddy, appeared out of nowhere and shoved him ungently towards the wagon where Geslin was readying a second target. "Shut up and do some work," he said.

He was slow enough that by the time he had his target propped up and ready for use, all nine of the other butts were ready as well. And there were forty archers standing a hundred paces distant, examining their spare strings and muttering about the damp.

Cuddy strung his bow with an economy of motion that belied long practice, and he opened the string that held the arrows he had in his quiver.

"Shall I open the dance?" he said.

He nocked, and loosed.

A few paces to his right, Wilful Murder, who fancied himself as good an archer as any man alive, drew and loosed a second later, contorting his body to pull the great war bow.

Bent put his horn to his lips and blew. "Cease!" he roared. He turned to Cuddy. "Kanny's still down range!" he shouted at the master archer.

Cuddy grinned. "I know *just* where he is," he said. "So does Wilful."

The two snickered as Kanny came from behind the central target, running as fast as his long, skinny legs would carry him.

The archers roared with laughter.

Kanny was spitting with rage and fear. "You bastard!" he shouted at Cuddy.

"I told you to work faster," Cuddy said mildly.

"I'll tell the captain!" Kanny said.

Bent nodded. "You do that." He motioned. "Off you go."

Kanny grew pale.

Behind him, the other archers walked up to their places, and began to loose.

The captain was late to the drill. He looked tired, and he moved slowly, and he leaned on the tall stone wall surrounding the sheepfold that Ser Hugh had converted to a tiltyard and watched the men-at-arms at practice.

Despite fatigue and the weight of plate and mail Ser George Brewes was on the balls of his feet, bouncing from guard to guard. Opposite him, his "companion" in the language of the tiltyard, was the debonair Robert Lyliard, whose careful fighting style was the very opposite of the ostentatious display of his arms and clothes.

Brewes stalked Lyliard like a high-stepping panther, his pole-arm going from guard to guard—low, axe-head forward and right leg advanced, in the Boar's Tooth; sweeping through a heavy up-cut to rest on his right shoulder like a woodcutter in the Woman's Guard.

Francis Atcourt, thick waisted and careful, faced Tomas Durrem. Both were old soldiers, unknighted men-at-arms who had been in harness for decades. They circled and circled, taking no chances. The captain thought he might fall asleep watching them.

Bad Tom came and rested on the same wall, except that his head projected clear above the captain's head. And even above the plume on his hat.

"Care to have a go?" Tom asked with a grin.

No one liked to spar with Tom. He hurt people. The captain knew that despite all the plate armour and padding and mail and careful weapon's control, tiltyard contests were dangerous and men were down from duty all the time with broken fingers and other injuries. And that was without the sudden flares of anger men could get when something hurt, or became personal. When the tiltyard became the duelling ground.

The problem was that there was no substitute for the tiltyard, when it came to being ready for the real thing. He'd learned that in the east.

He looked at Tom. The man had a reputation. And he had dressed Tom down in public a day before.

"What's your preference, Ser Thomas?" he asked.

"Longsword," Bad Tom said. He put a hand on the wall and vaulted it, landed on the balls of his feet, whirled and drew his sword. It was his war sword—four feet six inches of heavy metal. Eastern made, with a pattern in the blade. Men said it was magicked.

The captain walked along the wall with no little trepidation. He went into the sheepfold through the gate, and Michael brought him a tilt helmet with solid mesh over the face and a heavy aventail.

Michael handed him his own war sword. It was five inches shorter than Bad Tom's, plain iron hilted with a half-wired grip and a heavy wheel of iron for a pommel.

As Michael buckled his visor, John of Reigate, Bad Tom's squire, put his helmet over his head.

Tom grinned while his faceplate was fastened. "Most loons mislike a little to-do wi' me," he said. When Tom was excited, his hillman accent overwhelmed his Gothic.

The captain rolled his head to test his helmet, rotated his right arm to test his range of motion.

Men-at-arms were pausing, all over the sheepfold.

"The more fool they," the captain said.

He'd watched Tom fight. Tom liked to hit hard—to use his godlike strength to smash through men's guards.

His father's master-at-arms, Hywel Writhe, used to say *For good swordsmen, it's not enough to win. They need to win their own way. Learn a man's way, and he becomes predictable.*

Tom rose from the milking stool he'd sat on to be armed and flicked his sword back and forth. Unlike many big men, Tom was as fast as the tomcat that gave him his name.

The captain didn't strike a guard at all. He held his sword in one hand, the point actually trailing on the grass.

Tom whirled his blade up to the high Woman's Guard, ready to cleave his captain in two.

"Garde!" he roared. The call echoed off the walls of the sheep fold and then from the high walls of the fortress above them.

The captain stepped, moved one foot off line, and suddenly he had his sword in two hands. Still trailing out behind him.

Tom stepped off-line, circling to the captain's left,

The captain stepped in, his sword rising to make a flat cut at Tom's head.

Tom slapped the sword down—a *rabatter* cut with both wrists, meant to pound an opponent's blade into the ground.

The captain powered in, his back foot following the front foot forward. He let the force of Tom's blow to his blade rotate it, his wrist the pivot—sideways and then *under* Tom's blade.

He caught the point of his own blade in his left hand, and tapped it against Tom's visor. His two handed grip and his stance put Tom's life utterly in his hands.

"One," he said.

Tom laughed. "Brawly feckit!" he called.

He stepped back and saluted. The captain returned the salute and sidestepped, because Tom came for him immediately.

Tom stepped, then swept forward with a heavy downward cut.

The captain stopped it, rolling the blade well off to the side, but as fast as he could bring his point back on line, Tom was inside his reach—

And he was face down in sheep dip. His hips hurt, and now his neck hurt.

But to complain was not the spirit of the thing.

"Well struck," he said, doing his best to bounce to his feet.

Tom laughed his wild laugh again. "Mine, I think," he said.

The captain had to laugh.

"I was planning to chew on your toes," he said, and drew a laugh from the onlookers.

He saluted, Tom saluted, and they were on their guards again.

But they'd both shown their mettle, and now they circled—Tom looking for a way to force the action close, and the captain trying to keep him off with short jabs. Once, by thrusting with his whole sword held at the pommel, he scored on Tom's right hand, and the other man flicked a short salute, as if to say "that wasn't much." And indeed, Ser Hugo stepped between them.

"I don't allow such trick blows, my lord," Hugh said. "It'd be a foolish thing to do in a melee."

The captain had to acknowledge the truth of that assertion. He had been taught the Long Point with the advice *never use this unless you are desperate. Even then—*

The captain's breath was coming in great gasps, while Tom seemed to be moving fluidly around the impromptu ring. Breathing well and easily. Of course, given his advantages in reach and size, he could control most aspects of the fight, and the captain was mostly running away to keep his distance.

The last five days of worry and stress sat as heavily on his shoulders as the weight of his tournament helm. And Tom was very good. There was really little shame in losing to him. So the captain decided he'd rather go down as a lion than a very tired lamb. And besides, it would be funny.

So—between one retreat and the next blow—he swayed his hips, rotated his feet so that his weight was back, and let go the sword's hilt with his left hand. Eastern swordsmen called it "The Guard of One Hand."

Tom swept in with another of his endless, heavy, sweeping blows. Any normal man would have exhausted himself with them. Not Tom. This one came from his right shoulder.

This time, the captain tried for a *rebatter* defence—his sword sweeping up, one handed, coming slightly behind Tom's but cutting as fast as a falcon strikes its prey. He caught Tom's sword and drove it faster along its intended path as he stepped slightly off-line and *forward*, surprising his companion. His free left hand shot out, and he punched Tom's right wrist, and then his left hand was between the big man's hands, and Tom's aggressive pursuit of his elusive opponent carried him forward—the captain's left hand went deeper, and he achieved the arm lock, and twisted, in complete possession of the man's sword and shoulder—

And nothing happened. Tom was *not* rotated. In fact, Tom's rush turned into a swing, and the captain found himself swinging off Tom's elbow and the giant turned to the left, and again, and the captain couldn't let go without tumbling to the ground.

His master-at-arms had never covered this situation.

Tom whirled him again, trying to shake him off. They were at a nasty impasse. The captain had Tom's sword bound tight, and his elbow and shoulder in a lock too. But Tom had the captain's feet off the ground.

The captain had his blade free—mostly free. He hooked his pommel into Tom's locked arms, hoping it would give him the leverage to, well, to do what should have happened in the first place. The captain's sense of how combat and the universe worked had received a serious jar.

But even with both hands—

Tom whirled him again, like a terrier breaking a rat's neck.

Using every sinew of his not inconsiderable muscles, the captain pried his pommel between Tom's arms and levered the blade over Tom's head and grabbed the other side, letting his whole weight go onto the blade.

In effect, he fell, blade first, on Tom's neck.

They both went down.

The captain lay in the sheep muck, with his eyes full of stars. And his breath coming like a blacksmith's bellows.

Something under him was moving.

He rolled over, and found that he was lying entangled with the giant hillman, and the man was laughing.

"You're mad as a gengrit!" Tom said. He rose out of the muck and smothered the captain in an embrace.

Some of the other men-at-arms were applauding.

Some were laughing.

Michael looked like he was going to cry. But that was only because he had to clean the captain's armour, and the captain was awash in sheep dip.

When his helmet was off, he began to feel the new strain in his left side and the pain in his shoulder. Tom was right next to him.

"You're a loon," Tom said. He grinned. "A loon."

With his helmet off, he could still only just breathe.

Chrys Foliack, another of the men-at-arms who had hitherto kept his distance from the captain, came and offered his hand. He grinned at Tom. "It's like fighting a mountain, ain't it?" he asked.

The captain shook his head. "I've never—"

Foliack was a big man, handsome and red-headed and obviously well-born. "I liked the arm lock," he said. "Will you teach it?"

The captain looked around. "Not just this minute," he said.

That got a laugh.

Harndon Palace—The King

The king was in armour, having just trounced a number of his gentlemen on the tilt field, when his constable, Alexander, Lord Glendower—an older man with a scar that ran from his right eyebrow, all the way across his face, cleaving his nose from right to left so deeply as to make most men he met wince—and then down across his face to his mouth, so that his beard had a ripple in it where the scar had healed badly, and he always looked as if he was sneering—approached with a red-haired giant at his back.

Glendower's scar couldn't have suited a man worse as he was, as far as the king was concerned, the best of companions, a man little given to sneering and much to straight talk unlaced by flattery or temper. His patience with his soldiers was legendary.

"My lord, I think you know Ranald Lachlan, who has served you two years as a man-at arms." He bowed, and extended an arm to the red-bearded man, who was obviously a hillman—red hair, facial scarring, piercing blue eyes like steel daggers, and two ells of height unhidden by the hardened steel plate armour and red livery of the Royal Guard.

Ranald bowed deeply.

The king reached out and clasped his hand. "I'm losing you," he said warmly. "The sight of your great axe always made me feel safe," he laughed.

Ranald bowed again. "I promised Lord Glendower and Sir Ricard two years when I signed my mark," the hillman said. "I'm needed at home, for the spring drive."

Sir Ricard Fitzroy, so indicated, was the captain of the guard.

"Your brother is the Drover, I know," the king said. "It's a troubled spring, Ranald. Alba will be safer if your axe is guarding beeves in the hills, rather than guarding the king, safe in Harndon. Eh?"

Ranald shrugged, embarrassed. "There'll be fighting, I ha'e na' doot," he admitted. Then he grinned. "I have no doubt, my lord."

The king nodded. "When the drive is over?" he asked.

"Oh, I have reason to come back," he said with a grin. "My lord. With your leave. But my brother needs me, and there are things—"

Every man present knew that the things Ranald Lachlan wanted involved the Queen's secretary, Lady Almspend—not an heiress, precisely. But a pretty maid with a fair inheritance. A high mark for a King's Guardsman, commonly born.

The king leaned close. "Come back, Ranald. She'll wait."

"I pray she does," he whispered.

The king turned to his constable. "See that this man's surcoat and kit are well stored; I grant him leave, but I do not grant him quittance from my service."

"My lord!" the man replied.

The king grinned. "Now get going. And come back with some tales to tell."

Ranald bowed again, as ceremony demanded, and walked from the king's presence to the guardroom, where he embraced a dozen close friends, drank a farewell cup of wine, and handed the Steward his kit—his maille hauberk and his good cote of plates beautifully covered in the royal scarlet; his two scarlet cotes with matching hoods, for wear at court, and his hose of scarlet cloth. His tall boots of scarlet leather, and his sword belt of scarlet trimmed in bronze.

He had on a doublet of fustian, dark hose of a muddy brown, and over his arm was his three-quarter's tweed cloak.

The Steward, Radolf, listed his kit on his inventory and nodded. "Nicely kept, messire. And your badge…" The king's badge was a white heart with a golden collar, and the badges were cunningly fashioned of silver and bronze and enamel. "The king expressly stated you was to keep yours, as on leave and not quit the guard." He handed the badge back.

Ranald was touched. He took the brooch and pinned his cloak with it. The badge made his tweed look shabby and old.

Then he walked out of the fortress and down into the city of Harndon, without a backwards glance. Two years, war and peril, missions secret and diplomatic, and the love of his life.

A hillman had other loyalties.

Down into the town that grew along the river's curves. From the height of the fortress, the town was dominated by the bridge over the Albin, the last bridge before the broad and winding river reached the sea thirty leagues farther south. On the far side of the bridge, to the north, lay Bridgetown—part and not part of the great city of Harndon. But on this side, along the river, the city ran from the king's fortress around the curve, with wharves and peers at the riverside, merchants' houses, streets of crafts-men in houses built tall and thin to save land.

He walked down the ramp, leading his two horses past the sentries—men he knew. More hand clasps.

He walked along Flood Street, past the great convent of St. Thomas and the streets of the Mercers and Goldsmiths, and down the steep lanes past the Founders and the Blacksmiths, to the place where Blade Lane crossed with Armour Street, at the sign of the broken circle.

The counter was only as wide as two broad-built men standing side by side, but Ranald looked around, because the Broken Circle made the finest weapons and armour in the Demesne, and there were always things there to be seen. Beautiful things—even to a hillman. Today was better than many days—a dozen simple helmets stood on the counter, all crisp and fine, with high points and umbers to shade the eye, the white work fine and neat, the finish almost mirror bright, the metal blue-white, like fine silver.

And these were simple archer's helmets.

There was an apprentice behind the counter, a likely young man with arms like the statues of the ancient men and legs to match. He grinned and bobbed his head and went silently through the curtain behind him to fetch his master.

Tad Pyel was the master weapon smith of the land. The first Alban to make the hardened steel. He was a tall man with a pleasant round face and twenty loyal apprentices to show that the mild disposition was not just in his face. He emerged, wiping his hands on his apron.

"Master Ranald," he said. "Here for your axe, I have no doubt."

"There was some talk of a cote, of maille as well," Ranald added.

"Oh," Tad nodded absently to his apprentice. "Oh, as to that—Continental stuff. Not my make. But yes, we have it ready for you."

Edward, the apprentice, was shifting a wicker basket from the back, and Ranald opened the lid and looked at the river of gleaming mail, every ring riveted with a wedge so small that most of the rings looked as if they'd been forged entire. It was as fine as the hauberk he'd worn as a King's Man.

"This for thirty leopards?" Ranald asked.

"Continental stuff," the master replied. He didn't actually sniff, but the sniff was there. Then the older man smiled, and held out a heavy pole with the ends wrapped in sacking. "This would cut it as a sharp knife cuts an apple."

Ranald took it in his hands, and was filled with as sweet a feeling as the moment that a man discovers he is in love—that the object of his affection returns his feelings.

Edward cut the lashings on the sacking, revealing a sharp steel spike on one end, ferruled in heavy bronze, balancing an axe blade at the other end—a narrow crescent of bright steel, as long as a man's forearm, ending in a wicked point and armed with a vicious back-hook. All balanced like a fine sword, hafted in oak, with steel lappets to guard against sword cuts.

It was a hillman's axe—but incomparably finer, made by a master and not by a travelling smith at a fair.

Ranald couldn't help himself, and he whirled it between his hands, the blade cutting the air and the tip *not quite* brushing the plaster of the low room.

Edward flattened himself against the wall, and the master nodded, satisfied.

"The one you brought me was a fine enough weapon," the master said. "Country made, but a well-made piece. But the finish," he winced. And shrugged. "And I thought that the balance could be improved."

The spike in the butt of the haft was as long as a knight's dagger, wickedly sharp and three-sided.

Ranald just smiled in appreciation.

The master added two scabbards—a sheath of wood covered in fine red leather for the axe, and another to match for the spike.

Ranald counted down a hundred silver leopards—a sizeable portion of two years' pay. He looked admiringly at the helmets on the counter.

"They're spoken for," the master said, catching his eye. "And none of them would fit your noggin, I'm thinking. Come back in winter when my work is slow, and I'll make you a helmet you could wear to fight a dragon."

The air seemed to chill.

"Naming calls," Edward said, crossing himself.

"Don't know what made me say that," said the master. He shook his head. "But I'd make you a helmet."

Ranald carried his new maille out to his pack horse, who was not as fond

43

of it as he was, resenting the weight and the re-packing of the panniers it necessitated. He came back for the axe, and put it lovingly into the straps on his riding horse, close to hand. No one watching doubted that he'd handle it a dozen more times before he was clear of the suburbs. Or that he'd stop and use it on the first bush he found growing by the road.

"You ride today, then," the master said.

Ranald nodded. "I'm needed in the north," he said. "My brother sent for me."

The weapon smith nodded. "Send him my respects, then, and the sele of the day on you."

The hillman embraced the cutler, stepped through the door, and walked his horses back up the old river bank.

He stopped in the chapel of Saint Thomas, and knelt to pray, his eyes down. Above him, the saint was martyred by soldiers—knights in the Royal Livery. The scene made him uncomfortable.

He bought a pie from a ragged little girl by the Bridge Gate, and then he was away.

Harndon City—Edward

"There goes a fearsome man," said the master to his apprentice. "I've known a few. And yet as gentle as a lady. A better knight than many who wear spurs."

Edward was too smitten with hero-worship to comment.

"And where's our daring mercer?" asked the master.

"Late, your worship," said his apprentice.

Tad shook his head. "That boy would be late to his own funeral," he said, but his voice suggested he had nothing but praise for the mercer. "Pack the helmets in straw and take them round to Master Random's house, will you, Ned?"

No matter how kind your master is, there's no apprentice who doesn't relish a trip beyond the Ward. "May I have a penny to buy baskets?"

Master Thaddeus put coins in his hand. "Wish I'd made him a helmet," he said. "Where'd the thought of a dragon come from?"

Harndon Palace—the Queen

Desiderata sat primly on an ivory stool in the great hall, its stucco walls lined with the trophies taken by a thousand brave knights—the heads of creatures greater and smaller, and a very young dragon's head, fully the size of a horse, filling the northern wall beneath the stained glass window like a boat hull protruding from the sea. To her, it never quite looked the same way twice, that dragon—but it was huge.

She sat peeling a winter apple with a silver knife. Her hair was a halo of brown and red and gold around her—a carefully planned effect, as she sat in the pool of light thrown by the king's beloved rose window. Her ladies sat around her, skirts spread like pressed flowers on the clean checkerboard marble floor, and a dozen of the younger knights—the very ones who should have been tilting in the tiltyard, or crossing swords with the masters—lounged against the walls. One, the eldest of them by half a dozen years and some fighting, was called "Hard Hands" for his well-known feat of killing a creature of the Wild with a single blow of his fist. It was a story he often told.

The Queen disliked men who boasted. She made it her business to know who was worthy and who was not—indeed, she viewed it as her sacred role. She loved to find the shy ones—the brave men who told no one of their deeds. She thought less of the braggarts. Especially when they sat in *her* hall and flirted with *her* ladies. She had just determined to punish the man when the king came in.

He was plainly dressed, in arming clothes, he smelled like horses and armour and sweat, and she wrapped herself around him and his smell as if they were newly wed. He smiled down into her face and kissed her nose.

"I love it when you do that," he said.

"You should practise your tilting more often, then," she said, holding his arm. Behind the king, Ser Driant stood rubbing his neck, and behind him, Ser Alan, and the constable, Lord Glendower. She laughed. "Did you defeat these poor knights?"

"Defeat?" asked Driant. He laughed ruefully. "I was crushed like a bug in an avalanche, my lady. His Grace has a new horse that's bigger than a dragon."

Ser Alan shrugged. "I was unhorsed, yes, lady." He looked at Ser Driant and frowned. "I think it rude to suggest the king's *horse* rolled you on the sand," he said.

Driant laughed again. He was not a man who stayed downcast for long. "There's a great deal of me to hit the ground," he said, "and that ground is still frozen." He rubbed his neck again, peering past the Queen to her ladies sitting with their knights. "And you lads—where were you when the blows were being dealt and received?"

Hard Hands nodded appreciatively. "Right here in the warm hall, basking in the beauty of the Queen and all these fair flowers," he said. "What man goes voluntarily to fight on frozen ground?"

The king frowned. "A man preparing for war?" he asked quietly.

Hard Hands looked about him for support. He'd mistaken the bantering tone of conversation for permission to banter with the king.

The Queen smiled to see him humbled so swiftly.

"Out beyond the walls are creatures who would crack your armour to eat what lies within—or to drink your soul," said the king, and his voice rang through the hall as he walked beneath the rows of heads. "And alone of these fair flowers, Ser knight, *you* know the truth of what I say. You have faced the Wild." The king was not the tallest man in the room or the handsomest. But when he spoke like this, no other man could compare.

Hard Hands looked at the floor and bit his lip in frustration. "I sought only to entertain, Sire. I beg your pardon."

"Seek my pardon in the Wild," the king said. "Bring me three heads and I will be content to watch you flirt with the Queen's ladies. Bring me five heads and you may flirt with the Queen."

If you dare, she thought.

The king grinned, stopped by the younger man and clapped a hand on his shoulder. Hard Hands stiffened.

He did not want to leave the court. It was plain to see.

The king put his lips close to Hard Hand's ear, but the Queen heard his words. She always did.

"Three heads," the king whispered through the smile on his lips. "Or you will stay in your castle and be branded faithless and craven."

The Queen watched the effect on her ladies and held her peace. Hard Hands was quite a popular man. Lady Mary, who was known as "Hard Heart" had been heard to say that perhaps his hands were not so very hard, after all. Seated nearest to the Queen, she pursed her lips and set her mouth, determined not to show the Queen her hurt. Behind this vignette, the king waved to his squires and set off up the main stairs to his arming room.

When the king was gone, Desiderata sat back down on her stool and picked up her sewing—an arming shirt for the king. Her ladies gathered round. They felt her desire and closed themselves against the younger knights, who looked to Hard Hands for leadership. Or had. Now they were disconsolate at losing their leader. They left with the sort of loud demonstration that young men make when socially disadvantaged, and the Queen laughed.

Hard Hands stopped in the arch of the main door and looked back. He met her eye, and his anger carried clearly across the sun beams that separated them.

"I will come back!" he shouted.

The other young men looked afraid at his outburst, and pushed him out the door.

"Perhaps," purred the Queen. She smiled, much like a cat with a tiny piece of tail sticking out between its teeth.

The ladies knew that smile. They were silent, and the wisest hung their heads in real, or well-feigned, contrition, but she saw through all of them.

"Mary," said the Queen gently. "Did you let Hard Hands into your bed?"

Mary, sometimes called Hard Heart, met her eye. "Yes, my lady."

The Queen nodded. "Was he worthy?" she asked. "Answer me true."

Mary bit her lip. "Not today, my lady."

"Perhaps not ever—eh? Listen, all of you," she said, and she bent her head to her ladies. "Emmota—you are latest amongst us. By what signs do you know a knight worthy to be your lover?"

Emmota was not yet fully grown to her womanhood—fourteen years old. Her face was narrow without being pinched and a clear intelligence shone in her eyes. She was nothing next to the Queen, and yet, the Queen admitted to herself, the girl had something.

But in this instant, her wits deserted her, and she blushed and said nothing.

The Queen smiled at her, as she was always tender for the lost and the confounded. "Listen, my dear," she said softly. "Love only those worthy of your love. Love those who love themselves, and love all around them. Love the best—the best in arms, the first in the hall, the finest harpist, and the best chess player. Love no man for what he owns, but only for what he does."

She smiled at all of them. And then pounced. "Are you pregnant, Mary?"

Mary shook her head. "I did not allow him that liberty, my lady."

The Queen reached out and took Mary's hand. "Well done. Ladies, remember—we award our love to those who deserve us. And our bodies are an even greater prize than our love—especially to the young." She looked at each in turn. "Who does not yearn for the strong yet tender embrace? Who does not sigh for skin soft as fine leather over muscles as hard as wood? But get with child—" she locked eyes with Mary, "—and they *will* call you a whore. And you may *die*, bearing that bastard. Or worse, perhaps; find yourself living meanly, rearing his bastard child, while he rides to glory." She looked at the window. "If you are not locked away in a convent."

Emmota raised her head. "But what of love?" she asked.

"Make your love a reward, not a raw emotion," the Queen said. "Any two rutting animals feel the emotion, child. Here, we are only interested in what is *best*. Rutting is not best. Do you understand?"

The girl swallowed carefully. "Yes, I think so," she said. "But then—why would we ever lie with any man?"

The Queen laughed aloud. "Artemis come to earth! Why, because it is for the love of us that they face terror, girl! Do you think it is some light thing to ride out into the Wild? To sleep with the Wild, eat with it, live with it? To face it and fight it and kill it?" The Queen leaned down until her nose almost touched the sharp point of Emmota's nose. "Do you think they do it for the good of humanity, my dear? Perhaps the older ones—the thoughtful ones. They face the dangers for us all because they have seen the alternative." She shook her head. "But the young ones face the foe for just one thing—to be deemed worthy of you, my dear. And you control *them*. When you let a knight into your lap you reward him for his courage. His prowess. His *worth*. You must judge that it has been earned. Yes? You understand?"

Emmota gazed into the eyes of her Queen with worship. "I understand," she said.

"The Old Men—the Archaics of long ago—they asked 'Who shall guard the guardians?'" The Queen looked around. "We shall, ladies. We choose the best of them. We may also choose to punish the worst. Hard Hands was not deserving, and the king found him out. We should have known first—should we not? Did none of you suspect he was merely a braggart? Did none of you wonder where his prowess lay, that he made no show or trial of it?"

Mary burst into tears. "I protest, madame."

The Queen gave her a small embrace. "I relent. He is a good man-at-arms. Let him go prove it to the king. And prove himself worthy of you."

Mary curtsied.

The Queen nodded, and rose to her feet. "I go to attend the king. Think of this. It is our duty. Love—our love—is no light thing. It is be the crown of glory, available to the best and only the best. It should be hard won. Think on it."

She listened to them she went up the stairs—broad marble stairs of that the Old Men had wrought. They didn't giggle, which pleased her.

The king was in the Arming Room, with two squires—Simon and Oggbert, as like as two peas in a pod, with matching freckles and matching pimples. He was down to his shirt and his hose and his braes. His leg harnesses still lay on the floor having been removed, and each squire held a vambrace, wiping them down with chamois.

She smiled radiantly at them. "Begone," she said.

They fled, as adolescent boys do when faced with beautiful women.

The king sat back on his bench. "Ah! I see I have won your esteem!" he grinned, and for a moment he was twenty years younger.

She knelt and undid a garter. "You are the king. You, and you alone, need never *win* my esteem."

He watched her unbuckle the other garter. She buckled the two of them together and placed his leg harnesses together on a table behind her, and then, without hurry, she sat in his lap and put her arms around his neck and kissed him until she felt him stir.

And then she rose to her feet and unlaced her gown. She did it methodically, carefully, without taking her eyes off him.

He watched her the way a wolf watches a lamb.

The gown fell away leaving her kirtle—a sheath of tight silk from ankle to neck.

The king rose. "Anyone might come in here," he said into her hair.

She laughed. "What care I?"

"On your head be it, lady," he said, and produced a knife. He pressed the flat of the point against the skin of her neck and kissed her, and then cut the lace of her kirtle from neck to waist, the knife so sharp that the laces seemed to fall away, and his cut so careful that the blade never touched her skin through the linen shift beneath it.

She laughed into his kiss. "I love it when you do that," she said. "You owe me a lace. A silk one." Her long fingers took the knife from him. She stepped back and cut the straps of her shift at her shoulders and it fell away and she stabbed the knife into the top of the table so that it stuck.

He rid himself of his shirt and braes with more effort and far less elegance, and she laughed at him. And then they were together.

When they were done, she lay on his chest. Some of his hair was grey. She played with it.

"I am old," he said.

She wriggled atop him. "Not so very old," she said.

"I owe you more than a kirtle lace of silk," he said.

"Really?" she asked, and rose above him. "Never mind the shift, love— Mary will replace the straps in an hour."

"I was not being so literal. I owe you my life. I owe you—my continued interest in this endless hell that is kingship." He grunted.

She looked down. "Endless hell—but you love it. You *love* it."

The king pulled her down and hid his face in her hair. "Not as much as I love you."

"What is it?" she asked, playing with his beard. "You are plagued by something ...?"

He sighed. "One of my favourite men left me today. Ranald Lachlan. Because he has to make himself a fortune in order to wed your Lady Almspend."

She smiled. "*He* is a worthy man, and he will prove himself or die trying."

The king sighed. "Yes," he said. "But by God, woman, I was tempted to give him a bag of gold and a knighthood to keep him by me."

"And you would have deprived him of the glory of earning his way," she said.

He shrugged and said, "It is good that one of us is an idealist."

"If you are in a giving mood," she said, "might we have a tournament?"

The king was a strong man with a fighter's muscles, and he sat up despite her weight on his chest. "A tournament. By God, lady—is that what this was in aid of?"

She grinned at him. "Was it so bad?"

He shook his head. "I should be very afraid, were you to decide to do something I didn't fancy, inside that pretty head. Yes, of course we can have a tournament. But the wrong men always win, and the town's a riot for a week, and the castle's a mess, you, my dear, are a mess, and I have

49

to arrest men whose only crime was to drink too much. All that, for your whim?" He laughed.

Desiderata laughed, throwing her head back, and she read his desire in his eyes. "Yes!" she said. "All that for my whim."

He laughed with her. And then frowned. "And there are the rumours from the north," he said.

"Rumours?" she asked. Knowing full well what they were—war and worse in the northlands, and incursions from the Wild. It was her business to know them.

The king shrugged. "Never mind, love. We shall have a tournament, but it may have to wait until after the spring campaign."

She clapped her hands. Spring was, at last, upon them.

Chapter Three

Lissen Carak—The Red Knight

A my's Hob managed to get his nag to a gallop for long enough to reach the Captain in good time. The company was stretched out along the road in march order—no wagons, no baggage, no followers. Those were in camp with a dozen lances as guards.

"Lord—Gelfred says he's found its earth. Away in the forest. Trail and hole." Amy's Hob was a little man with a nose that had been broken as often as he'd been outlawed.

The scout held up his hunting horn, and in it was a clod of excrement.

The fewmets, thought the captain, wrinkling his nose in distaste. Gelfred's revenge for his impiety—sometimes close adherence to the laws of venery could constitute their own revenge. He gave the scout a sharp nod. "I'll just take Gelfred's word for it, shall I?" he said. He stood in his stirrups and bellowed "Armour up, people!"

Word moved down the column faster than a galloping horse. Men and women laced their arming caps and donned their helmets—tall bassinets, practical kettle hats, or sturdy barbutes. Soldiers always rode out armed from head to foot—but only a novice or an overeager squire rode in his helmet or gauntlets. Most knights didn't don their helmets until they were in the face of the enemy.

Michael brought the captain's high-peaked helmet and held it high over his head to slide the mail aventail, the cape that protected the neck and depended from the lower rim of the helmet, over his shoulders. Then he seated the helmet firmly on the padded arming cap, visor pinned up.

The captain motioned for his squire to pause and reached up to pull the ends of his moustache clear of the mail. He was very proud of his moustache. It did a great deal to hide his age—or lack of it.

Then Michael adjusted the fall of the aventail over his breastplate, checked the buckles under his arms, and pushed the gauntlets on to his master's hands, one at a time, while the captain watched the road to the north.

"How far up the road?" he asked Hob.

"A little farther. We'll cross the burn and then follow it west into the trees."

He had the second gauntlet on, and Michael unbuckled the captain's riding sword and took his long war sword from Toby, who was standing between them on foot, holding it out, a look of excitement on his plain face and a biscuit in his free hand.

Michael handed the shorter riding sword down to Toby, and girded him with the sword of war. Three and a half pounds of sharp steel, almost four feet long.

The weight always affected the captain—that weight at his side meant business.

He looked back, standing a little in his stirrups, feeling the increased weight of his armour.

The column had tightened up.

"How far?" he asked Hob.

"A league. Less. Not an hour's walk." Hob shrugged. His hands were shaking.

"Standard front, then. At my word—Walk!" called the captain. He turned to his squire. "Whistle. Not the trumpet."

Michael understood. He had a silver whistle around his neck. Carlus, the giant trumpeter and company armourer, shrugged and fell back.

The column shifted forward, into a walk, the horses suddenly eager, ears pricked forward and heads up. The chargers quivered with excitement—the lighter ronceys ridden by the archers caught the bug from the bigger horses. Along the column, the less able riders struggled to control their mounts.

Up a long hill they went, and then back down—to a burn running fast with the water of two days' rain. Hob led them west into the trees.

Now that they were at the edge of the Wild, the captain had time to note that the trees were still nearly bare. Buds showed here and there, but the north country was not yet in spring, and snow lay in the lee of the larger rocks.

He could see a long way in these woods.

And that meant other things could see him, especially when he was resplendent in mirror-white armour, scarlet and gilt.

He led them on for another third of a league, the column snaking along behind him, two abreast, easily negotiating the sparse undergrowth. The trees were enormous, their branches thick and long, but stretching out high above even Bad Tom's head.

But when an inner sense said that he was courting disaster—*imagine that taloned monster in among this column before we were off our horses and ready*— he raised his right fist to signal a halt and then spread his arms—always good exercise, in armour—and waved them downwards, once. *Dismount.*

He dismounted carefully, to Grendel's disgust. Grendel liked a fight. Liked to feel the hot squirt of blood in his mouth.

Not this time, the captain thought, and patted his destrier's shoulder.

Toby came and took his head.

"Don't go wandering off, young Toby," the captain said cheerfully. "All officers."

Michael, already off his horse and collected, blew a whistle blast. Then handed the captain a short spear with a blade as long as a grown man's arm at one end and a sharp spike at the other.

Jehannes and Hugo and Milus walked up, their armour almost silent.

"Gelfred has the beast under observation. Less than a league away. I want a spread line, heavy on the wings, light in the loins, and every man-at-arms with an archer tight to his back." The captain glanced about.

"The usual, then," said Jehannes. His tone suggested that the captain should have said as much.

"The usual. Fill the thing full of arrows and get this done." This was not the right moment to spar with Jehannes, who was his best officer, and disapproved of him nonetheless. He looked around for inspiration.

"Thick woods," Jehannes said. "Not good for the archers."

The captain raised his hand. "Don't forget that Gelfred and two of our huntsmen are out there," he said. "Don't let's shoot them full of arrows, too."

The rear two-thirds of the column came forward in an orderly mob and rolled out to the north and south, forming a rough crescent two hundred ells long, in three rough ranks—knights in the front rank, squires in the middle, both men covering an archer to the rear. Some of the archers carried six-foot bows of a single stave, and some carried heavy crossbows, and a few carried eastern horn bows.

The captain looked at his skirmish line and nodded. His men really were good. He could see Sauce, off to the north, and Bad Tom beyond her. What else could they do? Be outlaws? He gave them purpose.

I like them, he thought. *All of them. Even Shortnose and Wilful Murder.*

He grinned, and wondered who he would be, if he had not found this.

"Let's get this done," he said aloud. Michael blew two sharp blasts, and they were moving.

He'd counted two hundred paces when Gelfred appeared off to his left. He waved both arms, and the captain lifted a fist, and the line shuffled to a halt. A single shaft, released by a nervous archer, rattled through the underbrush and missed the huntsman by an ell. Gelfred glared.

Milus spat. "Get his name," he growled. "Fucking new fuck."

Gelfred ran to the captain. "It's big," he said. "But not, I think, our quarry. It is—I don't know how to describe it. It's different. It's bigger." He shrugged. "I may be wrong."

The captain weighed this. Looked into the endless trees. Stands of evergreen and alder stood denser than the big, older oaks and ashes.

He could feel it. It knew they were there.

"It's going to charge us," the captain said. He spoke as flatly as he could, so as not to panic his men. "Stand ready," he called. *To hell with silence.*

Behind him, Michael's breathing grew louder.

Gelfred spanned his crossbow. He wasn't wearing armour. Once he had a bolt on the stock, he stepped into line behind Michael.

The captain reached up and lowered his visor, and it fell across his face with a loud *snap.*

And then his vision was narrowed to the two long slits in his faceplate, and the tiny breathing holes that also gave him his only warning of any motion coming from below. His own breath came back into his mouth, warmer than the air. The inside of the helmet was close, and he could taste his own fear.

Through the slits, the woods went on and on, although they seemed darker and stiller than before.

Even the breeze had died.

Silence.

No bird song.

No insect noise.

Michael's breathing inside his dog-faced Thuruvian helmet sounded like the bellows in a forge running full-out at a fair. *His first time,* the captain thought to himself.

The line was shuffling a little. Men changed their stances—the veterans all had heavy spears, or pole-axes, and they shifted their weight uneasily. The crossbowmen tried to aim. The longbowmen waited for a target before they drew. No man could hold a hundred-pound weight bow for long at the full draw.

The captain could feel their fear. He was sweating into his armingcote. When he shifted, cold air came in under his arms and his groin, but the hot sweat ran down his back. His hands were cold.

And he could feel the tension from his adversary.

Does it have nerves too? Fear? Does it think?

No birds sang.

Nothing moved.

The captain wondered if anyone was breathing.

"Wyvern!" shouted Bad Tom.

It exploded from the trees in front of the captain—taller than a war horse, the long, narrow head full of back-curved teeth, scales so dark that they appeared black, so polished they seemed to be oiled.

It was fast. The damned things always were.

Its wave of terror was a palpable thing, expanding like a soap bubble around it—the full impact of it struck the captain and washed over him to freeze Michael where he stood.

Gelfred raised his crossbow and shot.

His bolt hit something and the creature opened its maw and screeched until the woods and their ears alike rang with its anger.

The captain had time to take his guard, spear high, hands crossed, weight back on his right hip. His hands were shaking, and the heavy spearhead seemed to vibrate like a living thing.

It was coming right for him.

They always do.

He had a long heartbeat to look into its golden-yellow eyes, flecked with brown—the slitted black pupil, the sense of its *alienness.*

Other archers loosed. Most missed—taking panicked shots at ranges far closer than they had expected. But not all did.

It ran forward over the last few yards, its two powerful, taloned legs throwing up clods of earth as it charged the thin line of men, head low and forward, snout pointed at the captain's chest. Wings half open, beating the air for balance.

Gelfred was already spanning his crossbow, confident that his captain would keep him alive for another few heartbeats.

The captain shifted his weight and uncrossed his hands—launching the hardest, fastest swing in his repertoire. Cutting like an axe, the spearhead slammed into the wyvern's neck, into the soft skin just under the jaw, the cut timed so that the point stopped against the creature's jawbone...and its charge rammed it onto the point, pushing it deeper and then through the neck.

He had less than a heartbeat to savour the accuracy of his cut. Then the captain was knocked flat by a blow from its snout, his spear lodged deep in the thing's throat. Blood sprayed, and the fanged head forced itself down the shaft of his spear—past the cross guard, ripping itself open—to reach him. Its hate was palpable—it grew in his vision, its blood lashed him like a rain of acid, and its eyes—

The captain was frozen, his hands still on the shaft, as the jaws came for him.

Afraid.

But his spearhead had wide lugs at the base, for just such moments as this and the wyvern's head caught on them, just out of reach. He had a precious moment—recovered his wits, put his head down, breaking the gaze—

—as in one last gout of blood, it broke the shaft, jaws open and lunged—

The hardened steel of his helmet took the bite. He was surrounded by the smell of the thing—carrion, cold damp earth, hot sulphur, all at once. It thrashed, hampered by the broken spear in its gullet, trying to force its jaws wider and close on his head. He could hear its back-curved teeth scrape, ear-piercingly, over his helmet.

It gave a growl to make his helmet vibrate, tried to lift him and he could feel the muscles in his neck pull. He roared with pain and held hard to the projecting stump of the shaft as the only support he had. He could hear the battle cries—loud, or shrill, depending on the man. He could hear the meaty sounds of strikes—he could *feel* them—as men's weapons rained on the wyvern.

But the creature still had him. It tried to twist his head to break his neck, but its bite couldn't penetrate the helmet for a firmer grip. Its breath was all around him, suffocating him.

He got his feet beneath him and tried to control his panic as the wyvern lifted him clean from the ground. He got his right hand on his heavy rondel dagger—a spike of steel with a grip. With a scream of fear and rage, he slammed it blindly into the thing's head.

It spat him free and he dropped like a stone to the frozen ground. His dagger spun away, but he rolled, and got to his feet.

Drew his sword.

Cut. All before the wave of pain could strike him—he cut low to high off the draw, left to right across his body and into the joint behind the beast's leg.

It whirled and before he could react, the tusked snout punched him off his feet. Too fast to dodge. Then threw back its head and screamed.

Bad Tom buried his pole-axe in its other shoulder.

It reared away. A mistake. With two wounded limbs, it stumbled.

The captain got his feet under him, ignored the fire in his neck and back, and stood, powering straight forward, coming at it from the side this time. It turned to flatten Bad Tom, and Jehannes, suddenly in front of it, hit it on the breastbone with a war hammer. Its face was feathered with barbs and arrows. There were more in the sinuous neck. Even as it turned and took another wound, in the moment that the head was motionless it lost an eye to a long shaft, and its body thrashed—a squire was crushed by a flick of the wyvern's tail, his back breaking and armour folding under the weight of the blow.

Hugo crushed its ribs with a mighty, two-handed overhead blow. George Brewes stabbed it with a spear in the side and left the weapon there while he drew his sword. Lyliard cut overhand into the back of its other leg; Foliack hammered it with repeated strokes.

But it remained focused on the captain. It swatted at him with a leg, lost its balance, roared, and turned on Hugo who had just hit it again. It closed its jaws on the marshal's head, and his helmet didn't hold, The bite crushed his skull, killing him instantly. Sauce stepped over his headless corpse and planted her spear in its jaw, but it flung her away with a flick of the neck.

The captain leaped forward again and his sword licked out. This time, his cut took one of the thing's wings clean off its body, as easy as a practice cut on a sapling. As the head turned and struck at him the captain stood his ground, ready to thrust for the remaining eye—but the head collapsed to the earth a yard from him, almost like a giant dog laying his head down at his master's feet, and the baleful eye tracked him.

He thrust.

It whipped its head up, away from the point of the sword, reared, remaining wing spread wide and thrashing the men under it, a ragged banner of the Wild—

—and died, a dozen bolts and arrows catching it all together.

It fell across Hugo's corpse.

The men-at-arms didn't stop hacking at it for a long time. Jehannes severed the head, Bad Tom took one leg off at the haunch, and two squires got the other leg at the knee. Sauce rammed her long rondel into every joint, over and over. Archers continued to loose bolts and arrows into the prone mound of its corpse.

They were all covered in blood—thick, brown-green blood like the slime from the entrails of a butchered animal, hot to the touch, so corrosive that it could damage good armour if not cleaned off immediately.

"Michael?" the captain said. His head *felt* as if it had been pulled from his body.

The young man struggled to get his maille aventail over his head, failed, and threw up inside his helmet. But there was wyvern blood on his spear, and more on his sword.

Gelfred spanned his crossbow one more time, eyes fixed on the dead creature. Men were hugging, laughing, weeping, vomiting, or falling to their knees to pray, others merely gazed blank-eyed at the creature. The wyvern.

Already, it looked smaller.

The captain stumbled away from it, caught himself, mentally and physically. His arming cote was soaked. He went instantly from fight-hot to cold. When he stooped to retrieve his dagger, he had a moment's vertigo, and the pain from his neck muscles was so intense he wondered if he would black out.

Jehannes came up. He looked—old. "Six dead. Sweet William has his back broken and asks for you."

The captain walked the few feet to where Sweet William, an older squire in a battered harness, lay crumpled where the tail and hindquarters had smashed him flat and crushed his breastplate. Somehow, he was alive.

"We got it, aye?" he said thickly. "Was bra'ly done? Aye?"

57

The captain knelt in the mire by the dying man's head. "Bravely done, William."

"God be praised," Sweet William said. "It all hurts. Get it done, eh? Captain?"

The captain bent down to kiss his forehead, and put the blade of his rondel into an eye as he did, and held the man's head until the last spasm passed, before laying his head slowly in the mire.

He was slow getting back to his feet.

Jehannes was looking to where Hugo's corpse lay under the beast's head. He shook his head. Looked up, and met the captain's eye. "But we got it."

Gelfred was intoning plainchant over the severed head. There was a brief flare of light. And then he turned, disgust written plain on his face. He spat. "Wrong one," he said.

Jehannes spat. "Jesu shits," he said. "There's another one?"

North of Harndon—Ranald Lachlan

Ranald rode north with three horses—a heavy horse not much smaller than a destrier and two hackneys, the smallest not much better than a pony. He needed to make good time.

Because he needed to make good time he went hard all day and slept wherever he ended. He passed the pleasant magnificence of Lorica and her three big inns with regret, but it was just after midday and he had sun left in the sky.

He didn't have to camp, exactly. As the last rays of the sun slanted across the fields and the river to the west, he turned down a lane and rode over damp manured fields to a small stand of trees on a ridge overlooking the road. As he approached in the last light, he smelled smoke, and then he saw the fire.

He pulled up his horses well clear of the small camp, and called out, "Hullo!"

He hadn't seen anyone by the fire, and it was dark under the trees. But as soon as he called a man stepped from the shadows, almost by his horse's head. Ranald put his hand on his sword hilt.

"Be easy, stranger," said a man. An old man.

Ranald relaxed, and his horse calmed.

"I'd share my food with a man who'd share his fire," Ranald said.

The man grunted. "I've plenty of food. And I came up here to get away from men, not spend the night prattling." The old fellow laughed. "But bad cess on it—come and share my fire."

Ranald dismounted. "Ranald Lachlan," he said.

The old man grinned, his teeth white and surprisingly even in the last light. "Harold," he said. "Folk around here call me Harold the Forester, though its years since I was the forester." He slipped into the trees, leading Ranald's packhorse.

They ate rabbit—the old man had three of them, and Ranald wasn't so rude as to ask what warren they'd been born to. Ranald still had wine— good red wine from Galle, and the old man drank a full cup.

"Here's to you, my good ser," he said in a fair mockery of a gentleman's accent. "I had many a bellyful of this red stuff when I was younger."

Ranald lay back on his cloak. The world suddenly seemed very good to him, but he remained troubled that there were leaves piled up for two men to sleep, and that there were two blanket rolls on the edge of the fire circle, for one man. "You were a soldier, I suspect," he said.

"Chevin year, we was all soldiers, young hillman," Harold said. He shrugged. "But aye. I was an archer, and then a master archer. And then forester, and now—just old." He sat back against a tree. "It's cold for old bones. If you gave me your flask, I'd add my cider and heat it."

Ranald handed over his flask without demur.

The man had a small copper pot. Like many older veterans Ranald had known, his equipment was beautifully kept, and he found it without effort, even in the dark—each thing was where it belonged. He stirred his fire, a small thing now the rabbit was cooked, made from pine cones and twigs, and yet he had the drink hot in no time.

Ranald had one hand on his knife. He took the horn cup that was offered him, and while he could see the man's hands, he said "There was another man here."

Harold didn't flinch. "Aye," he said.

"On the run?" Ranald asked.

"Mayhap," said Harold. "Or just a serf who oughtn't to be out in the greenwood. And you with your Royal Guardsman's badge."

Ranald was ready to move. "I want no trouble. And I offer none," he said.

Harold relaxed visibly. "Well, he won't come back. But I'll see to it that the feeling is mutual. Have some more."

Ranald lay under his cloak without taking off his boots and laid his dirk by his side. Whatever he thought about the old man, there were plenty of men who would cut another's throat for three good horses. And he went to sleep.

Harndon—Edward

Thaddeus Pyel finished mixing the powder—saltpeter and charcoal and a little sulphur. Three to two to one, according to the alchemist who made the mixture for the king.

His apprentices were all around him, bringing him tools as he demanded them—a bronze pestle for grinding charcoal fine, spoons of various sizes to measure with.

He mixed the three together, carried the mixture outside into the yard, and touched a burning wick to them.

The mixture sputtered and burned, with a sulphurous smoke.

"Like Satan cutting a fart," muttered his son Diccon.

Master Pyel went back into his shop and mixed more. He varied the quantities carefully, but the result was always the same—a sputtering flame.

The boys were used to the master's little ways. He had his notions, and sometimes they worked, and other times they didn't. So they muttered in disappointment but not in surprise. It was a beautiful evening, and they went up on the workshop roof and drank small beer. Young Edward, the shop boy and an apprentice coming up on his journeyman qualification, stared at the rising moon and tried to imagine *exactly* what the burning powder did.

In all his imagings it was something to do with a weapon, because at the sign of the broken circle, that's what they did. They made weapons.

Albinkirk—Ser John Crayford

Ser John was taking exercise. Age and weight had not prevented him from swinging his sword at his pell—or at the other four men-at-arms who were still willing enough to join him.

Since the young sprig had ridden through with his beautifully armed company, the Captain of Albinkirk had been at the pell three times. His back hurt. His wrists hurt. His hands *burned*.

Master Clarkson, his youngest and best man-at-arms, backed out of range and raised his sword. "Well cut, Ser John," he said.

Ser John grinned, but only inside his visor where it wouldn't show. Just in that moment, all younger men were the enemy.

"Ser John, there's a pair of farmers to see you." It was the duty sergeant. Tom Lickspittle, Ser John called him, if only inside his visor. The man couldn't seem to do anything well except curry favour.

"I'll see them when I'm done here, Sergeant." Ser John was trying to control his breathing.

"I think you'll want to—to see them now." *That was new.* Lickspittle Tom never questioned orders. The man gulped. "My lord."

That makes this some sort of emergency.

Ser John walked over to his latest squire, young Harold, and got his visor lifted and his helmet removed. He was suddenly ashamed of his armour—brown on many surfaces, or at least the mail was. His cote armour was covered in what had once been good velvet. How long ago had that been?

"Clean that mail," he said to Harold. The boy winced, which suited Ser John's mood well. "Clean the helmet, and find me an armourer. I want this recovered in new cloth."

"Yes, Ser John." The boy didn't meet his eye. Lugging armour around the Lower Town would be no easy task.

Ser John got his gauntlets off and walked across the courtyard to the guard room. There were two men—prosperous men; wool cotes, proper hose; one in all the greys of local wool, one in a dark red cote.

"Gentlemen?" he asked. "Pardon my armour."

The man in the dark red cote stood forward. "Ser John? I'm Will Flodden and this is my cousin John. We have farms on the Lissen Carak road."

Ser John relaxed. This was not a complaint about one of his garrison soldiers.

"Go on," he said, cheerfully.

"I kilt an irk, m'lord," said the one called John. His voice shook when he said it.

Ser John had been a number of places. He knew men, and he knew the Wild. "Really?" he said. He doubted it, instinctively.

"Aye," said the farmer. He was defensive, and he looked at his cousin for support. "There was tre of 'em. Crossing my fields." He hugged himself. "An' one loosed at me. I ran for ta' house, an' picked up me latchet and let fly. An' tey ran."

Ser John sat a little too suddenly. Age and armour were not a good mix.

Will Flodden sighed. "Just show it to him." He seemed impatient—a farmer who wanted to get back to his farm.

Before he even undid the string securing the sack, Ser John knew what he was going to see. But it all seemed to take a long time. The string unwinding, the upending of the sack. The thing in the sack had stuck to the coarse fabric.

For as long as it took, he could tell himself that the man was wrong. He'd killed an animal. A boar with an odd head, or some such.

But twenty years before Ser John had stood his ground with thousands of other men against a charge of ten thousand irks. He remembered it too damned well.

"Jesus wept. Christe and the Virgin stand with us," he said.

It was an irk, its handsome head somehow smaller and made ghastly having been severed from its sinuous body.

"Where, exactly?" he demanded. And turning, he ignored Tom Lick-spittle, who was a useless tit in a crisis. "Clarkson! Sound the alarm and get me the mayor."

Patience had never been the captain's greatest virtue, and he paced the great hall of the convent, up and back, up and back, his anger ebbing and flowing as he gained and lost control of himself. He suspected that the Abbess was keeping him waiting on purpose; he understood her motives, he read her desire to humble him and keep him off guard; and despite knowing that he was angry, and thus off guard.

Gradually, frustration gave way to boredom.

He had time to note that the stained glass of the windows in the clerestory had missing panels—some replaced in clear glass, and some in horn, and one in weathered bronze. The bright sunlight outside, the first true sign of spring, made the rich reds and blues of the glass glow, but the missing panes were cast into sharp contrast—the horn was too dull, the clear glass too bright, the metal almost black and sinister.

He stared at the window depicting the convent's patron saint, Thomas, and his martyrdom, for some time.

And then boredom and annoyance broke his meditation and he began to pace again.

His second bout of boredom was lightened by the arrival of two nuns in the grey habit of the order, but they had their kirtles on, open at the neck and with their sleeves rolled up. Both had heavy gloves on, tanned faces, and they bore an eagle on a perch between them.

An *eagle*.

Both of them bowed politely to the captain and left him with the bird.

The captain waited until they were clear of the hall and then walked over to the bird, a dark golden brown with the dusting of lighter colour that marked a fully mature bird.

"Maybe a little too fully mature, eh, old boy?" he said to the bird, who turned his hooded head to the sound of the voice, opened his beak, and said "*Raawwk!*" in a voice loud enough to command armies.

The bird's jesses were absolutely plain where the captain, who had been brought up with rich and valuable birds, would have expected to see embroidery and gold leaf. This was a Ferlander Eagle, a bird worth—

—worth the whole value of the captain's white harness, which was worth quite a bit.

The eagle was the size of his entire upper body, larger than any bird his father—the captain sneered internally at the thought of the man—had ever owned.

"*Raaaawk!*" the bird screamed.

The captain crossed his arms. Only a fool released someone else's bird—especially when that bird was big enough to eat the fool—but his fingers itched to handle it, to feel its weight on his fist. Could he even fly such a bird?

Is this another of her little games?

After another interval of waiting, he couldn't stand it any more. He pulled on his chamois gloves and brushed the back of his hand against the talons of the bird's feet. It stepped obligingly onto his wrist and it weighed as much as a pole-axe. More. His arm sank, and it was an effort to raise the bird back to eye level and place it back on its perch.

When it had one foot secure on the deerskin-padded perch, it turned its hooded head to him, as if seeing him clearly, and closed its left foot, sinking three talons into his left arm.

Even as he gasped, it stepped up onto its perch and turned to face him.

"Rawwwwwwwk," it said with obvious satisfaction.

Blood dripped over his gauntlet cuff.

He looked at the bird. "Bastard," he said. And he went back to pacing, albeit he now cradled his left arm in his right for twenty trips up and down the hall.

His third bout of boredom was broken by the books. He'd given them only a cursory glance on his first visit, and had dismissed them. They displayed the usual remarkable craftsmanship, superb calligraphy, painted scenes, gilt work everywhere. Worse, both volumes were collections of the *Lives of the Saints*, a subject in which the captain had no interest whatsoever. But boredom drove him to look at them.

The leftmost work, beneath the window of Saint Maurice, was well-executed, the paintings of Saint Katherine vivid and rich. He chuckled to wonder what lovely model had stood in a monk's mind, or perhaps a nun's, as the artist lovingly re-created the contours of flesh. Saint Katherine's face did not show torment, but a kind of rapture—

He laughed and passed to the second book, pondering the lives of the devout.

What struck him first was the poor quality of the Archaic. The art was beautiful—the title page had a capital where the artist was presented, sitting on a high stool, working away with a gilding brush. The work was so precise that the reader could see that the artist was working on the very title page, presented again in microcosm.

The captain breathed deeply in appreciation of the work, and the humour of it. And then he began to read.

He turned the page. He imagined what his beloved Prudentia would have said about the barbaric nature of the writer's Archaic. He could all but see the old nun wagging her finger in his mother's solar.

Shook his head.

The door to the Abbess's private apartments opened and the priest, hurried past, hands clasped together and face set. He looked furious.

Behind him, the Abbess gave a low laugh, almost a snort. "I thought you'd find our book," she said. She looked at him fondly. "And my *Parcival.*" She indicated the bird.

"I can't see how such a brutally bad transcription merited the quality of artist," he said, turning another page. "If that's your bird, you are braver than I thought."

"Am I?" she asked. "I've had him for many years." She looked fondly at the bird, who bated on his perch. "Can you not see why the book is so well wrought?" she asked with a smile that told him that there was a secret to it. "You do know that we have a library, Captain? I believe that our hospitality might extend as far as allowing you to use it. We have more than fifty volumes."

He bowed. "Would I shock you if I said that the *Lives of the Saints* held little interest for me?"

She shrugged. "Posture away, little atheist. My gentle Jesu loves you all the same." She gave him a wry smile. "I am sorry—I would love to spar with you all morning, but I have a crisis in my house. May we to business?" She waved him to a stool. "Still in armour," she said.

"We are still on the hunt," he said, crossing his legs.

"But you killed the monster. Don't think we are not grateful. In fact, I regret taking the tone I did, especially as you lost a man of great worth, and since you were so very effective." She shrugged. "And you have done your work before the new month—and before my fair opens."

He made a sour face. "My lady, I would like to deserve your esteem, and few things would give me greater pleasure than to hear you apologise." He shrugged. "But I am not here to spar, either. Unworthily, I assumed you kept me cooling my heels to teach me humility."

She looked at her hands. "You could use some, young man, but unfortunately, I have other issues before me this day or I would be happy to teach you some manners. Now, why do you say you do not deserve my regard?"

"We have killed a monster," he acknowledged. "But not the one that killed Sister Hawisia."

She jutted out her jaw—a tic he hadn't seen before. "I must assume that you have ways to know this. You must pardon me if I am sceptical. We have *two* monsters? I remember your saying the enemy seldom hunts alone this far from the Wild—but surely, Captain, you know that we are not as far from the Wild as we once were."

He wished for a chair with a back. He wished that Hugo were alive, and he hadn't been saddled with internal issues of discipline that should have been Hugo's. "May I have a glass of wine?" he asked.

The Abbess had a stick, and she thumped it on the floor. Amicia entered, eyes downcast. The Abbess smiled at her. "Wine for the captain, dear. And do not raise your eyes, if you please. Good girl."

Amicia slipped out the door again.

"My huntsman is a Hermetic," he said. "With a licence from the Bishop of Lorica."

She waved a hand. "The orthodoxy of Hermeticism is beyond my poor intellect. Do you know, when I was a girl, we were forbidden to use High Archaic for any learning beyond the *Lives of the Saints*. I was punished by my chaplain as a girl for reading some words on a tomb in my father's castle." She sighed. "You read the Archaic, then," she said.

"High and low," he answered.

"I thought as much... and there cannot be so many knights in the Demesne who can read High Archaic." She made a motion with her head, as if shaking off fatigue. Amicia returned, brought the captain wine and backed away from him without ever raising her eyes—a very graceful performance.

She wore that curious expression again. The one he couldn't read—it held both anger and amusement, patience and frustration, all in one corner of her mouth.

The Abbess had taken Parcival the eagle on her wrist, and she was stroking his plumage and cooing at him. While the arm of her throne-like chair helped support the great raptor, the captain was impressed by her strength. *She must be sixty*, he thought.

There was something about the Abbess—the Abbess and Amicia. It was not a similarity of breeding—two more different women could not be imagined, the older woman with an elfin beauty and slim bones, the younger taller, heavier boned, with strong hands and broad shoulders.

He was still staring at Amicia when the Abbess's staff thumped the floor.

The word *hermetic* rolled around the captain's busy brain, and curled itself in the corner of Amicia's mouth. But the staff took his attention.

"Assuming I believe you—what does your huntsman say?" the Abbess demanded.

The captain sighed. "That we got the wrong one. My lady, no one but a great Magus or a mountebank can tell us *why* the enemy acts as they do. Perhaps one of them is calling to others for reinforcements. Perhaps you have a nest of them. But Gelfred assures me that the signs left by Sister Hawisia's killer are *not* the same as those of the beast we slew and my men—all of them—are exhausted. It will take them a day to recover. They've lost a gallant leader, a man they all respected, so I am sorry, but we will not be very aggressive for a few days." He shrugged.

She looked at him for a long time, and finally crossed her hands on the top of her staff and laid her long chin on them. "You think I do not understand," she said. She shrugged. "I do. I do not believe you seek to cheat me."

He didn't know what to make of that.

"Let me tell you my immediate concerns," she said. "My fair opens in a week. The first week of the fair is merely local produce and prizes. Then the

Harndon merchants come upriver in the second week to buy our surplus grain and our wool. But in the second and third weeks of the fair, the drovers come down from the moors. That is when the business is done, and that's when I need my bridge and my people to be safe. You know why there is a fortress here?" she asked.

He smiled. "Of course," he said. "The fortress is merely to guarantee the bridge."

"Yes," she admitted. "And I have been lax in letting my garrison drop—' but if you will pardon an old woman's honesty, soldiers and nuns are not natural friends. Yet these attacks—I hold this land by knight service and garrison service, and I do not have enough men. The king will send a knight to dispense justice at the fair and I dread his discovering how my penny-pinching ways have put these lands at risk."

"You need me for more than just monster-hunting," he said.

"I do. I would like to purchase your contract for the summer, and I wonder if you have a dozen men-at-arms—archers, even—who could stay when you go. Perhaps men you'd otherwise pension off, or men who've been wounded." She shrugged. "I don't even know how to *find* a new garrison. Albinkirk used to be a fine town—and a place where such men could be found—but not anymore." She took a deep breath.

He nodded. "I will consider it. I will not pretend, since we are being honest with each other, that my company does not need a steady contract. I would like to recruit, too. I need men." He thought a moment. "Would you want women?"

"Women?" asked the Abbess.

"I have women—archers, men-at-arms." He smiled at her chagrin. "It's not so uncommon as it once was. It is almost accepted over the sea, on the Continent."

She shook her head. "I think not. What kind of women would they be? Slatterns and whores taught to fight? Scarcely fit companions for women of religion."

"You have a good point, my lady. I'm sure they are far less fit as companions then the sort of *men* who are attracted to a mercenary company." He leaned back, stretching his legs to ease the pressure on his lower back.

Their eyes met, sharp as two blades crossed.

She shrugged. "We are not adversaries. Rest if you must. Consider my offer. Do you need a service for the dead?"

For the first time, he allowed himself to feel warmth for the lady Abbess. "That would be greatly appreciated."

"Not all your men reject God as you do?" she said.

"Much the opposite." He rose to his feet. "Soldiers are as inclined to nostalgic irrationality as any other group—perhaps more so." He winced. "I'm sorry my lady, that was rude, in response to your very kind offer. We have no chaplain. Ser Hugo was a gentleman of good family who died in ✦

his faith, whatever you may think of me. A service for the dead would be very kind of you, and would probably do much to keep my people in order—ahem." He shook his head. "I appreciate your offer."

"You are really quite sweet in your well-mannered confusion," she said, also rising. "We will get along well enough, Ser Captain. And you will, I hope, forgive me if I counter your blatant lack of respect for my religion with an attempt to convert you to it. Whatever has been done to you, it was not Jesu who did it, but the hand of man."

He bowed. "That's just where you are wrong, my lady." He reached for her hand, which she offered, to kiss—but the imp in him could not be stopped, and so he turned it over and kissed her palm like a lover.

"Such a little boy," she said, but she was clearly both pleased and amused. "A rather wicked boy. Service tonight, I think, in the chapel."

"You will allow my company into the fortress?" he asked.

"Since I intend to employ you as my garrison," she replied, "I will, in time, have to trust you inside the walls."

"This is a sharp change of direction, my lady Abbess," he said.

She nodded and swept towards the inner door to the convent. "Yes it is," she said. She gave him a very straight-backed courtesy. "I know things, now."

He stopped her with his hand. "You said the Wild is closer now. I've been away. Closer how?"

She released a breath. "We have twenty farms which we have taken from the trees. There are more families here than when I was first a novice—more families. And yet. When I was young, nobles hunted the Wild in the mountains—expeditions into the Adacrags were a knight errant's dream. The convent used to host them in our guest house." She glanced out the window. "The border with the Wild used to be fifty leagues or more to the north and the west of us, and while the forest was deep, trustworthy men lived there." She met his eyes. "Now, my fortress is the border, as it was in my grandfather's time."

He shook his head. "The wall is two hundred leagues north of here. And as far west."

She shrugged. "The Wild is not. The king was going to push the Wild back to the wall," she said wearily. "But I gather his young wife takes all his time."

He smiled. And changed the subject. "Tell me what the book is?" he asked.

She smiled. "You will enjoy puzzling it out for yourself," she said. "I wouldn't want to deny you that pleasure."

"You are a wicked old woman," he said.

"Ah," she smiled. "You are beginning to know me, messire." She smiled, all flirtation, and then paused. "Captain, I have decided to tell you something," she said. She wasn't hestitant. She was merely careful. "About Sister Hawisia."

He didn't move.

"She told me that we had a traitor in our midst. And that she would unmask him. I was supposed to be at the farm that day. She insisted on going in my place." The Abbess looked away. "I'm afraid that monster was meant for me."

"Or your brave sister unmasked the traitor and he killed her for it. Or he already knew she intended to unmask him, and set a trap." The captain hadn't shaved in days, and he scratched absently under his chin. "Who knows of your movements and decisions, my lady?"

She sat back. Her staff smacked against the floor in real agitation. Their eyes met.

"I am on your side," he said.

She was fighting tears. "They are *my people*," she said. She bit her lip and gave her head a shake that moved the fine linen folds of her wimple. "Bah—I am not a schoolgirl. I will have to think, and perhaps look at my notes. Sister Miram is my vicar, and I trust her absolutely. Father Henry attends me at most hours. Sister Miram has access to everything in the fortress and knows most of my thoughts. John le Bailli is my factor in the villages and the king's officer for the Senechally. I will arrange that you meet them all."

"And Amicia," the captain said quietly.

"Yes. She attends me at most hours." The Abbess's eyes locked with the captain's. "She and Hawisia were not friends."

"Why not?" asked the knight.

"Hawisia was gently born, nobly born. She had great power." The Abbess looked out the window, and her bird bated slightly at her movement.

"Put him back on his perch, please?" she asked.

The knight collected the great bird on his fist and transferred his great weight to the perch. "Surely he is a royal bird?"

"I had a royal friend, once," said the Abbess, with a curl of her lips.

"And Amicia is not gently born?" the Red Knight prodded.

The Abbess met his glance and rose. "I will leave you to make such enquiries yourself," she said. "I find that I am uninterested in gossiping about my people."

"I have angered you," said the knight.

"Messire, creatures of the Wild are killing my people, one of them is a traitor and I have to hire sell-swords to protect me. Today *everything* angers me."

She opened the door, and he had a glimpse of Amicia, and then the door closed behind her.

Given an unexpected moment of freedom, he walked to the book. It stood under a window of Saint John the Baptist so he began to turn the pages, looking for the saint's story.

The Archaic was painful, stilted, ill-phrased, as if a schoolgirl had translated the Archaic to Gothic and then back, making grievous errors in both directions.

The calligraphy was inhuman in its perfection. In ten pages, he could not find a pen error. Who would labour so over such a bad book?

The secret of the book merged in his mind with the secret that hid in the corner of Alicia's downturned mouth, and he began to look more carefully at the lavish illuminations.

Facing the tale of Saint Paternus was a complex illustration of the saint himself, in robes of red, white and gold. His robes were richly embellished, and in one hand he held a cross.

In the other hand he held an alembic instead of an orb, and inside the alembic were minute figures of a man and a woman...

The captain looked back to the Archaic, trying to find the trace of a reference—was it heresy?

He stood up, releasing the vellum cover. *Heresy is none of my concern*, he thought. Besides—whatever that smug old woman was, she was no secret heretic. He walked slowly across the hall, his sabatons clinking faintly as he walked, and his mind still on the problem of the book. *She was right, damn her*, he thought.

Heading North—A Golden Bear

The mother bear swam until she could no longer swim, and then she lay up all day, cold to the bone and weary from blood loss and despair. Her cub sniffed at her and demanded food, and she forced herself to move to find some. She killed a sheep in a field and they fed on it; then she found a line of bee-hives at the edge of another field and they ate their way through the whole colony, eight hives, until both bears were sticky and drunk on sugar. She licked raw honey into the wounds the sword had made. Men were born without talons, but the claws they forged for themselves were deadlier than anything the Wild might give them.

She sang for her daughter, and called her name.

And her cub mewed like an animal.

When Lily was stronger, they went north again. That night, she smelled the pus in her wounds. She licked it and it tasted bad.

She tried to think of happier days—of her mate, Russet, and her mother's den in the distant mountains. But her slavery had gone on too long, and something was dimmed in her.

She wondered if her wound was mortal. If the warrior man had poisoned his claw.

They lay up another day and she caught fish, no kind she recognised, but something that tasted a little of salt. She knew that the great Ocean was salted, perhaps the river had a spring run of sea fish.

They were easy to catch, even for a wounded bear.

There were more hives at a field edge, whose outraged human guard lofted arrows at them from his stone croft. None of them struck home, and they slipped away.

She had no idea where she was, but her spirit said to go north. And the river flowed from her home, she could taste the icy spring run off. So she kept moving north.

The Great North Road—Gerald Random

Gerald Random, Merchant Adventurer of Harndon, looked back along the line of his wagons with the satisfaction of the captain for his company, or the Abbot for his monks. He'd mustered twenty-two wagons of his own, all in his livery colours, red and white, their man-high wheels carefully painted with red rims and white spokes; the sides of every wagon white with red trim, and scenes from the Passion of the Christ decorating every side panel, all the work of his very talented brother-in-law. It was good advertising, good religion, and it guaranteed that his carters would always form his convoy in order—every man, whether they could not read or figure or not, knew that the God Jesu was scourged by knights in their guard room, and *then* had to carry his own cross to Golgotha.

He had sixty good men, mostly drapers' and weavers' men, but a pair of journeymen goldsmiths and a dozen cutlers, and some bladesmiths and blacksmiths, a handful of mercers and grocers too, all armed and well armoured like the prosperous men they were. And he had ten professional soldiers he'd engaged himself, acting as his own captain—good men, every one of them with a King's Warrant that he had borne arms in the king's service.

Gerald Random had such a warrant himself. He'd served in the north, fighting the Wild. And now he was leading a rich convoy to the great market fair of Lissen Carak as the commander, the principle investor, and the owner of most of the wagons.

His should be the largest convoy on the road and the best display at the fair.

His wife Angela laid a long white hand on his arm. "You find your wagons more beautiful than you find me," she said. He wished that she might say it with more humour, but at least there *was* humour.

He kissed her. "I've yet time to prove otherwise, my lady," he said.

"The future Lord Mayor does not take his wife for a ride in the bed-carriage while his great northern convoy awaits his pleasure!" she said. She rubbed his arm through his heavy wool doublet. "Dinna' fash yourself, husband. I'll be well enough."

Guilbert, the oldest and most reliable-looking of the hireling swords-men, approached with a mixture of deference and swagger. He nodded—a compromise between a bow and a failure to recognise authority. Random took it to mean something like *I have served great lords and the king, and while you are my commander, you are not one of them.*

Random nodded.

"Now that I see the whole convoy," Guilbert nodded at it. "I'd like six more men."

Random looked back over the wagons—his own, and those of the gold-smiths, the cutlers, the two other drapers, and the foreign merchant, Master Haddan, with his tiny two wheel cart and his strange adult apprentice, Adle. Forty-four wagons in all.

"Even with the cutlers' men?" he asked. He kept his wife there by taking her hand when she made to slip away.

Guilbert shrugged. "They're fair men, no doubt," he said.

Wages for six more men—Warrant men—would cost him roughly the whole profit on one wagon. And the sad fact was that he couldn't really pass any part of the cost on to the other merchants, who had already paid—and paid well—to be in his convoy.

Moreover, he had served in the north. He knew the risks. And they were high—higher every year, although no one seemed to want to discuss such stuff.

He looked at his wife, contemplating allowing the man two more soldiers.

He loved his wife. And the worry on her face was worth spending more than the value of a cart to alleviate. And what would the profit be, should his convoy be taken or scattered?

"Do you have a friend? Someone you can engage at short notice?" he asked.

Guilbert grinned. It was the first time that the merchant had seen the mercenary smile, and it was a surprisingly human, pleasant smile.

"Aye," the man said. "Down on his luck. I'd esteem it a favour. And he's a good man—my word on it."

"Let's have all six. Eight, if we can get them. I have a worry, so let's be safe. Money is not all there is," he said, looking into his wife's eyes, and she breathed out pure relief. Some dark omen had been averted.

He hugged her for a long time while apprentices and journeymen kept their distance, and when Guilbert said he needed an hour by the clock to get his new men into armour—meaning they'd pawned theirs and needed to redeem it—Random took his wife by the hand and took her upstairs. Because there were so *many* things that were more important than money.

But the sun was still in the middle of the spring sky when forty-five wagons, two hundred and ten men, eighteen soldiers, and one merchant captain started north for the fair. He knew that he was the ninth convoy on the great road north—the longest to assemble, and consequently, the last that would reach Lissen Carak's great supply of grain. But he had the goods and the wagons to buy *so much* grain that he didn't think he'd be the loser, and he had a secret—a trade secret—that might make him the greatest profit in the history of the city.

It was a risk. But surprisingly for a man of money, as the lords called his kind, Gerald Random loved risk as other men loved money, or swords, or women, and he set his sword at his hip, his dagger on the other, with a round steel buckler that would not have disgraced a nobleman, and smiled. Win or lose, this was the moment he loved. Starting out. The dice cast, the adventure beginning.

He raised his arm, and he heard the sounds of men responding. He sent a pair of the mercenaries forward, and then he let his arm fall. "Let's go!" he called.

Whips cracked, and animals leaned into their loads, and men waved goodbye to sweethearts and wives and children and brats and angry creditors, and the great convoy rolled away with creaking wheels and jingling harness and the smell of new paint.

And Angela Random knelt before her icon of the Virgin and wept, the tears as hot as her passion of an hour before.

Lissen Carak—The Red Knight

Seven men had died fighting the wyvern. The corpses were wrapped in plain white shrouds because that was the rule of the Order of Saint Thomas, and they gave off a sickly sweet smell—corruption and zealous use of sweet herbs, and bitter myrrh burned in the censors that hung in the front of the chapel.

The whole fighting strength of his company stood in the nave, shifting uneasily as if facing an unexpected enemy. They wore no armour, bore no weapons, and some were very ill-dressed; not a few wore their arming cotes with mail voiders because they had no other jacket, and at least one man was bare-legged and ashamed. The captain was plainly dressed in black hose and a short black jupon that fitted so tightly that he couldn't bend over—his last decent garment from the Continent. His only nod to his status was the heavy belt of linked gold and bronze plaques around his hips.

Their apparent penury contrasted with the opulence of the chapel—even with the shrines and crosses swathed in purple for Lent, or perhaps the more so *because* the purple of Lent was so rich. Except that nearer to hand, the captain could see the edge of a reliquary peaking out from beneath its silken shroud, the gilt old and crazed, the wood broken. Tallow, not wax, burned in every sconce except the altar candelabra, and the smell of burning fat was sharp against the sweet and the bitter.

The captain noted that Sauce wore a kirtle and a gown. He hadn't seen her dressed as a woman since her first days with the company. The gown was fine, a foreign velvet of ruddy amber, somewhat faded except for one diamond shaped patch on her right breast.

Where her whore's badge was sewn, he thought. He glared at the crucified figure over the altar, his pleasant, detached mood destroyed. *If there is a god, how can he allow so much fucking misery and deserve my thanks for it?* The captain snorted.

Around him the company sank to their knees as the chaplain, Father Henry, raised the consecrated host. The captain kept his eyes on the priest, and watched him throughout the ritual that elevated the bread to the sacred body of Christ—even surrounded by his mourning company, the captain had to sneer at the foolishness of it. He wondered if the stick-thin priest believed a word of what he was saying—wondered idly if the man was driven insane by the loneliness of living in a world of women, or if he was consumed by lust instead. Many of the sisters were quite comely, and as a soldier, the captain knew that comeliness was in the eye of the beholder and directly proportionate to the length of time since one's last leman. Speaking of which—

He happened to catch Amicia's eye just then. He wasn't looking at her—he was very consciously not looking at her, not wanting to appear weak, smitten, foolish, domineering, vain...

He had a long list of things he was trying not to appear.

Her sharp glance said, *Don't be so rude—Kneel,* so clearly he almost felt he had heard the words said aloud.

He knelt. She had a point—good manners had more value than pious mouthing. If that was her point. If she had, indeed, even looked at him.

Michael stirred next to him, risked a glance at him. The captain could see that his squire was smiling.

Beyond him, Ser Milus was trying to hide a smile as well.

They want me to believe. Because my disbelief threatens their belief, and they need solace.

The service rolled on as the sun flared its last, nearly horizontal beams throwing brilliant coloured light from the stained glass across the white linen shrouds of the dead.

Dies iræ! dies illa
Solvet sæclum in favilla:
Teste David cum Sibylla!

The coloured light grew—and every soldier gasped as the blaze of glory swept across the bodies.

Tuba, mirum spargens sonum
Per sepulchra regionum,
Coget omnes ante thronum.

It's a trick of the light, you superstitious fools! He wanted to shout it aloud. And at the same time, he felt the awe just as they did—felt the increase in his pulse. *They hold the service at this hour to take advantage of the sun and those windows,* he thought. *Although it would be very difficult to time the whole service to arrange it,* he admitted to himself. *And the sun cannot be at the right angle very often.*

Even the priest had stumbled in the service.

Michael was weeping. He was scarcely alone. Sauce was weeping and so was Bad Tom. He was saying "Deo gratias" over and over again through his tears, his rough voice a counterpoint to Sauce's.

When it was all done, the knights of the company bore the corpses on litters made from spears, out of the chapel and back down the hill to bury them in the consecrated ground by the shrine at the bridge.

Ser Milus came and put his hand on the captain's shoulder—a rare familiarity—and nodded. His eyes were red.

"I know that cost you," he said. "Thanks."

Jehannes grunted. Nodded. Wiped his eyes on the back of his heavy firze cote sleeve. Spat. Finally met his eye too. "Thanks," he said.

The captain just shook his head. "We still have to bury them," he said. "They remain dead."

The procession left by the chapel's main door, led by the priest, but the Abbess was the focal point, now in severe and expensive black with a glittering crucifix of black onyx and white gold. She nodded to him and he gave her a courtly bow in return. The perfection of the Abbess's black habit with its eight-pointed cross contrasted with the brown-black of the priest's voluminous cassock over his cadaver-thin body. And the captain could smell the tang of the man's sweat as he passed. He was none too clean, and his smell was spectacular when compared with the women.

The nuns came out behind their Abbess. Virtually all of the cloister had come to the service, and there were more than sixty nuns, uniform in their slate grey habits with the eight pointed cross of their order. Behind them came the novices—another sixty women in paler grey, some of a more worldly cut, showing their figures, and others less.

They wore grey and it was twilight, but the captain had no difficulty picking out Amicia. He turned his head away in time to see an archer known as Low Sym make a gesture and give a whistle.

The captain suddenly felt his sense of the world restored. He smiled.

"Take that man's name," he said to Jehannes... "Ten lashes, disrespect."

"Aye, milord." Marshal Jehannes had his hand on the man's collar before the captain had taken another breath. Low Sym—nineteen, and no woman's friend—didn't even thrash. He knew a fair cop when he felt one.

"Which I was—" he began, and saw the captain's face. "Aye, Captain."

But the captain's eyes rested on Amicia. And his thoughts went elsewhere.

The night passed in relaxation, and to soldiers, relaxation meant wine.

Amy's Hob was still abed, and Daud the Red was fletching new arrows for the company and admitted to being "poorly," company slang for a hangover so bad it threatened combat effectiveness. Such a hangover would be punishable most days—the day after they buried seven men was not one of them.

The camp had its own portable tavern run by the Grand Sutler, a merchant who paid the company a hefty fee to ride along with his wagons and skim their profits when they had some to share. He, in turn, bought wine and ale from the fortress's stores, and from the town at the foot of Lissen Carak—four streets of neat stone cottages and shop fronts nestled inside the lower walls and called "The Lower Town." But the Lower Town was open to the company as well, and its tavern, hereabouts known as the Sunne in Splendour, was serving both in its great common room and out in the yard. The inn was doing a brisk business, selling a year's worth of ale in a few hours. Craftsmen were locking up their children.

That was not the captain's problem. The captain's problem was that Gelfred was planning to venture back to the tree line alone, while the captain had no intention of risking his most valuable asset without protection. And no protection was available.

Gelfred stood in the light rain outside his tent, swathed in a three-quarter length cloak, thigh high boots and a heavy wool cap. He tapped his stick impatiently against his boot.

"If this rain keeps up, we'll never find the thing again," he said.

"Give me a quarter hour to find us some guards," the captain snapped.

"A quarter hour we may not have," Gelfred said.

The captain wandered through the camp, unarmoured and already feeling ill-at-ease with his decision to dress for comfort. But he, too, had drunk too much and too late the night before. His head hurt, and when he looked into the eyes of his soldiers, he knew that he was in better shape than most. Most were still drinking.

He'd paid them. It improved his popularity and his authority, but it gave them the wherewithal to be drunk.

So they were.

Jehannes was sitting in the door of his pavilion.

"Hung over?" the captain asked.

Jehannes shook his head. "Still drunk," he answered. Raised a horn cup. "Want some?"

The captain mimed a shudder. "No. I need four sober soldiers—preferably men-at-arms."

Jehannes shook his head again.

The captain felt the warmth go from his heart to his cheeks. "If they are drunk on guard, I'll have their heads," he growled.

Jehannes stood up. "Best you don't go check, then."

The captain met his eye. "Really? That bad?" he said it mildly enough, but his anger came through.

"You don't want them to think you don't give a shit, do you, *Captain?*" Jehannes had no trouble holding his eye, although the marshal's were bloodshot and red. "This is not the moment to play at discipline, eh?"

The captain sat on an offered stool. "If something comes out of the Wild right now, we're all dead."

Jehannes shrugged. "So?" he asked.

"We're better than this," the captain said.

"Like fuck we are," Jehannes said, and took a deep drink. "What are you playing at? *Ser?*" He laughed grimly. "You've taken a company of broken men and made something of them—and now you want them to act like the Legion of Angels?"

The captain sighed. "I'd settle for the Infernal Legion. I'm not particular." He got to his feet. "But I will have discipline."

Jehannes made a rude noise. "Have some discipline tomorrow," he said. "Don't ask for it today. Show some humanity, lad. Let them be sad. Let them fucking *mourn.*"

"We mourned yesterday. We went to church, for god's sake. Murderers and rapists, crying for Jesus. If I hadn't seen it, I'd have laughed to hear about it." Just for a moment, the captain looked very young indeed—and confused, annoyed. "We're in a battle. We can't take a break to mourn."

Jehannes drank more wine. "Can you fight every day?" he asked.

The captain considered. "Yes," he said.

"You ought to be locked up, then. We can't. Give it a rest, *Captain.*"

The captain got to his feet. "You are now the constable. I'll need another marshal to replace Hugo. Shall I promote Milus?"

Jehannes narrowed his eyes. "Ask me that tomorrow," he said. "If you ask me again today, I swear by Saint Maurice I'll beat you to a fucking pulp. Is that clear enough?"

The captain turned on his heel and walked away, before he did something he'd regret. He went to Jacques—as he always did, when he'd reached bottom.

But his old valet—the last of his family retainers—was drunk. Even the boy Toby was curled up on the floor of the captain's pavilion, with a piece of rug pulled over him and a leg of chicken in one hand.

He looked at them for a long time, thought about having a temper-tantrum, and decided that no one was sober enough to bother. He tried to arm himself and found that he couldn't get beyond his chain hauberk. He put a padded cote over it, and took his gauntlets.

Gelfred had the horses.

And that is how the captain came to be riding with his huntsman, alone, on the road that ran along the river, sore back, pulled neck muscles, and all.

North of Harndon—Ranald Lachlan

Ranald was up with the dawn. The old man was gone, but had left him a deer's liver fried in winter onions—a veritable feast. He said a prayer for the old man and another when he found the man had thrown a blanket over his riding horse. He cleared the camp and had mounted up before the sun was above the eastern mountains.

It was a ride he'd done with the king a hundred times. Following the highway north along the Albin, except that where the great river wound like an endless snake, the highway ran as straight as the terrain would allow, deviating only for big hills and rich manors, and crossing the Albin seven times via the seven great stone bridges between Harndon and Albinkirk. Lorica was the first bridge. Cheylas was the second—a pretty town with red-tile roofs and round chimney-stacks and fine brick houses. He ate a big meal at the sign of the Irk's Head, and was out the door before the ale could tempt him to stay the night. He changed to his big hackney and rode north again, crossing Cheylas Bridge while the sun was high in the sky and making for Third Bridge as fast as his horse would go.

He crossed Third Bridge as darkness was falling. The Bridge Keeper didn't take guests—a matter of law—but directed him politely to a manor farm on the west bank. "Less than a league," the retired soldier said.

Ranald was pleased to find the man's directions were spot on, because the night was dark and cold, for spring. In the North, the Aurora played in the sky, and there was a feel to it that Ranald didn't like.

Bampton Manor was rich beyond a hillman's ideas of rich—but Ranald was used to how rich the southland was. They gave him a bed and a slice of game pie, and a cup of good red wine, and in the morning, the gentleman who owned the farms smiled at his offer of repayment.

"You are a King's Guardsman?" the young man asked. "I am—I would like to be a man-at-arms. I have my own harness." He blushed.

Ranald didn't laugh. "You'd like to serve the king?" he asked.

The young man nodded. "Hawthor Veney," he said holding out his hand.

His housekeeper bustled up with a bag. "Which I packed you a lunch," she said. "Good for a ploughman, good for a knight, I says."

Ranald bowed to her. "Your servant, ma'am. I'm no knight—just a servant of the king, going home to see my family."

"Hillman?" she said, and sniffed. It was a good sniff—it suggested that

77

hillmen themselves were not always good people, but that she'd already decided in his favour on the matter.

He bowed again. To young Hawthor, he said, "Do you *practise* arms, messire?"

Hawthor beamed, and the older housekeeper cackled. "It's all he does. Doesn't plough, doesn't reap, won't even attend the haying. Doesn't chase servant girls, doesn't drink." She shook her head.

"Goodwife Evans!" Hawthor said with the annoyance of a master for an unservile servant.

She sniffed again—another sniff entirely.

Ranald nodded. "Would you care to measure your sword against mine, young ser?"

In a matter of minutes they were armed and padded in jupons and gauntlets and helmets, standing in the farmhouse yard with a dozen labourers for an audience.

Ranald liked to fight with an axe, but service in the King's Guard required knowledge of the courtly sword. Four feet of steel. The boy—Ranald didn't think of himself as old, but found that Hawthor made him feel old with every comment he made—had a pair of training weapons, not too well balanced, probably made by a local man, a little heavy. But they were perfectly serviceable.

Ranald waited patiently in a garde. Mostly, he was interested in seeing how the boy came at him—a man's character was visible in his swordsmanship.

The boy stood his ground. He put his sword on his shoulder, and came forward in a position that fencing masters called "The Garde of the Woman." His stance was too open and he didn't seem to understand that he needed to cock the sword back as far as he could. *The sort of little error you would spot up when arms are your profession,* thought Ranald. But he liked how patient the boy was.

The boy closed with assurance, and launched his attack without a false preamble—no bobbing or weaving or wasting effort.

Ranald cut into the boy's attack and knocked his blade to the ground.

The boy didn't wait for the whole move, but back-stepped.

Ranald's sword licked out and caught him in the side of the head despite his retreat.

"Oh!" Hawthor said. "Well struck."

The rest was much the same. Hawthor was a competent lad, for a young man without a master-at-arms to teach him. He knew lots of wrestling and very few subtleties, but he was bold and careful, a superb combination for a man so young.

Ranald paused to get out of his heavy jupon and to write the boy a note. "Take this to Lord Glendower with my compliments. You may be asked to serve a year with the pages. Where are your parents?"

Hawthor shrugged. "Dead, messire."

"Well, if the goodwife can spare you," he said. And he was still smiling as he headed for the Fourth Bridge, at Kingstown.

North of Harndon—Harold Redmede

Harold Redmede looked down at the sleeping hillman with a smile. He packed his gear silently, left the hillman the better part of a venison liver, picked up his brother's gear as well, and humped it all to the stream.

He found his brother asleep under a hollow log with his threadbare cloak all about him. Sat and whittled, listening to the Wild, until his brother woke on his own.

"He was harmless," Harold said.

"He was a king's man, and thus a threat to every free man," said Bill.

Harold shrugged. "I've been a king's man," he said. It was an old argument, and not one likely to be resolved. "Here, have some venison and the cider I saved for you. I brought you fish hooks, twenty good heads for arrows and sixty shafts. Don't shoot any of my friends."

"An aristo is an aristo," Bill said.

Harold shook his head. "Bollocks to you, Bill Redmede," he said. "There's right bastards in the nobles and right bastards in the commons, too."

"Difference is that a right bastard commoner, you can break his head with your staff." Bill took a piece of his brother's bread as it was sliced off with a sharp knife.

"Cheese?" Harold asked.

"Only cheese I'll see this year." Bill sat back against a tree trunk. "I've a mind to go put a knife in your guest."

Harold shook his head. "No you won't. First, I drank with him, and that's that. Second, he's wearing mail and sleeping with a dirk in his fist, and I don't think you're going to off a hillman in his sleep, brother o' mine."

"Fair enough. Sometimes I have to remember that we must be fair in our actions, while the enemy is foul."

"I could still find you a place here," Harold said.

Bill shook his head. "I know you mean well, brother. But I am what I am. I'm a Jack. I'm down here recruiting new blood. It's going to be a big year for us." He winked. "I'll say no more. But the day is coming."

"You and your day," Harold muttered. "Listen, *William*. You think I don't know you have five young boys hid in the beeches north of here? I even know whose boys they are. Recruits? They're fifteen or sixteen winters! And you have an *irk* for a guide."

Bill shrugged. "Needs must when the de'il drives," he said.

Harold sat back. "I know irks is folks," he said, waving a hand. "I've met 'em in the woods. Listened to 'em play their harps. Traded to 'em." He leaned forward. "But I'm a forester. They kill other folks. Bill. If you're on their side you're with the Wild, not with men."

"If the Wild makes me free, mayhap I'm with the Wild." Bill ate more bread. "We have allies again, Harold. Come with me. We can change the world." He grimaced to himself. "I'd love to have a good man at my back, brother. We've some right hard cases, I'll admit to you." He leaned forward. "One's a priest, and he's the worst of the lot. You think I'm hard?"

Harold laughed. "I'm too fucking old, brother. I'm fifteen winters older than you. And if it comes to that—" He shrugged. "I'll be with my lord."

Bill shook his head. "How can you be so blind? They oppress us! They take our land, take our animals, grind us—"

"Save it for the boys, Bill. I have six foot of yew and a true shaft for any as tried to grind me. But that won't make me betray my lord. Who, I may add, fed this village himself when other villages starved."

"Farmers are often good to their cattle, aye," Bill said.

They looked at each other. And then both grinned at the same time.

"That's it for this year, then?" Harold asked.

Bill laughed. "That's it. Here, give me your hand. I'm off with my little boys for the greenwood and the Wild. Mayhap you'll hear of us." He got up, and his long cloak shone for a moment, a dirty white.

Harold embraced him. "I saw bear prints by the river; a big female and a cub." He shrugged. "Rare down here. Watch out for her."

Bill looked thoughtful.

"Stay safe, you fool," he said, and swatted him. "Don't end up eaten by irks and bears."

"Next year," Bill said, and was gone.

Lissen Carak—The Red Knight

Gelfred led them west along the river for miles, on a road that became increasingly narrow and ill-defined, until they had passed the point where they fought the wyvern and the road disappeared entirely. There were no longer any fields; the last peasant's cot was miles behind them, and the captain could not even smell smoke on the cool spring breeze, which instead carried an icy hint of old snow. The Abbess had not been exaggerating. Man had lost this land to the Wild.

From time to time Gelfred dismounted in patches of sunlight and drew his short, silver-tipped wand from his belt. He would take his rosary from his belt and say his beads, one prayer at a time, eyes flicking nervously to his captain, who sat impassively on his horse. Each time, he would lay the shrivelled, thorned stick of Witch Bane on the ground at his feet, and each time it pointed, straining like a dog on a leash.

Each time, they rode on.

"You use the power of grammerie to track the beasts?" the captain said, breaking the frosty silence. They were riding single file along a well-defined track, the old leaves deeply trodden. It was easy enough to follow, but the road was gone. And by almost any measure, they were in the Wild.

"With God's aid," Gelfred said, and looked at him, waiting for the retort. "But my grammerie found us the wrong beast. So now I'm looking for the man. Or men."

The captain made a face, but refused to rise to the comment about God. "Do you sense their power directly?" he asked. "Or are you following the same spore a dog would follow?"

Gelfred gave his captain a long look. "I'd like your permission to buy some dogs," he said. "Good dogs. Alhaunts and bloodhounds and a courser or two. I'm your Master of the Hunt. If that is true then I would like to have money, dogs, and some servants who are not scouts and soldiers." He spoke quietly, and his eyes didn't rest on the captain. They were always roaming the Wild.

So were the captain's.

"How much are we talking about?" the captain asked. "I love dogs. Let's have dogs!" He smiled. "I'd like a falcon."

Gelfred's head snapped around, and his horse gave a start. "You would?"

The captain laughed aloud. It was a sound of genuine amusement, and it rang like a trumpet through the woods.

"You think you are fighting for Satan, don't you, Gelfred?" He shook his head.

But when he turned to look at his huntsman, the man was down off his horse, pointing off into the woods.

"Holy Saint Eustace! All praise for this sign!" he said.

The captain peered off through the bare branches and caught the flash of white. He turned his horse—no easy feat on the narrow track between old trees—and he gasped.

The old stag was not as white as snow—that much was obvious, because he had a patch of snow at his feet. He was the colour of good wool, a warm white, and there were signs of a long winter on his hide—but he was white, and his rack of antlers made him a hart; a noble beast of sixteen tines, almost as tall at the shoulder as a horse. Old and noble and, to Gelfred, a sign from God.

The stag eyed them warily.

To the captain he was, palpably, a creature of the Wild. His noble head was redolent with power—thick ropes of power that seemed, in the unreal realm of phantasm, to bind the great animal to the ground, the trees, the world in a spider web of power.

The captain blinked.

The animal turned and walked away, his hooves ringing on the frozen ground. He turned and looked back, pawed the old snow, and then sprang over a downed evergreen and was gone.

Gelfred was on his knees.

The captain rode carefully through the trees, watching the branches overhead and the ground, trying to summon his ability to see in the phantasm and struggling with it as he always did when his heart was beating fast.

It had left tracks. The captain found that reassuring. He found the spot where the beast had stood, and he followed the prints to the place where it had turned and pawed the snow.

His riding horse shied, and the captain patted her neck and crooned at her. "You don't like that beast, do you, my honey?" he said.

Gelfred came up, leading his horse. "What did you see?" he asked. He sounded almost angry.

"A white hart. With a cross on his head. I saw what you saw." The captain shrugged.

Gelfred shook his head. "But why did *you* see it?

The captain laughed. "Ah, Gelfred—are you so very holy? Shall I pass word of your vow of chastity on to the maids of Lonny? I seem to remember one young lass with black hair—"

"Why must you mock holy things?" Gelfred asked.

"I'm mocking you. Not holy things." He pointed a gloved hand at the place where the stag had pawed the snow. "Run your wand over that."

Gelfred looked up at him. "I beg your pardon. I am a sinful man. I should not give myself airs. Perhaps my sins are so black that there is nothing between us."

The captain's trumpet laugh rang out again. "Perhaps I'm not nearly as bad as you think, Gelfred. Personally, I don't think God gives a fuck either way—but I do sometimes wonder if She has a wicked sense of humour and I should lighten up."

Gelfred writhed.

The captain shook his head. "Gelfred, I'm still mocking you. I have problems with God. But you are a good man doing his best and I apologise for my needling. Now—be a good fellow and pass your wand over the snow."

Gelfred knelt in the snow.

The captain winced at how cold his knees must be, even through his thigh high boots.

Gelfred spoke four prayers aloud—three Pater Nosters and an Ave Maria. Then he put his beads back in his belt. He raised his face to the captain. "I accept your apology," he said. He took the wand from his belt, raised it, and it snapped upright as if it had been struck by a sword.

Gelfred dug with his gloved hands. He didn't need to dig far.

There was a man's corpse. He had died slowly, from an arrow in the thigh that had severed an artery—that much they could reasoned from the blood that soaked his braes and hose into a frozen scarlet mass.

All of his garments were undyed wool, off white, well made. He wore a quiver that was full of good arrows with hardened steel heads—the captain drew them one by one and tested the heads against his vambrace.

Gelfred shook his head. The arrows alone were worth a small fortune.

The dead man's belt pouch had a hundred leopards or more in gold and silver, a fine dagger with a bronze and bone hilt and a set of eating tools set into the scabbard, and his hood and cloak were matching undyed wool.

Gelfred opened his cloak and took out a chain with an enamelled leaf. "Good Christ," he said, and sat back.

The captain was searching the snow using his sword as a rake, combing up old branches under the scant snow cover.

He found the bow after a minute. If was a fine war bow, heavy, sleek, and powerful—not yet ruined by the exposure to the snow.

Gelfred found the arrow that had killed him after assiduous casting, using his power profligately, casting it wider and wider. He had the body, had the blood, had the quiver. The connections were strong enough that it was only a matter of time, unless the arrow was a very long way away.

In fact, the arrow was near the road where they had left it, almost on their trail, buried in six inches of snow. Blood was still frozen to the ground where the arrow had been torn from the wound.

The arrow was virtually identical to the fifteen in the quiver.

"Mmm," said the captain.

They took turns watching the woods while the other stripped the corpse of clothes, chain, boots, belt, knife—of everything.

"Why didn't something eat him?" Gelfred asked.

"Enough power here to frighten any animal," the captain said. "Why didn't the man who killed him strip his corpse and take the arrows? And the knife?" He shook his head. "I confess, Gelfred—this is—" he snorted.

Gelfred didn't raise his eyes. "There's plenty of folk live in the Wild."

"I know *that*." The captain raised an eyebrow. "I'm from the north, Gelfred. I used to see Outwallers every day, across the river. There's whole villages of them." He shook his head. "We raided them, sometimes. And other times, we traded with them."

Gelfred shrugged. "He isn't an Outwaller." He looked at the captain as if he expected trouble. "He's one of those men and women who want to bring down the lords. They say we'll—that is, that they'll be free." His voice was detached and curiously non-committal.

The captain made a face. "He's a Jack, isn't he? The bow? The leaf brooch? I've heard the songs." He shook his head at his huntsman. "I know there's folk who want to burn the castles. If I were born a serf, I'd be out there with my pitchfork, right now. But Jacks? Men dedicated to fighting for the Wild? Who would fund them? How do they recruit? It makes no sense."

He shrugged. "To be honest, I'd always assumed the Jacks were made up by the lords to justify their own atrocities. Shows what a little youthful cynicism will get you."

Gelfred shrugged. "There are always rumours." His eyes slipped away from the captain's.

"You're not some sort of secret rebel, Gelfred?" The captain forced the other man to meet his eyes.

Gelfred shrugged. "Does it brand me a traitor to say that sometimes the whole sick wheel of the world makes me want to kill?" He dropped his eyes, and the anger went out of him. "I don't. But I understand the outlaws and the outwallers."

The captain smiled. "There. At last, you and I have something in common." He rolled the frozen corpse and used the dead man's sharp knife to slit his hose up the back. He cut the waistband of the man's linen braes, stiff with frozen blood, and took them as well. He got a sack from his heavy leather male that sat behind his saddle, and filled it with the dead man's belongings.

He tossed the purse to Gelfred. "Get us some dogs," he said.

Naked, the dead man didn't look like a soldier in the army of evil. The thought made the captain purse his lips. He leaned over the corpse—as white as the snow around it—and rolled it over again.

The death wound went in under the arm, straight to the heart, and had been delivered with a slim bladed knife. The captain took his time, looking at it.

"His killer came and finished him. And was so panicked, they didn't know their man was already dead."

"Already dead?" Gelfred asked.

"Not much blood. Look at his cote. There's the entry—there's the blood. But not much." The captain crouched on his heels. "This is a puzzle. What do you see, Gelfred?"

"His kit is better than ours," Gelfred said.

"Satan pays well," the captain shrugged. "Or perhaps he merely pays on time." He looked around. "This is not what we came for. Let's go back to the trail and look for the monster." He paused. "Gelfred, how can you conjure with Witch's Bane?"

Gelfred walked a few paces. "I've heard it can't be done," he said with a shrug. "But it can. It's like mucking out a stall—you just try not to get the shit on you."

The captain looked at his huntsman with a whole new appreciation. Sparring about religion had defined their relationship in the weeks since the captain had engaged him.

"You are potent," the captain said.

Gelfred shook his head eyes on the trees. "I feel that we've disturbed a balance," he said, ignoring the compliment.

The captain led his horse to a downed tree. He could vault into the saddle, but he felt sore in every limb, and his neck hurt where the wyvern had tried to snap it, and he was still more than a little hung over, and he used the downed tree to mount.

"All the more reason to keep moving," he said. "We're not in the Jack-hunting business, Gelfred. We kill monsters."

Gelfred shrugged. "My lord—" he began. He looked away. "You have power of your own. Yes?"

The captain felt a little frisson run down his back. *Run? Hide? Lie?*

"Yes," he said. "A little."

"Hmm," Gelfred said, noncommittally. "So. Now that I have eliminated the...the Jack from my casting, I can concentrate on the other creature." He paused. "They were bound together. At least," he looked scared. "At least, that's how it seemed to me."

The captain looked at his huntsman. "Why do you think someone killed the Jack, Gelfred?"

Gelfred shook his head.

"A Jack helps a monster kill a nun. Then, another man kills him." The captain shivered. The chainmail under his arming cote did a wonderful job of conducting the cold straight to his chest.

Gelfred didn't meet his eye.

"Not money. Not weapons." The captain began to look around. "I think we're being watched."

Gelfred nodded.

"How long had the Jack been dead?" the captain asked.

"Two days." Gelfred was sure, as only the righteous can be sure.

The captain stroked his beard. "Makes no sense," he said.

They rode back to the track, and Gelfred hesitated before facing west. And then they began to ride.

"The stag was a sign from God," Gelfred said. "And that means the Jacks are but tools of Satan."

The captain looked at his huntsman with the kind of look fathers usually have for young children.

Which, the captain thought, was odd, since Gelfred was ten years his senior.

"The stag was a creature of the Wild, every bit as much as the wyvern, and it chose to manifest itself as it did because it opposes whomever aids the Jacks." The captain shrugged. "Or so I suspect." He met his huntsman's eye. "We need to ask ourselves why a creature of the Wild helped us find the body."

"So you are an Atheist!" Gelfred asked. Or rather, accused.

The captain was watching the woods. "Not at all, Gelfred. Not at all."

The trail narrowed abruptly, killing their conversation. Gelfred took the lead. He looked back at the captain, as if encouraging him to go on, but the captain pointed over his shoulder and they rode on in silence.

After a few minutes, Gelfred raised a hand, slipped from the saddle, and performed his ritual.

The stick in his hand snapped in two.

"Holy Saint Eustace," he said. "Captain—it is right here with us." His voice trembled.

The captain backed his horse a few steps to get clear of the huntsman's horse and then took a heavy spear from its bucket at his stirrup.

Gelfred had his crossbow to hand, and began to span it, his eyes wide.

The captain listened, and tried to see in the phantasm.

He couldn't see it, but he could feel it. And he knew, with sudden weariness, that it could feel him too.

He turned his horse slowly.

They were at the top of a bank—the ground sloped sharply to the west, down to a swollen stream. He could see where the track crossed the stream.

On the eastern slope, towards the fortress, the ground fell away more slowly and then rose dramatically up the ridge they had just descended, and the captain realised that the ridge was littered in boulders—rocks big enough to hide a wagon, some so large that trees grew from the top of them.

"I think I may have been rash," the captain began.

He heard the sharp click as Gelfred's string locked into the trigger mechanism on his bow.

He was looking at an enormous boulder the size of a wealthy farmer's house. Steam rose over it, like smoke from a cottage fire.

"It's right there." He didn't turn his head.

"Bless us, Holy Virgin, now and in the hour of our deaths. Amen." Gelfred crossed himself.

The captain took a deep breath and released it softly, fighting his nerves. The ground between them and the rock was tangled with scrubby spruce, downed trees, and snow. Miserable terrain for his horse to cross in a fight. And he wasn't on Grendel—he was on a riding horse that had never seen combat.

Not wearing armour.

I'm an idiot, he thought.

"Gelfred," he said, without turning his head. "Is there more than one? What is downslope?"

Gelfred's voice was calm, and the captain felt a spurt of affection for the huntsman. "I believe there is another." Gelfred spat. "This is my fault."

"Is this our killer?" the captain asked. He was quite proud of his conversational tone. If he was going down, he would die like a gentleman. That pleased him.

Gelfred was also a brave man. "The one upslope is the killer," he said. "By the wounds of Christ, Captain—what *are* they?"

"Stick close," the captain said. "You're the huntsman, Gelfred. What are they?"

He began to ride forward, down the trail to the west. He passed Gelfred, who came in so tight behind him that the captain could feel the warmth of his horse. Down the steep slope to the stream, and he could no longer see the boulders, but he could hear movement—crashing movement.

Across the stream in a single leap of his horse. He could feel her terror. He could feel his own.

He rode five yards, holding his mount down to a trot by sheer force of will and knee. She wanted to bolt. Ten yards. He heard Gelfred splash across the stream instead of leaping it and he turned his horse. She didn't want to turn.

He put his spur into her right side.

She turned.

Gelfred's eyes were as wide as his horse's.

"Behind me," the captain said.

He was facing their back trail. He backed his horse again, judging the distance.

"I'm dismounting," Gelfred said.

"Shut up." The captain fought for enough mental control to enter the room in his head. Closed his eyes—forced them closed against the crashing sound from the top of the ridge to the east.

Prudentia?

She stood in the centre of the room, her eyes wide, and he ran to her, took her outstretched hand and pointed it over his shoulder.

"Katherine, Ares, Socrates!" he called. He ran to the door, grasped the handle, and turned the key while the room spun around him.

The lock clicked open and the door crashed back against his leg, throwing him from his feet so that he fell heavily on the marble floor. The breeze was an icy green wind, and on the other side of the door—

It was caught on his shoulder where he had fallen, and the gale was sliding him along the floor as it forced the door open.

He wondered what would happen if the door crashed back against its hinges. He wondered whether he could die in the small, round room.

Had to assume he could.

I rule here! he said aloud. He put a knee under himself, as he would if he was wrestling with a big man. Used the key for leverage. Pushed the door with his shoulder.

For a long set of heartbeats, it was like pushing a cart in mud. And then he felt the shift—minute—but the tiny victory lit his power like a mountebank's flare and he slammed the door closed as his net of power wove itself like a giant spider's web across the stream.

The horse was fighting him, and the thing was halfway down the hill, coming straight down the track, its bulk breaking branches on either side of the trail while its taloned feet gouged clods of earth out of the ground.

His mind shied away from looking at its head.

He couched his lance, timing his charge.

Horses are complex animals, delicate, fractious and sometimes very difficult. His fine riding horse was spirited and nervous on the best of days, and was now terrified, wanting only to flee.

Gelfred's crossbow loosed with a flat crack and the bolt caught the thing under its long snout and it shrieked. It slowed.

Thirty yards. The length of the tiltyard in his father's castle. Because this had to be just right.

The *adversarius*—the captain had never seen one, but had to assume that this was the fabled enemy of man—lengthened its loping stride to leap the brook.

A daemon.

The captain rammed his spurs into his mount. Sometimes, horses are simple. His riding horse exploded forward.

The adversarius leaped again at the edge of the stream, its hooked beak already reaching for his face, arms spread wide.

It seemed to slow as it crossed the water—vestigial wings a blur of angry motion, maned head with a helmet crest of bone curving above it, spraying spittle as the thing tried to snap at the fine web of Power he had cast over the near bank. It would only last a moment—already the daemon was blowing through the mild restraint the way a big child, angry and frightened, tears through spider web.

He tracked the thing's right eye with his lance tip like it was an opponent's crest; the brass ring; the upper left corner of the shield on the quintain. Held in place like an insect pinned to a page, it tried to rear back just as his spear point glanced off the ocular ridge and plunged into the soft tissue of the eye, the strong steel of the long spear head breaking the bone above and below the eye socket, driving the point deeper and deeper, the whole weight of the man and horse behind it.

His lance shaft snapped.

The creature's legs spasmed and its talons tore into his horse's forequarters, raking flesh and tendon from bone, flaying the poor animal while it screamed. The captain flew back over its rump on force of the impact, with no brace against his back from a tilting saddle. The horse reared and the talons eviscerated it, its guts spilling onto the road in a great gout.

The daemon got its feet on the ground and its forearms shredded the last of his web of power—

It turned from the ruin of his horse and he saw the damage he'd done, the angry orange of its remaining eye—no slit, no pupil. Nothing but fire. It *saw* him.

The terror of its presence pounded him like a hammer of spirit—for a moment, the terror was so pure in him that he had no self. He was only fear.

It came for him then, rising up fast on its haunches—and, like a puppet with the strings cut, it collapsed atop the corpse of his riding horse.

He gagged, clamped down on the vomit, failed, and heaved everything in his stomach down the front of his jupon. When he was done he was sobbing in the backwash of the terror.

As soon as he had any control over himself, he said "Ware! There's another!"

Gelfred approached him slowly, holding a cup in one hand and a cocked and loaded crossbow balanced carefully on his arms.

"It's been a long time." He shook his head. "I've prayed the whole rosary, waiting for you to recover." He was shaking. "I don't think the other one is coming."

The captain spat out the taste of vomit. "Good" he said. He wanted to say something witty. Nothing came. "Good." He took the cup. "How—long did I kneel here?"

"Too long," Gelfred said. "We need to ride."

The captain's hands shook so hard he spilled the wine.

Gelfred put his arms around him.

The captain stood in that unwanted embrace and shook. Then he washed in the creek. He felt violated. And different. He was suddenly afraid of everything. He didn't feel at all like a man who had faced a daemon, the greatest adversary to the rule of man, in single combat, and the adoration in Gelfred's eyes made him sick.

Tomorrow, I will no doubt be insufferable, he thought.

Gelfred cut the head from the daemon.

He threw up again, a stream of bile, and wondered if he could ever face a creature of the Wild again. His bones felt like jelly. There was something in the pit of his gut—something that had gone.

He knew exactly what this felt like: like being beaten by his brothers. Beaten and humiliated. He knew that feeling well. They'd been younger than him. They'd hated him. He'd made their lives a misery, when he learned that—

He spat.

Some things are best left unexamined. He held the line at that memory, and felt his fear recede a little, like the first sign the tide is in ebb.

It would pass, then.

Gelfred couldn't get the horse to bear the head. The captain didn't have enough concentration to conjure anything to help them with it. So they tied a rope to the head and dragged it.

It would be a long walk back to camp. And after an hour, something behind them began to howl, and the captain felt the hairs on the back of his neck rise.

Lissen Carak—Mogan

Mogan watched her cousin's killer as he mounted slowly and rode up the road.

Mogan was a hunter, not a berserker. Her cousin's death terrified her, and until she had understood it she was not going down to face the men on the road. Instead, she edged cautiously from rock to rock, keeping well out of their line of sight, and she watched them with her superb eyes, made for spotting the movement of prey a mile across the plains to the west.

When they were well clear of the scene of the fight, she trotted down the ridge.

Tunxis lay in a pitiful heap, his once mighty frame hunched and flattened by death, and there were already birds on the corpse.

They cut his head off.

It was horrendous. Mogan threw back her head and howled her rage and sorrow.

After her third howl, her brother came. He had four hunters with him, all armed with heavy war-axes or swords.

Thurkan looked at his nest-mate's corpse and shook his great head. "Barbarians," he spat.

Mogan rubbed her shoulder against his. "One man killed him. I chose not to try him. He killed our cousin so easily."

Thurkan nodded. "Some of their warriors are terrifying, little sister. And you had no weapon to open his armour."

"He had no armour," Mogan said. "But he had Power. Our Power."

Thurkan paused, sniffing the air. Then he walked to the edge of the stream, and back, several times, while his nestmates stood perfectly still.

"Powerful," Thurkan said. He paused and licked his shoulder where a mosquito had penetrated his armoured flesh. Insects. How he hated them. He batted helplessly with a taloned forefoot at the cloud that was gathering around his head. Then he bent over his cousin's form, raised his talons, and turned his cousin's corpse to ash in a flash of emerald light.

Later, as they ran through the forest, Thurkan mused to his sister. "This is not as Thorn thinks it to be," he said.

Mogan raised her talons to indicate her complete lack of interest in Thorn. "You seek to dominate him, and he seeks to dominate you, but as he is not of our kind your efforts are wasted," she said scathingly.

Thurkan took a hundred running steps before he answered. "I don't think so, little sister. I think he is the rising power of the Wild, and we must cleave to him. For now. But in this matter he is blind. This fortress,

The Rock. Here we are, masters of the woods from the mountains to the river—and he would have us leave our winnings to assault this one place. And now the Rock has a defender—one who is also a power of the Wild." Thurkan ran on. "I think Thorn is making an error."

"You seek his throat, and his power," Mogan said. "And it is we who wish to return to the Rock."

"Not if the cost is too high. I am not Tunxis." Thurkan leapt a log.

"How can the Rock have a defender who is one of us? And we not know him?" Mogan asked.

"I don't know," Thurkan admitted. "But I will find out."

Chapter Four

South of Lorica—Ser Gawin

awin Murien of Strathnith, known to his peers as Hard Hands, rode north along the Albin River in his armour, a knight bent upon errantry. And the further north he rode, the deeper his anger grew.

Adam, the elder of his two squires, whistled, bowed from his saddle to every passing woman, and looked at the world with whole-hearted approval. *He* was not sorry to be leaving the court of Harndon. Far from it. Far from the great hall, far from the rounds of dancing and cards and hunts and flirtation, squires lived in barracks under the absolute domination of the oldest and toughest. Younger men got little food and much work, and no chance of glory. Adam was the squire of a named and belted knight, and on errantry, he expected to have a chance to win his own place in song. At Harndon, all he got was black eyes and bad food.

Toma, the younger squire, rode with his head down. Adam could make nothing of him, beyond his mumbled answers and his clumsy work. He seemed young for his age and deeper in misery than a boy should be.

Gawin wanted to do something for him, but he was having a hard time seeing through his own anger.

It wasn't *fair*.

The words were meaningless. His oaf of a father had beaten any notion of fairness from him from birth. Gawin knew that the world gave you nothing but struggle. That you had to make your own luck. And a thousand more such aphorisms all with the same general message, but, by God and all the saints, Gawin had done his time, faced his monster and killed the literally damned thing in single combat with his gauntlets after his sword broke. He remembered it vividly, just as he remembered going to fight the damned thing out of sheer guilt.

I killed my brother.

It still made him sick.

He didn't want to have to face the foe again, not for all the pretty ladies in court and not for all the lands he stood to inherit. He was no coward. He'd *done it*. In front of his father and fifty other men. There probably weren't fifty knights in all Alba—from one end of the Demesne to the other—who had bested a daemon in single combat. He certainly hadn't wanted to.

But he had. And that should have been that.

But of course, the king hated him, as he hated all his brothers, hated his mother, loathed his father.

Fuck the king. I'll ride home to Pater.

Strathnith was one of the greatest fortresses in the Demesne. It was a citadel of the Wall, and the Muriens had held it for generations. The Nith was a mighty river—almost an inland sea—that defined the ultimate border between the Demesne and the Wild. His father ruled the fortress and the thousands of men and women who paid their taxes and depended on it for protection. He thought about the great hall; the ancient rooms, some built by the Archaics. The sounds of the Wild carrying across the broad river.

The constant bickering, the drunken accusations. The family fighting.

"Good Christ, I might as well go find a cursed monster and kill it," he said aloud. Going home meant returning to a life of constant warfare—in the field against the daemons, and in the hall against his father. And his brothers.

I killed my brother.

"They can have it," he said.

He'd been sent south, the young hero, to win a bride at court. To raise the family in the estimation of the king.

Another of his father's brilliant plans.

He had fallen in love, but not with a woman. Rather, he'd fallen in love with women. And the court. Music. Card games. Dice. Good wine and wit. Dancing.

Strathnith wasn't going to offer *any* of those things. He couldn't stop himself from thinking about it. In retrospect, maybe his loathsome brother had a point.

His mother—

He banished the thought.

"Lorica, m'lord," Adam sang out. "Shall I find us an inn?"

The idea of an inn helped douse his moment of self-doubt. Inns—good ones—were like miniature courts. A little rougher, a little more home-spun. Gawin smiled.

"The best one," he said.

Adam grinned, touched his spurs to his horse, and rode off into the setting sun. Drink. And maybe a girl. He thought fleetingly of Lady Mary, who so obviously loved him. A beautiful body, and, he had to admit, a fine wit. And the daughter of the Count. She was a fine catch.

He shrugged.

The sign of the Two Lions was an old inn built on the foundation of an Archaic cavalry barracks, and it looked like a fortress; it had its own curtain wall, separate from Lorica's town wall, and it had a tower in the north-east corner where any soldier could see the original gate had been. Built against the tower was a massive building of white plaster and heavy black beams, with a hipped thatch roof with expensive copper sheathing around the chimneys; glass windows opened onto the porches that ran all along the front and sunlit side, and four massive chimneys, all new masonry, rose out of the roof.

It was like a piece of the Palace of Harndon brought into the countryside. Lorica was an important town, and the Two Lions was an important inn.

Adam appeared to hold his horse. "A king's knight is very welcome here," he said through his grin. Adam liked to serve a great man—it rubbed off. Especially forty leagues north of the city.

A prosperous man, razor thin, wearing a fine woollen hood lined in silk and edged with silver crosses and a fur band, swept off the last and bowed to the ground. "Edard Blodget, m'lord. At your service. I won't call my inn humble—it's the best inn on the Highway. But I do like to see the king's knights."

Gawin was startled to see a commoner so well dressed and so frankly spoken—startled, but not displeased. He returned the bow, all the way to the ground. "Ser Gawin Murien," he said. "Knighthood doesn't necessarily make a man rich, Master Blodget. May I enquire—?"

Master Blodget gave a tight lipped smile. "Your own room for a silver leopard. Share with your squires for two cats more." He raised an eyebrow. "I can make it cheaper, m'lord, but it will be in a common room."

Gawin mentally reviewed his purse. He had a good memory, well-trained, and so he could almost literally see the contents—four silver leopards and a dozen heavy copper cats. And gleaming among them, a pair of rose nobles, solid gold, worth twenty leopards apiece. Not a fortune, by any means, but enough that he needn't stint on his first night on the road, or on the second.

"Adam will take care of it, then. I would prefer we were all in a room. With a window, if that's not too much to ask?"

"Clean linen, window, well-water, and stabling for three horses. The pack horse will cost another half a cat." Blodget shrugged, as if such petty amounts were beneath him, which they probably were. The Two Lions was at least a third of the size of the massive fortress of Strathnith, and was probably worth—Gawin tried to do the mathematics in his head—wished for his tutor—and finally arrived at a figure that had to be recklessly wrong.

"I'm flattered you came to greet me in person," Gawin said with another bow.

Blodget grinned from ear to ear.

Another thing I learned at court—men like to be flattered just as much as ladies, Gawin thought.

"I have a group of singers tonight, m'lord—on their way to court, or so they hope. Will you join us for dinner in the common room? It ain't a great hall—but it's not bad. And we'd be honoured to have you sit with us."

Of course, I'm as fond of flattery as the next man.

"We will join you for dinner and music," he said with a slight bow.

"Evensong at Saint Eustachios. You'll hear the bell," the innkeeper said. "Dinner follows the service directly."

Harndon City—Edward

Master Pyle appeared in the yard after evensong and asked for a volunteer.

Edward had a girl, but she worked, too. She would have to understand, because a chance to work with the master was every apprentice's dream.

The master mixed the powder differently this time. Edward didn't see how. But he moved a heavy iron pitch-bowl for repousse work into the yard, and cleared a lot of old rubbish—bits of ruined projects and soft wood for making temporary moulds and hordles—out of the way, in case they should catch fire. It wasn't skilled work, but he was still working for the master.

The smoke was thicker this time, and the flame burned whiter.

Master Pyle looked at it, fanning his face to get the evil smelling smoke to clear. He had a bit of a smile.

"Well," he said. He looked at Edward. "Are you ready for your examination, young man?"

Edward took a deep breath. "Yes," he said. And hoped that didn't sound too cocky.

But Master Pyle nodded. "I agree." He looked around the yard. "Clear all this up, will you?"

That night in the loft, the apprentices whispered. The older boys knew when the master was making progress. They could tell just by the way he held his head. And because rewards suddenly emerged from the master's purse, and boys got new work, and apprentices were suddenly tested to be journeymen. Lise, the eldest female cutler, had gone to the masters the week before. She'd passed.

And so Edward Chevins, senior apprentice and sometime shop boy, found himself up for journeyman. It was so sudden it made his head spin, and before the next morning was old enough to drink his beer, the Guild Hall had checked his papers, the Guild Masters examined him, his nerves were wracked, his hands shook—and he was left to sweat, alone, in a richly decorated room fit to entertain a king. It was plenty to overawe a seventeen-year-old blade smith.

Edward was a tall, gangly young man with sandy red hair and too many freckles. Standing under the stained glass of Saint Nicholas, he could think of twenty better answers he might have given to the question: "How do you achieve a bright, constant blue on a blade with a heavy forte and a needle point?"

He groaned. The other four boys who'd been tested with him looked at him with a mixture of sympathy and hope. It was too easy to believe that someone else's failure raised one's own hopes of success.

An hour later, the masters came into the hall. They all looked a little red in the face, as if they'd been drinking.

Master Pyle came and put a ring on his finger—a ring of fine steel. "You're made, boy," he said. "Well done."

Lorica—Ser Gawin

Gawin was awakened from his nap by the sound of men shouting in the courtyard. Angry voices have a timbre to them—especially when men mean violence.

Adam was at his bed. He had a heavy knife in his hand. "I don't know who they are, m'lord. Men from overseas. Knights. But—" Squires didn't speak ill of knights. It was never a good idea. So Adam shrugged.

Gawin rolled off his bed, wearing only his braes. He pulled a shirt over his head, and with Toma's help got his legs into his hose and his torso laced into his pourpoint and his hose tied on.

Down in the courtyard one voice sounded clear above the others. Accented, but powerful controlled, elegant. The words ended with a long, clear laugh that sounded like bells.

Gawin went to his window and threw it open.

There were a dozen armoured men in the courtyard. At least three were true knights, and wore armour as good as Gawin's own. Their men-at-arms were nearly as well armoured. It was possible they were *all* knights.

They all wore the same badge—a rose, gules, on a field d'or.

Not anyone he knew.

The leader with the magnificent laugh had silver-gilt hair and fine features—in armour, he looked like a statue of Saint George. He was *beautiful*.

Gawin felt ill-dressed and somewhat doltish in comparison.

Master Blodget stood in front of this saint with his hands on his hips.

"But," the knight had a smile on his face, "But that is the room I want, Master Innkeeper!"

Blodget shook his head. "There's a gentleman in that room—a belted king's knight, in that room. First come, first served, m'lord. Fair is fair." The knight shook his head. "Throw him out, then."

Toma had his master's doublet and helped him into it. While Adam did the laces, Toma fetched his riding sword.

"Follow me," Gawin snapped at the scared boy, and sprang down the stairs. He went through the common room—empty, because every man in the inn was in the courtyard watching the fun.

He stepped through the door and the knight turned to look at him. He smiled.

"Perhaps I don't wish to leave my room," Gawin called. He hated that his voice wavered. There was nothing to fear, here—just a misunderstanding, but the kind wherein a knight had to make a good show.

"You?" he asked. His tone of disbelief wasn't mocking—it was genuine. "You are a king's knight? Ah—Gaston, they need us here!"

Closer up, the men in the courtyard were huge. The smallest of them was a head taller than Gawin, and he was not a small man.

"I have that honour," Gawin said. He tried to find something wittier to say, but he was more interested in defusing the tension than in scoring points.

The one called Gaston laughed. The rest laughed too.

The beautiful knight leaned down from his saddle. "Have your man clear your things from that corner room," he said. And then, in a particularly annoying tone, he added, "I would esteem it a favour."

Gawin found that he was angry.

"No," he said.

"That was ill-said, and not courteous," the knight answered him with a frown. "I shall have it. Why make this difficult? If you are a man of honour then you may cede it to me with a good grace, knowing I am a better man than you." He shrugged. "Or fight me. That would be honour too." He nodded to himself. "But to stand here and tell me I can't have it; that makes me angry."

Gawin spat. "Then let us fight, ser knight. Give me your name and style, and I will name the weapons and the place. The king has announced a tournament in a two months, perhaps—" Even as he spoke, the man was dismounting.

He gave his reins to Gaston and turned, drawing his sword—a four-foot long war sword. "Then fight."

Gawin squeaked. He wasn't proud of the squeak, but he was unarmoured and had only his riding sword—a good blade, but a single handed weapon whose only real purpose was to mark your status in life and keep riff-raff at arm's length.

"Garde!" the man called.

Gawin reached out and drew his sword from the scabbard Toma held, and brought it up in a counter cut that just stopped his opponent's first heavy overhand blow. Gawin had time to bless his superb Master at Arms— and then the giant cut at him again and he slipped to the side, allowing the heavier sword to slide off his own like rain off a roof.

The bigger man stepped in as quick as a cat and struck him in the face with one gauntleted hand, knocking him to the ground. Only a turn of his head saved him from spitting teeth. But he was a knight of the king—he rolled with the impact, spat blood, and came to his feet with a hard cut at his opponent's groin.

A single-handed sword has advantages in a fight with a heavier sword. It is quicker, even if the wielder is smaller.

Gawin funnelled his anger into his sword and cut—three times, on three different lines, trying to awe the giant with a flurry of blows. The sword rang off the mirrored finish of his opponent's armoured wrist on the third cut. It was a fight ending blow.

If his opponent wasn't covered in steel.

The giant attacked, drove him back two steps, and then Toma screamed. The boy had been unprepared for a fight and stood frozen, but now tried to turn and run he'd became entangled with his master's defensive flurry. Gawin almost fell, and the bigger man's long sword licked out, caught his, and drove his thrust deep into Toma.

He kicked Gawin in the groin when he turned to look at Toma, whose head was cut nearly in half by the blade. Gawin fell, retching with the pain, and the big knight showed no mercy; knelt on his back, and pushed his nose into the mud in the courtyard. He stripped the sword from Gawin's hand.

"Yield," he said.

Northerners were reputedly stubborn and vengeful. Gawin, in that moment, swore to kill this man, whomever he might be, if it cost him his life and his honour to do it.

"Fuck yourself," he said through the mud and blood in his mouth.

The man laughed. "By the law of arms, you are my prisoner, and I will take you to your king to show him how very much he needs me."

"Coward!" Gawin roared. Even as part of his mind suggested that slumping in pretended swoon might be the wiser course.

A gauntleted hand rolled him over and pulled him up. "Get your things out of my room," he said. "I will pretend I did *not* hear you say such a thing to me."

Gawin spat blood. "If you think you can take me to the king and *not* be bound for murder—"

The blond man sniffed. "You killed your own squire," he said. He allowed himself just the slightest smile at the words and, for the first time, Gawin was afraid of him. "And calling a man who has bested you in a test of arms 'coward' is poor manners."

Gawin wanted to speak like a hero, but rage, sorrow, fear, and pain spat his words out "You killed Toma! You are no knight! Attacking an unarmoured man? With a war sword? In an *inn*?"

The other man frowned. He leaned close.

"I should strip you and have you raped by the grooms. How dare you call me—me!—an unfit knight? Little man, I am Jean de Vrailly, I am the greatest knight in the world, and the only law I recognise is the law of Chivalry. Yield to me, or I will slay you where you stand."

Gawin looked into that beautiful face—unmarred by anger, rage, or any other emotion—and he wanted to spit in it. His father would have.

I want to live.

"I yield," he said, and hated himself.

"All these Alban knights are worthless," de Vrailly laughed. "We will rule here."

And then they all dismounted, leaving Gawin alone in the courtyard with the body of his squire. The boy was quite dead.

I killed him, Gawin thought. *Sweet Christ.*

But it wasn't over yet, because Adam was a brave man, and he died alone in the doorway of their corner room.

One of the foreigners threw all his kit through the window after he heard his squire die. They laughed.

Gawin knelt on the stones by Toma and, after an hour, when the bells rang for evensong, the innkeeper came to him.

"I've sent for the sheriff and the lord," he said. "I'm so sorry, m'lord."

Gawin couldn't think of anything to say.

I killed my brother.

I killed Toma.

I have been defeated and yielded.

I should have died.

Why had he yielded? Death would have been better than this. Even the innkeeper *pitied* him.

Lorica—de Vrailly

Gaston was wiping the blood from his blade, fastidiously examining the last four inches where he'd hacked repeatedly into the young squire's guard, battering his defences until he was overwhelmed and then dead. His blade had taken some damage in the process and would need a good cutler to restore the edge.

De Vrailly drank wine from a silver cup while his squires removed his armour.

"He cut you, the man in the courtyard," Gaston said, looking up from his task. "Don't try to hide it. He cut you."

De Vrailly shrugged. "He was swinging wildly. It is nothing."

"He got through your guard." Gaston sniffed. "They aren't really so bad, these Albans. Perhaps we will have some real fights." He looked at his cousin. "He hit you hard," he pointed out, because de Vrailly was rubbing his wrist for the third time in as many minutes.

"Bah! They have little skill at arms." De Vrailly drank more wine. "All they do is make war on the Wild. They have forgotten how to fight other men." He shrugged. "I will change that, and make them better at defeating the Wild as I do. I will make them harder, better men." He nodded to himself.

"Your angel has said this?" Gaston asked, with obvious interest. His cousin's encounter with an angel had benefited the whole family, but it was still a matter that puzzled him.

"My angel has commanded it. I am but heaven's tool, cousin." De Vrailly said it without the least irony.

Gaston took a deep breath, looking for his great cousin to show a little humour, and found none. "You called yourself the best knight in the world," he said, trying to raise a smile.

De Vrailly shrugged as Johan, his older squire, unlaced his left rerebrace and began to remove the arm harness over the wound on his wrist. "I am the greatest knight in the world," he said. "My angel chose me *because* I am the first lance in the East. I have won six battles; I have fought in twelve passages of arms and never been wounded; I have killed men in every list in which I've fought; in the melee at Tours—"

Gaston rolled his eyes. "Very well, you are the best knight in the world. Now tell me why we've come to Alba, besides bullying the locals."

"Their king will proclaim a tournament," de Vrailly said. "I will win it, and emerge as the King's Champion." He nodded, "and then I will be the king, to all intents and purposes."

"The angel has said this?" Gaston asked.

"You question my angel, cousin?" De Vrailly frowned.

Gaston rose and sheathed his sword. "No, I merely choose not to believe everything I'm told—by you or any other man."

De Vrailly's beautiful eyes narrowed. "Are you calling me a liar?"

Gaston smiled a crooked smile. "If we continue like this we will fight. And while you may be the best knight in the world, I believe I have bloodied your knuckles more than once—eh?"

Their eyes crossed, and Gaston saw the glitter in de Vrailly's. Gaston held his gaze. Few men could do it. Gaston had the benefit of a lifetime of practice.

De Vrailly shrugged. "You couldn't have asked this before we left home?" he asked.

Gaston wrinkled his nose. "When you say fight, I fight. Yes? You say:

gather your knights, we go to conquer Alba. I say: lovely, we shall all be rich and powerful. Yes?"

"Yes!" de Vrailly said, through his smile.

"But when you tell me that an Angel of God is giving you very specific military and political advice—" Gaston shrugged.

"We are to meet the Earl of Towbray in the morning. He will engage us in his mesne. He desires what my angel desires." For the first time, de Vrailly seemed to hesitate.

He pounced. "Cousin—*what does your angel desire?*"

De Vrailly drank more wine, put the cup down on the sideboard, and shrugged out of his right arm harness as his younger squire opened the vambrace. "Who can know what an angel desires?" he said quietly. "But the Wild here must be *destroyed*. That's what the king's father intended. You know they burned swathes of the wood between the towns to do it? They waited for windy days and set fires. The old king's knights fought four great battles against the Wild—and what I would give to have been part of that. The creatures of the Wild came forth to do battle—great armies of them!" His eyes shone.

Gaston raised an eyebrow.

"The old king was victorious in the main, but eventually, he sent to the East for more knights. His losses were fearsome." De Vrailly looked as if he could see it happening. "His son—now the king—has fought well to hold what his father gained, but he takes no new land from the Wild. My angel will change that. We will throw the Wild back beyond the wall. I have seen it."

Gaston released a long-held breath. "Cousin, just how fearsome were these losses?"

"Oh, heavy, I suppose. At the Battle of Chevin, King Hawthor is said to have lost fifty thousand men." De Vrailly shrugged.

Gaston shook his head. "Numbers that large make my head ache. That's the population of a large city. Have they replaced their losses?"

"By the good Saviour, no! If they had, do you think we could challenge for the rulership of this land with three hundred lances?"

Gaston spat. "Good Christ—"

"Do not blaspheme!"

"Your angel wants us to take this realm with three hundred lances so that he can launch a war against the Wild?" Gaston stepped close to his cousin. "Should I slap you to wake you up?"

De Vrailly rose to his feet. With a gesture, he dismissed his squires. "It is not seemly that you question me on these matters, cousin. It is enough that you summoned your knights and now you follow me. Obey me. That is all you need to know."

Gaston made a face like a man who has discovered a bad smell. "I have always followed you," he said.

De Vrailly nodded his head.

"I have also saved you from a number of mistakes," Gaston added.

"Gaston," de Vrailly's voice suddenly softened. "Let us not disagree. I am advised by heaven. Do not be jealous!"

"Then I should like to meet your angel," Gaston said.

De Vrailly narrowed his eyes. "Perhaps," he said, "perhaps my angel is only for me. After all—I alone am the greatest knight."

Gaston sighed and moved to the window where he looked down at the lone figure kneeling on the smooth stones of the courtyard. The bodies had been taken, laid out and wrapped in linen ready for burial, but still the Alban knight knelt in the courtyard.

"What do you plan to do with that man?" Gaston asked.

"Take him to court to prove my prowess. Then I'll ransom him."

Gaston nodded. "We should offer him a cup of wine."

De Vrailly shook his head. "He does penance for his weakness—for the sin of pride, in daring to face me, and for his failure as a man-at-arms. He should kneel there in shame for the rest of his life."

Gaston looked at his cousin, his face half turned away. He fingered his short beard. Whatever he might have said was interrupted by a knock on the door. Johan put his head in.

"An officer of the town, *monsieur*. To see you."

"Send him away."

After a pause in which Gaston poured himself wine, Johan reappeared. "He says he must insist. He is *not* a knight. Merely a well-born man. He is not in armour. He says he is the sheriff."

"So? Send him away."

Gaston put a hand on his cousin's shoulder. "Their sheriff's are king's officers, are they not? Ask him what he wants."

Johan could be heard speaking, and then shouting, and then the door slammed open. Gaston drew his sword, as did de Vrailly. Their gentlemen poured in from adjoining rooms, some still fully armed.

"You are Jean de Vrailly?" asked the newcomer, who didn't seem to care that he was surrounded by armed foreigners who topped him by a head or more. He was in doublet and hose, with high boots and a long sword belted at his waist. He was fiftyish and running to fat, and only the fur on his hood, his bearing and the sword at his hip suggested he was a man of any consequence. But he glowered.

"I am," de Vrailly answered.

"I arrest you in the name of the king for the murder of—"

The sheriff was knocked unconscious with a single blow from Raymond St. David, who let the body fall to the floor. "Bah," he said.

"They are soft," de Vrailly said. "Did he bring men-at-arms?"

"Not one," Raymond said. He grinned. "He came alone!"

"What kind of a country is this?" Gaston asked. "Are they all insane?"

In the morning, Gaston's retainers collected the dull-eyed Alban knight from the courtyard and packed him onto a cart with his armour; his horses were tethered behind. He tried to engage the Alban in conversation and was repelled by the man's look of hatred.

"Destriers," his cousin commanded. There was a lot of grumbling at the order—no knight liked to ride his war horse when the occasion didn't demand it. A good war horse, fully trained, was worth the value of several suits of armour—and a single pulled muscle, a strain, a cut, or a bad shoe was an expensive injury.

"We must impress the earl."

De Vrailly's household knights formed up in the inn's great courtyard while the lesser men-at-arms prepared in the field outside the town. They had almost a thousand spears, as well as three hundred lances. Gaston had already been out the gate, seen to the lesser men, and was back.

The innkeeper—a surly, sharp faced fellow—came out and spoke to the Alban knight on the cart.

De Vrailly grinned at him, and Gaston knew there would be trouble.

"You!" de Vrailly shouted. His clear voice rang across the courtyard. "I take issue with your measure of hospitality, Ser Innkeeper! Your service was poor, the wine bad, and you attempted to interfere in a gentleman's private matter. What have you to say for yourself?"

The rat-faced innkeeper put his hands on his hips. Gaston shook his head. He was actually going to *discuss it* with a knight.

"I—!" he began, and one of de Vrailly's squires, already mounted, reached out and kicked him. The kick caught him in the side of the head and he fell without a sound.

The other squires laughed and looked to de Vrailly, who dropped a small purse on the unconscious man. "Here's *money*, innkeeper." He laughed. "We will teach these people to behave like civilized people and not animals. Burn the inn!"

Before the last wagon of their small army had pulled out onto the road, a column of smoke was rising over the town of Lorica, and high into the sky.

An hour later, Gaston was at his cousin's side when they met the Earl of Towbray and his retinue where the Lorica road crossed the North road. The man had fifty lances—a large force for Alba. The earl was fully armoured and wore his helmet. He sent a herald who invited *The Captal de Vrailly and all those who attend him* to ride forward and meet the earl under the shade of a large oak that grew alone at the crossroads.

Gaston smiled at the earl's caution. "Here is a man who understands how the world works," he said.

"He grew up among us," de Vrailly agreed. "Let us ride to meet him. He has six lances with him—we shall take the same."

The earl raised his visor when they met. "Jean de Vrailly, Sieur de Ruth?" he asked.

De Vrailly nodded. "You do not remember me," he said. "I was quite young when you toured the east. This is my cousin Gaston, Lord of Eu."

Towbray clasped hands with each in turn, gauntleted hand to gauntleted hand. His knights watched them impassively, visors closed and weapons to hand.

"Did you have trouble in Lorica?" the earl asked, pointing at the column of smoke on the horizon.

De Vrailly shook his head. "No trouble," he said. "I taught some lessons that needed to be learned. These people have forgotten what a sword is, and forgotten the respect due to the men of the sword. A poor knight challenged me—I defeated him, of course. I will take him to Harndon and ransom him, after I display him to the king."

"We burned the inn," Gaston interrupted. He thought it had been a foolish piece of bravado, and he was finding his cousin tiresome.

The earl glared at de Vrailly. "Which inn?" he asked.

De Vrailly glared back. "I do not like to be questioned in that tone, my lord."

"The sign of two lions. You know it?" Gaston leaned past his cousin.

"You burned the Two Lions?" The earl demanded. "It has stood there forever. Its foundations are Archaic."

"And I imagine they are still there for some other peasant to build his sty upon." De Vrailly frowned. "They scurried like rats to put out the fire, and I did nothing to stop them. But I was offended. A lesson needed to be made."

The earl shook his head. "You have brought so *many* men. I see three hundred knights—yes? In all of Alba there might be four thousand knights."

"You wanted a strong force. And you wanted me," de Vrailly said. "I am here. We have common cause—and I have your letter. You said to bring all the force I could muster. Here it is."

"I forget how rich the East is, my friend. Three hundred lances?" The earl shook his head. "I can pay them, for now, but after the spring campaign we may have to come to another arrangement."

De Vrailly looked at his cousin. "Indeed. Come spring we will have another arrangement."

The earl was distracted by the cart in the middle of the column.

"Good Christ," he said suddenly. "You don't mean that Ser Gawin Murien is your prisoner? Are you *insane*?"

De Vrailly pulled his horse around so hard Gaston saw blood on the bit.

"You will not speak to me that way, my lord!" De Vrailly insisted.

The earl rode down the column, heedless of his men-at-arms' struggle to stay with him. He rode up to the wagon.

Gaston watched his cousin carefully. "You will not kill this earl just because he annoys you," he said quietly.

"He said I was insane," de Vrailly countered, mouth tight and eyes glittering. "We can destroy his fifty knights with a morning's work."

"You will end with a kingdom of corpses," Gaston said. "If the old king really lost fifty *thousand* men in one battle a generation ago, this kingdom must be almost empty. You cannot kill everyone you dislike."

The earl had the Alban knight out of the cart and on horseback before he rode back, his visor closed and locked and his knights formed closely behind him.

"Messire," he said, "I have lived in the East, and I know how this misunderstanding has sprung up. But in Alba, messire, we do not keep to *The Rule of War* at all times. In fact, we have something we call the *The Rule of Law.* Ser Gawin is the son of one of the realm's most powerful lords—a man who is my ally—and Ser Gawin acted as any Alban would. He was not required to be in his armour at that hour—not here, and not when taking his ease at an inn. He is not in a state of war with you, messire. By our law, you attacked him perfidiously and you can be called to law for it."

De Vrailly made a face. "Then your law is something that excuses weakness and devalues strength. He chose to fight and was beaten. God spoke on the matter and no more need be said."

The earl's eyes were just visible inside his visor and Gaston had his hand on his sword; while the earl was speaking reasonably, his hand was on the pommel of an axe at his saddle bow. His knights all had the posture—the small leaning forward, the steadying hand on a horse's neck—of men on the edge of violence. They were one step away from a disaster of blood. He could sense it.

"You will apologise to him for the barbaric deaths of his squires, or our agreement is at an end." The earl's voice was firm, and his hand was steady on his axe. "Listen to me, messire. You *cannot* take this man to court. The king has only to hear his story and you will be arrested."

"There are not enough men-at-arms in this country to take me," de Vrailly said.

The earl's retainers drew their swords.

Gaston raised his empty, armoured hands and interposed his horse between the two men. "Gentlemen! There was a misunderstanding. Ever it has been so, when East meets West. My cousin was within his rights as a knight and a seigneur. And you say this Ser Gawin was also within his rights. Must we, who have come so far to serve you, my lord Earl—must we all pay for this misunderstanding? As it pleases God, we are all men of good understanding and good will. For my part, I will apologise to the young knight." Gaston glared at his cousin.

The beautiful face showed understanding. "Ah, very well," he said. "He is the son of your ally? Then I will apologise. Although, by the good God! He needs training in arms."

Gawin Murien had recovered enough of his wits to pack his armour onto one horse and mount another. Then he followed the earl through the column, the way a child follows his mother.

The earl raised his visor. "Gawin!" he called out. "Lad, the foreign knights—they come from different customs. The Lord de Vrailly will apologise to you."

The Alban was seen to nod.

De Vrailly halted his horse well out of arm's reach, while Gaston rode closer. "Ser Knight," he said, "for my part, I greatly regret the deaths of your squires."

The Alban knight nodded again. "Very courteous of you," he said. His voice was flat.

"And for mine," de Vrailly said, "I forgive your ransom, as the earl insists that by your law of arms, I may have encountered you unfairly." The last word was drawn from him as if by a fish hook.

Murien looked a less-than-heroic figure in his stained cote-hardie and his hose ruined by a night of kneeling in the courtyard. He didn't glitter. In fact, he hadn't even put his knight's belt back on, and his sword still lay on the bed of the wagon.

He nodded again. "I hear you," he said.

He turned his horse, and rode away.

Gaston watched him go, and wondered if it would have been better for everyone if his cousin had killed him in the yard.

Chapter Five

Harndon Palace—Harmodius

Harmodius Magus sat in a tower room entirely surrounded by books, and watched the play of the sun on the dust motes, as it shone through the high, clear glass windows. It was April—the season of rain but also the season of the first serious, warm sun—when the sunlight finally has its own colour, its own richness. Today, the sky was blue and a cat might be warm in a patch of sunshine.

Harmodius had three cats.

"Miltiades!" he hissed, and an old grey cat glanced at him with weary insolence.

The man's gold-shod stick licked out and prodded the cat, whose latest sleeping spot threatened the meticulously drawn pale blue chalk lines covering the dark slate floor. The cat shifted by the width of its tail and shot the Magus a disdainful look.

"I feed you, you wretch," Harmodius muttered.

The light continued to pour through the high windows, and to creep down the whitewashed wall, revealing calculations in chalk, silver or lead pencil, charcoal, even scratched out in dirt. The Magus used whatever came to hand when he felt the urge to write.

And still the light crept down the wall.

In the halls below, the Magus could sense men and women—*a servant bringing a tray of cold venison to his tower's door; a gentleman and lady engaged in a ferocious tryst that burned like a small fire almost directly under his feet—where was that? It must be awfully public—and the Queen, who burned like the very sun.* He smiled when he brushed over her warmth. Oftimes, he watched others to pass the time. It was the only form of phantasm he still cast regularly.

Why is that? he wondered, idly.

But this morning, well. This morning his Queen had asked him—challenged him—to do something.

Do something wonderful, Magus! she had said, clapping her hands together.

Harmodius waited until the sun crossed a chalk line he had drawn, and then raised his eyes to a particular set of figures. Nodded. Sipped some cold tea that had a film of dust—what was that dust? Oh—he had been grinding bone for oil colour. He had bone dust in his tea. That wasn't entirely disgusting.

All three cats raised their heads and pricked their ears.

The light intensified and struck a small mirror with the image of Ares and Taurus entwined on the ivory back—and then shot across the floor in a focused beam.

"Fiat lux!" roared the Magus.

The beam intensified, drawing in the light around it until the cats were cast in shadow while the beam sparkled like a line of lightning—passing above the chalk designs, through a lens, and into a bubble of gold atop his staff. Unnoticed by him, it struck a little off centre and a tiny fragment of the white beam slid past the staff to dance along the far wall, partially reflected by the golden globe, partly refracted by the mass of energy seething inside the staff itself. The intense light flicked up sharply, licked at gilding of a triptych that adorned the sideboard, struck a glass of wine abandoned hours before. And, still focused, it passed across the east wall, its rapid passage burning away a dozen or more characters of a spell written in an invisible, arcane ink, hidden under the paint.

The older cat started, and hissed.

The Magus felt suddenly light headed, as if at the onset of a fever or a strong head-cold. But his mind was abruptly clear and sharp, and the staff was giving off the unmistakable aura of an artefact filling with power. He saw the rogue light fragment and deftly moved the mirror and the focus to touch the staff perfectly.

He clapped his hands in triumph.

The cats looked around, startled, as if they had never seen his room before—and then went back to sleep.

Harmodius looked around the room. "What in the name of the triad just happened?" he asked.

He didn't need rest. Even after casting a powerful *phantasm* like the last, the feeling of the *helios* in his staff made him tingle with anticipation. He'd promised himself that he'd wait a day...perhaps two days...but the temptation was strong.

"Bah," he said aloud, and the cats flicked their ears. He hadn't felt so alive in many years.

He took a heavy flax mop and scrubbed the floor, eliminating every trace of the complex chalk pattern that had decorated it like an elaborate Southern rug. Then, despite his age and his heavy robes, he was down on his knees with a square of white linen, scrubbing even the cracks between the slate slabs until there was not a trace of pale blue chalk. However eager he was, he was also fastidious about this—that no trace of one phantasm should linger while he performed another. Experience had taught him that lesson well.

Then he went to a side table and opened the drawer, wherein was laid a box of ebony bound in silver. The Magus loved beautiful things—and when the consequences of bad conjuring were soul-destruction and death, the presence of beautiful things help reassure and steady him.

Inside the box lay a nested set of instruments made of bronze—a compass, a pair of calipers, a ruler with no markings; a pencil which held silver suspended in alum and clay and wax, blessed by a priest.

He wrapped a string around the pencil, measuring the length against the ruler, and began to pray. "O, Hermes Trismegistus," he began, and continued in High Archaic, purifying himself, clearing his thoughts, invoking God and his son and the prophet of the magi while another part of his mind calculated the precise length of string he would need.

"I should not do this today," he told the fattest cat. The big feline didn't seem to care.

He knelt on the floor, not to pray, but to draw. Putting a sliver of wood into a slot in the slate, he used the string, shaking with the tension in his hands, to guide his hand through a perfect circle, and into the circle, with the help of the ruler and a sword, he inscribed a pentagram. He wrote his invocation to God and to Hermes Trismegistus in High Archaic around the outside, and only the clamour of the cats for their noonday feast kept him from attempting his work right there and then.

"All three of you are man's best practice for dealing with demons," he said as he fed them fresh salmon, new caught in the River Albin and sold in the market.

They ignored him and ate, and then rubbed against him with loud protests of eternal love.

But his words gave him pause, and he unlocked the heavy oak door to the tower chamber and walked down one hundred and twenty-two steps to his sitting room where Mastiff, the Queen's man, sat reading in an armchair. The man leapt to his feet when the Magus appeared.

The Magus raised an eyebrow and the man bowed. But Harmodius was in a hurry—a hurry of passion—and little incivilities would have to wait. "Be so kind as to hurry and beg the Queen's indulgence: would she do me the kindness to pay me a visit?" he asked, and handed the man a plain copper coin—a sign between them. "And ask my laundress to pay me a visit." He handed over a handful of small silver change. Some of the coins were as small as sequins.

Mastiff took the coins and bowed. He was used to the Magus and his odd ways, so he hurried off as if his life depended on the journey.

The Magus poured himself a cup of wine and drank it off, stared out the window, and tried to convince himself to let it go for a day. Who would care?

But he felt ten years younger, and when he thought of what he was about to prove he shook his head, and his hand trembled on the cup.

He heard her light step in the hall, and he rose and bowed deeply when she entered.

"La," she said, and her presence seemed to fill the room. "I was just saying to my Mary—I'm bored!" She laughed, and her laugh rose to the high rafters.

"I need you, your Grace," he said with a deep bow.

She smiled at him, and the warmth of it left him more light headed still. Afterwards, he could never decide whether lust played a part in what he felt for her; the feeling was strong, possessive, awesome, and dangerous.

"I am determined to work a summoning, your Grace, and would have you by me to steady my hand. I hope it will be wonderful." He bowed over hers.

"My dear old man, she looked at him tenderly. He felt in her regard a flaw—she pitied him. "I honour your efforts, but don't tax yourself to impress me!"

He refused to be annoyed. "Your Grace, I have made such summonings many times. They are always fraught with peril, and like swimming, only a fool does such a thing alone." In his mind's eye, he imagined swimming with her, and he swallowed heavily.

"I doubt that I can do anything to support a mighty practitioner such as you—I, who only feel the sun's rays on my skin, and you, who feel his power in your very soul." But she went to the base of the long staircase eagerly and led him to the top, her feet lighter on the treads than his by half a century. And yet he was not breathing hard when they reached the top.

She kicked off her red shoes on the landing and entered his chamber carefully, barefoot, avoiding the precise markings on the floor. She paused to look at them. "Master, I have never seen you work something so—daring!" she said, and this time her admiration was unfeigned.

She went to stand in the sun which now covered the east wall instead of the west. She stood there studying the equations and lines of poetry, and then she began to scratch the ears of the old fat cat.

He purred a moment, sank his fangs into her palm, and mewed when she swatted him with her other hand.

Harmodius shook his head and poured honey on the punctures the cat had left. "I've never known him to bite before," he said.

She shrugged with an impish smile and licked the honey.

He, too, removed his shoes.

He went to his wall of writing and pushed his nose close, reading two lines written in silver pencil. Then, taking up a small ebony wand, he wrote the two lines in the air, and left letters of bright fire behind—thinner than the thinnest hair, and yet perfectly visible from where either of them stood.

"Oh!" said the Queen.

He smiled at her. He had the briefest temptation to kiss her and another desire, equal but virtually opposite, to back out of the whole thing.

She reminded him of—

"Bah," he said. "Are you ready, your Grace?"

She smiled and nodded.

"Kaleo se, CHARUN," the Magus said, and the light over the pentagram paled.

The Queen took a step to the right, and stood in the full beam of the sun from the high windows, and the old cat rubbed against her bare leg.

Shadow began to fill the pentagram. The Magus took up his staff, and held the hollow golden end like a spear point between himself and the inscribed sign on the floor.

"Who calls me?" came a whisper from the fissure in light that flickered like a butterfly above the pentagram.

"KALEO," Harmodius insisted.

Charun manifested beneath the shadow. The Magus felt his ears pop, and the sun seemed dimmed.

"Ahhh," he hissed.

"Power for knowledge," Harmodius said.

The shadows were drawn into a creature that was like a man, except he was taller than the highest bookcase, naked, a deep white veined in blue like old marble, with tough, leathery wings that swept majestically from well above his head to the floor in a perfect arc that any artist would have admired.

The smell he brought with him was alien—like the smell of lye soap being burned. Neither clean nor foul. And his eyes were a perfect, black blank. He carried a sword as tall as a man and wickedly barbed, and his head held both alien horror and angelic beauty in one—an ebony-black beak inlaid with gold; huge, almond shaped eyes, deep and endless blue like twin sapphires, and a bony crest filled with hair, like the decoration on an Archaic helmet.

"Power for knowledge," Harmodius said again.

The demon's blank eyes regarded him. Who knew what they thought? They seldom spoke, and they didn't often understand what a magus asked.

And then, as swiftly as an eagle seizes a rabbit, the sword shot out and cut the circle.

Harmodius's eyes narrowed, but he had not lived as long as he had by giving in to panic. "*Sol et scutum Dominus Deus,*" he said.

The second strike of the sword licked out through the circle but rang off the shield that had formed over the demon. The creature looked at the shield, glowing a bubbly purple shot with white, and began to prod it with the sword. Sparks began to cascade down the sides of the shield, shaped like a bright bell of colour suspended over the daemon. Smoke began to rise from the floor.

Harmodius struck his staff against the edge of the circle where the sword had cut his pattern. "*Sol et scutum Dominus Deus!*" he roared.

The rift in the circle closed, and the creature reared back and hissed.

The Queen leaned in towards it, and Harmodius felt a pang of pure terror that she would unwittingly cross the circle. But he could not say anything to her. To do so would be to betray the energy of his summoning—his entire will was bent on the creature that had manifested, and the circle, the pentagram, and the shield.

He was, he realised, juggling too many balls.

He considered letting the shield go—right up until the demon breathed fire.

It blossomed like a flower, flowing to cover the entire surface of the shield, and the room was suddenly hot. The fire could not pass the shield—but the heat from it could, and the deamon's heat changed the contest of wills utterly. Even as he began to consider the possibility that he might be defeated, Harmodius's mind viewed this fact with fascination. Despite the shield, he could smell the creature, and he could feel the heat.

As suddenly as they had appeared, the flames retreated from the edges of the circle and fled back into the creature's mouth. The heat dropped perceptibly.

Desiderata leaned in until her nose touched the unsolid surface of the shield. And she *laughed.*

The demon turned to her, head cocked, for all the world like a puppy. And then he laughed back.

She curtsied, and then began to dance.

The demon watched her, rapt, and so did the Magus.

She expressed herself in her hips, and in the rise of her hands above her head as she danced a mere dozen steps—a dance of spring, naïve and unflawed by practice.

The creature inside the bubble of power shook his head. "*Eyah!*"

He took a step towards her, and his head touched the edge of the pentagram, and he howled with rage and swept his sword across the sigil, cutting a gouge in the slate floor that broke the circle.

She extended a foot and crossed her toes over the break, and it was healed.

Harmodius breathed again. Quick as a terrier after a rat, he struck his staff through the shield and poured the power he had collected from his phantasm into the demon.

It whirled from the Queen to face the Magus, sword poised—but took no action. Its mighty chest rose and fell. Its aspect changed, suddenly—it rose into the air, glowing white, an angel with wings of a swan, and then it fell to the slate floor and its writhing changed to the hideous controlled motion of a millipede larger than a horse, cramped in the confines of the shield. Harmodius raised his wand, joy surging though his heart—the pure joy of having truly tested a theory and found it to contain more gold than dross.

Harmodius's took his staff from the circle and spat "*Ithi!*"

The pentagram was empty.

Harmodius was too proud to slump. But he went to the Queen's side and threw his arms around her with a familiarity he never knew he dared.

She kissed him tenderly.

"You are an old fool," she said. "But a brilliant, brave old fool, Harmodius." Her smile was warm and congratulatory. "I had no idea—I've never seen you do anything like it."

"Oh," he said, into the smell of her neck—and a galaxy of new learning occurred to him in that moment. But he backed away and bowed. "I owe you my life," he said. "What are you?"

She laughed, and her laugh threatened to mock all evil straight out of fashion. "What am I?" she asked. She shook her head. "You dearest old fool."

"Still wise enough to worship at *your* feet, your Grace." He bowed very low.

"You are like a boy who attacks a hornet's nest to see what will come out. And yet I smell the triumph of the small boy on you, Harmodius. What have we learned today?" She subsided suddenly into a chair, ignoring the scrolls that covered it. "And where did this sudden burst of daring come from? You are a byword for caution in this court." She smiled, and for a moment, she was not a naïve young girl, but an ancient and very knowing queen. "Some say you have no power, and are a sort of Royal Mountebank." Her eyes flicked to the pentagram. "Apparently, they are wrong."

He followed the wave of her hand and hurried to pour her wine. "I cannot say for certain sure what we learned today," he said carefully. Already his careful manner was reasserting itself. But he *knew* he was right.

"Talk to me as if I was a student—a stupid squire bent on acquiring the rudiments of hermeticism," she said. She sipped his wine and her look of contentment and the flinging back of her head told him that she, too had known a moment of terror. She was mortal. He was not always sure of that. "Because I can use power, I think you assume that I know how it functions. That we have the same knowledge. But nothing can be further from the truth. The sun touches me, and I feel God's touch, and sometimes, with his help, I can work a miracle." She smiled.

He thought that her self-assurance could, if unchecked, make her more terrifying than any monster.

"Very well, your Grace. You know there are two schools of power—two sources for the working of any phantasm." He laid his staff carefully in a corner and then knelt to wipe the pentagram from the floor.

"White and black," she said.

He glared at her.

She shrugged with a smile. "You are so easy, my Magus. There is the power of the sun, pure as light, unfettered, un-beholden—the very sign of the pleasure of God in all creation. And there is the power of the Wild—for which, every iota must be exchanged with one of the creatures that possess it, and each bargain sealed in blood."

Harmodius rolled his eyes. "Sealed. Bargained for. Blood does not really enter into it." He nodded. "But the power is there—it rises from the very ground—from grass, from the trees, from the creatures that live among the trees."

She smiled. "Yes. I can feel it, although it is no friend to me."

"Really?" he asked, cursing himself for a fool. Why had he *not* asked the Queen earlier? A safer experiment sprang to his mind. But what was done was done. "You can feel the power of the Wild?"

"Yes!" she said. "Stronger and weaker—even in those poor dead things that decorate the hall."

He shook his head at his own foolishness—his hubris.

"Do you sense any power of the Wild in this room?" he asked.

She nodded. "The green lamp is an artefact of the Wild, is it not? A faery lamp?"

He nodded. "Can you take any of the power it pours forth and use it, your Grace?"

She shuddered. "Why would you even ask such a thing? Now I think you dull, Magus."

Hah, he thought. *Not so hubristic as all that.*

"And yet I conjured a powerful demon of the abyss—did I not?" he asked her.

She smiled. "Not one of the greatest, perhaps. But yes."

"Allied to the Wild—would you say?" he asked.

"*God is the sun and the power of the sun—and Satan dwells in the power of the Wild.*" She sang the lines like a schoolgirl. "*Daemons must use the power of the Wild. When Satan broke with God and led his legions to hell, then was magic broken into two powers, the green and the gold. Gold for the servants of God. Green for the servants of Satan.*"

He nodded. Sighed. "Yes," he said. "But of course, it is more complicated than that."

"Oh, no," she said, showing that glacial self-assurance again. "I think men often seek to overcomplicate things. The nuns taught me this. Are you saying that they lied?"

"I just fed a demon with the power of the sun. I conjured him with the power of the sun." Harmodius laughed.

"But—no, you banished him!" Her silver laugh rang out. "You tease me, Magus!"

He shook his head. "I banished him after feeding him enough power to make him *grow*," the Magus said. "Pure Helios, which I drew myself using my instruments—lacking your Grace's special abilities." *Whatever they may be.*

She gazed at him, eyes level, devoid of artifice or flirtation, mockery or subtle magnetism or even her usual humour.

"And this means?" she asked, her voice a whisper.

"Ask me again, your Grace, after I conjure him back a week hence. Tell me you will stand at my side that day—I'm beholden to you, but with you—"

"What do you seek, Magus? Is this within the circlet of what the church will countenance?" She spoke slowly, carefully.

He drew a breath. Released it. *Sod the church*, he thought. And aloud he said, "Yes, your Grace." *No, your Grace. Perhaps not. But they're not scientists. They're interested in preserving the status quo.*

The Queen gave him a beautiful smile. "I am just a young girl," she said. "Shouldn't we ask a bishop?"

Harmodius narrowed his eyes. "Of course, your Majesty," he said.

The North Road—Gerald Random

Random's convoy moved fast, by the standards of convoys—six to ten leagues a day, stopping each night at the edge of a town and camping in pre-arranged fields, with fodder delivered to their camp along with hot bread and new-butchered meat. Men were happy to work for him because he was a meticulous planner and the food was good.

But they had a hundred leagues to go, just to make Albinkirk, and another forty leagues east after that, to the fair, and he was later than he wanted to be. Albinfleurs—little yellow balls of sweet-scented, fuzzy petals that grew only on the cliff edges of the great river—were blooming in the hayfields that lined the roads; and when they were on his favourite sections of road—the cliff-edge road along the very edge of the Albin which ran sixty feet or more below them in the vale—the Albinfleurs were like stripes of yellow below him and layers of yellow on the cliffs nearly a mile distant on the other side. It was years since he'd left late enough to see the Albinfleurs. They didn't grow in the north.

But after three glorious days of solid travel, they came to Lorica, and the Two Lions. His usual stop and supplier of bread and forage was a smoking hulk. It took him a day to establish a new supplier and get the material he needed, and the story of how the inn had been burned and the sheriff beaten by foreigners angered him. But the innkeeper had sent to the king, and stood in his yard with a bandaged head watching workmen with a crane lift the charred rooftrees off the main building.

He used one of his precious mercenaries to send a message about the killings back to the Guild Master in Harndon. Harndoners didn't usually concern themselves with the doings of the lesser towns. But this was business, friendship, and basic patriotism all in one package.

The following day not one but two of his wagons broke spokes on their wheels—one so badly that the wooden wheel split and the iron tyre popped off the wheel. That meant finding a smith and wheelwright and forced him to go *back* to Lorica, where he had to stay in an inferior inn while his convoy crept north without him. He had to do it himself—the men in Lorica knew him but none of his hirelings, not Judson the draper, nor any of the other investors.

In the morning, the two wagons were ready to move, and he grudgingly paid the agreed fee for making two apprentice wheelwrights and a journeyman work by rush light through the night. Plus an extra silver leopard to the blacksmith for getting the tyre on before matins.

He finished his small beer and mounted his horse, and the smaller train was on the road as soon as he'd taken the Eucharist from a friar who said Mass at a roadside shrine. That roadside Mass was full of broken men and women—wastrels, a pair of vagabonds, and a troop of travelling players. Random had never been troubled by the poor. He gave them alms.

But the broken men worried him, for both his convoy and his purse. There were four of them, although they didn't seem to be together. Random had never been robbed by men he'd just attended Mass with, but he didn't take any chances, either. He mounted, exchanged meaningful glances with his drovers, and the carts moved on.

One of the broken men followed them on the road. He had a good horse and armour in a wicker basket, and he seemed listless. Random looked back at him from time to time.

Eventually, the man caught them up. But he hadn't put on his armour and he didn't even seem to know they were there. He rode up, slowly catching and then overtaking them.

Harndoners traditionally called the men they'd attended Mass with that day Brother or Sister, and so Random nodded to the stranger.

"The Peace of God to you, Brother," he said, a little pointedly.

The man looked startled to be addressed.

In that moment, Random realised he wasn't a broken man at all but a dirty gentleman. The differences were clear in his quality—the man had a superb leather-covered jupon worth a good twenty leopards, even covered in dirt. Hip boots with gold spurs. Even if they were silver gilt, they were worth a hundred leopards by weight.

The man sighed. "And to you, messire."

He rode on.

Random hadn't come to relative riches in the cut-throat world of Harndon's shippers and guilds without having some willingness to grab at Fortuna's hairs. "You're a knight," he said.

The man didn't rein in, but he turned his head and, feeling the weight shift, his horse stopped.

The man turned to look at him, and the silence was painful.

What have we here? Random wondered.

Finally, the young man—under his despair, the man was younger than Random by a generation—nodded.

"I am a knight," the young man said, as if confessing a sin.

"I need men," Random said. "I have a convoy on the road and if you wear spurs of gold, I'd be honoured to have you. My convoy is fifty good wagons headed north to the fair, and there's no dishonour in it. I fear only bandits and the Wild."

The man shook his head minutely and turned away, and his horse ambled on, a good war horse which was over-burdened with man and armour, the weight ill-distributed and ruining the horse's posture.

"Are you sure?" Random asked. It never hurt to try.

The knight kept riding.

Random let his drovers stop for lunch, and then they pushed on—into the evening and even a little after dark.

In the morning, they rose and were moving on before the sun was a finger above the river which curved, snake-like, to the east. Later in the morning they descended into the vale and crossed the Great Bridge, the edge of the Inner Counties. He had a fine meal at the Crouching Cat with his drovers, who were honoured by his willingness to join them and pleased to eat so good a meal.

After lunch they crossed Great Bridge, twenty-six spans built by the Archaics and painstakingly maintained. And then climbed the far bank for an hour, with the drovers leading the horses. They crested the far bank, and Random saw the knight again, kneeling at a roadside chapel, tears cutting deep channels in the road-dust on his face.

He nodded to him, and rode on.

By evening he caught up the rest of the convoy, already in camp, and he was welcomed back by the men he'd left. His drovers regaled their peers with the minutiae of their days, and Guilbert saluted and told him how the column had proceeded, and Judson was resentful that he was back so soon.

Business as usual.

A little after dark, one of the goldsmith boys came to his wagon and saluted like a soldier. "Messire?" he asked. "There's a knight asking for ye." The boy had a crossbow on his shoulder, and was obviously puffed with pride at being on watch, on convoy, and in such an important role. *Henry Lastifer*, the name floated up from the merchant's storehouse of ready knowledge.

Random followed the boy to the fire. Guilbert was there, and Old Bob, another of the men-at-arms.

And the young knight from the road, of course. He was sitting, drinking wine. He rose hurriedly.

"May I change my mind?" he blurted.

Random smiled. "Of course. Welcome aboard, Ser Knight."

Guilbert smiled broadly. "M'lord, is more like. But he's the king's mark. And that's a sword." He turned to the knight. "Your name, m'lord?"

The young man waited so long it was obvious he was going to lie. "Ser Tristan?" he said, wistfully.

"Fair enough," Guilbert said. "Come wi' me, and we'll see to it you have a place to sleep."

"Mind you," said Random. "You work for Guilbert and then for me. Understand?"

"Of course," said the young man.

What am I getting myself into? Random thought. But he felt satisfied with the man, broken or not. King's knights were trained to a high level— especially trained to fight the Wild. Even if the young man was a little addled... well, no doubt he was in love. The gentry were addicted to love.

He slept well.

North of Lorica—Bill Redmede

Bill Redmede led his untrained young men up the trail. Their irk stayed well ahead, moving like smoke through the thick trees. He tended to return to the column from the most unexpected directions, even for a veteran woodsman like Bill.

The lads were all afraid of him.

Bill rather liked the quiet creature, which spoke only when it had something to say. Irks had something about them. It was hard to pin down, but they had some kind of nobility

"Right files watch the right side of the trail," Bill said, automatically. "Left files watch the *left* side." Three days on the trail and all he did was mother them.

"I need a break," whined the biggest and strongest of them. "Christ on the Cross, Bill! We're not boglins!"

"If you was, we'd move faster," Redmede said. "Didn't you boys do any *work* on the farm?"

It was worse when they made camp. He had to explain how to raise a shelter. He had to stop them from cutting their twine, and teach them how to make a fire. A *small* fire. How to be warm, how to be dry. Where to take a piss.

Two of them sang while they worked, until he walked up and knocked one to the ground with a blow of his fist.

"If the king catches you because you are *singing*, you will hang on a gibbet until the crows pick your bones clean and then the king's fucking sorcerer will grind your bones to make the colours for his paints," Bill said.

The angry silence of wronged young men struck him from all sides.

"If you fail, you will die," he said. "This is not a summer lark."

"I want to go home," said the biggest man. "You're worse than an aristo." He looked around. "And you can't stop all of us."

The irk materialised out of the dusk. He looked curiously at the big man. Then he turned to Bill. "Come," he said in his odd voice.

Bill nodded to them, the debate now unimportant. "Don't go anywhere," he said, and followed the irk.

They crossed a marsh, over a low ridge, and then down to a dense copse of spruce.

The irk turned and made a motion with its head. "Bear," it said. "A friend. Be kind, Man."

Near the centre of the spruce was a great golden bear. It lay with its head in its paws, as if it was resting. A beautiful cub stood licking its face.

As Bill come up, the bear stirred. It raised its head and hissed.

Bill stepped back, but the irk steadied him, and spoke in a sibilant whisper.

The bear rolled a little, and Bill could see it had a deep wound in its side, full of pus—pus was dryed on either side of the wound, and it stank.

The irk squatted down in a way a man could not have done. Its ear drooped—this was sadness, which Bill had never seen in an irk.

"The bear dies," the irk said.

Bill knew the irk was right.

"The bear asks—can we save her cub?" The irk turned and Bill realised how seldom the elfin creature had met his eyes, because in that moment, the irk's gaze locked with his, and he all but fell into the forest man's regard. His eyes were huge, and deep like pools—

"I don't know a thing about bears," Bill said. He squatted by the big mother bear. "But I'm a friend of any creature of the Wild, and I give you my word that if I can get your cub to other golden bears, I will."

The bear spat something, in obvious pain.

The irk spoke—or rather, sang. The line became a stanza, full of liquid rhymes.

The bear coughed.

The irk turned. "The cub—her mother named her for the yellow flower."

"Daisy?"

The irk made a face.

"Daffodil? Crocus? I don't know my flowers."

"In water." The irk was frustrated.

"Lily?"

The irk nodded.

So he reached out a hand to the cub, and the cub bit him.

Lissen Carak—The Red Knight

The captain was so tired and so drained by the fear that it was all he could do to push one boot in front of the other as the trail became a track and the track became a road.

Nothing troubled them but the coming darkness, their exhaustion, and the cold. It was late in the day and increasingly clear that they would have to camp in the woods. The same woods which had produced a daemon and a wyvern.

"Why didn't it kill us?" the captain asked. *Two daemons.*

Gelfred shook his head. "You killed that first one. Pretty. Damn. Fast." His eyes were always moving. They had reached the main road, and Gelfred pulled up on his horse's reins. "We could ride double," he said.

"You'll lame that horse," the captain snapped.

"You *cast a spell.*" Gelfred wasn't accusatory. He sounded more as if he was in pain.

"Yes," the captain admitted. "I do, from time to time."

Gelfred shook his head. He prayed aloud, and they rode on until a drizzle began and the light began to fade.

"We'll have to stand watches," the captain said. "We are very vulnerable." He could barely think. While Gelfred curried the poor beast, he gathered firewood and started a fire. He did everything wrong. He gathered bigger wood and had no axe to cut it; then he gathered kindling and broke it into ever smaller and better sorted piles. He knelt in his shallow fire-pit and used his flint and steel, shaving sparks onto charred cloth until he had an ember.

Then he realised that he hadn't built a nest of tow and bark to catch the ember.

He had to start again.

We're a pair of fools.

He could *feel* that the woods were full of enemies. Or allies. It was the curse of his youth.

What exactly have I stumbled into? he asked himself.

He made a little bird's nest of dry tow and birchbark shreds, and made sparks again, his right hand holding the steel and moving precisely to strike the flint in his left hand. He got a spark, lit the char—

Dropped it into the tow and bark—

And blew.

The fire caught.

He dropped twigs on the blaze until it was steady, and then built a cabin of dry wood, carefully split with his hunting knife. He was very proud of his fire when he'd finished, and he thought that if the Wild took him here, at least he'd started the damned fire first.

Gelfred came and warmed his hands. Then he wound his crossbow. "Sleep, Captain," he said. "You first."

The captain wanted to talk—he wanted to think, but his body was making its own demands.

But before he could go to sleep he heard Gelfred move, and he was out of his blankets with his sword in his fist.

Gelfred's eyes were big in the firelight. "I just wanted to move the head," he said. "It—it's hard to have it there. And the horse hates it."

The captain helped to move the head. He stood there, in the dark, freezing cold.

There was something very close. Something powerful.

Perhaps building the fire had been a mistake, like coming out into the woods with just one other man.

Prudentia? Pru?

Dear boy.

Pru, can I pull the Cloak over this little camp? Or will I just make a disturbance in casting?

Cast quietly, as I have taught you.

He touched her marble hand, chose his wards and gardes, and opened the great iron door to his palace. Outside was a green darkness—thicker and greener than he liked.

But he took carefully from the green, and closed the door.

He staggered with the effort.

Suddenly he couldn't stay upright. He fell to his knees by the daemon's head.

The darkness was thick.

The head still had something of its aura of fear about it. He knelt by it—knees wet in the damp, cold leaves, and the cold helped to steady him.

"M'lord?" Gelfred asked, and he was obviously terrified. "M'lord!"

The captain worked on breathing for a moment.

"What?" he whispered.

"The stars went out," Gelfred said.

"I cast a little—concealment over us," the captain said. He shook his head. "Perhaps I mis-cast."

Gelfred made a noise.

"Let's get away from this thing," the captain said, and he got to his feet, and together the two men stumbled over tree roots to their tiny fire.

The horse was showing the whites of its eyes.

"I have to sleep," he said.

Gelfred made a motion in the dark. The captain took it for acceptance.

He slept from the moment his head went down, despite the fear, to the moment Gelfred woke him with a hand on his shoulder.

He heard the hooves.

Or talons.

Whatever it was, he couldn't see the thing making the noise. Or anything else.

The fire was out and the night was too dark to see anything. But something very large was moving—just an arm's length away. Maybe two.

Gelfred was right there, and the captain put a hand on his shoulder to steady them both.

Skerunch.

Snap.

Tick.

And then it was past them, moving down the hill to the road.

After an aeon, Gelfred said "It didn't see us or smell us."

The captain said *Thanks, Pru.*

"My turn to watch," he said.

Gelfred was snoring in ten minutes, secure in his lord in a way the captain could not be in himself.

The captain stared into the darkness, and it became his friend more than his foe. He watched, and as he watched, he felt his heartbeat settle, felt his pains fade. He made an excursion into his palace of memory—reviewing sword cuts, castings, wards, lines of poetry.

Beyond the bubble of his will the night passed slowly. But it did pass.

Eventually, the faintest light coloured the eastern sky, and he woke Gelfred as gently as he could. He lowered his ward when they were both awake and armed, but there was nothing waiting for them, and they found the horse, and the head.

Just around the clearing where they'd slept, a pair of deep tracks—cloven, with talons and a dew claw—pierced the forest leaf mold.

Gelfred started. The captain watched as he followed the tracks—

"Are we borrowing trouble, Gelfred?" he asked, following a few paces behind.

Gelfred looked back and pointed at the ground in front of him. When the captain joined him, he saw multiple tracks—perhaps three sets, or even four.

"What you fought yesterday. Four sets of prints. Here's one moving more slowly. Here's two moving fast—here they pause. Sniffing." He shrugged. "That's what I see."

Curiosity—the kind that gets cats killed—pulled the two of them forward. In ten more steps, there were eight or ten sets of tracks, and then, in another ten steps—

"Sweet Son of Man and all the angels!" Gelfred said.

The captain shook his head. "Amen," he added. "Amen."

They stood on a bank over a gully wide enough for a pair of wagons and a little deeper than the height of a man on a horse. It ran from west to east. The base was clear of undergrowth, like a—a road.

The whole gully was a mass of churned earth and tracks.

"It's an army!" Gelfred said.

"Let's move," said the captain. He turned and ran back to their clearing and settled his gear on the poor horse.

Then they were moving.

For a while, every shadow held a daemon—until they passed it. The captain didn't feel recovered; he was cold, hungry, and afraid even to make tea. The horse was lame from the cold and from being insufficiently cared for on a cold, damp spring night, and they rode her anyway.

It turned out they didn't have to go very far, which probably saved her life. The camp's sentries must have been alert, because a mile from the bridge, they were met by Jehannes leading six lances in full armour.

Jehannes's eyes were still bloodshot, but his voice was steady.

"What in the name of Satan were you doing?" Jehannes demanded.

"Scouting," the captain admitted. He managed to shrug, as if it was a matter of little moment. He was very proud of that shrug.

Jehannes looked at him with the look that fathers save for children they intend to punish later—and then he caught sight of the head being dragged in the mud. He rode back to look at it. Bent over it.

His wide and troubled eyes told the captain that he had been right.

Jehannes turned his horse with a brutal jerk of the reins.

"I'll alert the camp. Tom, give the captain your horse. M'lord, we need to inform the Abbess." Jehannes's tone had changed. It wasn't respectful, merely professional. This was now a professional matter.

The captain shook his head. "Give me Wilful's horse. Tom, stay at my back."

Wilful Murder dismounted with his usual ill grace and muttered something about how he was always the one who got screwed.

The captain ignored him, got a leg over the archer's roncey with a minimum of effort, and set off at a fast trot, Wilful holding onto another man's stirrup leather and running full out, and then they stretched to a racing gallop across the last furlongs, with Wilful seeming to run alongside in ten league boots.

The guard had already turned out at the camp gate—a dozen archers and three men-at-arms, all in their kit and ready to fight. For the first time since he'd set his spear under his arm the day before, the captain's heart rose a fraction.

The head dragged in the dirt behind Gelfred's horse left a wake of rumour and staring.

The captain pulled up before his pavilion and dropped from the saddle. He considered bathing, considered washing the clots of ordure from his hair. But he wasn't positive he had the time.

He settled for a drink of water.

Jehannes, who had paused to speak to the Officer of the Watch, rode up, tall and deadly on his war horse.

Two archers—Long Sam and No Head, were ramming the head down on a stake.

The captain nodded at them. "Outside the main gate," he said. "Where every cottager can see it."

Jehannes looked at it for too long.

"Double the guard, put a quarter of the men-at-arms into harness round the clock as a quarter-guard, and draft a plan to clear the villages around the fortress," the captain said. He was having trouble with words—he couldn't remember being so tired. "The woods are full—*full* of the Wild. They have amassed an army out there. We could be attacked any moment." He seized an open inkwell on his camp table and scrawled a long note. He signed it in big capitals—good, educated writing.

The Red Knight, Captain.

"Get two archers provisioned and mounted as fast as you can—a pair of good horses apiece, and on the road. Send them to the king, at Harndon."

"Good Chryste," said Jehannes.

"We'll talk when I've seen the Abbess," the captain called, and Toby brought up his second riding horse, Mercy. He mounted, collected Bad Tom with a glance, and rode up the steep slope to the fortress.

The gate was open.

That was about to change.

He threw himself from Mercy and tossed the reins to Tom, who dismounted with a great deal less haste. The captain ran up the steps to the hall and pounded on the door. The priest was watching from his chapel door, as he always watched.

An elderly sister opened it and bowed.

"I need to see the lady Abbess as soon as may be," the captain said.

The nun flinched, hid her eyes and closed the door.

He was tempted to pound on it with his fists again, but chose not to.

"You and Gelfred killed that thing?" Bad Tom asked. He sounded jealous.

The captain shook his head. "Later," he said.

Bad Tom shrugged. "Must have been something to see," he said wistfully.

"You're—listen, not now, eh? Tom?" The captain caught himself watching the windows in the dormitory.

"I'd ha' gone wi' you, Captain," Tom said. "All I'm saying. Think of me next time."

"Christ on the cross, Tom," the captain swore. It was his first blasphemous oath in a long time, so naturally, he uttered it just as the frightened, elderly nun opened the heavy door.

Her look suggested she had heard a few oaths in her day. She inclined her head slightly to indicate that he should follow her so he climbed the steps and crossed the hall in her wake, to the doorway he'd never passed through but from whence wine had been served, and stools brought.

She led him down a corridor lined with doors and up a tightly winding stair with a central pillar of richly carved stone, to an elegant blue door. She knocked, opened the door and bowed.

The captain passed her, returning her bow. He wasn't too tired for courtesy, it appeared. His mind seemed to be coming back to him and he found that he was sorry to have blasphemed in the hearing of the nun.

It was like the feeling returning to an arm he'd slept on—the gradual retreat of numbness, the pins and needles of returning awareness, except that it was emotion returning, not his senses.

The Abbess was sitting on a low chair with an embroidery frame. Her west window caught the mid-day rays of the spring sun. Her scene showed a hart surrounded by dogs, a spear already in his breast. Bright silk-floss blood flowed down his flank.

"I saw you come in. You lost your horse," she said. "You stink of phantasm."

"You are in great peril," he replied. "I know how that sounds. But I mean it, just the same. This is not a matter of a few isolated creatures. I believe that some force of the Wild seeks to take this fortress and the river crossing. If they cannot take it by stealth and subterfuge, they will come by direct assault. And the attack could come at any hour. They have massed, in large numbers, in your woodlands."

She considered him carefully. "I assume this isn't a dramatic way of increasing your fee?" she asked. Her smile was subtle, betraying fear and humour in the same look. "No?" she asked, with a catch in her voice.

"My huntsman and I followed the spore—the Hermetical spore—of the daemon that murdered Hawisia," he said.

She waved him to a stool, and he found a cup of wine sitting on the side table. He drank it—the moment the cup touched his lips, he found that he was tilting it back, feeling the acid fire rush down his gullet. He put the cup back down, a little too hard, and the horn made a click on the wood that caused the Abbess to turn.

"It is bad?" she asked.

"We found a man's corpse first. He was dressed as a soldier—as a *Jack*." He took a deep breath. "Do you remember the Jacks, Abbess?"

Her eyes wandered far from him, off into another time. "Of course," she said. "My lover died fighting them," she said. "Ah, there's a reason for penance. My lover. Lovers." She smiled. "My old secrets have no value here. I know the Jacks. The secret servants of the Enemy. The old king exterminated them." She raised her eyes to his. "You found one. Or at least you showed me a leaf."

"Dead. Looked as if he had been killed, quite recently, by one of his own." The captain found a flagon of wine and poured a second cup. "I'm going to wager that he died a few hours after Sister Hawisia. Killed by another of his kind, as if that makes sense." He shook his head. "Then we went west, still following the spore." He sat down again, a little too hard.

She watched him.

"Then we found the creature." He stared at her. "An adversarius. You know what they are?" he asked.

"Every person of my generation knows what they are." She covered her eyes with her hand for a moment. "Daemons. The Wardens of the Wild."

He let another long breath go. "I thought they had been exaggerated." He looked out the window. "At any rate, there were two of them. I can only assume that the Jacks and the daemons are working together. If they are, this cannot be a random incident—I believe they're the harbingers of an attack, testing your strength, and I assume that your fortress is the target. It certainly has immense strategic value. I need to ask you to let my troops in, close the gates, place yourself in a posture of defence, and victual the fortress—call in your people, of course. And send word to the king."

She looked at him for a long time. "If you planned to take my fortress yourself . . ." she said. And left it there.

"My lady, I agree that it would be a brilliant stratagem. I even agree that I might try something like. I have fought in the East—we did such things there." He shrugged. "This is my country, my lady. And if you doubt me—and you have every reason to doubt me—you have only to look at what my archers are putting up outside the gates of our camp."

She looked out the window.

"You could tell me that there's an angel of the Lord outside the gates of your camp, telling your archers that I'm the most beautiful woman since Helen, and I couldn't see it well enough to believe you," she said. "But—I have seen you. I can smell the power on you. And—now I understand other things I have seen."

"You are an astrologer," he said. *I am slow*, he thought.

"Yes. And you are very difficult to read, as if—as if you have some protection from my art." She smiled. "But I am no novice, and God has given me the power to look at souls. Yours is rather curious—as I expect you know."

"Oh, God has been very good to me," he said.

"You mock and are bitter, but we face a crisis, and I am not your spiritual mother." Her voice changed, becoming sharper, and yet deeper. "Although

I would be, if you would let me in. You need His spirit." She turned away. "You are armoured in darkness. But it is a false armour, and will betray you."

"So people tell me," he said. "Yet it's served me well so far. Answer me this, Abbess. Who else was at that manor?"

The Abbess shrugged. "Later…"

The captain looked at her for a long time. "Who *else* was there?"

She shook her head. "Later. It is not the issue now, when I have a crisis of my tenure. I will not fail. I will hold this place."

He nodded. "So you will put this fortress in a posture of defence?" he asked.

She nodded. "This minute." She raised a hand bell and rang it.

The elderly nun came immediately.

"Fetch the gate warder and the sergeant at arms. And ring the alarm," the Abbess ordered in a firm voice. She went to the mantel on her fireplace, and opened a small box of ivory carved in the Cross of the Order of Saint Thomas. In it was a slip of milk-white birch bark.

"You're sure about this?" she whispered.

"I am," he said.

"I need to share your assurance," she said.

He sat back. "I could not make this up. You say you smell the power of the phantasm on me—"

"I believe that you have met and defeated another monster. It is possible that you found a dead Jack." She shrugged. "It is possible I have a traitor inside my walls. But once I cast this summoning, the Master of My Order will come with all his knights. He will probably demand that the king raise an army."

"That's is just about what is required here," said the Red Knight.

"I cannot have them come to my aid for nothing," she said.

The Red Knight sat back. His back hurt, and his neck hurt, and he felt the dull anger of complete fatigue. He bit back a retort, and then another.

"What will satisfy you?" he asked.

She shrugged. "I believe you. But I must be sure."

He nodded. Irrationally angry.

"Fine," he said. He rose, and bowed.

She reached for his hand.

He stepped back. "No time like the present," he spat.

"Captain!" she said. "You are not a small child."

He nodded, held onto his anger, and stalked out.

"What did she say?" Tom asked.

"She wants us to find their army, not just the signs of it," the captain said.

Tom grinned. "That will be a mighty feat of arms," he said.

Ser Milus had the banner, and the rest of his entourage was ready to mount. But the sergeant at arms stood in the gate with only the postern open. They would have to walk their horses out the gate. Even while cursing this delay, the captain commended the old witch. She took his warning seriously.

"Captain!"

He turned to see Amicia running barefoot across the courtyard.

"Let's go," Tom grunted. "I'll get a convoy together."

"Twenty lances," the captain said.

"Aye," said Tom. He winked as he left.

Amicia reached him. He felt her through the aether as she came up. He could smell her, an earthy, female smell, clean and bright, like a new sword. Like a taste of the Wild.

"The Abbess sends this," she said levelly. She held out a small scroll. "She says she will take immediate steps, so you are not to think yourself ignored."

He took the scroll from her hand.

"Thank you," he said. He managed a smile. "I am tired and difficult."

"You have fought for your life," she said. Her eyes held his. "There is no fatigue like that of fear and war."

He might have denied it. Knights don't admit to fear. But her gentle voice held an absolute certainty. It was healing. It was forgiving.

It was admiring.

He realised that he had been holding her hand the whole time. She flushed, but did not snatch it away.

"Lady, your words are a tonic to a tired man." He bowed and kissed her hand. It *was* a tonic. That or she had cast a spell on him unnoticed.

She laughed. "I am no lady, but a simple novice of this house," she said.

He tore himself away from her, or they might have stood far too long in the courtyard, with the first sun of the spring resting on them.

He read the scroll as he rode down the gravel path from the main gate to the Lower Town. Much of the path was walled, and some of it paved, making a fortified road, itself a defence.

Someone had put a great deal of money into this fortress.

He cantered through the town. His shoulder didn't hurt at all. But his right hand tingled for another reason entirely, and he laughed aloud.

Harndon Palace—Desiderata

Desiderata led her knights and ladies out into the spring.

It was early days yet, and even the heartiest of her bold young friends would not slip into the river naked today. But it was warm enough to ride fast, and to lay a picnic out on blankets.

Lady Mary directed the laying out of the food. Spontaneity, with Desiderata, often involved careful preparation and a great deal of work. Usually by Lady Mary.

Lady Rebecca Almspend, the Queen's bookish secretary, sat behind her, ticking items off as they were unpacked. They were old allies and childhood friends.

Rebecca kicked off her shoes. "It *is* spring," she said.

Mary smiled at her. "When a young man's fancy turns to war," she said.

"Too true. They've left us for the first foe in the field, and that is enough to turn any girl's head." Rebecca frowned. "I think he'll offer for me. I thought he might before he left."

Mary pursed her lips, looking at the two stone jars of marmalade—the Queen's favourite. She could eat a great deal of marmalade. "Did we really bring just two jars?"

"Honestly, Mary, the stuff costs the earth—oranges from the south? White sugar from the Islands?" Rebecca tossed her head. "She'll have no teeth when she's thirty."

"No one would notice," Mary said.

"Mary!" Rebecca was appalled to find her friend weeping. She slipped off her stump, and threw her arms around Mary. She was widely known as *sensible*, which seemed to mean that all of them could cry on her shoulders. In this case, she stood with her stylus in one hand and her wax tablet in the other, clutched to her friend's back, feeling a little foolish.

"He left without so much as a good-bye!" Mary said, fiercely. "Your hillman loves you, Becca! He'll come back for you, or die in the attempt. Murien only loves himself, and I was a fool—"

"There, there," Rebecca muttered. Over by the willows that lined the river, there was laughter—the flash of the queen's hair.

"Look, she has her hair down," Mary said.

They both laughed. The Queen tended to let her hair down out of its coif at the least excuse.

Rebecca smiled. "If I had her hair, I'd let it down too."

Mary nodded. She stepped back from their embrace and wiped her eyes. "I think we're ready. Tell the servants to start laying plates." She looked around at the trees, the angle of the sun. It was beautiful—as spring-like as could be imagined, like a scene in an illustrated manuscript.

At her word, Mastiff, the Queen's man, stepped out from behind a tree and bowed. He snapped his fingers, and a dozen men and women moved with the precision of dancers to lay out the meal. They were done in the time it would take a man to run to the river.

Mary touched Mastiff's elbow. "You work miracles, as always, ser," she said.

He bowed, obviously pleased. "You are too kind, my lady," he said. He and his team melted back into the trees, and Mary summoned the Queen and her friends to lunch.

The Queen was barefoot, lightly clad in green with her hair free down her back and her arms bare in the new sun. Some of the young men were fully clad, but two of them, both knights, wore simple homespun tunics and no leggings, like peasants or working men. The Queen seemed to be favouring them—and the short tunics and bare legs did show off their muscles to good advantage.

When they sat on the new grass to eat, though, they had to fold their legs very carefully. This made Mary smile, and meet Rebecca's eye who grinned and looked away.

Lady Emmota, the youngest of the Queen's lady's, had her hair down as well, and when the Queen sat, Emmota sat next to her and the Queen pulled the girl to lie down with her head in the Queen's lap. The Queen stroked her hair. The young girl gazed at her with adoration.

Most of the young knights were unable to eat.

"Where is my lord?" asked the Queen.

Lady Mary curtsied. "And it please you, he is hunting, and said he might join us for lunch if the hart allowed him."

The Queen smiled. "I am second mistress to Artemis," she said.

Emmota smiled up at her. "Let him have his blood," she said.

Their eyes met.

Later, while the young men fenced with their swords and bucklers, the women danced. They wove wreaths of flowers, and danced in rings, and sang old songs that were not favoured by the church. As the sun began to sink, they were flushed, and warm, down to their kirtles, and now all of them were barefoot in the grass, and the knights were calling for wine.

The Queen laughed. "Messires," she said, "none of my ladies will get a green back for the quality of your fencing, however much we ladies may be affected by the rising sap of spring."

The women all laughed. Some of the men looked crestfallen. A few—the best of them—laughed at themselves and their fellows alike, but none of them answered her.

Rebecca put a hand on Mary's bare arm. "I miss him too," she said. "Gawin would have given her a witty answer."

Mary laughed. "I love her—and she's right to speak. Emmota will fall into the first strong arms that will have her. It's all the light and the warmth and the bare legs." At a motion from the Queen, she walked over and offered a hand to draw the Queen to her feet. The Queen kissed her lady.

"You arrange everything so well, Mary." She took her hands. "I hope you had a pleasant day as well."

"I am easily pleased," Mary said, and the two women smiled at each other, as if enjoying a private joke.

Riding back, they rode three abreast, with the Queen flanked by Lady Mary and Lady Rebecca. Behind them, Emmota rode between two young knights, her head back, laughing.

"Emmota is vulnerable," Mary said carefully.

The Queen smiled. "Yes. Let us break up these laughs and long glances. It is far too early in the season."

She straightened her back and gave her horse a check, turned in her saddle like a commander in a tapestry.

"Gentles! Let us race to the Gates of Harndon!"

Ser Augustus, one of the young men in a peasant's smock, laughed aloud. "What is the forfeit?" he called.

"A kiss!" called the Queen, and she gathered her horse under her.

One of the squires blew a horn, and they were away into the fading spring light in a riot of colour and noise, the last of the sun on brilliant greens and blues and brght scarlet, gold and silver.

But the Queen's kiss was never in danger. Her southern mare seemed to scarcely touch the road as she skimmed along, and the Queen was the first horsewoman in her court—back straight, shoulders square, hips relaxed, and the two of them seemed like a single creature as they led the excited pack of young courtiers along the road, over the bridge, and up the long hill, recently lined with fine houses, to the gates of the city.

The Queen touched her crop to them, first of all the pack by two lengths, and Lady Rebecca was second, flushed and delighted at her own prowess.

"Becca!" cried the Queen in delight. As the others rode up, she kissed her secretary. "You are riding more for your hillman?"

"Yes," she said modestly.

The Queen beamed at her.

"Are you the Queen, or has some wild hussy stolen the Queen's horse?" said a voice from inside the gate, and Diota emerged. "Put your hair up, *my lady*. And put some decent clothes on."

The Queen rolled her eyes.

Lissen Carak—The Red Knight

The Red Knight drank off a cup of wine from the saddle. He handed the cup down to Toby.

"Listen up, messires," he said. "Gelfred—we have to assume their camp is between us and Albinkirk."

Gelfred looked around. "Because we didn't come across it last night, you mean?"

The captain nodded. "Exactly. Let's look at this for a moment. The farm that was hit was east of the fortress."

Ser Jehannes shrugged. "You found the dead Jack west of here, though. And it stands to reason he was returning to camp."

The captain looked at him for a moment, and then shook his head. "Damn," he said. "I hadn't thought of that."

Bad Tom leaned in. "Can't be south. They can't be across the river."

"West and north, I'm thinking," said Gelfred. "I'm sensing there's a high ridge that way, that runs parallel to the ridge that the fortress is on."

"This could take days," Ser Jehannes said.

The captain seemed to glow with vitality, an impossible feat for a man who had fought two monsters in three days.

"Messires," he said, "This is what we do. All the men-at-arms in the centre, in one group. Pages will ride ahead, ten horse lengths between men. We will stop whenever I whistle, and dismount. And *listen*. The archers will follow well to the rear, also in a long skirmish line. In the event of a fight, the archers will close on the battle and the men-at-arms will remain under my command. Because we are *not* going out to fight. We are going out to find evidence of a force of the Wild mustering. The only occasion to fight will be to rescue one of our scouting parties." His voice was clipped, professional, and had the self-assurance of a prince. Even Jehannes had to admit his plan was correct.

"Gelfred, when we locate their camp, we will make a brief demonstration." He grinned. "To occupy their attention." He winked at Cuddy, who nodded.

"I'm thinking you mean an archery demonstration," he said.

The captain nodded and continued. "You and your men will conceal yourselves nearby and report what happens when we leave. We will withdraw due east, and come down into the Vale of the Cohocton. If there is pursuit, they will have the sun in their eyes." The captain looked at Cuddy. "If we are pursued—"

"I dismount the lads and ambush your pursuers. If I ain't been hit myself." He nodded. "I know the game."

The captain clapped his armoured shoulder. "Everyone see it?"

His squire, Michael, was pale. "We're going out into the woods, looking for an army of creatures of the Wild?" he asked.

The Red Knight smiled. "That's right," he said.

As their leader turned his war horse and raised his baton to give an order, Jehannes turned to Tom. "He's drunk."

"Nah. He's a loon, like I am. He wants a fight. Give him his head." Tom grinned.

"He's drunk!" Jehannes repeated.

Ser Milus shook his head. "Only on love," he said.

Jehannes spat. "Worse and worse."

They rode west first, and the road was very familiar. As soon as they reached the edge of the woods, the pages split off, riding ahead, their skirmish line widening and widening to the north. The men-at-arms turned into the woods behind them in a compact mass, and then came the archers. Gelfred rode with the captain, and his scouts were nowhere to be seen.

After enough time to terrify most of the pages, who rode in fear of imminent ambush by unimaginable monsters, the captain's whistle rang out.

Every man reined in his horse and slipped to the ground.

They were still for a long time.

The captain's whistle sounded again, two long blasts.

They mounted and rode forward. It was late afternoon. The sky had patches of blue, and a man could be warm from the sun, the weight of his harness, and his nerves.

Or cold, from the same causes.

Men tire quickly when they are scared. A patrol in hostile terrain is the most tiring thing a soldier can do short of violence. The captain blew his whistle each time he had completed a silent count to fifteen hundred. Stopping gave his men a rest.

The sun began to slant more, and the light grew redder. The sky to the west was clear.

They began to climb Gelfred's ridge, and the tension began to grow.

About halfway up the ridge, the captain's whistle sounded, and the company dismounted.

The captain motioned to Michael, who stood at his shoulder.

"Whistle: horseholders."

Michael nodded. He took off his right gauntlet, picked up the silver whistle on the cord around his neck, and blew three long and three short notes. After a pause, he blew the same call again.

All around them, men-at-arms handed their horses to squires. Behind them, at the base of the hill, every sixth archer took the horses of his mates and led them to the rear.

The captain watched it all, wondering if the pages, who he couldn't see, were also obeying.

He could *feel* the enemy. He could smell the green of the Wild. He listened, and he could almost hear them. Idly, he wondered why Amicia smelled like the Wild.

There was a distant trumpeting noise, like the belling of a hart.

"Jehannes, you have the men-at-arms. I'm going to take command of the pages. Michael, on me." He handed his reins to Toby and started up the hill. His harness was almost silent, and he moved fast enough to leave Jehannes's protests behind.

Bad Tom stepped out and followed him.

The hill was steep, and the pages were two hundred paces further up the ridge. He breathed in relief when he saw them—too clumped up, but all dismounted, and he passed a boy of fifteen with six horses headed down the hill.

Climbing a steep ridge in armour reminded him of just how little sleep he'd had since the first fight, against the wyvern, but through his fatigue he could still feel the place on his fingers where Amicia had touched him.

Michael and Tom had trouble keeping up with him.

He reached the pages. Jacques had them spreading out already. He smiled at the captain.

"Nice job," he whispered.

"We're going to the top, I take it?" asked Jacques.

The captain looked right and left. "Yes," he said. He motioned to Michael, who gave one whistle blast.

The pages were lightly armed. They weren't woodsmen, but they slipped up the hill like ghosts, at a pace that left the captain breathless. The hill steepened and steepened as they climbed, until the very top was almost sheer, and the pages hauled themselves up from tree to tree.

There was a scream, a wicked hiss of arrows, a boy of no more than sixteen roared, "For God and Saint George!" and there was the unmistakable sound of steel on steel.

An arrow, nearly spent, rang off the captain's helmet.

Suddenly, he had the spirit to run to the crest of the hill. The trees were dense, and branches reached for him, but a man in armour can run through a thicket of thorns and not take a scratch. He grabbed a slim oak, pulled with all his strength, and found himself at the top.

There was a small hollow, with a fire hidden by the bulk of the hill, and a dozen men.

Not men.

Irks.

Like men, but thinner and faster, with brown-green skin like bark, almond eyes and pointed teeth like wolves. Even as the captain stopped in surprise, an arrow rang off his breastplate and a dozen pages burst from the trees to the right of the irks around the fire and charged.

The captain lowered his head and ran at the irks, too.

They loosed arrows and fled away north, and the pages gave chase.

The captain stopped and opened his visor. Michael appeared at his side, sword out, buckler on his left hand. He could smell woodsmoke, lots of woodsmoke.

"We've found them!" Michael said.

"No. A dozen irks is not an army of darkness," said the captain. He looked at the sky.

Tom came up behind him.

"Tom? We have an hour of good light. The pages are running down their sentries." He looked at the veteran man-at-arms. He shrugged. "I don't really know all that much about fighting the Wild," he admitted. "My instinct is to keep going forward."

Tom nodded. "It's the Wild," he said. "They never have a reserve. Yon won't have anything like a quarter guard." He shrugged.

The captain knew the decision they made now was pivotal. Any losses out here didn't bear thinking about. Caution would dictate—

He thought of her touch on his hand. Her admiration.

He turned to Michael. "Tell the archers to prepare an ambush half a league back. men-at-arms to guard the horses at the base of the ridge. This is the pages only. Understand?"

Michael nodded. "I want to come with you."

"No. Give me your whistle. Now move! Tom, with me."

They ran down the northern side of the ridge, toward the sound of screams and fighting.

Later, the captain admitted that he'd let the pages get too far ahead of him. The deep woods and fading light made it almost impossible to maintain communications.

He ran down the ridge with Tom beside him, crashing recklessly through thickets. He all but fell into a steep-sided vale; a small stream that cut deeply into the side of the ridge. It was easier to go east, so he followed it, passing three corpses—all irks.

At the base of the ridge, with his breath coming in great shuddering gasps, there was a shallow stream and, on the far side, a path. And along the path—

Tents. But no pages.

There were fifty men, most of them stringing bows.

The captain stopped. He'd made enough noise coming down the ridge to catch their attention but with the sun at his back, despite his armour, they were easier for him to see than he was for them.

Tom and Jacques and a dozen pages who had followed them down the hill slipped in behind old trees. There were screams off to the west—screams and something else.

"Fucking Jacks," Jacques said.

The men across the stream turned, almost as one. A small horde of boglins and irks bolted down the path from the west. It was odd to see the monsters of myth running.

The Jacks began to shuffle.

Several of them drew their great bows and shot west.

The captain looked around. "Follow me," he said. "Make a *lot* of noise."

They all looked at him.

"One. Two. Three." He broke cover, and bellowed "THE RED KNIGHT!"

The effect was electric. The captain was south of and slightly behind the line of Jacks, and they had to look over their shoulders to see him. Immediately, men began to flee with the boglins and the irks.

The pages behind him roared his battlecry, and Bad Tom roared his— "Lachlan for Aa!"

There are different types of soldier. Some men are trained to stand under fire, waiting for their turn to inflict death. Others are like hunters, slipping from cover to cover.

The Jacks were not of a mind to stand and fight. It wasn't their way.

One arrow, launched from a mighty bow, slammed into the captain's scarlet surcote, punched through it, and left a dent a finger deep and bruised him like a kick from a mule. And then the Jacks were gone.

The captain grabbed Bad Tom by the shoulder. "Stop!" he roared.

Tom's eyes were wild. "I have nae' wet my sword!" he shouted.

The captain kept a hand on him, like a man calming a favourite dog. He blew the recall on the whistle—three long blasts, and then three more, and then three more.

The pages stopped. Many wiped their swords on dead things, and all of them drank from their water bottles.

From the east came a long scream. It was an alien sound, and it sobered them.

"Up and over the ridge. Straight back the way we came, tight and orderly. Now." The captain pointed his sword up the ridge. "Stay by the stream!" he called.

Now there was a baying and roaring in the woods to the east. Roaring, infernal screams, and something else, something that was huge and terrible and fell, and as tall as the trees.

He turned to run up the ridge.

Tom was still at his shoulder. "I have nae killed a one!" he said. "Just let me kill one!"

Suiting action to word, Tom turned as a gout of green fire smashed into the ground, not two horselengths from Tom's outstretched sword. It exploded with a roar and suddenly the very stones seemed to be on fire.

Tom smiled and raised his sword.

"Tom!" the captain screamed. "This is not the time!"

Boglins and irks were crossing the stream at the foot of the ridge, led by a golden bear, as tall as a war horse and shining gold like the sun. When it roared, its voice filled the woods like a storm wind.

"What the *fuck* is that?" asked Tom. "By god, I want a cut at that!"

The captain pulled hard at the hillman's arm. "With me!" he ordered, and ran.

Grudgingly, Tom turned and followed him.

They made the top of the ridge. The bear was not charging them, it seemed content to lead the boglins and the irks. But behind them came something far worse. And much larger.

The pages had waited for the captain a little way down the ridge, in itself an act of fine discipline and bravery. But as soon as he caught them up, they turned and ran for the base and their horses.

The captain could barely move his steel clad feet, and never had leg armour seemed so pointless, so heavy, as it did when the first of the enemy began to crest the hill behind him. They were close.

West of Lissen Carak—Thorn

Thorn's initial reaction to the assault on his camp was panic. It took him long minutes to recover from the shock and when he did, the sheer effrontery of it filled him with an irrational rage. As he reached out through his creatures, he was shocked to find how pitiful and few were his human attackers. A few dozen of them, and they had sent his Jacks running down the path, broken fifty irks, and killed an outpost of boglins who were caught napping after a feed.

He stopped the rout by killing the first irk to pass him, in spectacular style. The creature exploded in green fire, raining burning flesh on the others, and the Magus raised his hoary arms and the rout stopped.

"You fools!" he roared at them. "There are fewer than fifty of them!" He wished he had his daemons but they were already scouting Albinkirk. His wyverns were close, but not close enough. He poured his will into two of the golden bears and sent his forces up the ridge after the raiders. His Wild creatures would be far more nimble in the woods then mere men. The bears were faster than horses on their home ground.

One of the boglin chiefs stood at his side, his milk-white chiton all but glowing in the setting sun.

"Tell your people that they will feast. Anything they catch is for their own."

Exrech saluted with a sword. He released a cloud of vapour—part power and part scent. And then he was away, racing loose-limbed up the ridge with boglins following like a brown tide at his heels.

West of Lissen Carak—The Red Knight

The captain tried to be the last man, shoving his flagging pages along before him by force of will, but the weaker among them were used up. One, a little plumper than he ought to have been, stopped to breathe hard.

The enemy were fifty paces away. Closer with every heartbeat.

"Run!" roared Tom.

The boy threw up, looked behind him and froze.

A boglin paused and shot him with an arrow.

He screamed and fell, kicking, into his own vomit.

Tom heaved the writhing boy over his shoulders and ran. His sword licked out—caught an irk in the top of the knee, and the thing screamed and fell, clutching at the wound.

The captain paused—they were trying to surround him. He punched at the nearest and impaled him, took two cuts on his leg armour, and suddenly it *had* been worth it to wear the stuff all afternoon.

There were, in moments, *hundreds* of boglins. They seemed to boil up out of the ground in terrifying numbers. They moved like ants and covered the forest floor as fast as he could back away. Their armoured heads rose above his knight's belt.

Behind him, he heard a trumpet call and Cuddy's voice, as clear as on parade, called "Nock! And Loose!"

The captain was still on his feet, but there was a sharp pain in his left thigh where a boglin was trying to sink its jaws into his flesh, and his legs were all but immobilized by the press of creatures when something reached for his soul through the aether.

He panicked.

He couldn't see. The brown boglins were everywhere, clamping onto him, and he wasn't fighting anymore, he was just trying to keep his feet, and the pressure of the phantasm was bearing down harder and harder on his soul.

Then, even through his helmet and his fear, he could hear the hiss of the warbow arrows, like the fall of vicious sleet.

The arrows hit.

Three of them hit him.

West of Lissen Carak—Thorn

Thorn paused at the top of the ridge to watch the last moments of the raiding party. The boglins weren't as fast as the irks, but the irks were running the enemy down. The tide of boglins would finish the fight.

Any fight.

He prepared a casting, gathering the raw force of nature to him through a web of half-rational portals and paths.

At the base of the ridge, one of the fleeing raiders paused.

Thorn reached out for him, grasped him and felt his will slip off the man like claws around a stone.

And then fifty enemy archers stood up from concealment, and began to fill the air with wood and iron.

West of Lissen Carak—The Red Knight

The captain was hit more than a dozen times more. Every strike was like being kicked by a mule. Most fell on his helmet, but one ripped across his inner thigh, cutting through his hose and his braes. He was blind with pain, dazed by the repeated impacts.

But he was armed cap à pied in hardened steel armour, and the boglins trying to kill him were not.

When every one of Cuddy's archers had loosed six shafts, the V-shaped space between the arms of the ambush was silent. Nothing was left alive.

Cuddy ordered his men forward to collect their shafts as the captain raised his visor, aware that there was still something—

At the top of the hill, the figure of horror stepped out where they could all see him, and raised his arms—

He still functioned through the panic because he'd been afraid so damned often he was used to it now.

The captain touched Prudentia's hand. Above his head, the three great levels of his palace spun like gaming wheels.

"Don't open the door!" Prudentia said. "He's right there!"

Faced with imminent immolation, the captain opened the door.

There was an entity of the Wild. Right outside the door to his mind.

He made a long, sharp dagger of his will and punched it into the entity, leaning out through the door to do so.

Prudentia caught him.

The door slammed shut.

"You're insane," she said.

In the world the great figure stumbled. It didn't fall, but the intensity of its gathered power stumbled with it. And dissipated.

"To horse!" he captain roared. Behind the monstrous figure on the ridge he could see thrashing tentacles approaching and fresh hordes of monsters.

The massive thing, like two twin trees, reared up and a flash of green fire covered the hillside. It fell shorter than it might have, or more men might have died, but archers were reduced to bones—a page burned green like a hideous barn-lamp for three heartbeats before vanishing—and dozens of wounded creatures on the ground were immolated as well.

Behind him, men were mounting—pages and archers hurried horses to their riders. This was their most practised movement: escape.

But the captain's sense of the enemy was that he'd get one more gout of fire in.

He got a leg over Grendel's saddle and

Passed back into the palace.

"Shield, Pru!" he called. He pulled raw power from the sack hanging on her arm as the sigils turned above them—Xenophon, St. George, Ares.

The first spell any magister learned. The measure of an adept's power.

He made a buckler, small and nimble, and threw it far forward, into his adversary's face.

Behind him, the corporals ordered men into motion, but they needed no urging, and the company moved away, down the hill.

The captain turned Grendel and rode, running as fast as the heavy horse would allow—

The two-horned thing in the woods reached out with his staff—

The captain's shield—his very strongest, smallest, neatest casting—vanished like a moth in a forge fire.

The captain felt his shield go—felt it vanish—had a taste of the sheer power of his adversary—but training told.

Quick as a cat pouncing, the captain spun his horse to face the foe and *reached in and cast again—a wider arc to cover horse and rider*

The green fire ran across the ground like a rising tide, immolating everything that lay in its path—scarring trees, reaping grass and flowers, boiling squirrels in their own skin. It struck the air in front of Grendel's chamfron—

It was like watching a sand-castle give way under the power of the waves.

His second shield was weaker, but the green fire had crossed hundreds of paces of ground and its puissance was ebbing—and still it eroded the shield—slowly, and then more quickly as Grendel half-reared in panic, alone in a sea of incandescent green.

He put everything he had—every shred of stored power

He could smell burning leather, and he could see—trees. Upright and black.

Grendel screamed and bolted.

All he wanted to do was sleep, but Cuddy needed reassurance. "You was in full harness—" said the Master Archer.

"It was the right decision," the captain agreed.

"I can't believe we hit you so many times," Cuddy said, shaking his head. Even as he spoke, Carlus, the armourer and company trumpeter, was working with heat and main strength to get the dents out of the captain's beautiful helmet.

"I'll be more careful to whom I give extra work details in future," the captain agreed.

Cuddy left the tent, still muttering.

Michael got his captain out of the rest of his armour. The breast plate was badly dented in two places. The arm harnesses were untouched.

"Wipe my blade first," muttered the captain. "Boglins; I've heard their blood is caustic."

"Boglins," Michael said. He shook his head. "Irks. Magic." He took a deep breath. "Did we win?"

"Ask me that in a month, young Michael. How many did we lose?"

"Six pages. And three archers, in the retreat when yon *thing* began to rain fire on us." Michael shrugged.

Their retreat had become a rout. Most of the men had ridden back to camp almost blind with terror, as more and more monsters crested the ridge and entered the field, following that fire-raining figure of terror.

"Well." The captain allowed his eyes to close for a moment and then jolted awake. "Son of a bitch. I have to tell the Abbess."

"They might attack us again, any moment," Michael said.

The captain gave him a hard look. "Whatever they are, they aren't so different from us. They know fear. They do not want to die. We hurt them today." *They hurt us, too. I was too rash. Damn it all.*

"So now what happens?" Michael asked.

"We scurry into the fortress. And that thing comes and lays siege to us." The captain got slowly to his feet. For a moment, absent the weight of his harness, he felt as if he could fly. Then the fatigue settled again like an old and evil friend.

"Attend me," he said.

The Abbess received him immediately.

"It seems you were correct. Your men look badly beaten." She averted her eyes. "That was unworthy," she allowed.

He managed a smile. "My lady, you should see the state they're in."

She laughed. "Is that cockiness or truth?"

"I think we killed a hundred boglin and fifty irks. Perhaps even a few Jacks. And we kicked the hornet's nest." He frowned. "I saw their leader—a great horned creature. Like a living tree, but malevolent." He shrugged, trying to forget his panic. Tried to keep his voice light. "It was huge."

She nodded.

He put that nod away for future consideration. Even in his fatigue, he caught that she knew something.

She went to the mantel of her chimney and picked up her curious ivory box. This time, she opened it and took the slip of bark between her hands. It turned jet-black. He felt her casting. Then she threw it in the fire.

"What shall I do now?" the captain asked. He was too tired to think.

She pursed her lips. "You tell me, Captain," she said. "You are in command."

Lissen Carak—Father Henry

Father Henry watched the mercenary come down the steps of the Great Hall with the Abbess on his arm, and his skin crawled to watch that spawn of Satan touch her. The man was young and pretty, for all his bruises and the dark circles under his eyes, and he had an air about him that Father Henry knew in his soul was all pretence; the sham of concern and the worm of falsity.

The big mercenary barked a laugh. And then the sergeant at arms and the master warder both appeared from the donjon tower.

Father Henry knew his duty—knew that he could not allow major decisions to be made without him. He walked forward to join them.

The Abbess gave him a look that he suspected was meant to drive him away, but he schooled his face to hide his feelings and bowed to the loath-some killer and his minion.

The master warder rolled his eyes. "Nothing for you here, Father," he said. The old soldier had never liked him, had never made a confession.

The mercenary returned his bow pleasantly enough, but the Abbess didn't introduce him or let any one else do so. She indicated the mercenary. "The captain is now the Commander of this fortress. I expect all of you to give him your ready obedience."

The master warder nodded and the sergeant at arms, who commanded the tiny garrison, merely bowed. A possible ally, then.

"My lady!" Father Henry rallied his arguments. His thoughts were a riot of confused images and conflicting motives, but they were united by the knowledge that *this man must not be given command of the fortress.* "My lady! This man is an apostate, an unrepentant sinner, a bastard child of an unknown mother by his own admission."

The mercenary now looked at him with reptilian hate.

Good.

"I've never suggested my mother was unknown," he said with mild condescension.

"You cannot allow this piece of *scum* into our fortress," the priest said. He was too vehement, he could see them closing their minds against him. "As your spiritual adviser—"

"Father, let us continue this conversation at a more seemly time and place," the Abbess said.

Oh, how he hated her tone. She spoke to him—him, a man, a *priest*—as if he was an errant child and just for a moment the quality of his rage must have shown through, because all of them—except the mercenary—took a step back.

The mercenary, on the other hand, looked at him as if seeing him for the first time, and gave a sharp nod.

"I feel you are making a grave error, my lady," the priest began again, but she turned on him with a speed that belied her years and put her hand on the pectoral cross he wore.

"I understand that you disagree with my decision, Father Henry. Now please *desist.*" Her tone of ice froze him in place.

"I will not stop while the power of the Lord—"

"*Me Dikeou!*" she hissed at him.

The bitch was using arcane powers on him. And he found himself unable to speak. It was as if his tongue had gone to sleep. He couldn't even form a word in his mind.

He staggered back, scarred hands over his mouth, all of his suspicions confirmed and all of his petty errors transformed into acts of courage. She had used witchcraft against him. She was a witch—an ally of Satan. Whereas he—

She turned to him. "This is an emergency, Father, and you were warned. Return to your chapel and do penance for your disobedience."

He fled.

North of Lissen Carak—Thorn

Thorn strode east as fast as his long legs would carry him, a swarm of faeries around his head like insects, feeding on the power that clung to him like moss to stone. "We continue," he said to the daemon at his side.

The daemon surveyed the wreckage of tents and the scatter of corpses. "How many did you lose?" he asked. His crest moved with agitation.

"Lose? Only a handful. The boglins are young and unprepared for war." The great figure shook like a tree in the wind.

"You took a wound yourself," Thurkan said.

Thorn stopped. "Is this one of your dominance games? One of them distracted me. He had a little magic and I was slow to respond. It will not happen again. Their attack had no real affect on us."

The great figure turned and shambled east. Around him, irks and boglins and men packed their belongings and prepared to march.

Thurkan loped alongside, easily keeping pace with the giant sorcerer. "Why?" he asked. "Why Albinkirk?"

Thorn stopped. He despised being questioned, especially by a trouble-maker like Thurkan, who saw himself—a mere daemon—as his peer. He longed to say, "Because I will it so."

But this was not the moment.

"Power summons power," he said.

Thurkan's head-crest trembled in agreement. "So?" he asked.

"The irks and boglin hordes are restless. They have come here—was that at your bidding, daemon?" Thorn leaned at the waist. "Well?"

"Violence summons violence," Thurkan said. "Men killed creatures of the Wild. A golden bear was enslaved by men. It cannot be borne. My cousin was murdered; so was a wyvern. We are the guardians. We must act."

Thorn paused, and pointed his staff. They were passing to the north of the great fortress; it was just visible from here, high on its ridge to the south.

"We will never take the Rock with the force we have," Thorn said. "I might act to destroy it, or I might not. This is not my fight. But we are allies, and I will help you."

"By leading us away from that which we wish to reclaim?" snapped the daemon.

"By unleashing the Wild against a worthy goal. An *attainable* goal. We will strike a blow that will rock the kingdoms of man, and that will send a signal throughout the Wild. Many, many more will come to us. Is this not so?"

Thurkan nodded slow agreement. "If we burn Albinkirk, many will know it and many will come."

"And then," said Thorn, "we will have the force and the time to act against the Rock, while the men worry over smoking ruins."

"And you will be many times more powerful than you are now," Thurkan said suspiciously.

"When you and yours can again drink from the spring of the Rock, and mate in the tunnels beneath the Rock, you will thank me," Thorn said.

Together, they began to walk east.

Chapter Six

Prynwrithe—Ser Mark Wishart

Two hundred leagues and more south of the Cohocton, well west of Harndon, the Priory of Pynwrithe was a beautiful castle rising from a spur of solid rock, a hundred years old, with high battlements, four slim towers with arched windows, topped in copper-gilt roofs, and a high arched gate that made some visitors exclaim that the whole must have been built by the Faery.

Ser Mark Wishart, the Prior, knew better. It had been built by a rich thug, who had given it to the church to save his soul.

It was a very comfortable place to live. A dream for a soldier who had lived most of his life having to sleep on the cold hard ground. The Prior was standing in his shirt, in front of a roaring fire, with a piece of bark in his hand—a small piece of birch bark, which had just turned almost perfectly black. He turned it over and over in his hands, and winced at the pain in his shoulder. The she-bear had hurt him badly.

It was a chilly morning, and from the glazed glass window, he could see that there had been a frost—but a mild one. Spring was in the air. Flowers, crops, new life.

He sighed.

Dean—his new servant boy—appeared with a cup of small beer and his clean mantle. "My lord?" he said, an evocative question, for two words.

The boy was far too intelligent to spend his life pouring hippocras for old men.

"Hose, braes, double, and a cote, lad," the Prior said. "Summon the marshal and my squire."

Thomas Clapton, the Marshal of the Order of Saint Thomas of Acon, was in his solar before the Prior had his hose laced to his doublet—something he could not get used to allowing a servant to do.

"My lord," the marshal said, formally.

"What's our fighting strength, right now?" the Prior asked.

"In the priory?" the marshal asked. "I can find you sixteen knights fit to ride this morning. In the Demesne? Perhaps fifty, if I give you the old men and boys."

The Prior lifted the birchbark and his marshal went pale.

"And if we make knights of all our squires who are ready?" Ser Mark asked.

The marshal nodded. "Then perhaps seventy." He rubbed his beard.

"Do it," said Ser Mark. "This isn't some minor incursion. She would never call us unless it was war."

Harndon Palace—Harmodious

Harmodious cursed his age and peered into the silver mirror, looking for any redeeming features and finding none. His bushy black and white eyebrows did not recommend him as a lover and nor did his head; he was bald on top with shoulder length white hair, the ruined skin of age and slightly stooped shoulders.

He shook his head, more at the foolishness of desiring the Queen than at his reflection. He admitted to himself that he was happy enough with his appearance, and with its reality.

"Hah!" he said to the mirror.

Miltiades rubbed against him, and Harmodius looked down at the old cat.

"The ancients tell us that memory is to reality as a seal in wax is to the seal itself," he said.

The cat looked up at him with aged disinterest.

"Well?" he asked Miltiades. "So is my memory of the image of myself in the mirror a new level of removal? It's the image of an image of reality?" He chuckled, pleased with the conceit, and another came to him.

"What if you could perform a spell that altered what we saw between the eye and the brain?" he asked the cat. "How would the brain perceive it? Would it be reality, or an image, or an image of an image?"

He glanced back at the mirror. Pursed his lips again and began to climb the stairs. The cat followed him, his heavy, four-foot gait an accusation and a complaint about overweight infirmity.

"Fine," Harmodius said, and turned to scoop Miltiades up, putting a hand in the middle of his back at the pain. "Perhaps I could exercise more," he said aloud. "I was a passable swordsman in my youth."

The cat's grey whiskers twitched a reproach.

"Yes, my youth was quite some time ago," he said.

Swords, for example, had changed shape since then. And weight.

He sighed.

At the top of the stairs he unlocked the door to his sanctum and reset the light wards he'd left on the place. There was very little to guard here, or rather, his books and many artefacts were supremely valuable, but it was the king that guarded them, not the lock and the wards. If he ever lost the king's confidence—

It didn't bear thinking about.

Wanting Desiderata must be the common denominator of the entire court, he thought and laughed, mostly at himself, before going to the north wall where shelves of Archaic scrolls, many of them gleaned from daring raids into the necropoli of the distant southlands, waited for him like pigeons in a cote. *I used to be a very daring man.*

He deposited Miltiades on the ground and the cat walked heavily to the centre of the room and sat in the sun.

He began to read on the origins of human memory. He picked up a day-old glass of water and drank from it, tasting some of yesterday's flames and a little chalk, and said "Hmm," a dozen times as he read.

"Hmmm," he said again, and carefully re-rolled the scroll before sliding it back into the bone tube that protected it. The scroll itself was priceless—one of perhaps three surviving scrolls of the Archaic Aristotle, and he always meant to have it copied but never did. He was tempted, sometimes, to order the destruction of the other two, both held in the king's library.

He sighed at his own infantile pride.

The cat stretched out in the sun and went to sleep.

The other two cats appeared. He didn't know where they had been—and suddenly wasn't sure he could remember when he'd adopted them, or where they had sprung from at all.

But he had found the passage that he remembered, about an organ in the tissue of the brain that transmitted the images from the eye for the mind.

"Hmm," he said to himself with a smile, and reached down to pat the old cat who bit his hand savagely.

He jerked his bloody hand back and cursed.

Miltiades got up, walked a few steps and settled again. Glared at him.

"I need a corpse. Perhaps a dozen of them," he said, flexing his fingers and imagining the dissection. His master had been quite enamored of dissection...and it had not ended well.

It had led him to make a stand with the Wild at the Field of Chevin.

The old memory hurt, and Harmodius had an odd thought—he thought *when did I last think about the fight at Chevin?*

It poured into his mind like an avalanche, and he staggered and sat under the impact of the memories—the strange array of the enemy, with Jacks on the flanks and all their monstrous creatures in the centre, so that the kingdom's knighthood was raked with arrows as they rode forward through the waves of terror to face the creatures of the Wild.

His hands shook.

And his master had stood with them. And thrown carefully considered workings designed to baffle and deceive, that had led the king's archers to loose their shafts into their own knights, and to fight each other—

And so I attacked him. Harmodius didn't treasure the memory, or that of the king begging him to do *something.* The suspicion of the barons, each assuming he would betray them and join the Wild as well.

His master's eyes when they locked wills.

He cast, and I cast. Harmodius shook his head. *Why did he join our enemy? Why? Why? Why? What did he learn when he began to dissect the old corpses?*

Why have I not thought on this before?

Shrugged. "My hubris differs from his hubris," he said to his cats. "But I pray to God that he may yet see the light." At least enough to reduce him to a small mound of ash, he continued in his head. A really powerful light. Like a lightning bolt.

Some things were best not said aloud, and naming could most definitely call. He had triumphed over his master, but no corpse had ever been found, and Harmodius knew in his bones that his mentor was still out there. Still part of the Wild.

Enough of this, he thought, and reached for another scroll on memory. He scanned it rapidly, took a heavy tome of grammerie down from a high shelf, referred to it, and then began to write quickly.

He paused and tapped his fingers rapidly on an old beaker while trying to think who could provide him with fresh corpses for his work. No one in the capital. The town was too small, the court too full of intrigue and gossip.

"Who would feed you if I took a trip?" he asked. Because, already, his pulse was racing. He hadn't left his tower in—he couldn't remember when he'd last left Harndon.

"Gracious Divinity, have I been here since the battle?" he asked Miltiades.

The cat glared at him.

The Magus narrowed his eyes suddenly. He couldn't remember this cat as a kitten, or where the cat had come from. There was something out of step in his memories.

Christ, he thought, and sat in a chair. He could remember picking the kitten out of the dung heap by the stables, intending to dissect it. But he hadn't.

How had he lost that memory?

Was it even a true memory?

A spear of pure fear lunged through his soul. The beaker crashed to the floor, and all the cats jumped.

I have been ensorcelled.

He drew power quickly, in a whispered prayer, and performed a small and subtle working with it. Indeed, it was so subtle it scarcely required power.

The tip of his staff glowed a delicate shade of violet, and he began to move it around the room.

The violet remained steady for some time until, as he paused with the staff held up, to look at his own chalk marks on one wall, the tip flared pink and then a deep, angry red.

He waved it again.

Red.

He leaned closer to the wall. He moved the tip of the staff back and forth in ever smaller arcs, and then he muttered a second casting, speaking stiffly the way a man does when he fears he's forgotten his lines in a play.

A line of runes was suddenly picked out in angry fire-red. Wild runes, concealed under the paint on the wall.

Across the middle was a scorch mark that had erased a third of the writing.

"By the divine Christ and Hermes saint of Magisters," he said. He staggered back, and sat, a little too suddenly. A cat squalked and twitched its tail out from beneath him.

Someone had placed a binding spell on the walls of his sanctum. A binding laid on him.

On a hunch, he placed his staff where he had positioned it yesterday, to power it. He sighted along the line from his crystal to the head of the staff—

"Pure luck." he said. "Or the will of God."

He stood in thought. Then he took a deep breath. Sniffed the air.

He gathered power slowly and carefully, using a device he had in the corner, using an ancient mirror he had on a side table, using in the final instance a vial filled with shining white fluid.

In the palace of his mind, on a black and white tiled floor like an infinite chessboard, pieces moved—like chess pieces and yet not like. There were pawns and rooks and knights, but also nuns and trees and ploughs and catapults and wyverns. He slowly resolved them into a pattern, each piece positioned on a tile of its own.

He poured his gathered power slowly out on the altar in the centre of the floor.

With the casting hovering, potent with a will to locate but still un-realised, in his mind, he climbed the twenty steps from his sanctum to the very top of his tower. He opened the door and stepped out onto a wooden hoarding, like a massive balcony, that ran all the way around the top of the tower. The spring sun was bright and the air was clear but the breeze was cold.

He saw the sea to the south-east. Due south, Jarsey spread like a story-book picture of farms and castles, rolling away for leagues. He raised his arms and released his phantasm.

Instantly, he felt the power behind him, in the north.

No surprise there.

He walked slowly around the hoardings, his staff thumping hollowly on the wooden planks. His eyes stayed on the horizon. He looked due west, and there was, to his great enhanced vision, a faint haze of green off to the west along the horizon. Just as it ought to be, where the Wild held sway. But the border was farther than a man could ride in five days on a good horse, and the tinge of green stemmed from the great woods beyond the mountains. A threat—but one that was always there.

He walked around the tower.

Long before he reached the northernmost point, he saw the bright green flare. His spell was potent and he used it carefully, tuning his vision to get every scrap of knowledge from his altered sight.

There it was.

He refined the casting, so that instead of a complex web of lenses bounc-ing light, he reduced his effort to a single shining green strand, thinner than a strand of a spider web, running from the north directly to his tower. He had no doubt it ran to the very runes on his wall.

Damn.

"Was I fantasising about the Queen a moment ago?" he asked the wind. "What a fool I have been."

He didn't sever the strand. But he let go most of the Aethersight that had allowed him to see the threats displayed, and he reduced that, too, until he could just see the glimmer of his thread. Now his great phantasm took almost no golden light to power it.

He strode down into the tower with sudden purpose, and carefully shut the door behind him.

He picked up his staff, took the first wands to come under his hand and a heavy dagger with a purse, and went back out of his library, leaving the door wide open. He went down one hundred and twenty-two steps to the floor below, picked up a heavy cloak and a hat and fought the urge to pause there. He walked through the open door and shut it behind him, aware that all three cats were watching him from the top of the stairs.

He longed for an ally and, at the same time, doubted everything.

But he had to trust someone. He chose his Queen, stopped at the writing desk beyond the door and wrote.

Urgent business calls me to the north. Please tell the king that I have the gravest fears that I have been manipulated by an ancient enemy. Be on your guard.
 I remain your Majesty's least humble servant,
Harmodius

He walked rapidly to the head of the twisting stairs and started down them, cursing his long staff and making as much haste as he could. He was trying to remember when he had last come down the stairs. Had it been yesterday?

He cast a very minor working ahead of him, now afraid that there might be spells to prevent his departure, but he could see nothing. That didn't help. If his fears were correct, his eyes might betray him, or be a tool of the enemy. Did his vision in the aether function in the same manner as natural sight?

Richard Plangere used to ask us, "What is this natural of which you speak" and we'd all be silent.

Richard Plangere, the spell on my wall stinks of you.

Caught up in his thoughts, Harmodius almost missed a step. His foot slipped, and for a moment he hung at the edge of a forty-foot fall to the cobblestones below, and the only enemy he was fighting was old age and memory. He got the rest of the way down the stairs with nothing worse than a pain in his side from walking too fast.

His tower opened on the main courtyard, fifty paces on a side and lined with the working buildings of the king's government, although there were more of those down along the west wall as well, where there high windows looked down on the mighty river.

He walked to the stable. Men and women bowed deeply at his approach. His actions were scarcely secret, and he wondered briefly if he would have been better served leaving in the dark of night. Anyone could be an informant. Equally, he feared to go back to his chambers.

What am I afraid of?

Have I lost my mind?

He built a mental compartment around his chambers and all his associated thoughts and fears and closed the door on them. *I may be at the edge of madness, or I may have just discovered a terrible secret,* he thought.

There were two grooms in the stable, working quickly and efficiently to unsaddle a dozen royal horses in hunting tack. They stopped when they saw the Magus.

He tried a smile. "I need a horse," he said. "A good one, for a journey."

Both of them looked at him as if he was insane.

Then they looked at each other.

Finally, the older nodded. "Whatever you like, m'lord," he said. "I can gi' you a courser—a fine big mare callit Ginger. If it please you?"

Harmodius nodded, and before he could grow any more afraid a big bay was led out, a light saddle on her back. Harmodius looked up at that saddle with an old man's despair, but the younger groom had anticipated his look and moved to help, bringing him a stool.

Harmodius stepped up on the stool and forced his leg up over the horse's back.

The ground seemed a long way down.

"Thank you, lad," Harmodius said. The boys handed him up his staff, two wands, and his purse, dagger, and cloak. The elder boy showed him how to stow it all behind the saddle.

"See that this note makes it to the Queen. Deliver it in person. This is my ring, so you may reach her—every guard in the palace should know it. Do you understand me, boy?" he asked, and realised that he was a figure of terrible fear to these two boys. He tried on a smile. "You'll get a reward."

The younger smiled bravely. "I'll take it, Master."

"See you do." He nodded.

And then they were gone, and he was riding.

He rode through the gate without so much as a nod from the two Royal Guardsmen who stood there, either scanning the approach or sound asleep. The brims of their ornate helmets hid their eyes.

His horse's hooves rang hollowly against the drawbridge. The palace and its surrounding castle was merely the citadel in an extensive series of works—three rings of walls and two other castles—that towered above the ancient city of Harndon. Twice in Alba's history the entire Demesne had been reduced to the people that could huddle inside these walls.

When the Wild came.

He rode down the slope of the castle mound into High Street—the main street of the city of Harndon, that ran from gate to gate until it became the High Road and passed through the countryside, out to the town of Bridge where it crossed the mighty river, in the first of seven bridges. The river ran like a great snake from the north to the south of Alba, while the road cut straight across it.

Here the road was a steep street lined with magnificent white-walled houses, each as tall and turreted as small castles. They were adorned in gilt and black iron with red or blue doors, tile or copper roofs, marble statuary painted and unpainted, and windows, clear or stained, high or wide. Each house was a palace and had its own character.

I used to dine here. And here. How long have I been under?

The pressure in his chest eased as Harmodius rode down the hill, looking at the palaces of courtiers and great knights and wondering how it was that he had never visited any of them.

He rode through the Inner Gate without glancing at the guards. It was chilly in the wind, and he struggled with his cloak as he rode through Middle Town, and peered out into the High Cheaping, the city's principal market. The Cheaping was a market square two or three times the size of the courtyard of the castle, and packed with stalls and the bustle of commerce. He watched it as he passed, and then he was into the lower town, the Cheaping in local dialect, crossing Flood Street at the Bridge Gate, and his heart began to beat faster. He saw no threat—but he expected one.

The men at the Bridge Gate had all of their attention on a magnificent retinue of knights and armoured men-at-arms entering the city. Harmodius looked at it from under his hood, trying to make out the blazon and guess whom the lord might be—not anyone he had ever seen at court. A tall man, heavy with muscle.

The guards clearly wanted no part of making the decision to let the giant and his men into the town. Nor did they have any attention to spare for solitary old men riding out.

The knight commanding the retinue did, though, and turned to watch him as he rode by. His glance sharpened—and then the Lieutenant of the Lower Gate appeared, armoured head to toe and holding not a wax tablet and stylus but a pole-axe, with four more knights at his back. The foreigner stiffened, and Harmodius rode past him while he was distracted.

Through the gate, down the slope past the lesser merchants who were only allowed to display their wares outside the walls—in the Ditch, as men liked to call it. He rode past the mountebanks, the players, and the workmen building bleachers and barriers for the Whitsunday Play.

He pursed his lips and touched his heels to the horse's flanks, and the mare, delighted to be out in the spring and bored by the pace, sprang forward.

Harmodius cantered along beside the market and continued past the outer ring of homes, the poorest still associated with the city, and past the first fields, each surrounded by a ring of rocks and old, painstakingly cleared tree stumps. The soil here was not the best. He cantered along the road for a further half a mile, pleased with his horse but still in the grip of fear, and came to the bridge.

Still no one challenged him.

He crossed the first great span, stopped, spat into the river, and worked two powerful spells while he was safe in the bright sunshine at the centre of the bridge. Hermeticism functioned best in sunlight; while most workings of the Wild couldn't cross running water without enormous effort or the water's Hermetic permission. There was no power on earth that could take him in bright sunlight, in the middle span of flowing fresh water.

And if there was such a power, he had no chance against it anyway.

Then he went the rest of the way across and took the road north.

The Behnburg Road, East of Albinkirk—Robert Guissarme

Robert Guissarme was tall and cadaverously thin despite his intake of mutton and ale. Men said that his appetite for food was only exceeded by his appetite for gold. He called his company of men a *Company of Adventure*, like the best Eastern mercenaries, and he dressed well in leather and good wool, or in bright armour made by the best Eastern smiths.

No one knew much of his birth. He claimed to be the bastard son of a great nobleman, whom he was careful never to name—but he was known from time to time to lay a finger to his nose when a great man passed him on the road.

His sergeants feared him. He was quick to anger, quick to punish, and as he was the best man-at-arms of his company none of them wanted to cross him. Especially not right now; he was sitting fully armed on his charger, in deep fog, looking at a pair of peddlers who had passed them the night before, and who now stood in the middle of the road. They had been carefully butchered, flayed, and then set on posts in the road so that their heads seemed locked in endless screams of abject agony.

Since yesterday, he had pushed his convoy north-west along the bad road that connected Albinkirk to the east—to the Hills, and then over the mountains to Morea, and the land of the Emperor. He'd started his convoy in Theva, the city of slavers, and had pushed his men so hard that their horses began to fail. As for the long chain of slaves that was their principal cargo—he no longer cared much whether they lived or died. They had been entrusted to him in Theva; a long line of broken men and women—some pretty, some ugly, and all with the blank despair of the utterly beaten human being. He'd been told that they were a valuable consignment, being skilled slaves—cooks, menservants, housemaids, nurses, and whores.

His company had treated them well enough on the long trip west. Well enough, despite the frowns of the Emperor's Knight—a pompous bastard too proud to share his meals with a mere *mercenary*. After Albinkirk the man would no longer be his problem.

But when they passed Behnburg, the last town before Albinkirk, and found the town's garrison and population huddled within their walls in fear of un-named terrors, he'd started to hurry west, leaving the rest of the spring flood of merchants to hurry along in his wake. A dozen with wagons and good horses had paid him in gold to stay with his convoy.

He'd only taken the job transporting slaves to pay his passage—rumour had it that the fortress convent at Lissen Carak was offering payment in gold for monster-hunting work, and Guissarme needed the work. Or his company did.

Or perhaps they could manage a little longer. He sat his charger, at eye level with the corpses who had been killed, he now saw, by the act of their impaling.

He'd heard of impalement. Never seen it before. He couldn't tear his eyes away.

He was still gazing at them, rapt, when the arrows began to fall.

The first hit his horse. The second struck his breastplate with enough force to unseat him and sprang away and then he was falling. Men were screaming around him, and he could hear his corporals shouting for order. Something struck him in the groin and he felt a hot, rapidly spreading damp. Heard the sound of hooves—heavy horses moving fast, although with an odd rhythm. He couldn't see well.

He tried to raise his head, and *something* crouched over him, coming for his face—

The Behnburg Road, East of Albinkirk—Peter

Peter watched the arrows fly from the woods that lined the road with a sort of hopeless, helpless anger.

It was so *obvious* an ambush. He couldn't believe anyone had walked into it.

Chained by the yoke around his neck to the women front and back, he couldn't run.

He didn't have the words, but he tried all the same.

"Fall down!" he shouted. "Down!"

But the panic was already coming. The terror—he'd never felt such terror. It came directly behind the arrows, and washed over him like dirty water leaving fear behind. The two women to whom he was bound ran in different directions, stumbled, and fell together, taking him to the ground with them.

The arrows continued to fall on the soldiers, who mostly died. Only a small knot of them were still fighting.

Something—he couldn't see very well in the late morning ground fog—something came out of the fog moving as fast as a knight on a horse and slammed into the column. Men and horses screamed anew, and the terror increased to the point where his two companions simply curled into balls.

Peter lay still and tried to make his head work. Watched the creatures coming at the column. They were daemons. He had heard of them in his home, and here they were, and they were feeding on the corpses. Or perhaps the living.

A wyvern fell from the sky on the blonde woman ahead of him, its beaked head ripping at her guts. The woman behind him shrieked and got to her knees, arms extended, and a gout of pure green passed inches over

Peter's head and slammed into the thing, which gave off an overpowering smell of burning soap.

It pivoted on its hips like a dancer, the action ripping the screaming woman under its forefoot in two and snapping the chain that connected the slaves. The end of the chain whipped around the creature's leg.

The wyvern unwound the chain fastidiously, using a talon, and the woman at Peter's back cast again, two handfuls of raw spirit shot out with an hysterical scream. The wyvern screamed back as it was hit, hundreds of times as loud, snapped its wings open and flung itself on the woman.

Peter rolled beneath it, the newly snapped end of the chain running through his yoke, which caught on a tree root and wrenched his neck. Free, he was on his feet and running into the fog.

A flash, and he was thrown flat. Silence—he got to his feet and ran on, and only after a hundred panicked steps did he realise he was deaf and the shirt on his back was charred.

He ran on.

His mouth was so dry he could not swallow, and his thighs and calves burned as if they, too, had been burnt. But he ran until he crossed a deep stream, and there he drank his fill and lay gasping until he passed out.

Albinkirk—Ser Alcaeus

Ser Alcaeus rode up to Albinkirk on a blown horse, with his destrier trotting along behind him. He'd lost his squire and his page in the fighting but his valet, a boy too young to swing a sword to any effect, had somehow survived with the pack horse.

Alcaeus pounded on the town's west gate with his sword hilt. A pair of scared looking guards opened the main gate the width of one horse to let him in.

"There is an army of the Wild out there," Alcaeus gasped. "Take me to your captain."

The captain of the town was an old man—at least as fighters went—grey bearded and tending to fat. But he was booted and spurred, wearing a hauberk of good iron rings and a belt that showed his paunch to unfortunate effect.

"Ser John Crayford," he said, holding out a hand.

Ser Alcaeus thought it unlikely that the man had ever been knighted. And he wondered how such an ill-favoured lout had come to command such an important post.

"I was with a convoy of fifty wagons on the Behnburg Road," Alcaeus said. He sat suddenly. He hadn't intended to sit, but his legs went out from under him.

"The Wild," he said. He tried to sound sane and rational and like a man whose word could be trusted. "Daemons attacked us. With irks. A hundred, at least." He found that he was having trouble breathing.

It was difficult even telling it.

"Oh, my God," he said.

Ser John put a hand on his shoulder. The man seemed bigger somehow. "How far, messire?" he said.

"Five leagues." Alcaeus took a deep breath. "Maybe less. East of here."

"By the Virgin!" the Captain of Albinkirk swore. "East, you say?"

"You believe me?" Alcaeus said.

"Oh, yes," said the captain. "But east? They went *around* the town?" He shook his head.

Alcaeus heard boots on the steps outside. He raised his head and saw the same man who'd let him into the city, with a pair of lower-class men.

"They say there's boglins in the fields, Ser John." The sergeant shrugged. "That's what they say."

"My daughter!" the younger man shouted. It was more like a shriek than a shout. "You have to save her."

Ser John shook his head. "I'm not taking a man out that gate. Steady, man." He poured the man a cup of wine.

"My *daughter*!" the man said in anguish.

Ser John shook his head. "I'm sorry for your loss," he said, not unkindly. He turned to the sergeants. "Sound the alarm. Bar the gates. And get me the mayor and tell him I'm imposing martial law. *No one is to leave this town.*"

East of Albinkirk—Peter

Peter woke at a jerk of his heavy yoke. It was a hand-carved wooden collar with a pair of chains that ran down to his hands, allowing some movement, and a heavy staple for attaching him to other slaves, and he'd slept in it.

Two Moreans, easterners with scrips and heavy backpacks, wearing hoods and the air of men recently released from fear, stood over him.

"One survived then," the taller one said, and spat.

The shorter one shook his head. "Hardly a fair return on the loss of our cart," he said. "But a slave's a slave. Get up, boy."

Peter lay in abject misery for a moment. So, naturally, they kicked him.

Then they made him carry their packs, and the three of them started west along a trail through the woods.

His despair didn't last long. He had been unlucky—or perhaps he had been lucky. They fed him; he cooked their meagre food and they let him have some bread and a little of the pea soup he'd made them. Neither of them were big men, or strong, and he thought he could probably kill them both, if only the yoke came off his shoulders.

But he couldn't get it off. It had been his constant companion for a month of walking over snow and ice, sleeping with the cold and hellish thing while the soldiers raped the women to either side of him and waiting to see if they would take a turn on him.

He bruised his wrists again and again trying get free of the thing. He daydreamed of using it as a weapon to crush these puny men.

"You're a good cook, boy," the taller man said, wiping his mouth.

The thin man frowned. "I want to know what happened back there," he said, after drinking watered wine from his canteen.

The thicker man shrugged. "Bandits? Cruel bastards, no doubt. I never saw a thing—I just heard the fighting and—well, you ran, too."

The thinner man shook his head. "The screams," he said, and his voice shook.

They sat and glowered at each other, and Peter looked at them and wondered how they managed to survive at all.

"We should go back for our cart," said the thinner man.

"You must've had a bump on the head," the fatter one said. "Want to be a slave? Like him?" he gestured at Peter.

Peter hunched by the fire and wondered if lighting it had been a good idea, and wondered how these two could be so foolish. At home, they had had daemons. These idiots must know of them too.

But the night passed—a night in which he never slept, and the two fools slumbered after tying his yoke to a tree. They snored, and Peter lay awake, waiting for a hideous death that never came.

In the morning, the easterners rose, pissed, drank the tea he'd made, ate his bannock and started west.

"Where'd you learn to cook, boy?" the thicker man asked him.

He shrugged.

"Now that's a saleable skill," the man said.

The Toll Gate—Hector Lachlan

Drovers hated tolls. There was no way to love them. When you have to drive a huge herd of beasts—mostly cattle, but small farmers put in parcels of sheep, and even goats as well—representing other men's fortunes, across mountain, fen, fell, swamp and plain, through war and pestilence, tolls are the very incarnation of evil.

Hector Lachlan had a simple rule.

He didn't pay tolls.

His herd numbered in the hundreds, and he had as many men as a southern lord had in an army; men who wore burnies of shining rings and carried heavy swords and great axes slung from their shoulders. They looked more like the cream of a mercenary army than what they were. Drovers.

"I didn't mean to cross you, Lachlan!" the local lordling pleaded. He had that tone, the one Hector hated the most—wheedling bluster, he called it, when a man who had pretended he was cock of the north started begging for his life.

Hector hadn't even drawn the great sword that sat across his hip and rump. He merely leaned his forearm on the hilt. He stroked his moustache idly and ran a hand through his hair, looked back down the long, muddy train of cattle and sheep that extended behind him, as far as the eye might see on the mountain track.

"Just pay me the toll. I'll—see to it you ha' the coins back soon enough." The other man was tall, well-built, and wearing a chain hauberk worth a fortune, every link riveted closed, strong as stone.

He was afraid of Hector Lachlan.

But not afraid enough to let the long convoy of beasts past. He had to be seen to try and collect the toll. It was the way, in the hills, and his own fear would make him angry.

Sure enough, even as Hector had the thought, he saw the man's face change.

"Be damned to you, then. Pay the damned toll or—"

Hector drew his sword. He wasn't hurried by his adversary's anger, fear, or the fifty armed men at his back. He drew the long sword at his own pace, and allowed the heavy pommel to rotate the sword in his hand, so that the point aimed unwaveringly at the other man's face.

And punched the needle sharp point through the other man's forehead with all the effort of a shoemaker punching a hole in leather. The armoured man crumpled, his eyes rolling up. Already dead.

Hector sighed.

The dead man's retinue stood rooted to the ground in shock—a shock that would last a few more heartbeats.

"Stop!" Hector said. It was a delicate art—to command without threatening them and provoking the very reaction he sought to avoid.

The body crashed to the ground, the dead man's heels thrashing momentarily.

"None of ye need to die," he said. There was a thread of the dead man's blood on the tip of his sword. "He was a fool to demand a toll of me, and every man here knows it. Let his tanist take command, and let us hear no more about it." Lachlan got the words out, and for a moment the men he was facing teetered on the knife-edge of doubt and greed and fear and loyalty—not to the dead man but to the code that required them to avenge him.

The code won.

Lachlan heard the grunt that signified their refusal, and he had both hands on his sword, swinging a heavy overhand blow at the nearest man. He had a sword in his hand, but was too slow to save his own life; the heavy swing batted his parry aside and cut through his skull from left eyebrow to right jaw, so that the top of his head spun away, cleanly severed.

Hector's own men started to come forward, abandoning their places with his herd. Which meant that when this was over, with all the attending noise, violence, blood and ordure, a day would be lost while they collected all the beasts who ran off into the glens and valleys.

Someone—some ancient philosopher Lachlan couldn't remember from the days when a priest came to teach him letters—had said that the hillmen would conquer the world, if only they would ever stop fighting among themselves.

He pondered that as he killed his third man of the day, as his retinue charged with a shout, and as the doomed men of the toll gate tried to make a stand and were cut down.

Lissen Carak—The Red Knight

The camp below the Abbey vanished as quickly as it had appeared, the tents folded and packed into the wagons, the wagons double-teamed and hauled up the steep slope into the fortress.

The first chore that faced all of them was billeting the company. Captain and Abbess walked quickly through the dormitory, the great hall, the chapel, the stables, and the storehouses, adding, dividing, and allocating.

"I will need to bring all my people in, of course," the Abbess said.

The captain bit his lip and looked at the courtyard. "Eventually, we may have to re-erect our tents here," he said. "Will you use the Great Hall?"

"Of course. It's being stripped even now," she said. She shrugged. "It is Lent—all of our valuables are put away already."

One of the company's great wagons was just crossing the threshold of the main gate. Its top just fitted under the lintel.

"Show me your stores and all your storage places," he said.

She led him from cellar to cellar, from store room to the long, winding, airless steps that led deep into the heart of the living rock under their feet, to where a fresh spring burbled away into a pool the size of a farm pond. She was slower coming back up the winding steps than she had been going down.

He waited with her when she stopped to rest.

"Is there an exit? Down there?" he asked.

She nodded. "Of course—who would hollow out this mountain and not make one? But I haven't the strength to show you." They reemerged through the secret door behind the chapel altar, and the Abbess was immediately surrounded by grey-clad sisters, each demanding her attention—matters of altar care, of flowers for the next service, of complaints about the rain of blasphemous oaths falling from the walls, now fully manned.

"All you cock suckers get your fucking arses in armour or I'll chew off the top of your sodding skulls and fuck your brains," Bad Tom was dressing down a dozen men-at-arms just going onto the wall. His tone was conversational and yet it fell into a moment of silence and was carried everywhere inside the fortress.

An older sister stared at her Abbess in mute appeal.

"Your sisters are silent," the captain said.

The Abbess nodded. "All are allowed to speak on Sundays. Novices and seniors may speak when they are moved to—which is seldom for seniors and often for novices." She made a gesture with her hands. "I am their ambassador to the world." She pointed at the cowled figure who followed her. "This is Sister Miram, my chancellor and my vicar. She is also allowed to speak."

The captain bowed to Sister Miram, who inclined her head slightly.

The Abbess nodded. "But she prefers not to."

Whereas you—the captain thought that perhaps she liked to speak more than she let on, and liked to talk to him, to have an adult to spar with. Yet he did not doubt her piety. To the captain, piety came in three brands—false piety, hypocritical piety, and hard won, deep and genuine piety. He fancied that he could tell them apart.

At the far end of the chapel stood Father Henry. He looked harried—hadn't bathed or shaved, the captain suspected. He looked at the Abbess. "Your priest is in a bad way," he said.

He knew that she had cast a phantasm on him last night. She'd done it expertly, and so revealed she was more than a mere mathematical astrologer. She was a magus. She'd probably known the instant he cast his glamour in her yard, and on her sisters.

And she was not the only magus. There were wheels within the wheels that powered this situation. He looked at Sister Miram, his sense of power reaching tentatively towards her, like a third hand.

Aha. It was as if Sister Miram had slapped that hand.

The Abbess was looking at the priest. "He's in love with me," she said dismissively. "My final lover. Gentle Jesu, might you not have sent me someone handsome and gentle?" She turned and smiled wryly. "I suspect he was sent me as a penance. And a reminder of what—of what I was." She shrugged. "The Knights of our Order didn't send us a priest last winter, so I took him from a local parish. He seemed interesting. Instead, I find he's—" She paused. "Why am I telling you this, messire?"

"As your captain, it is my duty to know," he said.

She considered him. "He's a typical ignorant parish priest—can scarcely read Archaic, knows the Bible only from memory, and thinks women are less than the dirt on his bare feet." She shook her head. "And yet he came here, and he is drawn to me."

The captain smiled at her, took her right hand between his and kissed it. "Perhaps *I* am your last lover," he said.

As he did it, he saw the priest squirm. *Oh, my, what fun.* The man was loathsome, but his piety was probably genuine too.

"Should I box your ears for that? I understand that's the fashion," the Abbess said. "Please desist, Captain."

He retreated as if she'd struck him. Sister Miram was frowning.

To regain his composure, he summoned Jehannes and Milus. "Get the drovers to dismantle the wagons. Put the hardware in the cellars—Abbess, we're going to need some guides."

The Abbess sent for the old garrison—eight non-noble men-at-arms hired at the Great Fair a dozen years before. They were led by Michael Ranulfson, a grizzled giant with gentle manners, the sergeant at arms the captain had met briefly the night before.

"You know that I've placed the captain in charge of our defence," she said. "His men need help moving in, and guides to the storerooms. Michael—I trust them."

Michael bowed his head respectfully, but his eyes said *on your head be it.*

"How are you set for hoardings?" the captain asked. "Do you have pre-cut lumber?"

The old sergeant at arms nodded. "Aye. Hoardings, portable towers, a pair of trebuchets, some smaller engines." He rolled his head on his neck, as if trying to rid himself of a stiffness. "When you are in garrison, you may as like do a good job of work."

The captain nodded. "Thanks, Ser Michael."

"I'm no knight," Michael said. "My da was a skinner."

The captain ignored his statement to look at Jehannes. "As soon as the lads are unpacked, give this man fifty archers and all the riff-raff and get the hoardings up while the men-at-arms stand to."

Jehannes nodded, obviously in full agreement.

"Store the dismantled wagons wherever the hoardings are now," the captain said. "And then we'll start on patrols to fetch in the peasants. Gentlemen, this place is going to be packed as tight as a cask of new-salted mackerel. I want to say this in front of the Abbess. There will be no rape and no theft by our men. Death penalty on both. My lady, I can't do much about casual blasphemy, but an effort will be made—you understand me, gentlemen? Make an effort."

She nodded. "It is Lent," she said.

Jehannes nodded. "I gave up wine," he said, and then stared at the floor.

"Jesu does not care what you give up, but rather, what you give him," Sister Miram replied, and Jehannes smiled shyly at her.

She returned his smile.

The captain released a heavy sigh. "Ladies, you may well cure all of our souls yet, but it must wait until the hoardings are up and all your people are safe. Michael, you are in charge of them. I recommend that my men live in the towers and galleries—if we have time, we'll build them beds."

"My people will go four to a room," the Abbess said. "I can take the older girls and single women from the farms into the dormitory, and all the men and their families will go in the hall. Overflow into the stables."

Michael nodded. "Yes, my lady," he replied. He turned to the captain. "I'm at your orders." He looked back and forth. "Will we hold the Lower Town?"

The captain stepped up onto the gate wall and looked down at the four streets of the town, a hundred feet below.

"For a little while," he said.

Albinkirk—Ser Alcaeus

Ser Alcaeus passed a bad night and drank too much wine in the morning. The man whose daughter had been abducted sat in the garrison barracks and wept, and demanded that the garrison send out a sortie to her rescue.

The mayor agreed with him, and hot words were exchanged.

Alcaeus didn't want any part of it. They were too alien—the commoners were both too servile and too free, and Ser John was no knight. Even the churches were wrong. Mass was said in low Archaic.

It was disorienting. Worse than the convoy of slaves had been, because he could ignore them.

Mid-morning, as he finished his ablutions—he, the Emperor's cousin, washing without so much as a servant or slave to help him—he heard the mayor's shrill voice in the guardroom, demanding that Ser John come out.

Alcaeus dressed. He had spare shirts because the boy had saved his packhorse, and he'd see the page richly rewarded for it.

"Come out of your hole, you doddering old coward!" shrieked the mayor.

Alcaeus was trying to lace his cuffs by himself. He *had* done his own in the past, but not since he became a man. He had to press his right hand against the stone of the castle wall and pin the knot in place.

"Master Mayor?" he heard. It was Ser John, his voice calm enough.

"I demand that you gather all the useless mouths you call your garrison and go out and find this man's daughter. And open the gates—the grain convoys are on their way. This town needs money, though I'm sure you've been too *drunk* to notice." The mayor sounded like a fishwife—a particularly nasty one.

"No," said the captain. "Was that all?"

Alcaeus couldn't, in that moment, decide exactly what he thought of the knight. Over-cautious? But memories of yesterday's ambush were still burned onto the backs of his eyelids.

He reached for his boots—uncleaned, of course. He pulled them on, and fought with all the buckles, his head suddenly full of irks and boglins and worse things. The road. The confusion.

He had been trained to fight the Wild. Until yesterday, he'd only fought other men—usually one to one, with knives, at court.

The images in his head made him shudder.

"I order you!" the mayor screamed.

"You can't order me, Master Mayor. I have declared martial law, and I, not you, am the power here." Ser John sounded apologetic rather than dismissive.

"I represent the *people* of the town. The burgesses, the merchants, and the artisans!" The mayor's voice sank to a hiss. "You don't seem to understand—"

"I understand that I represent the king. And you do not." Ser John's voice remained level.

Alcaeus had made his decision. He was going to go support the low-born knight. It didn't matter what the two men were debating—it was their manners. Ser John was knightly. He might even survive at court.

Alcaeus tested his feet in his boots, and took his heavy dagger and put it in his belt. He never left his rooms without a dagger. Then he went out into the hall—a hall crowded with garrison soldiers listening to the argument in the main room below. He ran light-footed down the stairs.

He'd missed an exchange. When he entered, the mayor, red-faced, thin and tall and blond as an angel, was silent, his mouth working.

Ser Alcaeus went and stood behind the old knight. He noted that the mayor wore a rich doublet of dark blue velvet trimmed in sable, and a cap to match, embroidered with irks and rabbits. He smiled—his own silk doublet was worth about fifty times the value of the mayor's.

The irks in the mayor's cap were ironic, to say the least.

"This is Ser Alcaeus," Ser John said. "The Emperor's ambassador to our king. Yesterday his convoy was attacked by *hundreds* of Wild creatures."

The mayor shot a venomous glance at him. "So you say. Go do your *fucking* job, sell-sword. Aren't you even a little humiliated to think that this man's daughter is the plaything of monsters while you sit and drink wine?"

The man—who stood behind the mayor with a dozen other men—gave a sob and sank to a wooden bench, his fist in his mouth.

"His daughter has been dead since yesterday and I won't risk men to look for her corpse," Ser John said with casual brutality. "I want all the woman and children moved to the castle immediately, with victuals."

The mayor spat. "I forbid it. Do you want to panic the town?"

Ser John shrugged. "Yes," he said. "In my professional opinion—"

"You *have* no professional opinion. You were a sell-sword—what? Forty years ago? And then a drinking crony of the king's. Very professional!" The mayor was beside himself.

Alcaeus realised the man was afraid. Terrified. And that terror made him belligerent. It was a revelation. Alcaeus was not, strictly speaking, a *young* man. He was twenty-nine, and he thought he knew how the world worked.

Yesterday had been a shock. And now today was a shock too. He watched the fool mayor, and watched Ser John, and understood something of their quality.

"Messire mayor?" he asked in his stilted Gothic. "Please—I am a stranger here. But the Wild is real. What I saw was real."

The mayor turned and looked at him. "And who in God's name are you?" he asked.

"Alcaeus Comnena, cousin to the Emperor Manual, may his name be praised, the drawn sword of Christ, the Warrior of the Dawn." Alcaeus bowed. His cousin was too old to draw a sword but his titles rolled off the tongue, and he was annoyed by the mayor.

The mayor was, for all his belligerence and terror, a merchant and an educated man. "From Morea?" he asked.

Alcaeus thought of telling this barbarian what he thought of their casual use of Morea for the Empire. But he didn't bother. "Yes," he shot back.

The mayor drew a breath. "Then if you are a true knight, *you* will go and rescue this man's daughter."

Alcaeus shook his head. "No. Ser John is correct. You must call in your out-farmers and move the people into the castle."

The mayor shook his fist. "The *convoys* are coming. If we close the gates, this town will *die*!" He paused. "For the love of God! There's *money* involved."

Ser John shrugged. "I hope the money helps when the boglins come," he said.

As if on cue, an alarm bell sounded.

After the mayor pounded out of the castle, Alcaeus went out on the wall and saw two farms burning. Ser John joined him. "I told him to bring the people in last night," he muttered. "Fucking idiot. Thanks for trying."

Alcaeus watched the plumes of smoke rise and his stomach did flips. Suddenly, again, he was seeing those the irks under his horse. He had once, single-handed, fought off four assassins who were going for his mother. Irks were much, much worse. He tasted bile.

He thought of lying down.

Instead, he drank wine. After a cup, he felt strong enough to visit his page, who was recovering from terror in the resilient way teenagers so. He left his page to cuddle with a servant girl and walked wearily back to the guard room, where there was an open cask of wine.

He was on his fourth when Ser John's fist closed around his cup. "I take it you are a belted knight," Ser John said. "I saw your sword, and you've used it. Eh?"

Ser Alcaeus got up from his chair. "You dared draw my sword?" he asked. At the Emperor's court touching a man's sword was an offence.

The old man grinned mirthlessly. "Listen, messire. This town is about to be attacked. I never thought to see it in my lifetime. I gather you had a bad day yesterday. Fine. Now I need you to stop draining my stock of wine and get your armour on. They'll go for the walls in about an hour, unless I miss my guess." He looked around the empty garrison room. "If we fight like fucking heroes and every man does everything he can, we might just make it—I'm still trying to get that fool to send the women into the castle. This is the Wild, Ser Knight. I gather you've tasted their mettle. Well—here they come again."

Ser Alcaeus thought that this was a far, far cry from being a useful functionary at his uncle's court. And he wondered if his true duty, given the message he had in his wallet, was to gather his page and ride south before the roads closed.

But there was something about the old man. And besides, the day before he'd run like a coward, even if he'd had the blood of three of the things on his sword first.

"I'll arm," he said.

"Good," Ser John said. "I'll help, and then I'll give you a wall to command."

Abbington-on-the-Carak—Mag the Seamstress

Old Mag the seamstress sat in the good, warm sunshine on her doorstep, her back braced against the oak of her door frame, as she had sat for almost forty years of such mornings. She sat and sewed.

Mag wasn't a proud woman, but she had a certain place, and she knew it. Women came to her for advice on childbirth and savings, on drunken husbands, on whether or not to let a certain man visit on a certain night. Mag knew things.

Most of all, she knew how to sew.

She liked to work early, when the first full light of the sun struck her work. The best time was immediately after Matins. If she managed to get straight to her work—and in forty years of being a lay sister, helping with the altar service in her village church, of tending to her husband and two children she had missed the good early morning work hours all too often.

But when she got to it—when cooking, altar service, sick infants, aches and pains, and the will of the Almighty all let her be—why, she could do a day's work by the time the bells rang for Nones in the fortress convent two leagues to the west.

And this morning was one of those wonderful mornings. She'd been the lay server at church, which always left her with a special feeling, and she had laid flowers on her husband's grave, kissed her daughter in her own door yard and was now home in the first warm light, her basket by her side.

She was making a cap, a fine linen coif of the sort that a gentleman wore to keep his hair neat. It wasn't a difficult object and would take her only a day or two to make, but there were knights up at the fortress who used such caps at a great rate, as she had reason to know. A well-worked cap that fit just so was worth half a silver penny. And silver pennies were not to be sneered at, for a fifty-three-year-old widow.

Mag had good eyes, and she pricked the fine linen—her daughter's linen, no less—with precision, her fine stitches as straight as a sword blade, sixteen to the inch, as good or better as any Harndon tailor's work.

She put the needle into the fine cloth and pulled the thread carefully through, feeling the fine wax on the thread, feeling the tension of the fine cloth, and aware that she pulled more than the thread with each stitch—every one gathered a little sun. Before long, her line of stitches *sparkled*, if she looked at it just so.

Good work made her happy. Mag liked to examine the fine clothes that came through to Lis the laundress. The knights in the fortress had some beautiful things—usually ill-kept but well made. And many less well-made clothes, too. Mag had plans to sell them clothes, repairs, darning—

Mag smiled at the world as she stitched. The sisters were, in the main, good landlords, and much better than most feudal lords. But the knights and their men brought a little colour to life. Mag didn't mind hearing a man say fuck, as long as he brought a little of the outside world to Abbington-on-the-Carak.

She heard the horses, and her eyes flicked up from her work. She saw dust rising well off to the west. At this hour, it could never bode well.

She snorted and put her work in her basket, carefully sheathing her best needle—Harndon work, there was no local man who could make such—in a horn needle case. No crisis was so great that Mag needed to lose a needle. They were harder and harder to get.

More dust. Mag knew the road. She guessed there were ten horses or more.

"Johne! Our Johne!" she called. The Bailli was her gossip, and occasionally more. He was also an early riser, and Mag could see him pruning his apple trees.

She stood and pointed west. After a long moment, he raised an arm and jumped down from the tree.

He dusted his hands and spoke to a boy, and heartbeats later that boy was racing for the church. Johne jumped the low stone wall that separated his property from Mag's and bowed.

"You have good eyes, m'ame." He didn't smirk or make any obvious gesture, which she appreciated. Widowhood brought all sorts of unwelcome offers—and some welcome ones. He was clean, neat, and polite, which had become her minimum conditions for accepting even the most tenuous of male approaches.

She enjoyed watching a man of her own age who could still jump a stone wall.

"You seem unconcerned," she murmured.

"To the contrary," he said quietly. "If I were a widowed seamstress I would pack all my best things and be prepared to move into the fortress." He gave her half a smile, another bow, and sprang back over the wall. "There's been trouble," he added.

Mag didn't ask foolish questions. Before the horses rode into their little town square, shaded by an ancient oak, she had two baskets packed, one of work and one of items for sale. She filled her husband's travelling pack with spare shifts and clothes, and took her heaviest cloak and a lighter cloak—for wearing and sleeping, too. She stripped her bed, took the bolster and rolled the blankets and linens tightly around it to make a bundle.

"Listen up!" called a loud voice—a *very* loud voice—from the village square.

Like all her neighbours she opened the upper half of her front door and leaned through it.

There were half a dozen men-at-arms in the square, all mounted on big horses and wearing well-polished armour and scarlet surcotes. With them were as many archers, all in less armour with bows strapped across their backs, and as many valets.

"The lady Abbess has ordered that the good people of Abbington be mustered and removed into the fortress immediately!" the man bellowed. He was tall—huge, really, with arms the size of most men's legs, mounted on a horse the size of a small house.

Johne the Bailli, walked across the square to the big man-at-arms, who leaned down to him, and the two spoke—both of them gesturing rapidly. Mag went back to her packing. Out the back she scattered feed for her chickens. If she wasn't here for a week, they'd manage, longer, and they'd all be taken by something. She had no cow—Johne gave her milk—but she had her husband's donkeys.

My donkeys, she reminded herself.

She'd never packed a donkey before.

Someone was banging at her open door. She shook her head at the donkeys, who looked back at her with weary resignation.

The big man-at-arms stood on her stoop. He nodded. "The Bailli said you'd be ready to move first," he said. "I'm Thomas." His bow was sketchy, but it was there.

He looked like trouble from head to foot.

She grinned at him, because her husband had looked like trouble, too. "I'd be more ready if I knew how to pack a donkey," she said.

He scratched under his beard. "Would a valet help? I want people moving in an hour. And the Bailli said that if people saw you packed, they'd move faster." He shrugged.

Off to the right, a woman screamed.

Thomas spat. "Fucking archers," he snarled, and started back out the door.

"Send me a valet!" she shouted after him.

She got a produce basket down from the shed and began to fill it with perishable food, and then preserves. She had sausage, pickles, jam, that was itself valuable—

"Good wife?" asked a polite voice from the doorway. The man was middle-aged, and looked as hard as rock and as sound as an old apple. Behind him was a skinny boy of twelve.

"I'm Jaques, the captain's valet. This is my squire, Toby. He can pack a mule—I reckon donkeys ain't much different." The man took his hat off and bowed.

Mag curtsied back. "The sele of the day to you, ser."

Jacques raised an eyebrow. "The thing of it is, ma'am—we're also to take all your food."

She laughed. "I've been trying to pack it—" Then his meaning sunk in. "You mean to take my food for the garrison."

He nodded. "For everyone. Yes." He shrugged. "I'd rather you made it easy. But we will take it."

Johne came to the door. He had a breast and back plate on and nodded to Jacques. To Mag, he said, "Give them everything. They are from the Abbess, we have to assume she will repay us." He shrugged. "Do you still have Ben's crossbow? His arming jack?"

"And his sword and dagger," Mag said. She opened her cupboard, where she kept her most valuable things—her pewter plates, her silver cup, her mother's gold ring, and her husband's dagger and sword.

Toby looked around shyly, and said to Jacques, "This is a rich place, eh, master?"

Jacques smiled grimly and gave the boy a kick. "Sorry, ma'am. We has some bad habits from the Continent, but we won't take your things."

But you would under other circumstances, and anything else you fancied, she thought.

Johne took her by her shoulders. It was a familiar, comfortable thing, and yet a little too possessive for her taste, even in a crisis.

"I have a locking box," he said. "There's room in it for your cup and ring. And any silver you have." He looked into her eyes. "Mag, we may never come back. This is war—war with the Wild. When it's done, we may not have homes to return to."

"Gentle Jesu!" she let slip. Took a shuddering breath, and nodded. "Very well." She scooped up the cup and ring, tipped over a brick in her fireplace and took out all her silver—forty-one pennies—and handed it all to the bailli. She saved out one penny, and she gave it to Jacques.

"This much again if my donkeys make it to the fortress," she said primly.

He looked at it for a moment. Bit it. And flipped it to the boy. "You heard the lady," he said. He nodded to her. "I'm the captain's valet, ma'am. A piece of gold is more my price. But Tom told me to see to you, and you are seen to." He gave her a quick salute and was out her door, headed for Simon Carter's house.

She looked at the boy. He didn't seem very different from any other boy she knew. "You can load a donkey?" she asked.

He nodded very seriously. "Do you—" he looked around. He was as skinny as a scarecrow and gawky the way only growing boys can be. "Do you have any food?" he asked.

She laughed. "You'll be taking it all anyways, won't you, my dear?" she asked. "Have some mince pie."

Toby ate the mince pie with a determination that made her smile. While she watched him, still packing her hampers, he ate the piece he was given and then filched a second as he headed for her donkey.

A pair of archers appeared next. They lacked something that Ser Thomas and Jacques the valet had both possessed. They looked dangerous.

"What have we here?" asked the first one through the door. "Where's the husband, then, my beauty?" His voice was flat, and so were his eyes.

The second man had no teeth and too much smile. His haubergeon was not well kept, and he seemed like a half-wit.

"Mind your own business," she said, her voice as sharp as steel.

Dead-eyes didn't even pause. He reached out, grabbed her arm, and when she fought him he swept her legs out from under her and shoved her to the floor. His face didn't change expression.

"House's protected," said the skinny boy said from the kitchen. "Best mind yourself, Wilful."

The dead-eyed archer spat. "Fuck me," he said. "I want to go back to the Continent. If I wanted to be a nurse-maid—"

Mag was so stunned she couldn't react.

The archer leaned down and stuck his hand in the front of her cote-hardie. Gave her breast a squeeze. "Later," he said.

She shrieked, and punched him in the crotch.

He stumbled back, and the other one grabbed her hair, as if this was a practised routine—

There was a sharp *crack* and she fell backwards, because the archer had released her. He was kneeling on the floor with blood pouring out of his face. Thomas was standing over him, a stick in his hand.

"I tol' 'em that this house was protected!" the thin boy shouted.

"Did you?" The big man said. He eyed the two archers.

"We was gentle as lambs!" said the one with dead eyes.

"Fucking archers. Piss off and get on with it," the big man said, and offered her a hand up.

The two archers got to their feet and went out the back to collect her chickens and her sheep and all the grain from her shed, all the roots in her cellar. They were methodical, and when she followed them into the shed, the dead-eyed one gave her a look that struck fear into her. He meant her harm.

But soon enough the boy had her donkeys rigged and loaded, and she put her husband's pack on her back, her two baskets in her arms, and went out into the square.

From where she stood, her house looked perfectly normal.

She tried to imagine it burned. An empty basement yawning at the sun. She could see the place where she rested her back when she sewed, rubbed shiny with use, and she wondered if she would ever find such a well-lit spot.

The Carters were next to be ready—they were, after all, a family of carters with two heavy carts of their own and draught animals, and six boys and men to do the lifting. The bailli's housekeeper was next, with his rugs—Mag had lain on one of those rugs, and she blushed at the thought. She was still mulling over her instinctive use of his name—his Christian name—

The Lanthorns were the last, their four sluttish daughters sullen, and Goodwife Lanthorn, in her usual despair, wandered the village's column of animals, begging for space for her bag and a basket of linen. Lis the laundress was surrounded by soldiers, who competed to carry her goods. But she knew many of them by name, having washed their linens, and she was both safely middle-aged *and* comely, an ideal combination in the soldiers' eyes.

At last the Lanthorns were packed—all four daughters eyeing the soldiers—and the column began to move.

Three hours after the men-at-arms rode into Abbington, the town was empty.

Albinkirk—Ser Alcaeus

Ser John gave him a company of crossbowmen—members of the town's guilds, all of them a little too shiny in their guild colours. Blue and red predominated, from the furriers, the leading guild of Albinkirk. He might have laughed to think that he, cousin to the Emperor, was commanding a band of common-born crossbowmen. It would have amused him, but...

They came at sunset, out of the setting sun.

The fields looked as if they were crawling with insects and then, without a shout or a signal the irks changed direction and were coming up the walls. Ser Alcaeus had never seen anything like it, and it made his skin crawl.

There were daemons among them, a dozen or more, fast, lithe, elegant and deadly. And they simply ran up the walls.

His crossbowmen loosed and loosed into the horde coming at them, and he did his best to walk up and down behind them on the crenellations, murmuring words of encouragement and praising their steadiness. He knew how to command, he'd just never done it before.

The first wave almost took the wall. A daemon came right over and started killing guildsmen. It was nothing but luck that its great sword bounced off a journeyman armourer's breastplate and the man's mates got their bolts into the lethal thing. It still took four more men down while it died, but the sight of the dead daemon stiffened the guildsmen's spines.

They staved off the second wave. The daemons had grown careful and led from the back. Alcaeus tried to get his crossbowmen to snipe at them, but there was never a moment when they could do anything but fight the most present danger.

A guild captain came to him where he was standing, leaning heavily on his pole-axe because he knew enough not to waste energy in armour. The man saluted.

"M'lord," he said. "We're almost out of bolts. Every lad brings twenty."

Ser Alcaeus blinked. "Where do you get more?"

"I was hoping you would know," said the guild officer.

Ser Alcaeus sent a runner, but he already knew the answer.

The third wave got over the walls behind them, they heard it go. The sounds of fighting changed, there was sudden shrieking and his men started to look over their shoulders.

He wished he had his squire—a veteran of fifty battles. But the man had died protecting him in the ambush and so he had no one to ask for advice.

Ser Alcaeus set his jaw and prepared to die well.

He walked along the wall again as the shadows lengthened. His section was about a hundred paces, end to end—Albinkirk was a *big* town, even to Ser Alcaeus who hailed from the biggest city in the world.

He stopped when he saw three of his men looking back at the town.

"Eyes front," he snapped.

"A house on fire!" some idiot said.

More men turned and, just like that, he lost them. They turned, and then there was a daemon on the wall, killing them. It moved like fluid, passing through men, round them, with two axes flashing in its taloned hands—even as Alcaeus watched, one of the daemon's taloned feet licked out to eviscerate a fifteen-year-old who'd had no breastplate.

Alcaeus charged. He felt the fear that it generated—but in Morea knights trained for this very thing, and he knew the fear. He ran through it, blade ready—

It hit him. It was faster by far, and an axe slammed into his arm. He was well-trained and caught much of the blow. His small fortune in plate armour ate the rest, and then he was swinging.

It had to pivot to face him. The twitch of its hips took a heartbeat, and he swung his pole-axe up from the garde of the boar, like a boy swinging a pitchfork at haying, but with twice the speed.

Ser Alcaeus was as shocked as the daemon when his axe caught the other creature's axe-hand and smashed it. Ichor sprayed and its axe fell. It slashed at him with the left, turned and kicked him with a taloned foot. All four talons bit through his breastplate and knocked him flat, but none reached him through his mail and padded arming cote.

A crossbow struck the daemon. Not a bolt but the bow itself, swung by a terrified guildsman.

The daemon bounded onto the wall, scattering defenders, and jumped. Alcaeus got to his feet. He still had his pole-axe.

He was proud of himself for two breaths, and then he realised that the town behind him was afire, and there were two more daemons on the wall with him, and irk arrows were suddenly everywhere. Worse, they were coming from the town.

He had a dozen men by him, including the stunned looking man who'd hit the daemon with his crossbow. The rest of his fools were leaving the wall, running for their houses.

He shook his head and cursed. They were surrounded, half his men gone, and it was growing dark rapidly.

He made his decision. "Follow me!" he called, and ran along the wall. He was headed for the castle, which towered over the western end of town by the river gate. It had its own defensive walls.

The whole town was falling. It was the only place to make a stand.

When he paused to breathe, Albinkirk was afire from south to north, and a sea of Wild creatures were running through the streets. He knew the difference between the irks—elfin and gnarled and satanic in the firelight—and the boglins, with their leather midsections and their oddly-jointed arms. He'd studied pictures. He'd trained for this, but it was like a nightmare. He was running *again* with the half dozen of his crossbowmen who stuck with him. The rest ran off into the town despite his admonitions. One died at their feet, ripped to pieces by boglins and consumed by something worse.

He could see the river, and the castle, but the next section of wall was crowded with enemies. The streets below were worse.

But at the edge of the firelight, he could see a company of soldiers with spears still holding one street, a crowd of panicked refugees behind them pressing on the castle gates.

Unbeckoned, a thought whispered into his head.

Time to earn your spurs.

"Let me go first," he said to his crossbowmen. "I will charge. You will follow me and kill anything that gets past me. You understand?"

He longed, just for a second, for wine and his lyre, and for the feeling of a woman's breast under his hand.

He raised his pole-axe.

"Kyrie Eleison!" he sang, and charged.

There were perhaps sixty boglins on the wall. It was too dark to count, and he wasn't that interested.

He smashed into them, taking them by surprise. The first one died, and after that nothing went right. His pole-axe fouled in the boglin; his blow had caught the thing in an armpit, and it fell off the wall taking his precious weapon with it.

He was instantly surrounded.

He got a dagger unsheathed with a practised *flick*—because a bastard cousin of the Emperor does not survive long at court without being able to use a dagger expertly, in or out of armour—and then they piled on him and he was all but buried standing up.

His right arm began stabbing largely of its own accord.

A tremendous blow knocked him forward, and he stumbled a few steps smashing pieces of boglin beneath his feet—suddenly panicked that he would fall off the wall. Panic powered his limbs, he spun and felt his steel-clad back slam into the crenellations. Suddenly his arms were free, and the thing trying to open his visor was the top priority, and then it was gone too and he was clear.

His right arm was slick with green-brown blood. He took up the low guard—All Gates are Iron—with his dagger back over his right hip, left fist by his left hip, looking over his left shoulder.

A boglin threw a spear at him.

He blocked it with his left hand, and stumbled forward into them. His breath was coming in great bursts, but his brain was clear, and he rammed the point of his heavy dagger into the first one, right through its head, and ripped it out again. His armoured fist snapped out in a punch and smashed the noseless face of a second.

The next two boglins were folded over their midriffs, shot with bolts. He stepped past them, his dagger switching hands with a dexterity his uncle's master of arms would have approved of, he was drawing his sword right-handed as he advanced.

The boglins began to back away.

He charged them.

They had their own gallantry. One creature gave its life to trip him, and died on his dagger as he fell. He rolled on a shoulder, but then there was nothing under his feet—

He hit a tiled roof, slid, hit a stone lintel with his armoured shoulder, flipped...

And landed in the street, on his feet. He still had both sword and dagger and took the time to thank God for it.

Above him, on the wall, the boglins were staring at him. "Follow me!"

he shouted to his men. He hadn't meant to come down to the street—but from here he could see irks coming along the wall from behind his archers.

Two made the jump. The rest froze, and died where they stood.

The three of them ran for the castle, which was lit up as if it was a royal palace ready for a great event. Albinkirk was ablaze, and the streets were carpeted with dead citizens and their servants and slaves.

It was a massacre.

He ran as well as he could in sabatons. His two surviving archers ran at his heels, and they killed the only two enemies they found, and then they were in the open street in front of the castle's main gate.

The spearmen were still holding the street.

The gate was still shut.

And the three of them were on the wrong side of the fighting.

He flipped up his visor. He no longer cared that he might die; he had to breathe. He stood there for as long as it took for his breathing to slow— bent double, he was easy meat for any boglin or irk who wanted him.

"Messire!" shouted the panicked crossbowmen.

He ignored them.

It seemed like eternity, but he got his head back up after he vomited on the cobbles. There was a half-eaten young boy at his feet, his body cast aside after his legs had been gnawed to the bone.

Across the square, the spearmen were barely holding. There were fifteen of them, or perhaps fewer, and they were holding back a hundred irks and boglins. The Wild creatures weren't particularly enthusiastic—they wanted to loot, not fight. But they kept pressing in.

Alcaeus pointed across the small square. "I'm going into that," he said to the crossbowmen. "I intend to cut my way through to the spearmen. Die here or die with me—it's all one to me." He looked at the two scared boys. "What are your names?" he asked.

"James," said the thin one.

"Mat," said the better accoutered one. He had a breastplate.

"Span, then. And let's do this thing," he said.

He knew that he didn't want to do it—and he knew that if he didn't make himself go then he'd die right here, probably still trying to catch his breath.

"Holy Saint Maurice, stand with me and these two young men," he said. And then, to the boys, "Walk right behind me. When I say to loose, kill the creatures closest to me." He began to walk around the edge of the square.

Off to the right a pack of irks were fighting over bales of furs. He ignored them.

A daemon loped into an alley, chasing a screaming, naked man, and he ignored it, too. He kept walking, hoarding his strength, sabatons making a grim metallic sound on the bloody stones.

He didn't look back. He just kept going, under a tree hanging over a house wall, and then along a stone bench on which, in happier days, drunks had no doubt passed out.

When he was ten paces from the back of the enemy mob, he shrugged. He wanted to pray, but nothing came to his mind but the sight of a beautiful courtesan in Thrake.

"Loose," he said.

Two bolts snapped into the mass of Wild flesh, and he followed them in, his sword and dagger flashing.

The lowest caste of boglins had no armour, but just their soft leather carapaces, and he cut them open, slammed them to earth, and crushed them with his fists. One.

Two.

Three.

Four.

Five.

He couldn't breathe. He couldn't see. He had no more to give—

—but he struck blindly, and something caught his dagger hand and threw him to the ground.

He rolled to his feet, because he was a knight, as an irk—one of the deadly ones—slammed a spear into his midriff. He went backwards and suddenly there were men all around him—

Men!

He was in among the spearmen. It put power into his limbs, and he got up again, his sword rising and falling.

He could see the thin crossbowman, James, still standing. The boy had flattened some of the things with his crossbow, and now had his side sword in his hand.

The creatures, panicked by even this very small attack from their rear, were flinching away from them both.

Ser Alcaeus gathered himself. One more time.

He tottered forward, and swung—one.

Two.

Three times. In those swings two boglins went down. The big irk flinched, turned, and hopped back.

The two hellish things feeding on the older boy died on James's sword, and then abruptly the square cleared.

Behind them huddled two hundred shocked survivors.

The men on the castle walls finally opened the gate. Or perhaps were ordered to, now it was safer, and people flooded through, utterly panicked. More died, trampled by others, than at the Wild's hands—the crush of women panicked beyond the capacity for anything but herd animal flight.

The spearmen backed up after them, step by step.

Step.

By.

Step.

In the shadowed streets beyond the square a pair of daemons rallied their own panicked forces, and added irk archers—good ones. Using the light of the burning town, the irks began to loose long shots across the square. Their elfin bows were light but deadly.

Ser Alcaeus couldn't cover them all. He was almost immune to their hits but the shafts hurt when they struck his helmet or his greaves, and he was already beyond normal pain, beyond normal fatigue. He looked to the right and left and found that he had reached the gate. The guards were trying to close it; he was trying to back in. But the crush of injured men and trampled corpses underfoot was jamming them open as the enemy made their charge.

He was able to get his sword arm up in time; he managed to cover himself against a daemon's heavy sword, and then old Ser John was there. He had a mace. It had a five-foot handle.

He used it well.

He stepped out past Ser Alcaeus, bouncing on the balls of his feet as if eager for the contest, and his mace moved like a piston. The daemons flinched back from his strike. A boglin died. Another daemon took a blow in the torso and staggered and the mace hit its foot, shattering the bone. It screamed as it went down.

It wasn't glorious work but Alcaeus bent and grabbed the corpse of a trampled woman and threw it out into the darkness.

The gate moved.

He got his hands under a dead boglin's skull and threw the corpse into its fellows.

The gate moved another hand's breath.

"Ser John!" he shrieked. His voice was hoarse and cracked.

The old knight bounced, cut, and suddenly bounded back.

Alcaeus stumbled after him.

The gates slammed shut. Terrified sergeants slammed the timbers home into the sockets that held them, and blows rained on the outside surface of the gate from the creatures outside. One irk, braver or craftier than the rest, ran up the gate and got a leg over before one of Ser John's archer's spiked it to the wooden hoardings with a clothyard shaft. The professionals on the wall held—the wave failed, and died.

Ser John fell to his knees. "Too gods-damned old for this," he said, staring at the courtyard full of refugees.

But the gate held. The wall held.

Alcaeus tottered to a pillar in the colonnade and tried to open his face-plate, but he couldn't raise his arms. He hit his head on the colonnade. He couldn't breathe.

Strange hands flipped the catches of his visor and lifted it. Air flooded him. Sweet, wonderful air, tainted only with the harsh screams of people too maddened by fear to do anything else.

It was James the crossbowman. "I've got it," he said. "Just stand still." The boy hauled the helmet right off his head.

He pulled off the gauntlets. And Alcaeus slumped to the ground, his back against the colonnade.

Ser John appeared in front of him. "I need you on the walls."

Alcaeus groaned.

The boy stood in front of him. "Let him breathe! He saved everyone!"

Ser John snorted. "They ain't saved until they's saved, boy. Ser knight? To the walls."

Alcaeus reached out a hand.

Ser John caught it, and pulled him to his feet.

Harndon City—Edward

Master Pyel's first commission for him was the dullest project he could imagine. It was something he could have done when he was fourteen.

He was to take twenty iron bars and make staves like barrel staves, then forge-weld them into a single column with bands to keep the staves together. Bands every handspan. Inside diameter to be a constant diameter of one inch.

Dull.

Still, he was smart enough to know that Master Pyle wouldn't have given him the work if it didn't matter. He was careful with his measurements, and he decided to construct a mandrel to keep the *insides* of the staves equidistant while he forge-welded them. That took time, too. He planished the mandrel and then polished it endlessly.

He had a moment of deep satisfaction when another journeyman, Lionel, grinned. "You know," he drawled, obviously relishing the moment. "You can order an apprentice to do that."

I'm a fool, he thought, happily. He left Ben the shoemaker's boy to use pumice on his lovely mandrel while he went out into the evening to fence with his mates and show Anne his ring. Better, to show Anne's parents. Apprentices didn't marry—but a journeyman was a person of consequence. He was a man.

The next morning, he had the mandrel ready, thanked the apprentice like a good master, and then whipped the forge welds into shape, smoothing both inside and outside. It turned out to be more finicky than he had expected, and took him all day.

Master Pyle looked at the result and slammed it against the oak tree in the yard. The welds held. He smiled. "You made a mandrel," he said.

"Had to," replied Edward.

Master Pyle made a face. "My design is flawed," he said. "How're your casting skills?"

Edward shrugged. "Not that good, Master," he admitted.

The next morning when the sun rose, he was down by the river, casting bells with the Foibles—rivals, but friends.

Lissen Carak—The Red Knight

Hundreds of leagues to the north, the same sun rose on a fortress which was complete in every warlike respect—high wooden hoardings crowned the turrets and curtain walls, and a major engine of war stood atop every tower: the donjon tower bore the weight of a trebuchet, and smaller mangonels and ballistae decorated the smaller towers.

Aside from a dozen men on duty, the garrison, who had laboured two days and nights by torchlight, lay asleep in heaps of straw. The dormitory was full of local people and so was the hall and the stable.

Sauce awakened the captain because there was movement down by the river. He had placed a garrison of ten archers, three men-at-arms and a pair of knights in the tower at the bridge under Ser Milus's command the evening before. They had their own food and a mirror with which to signal, and this morning they were apparently flashing away merrily.

Ser Jehannes had gone with them, as a mere man-at-arms. He had gone without comment and left no note. The captain awoke to find it still on his mind.

"Damn him," he said, staring at the newly whitewashed plaster over his head. Jehannes had always disliked him because he was young and well-born.

As far as the captain saw it, Messire Jehannes could have both his birth and his youth. He lay on his bed, his breath steaming in the air, and found himself growing angrier and angrier.

"Damn who?" asked Sauce. She flashed him a smile that was probably meant to be winsome. She was an attractive woman, but the missing front teeth and the scar on her face tended to made her winsome look slightly savage.

Sauce and the captain went backaways. The captain considered confiding in her—but he was the captain, now. Everyone's captain.

He got his feet on the cold stone instead. "Never mind. Call Toby for me, will you?"

She leered. "I'm sure I could dress you, mesself."

"Maybe you could and maybe you can't, but neither will get me moving fast enough." He stood up, naked and she swatted at him with her gloves and went out calling for Toby.

Toby and Michael arrived together, Toby with clothes, Michael, sleepy to the point of clumsiness, with a cup of steaming wine.

The captain armed himself in the ruddy light of the new sun, Michael fumbling with buckles and laces so that it seemed to take twice as long as arming usually did and he almost regretted sending Sauce away. But he ran lightly down the steps to the great courtyard and patted Grendel's nose when he was led out. He took the tall bassinet on his head, pulled steel gauntlets over his hands, and vaulted into Grendel's war-saddle. He was giving his men a good example—he was also riding out of a fortress into the unknown.

It occurred to him as he ducked his head to pass through the narrow postern—he had ordered that the main gate be shut for the duration—that if nothing attacked them, he was going to look a ripe fool. Followed by the image of a taloned foot ripping the guts out of his riding horse, which made his stomach lurch and his throat go cold.

He rode down the steep road, leaning well back into the comforting buttress of his war-saddle, with Wilful Murder, Sauce, Michael Rankin and Gelfred all fully armed at his back. At the base of the hill he turned away from the bridge and rode west—not onto the narrow track he'd followed and fought the daemon, but around the base of the fortress.

He rode slowly around it, looking up so hard that his neck hurt, examining his hoardings from their attackers' perspective. The fortress was a hundred feet above him, huge, imposing and very, very far away.

After he passed the donjon the first trebuchet released. He heard the crack of the wood base of the counter-weight striking its restraint and saw the rock pause at the height of its arc. Then it fell with a crash well to the west.

The captain turned to Wilful Murder. "Go and put an orange stake on it, Will. They won't loose again."

"It's always me," Wilful grumbled and did as he was told.

The rest continued to ride around the base of the fortress. Two other engines released, and both times the captain sent Wilful off to mark the fall of shot.

"Tough nut," Sauce said, suddenly.

"Some of our enemy have wings," the captain replied and he nodded heavily, because he was in full harness and couldn't really shrug well. "But yes. With our company on the walls and all the defences up we should be able to hold until we starve." He looked beyond her. "We'll lose the Lower Town first, then Bridge Castle." He shrugged. "But the—the king will come first."

With that, he leaned his weight forward and led them at a slow, lumbering canter across the fields to the Bridge Castle.

Milus met him, also fully armoured, at the tower gate. Behind him, on the bridge, were a dozen heavy wagons laden with goods and fifty or more men and women all pale as parchment. Merchants.

"Come for the fair," Milus said. He made a face. "They say there's five convoys behind them."

The captain turned and looked at Michael, who grimaced. "We don't even have all the farmers in," he said. "Fifty, you say? And their wagons?"

"And I'll bet they don't have any food," the captain said. "I'll guess they have carts full of cloth and luxury goods, because they've come to *buy* grain." He looked around. "How many more mouths can you take, Milus?"

The older knight narrowed his eyes. "I can take all of 'em," he admitted. "And thirty more like 'em. But I'll need more grain, more salt meat, more of everything to do it. Except water. We've plenty of that, out of the river."

Back up the hill he went to report to the Abbess. A heavy military wagon was raised from the cellars and reassembled, then loaded to heaping with food and provender, and hand-hauled down the steep slope, teams of men on gate winches letting it down a few feet a time. The captain disarmed, handing his harness to his squire. His hips were screaming, and once it was finally off he felt light enough to fly away.

Even as they increased the supplies to the lower fort, more merchants arrived. Some were angry at the interruption of trade, and some were clearly already terrified. The captain went back down the hill and wasted the morning trying to calm them. He finally told them to send a deputation up the hill to the Abbess.

Then he made the climb back up to the fortress to hide in his Commandery, a small cell with a door directly onto the courtyard and a pair of arched windows separated by a fluted column. Open, the windows let in a spring breeze carrying the scent of wildflowers and jasmine, and he could see fifteen leagues to the east over the low hills.

Today, instead of turning to the parchment scrolls full of accounts that awaited him, he unbuckled his sword and hung it on the man-high bronze candelabra and leaned his elbows on the sill of the leftmost window.

Booted footsteps announced Michael. "Your armour," the young man said quietly.

The captain turned to see two archers with a heavy wicker basket, and his valet with an armload of dressed lumber. While he watched, the archers argued about which pre-cut peg went in which hole and the valet stared off into space while idly providing the correct piece, even when the archers asked for the wrong thing. Before the sun had moved the width of a finger, they had assembled a rack for the captain's armour, man sized, a little taller than the man himself, and Michael dressed the heavy wooden form carefully. A good arming rack could speed a man into his harness by precious minutes. And with every inch of the fortress convent crammed to capacity and past it with soldiers and refugeees, his office was his sleeping room.

When the archers and the valet went back out, the noise vanished and the captain returned to his window.

"Will that be all, ser?" Michael asked.

"Well done, Michael," the captain said.

The younger man jumped as if he'd been bitten. "I—that is—" he laughed. "Your valet, Jacques, did most of it."

"The more credit to you that you give him credit," the captain observed.

Emboldened, Michael came forward and, very slowly, leaned into the right hand window. His stealthy progress was not unlike that of a convent cat the captain had observed that morning, which had been intent on stealing a piece of cheese. He smiled. It took Michael as long to rest in the window as it had for the three men to build the armour rack. "We're fully provisioned," Michael said carefully.

"Hmm. No commander facing a siege ever admits being 'fully provisioned,'" the captain said.

"So now we wait?" Michael asked.

"Are you a squire or an apprentice captain?" the captain asked.

Michael stood up straight. "My pardon, ser."

He grinned wickedly. "I don't mind an intelligent question, and especially not when it helps me think. I do have to think, young Michael. Plans don't just come full-blown into my head. Next we're going to use a powerful magic, something potent, grave and dire. The Archaics used it well and often. All the histories describe it, and yet no romance of chivalry ever mentions it."

Michael pulled a face that told the captain he'd wit to tell when he was being baited.

"What spell?" he asked.

"No spell," the captain advised. "But it's a kind of magic nonetheless. We're provisioned and armed, we've repaired our fortifications, and the enemy are not yet at the gates. So what shall we do?"

"Compel the rest of the peasants into the walls?" Michael asked.

"No. That's done."

"Build outworks?"

"We lack the force to man them, so no." The captain paused. "Not so bad, though."

Michael's frustration was obvious. "Summon a tame daemon?" he asked.

The captain scratched his pointed beard. "No," he said. "Although if I knew how to I might."

Michael shrugged.

"Two words," the captain encouraged him.

Michael shook his head. "Higher walls?" he asked, knowledge of his own inadequacy making him sound petulant.

"No."

"More arrows?"

"Not bad, but no."

"Find allies?" Michael asked.

The captain was silent a moment at that, looking east. "We have already summoned our allies, but that's not bad at all," he said. "A very useful thought, and one that I may pursue." He looked at the fashionably green-clad scion of the aristocracy and added. "But no."

"Damn," Michael said. "Can I give up?"

"As squire, or as apprentice captain?" the captain asked. "You started this, not me." The captain picked up the short baton of office that he almost never carried. It had belonged to the previous captain, and had some history and authority to it—enough that the captain suspected it might have a touch of phantasm about it. "You have thirty-one lances, give or take; sixteen elderly but competent sergeants and one well-constructed, if elderly, fortress on good ground. You must defend a ford, a bridge, a constant flow of terrified merchants and a vulnerable Lower Town with inadequate walls. Tell me your plan. If it's good enough, I'll claim it's my own and use it. There are stupid answers but there's no right answer. If your answer is good, you live and make a little money. If your answer is bad, you fail and die and just for extra points, a lot of harmless people, some actual nuns and a bunch of farmers will die with you." The captain had an odd look in his eyes. "Let's hear it."

Michael had sprouted enough hairs on his chin that it might honestly be called a beard and he played with them for a while. "All in our current situation? Fully provisioned and so on?"

The captain nodded.

"Send messengers for aid. Enlist allies from local lords. Button up the fortress, tell the merchants to go hang themselves, and prepare for the enemy." Michael looked out over the woods to the east while he thought on.

"Messengers sent. Allies cost money and our profit on this is slim as it is. We were in pretty desperate straits before we got this job. And those merchants represent a source of cash to us. I leave aside the morality of the thing. We can make them pay for protection and split the money with the abbess. Fair is fair—it's her fortress and our steel." The captain's gaze was out the window, on the distant woods.

The sun moved in the sky.

"I give up," Michael admitted. "Unless it's something very simple like more rocks for siege engines, or more water."

"I think I'm glad that you can't find it, lad, because you have a brain and your family has a lot of war craft. And if you don't see it, perhaps *they* won't see it either." The captain pointed out the window.

"They? The Wild?" Michael asked quietly.

The captain scratched at his beard again. "Active patrolling, Michael. Active patrolling. Starting in about six hours, I'm putting our lances out in fast-moving patrols. In all directions, but mostly east. I want to be familiar with the terrain, to relocate our foe, and then I'm going to ambush, harass, irritate, and annoy him and his minions until they go elsewhere looking for easier prey. If they choose to come here and lay siege to us I intend to have them leave a trail of blood—or whatever they have for blood—through that forest."

Michael was looking at his hands, which were trembling. "You intend to go out into the Wild?" he asked, incredulous. "Again?"

"If the initiative is in the woods, I'll seize it in the woods," said the captain. "You think the enemy are ten feet tall and made of adamantine. I think they have a corps of men as servants, archers and woodsmen, who have so little war-craft that I can see the smoke of their dinner fires from here." The captain put a hand on his squire. "And ask yourself—why is the main body of our enemy to the *east*?" He looked out. "Gelfred is out there right now," he said quietly.

Michael whistled. "Blessed Saint George. Have they passed us by?"

The captain smiled. "Well guessed, young Michael. Our enemy has bypassed us—a tribute to our preparations and our little raid. But there's a reason you don't bypass a fortress, and I'm about to teach him. Unless," he smiled, and just for a moment, he showed his youth. "Unless it's all a fucking trap."

Michael swallowed.

"Anyway, his human allies are right there as well—to the east. Don't point. I suspect that some of the birds are spies." The captain turned away.

"Then they can see everything we do!" Michael said.

"Everything," the captain said with evident satisfaction. "Go to the refectory, find some parchment, write me a list of all of your notions for the defence of this position, and then go polish something." He smiled. "But first, get me some wine."

"I was afraid," the squire blurted. "In the fight with the wyvern—I was so afraid I could barely move." He breathed heavily. "I can't stop thinking about it."

The captain nodded. "I know," he said.

"But it will get better, won't it? I mean—I'll get used to it. Won't I?" he asked.

"No." The captain shook his head. "Never. You never get used to it. You shake, vomit, foul your braes, piss yourself, whatever you do, every fucking time. What you get used to is the power of the fear, the onset of the terror. You learn you can face it. Now get me some wine, drink a couple of cups yourself, and get back to work."

"Yes, m'lord."

There was a constant flow of men and materiel up and down the hill, from the top of the fortress to Bridge Castle. The war engines on the towers lofted practice rounds into the fields, and trusted corporals took patrols out into the farmland—careful, wary patrols on fast horses. The closest farmers had responded well enough to the alarm bells and yesterday's summons, and Abbington, the biggest of the hamlets, was clear, but the more distant had only sent children to ask for more information, and none of them had brought in any of their precious grain unless the soldiers had brought it themselves. The patrols either went to fetch in the timid or led out farmers who had believed it was merely a drill.

And the more prosperous yeoman had other questions.

"Who is going to pay for our grain?" demanded a strong middle-aged man with an archer's forearms and a handsome head of brown hair. "This is my treasure, ser knight—my precious store. What we scrimp and save up over the winter turns to silver when the merchants come in the spring. Who's paying for it now?"

The captain directed all such questions, firmly and quietly, to the Abbess.

As the sun set on the third full day the cellars were bursting with grain. A further hundredweight lay at the foot of the track that ran up the hill to the fortress where a cart had broken loose and smashed to pieces, and now every wagon up or down ran with ropes attached to the gate winches—and the main gate had stood open all day.

The hundredweight of grain had the curious effect of dragging birds out of the sky to eat the free bounty. Archers, led by Gelfred, netted them.

The fortress was so packed with people that there were men and women planning to sleep on the stone flags on straw despite the briskness of the evening. Torches burned all around the courtyard and a bonfire burned in the centre, the flickering orange light reflecting off the towers, the donjon and the sparkling dormitory windows. Chickens—hundreds of chickens—ran about the courtyard and the rocks on the ridge below the gate. Pigs rooted in the convent garbage at the base of the cliff, nigh on two hundred of them. The convent sheepfold, hard against the eastern walls, was also full to bursting and in the last light a man standing in the Abbess's solar could see the glitter of a dozen men-at-arms and as many archers, bringing in another thousand sheep from the eastern farms.

The captain stood in the Abbess's solar and watched patrols, the sheep, and the formal closing of the gate. He followed Bent's craggy form as the big archer changed the watch in the donjon, marching the off-going watch around the whole circuit as he collected them and put fresh men in their places. It was an impressive and efficient ceremony, and it had the right effect on the villagers, most of whom had never seen so many armed men in their lives.

The captain sighed. "In an hour's time a virgin will have been deflowered and a husbandman will have lost his farm at dice," he said.

"You have a virgin in mind?" the Abbess asked.

"Oh, I'm quite above such earthy concerns." The captain continued to watch, and he was smiling.

"Because you are worried, you mean. You must be worried that nothing has come at us yet," the Abbess said.

The captain pursed his lips and shook his head. "I'd rather be a ripe fool, the laughing stock of every soldier in Alba," he said, "then face a siege by those things. I don't know where they are yet or why they let us get everyone under cover. In my dark moments I think our walls are already undermined, or they have a legion of traitors inside the walls—" He raised a hand, making a warding-off motion. "But in truth, I can only hope they know as little of us as we know of them. The day before yesterday we were easy meat. Today, if sheer fear doesn't break us, we could hold for a year." He glanced at her worried face.

She shrugged. "How old are you, Captain?"

He was clearly uncomfortable with the question.

"How many sieges have you seen?" she asked. "How many Wild creatures have you faced in combat?" She turned towards him and stepped forward, boring in on her target. "I'm a knight's daughter, Captain. I know these are not polite questions, but by God I feel I deserve to know the answer."

He leaned against the wall. Scratched under his chin for a moment, staring off into space. "I've killed more men than I have monsters. I've stood one siege and, to be fair, we broke it in the second month. I'm—" He turned his head and met her eye. "I'm twenty."

She made a sound between a satisfied hrmmf and a snort.

"But your divination told you that." He straightened from the wall. "I'm young, but I've seen five years of unending war. And my father—" He paused, and the pause became a silence.

"Your father?" she asked quietly.

"Is a famous soldier," he finished, his voice very quiet.

"I've entrusted my defences to a child," the Abbess said, but she pursed her lips in self-mockery.

"A child with a first rate company of lances. And there is, truly, no better sell-sword captain in Alba. I know what I'm doing. I've seen it and done it before, and I've studied it, unlike the rest of my breed. I've studied them all—Maurikos and Leo and Nikephoros Phokas, even Vegetius. And if I may say so, it's too late to change your mind now."

"I know," she said. "I'm afraid." She drank her wine and, quite spontaneously, she took his hand. "I'm fifty," she admitted. "I've never withstood a siege, myself." She let his hand go and bit her lip. "Are you afraid?"

He took her hand again and kissed it. "Always. Of everything. My mother made me a coward. She taught me, very carefully, to fear *everything*. Starting with her. See? You are become my confessor." He smiled crookedly. "I am the world's expert at overcoming fear. Cowardice is the best school for courage, I find."

She had to smile. "Such a wit. Vade retro!"

He nodded. "I'm too tired to get out of the chair."

Their laughter and light conversation lasted through the rest of her wine, and his. Finally she said, after looking out the window, "And what do you fear most?"

"I fear failure," he said. He laughed at his own words. "But alone of the people in this fortress, I have no fear of the Wild whatsoever."

"Are you posturing?" she asked.

He stared into her fire for a little. "No," he said with a sigh. "I need to go look at the watch. I have tried something reckless tonight. I need to make sure my people are ready for it. You know that your enemy is using animals to watch us—yes?"

"Yes," she said, very quietly.

"Do you know anything else, my lady? Anything that would help your very young captain save your walls?" He leaned toward her.

She looked away. "No," she said.

He put his wine cup on the oak sideboard with a click. "I told you the truth."

"Let us have a few moments to marshal our forces," she said with a wan smile. "Go see to your watch. My few tawdry secrets are not in any way germane to our siege."

He bowed, and she waved him away, so he went out into the stairwell. It was dark.

Her door closed, and he began to feel his way down the stone steps when a hand closed on his.

He knew her in a moment, and pulled the hand to his lips—faster than she could take it away. He heard her sigh.

That moment he considered crushing her against the stone wall. But it occurred to him that she must be there by the Abbess's commission, and it would be rude, to say the least, to attack the novice outside the Abbess's door. Or something like that went through his head—before her lips came down on his and her hands pushed against his shoulders.

His heart pounded. His mind went blank.

He could feel her power, now. As their bodies moved together—her tongue probing his—they were *generating* power.

She broke their kiss and stepped away—a sudden absence of warmth in the dark—and said "Now we are even." She took his hand. "Come."

She led him down the dark stone steps. Across the hall—the bonfires in the courtyard made the stained glass figures flicker and wriggle as if they were animated, and fitful rainbows played across the hall floor. After the complete darkness of the Abbess's solar stairwell, the hall seemed well enough lit.

She was taking him to the books. Halfway across the hall they kissed again. No one could have said which of them initiated it. But when his hand moved across her bodice, she stepped away.

"No," she said. "I want to show you this, and I am not your whore."

But she kept his hand. Led him to the book. "Have you seen it?" she asked.

"Yes."

"Did you understand?" she asked, flipping the pages.

"No," he admitted. There is nothing a young man enjoys less than telling the object of his affection how little he knows.

Her not-quite-a-smile played somewhere in the corner of her mouth. "You are one of us, are you not? I can feel you."

His eyes were on hers, but when she looked at the book he looked too. Looked at the alembic in St. Pancreas's hand. And followed the saint's pointing finger to a diagram, lower on the page—a tree.

He flipped to another page, where another saint pointed—this time to a cloud.

"Is this a test?" he asked.

She smiled. "Yes.

"Then I guess the book is a code. The shapes that the saints point to indicate the shape of a template that, when covering the text, will indicate what the reader should read." He ran his finger over the text across from St. Eustachios. "It is a grimoire."

"A fantastically detailed, internally coded, referential grimoire," she said, and then bit her tongue which he found, just at that moment, intensely erotic. He reached to kiss her, but she made the dismissive motion women make when boys are tiresome. "Come," she said.

He followed her across the hall. He was conscious, at a remove, that he had a watch to oversee; a siege to command. But her hand in his held such promise. It was smooth, but rough. The hand of a woman who worked hard. But still smooth; like the surface of good armour.

She dropped his hand the moment she opened the courtyard door, and they were in the light again.

He wanted to say something to her—but he had no idea *what* he wanted to say.

She turned and looked back at him. "I have one more thing to show you," she said.

Even as she spoke, she pulled a cowl of *not-seeing* around herself.

He was being tested in another way.

He reached into the palace of his memory and did the same. He was there for long enough to see Prudentia looking at him with ferocious disapproval, and that the green spring outside his iron door was building up into a storm of epic proportions.

And then they slipped across the courtyard. They were scarcely invisible—one of the Lanthorn girls, spinning in a reel with a young archer, saw the captain clearly because she was dancing and she deftly avoided him as she whirled.

But he was not interrupted as he passed.

She stopped at the iron-bound dormitory door and he manipulated his phantasm so that it linked to hers. It was a very intimate thing to do—something he had never done with anyone but Prudentia, and which the sight of her had reminded him of.

She used to say that the mind was a temple, an inn, a garden, and an outhouse, and that casting with another magus partook of worship, intimate conversation, sex, and defecation.

But as his power reached to hers, hers accepted it, and they were linked.

He winced.

She winced as well.

And then they were in the dormitory, standing in a small hall where, on his former visit, older nuns had sat to read or to do needlework. There was light here. Most of the nuns were out in the yard, but two still sat quietly.

"Look at them," Amicia said. "Look."

He didn't have to look too hard. Tendrils of power played about them.

"All of you have the power?" he asked.

"Every one of us," she said. "Come."

"When will I see you again?" he managed, as she led him along the northern curtain behind the stable block. An apple tree grew there, in a stone box set into the wall. There was a bench around it.

Amicia settled onto the bench.

He was too befuddled to seek to kiss her, so he simply sat.

"All of you are witches?" he asked.

"That's an ugly word for *you* to use, man-witch," she said. "Sorcerer. Warlock." She looked out over the wall.

Far to the east he saw the barest smudge of orange, and it instantly recalled him to his duty. "I must go," he said. He wanted to impress her—he wanted not to seem to need to impress her. "I've sent people to do something I should have done myself," he blurted.

She didn't seem to pay him any heed. "I thought that you needed to know what the stakes were," she said. "I don't think *she* is going to tell you. This is a place of power. And the Masters of our Order have filled it with women of power, and with powerful artefacts. Now it shines like a beacon."

He felt blind and foolish at her words. But Prudentia's rules—on the use of power, on using the sight of power—which were wisdom in a world that distrusted the magi, had deprived him of this insight.

"That, or she meant me to tell you," Amicia added. Her head slumped for the first time that evening.

"Or she expected me to reason it out for myself," he said bitterly. He felt the time flowing away as if he had an hourglass in his hand—he felt tonight's raid slipping west into the trees, and he felt the lack of alertness on his watch, and sensed a thousand forgotten details, like a tendril of power attached to his soldiers that was pulling him from her side. And the glow far in the east—what was that?

And then he felt her, and it was like a chain that tethered him to the bench.

"I must go," he said again. But youth, and his hand, betrayed him, and he was again in her arms or she in his.

"I do not want this," she said as she kissed him again.

So he broke free. Broke the binding between them with a thought, and stepped away. "Do you often come here?" he asked, his voice hoarse. "To the tree?"

She nodded, barely perceptible in the odd light.

"I might write to you," he said. "I want to see you again."

She smiled. "I imagine you'll see me every day," she said. "I don't want this. I don't need it. You don't know me. We should walk away."

"If I strike you now we can end as we started," he said. "With a kiss and a blow. But you want me as I want you. We are *bonded*."

She shook her head. "That sort of thing is for children. Listen, *Captain*. I have been a wife. I know how a man feels between my legs. Ah! You wince. The novice is not a virgin. Shall I go on? I lived across the wall. I was an Outwaller. No, look!" She peeled back the collar of her gown, and her shoulder was covered in tattoos.

Bathed in the distant firelight her shoulder gleamed, and all he felt was desire.

"I was taken young, and grew to womanhood among them. I had a husband—a warrior, and we might have grown old together, he as war chief and I the shaman. Until the Knights of the Order came. They killed him, they took me, and here I am. And I do not need rescuing. I *live* in the world of spirit. I have come to love Jesus. Every time I kiss you, I hurtle backwards in my life to another place. I cannot be with you. I will not be a mercenary's whore. I sacrificed myself this evening so that you could see what you are so obviously blind to—because you are so very afraid of your power." She turned her head. "Now go."

The lines of power to his soldiers were taut as cables. He was ignoring his duty. It was like a broken bone—a scream of pain. But he couldn't let what was between them rest.

"You wanted me as much as ever I wanted you, from the moment your eyes met mine. Don't be a hypocrite. You sacrificed yourself this evening? Rather, you craved this evening and built yourself a reason to let yourself have it." Even as he spoke the words, he cursed himself for a fool. It was not what he wanted to say.

"You have no idea what I do or do not want," she said. "You have no idea the life I have led."

He took a half-step away—the sort of half-step a swordsman takes when he changes from defence to attack. "I grew up with five brothers who hated me, a father who ignored and despised me, and a doting mother who wanted to make me a tool of her revenge," he hissed. "I grew up across the river from your Outwaller villages. When I looked out of my tower I saw you Outwallers in the land of freedom. You had a husband who loved you? I had a succession of sweethearts placed in my bed by my mother to spy on me. You would have been an Outwaller shaman? I was being trained to lead armies of the Wild to crush Alba and rid the earth of the king. So that my mother could feel avenged. Knights of the Order came for you? My brothers ganged up to beat me, to please my supposed father. It was *good fun.*" He found that his voice was rising and spittle flew from his mouth.

So much for self-control; he had said too much. Far too much. He felt sick.

But he was not done. "But *fuck that*. I am not the Antichrist, even if God himself decrees I should be. I will be what I will, not what anyone else wills, as can you. Be what you choose. You love Jesus?" he asked, and something black passed into his mind. "What has he done for you? Love me instead."

"I will not," she said, quite calmly.

He didn't will himself to walk away. He didn't feel a thing—he didn't feel an urge to reply. It was like being cut with a very sharp sword, and watching your arm fall to the ground.

The next he knew, he was standing in the guard box over the gate.

Bent, the duty archer, stood with his arms crossed. When he saw the captain he twirled his moustaches. "You've sent out a sortie," he said. "Or somewhat similar. I can't find Bad Tom or half the men-at-arms for duty."

"It's about to happen," the captain said, mastering himself. "Tell the watch to be alert. Tell them—"

He looked up. But the stars were silent and cold.

"Tell them to be alert," he said, at a loss. "I have to attend the Abbess."

He got himself to the jakes and threw up. Wiped his chin on an old handkerchief and threw it after his puke, which would have scandalized a laundress. And then he pulled himself up straight, nodded, as if to an invisible companion, and walked back into the hall.

The Abbess was waiting for him.

"You met with my handmaiden," she said.

His armour was adamantine. He smiled. "A merry meeting," he said.

"And you saw to your guards," she said.

"Not enough," he said. "Lady, there are too many secrets here. I do not know what the stakes are. And perhaps I am simply too young for this." He shrugged. "But we have two foes—the enemy outside and the enemy within. I wish you would tell me what you know."

"If I told you everything I knew you would scourge me with whips of fire," said the Abbess. "It is a passage in the Bible on which I often ponder." She rose from her throne and crossed the hall to the book. "You have solved this riddle?" she asked.

"Using the enormous hints provided," he answered.

"It was not my place to tell you," she said. "When our kind swear oaths, those oaths bind our power."

He nodded.

"You are as tense as a bowstring," she said. "Is that the effect of Amicia?"

"I have played a trump card tonight," he admitted. "And I let my tryst interfere with duty. Things are not done as I would like on an evening when I have taken a gamble that now seems reckless." He paused, and said what he had boiling inside him. "I do not enjoy being toyed with."

The Abbess picked up her onyx rosary and adjusted her wimple. She shrugged. "No one does," she said dismissively. "I don't deal in the imagery of gambling," she said. "But perhaps we can do some good, and by our presence prevent the dicing and the deflowering you were worried about," she said. "Let's walk among our people, Captain."

They walked out, and she put a hand on his arm, very much the lady, and a veiled sister came and carried her train, which was longer and more ornate than any other sister's in the convent. Indeed, the captain suspected that her habit was far from the rule as laid down for sisters of Saint Thomas. She was a rich and powerful woman who had somehow turned to this life.

When they entered the courtyard all conversation stopped. A ring of dancers moved to the sound of a pair of pipes and a psalter played by none other than the captain's squire. The musicians continued to play, and the dancers paused, but the Abbess gave them a firm nod of approval and the dancing continued.

"When will they come at us?" the Abbess asked quietly.

"Never, if I have my way," the captain said pleasantly.

"It's better to make your money without fighting?" she asked.

"Always," he said, bowing deeply to Amicia, who stood watching the dancers. She nodded coolly in return. But he had armed himself against her and he continued without a pause. "But I also like to win. And winning requires some effort."

"Which you will make eventually?" she said. But she smiled. "We spar so naturally I might have to do some penance for flirtation."

"You have a gift for it that must have won you many admirers," he said gallantly.

She struck the back of his hand with her fan. "Back in the ancient times when I was young, you mean?"

"Like all beautiful women, you seek to make an insult of my flattery," he returned.

"Stand here. Everyone can see us here." She nodded to Father Henry, who was standing hesitantly between the chapel and the steps to the Great Hall.

The captain thought that the man was a-boil with hostility. A year ago, the captain, in one of his first acts on taking command, had executed a murderer in the company—an archer who had started to kill his comrades for their loot. Torn had been a non-descript man, an outlaw. The captain eyed the priest. He had something of the same look. It wasn't really a look. A feel. A smell.

"Father Henry, I don't believe that you've been properly introduced to the captain." She smiled, and her eyes flashed—a glimpse of the woman she had been, who knew that a flash of her eyes would restore any admirer to obedience. A predator who liked to play with her food.

Father Henry offered a long hand to shake. It was moist and cold. "The Bourc, his men call him," he said. "Do you have a name you prefer?"

The captain was so used to dealing with petty hostility that it took a moment to register. He turned his full attention on the priest.

The Abbess shook her head and pushed the priest by the elbow. "Never mind. I will speak to you later. Begone, ser. You are dismissed."

"I am a priest of God," he said. "I go where I will, and have no master here."

"You haven't met Bad Tom," the captain said.

"You have a familiar look about you," Father Henry added. "Do I know your parents?"

"I'm a bastard, which you've already found cause to mention," the captain said. "Twice, man of God."

The priest withstood his glare. But his eyes were as full of movement as a man dancing on coals. After too long a pause, the priest turned on his heel and walked away.

"You go to great lengths to hide your heredity," the Abbess noted.

"Do you know why?" the captain asked.

The Abbess shook her head.

"Good," said the captain. His eyes were on the priest's back. "Where did he come from? What do you know about him?"

The dance had finished, and men were bowing, women dipping deep courtesies. Michael had just noted that his lord had witnessed his troubadour skills and flushed deep red in the torchlight, and the Abbess cleared her throat.

"I told you. I took him from the parish," the Abbess murmured. "He has no breeding."

The sky to the east lit up, as if from a flash of lightning, but the flash lasted too long and burned too red, for as long as it took a man to say a Pater Noster.

"Alarm!" roared the captain. "Gate open, all crossbows armed, get the machines loaded. Move!"

Sauce had been watching the dancers. She paused, confusion written on her face. "Gate *open*?" she asked.

"Gate open. Get a sortie ready to ride, you'll be leading it." The captain pushed her towards her helmet.

Most of his men were already moving, but if he hadn't been beguiled by the evening's revelations, they'd have been in their armour already.

Already, a dozen men-at-arms stood by their destriers in the torchlit gateway, their squires and valets scrambling to arm them. Archers scrambled from the courtyard onto the catwalks around the curtain walls, some even bare-arsed in the light of the courtyard fires, their hose down and their shirttails dangling.

There was a second flash of fire to the east, half as long as the last.

The captain was grinning. "I hope you didn't need olive oil for anything really important," he said, and squeezed her arm in a very familiar way. "May I take my leave? I should be back with you before the next bell."

She eyed him in the fire-lit darkness. "This is your doing, and not the enemy's?" she asked.

He shrugged. "I hope so," he said. Then he leaned close. "Hellenic fire. In their camp. Or so I hope."

North of Harndon—Harmodius

Dissection is one of those skills a man never really forgets. Harmodius had exhumed the corpse himself—not much of a risk, given the haste with which it had been buried.

He was only interested in the brain, anyway. Which was as well, as the thorax was badly damaged and the central body cavity was largely empty. Something had eaten the guts.

Harmodius was above such feelings as nausea. Or so he kept telling himself. A steady spring rain fell on his back, darkness was falling, and he was in the midst of the northern wilderness, but the body was there for the taking and it was, after all, what had started him on this mad-cap chase. That, and the firm and magnetic draw of the power. Power like a beacon.

He took out a hunting trousseau—a pair of very heavy knives and half a dozen smaller, very sharp ones—and quickly and accurately flensed the skin from the dead man's skull, folded the flaps back, took a trepan from his pack, and lifted a piece of skull the size of a triple leopard of solid silver.

The light was failing, but it was still clear the brain-matter was rotting.

Harmodius took an eating knife from his purse, pulled out the sharp pick, and dug around carefully. He used the tip of the knife to cut away small portions of the rotting material—

He spat out a mouthful of salty saliva. "I will not vomit," he declared aloud. Dug again.

It was too damned dark. He pulled a candle from his increasingly upset horse's pack, and lit it with sorcery. There was no breeze at all, and the candle hissed in the light rain. He lit two more, squandering the beeswax.

He trepanned again, but it was no use. The brain-matter was too rotten. Or his theory was entirely wrong. Or rather, Aristotle's theory was entirely wrong.

The Magus left the body where it was, lying half exhumed in the rain. He washed his hands in the creek at the base of the hill, repacked his knives, extinguished the candles, and reloaded his horse, who now shied at every noise. He reached out, and felt the power gathering the north.

Jesu Christe

The Magus paused, one booted foot already in a stirrup. There was something—

The creature gave itself away with a growl, and his mare bolted. Harmodius managed to get a hand on the saddle-bow and clung on for a furlong until the frightened animal turned. Harmodius rode the turn, using the force of her movement to help get his leg over the saddle at last. The moon was new and distant, the rain was covering the stars, and the night was dark. He prayed, rapidly and incoherently, that his mare stayed on the road.

He got his right foot in the stirrup and the reins in his left hand, and he pulled on them. Ginjer did *not* obey.

He reined in sharply, and felt for the baton he used as a riding whip. It took him what seemed hours to locate it in his belt, and hours more, apparently, to press it to her neck, a trick he'd learned from a knight.

He cast a simple thought, a phantasm that allowed him to see in the dark.

What he saw froze his blood. The horse balked, and he almost went over the cantle.

"Sweet Jesu!" he said aloud.

Something was standing in the road, waiting for him.

Off to his left, the north-west, the sky erupted—a long orange flash. Its dim light further illuminated the familiar—too familiar—shape of the creature standing on the road.

It tossed the corpse aside and loped at him. But he had time to feel the convulsion in the northern power first. To ponder, for an instant, the fact that the long flash of orange beyond the horizon had reached him long before the convulsion of power, a matter of great interest to a hermeticist. He had never fully investigated the effects of distance on power—

It was a form of panic, to spin off thought after thought, none of them connected to the monster on the road ahead of him, or the wave of terror that it emitted like a fist of fear.

"*Adeveniat regnum tuum,*" the Magus spat.

A lance of fire sprang from his riding stick to the winged creature, whose head was bathed in flame for as long as man might draw a deep breath. The liquid parts of the creature's head vaporized and its skull exploded, lit by the intense flame of the lance of fire.

The fire went out, apart for some pale blue flames that licked at the creature's neck for a few heartbeats before sizzling out.

Silence fell, in which the creature's tail lashed the ground—*thump, thump, thump*—and then was still.

The silence went on, and on. The night smelled of singed hair and burnt soap.

The Magus drew a deep breath. Raised his riding crop and blew gently on the silver rune set in the gold cap. He smiled to himself, despite the fatigue that settled on his shoulders like a haubergeon of mail, and allowed himself a single "heh."

He watched the northern horizon as the fire flickered there again, then dismounted and walked through the darkness to the creature's side and muttered "Fiat lux." His light was blue and pale, but it sufficed.

He made a clucking sound, reached out into the night with his senses, recoiled from what he found there and ran for his horse.

East of Lissen Carak—Peter

Peter lay in a state of angry exhaustion and watched the pale fire flicker in the distant west. He had to tear his eyes away from it and watch the darkness to be sure that the whole thing wasn't just his imagination. But it was true—above the endless trees, somewhere to the west, there was a great fire. So great, it reflected from the cliff face above him in long flashes of light.

His two "masters" slept through it.

He struggled with his yoke again, surrendered again, and fell asleep.

Awoke to the smaller man kneeling beside him.

"Cook," he said. "Wake up. Something is out here with us," he added. There was fear in his voice.

"What the fuck are you doing?" asked the other Morean.

"I'm letting him out of this yoke," said the smaller man. "I'm not going to run and leave him to die. Jesu—I'm a better man than that."

"He's a pagan, or a heretic, or some such filth. Leave him." The first man was loading the mule as fast as he could. It was dark, but not true dark—the first pale light of morning. And something heavy was moving in the bush.

"I am a Christian man," Peter said.

"See?" said the smaller man. He fumbled with the chains. Grunted.

"Come on!" shouted his friend.

The shorter man pulled again, slammed the yoke against a rock, and scrambled to his feet. "Sorry," he said. "We don't have the key." And he followed his mate into the woods, leaving Peter lying on the ground.

He lay there and waited to die.

But no one came for him, and you can only be so terrified for so long.

He got to his feet and stumbled over a stump he'd made himself the night before. The axe handle bruised his shin. The idiots had left their axe.

He plucked it from the stump. He went through the camp, over the broken ground in the near dark—camp was too strong a word for a place where three men had built a fire the size of a rabbit and lain on the bare ground. But by the fire he found an earthenware cup, still intact, and a tinderbox with both char cloth, flint and a steel.

Peter knelt on the ground and prayed to God. He managed a bittersweet thanks, and then he put the cup and the tinderbox into the front of his shirt, tied them in place, and made his way to the road, just a few horse lengths to the north. It was the main road from the eastern seaports to the Albin Plains. He knew that much.

To the east lay civilization and safety—and slavery.

To the west lay the Albin River and the Wild. Peter had seen the Wild, red in tooth and claw. And it had not enslaved him. So he shouldered the axe and headed west.

Harndon Palace –Desiderata

She read the note with ill-concealed irritation. "He gave this to you when?" she asked the terrified boy.

"Yesterday, r'Grace," he mumbled. "Which—er—cook sent me to Cheapside and me mum was sick—"

She looked at him. She was annoyed—she loved the useless old Magus the way she loved her magnificent Eastern riding horse, and his recent display of *real* power made him even more exciting.

"An he took a horse—a fine horse—r'Grace. Had leather bags—had hisn staff." The boy's desire to please was palpable, and she relented.

She turned to Lady Almspend and motioned at her waist. "Give the boy a leopard for his pains and send Mastiff to the Magus's rooms in the tower. I would like a full report." She made a face. "Sir Richard?"

Sir Richard Fitzroy was the old king's bastard son, a handsome man, a fine knight, and a reliable messenger. He doted on the Queen, and the Queen appreciated his stability.

He was attending her, obviously courting Lady Almspend now that his low-born rival was gone.

She beckonned to him. "Sir Richard—I need a private word with the king," she said.

"Consider it done," he allowed, and bowed himself out.

East of Albinkirk—Gerald Random

Gerald Random woke to hear Guilbert Blackhead rapping for entrance to his tent—knocking on the tent's cross-pole with his sword hilt. Random was on his feet in an instant, dagger in hand, and he was awake in another.

"What is it?" he asked, fumbling for the hooks and eyes that would open the flap.

"No idea. But you had better see it." Guilbert's urgency was carried fluently.

Random was out of the tent in another few heartbeats.

They were camped in a narrow meadow on the banks of the Albin, and the great river was in full flood, running fast and deep and almost silent, the black water sullen in the damp night air. They'd been hit by rain squalls again and again all day, and men and animals were still as wet and as sullen as the water.

Far off, north-east, the first crags of the mountains should have been visible, but low clouds drifted right over them, obscuring them for minutes at a time and then clearing just as rapidly, keeping the grass and the trees full of water.

As the next low cloud passed by, the Adnacrag Mountains loomed even in the darkness. Random thought that they might make the fortress town of Albinkirk in four more days. It was not the distance but the condition of the road at this time of year which delayed them. The river road, with its stone bridges and deep stone foundations built by the Archaics, was the only one a sane man would travel with heavy wagons. Every other road was fetlock deep in mud. But all the same, it was not easy.

There was an orange glow to the north.

"Just watch," Guilbert said.

After six days on the road Random had the warrant-man's measure—careful, cautious, and thorough. Perhaps not the man for a deed of daring, but just the sort of man to work a convoy. The guard posts were always manned and constantly checked.

Whatever he was trying to show the merchant, it was important.

Random watched a flicker—was it more than that? North-west, towards the fair. Perhaps—but they were too far for the fair to be visible. It was fifty leagues away or more—they were not yet to Albinkirk.

"There!" said the mercenary.

There was, just for a moment, a pinpoint of light that burned like a star above the glow of Albinkirk.

Random shrugged. "That's all?" he asked.

Guilbert nodded, clearly unhappy about it.

"I'm for bed, then," Random said. "Wake me if we're attacked," he added. He wished, later, that he hadn't been quite so snappish.

Lissen Carak—Mag the Seamstress

Mag the seamstress sat on a barrel, staying out of the way. The day had passed well enough—she'd helped Lis wash shirts and been paid in solid coin for her work; had remembered her skills at avoiding pinching fingers, or delivering a slap where it was needed. The mercenaries were like nothing she'd ever seen—aggressive beyond anything a town of peasants had to offer.

She knew that, had the circumstances differed, they'd have killed her sheep, taken her chickens, her silver, and probably raped and killed her as well. These were hard men—bad men.

But they shared their wine and danced in the evening, and she had a hard time seeing them for what they probably were. Thieves and murderers. Because the Abbess said the Wild was going to attack them, and these men were all they had as defenders, and Mag thought...

Whatever she thought, she must have drifted off after the flashes in the sky. And suddenly they came out of the darkness in blackened armour, led by Thomas, who she now knew was Ser Thomas, riding hard on a destrier covered in sweat; six men-at-arms, twenty archers and some armed valets, all galloping up the twisting road and through the gate almost at her feet.

Bad Tom was the first off his horse, and he bent his knee to the captain. "Just as you said," he panted. "We *fucked* 'em." He rose stiffly.

The captain embraced the bigger man. "Go get your harness off and get a drink," he said. "With my thanks, Tom. Well done."

"And who's gonna take the lamp-black off my mail?" complained one of the archers—the one with dead eyes. He looked up, and his terrifying eyes found her unerringly with their promise of violence.

He grinned at her. The other men called him Will, and she'd learned it stood for Wilful Murder, of which he had apparently been convicted.

She flinched.

"How was it?" asked the captain.

Thomas laughed his huge laugh. "Gorgeous, Cap'n!" he said, and swung down.

The other men laughed, a little wildly, as Mag knew men she knew that Thomas was really laughing, and the others had endured something sharp and horrible.

They'd survived it, and triumphed.

The captain embraced the big man again, and shook his hand. He went among the archers, helping them dismount and giving each his hand, and Mag saw the Abbess was right next to him and that she was *blessing* them.

She clapped her hands and just managed not to laugh.

Harndon Palace—Desiderata

As evening fell, Desiderata watched the foreign knight with the pleasure of a connoisseur for a true artist. He was tall—a head taller than every other man in the great hall—and he moved with a grace that God only bestowed on women and exceptional athletes. His face was like that of a saint—bright gold hair and sculpted features that were not *quite* too fine for a man. His red jupon fitted to perfection, his white hose were silk, not wool, and the wide belt of gold plaques on his slim hips was a mute testament to riches, privilege, and bodily power.

He bowed deeply before the king, sinking all the way to one knee with graceful courtesy.

"My lord King, may I present the noble Jean de Vrailley, Captal de Ruth, and his cousin Gaston D'Albret, Sieur D'Eu." The herald proceeded to name their coats of arms and their heraldic achievements.

Desiderata already knew the foreign knight's achievements.

She watched his eyes, and he watched the king.

The king scratched his beard. "It is a long way from the *Grand Pays*," he said. "Is all of Galle at peace, that you can bring so many knights to my lands?" He said the words easily, and yet his eyes were hard and his face blank.

De Vrailly remained on one knee. "An angel commanded me to come and serve you," he said.

His sponsor, the Earl of Towbray, turned sharply.

Desiderata extended her sense—her warmth, as she thought of it— towards him, and the foreign knight burned like the sun.

She inhaled, as if to inhale his warmth, and the king glanced at her.

"An angel of God?" the king asked. He leaned forward.

"Is there another kind?" de Vrailly asked.

Desiderata had never heard a man speak with such simple arrogance. It *hurt* her, like a physical blemish on a beautiful flower. And yet, like many blemishes, it had its own fascination.

The king nodded. "How do you intend to serve me, Ser Knight?" he asked.

"By fighting," de Vrailly said. "By making unrelenting war upon your enemies. The Wild. Or any men who oppose you."

The king scratched his beard.

"An angel of God told you to come and kill my enemies?" he asked. Desiderata thought the knight spoke with irony but she couldn't be sure. De Vrailly blinded her in some strange way. He filled the room.

She closed her eyes and she could still sense him.

"Yes," he said.

The king shook his head. "Then who am I to deny you," he said. "And yet I sense that you, in turn, desire something of me?"

De Vrailly laughed, and the sweet musical sound of it filled the room. "Of course! I would be your heir in exchange, and this kingdom shall, after you, be my own."

The earl staggered as if he had been struck.

The king shook his head. "Then, angel or no, I think it would be best if you went back to Galle," he said. "My wife will bear me an heir of my body, or I will appoint my own choice."

"Of course!" de Vrailly said. "But of course, my king!" He nodded, his eyes shining. "But I will prove myself and become your choice. I will serve you, and you will see that there is no one like me."

"And you know this because an angel told you."

"Yes," said Jean de Vrailly. "And I offer to prove it on the body of any man you send against me, on horse or foot, with any weapon you care to name."

His challenge, delivered in his sweet angelic voice from the bended knee of the suppliant, had all the authority of a decree. Men flinched from it.

The king nodded, as if satisfied.

"Then I look forward to placing my lance against yours," he said. "But not as a challenge to your angel. Merely for the pleasure of the thing."

Desiderata saw the perfect knight exchange a glance with his cousin. And she had no idea what thought they shared, but they were pleased. Pleased with themselves, and perhaps pleased with the king. It warmed her, so she smiled.

Gaston, the Sieur D'Eu, smiled back at her, but the golden de Vrailly, never took his eyes from the king. "I should love to match lances with you, sire," he said.

"Well, not tonight. It's too dark. Perhaps tomorrow." The king looked at the Earl of Towbray and nodded. "I thank you for bringing me this splendid man. I hope I have the revenue to keep him and his army!"

The earl chewed his moustache for a moment, and then shrugged. "My pleasure, your Majesty," he replied.

Lissen Carak—The Red Knight

"God be with you," the Abbess said quietly, laying her hands on Wilful Murder's head, and he flinched.

She caught the captain's eye as the narrow gateway began to clear.

"Any pursuit?" he asked Ser George Brewes, the rear file leader—a man ready to be a corporal. One of Jehannes's cronies, not one of Tom's. Still waiting in the gate, aware it was open, eyes on the darkness outside.

Brewes shrugged. "How would I know?" he asked. But he relented. "I wouldn't think it." He shook his head. "We lit ten farms' worth of the woods, and sent the fire downwind right at their camp."

"How many Jacks?" the captain asked.

"At least a hundred. Maybe thrice that—there's no proper counting in the dark, ser." Brewes shrugged. "M'lord," he added, as an afterthought.

A pair of valets and an archer came up and began to winch the main gate shut.

"Ware!" shouted a voice from the highest tower, the one over the nuns' dormitory, and the captain heard the unmistakable sound of a crossbow snapping off a shot.

Something passed over the moon.

Thankfully every man was on the walls and alert, or it might have been worse when the wyvern came down into the courtyard on wings a dozen ells wide, and its claws wreaked ruin among the unarmoured dancers and singers and merry-makers, but before the screams started it sprouted a dozen bolts, and it raised its head and screeched a long cry of anger and pain, and leapt back into the air.

The captain saw Michael, unarmoured, hurdle a pair of corpses and draw his heavy dagger, flinging himself at the wyvern's back as it lifted into the air. Its tail flicked—and slammed full force into the squire's hip. Michael screamed in pain and was thrown a horse's length to the stone.

The Red Knight didn't waste the time provided by his squire. He was down from the gatehouse, sword in gloved hand, before Michael's scream had echoed off the stable walls and the chapel.

The wyvern whirled to finish the squire, and Bad Tom stepped between the monster and its prey. The big man had a long, heavy spear in hand, and he attacked, thrusting for the thing's head. It was fast—but its sinuous neck served the creature as a man's torso serves a man, and when it flicked its head to avoid the spear, it could neither strike nor rise into the air until it had its balance back.

Bad Tom stepped in closer, shortened his grip on the spear and struck hard, thrusting the spear brutally into the thing's chest where the neck met its underbelly.

Long shafts began to feather the thing's wings and abdomen.

It screamed and leaped into the air, wings beating hard, slamming its tail at Tom, but the big man jumped high and cleared the lashing tail by a fraction. But he missed the flicker of a wing in the dark, and the wingtip creased his backplate and slammed him to the ground.

The archers on the walls loosed shaft after shaft. Wilful Murder stood a horse's length away, drawing shafts from the quiver at his hip and loosing carefully—aiming for any vulnerable part.

The bonfire in the courtyard illuminated their target, and the wickedly forged arrowheads cut into the beast's hide like chisels through wood as the sparks from the courtyard fires rose like fireflies in the weakening wingbeats.

The captain was behind and above it when it leaped for the air, and he leaped too. He hit its neck and his sword whipped around its throat. His left hand grabbed the sword at the other side and he let himself drop, his sword become a vicious fulcrum, dragging the wyvern's head down. It lost height and crashed on the steps of the chapel, his sword deep in the soft underside the neck, its jaws unable to reach him, the wyvern injuring itself as its head slammed into the steps again and again in fury and panic.

A lone crossbowman ran along the parapet, leaped down to the courtyard, stumbled, righted himself, and loosed his heavy weapon into the wyvern's head from a distance of a few feet. The power of the bolt snapped its head back, and the captain rolled to his left, loosed his left hand, and got to his feet, his heavy blade already lashing out for the neck—again, and again, and then, when the head came up, he caught the blade in his left hand again, and slashed down into the creature's head, his blade sliding down its armoured scales to slice softer flesh. He made ten strokes in as many heart beats, and the head suddenly snapped back, the whole beast rolled like a man and the brave crossbowman died when the mighty claws took him round the waist and tore him in half.

"There's another!" shouted Tom, off to his left.

The tip of the thrashing tail caught his right ankle and ripped his feet from under him, and the captain cursed that he was not in armour.

He hit his head on a chapel step and lost an instant.

The wyvern reared over him.

A woman—the seamstress—appeared out of the darkness on his right, and threw a barrel at the monster—clipped the thing's head, and it lost its balance, and one of his engineers loosed a scorpion into it.

The power of the scorpion shaft was so great that it took the creature's neck and punched it *through* the chapel doors so hard that where the creature's head smashed into the stone the lintel cracked. He heard its neck break. The shaft did a hundred leopards' damage inside the chapel, the wyvern's death struggles did a hundred more, and a river of gore spoiled the sacred carpet on the marble floor.

The captain got to his feet and found that he'd kept his sword. His chamois gloves were ruined and his left hand was bleeding where he'd grabbed the blade too high, above the area left dull for such purposes. He'd twisted his ankle, and he had to blink rapidly bring the world, spinning around him, back into focus.

The thing twitched, and he buried his point in the eye he could reach.

The courtyard fire glimmered on the belly of the second wyvern.

Forty archers threw shaft after shaft, so that the fortress seemed to have a new column of sparks rising into the fire-lit monster, and something happened—not suddenly, like the strike of the siege shaft, but gradually the wyvern's wings tore, holed, it lost lift and screamed in fear as the men below brought it down and it realised there was no escape from the deadly upwards rain of steel. It slipped lower and lower, wings beating more frantically, turned sharply and suddenly one mighty wing failed. It plummeted to the hillside and crashing down with such weight and speed that the captain felt the steps shake under his boots.

"Sortie!" the captain shouted. He meant to shout, but it came out as more of a croak...although it was understood, and his eight armoured knights had the gate open and were away down the road, led by Sauce.

As the courtyard stilled it showed twenty dead people—dead or terribly maimed. A girl of fifteen or so screamed and screamed, and the woman who had thrown the barrel bent and gathered her into her arms.

A child tried to drag himself by his arms, because he had no legs.

Nuns were suddenly pouring from their dormitory—ten, twenty, fifty women, surrounding the injured and the dead in a storm of grey wool and clean linen, spreading out to access the scale of the dead, injured and traumatised. The captain slumped against a wall, his right leg a torrent of pain, and wished he could just slide into unconsciousness.

She screamed again and again. His eyes flickered to her but only after a long look did he see that most of the left side of her upper torso was *gone*. He couldn't believe she was alive, or screaming. The woman who had saved his life was covered in her blood—shiny with it, trying to help her—and there was *nothing* to be done.

He wished the screaming woman would just die.

A pair of nuns wrapped her tight in a sheet, round and round, and the sheet turned red as fast as they could wrap another layer, and still she screamed, becoming one voice amongst a chorus of anguish that filled the night.

He staggered up and stumbled to Michael, who lay crumpled against the chapel.

The boy was alive.

He looked around for Amicia. She had been standing right there—there, where the woman screamed. But she was gone. He shouted for a sister—for anyone—and four responded. They ran their hands carefully over him before lifting him away from Michael.

Men were shouting now. Even over the screams, their shouts were triumphant, but he ignored them and dragged himself over to Tom.

Tom was sitting against the stable. "Backplate took it," he said with a grin. "Christ, I thought I was done." He pointed at the sword. "Nice trick, that."

"Half-sword versus wyvern," the captain said. "A standard move. All the best masters teach it." He stripped away the ruin of his left glove and wrapped it tight around his cut. "I just need more practice."

Tom chuckled. "Sauce just killed t'other, I'll wager," he said, pointing at the cheering archers.

Sure enough, the next moments brought the mounted sortie back through the main gate, dragging the head of the second wyvern. Brought to earth by fifty arrows, it had died on their lance tips without injuring a single human.

Tom nodded. "That was well done, Captain."

The captain shrugged. "We were ready, we laid our trap, you burned their camp and surprised them, and they *still* killed our people." He shook his head. "I wasn't ready enough. I was caught lollygagging."

Tom shrugged back. "They killed a lot of people." He raised an eyebrow. "But not many of *our* people."

"You're a hard bastard, Tom Mac Lachlan."

Bad Tom shrugged, obviously taking it as a compliment, then something caught his eye in the chapel. He wrinkled his nose as if he'd smelled something bad.

"What?" asked the captain.

"Ever notice how they're always smaller when they're dead?" Tom asked. "It's just the fear that makes 'em seem so big."

The captain nodded. He was looking at the wyvern too, and he had to admit that it *was* smaller than it had seemed in the fight. And it looked different. Paler. A mass of wounds and cuts and barbs.

Almost pitiful.

Tom smiled and started to get to his feet, and the Abbess was there.

He expected anger or recriminations from her, but she merely extended a hand and took his.

"Let us heal your people," she said.

The captain nodded, still pressing his glove tight around his hand. There was a lot of blood. She got an odd look on her face, just before he fainted in her arms.

Albinkirk—Ser Alcaeus

Deep in the marches of the next night, the enemy attacked the castle of Albinkirk.

Ser Alcaeus had passed beyond fatigue. He was in a world lived one heartbeat at a time, and events passed him in a series of illuminated flashes, as if lightning was playing on all of them.

There were some assaults on the walls of the castle, but unlike the low stone curtain walls of the town the castle walls were too high and too well maintained for the flood of Wild creatures to climb. The handful of beasts who made it to the top were killed.

But every attack cost him a little more.

One flash was a fight with an irk—a tall, thin, beautiful creature with a hooked nose like a raptor's beak and chain armour as fine as fish scales that turned his sword again and again. And when, by dint of desperate strength, he knocked it to the stones, and its helmet spun away, the irk's eyes begged for mercy. Like a man's.

Alcaeus would remember that. Even as his dagger terminated it he registered that it, too, had humanity.

...and what followed was worse.

Because something came.

It was huge and foreboding, out in the horrifying fire-lit ruins of the town. It strode forward with a hideous shambling gait, and it was as tall as the city wall or taller.

It was *alive*.

And now it raised its staff—the size of a mounted knight's heavy lance, or bigger—and a line of white-green fire struck the castle wall. The stone deflected in it a wash of white-green fire for as long as the terrified men on the wall might have counted to ten.

And then there was a rending *crack* and the wall breached, about ten paces to the left of the gate. The whole wall moved. Men fell—chunks of flint fell to crush the creatures below.

Then the monster raised its arms and seemed to call the stars down from the heavens, and as they began to plummet, Alcaeus fought not to fall on his face and hide.

The stars screamed down from the clear sky, falling to earth with an eerie, unearthly wail, and struck. One struck out in the fields, killing a wave of boglins. One struck in the centre of the town, and the cloud of fire reached into the heavens. The whole castle moved, and a cloud of dust reached like a fist into the heavens.

The third struck the castle wall mere feet from the great crack, and an enormous piece of masonry and stone fell outward with a crash.

Alcaeus ran for the breach, and found himself with another armoured man—Cartwright, he thought, or the Galle, Benois. The breach was narrow—two men wide.

They filled it with their bodies.

And the enemy came for them.

At some point, Benois fell. He was stunned, and Alcaeus tried to cover him, but the enemy reached a hundred hands and talons for his feet, sank claws into his flesh and dragged him to the edge of the wall, inch by inch. He screamed, unmanned with horror, and tried to rise. Boglin weapons cut him in the soft places not covered by armour, peeled his plate away.

They were eating him alive.

Alcaeus struck and struck again, powered by desperate fear, and he straddled the screaming man's body and cut and cut.

It wasn't enough. And then Benois grabbed at *his* ankles.

He ripped himself clear, and leaped back into the uncertain footing of the breach, and Benois was gone, a pile of hellspawn feeding on him, his armour torn open—

Alcaeus made himself breathe.

Suddenly Ser John was there with his mace. The five foot weapon moved like a goodwife's broom on a new spring morn, and he shattered first the boglins around them, and then Benois's skull.

There was a flash of light to the east—a distant *whump* of displaced air. A column of flame leaped up perhaps a league away. Perhaps two.

Then another—even greater.

The creatures of the Wild faltered, looked over their shoulders, and the fury of their assault rapidly abated.

Albinkirk—Thorn

In an instant, Thorn knew that something had gone wrong.

He'd drained himself by calling even the smallest stones from the heavens. It was a showy, inaccurate and inefficient working, but it had spectacular results when it worked. And he loved to cast it, the way a strong man loves to show his strength.

The daemons were impressed, and that alone was worth the fatigue. Better, the town was utterly destroyed and it had been far, far easier than even he had hoped.

I have grown so strong, he thought. What he had planned as a mere diversion had become a triumph. She would hear of it and cower in fear.

Perhaps taking the Rock is worth doing after all. Perhaps I will refashion myself as a warlord.

But the twin pillars of fire behind him came from his camp—the camp where his greatest allies, the irks and the boglins, stored their food and their belongings and their slaves and their loot. And it was afire.

He had left his most trusted troops had been left to guard it.

He turned with his army and strode for it.

Without his willing it, the bulk of his Wild creatures turned and followed him. They had no discipline, and they went like a shoal of fish—

Albinkirk—Ser Alcaeus

Alcaeus watched them go, slumped against the wall. The Gallish man-at-arms looked like a butchered animal, his bones stripped. The boglins had feasted on him.

The sun was rising, and the lower town was an abattoir of horrors. In the main square irks had taken the time to carefully flay a man and hang him on a cross. He was still alive.

James the crossbowman stepped into the breach. He took a long look, raised his weapon and shot the crucified man. It was a good shot, given the range. The man's screaming, skinless head dropped, and he was silent.

Ser John was slumped against the other wall. James helped the old man get his visor up. He winked.

He *winked.*

In that moment the old knight became a hero, in Ser Alcaeus's estimation.

Alcaeus had to smile back, despite so many things. The loss of Benois hurt. The feel of the man's hands on his ankles—

"I need you to ride to the king," Ser John said. "Right now, while whatever miracle this respite may be lasts."

Alcaeus must have agreed with him, because an hour later he was on his best horse, unarmoured, and galloping south. It was a desperate gamble.

He was too tired to care.

Chapter Seven

South of Albinkirk—Master Random

"**G**ates of Albinkirk are broken, ser," Guilbert reported. He shrugged. "There's fires burning in the town and it looks like a fucking fist, beg your pardon, punched the cathedral. King's banner still flies over the castle but none answered my hail."

John Judson, worshipful draper, and St. Paul Silver, a goldsmith, drew their horses closer to Random where he sat with Old Bob, Guilbert's friend and the last man he'd hired, a bald, ruddy skinned drunkard whose voice and carriage suggested that the spurs on his heels were actually his.

Old Bob was the oldest man in the company, and had a much-broken nose, bumpy with knots of erupting flesh. His straggly salt and pepper hair erupted from a narrow zone around his ears and was always dirty, but the man's eyes were deep and intelligent and a little disturbing, even to a man as experienced as Gerald Random.

He wore good armour, and he wore it all the time.

"That's what the peasants said yesterday," Old Bob noted calmly.

Random looked at the other merchant venturers. "Albinkirk in ruins?" he asked. "I've fought up here, friends. The border is a hundred leagues farther north, and even then—the Wild is west and north of us, not here."

"Something did this, all the same," Judson said. The corners of his lips were white, the lips themselves drawn tight. "I say we go back."

Paul Silver wore high boots like a gentleman. Goldsmiths were often better dressed than their customers. It was the way of the world. But Silver had also served the king and wore a heavy sword, an expensive weapon meticulously kept ready for battle. "We'd be fools to ignore that something is going on," he agreed. "But bad as this is I'm not sure it means a convoy of nearly fifty wagons should turn back."

Albinkirk rose on a high hill at the next great bend in the river. Ships would make it this far north, later in the summer when the floods were done and all the ice was out of the mountains—when the run off wasn't carrying whole pine trees, big enough to stove in a round ship, down mountainsides and out into the great river. Albinkirk was the northernmost town that could be reached by ship, and yet the southernmost at the edge of the Great Forest that covered the mountains. Once it had hosted the Great Fair, but poor management and rapacious tolls had forced it to move further east, to the convent at Lissen Carak.

Today Albinkirk was a corpse, red-tile roofs looking grey and old, or fire-blacked, in the distance, and the spire of the cathedral gone.

"What's happened to the cathedral?" Random asked.

Old Bob made a face. "They was attacked by dragons." He shrugged. "Or Satan himself."

Random took a deep breath. This was the sort of moment for which he lived. The great decision. The gamble.

"We could leave the road. Turn east on this side of the river and use the bridge at Lissen Carak," he found himself saying. "Keep the river between us and Albinkirk."

"A river won't stop wyverns," Old Bob said.

"Not much choice anyway," Guilbert said. "The gates are shut, so we can't exactly take the High Road."

"They should *want* us in that town," Random said.

Judson watched him, and his face held something Random didn't recognise—horror? Fear? Curiosity?

But finally the man worked up his courage and spoke his mind. "I'll be taking my wagons back south," he said carefully.

Random nodded. Judson had the second largest contingent—eight wagons, a sixth of the total.

"I reckon I'll take my share of the sell-swords, too," Judson said.

Random thought for a fraction of a heart beat and shook his head. "How do you reckon that, messire?"

Judson shrugged, but his eyes were angry. "I paid for eight wagons to join your convoy," he said. "I reckon that's a quarter the cost of the sell-swords, so I'll take four of them. Six would be better."

Random nodded. "I see," he said. "No, and you know it doesn't work that way. You joined my convoy for a fee. If you leave it—that's on you. You didn't purchase a share, you purchased a place."

"You think the King's Court will see it that way?" Judson asked. Fear had made him bold. "I'll be back in a few days, telling my story." He shrugged and looked away. "Give me my half-dozen swords, and I'll say nothing."

Judson looked at Paul, and then he leaned forward. "You want to be Lord Mayor, Random? Start playing the game."

Random looked at him, and then shook his head. "No. I won't quarrel with you, and I won't give you a sword, much less six. Go your own way. It should be safe enough."

"You'd send me back without a single man?" Judson demanded.

"I'm not sending you back. You're going. Your decision." Random looked at Guibert and Old Bob. "Unless one of you has cold feet too?"

Old Bob scratched something unspeakable on his nose. "Going on ain't going to be good," he said. "But I don't need to go back."

Guilbert looked at the older man. "What's not going to be good?" he said. "What in hell's name are you on about?"

"Wyverns," said the old man. "Daemons, irks and boglins." He grinned, and he looked truly horrific. "The Wild lies ahead."

Harndon Palace—Desiderata

The lists were pristine—the gravel carefully tended and unmarked, the barriers crisp and white with new lime, like a farmer's dooryard fence except for the fancy red posts at either end, each topped with a brightly polished brass globe the size of a man's fist.

The stands were virtually empty. The Queen sat in her seat, her ladies around her, and her young knights in the lower tiers of the seats, tossing early flowers to their favourite ladies.

There were professional spectators—a dozen men-at-arms, most from the castle garrison of archers. Word had spread quickly, and the rumour was that the king had been challenged by this foreign knight and meant to show him a thing or two.

Desiderata watched her husband sitting quietly by the little wooden shack where he had armed. He was drinking water. His hair was long and well kept, but even at this distance, she could see the grey in the dark brown.

At the other end of the lists, his opponent's hair was an unmarked gold, the gold of sunset, of polished brass, of ripe wheat.

Ser Jean finished whatever preparations he was making and had a quiet word with his cousin, while his squire held the biggest war horse the Queen had ever seen—a beautiful creature, tall and elegant of carriage, its gleaming black hide unrelieved by marks of any kind, with a red saddle and blue furniture all pointed in red and gold. Ser Jean's arms, a golden swan on a field of red and blue, decorated the peak of his helm, the tight, padded surcote over his coat armour, the heavy drapery over the rump of his horse, and the odd little shield, curved like the prow of a war-galley, that sat on his left shoulder.

It was a warm day. Perhaps the first truly warm day of spring, and the Queen bathed in the sun like a lioness and gave forth a glow of her own that bathed her ladies and even the knights on the seats below her.

Today the foreign knight glanced up at her quite frequently, as was her due.

She looked back at the king. By comparison, he looked small and just a little dingy. His squires were the best in the land, but he *liked* his old red arming cote and his many-times-repaired plate, fashioned in the mountains far across the ocean when hardened steel was a new thing and carefully repaired by his armourer ever since. He *liked* his old red saddle with the silver buckles, and if they left traces of black tarnish on the leather, it was still a fine saddle. Where the foreign knight was new and shone from top to toe, her king was older—worn.

His war horse was smaller too—Father Jerome, the king called him, and he was veteran of fifty great jousts and a dozen real fights. The king had other, younger, bigger horses, but when he went to fight for real he rode Father Jerome.

The herald and the master of the list called them to action. It was friendly play—the spears were bated. Desiderata saw Gaston, the foreign knight's friend, say something to the king, pointing to his neck, with a bow.

The king smiled and turned away.

"He's not wearing his gorget under his aventail," Ser Driant said in her ear. "Young Gaston asks why, and requests that the king wear it." He nodded in approval. "Very proper. His man wishes to fight hard, and he doesn't want to be accused of injuring the king. I'd feel the same way myself, if the king had challenged me."

"The king did *not* challenge him," Desiderata said.

Ser Driant gave her a queer look. "That's not what I heard," he said. "Still, I suspect the king will tip him in the sand and that will be that."

"Men say that man is the best knight in the world," the Queen replied, a little coldly.

Ser Driant laughed. "Men say such things about any pretty knight," he said. He looked at Ser Jean, mounting with a vault and taking his lance. "Mind you, the man is the size of a giant."

The Queen felt a mounting unease, such as she had never experienced watching men fight. This was her place—her role. It was her duty to be impartial as the armoured figures crashed together, and to judge the best of them. To forget that one was her lover and king and the other an ambitious foreigner who had all but accused her of being barren.

She should judge only their worthiness.

But as the two men manoeuvred their horses on either side of the barrier, she felt a band tighten around her heart. He had forgotten to ask for her favour, and she almost lifted the scarf she held in her hand.

She couldn't remember the last time she'd watched men fight without bestowing her favour on one, or perhaps both.

Ser Jean wore a foreign type of helmet, a round-faced bascinet with a low, round brow and a heavy dog-faced visor with the Cross of Christ in brass and gold.

The king wore the high-peaked helmet more typical of Albans, with a pointy visor that men called pig-faced but which always reminded the Queen of a bird—a mighty falcon.

Even as she watched, he flicked the visor down and it closed with a click audible across the field.

There was a stir up in the castle yard—soldiers craning their necks, others moving to the walls, while still others jammed up at the gate beyond which were sounds of shouting and galloping horses.

The Queen did not often pray. But as she watched the king she put her right hand to the rosary around her neck and prayed to the Queen of Heaven, asking her for grace—

Two horses flashed past the gate, galloping along the cobbled road to the lists down by the moat yard, their riders shouting and horseshoes striking sparks that leapt even in the sunlight.

She could feel the gathering of powers in the tiltyard, exactly as she had been able to feel the first gathering of Harmodius's not inconsiderable power, but this was power of another order—like bright white light on a dark day.

The foreign knight touched his spurs to his horse.

The king spurred Father Jerome, almost in the same instant. In another time, she would have applauded.

The two messengers were racing along the moat road, neck and neck, as king and knight charged each other—

—and Ser Jean's horse shied beneath him as a great horse fly sunk its sting far into the black horse's unprotected nose, where the soft lips emerged from beneath the chamfron.

The war horse balked, missed a stride, and half-reared, half-turned from the barrier. Ser Jean fought for his seat, tried to force his mount's head back to the barrier, but he was hopelessly out of line and now too slow to strike with real force. He raised his lance and then cast it aside as his pained horse reared again.

The king came on at full tilt, back straight, Father Jerome perfectly collected under him, lance aimed like a swift arrow from some ancient god's bow. A foot short of Jean de Vrailly's prow-shaped shield his lance tip swept up, plucked the swan from his helmet, and then the king thundered by, his lance dropping again to strike the brass globe on the last post of the lists. He struck it squarely, so hard that it ripped from its post and flew through the air to bounce and roll past Ser Gaston, past the two messengers thundering up the rise to the lists, and into the moat.

The Queen applauded...and yet felt that the king—she tried to keep the thought in check—that he might have voided his lance and passed his opponent without taking his crest. It would have been a generous act, and such things were done, between friends, when a knight was obviously struggling with his horse.

De Vrailly rode back toward his own end, back straight, horse now firmly under control.

A dozen royal archers ran to get between the king and the two riders, who were bearing down on him with intent, shouting but their words indistinct. They both held scrolls, the colourful ribbons dangling.

The archers parted to let them through when the king opened his faceplate and beckoned to the messengers. He was grinning like a small boy in his victory.

The Queen wasn't sure whether this was the outcome of her prayer or not, and so she prayed again as the messengers reached the king, dismounting to kneel at his feet even as his squires began to take his armour.

At the same end of the lists, only a few feet away, Jean de Vrailly dismounted. His cousin spoke sharply to him, and the tall knight ignored the smaller man, and drew his sword—almost too fast to follow.

His cousin slapped him—hard—on the elbow of his sword arm, and the foreign knight fumbled his sword—the only clumsy movement she'd ever seen him make. He turned on his cousin, who stood his ground.

The Queen knew unbridled rage when she saw it, and she held her breath, a little shocked to see the Galle so out of control—but even as she watched, the man mastered himself. She saw him incline his head very slightly to his cousin, as if acknowledging a hit in the lists.

He turned and spoke to one of his squires.

The man collected the mighty horse's reins and began to strip its barding with the help of a pair of pages.

She lost the action for a moment while she tried to take in what she had seen.

Suddenly the king was by her side.

"He's very angry," the king said, while bowing over her hand. He sounded content with his opponent's anger. "Listen, sweeting. The fortress at Lissen Carak is under attack by the Wild. Or so both these two messengers say."

She sat up. "Tell me!" she demanded.

Ser Gaston came up, approaching the king with the deference that his cousin never seemed to show even when kneeling.

"Your Grace—" he began.

The king raised a hand. "Not now. The joust is over for the day, my lord, and I thank your cousin for the sport. I will be riding north with all my knights as soon as I can gather them. One of my castles, and not the least of them, is under attack."

Ser Gaston bowed. "My cousin requests that he might ride one course against you." He bowed. "And he wishes your Grace to know that he honours your Grace's horsemanship—he sends you his war horse, in hopes your Grace might school him as well as your own is schooled."

The king smiled like a boy who's been well-praised by a parent. "Indeed, I love a horse," he said. "I do not claim the good knight's horse and arms, you understand—but if he offers." The king licked his lips.

Ser Gaston nodded to where the squire was leading the now-unarmed horse. "He is yours, your Grace. And he asks that he be allowed to take another horse and have another course with your Grace."

The king's face closed like the visor of his helmet had clicked down. "He has ridden one," the king said. "If he wishes another chance to prove himself, he may gather his knights and ride with me to the north." The king seemed on the verge of saying more, and then he steadied himself. But he allowed himself a small, kingly smile and said, "And tell him that I'll be happy to loan him a horse."

But Gaston bowed. "We will ride with you, your Grace."

But the king had already dismissed him, and turned to the Queen.

"It's bad," he said. "If the writer of this letter knows his business, it's very bad. Jacks. Daemons. Wyverns. The might of the Wild has joined against us."

At the names, all of her ladies crossed themselves.

The Queen rose to her feet. "Let us help these worthy gentlemen," she said to her ladies. She rose and kissed the king's face. "You will need carts, provender, supplies, canteens and water casks. I have the lists to hand. You gather your knights, and I'll have the rest ready to follow you before noon." In a moment, the winds of war—actual war, with all it implied about glory and honour and high deeds—blew away her fancy for the foreign knight.

And her lover was the *king*. Going to war with the Wild.

He looked into her eyes with adoration. "Bless you!" he whispered. And her king turned, and shouted for his constable. And the Earl of Towbray, who was ready to hand.

Towbray had the grace to give the king a wry smile. "How convenient that I have all my armed strength to hand, your Grace. And that you have summoned your knights to a tournament."

The king usually had no time for Towbray, but just for a moment they shared something. The king clapped the other man's shoulder. "If only I *had* planned it," he said.

Towbray nodded. "My knights are at your service."

The king shook his head. "That's the trouble with you, Towbray. Just when I've found reason to despise you, there you are doing something to help. And unfortunately a year hence, you'll do something to spoil it again."

Towbray bowed. "I am what I am, your Grace. In this case, your Grace's servant."

He glanced at the Queen.

She didn't see his look, already busy with a list of long-bodied wagons available in the town of Harndon.

But the king followed Towbray's glance, and his lip curled.

Towbray had been watching the king, too. It was easy to dismiss him—he didn't seem to have any finer feelings, or to have any purpose beyond the tilt field and his wife's bed.

And yet here was the Wild, launching an attack, and the king *just happened* to have already summoned his host. That kind of luck seemed to happen to the king all the time.

Lissen Carak—The Red Knight

The captain woke in the Abbey infirmary, his head on a feather pillow, his hands—the left heavily wrapped in bandages—laid neatly on a white wool blanket atop a fine linen sheet. The sun shone through the narrow window well over his head and the shaft of light lit Bad Tom, snoring in the opposite bed. A young boy lay with his face to the wall in the next bed, and an older man with his whole head wrapped in linen opposite him.

He lay still for a moment, oddly happy, and then it all came back to him in a rush. He shook his head, cursed God, sat and got his feet on the floor.

His movement caused the duty sister to raise her head. He hadn't noticed her. She smiled.

Amicia.

"Aren't you afraid to be alone with me?" he asked.

Her composure was palpable, like armour. "No," she answered. "I am not afraid of you, sweet. Should I be?" She rose to her feet. "Besides, Tom is only just asleep and old Harold—who has leprosy—sleeps very lightly. I trust you not to disturb them."

The captain winced at the word trust. He leaned towards her—she smelled of olive oil and incense and soap—and had to fight the urge to put his hands on her hips, her waist—

She cocked her head a little to one side. "Don't even think it!" she said, sharply, but without raising her voice.

His cheeks burned. "But you like me!" he said. It seemed to him one of the stupidest things he'd ever said. He gathered himself, his dignity, his role as the captain. "Tell me why you always fend me off?" he asked, his voice controlled, light hearted, and false. "You didn't fend last night."

She met his look, and hers was serious, even severe. "Tell me why you curse God on rising?" she asked.

The silence between them lasted a long time, during which he even considered telling her.

She took his left hand and started to unwrap the bandage. That hurt.

A little later, Tom opened one eye. The captain did not particularly enjoy watching him admire her hips and her breasts as she moved with her back and side to him.

He winked at the captain.

The captain did not wink back.

After she'd put a oregano poultice on his hand and wrapped it in linen, she nodded. "Try not to seize the sharp bits when fighting grim beasts in future, messire," she said.

He smiled, she smiled, their silence forgotten, and he left feeling as light as air. It lasted all the way down the steeply turning stairs, until he saw the twenty-three tight-wrapped white bundles under an awning in the otherwise empty courtyard.

In the aftermath of the battle, the Abbess had ordered all of her people to stay indoors. No one would sleep in the open air, no matter how balmy and spring-laden it was. Services were held in a side chapel—the main chapel was now sleeping quarters.

He passed under the arch to his Commandery, and found Michael, who was busy writing, with Ser Adrian, the company's professional clerk. Michael rose stiffly and bowed. Adrian kept writing.

The captain couldn't help but smile at his squire, who was obviously alive and *not* one of the bundles in the courtyard. His face asked the question.

"Two broken ribs. Worse than when I tried to ride my father's destrier," Michael said ruefully.

"In a business where we take daring and courage for granted, yours was a brave act," the captain said, and Michael glowed. "Stupid," the captain continued, putting a hand on the young man's shoulder, "and a little pointless. But brave."

Michael continued to beam with happiness.

The captain sighed and went to his table, which was stacked high with scrolls and tubes. He found the updated roster. It was due the first of every month, and tomorrow was the first of May.

Why had he even considered telling her why he cursed God?

People were often stupid, but he wasn't used to being one of them.

He read through the roster. Thirty-one lances—thirty, because Hugo was dead and that broke his lance. He needed a good man-at-arms—not that there seemed to be any to be found in this near wilderness. There must be local knights—younger sons eager for glory, or for a little cash, or with a pregnancy to avoid.

The whole stack of paperwork made him tired. But he still needed men, and then there was the Wild to consider as well.

"I need to talk to Bad Tom when he's well enough. And to the archers from last night. Who was most senior?" he asked.

Michael took a deep breath. The captain knew he was testing the bounds of the pain against the inside of the bandage with that breath—knew this from having broken so many ribs himself.

"Long Paw was the senior man. He's awake—I saw him eating." Michael rose to his feet.

The captain held up a hand. "I'll see him with Tom. If he can leave the infirmary." His hand was throbbing. He initialled the muster roll. "Get them, please."

Michael paused, and the captain swallowed a sigh of irritation. "Yes?"

"What—what happened last night?" Michael shrugged. "I mean, all the men feel we won a great victory, but I don't even know what we did. Beyond killing the wyverns," he said, with the casual dismissiveness of youth.

The captain felt like yelling, *We killed two wyverns, you useless fop.* But he understood the boy's attitude, albeit unspoken.

The captain sat carefully in a low backed folding chair made of a series of arches linked at the base—it was a beautiful chair with a red velvet cushion which welcomed him, and he leaned back. "Are you the apprentice captain asking? Or my squire?"

Michael raised an eyebrow. "I'm the apprentice captain," he said.

The captain allowed the younger man a small smile. "Good. Tell me what you *think* we did."

Michael snorted. "Saw that coming. Very well. All day we sent out patrols to gather in farmers. I didn't realise it at the time, but more patrols went out than came back."

The captain nodded. "Good. Yes. We're being watched, all the time. But the creatures watching us aren't very bright. Do you have any of the power?"

Michael shrugged. "I studied it but I can't hold all the images in my mind. All the phantasms."

"If you capture a beast and bend it to your will, you can look through its eyes—it's a potent phantasm but it is wasteful. Because you must first overcome the will of another creature—a massive effort, there—and then *direct* that effort. And in this case you must do so over distance."

Michael listened, utterly fascinated. Even Ser Adrian had stopped writing.

The captain glanced at him, and the clerk shook his head and started to get to his feet. "Sorry," he mumbled. "No one ever talks about this stuff."

The captain relented. "Stay. It is part of our lives and our way of war. We use scouts because we don't have a magus to use birds. Even if we did I'd rather use scouts. They can observe and report, can make judgments as to numbers, can tell if they see the same three horses every day. A bird can't make those judgments, and the magus's perceptions of whatever the bird sees is filtered through—something." The captain sagged. "I don't know what, but I imagine it as a pipe that's too small for all the information to get through, as if everything is seen through water or fog."

Michael nodded.

"The Wild has no scouts, so I guessed that our enemy was using animals as spies. We have trapped a lot of birds, and then I misled him." The captain crossed his hands behind his head.

"And with cook fires. You told me so." Michael leaned forward.

"Gelfred isn't down at the Bridge Castle, not much anyway. He's out in the woods, watching their camps. He has been since we realised the bulk of the Wild army had gone around us. Want to talk about brave? I sent patrols out with a weapon—something the Moreans make. Olive oil, ground oil, whale oil will do—bitumen, if you can get it, plus sulphur and saltpeter. There's dozens of mixtures and any artificer knows them. It makes sticky fire."

Michael nodded. The clerk crossed himself.

"Even the creatures of the Wild sleep. Even the adversarius is just a creature. And when they gather to attack men—well, it stands to reason that they must have a camp. Do they talk? Do they gather at campfires? Play cards? Fight amongst themselves?" The captain looked out of the window. "Have you ever thought, Michael, that we are locked in a war without mercy against an enemy we don't understand at all?"

"So you've watched them, and attacked their camp," Michael said with satisfaction. "And we hit them hard." Now Michael was smiling.

"Yes and no. Perhaps we didn't touch them," the captain said. "Perhaps Bad Tom and Wilful Murder put some fire on some meaningless tents, and then they followed our boys back and hit us harder—killing twenty-three people for the loss of just two wyverns," the captain said.

Michael's smile froze. "But—"

"I want you to see that victory and defeat are a question of perception, unless you are dead. You know every man and woman in the company—in this fortress—feels we won a great victory. We fired the enemy's camps, and then we killed a pair of his most fearsome monsters in ours." The captain got to his feet as Michael nodded.

"And because of this perception, everyone will fight harder and longer, and be braver, despite my fucking mistake to allow civilians into the courtyard which cost us twenty-three lives. Despite that, we're *winning*." The captain's eyes locked on Michael's. "Do you see?"

Michael shook his head. "It wasn't your fault—"

"It was my fault," the captain said. "It's not my moral burden—I didn't kill them. But I could have kept them alive if I hadn't been distracted that evening. And keeping them alive is my duty." He stood up straight and picked up the baton of the command. "Best know this, if you want to be a captain. You have to be able to look reality in the eye. I fucked their lives away. I can't go to pieces about it, but neither can I forget it. That's my job. Understand?"

Michael nodded and gulped.

The captain made a face. "Excellent. Here endeth the lesson about victory. Now, if it is not too much trouble, I'd like Long Paw and Bad Tom, please."

Michael stood and saluted. "Immediately!"

"Harumf," said the captain.

Long Paw was fifty, his once red hair mostly grey and a mere tonsure around a bald pate, with an enormous moustache and long sideburns so that he had more hair on his face than on his head. His arms were unnaturally long and despite his status as an archer and not a man-at-arms, he was reputed the company's best swordsman. The rumour was he had once been a monk.

He clasped hands with the captain and grinned. "That was a little too exciting."

Bad Tom came in after him, a head taller than either the captain or the archer, his iron grey hair curiously at odds with his pointed black beard. His forehead had a weight of bone that made his head look like the prow of a ship, and no one would call him a handsome man. He looked scary, even in broad daylight, dressed in nothing but a shirt and an infirmary blanket. He clasped hands with the captain and the archer, grinned at Ser Adrian, and settled every inch of his gigantic frame into one of the arched chairs.

"Good plan," he said to the captain. "I had fun."

Michael slipped in. No one had invited him, but his face suggested that no one had told him he couldn't come, either.

"Get us all a cup of wine," the captain said, which indicated that he was welcome enough.

When five horn cups were on five chair arms, and when Ser Adrian had his lead poised to write, Tom tasted his wine, leaned back and said, "We hit 'em hard. Not much to say—worst part was getting there. The lads was fair skittish, and every shadow had a boglin or an irk in it, and I thought once I was going to have to cut Tippit in half to shut him the fuck up. So I leaned over him—"

Long Paw grinned. "Leaned over him with that giant dagger in his fist!"

"And Tippit pissed himself," Bad Tom said with evident satisfaction. "Call him Pishit from now on."

"Tom," Long Paw cautioned.

Tom shrugged. "If he can't cut it he should go weave blankets or cut purses. He's a piss poor archer and one day he's going to get a man killed. Anyway, we rode most of the way there, and we moved fast, 'cause you said—" Bad Tom paused, obviously at a loss for the words.

"Your only stealth will be speed." *One of Hywel's many aphorisms.*

"That's what you said," Tom agreed. "So we didn't sweat it too much, but went for them. If they had sentries, we never saw 'em, and then we were in among their fires. I slit a lot of sleeping cattle," he said, with a horrible smile. "Stupid fucks, asleep with a killer among them."

Remorse was not in Tom's lexicon. The captain winced. The big man looked at Long Paw. "I got busy. You tell it."

Long Paw raised an eyebrow. "All the archers had an alchemical on our backs. I threw mine in a fire—to start the ball, so to speak." He nodded. "They were *spectacular*. If that's the word." Long Paw was obviously proud of it.

Tom nodded. "Made us plenty of light," he said, and the words, combined with his look, were horrible enough that Long Paw looked away from him. "We didn't see no tents. But there was men sleeping on the ground, critters too. And beasts—horses, cattle, sheep. And wagons, dozens of them. They've been hitting the fair convoys, or I'm a Galle."

The captain nodded.

"We burned it all, killed the animals, and then any critter we come across too."

"What critters? Boglins? Irks? Tell me," the captain asked, and the words just hung there, between them.

Tom made a face. "Little ones. Boglins and irks mostly. You know. Nightmares and daemons pursued us. Fucking daemons are fast. I fought a golden bear, sword to its axe and claws." He blew his nose into his hand and flicked the contents out the window. "But I didn't get to fight a daemon," he said regretfully.

The captain wondered if, in the entire world, there was another man who could regret not having met a creature that projected terror.

Bad Tom was not like other men.

"How many? Total? What are we still up against?" the captain asked.

Long Paw shrugged. "Dark and fire, Cap'n. My word ain't worth shit— but I say we killed maybe fifty men and more creatures." He shrugged. "And all we really did was kick the ant hill."

Tom gave Long Paw a look of appreciation. "What he said," Tom admitted. "We kicked the ant hill. But we kicked it hard."

Michael sputtered. "You two killed fifty *Jacks*?" he asked.

Tom looked at him as if he'd discovered a bad smell. "We had help, younker. And it weren't all *Jacks*. I killed I don't know how many—five? Ten?—before I realised they was all yoked together. Poor fucks."

Michael made a choking sound. "Captives?" he managed.

Tom shrugged. "Got to think so."

Michael's outrage showed, and the captain raised a hand. Pointed at the door. "More wine," he said. "And take your time."

Long Paw shook his head as the young man slammed out. "Not for me, Captain. It'll send me to sleep."

"I'm done, anyway," the captain said. "Better result than I thought. Thanks."

Long Paw clasped his hand again. "One for the books, Cap'n."

The clerk looked at his pencil scrawl. "I'll just copy this out for fair," he said, exchanging a parting look with Long Paw and heading for the door himself.

His departure left the captain alone with Bad Tom, who stretched his naked legs out beneath his blanket and took a long drink of his wine.

"That Michael's too soft for this life," Tom said. "He tries, and he ain't worthless, but you should let him go."

"He doesn't have anywhere *to* go," the captain said.

Tom nodded. "I'd wondered." He took another sip and grinned. "That girl—the nun?"

The captain looked blank.

Tom wasn't fooled for a moment. "Don't give me that. Asking you why you curse God. Listen, you want my advice—"

"I don't," the captain said.

"Get a knee between her legs and keep it there 'til you're inside her. You want her—she wants you. I'm not saying rape her." Tom said this with a professional authority that was more horrible than his admission of killing the captives. "I'm just saying that if you get it done, you can have a warm bed as long as you're here." He shrugged. "A warm bed and a soft shoulder. Good things for a man in command. None of the lads will blame you." His unspoken thought came through, too. *Some of the lads might see you in a better light for it.*

Tom nodded at the captain, and the captain felt a black rage boil up inside him. He worked on it—trying to shape it, trying to plug it. But it was like the brew they'd sent against the enemy—oily black, and when it hit fire—

Bad Tom took a deep breath and stepped back. "Beg your pardon, Captain," he said. He said it with as much assurance as he'd suggested everything else. "Overstepped, I expect."

The captain swallowed bile. "Are my eyes glowing?" he asked.

"Little bit," Tom said. "You know what's wrong with you, Captain?"

The captain leaned on the table, the burst of rage dying away and leaving fatigue and a headache of Archaic proportions. "Many things."

"You're a freak, just like me. You ain't like them. Me—I take what I want and let the rest go. You want them to love you." Tom shook his head. "They don't love the likes of us, Captain. Even when I kill their enemies, they don't love me. Eh? You know what a sin-eater is?"

That came out of nowhere. "I've heard the name."

"We have 'em up in the hills,. Usually some poor wee bastard with one eye or no hands or some other freak. When a man dies, or sometimes a woman, we put a piece of bread soaked in wine—they used to soak it in blood—on the corpse. Goes on the stomach and the heart. And the poor wee man comes and eats the bread, and takes all the dead's sin on them. So the dead un goes off to heaven, and the poor wee man goes to hell."

Tom was far away, in memory. The captain had never seen him that way before. It was odd, and a little scary, to be intimate with Bad Tom.

"We're sin-eaters, every one of us," Tom said. "You and me, sure—but Long Paw an' Wilful Murder and Ser Hugo and Ser Milus and all the rest. Sauce too. Even that boy. We eat their sin. We kill their enemies, and then they send us away."

The captain had a flash of the daemon eviscerating his horse. *We eat their sin.* Somehow, the words hit him like a thunderclap, and he sat back. When he was done with the thought—which cascaded away like a waterfall, taking his thoughts in every direction—he realised the shadows had changed. His wine was long gone, Bad Tom was gone, his legs were stiff, and his hand hurt.

Michael was standing in the doorway with a cup of wine in his hand.

The captain dredged a smile out of his reverie, shrugged and took the wine.

He drank.

"Jacques went down to Bridge Castle with grain and came back with a message for you from Messire Gelfred," Michael said. "He says it's urgent he speak to you."

"Then I'll have to put my harness on," the captain said. He sounded whiney, even to himself. "Let's get it done."

The Albinkirk Road—Ser Gawin

He had lost track of time.

He wasn't sure what he was any more.

Gawin rode through another spring day, surrounded by carpets of wildflowers that flowed like morning fog beneath his horse, rolling away in clumps and hummocks, a thousand perfect flowers in every glance, blue and purple, white and yellow. In the distance, all was a carpet of yellow green from the haze of sun on the mountainsides that were coming closer every day, their peaks woven like a tapestry in and out of the stands of trees that grew thicker and closer every mile.

He'd never had the least interest in flowers before.

"Ser knight?" asked the boy with the crossbow.

He looked at the boy, and the boy flinched. Gawin sighed.

"Ye weren't moving," the boy said.

Gawin pressed his spurs to his horse's side, and shifted his weight, and his destrier moved off. His once-handsome dark leather bridle was stained with the death of fifty thousand flowers, because Archangel ate every flower he could reach as soon as he'd figured out that the once fierce hands on the reins weren't likely to stop him eating. That's what his misery meant to his war horse—more flowers to eat.

I am a coward and a bad knight. Gawin looked back at a life of malfeasance and tried to see where he'd gone wrong, and again and again he came back to a single moment—torturing his older brother. The five of them ganging up on Gabriel. Beating him. The pleasure of it—his screams—

Is that where it started? he asked himself.

"Ser knight?" the boy asked again.

The horse's head was down, and they'd stopped again.

"Coming," Gawin muttered. Behind him, the convoy he was not guarding rolled north, and Gawin could see the Great Bend ahead, where the road turned to head west.

West towards the enemy. West, where his father's castle waited full of his mother's hate and his brother's fear.

Why am I going west?

"Ser knight?" the boy asked. This time, there was fear in his voice. "What's that?"

Gawin shook himself out of his waking dream. The goldsmith's boy— Adrian? Allan? Henry?—was backing away from a clump of trees just to his left.

"There's something there," the boy said.

Gawin sighed. The Wild was *not* here. His horse stood among wildflowers, and last year this field had been ploughed.

Then he saw the sickly-pale arm, light brown, shiny like a cockroach, holding a stone-tipped javelin. He saw it and it saw him in the same moment, and he leaned to the left with the habit of hard training and ripped his long sword from its scabbard.

The boglin threw its weapon.

Gawin cut the shaft out of the air.

The boglin gave a thin scream of anger, balked of its prey, and the goldsmith's boy shot it. His crossbow loosed with a snap and the bolt went home into the creature with a slurpy thud and came straight out the other side in a spray of gore, leaving the small horror to flop bonelessly on the wildflowers for as long as a trout might take to die, making much the same gasping motions with its toothless mouth, and then its eyes filmed over and it was gone.

"They always have gold," the goldsmith's boy said, taking a step towards it.

"Step back, young master, and load that latch again." Gawin was shocked at his voice—calm, commanding. Alive.

The boy obeyed.

Gawin backed Archangel slowly, watching the nearest woods.

"Run for the wagons, boy. Sound the alarm."

There was more movement, more javelin heads, a flash of that hideous cockroach brown, and the boy turned and ran.

Gawin slammed his visor down.

He wasn't in full armour. Most of it was in a goldsmith's wagon, wrapped in tallow and coarse sacking in two wicker baskets because he had no squires to keep it. And because wearing it might have meant something.

So he was wearing his stained jupon, his boots, his beautiful steel gauntlets and his bassinet, riding a horse worth more than three of the wagons full of fine wools he was protecting. He backed Archangel faster, sawing the reins back and forth as his destrier all but trotted backwards.

The first javelin came out of the woods, high. He had his sword in his right hand, all the way down by his left side, the position his father's master at arms had taught him. He could hear the man saying "Cut up, mind! Not into your own horse, ye daft thing!"

He cut up, severing the weapon's haft and breaking its flight.

Behind him, he heard the boy yelling "To arms! To arms!"

He risked a long glance back at the convoy. It was hard to focus through the piercing of his visor, hard to pick up distant movement, but he thought he could see Old Bob directing men in all directions.

He turned back to see the air full of javelins, and he cut—up, down, up again as fast as thought. A javelin haft caught him in the side of his head and rang his helmet like a bell, even with his padded arming cap. He smelt his own blood.

Turned his horse's head—because once they'd all thrown, he had a moment to get around, and get away.

Two of them were running for him. They were fast, moving like insects—so low to the ground that they were a danger to horses' legs. Archangel reared, pivoted on his hind legs, and a powerful forefoot shot out like a boxer's punch.

Gawin flicked his sword out along his fingers, lengthening his grip until he was holding only the disc-shaped pommel and, in the same motion, made a wrist cut down and back.

Archangel's boglin popped like a ripe melon, its chest and neck caving in with a dull thud and a fine spray of ichor. Gawin's screeched as the cold iron pierced its hide—iron was poison to its kind, and it screamed its hate as its tiny soul rose from its corpse like a minute thundercloud that dissipated on the first whiff of breeze.

All at once they were away, the big horse galloping easily over the wildflowers. Gawin had trouble breathing. His visor seemed to cut all the air from his lungs and his chest was tight.

As he rode, he could see there were other knots of the things—perhaps four or five groups of them spread across the flowers like shit stains on a pretty dress, and suddenly he was filled with a fey energy, a will to do a great deed and die in the accomplishment.

I am a knight, he thought fiercely.

Gawin sat up in the saddle, holding his long, sharp sword with new purpose, and he turned Archangel and raised it at the boglins. Something dead within him rekindled as the sun lit the blade like a torch.

He felt the touch of something divine, and he saluted as if riding in a tournament.

"Blessed Saint George," he prayed, "let me die as I wish I had lived."

He put his spurs to Archangel—gently, a nudge rather than a rake—and the great horse thundered forward.

The boglins scattered. Javelins flew past and then he was among them, through them, using his knees to turn Archangel in a long curve toward the next clump, who were already running for the trees.

Gawin had no plans to survive so he thundered after them, slaying any that stood or were merely too slow to escape, leaning far out from the saddle—

Something called from inside the wood—a wail that froze his blood.

It was out of the woods and at him in heartbeats.

Archangel was ready, pivoted his whole great bulk as Gawin's weight shifted so that the war horse moved like his own feet in a fight, and the huge enemy—scent of burned hair and soap and old ashes—shot past. One taloned arm stretched out like an angry cat's paw, reaching for Archangel's neck, but the war horse was fast, and some steel-shod forefoot smashed the taloned hand with lethal precision.

The thing screamed, its left talon hanging limply, the bones broken. It rose on its hind feet, raised its right claw, and fire shot from its outstretched talons—a beam of fire that caught his body where the mail aventail of his helmet hung over his padded jupon. It had no pressure, no impact, and Gawin ducked his head, putting the peak of his helmet into the flame by instinct rather than training. His left eye flared with pain even as the first cold knife of agony pierced his left shoulder. His body, with no guidance from his mind, cut down blindly with the sword.

His blow was weak and badly directed—the edge of the blade didn't even bite into the thing's hide—but the sword's weight fell on its brow ridge, and it stumbled.

Archangel shouldered it. Gawin almost lost his seat, his back and rump crashing into the high-backed saddle as his war horse made its own fighting decisions and leaped forward, bearing down the monster again with weight and momentum, so that the creature's stumble was more off balance and the horse landed two more blows with its steel-shod forefeet, forcing the creature onto all fours. It roared with pain as it put weight on the broken limb.

And then the grass was full of boglins thrusting their stone-tipped spears at him, and some of them scoring hits. The deerskin of his padded jupon turned a few and the damp sheep's wool stuffing turned others, but at least one punched straight through and into his skin. Unthinking, he touched his spurs to Archangel and the great horse responded with a mighty leap forward, and then they were running free.

Gawin turned him in a wide circle. He couldn't see from his left eye, and the pain in his side was so great that he could scarcely feel it—or anything else.

I want that thing, he thought. *Let them take that head back to Harndon and show it to the king, and I will be content.*

He got Archangel around. The horse had at least two wounds—both from javelins. But like his rider he was trained to fight hurt, and went at his prey with all the spirit he could have asked.

But the monster was running—weight forward, low to the ground, only three legs working, a dozen boglins gathered tight around it in the strong sunlight, as they fled into the trees.

Gawin reined up—surprised at himself. Death lay waiting in those trees. But it was one thing to fight to the death out here under the sun, and another to follow the Wild into the waiting trees and die alone—and for nothing. He reined up, and looked at the litter of broken boglins, and his view of them suddenly narrowed—he tasted salt in his mouth, and copper, and—

Lorica—Ser Gaston

Lorica again.

Gaston spat the foreign name as he watched the grey stone walls approach. He flicked a look at his cousin, who was riding serenely at his side.

"We are going to be arrested," Gaston said.

Jean made a face. "For what?" he asked. He laughed, and at the silvery peel of his laughter, other men smiled all down the column. Their contingent was third; first the king's household, then the Earl of Towbray's, and then theirs. They had more knights than the king and the earl together.

"We killed the two squires. I locked the sheriff in a shed. You burned the inn." Gaston winced as he said the last. Ten days in Alba and he was beginning to appreciate just how poor their behaviour had been.

Jean shrugged. "No one of worth was involved except the knight," he said. His voice rode the edge of a sneer. "And he has chosen not to take exception. He has shown especial wisdom in this, I think."

"Nonetheless, the king will learn exactly what happened in the next hour or so," Gaston said.

Jean de Vrailly gave his cousin a sad smile. "My friend, you have much to learn of the workings of the world. If we were in the least danger, my angel would have told me. And it seems to me that our knights make up the best part of this column—bigger, better men in superb armour on fine horses. We can always fight. And if we fight, we will win." De Vrailly shrugged again. "You see? Simple."

Gaston considered taking his own men and riding away.

The captain rode through the postern gate of the Bridge Castle with no one but Michael, also mailed and armed. They'd ridden out of the upper postern of the fortress with a minimum of fuss—two men-at-arms on detail. But the captain rode fast and hard down the ridge because the sky was full of crows to the west. He noted there wasn't a bird to be seen over the fortress or the castle.

He dismounted in the Bridge Castle courtyard, where big merchant wagons were parked hub-to-hub leaving just room for a sortie to form up. As the captain looked around he realised that all the wagons were occupied. The merchants were living in them. No wonder Ser Milus said he had room. Over by the main tower, dogs whined and barked—four brace of good hounds. He stopped and let them smell him. Dogs made him smile with their enthusiastic approval. All dogs liked him.

Cleg, Ser Milus's valet, came and led him into the main tower, where the garrison had their quarters on the ground floor—plenty of paliasses of new straw, with six local women and another half-dozen company trulls sitting on the floor and sewing. They were making mattresses—there were twenty ells of striped sacking already measured and cut, as the captain had seen done in a dozen countries. Clean sacks made good mattresses while dirty linen spread disease—any soldier knew it.

The women rose to their feet and curtsied.

The captain bowed. "Don't let me disturb you, ladies."

Ser Milus took his hand and a pair of archers—older, steady men, Jack Kaves and Smoke, pushed the merchants away. Three of them were waving scrolls.

"I protest!" the taller man called. "My dogs—"

"I'll take you to law for this!" called a stout man.

The captain ignored them and went up a set of tight steps to the uppermost floor, where tents had been used to partition the tower into sleeping quarters for officers.

Ser Jehannes nodded curtly to the captain. He nodded back.

"Ready to move back up the hill?" the captain said.

Jehannes nodded. "Do I owe an apology?"

The captain lowered his voice. "I pissed you off, and you sulked about it. I need you. I need you at the fortress, giving orders, kicking arses and taking names."

Jehannes nodded. "I'll go back up with you." He looked over to Gelfred, and indicated the huntsman with a nod. "It's bad."

"No one ever summons me for good news." The captain was relieved that he hadn't lost his most senior man forever, and clapped the man on the back hoping it was the right gesture. "I'm sorry," he said.

Jehannes paused. "I am also sorry," he said. "I am differently made to you, and I lack your certainty." He shrugged. "How is Bent doing?"

"Very well indeed." Bent was the archer in Ser Jehannes's lance—and also the most senior archer in the fortress.

"I'll send you Ser Brutus," the captain said to Milus, who grinned.

"You mean you're trading me the best knight in the company for a kid with an archer he can't control?" He laughed. "Never mind—Jehannes outranked me and never did any work anyway."

The captain thought—not for the first time—how sensitive his mercenaries were. Jehannes had chosen to go to the castle garrison as a mere man-at-arms rather than go to the fortress with the captain, because he was angry. And everyone knew it, because there was no privacy, in a camp or in a garrison. And now that he and the captain had made it up everyone was very gentle about it. The teasing would start later. The captain thought it remarkable that such men had so much tact, but they did.

Gelfred was waiting, and from his expression, he was about to explode.

The captain went into his "room" and sat at the low camp table on a leather stool. Gelfred beckoned to the other two officers, and both came in. Jehannes paused in the doorway and spoke to someone just outside the tent flap wall. "Clear this floor," he said.

They heard men grumbling, and then Marcus, Jehannes's squire, said in his guttural accent, "All clear, sers."

Gelfred looked around. "Not sure where to start."

"How about the beginning? And with a cup of wine?" The captain tried to be light hearted, but the others looked too serious.

"The merchants came in—two of them had animals." Gelfred shrugged. "I'm telling this badly. Two of them had a dozen good falcons and some dogs. I took the liberty of securing them. Aye?"

A dozen good falcons and some hunting dogs would be worth a fortune. No wonder the merchants were so incensed.

"Go on," the captain said.

"Today is the first morning I've been here." Gelfred cleared his throat. "I've been in the woods."

"You did a beautiful job," the captain said. "Tom hit their camp just right—didn't even see a guard."

Gelfred smiled at the praise. "Thanks. Anyway. Starting this morning, I—" He looked at Ser Milus. "I started flying the hawks against the birds— those that watch the castle." He shrugged. "I know this sounds lame—"

"Not at all," said the captain.

Gelfred breathed a sigh of relief. "I was afraid you'd think me mad. Will you trust that I can see—I can *see*—that some of the animals are servants of the Enemy?" He whispered the last part.

The captain nodded. "Yes. I believe it. Go on."

Jehannes shook his head. "It sounds blasphemous to me," he said.

Gelfred put his hands on his hips in exasperation. "I have a licence from the *Bishop*," he said.

The captain shrugged. "Get on with it, Gelfred."

Gelfred brought out a game bag. It was stiff with blood, but then game bags generally were.

He extracted a dove—a very large specimen indeed—laid it on the camp table, and stretched out its wings.

"The gyrfalcon took it down about two hours ago," he said. "No other bird we have is big enough."

The captain was staring at the message tube on the bird's leg.

Gelfred nodded. "It came *out* of the abbey, Captain," he said.

Milus handed him a tiny scroll no larger than his smallest finger. "Low Archaic," he said. "Has to limit the suspects."

The captain ran his eyes over the writing. Neat, precise, and utterly damning—a list of knights, men-at-arms and archers; numbers, stores and defences. But no description. Nothing with which to catch a spy.

"Limit the suspects in a convent?" the captain said bitterly. "A hundred women, *every one of whom can read and write low Archaic*." And use power.

One of whom he knew was an Outwaller.

Gelfred nodded. "We have a traitor," he said, and the captain's heart sank.

The captain leaned his head on his hand. "This is why you needed to meet me here," he said.

Gelfred nodded. "The traitor isn't here," he said. "The traitor is in the fortress."

The captain nodded for a while, the way a man will when he's just heard bad news and can't really take it all in. "Someone killed the Jack in the woods," he said. His eyes met Gelfred's. "Someone stabbed Sister Hawisia in the back."

Gelfred nodded. "Yes, my lord. Those are my thoughts, as well."

"Someone co-operated with a daemon to murder a nun." The captain scratched under his beard. "Even by my standards, that's pretty bad."

No one smiled.

The captain got to his feet. "I'd like to have you hunt our traitor down, but I need you out in the woods," he said. "And it is going to get worse and worse out there."

Gelfred smiled. "I like it." He looked around. "Better than in here, anyway."

Lorica—Ser Gaston

Outside the town, a deputation of ten wagons full of forage, four local knights, and the town's sheriff waited under the Royal Oak. The king rode up and embraced the sheriff, and the king's constable accepted the four young knights and swore them to their duty. The quartermaster took charge of the wagons.

The sheriff was midway through telling the king of the burning of the Two Lions when he turned white, then red.

"But that is the man!" he said. "Your Grace! *That* is the man who ordered the inn burned!" He pointed at de Vrailly.

De Vrailly shrugged. "Do I know you, ser?" he asked, and rode to the king, the sheriff, and the other member's of the Royal Household gathered under the great tree.

The sheriff sputtered. "You— Your Grace, *this* is the miscreant who ordered the inn burned! Who allowed the innkeeper to be beaten, a loyal man and a good—"

De Vrailly shook his head mildly. "You call *me* a miscreant?"

The king put his hand on de Vrailly's bridle. "Hold hard, my lord. I must hear this accusation." The king glared at his sheriff. "However baseless it is."

"Baseless?" the sheriff shouted.

De Vrailly smiled. "Your Grace it is true. My squires kicked the worthless *paysant* and burned his inn as a lesson for his insolence." He raised his left eyebrow just a hair—his beautiful nostrils flared, and his lips thinned.

The king took a deep breath. Gaston watched him very carefully. He had already loosened the sword at his hip in its sheath. Not even de Vrailly would get away this time. The king's justice could not be seen as weak in front of his own people, his vassals and his officers.

De Vrailly is insane, Gaston thought to himself.

"Ser knight, you must explain yourself," the king said.

De Vrailly raised both eyebrows. "I am a lord, and I have the High Justice, the Middle Justice, and the Low Justice right here in my scabbard. I need no man's leave to take a life. I have burned more peasants' cots than a boy has pulled the wings off flies." De Vrailly shook his head. "Take my word, your Grace: the man received due payment for his foolishness. Let us hear no more about it."

The sheriff put his hands on the pommel of his saddle as if to steady himself. "I have never heard the like of this. Listen, your Grace—this pompous foreigner, this so-called knight, also killed two squires of Ser Gawin Murien, and then, when I approached him, had me beaten. I was thrown into a shed, tied and bound. When I was rescued, I found the inn burned."

Gaston pushed his horse into the angry group. "Your words in no way prove my lord's guilt," he insisted. "You did not witness any of these things, yet now pronounce them truth."

"You were the one who hit me!" the sheriff said.

Gaston had to restrain himself from shrugging. *You are an ineffective, useless man and a shame on your king—and you were in my way.* But he smiled, glanced at the king, and offered his hand. "For that I apologise.

My cousin and I were newly landed, and failed to understand the laws of these parts."

The king was firmly in the cleft stick of conflicting emotions, goals and needs—his indecision showed clearly on his face. He needed Jean de Vrailly's three hundred knights and he needed to be seen to give justice. Gaston willed the sheriff to take his hand and clasp it. He *willed* it, and so did the king.

"Messire, my cousin and I have joined the king to ride against the Wild." Gaston's voice was low, urgent and yet soothing. "I *beg* your forgiveness before we go into battle."

Gaston prayed that the king wasn't looking at his cousin, whose expression at the word *beg* would have curdled milk.

The sheriff sniffed.

The king's shoulders began to relax.

Almost as if against his will, the sheriff of Lorica took Gaston's hand and clasped it. He left his glove on, which was rude enough, and he didn't meet Gaston's eye.

But the king seized the moment. "You will pay reparations to the town and to the innkeeper," he said. "The sum to be the full value of the inn and all of its goods and chattels. The sheriff will investigate the value and send a writ." The king turned in his saddle to address the Captal de Ruth. "You, who have announced your willingness to serve me, will first serve my sentence on this: your wages and those of all of your knights will be paid, in lieu of fine, to the innkeeper and to the town until the value set by the sheriff has been discharged."

Jean de Vrailly sat on his horse, his beautiful face still and peaceful. Only Gaston knew he was considering killing the king.

"We—" he began, and the king turned in his saddle, showing some of the flexibility he had showed jousting.

"Let the captal speak for himself," the king said. "You are glib in your cousin's defence, my lord. But I must hear him speak his acceptance for himself."

Gaston thought, *He is very good at this. He has understood my cousin better than most men, and he has found a way to punish him while keeping him close and using his prowess against his enemies. Jean and his angel will not dominate this king in an afternoon.* Outwardly, he bowed.

And glared at Jean.

Jean bowed as well. "I came to fight your enemies, your Grace," he said in his charming accent. "At my own expense. This *ordinance* makes little difference to me."

Gaston winced.

The king looked around him, gathering eyes, gathering the opinions men cast with their body language, in subtle facial expressions, in the fretting of their horses. He pushed his tongue against his teeth—which Gaston had already come to read as a tic of frustration.

"That is not sufficient," the king said.

De Vrailly shrugged. "You wish me to say that I accept your law and your writ?" he said, and contempt dripped from every word.

Here we go, Gaston thought.

The Earl of Towbray pushed his horse between the king and the captal. "This," he said, "is my fault."

Both the king and de Vrailly looked at him as if he'd come between them in the lists.

"I invited the Captal to Alba to serve me, and I failed—even after a youth spent fighting on the Continent—to understand how he would see us." The earl shrugged. "I will bear the cost, for my mistake."

De Vrailly had the good grace to appear surprised. "But—no!" he said suddenly. "But I insist! I must bear it."

The king was looking at the Earl of Towbray the way a man might look at a rare flower suddenly discovered on a dung hill.

Gaston remembered to breathe.

And in moments men were chattering with relief, the convoy was forming up, and Gaston could ride to his cousin's side.

"This is *not* what the angel told me would happen," he said.

Gaston raised an eyebrow.

De Vrailly shrugged. "But it will suffice. It irks me, cousin, to hear you crawl to a creature like that *sheriff*. You must avoid such things, lest they form a habit."

Gaston sat still for a moment, and then leaned forward. "It irks me, cousin, to hear you put on airs before the King of Alba. But I assume you cannot help yourself." He turned, and rode back to his own retinue, and left Jean to ride by himself.

West of Lissen Carak—Thorn

Thorn was dimly conscious of his body while he sat beneath the giant holm-oak and reached out over the sea of trees. He was aware of himself at the centre; of the fear and anger from the Jacks; the restive arrogance of the qwethnethogs; the mourning of the winged abnethogs; the distant presence that heralded the arrival of the Sossag people from the north, across the wall. He was aware of every tree past its tenth season; of the large patches of iris flowers; of the wild asparagus growing by the river where a man had built a cottage a century before; of the cattle that his raiders had taken to feed the Jacks; of the tuft-eared lynx that was both terrified and angered to have his army camped in its territory, and of the thousand other presences rolling away to the limits of his *kenning*.

He sympathised with the lynx. Unknowable, powerful creatures with filthy thoughts and polluted bodies, dirty with fear and hate, had come to his woods and fired his camp, terrifying his allies, destroying his trees and making him seem weak. The greater qwethnethogs would question whether he was worthy of service—the very strongest might even waste themselves and their energy on a challenge for mastery.

It was difficult for a Power of the Wild to have trusted lieutenants. But he would continue to attempt such relationships, for the good of the Wild and their cause.

He rose from beneath his tree and walked into camp, scattering lesser creatures and frightening the Jacks. He walked west, to the handful of golden bears who had allied themselves with him and had made huts of brush and leaves. He nodded to Blueberry, a huge bear with blue eyes.

The bear rose on his haunches. "Thorn," he said. The bears were afraid of nothing, not even him.

"Blueberry," Thorn said. "I wish to recruit more of your people. Let me have the child and I will take it to the ice caves."

Blueberry thought for a moment. "Yes," he said. "Better food, and females. Well thought." Sunset, the largest of the bears, brought the cub. She was small enough for Thorn to carry easily and mewed at him when he took her. He stroked her fur, and she bit at him, tasted his odd flesh, and sneezed.

He left the bears without another word and started north. When he stretched his legs, he moved faster than a galloping horse, and he could travel that fast for as long as he wished. He cradled the little bear and moved faster still.

Before the sun had dipped a finger's breadth, he was too far from his camp to hear the thoughts of his allies, or to smell the fires of the men who had chosen to serve him. He crossed a series of beaver meadows, enjoying their health, feeling the trout in the streams and the otters in the banks, and he crossed a big stream flowing south from the Adnacrags. There he turned and followed the banks north, into the mountains. Leagues flew by. Thorn drew power from the hills, valleys, water, and the trees. He drew more than power.

He drew inspiration.

War was not his choice. It had been an accident. But if he had to make war now, he needed to remind himself *why*. He would make war for this. For the wilderness. To keep it clean.

And, of course, for himself. He was growing more powerful with every creature which chose to come and follow him.

The stream began to climb, faster and faster—up a great ridge, and then down, and then up again. He was in the foothills now, and his passage was like a strong wind in the trees. Deer looked up startled. Afraid.

Birds fled.

He knew the valley he wanted—the valley of the creek that the Sossag called the Black, that flowed from the ice caves under the mountains. It was a special place, almost as imbued with power as the Rock.

The bears ruled it.

He climbed a steep path, almost a road, from the stream to the top of the ridge, and waited. He was fifty leagues from his army. He set the bear on the ground and waited.

The sun began to set behind him and he let his mind wander, wondered if the enemy would try to raid his camp again. It occurred to him, now that he was far from the problem, that the enemy captain must have someone watching his camp. *Of course.* How else would he have known where to attack. *He must be using animals as spies.*

It was suprising how much clarity he could achieve when he was not bombarded with the chaos of other creatures.

"Thorn."

The speaker was old, a bear who had lived more then a century. He was called Flint, and he was acknowledged as a Power. He stood almost as tall as Thorn, and while he had white at his ears and muzzle, his body was strong and firm as a new apple in fall.

"Flint."

The old bear reached out and the little bear ran to him.

"Her mother was enslaved and tortured by men," Thorn said. "To be fair, she was then rescued by other men, and brought to Blueberry at my camp."

"Men," said Flint. Thorn could feel the old bear's anger, and his power.

"I have burned Albinkirk," Thorn said, and realised what a pointless boast it was. Flint would know.

"With stars from the sky," Flint said. His deep voice was like the sound of a rasp cutting into hardwood.

"I have come to ask—" Faced with Flint, it was suddenly difficult to explain. Bears were well known for their complete contempt for organisation. For government. Rules. War. Bears would kill when roused. But war repelled them.

"Do not ask," Flint said.

"What I do—" Thorn began.

"Has nothing to do with bears," Flint said. He nodded. "This is the cub of Sunbeam, of the Clan of the Long Dam. Sunbeam's brother will no doubt come and avenge her." The old bear said this with obvious sadness. "As will his friends." Flint picked up the cub. "They are young, and understand nothing. I am old. I see you, Thorn. I know you." He turned his back and walked away.

All at once Thorn wanted to chase down the old bear and sit at his feet. Learn. Or protest his—not his innocence, but his intentions.

But another part of him wanted to turn the old bear to ash.

It was a long walk back to camp.

Sister Miram was missing her favourite linen cap, and she took the moments between study of High Archaic and Nones to visit the laundry. She raced down the steps of the north tower—for a large woman, she was very fast—but then a flash of intuition made her pause at the door to the laundry. Six sisters laboured away, their hands and faces red, stripped to their shifts in the heat of the room. A dozen local girls worked with them.

Lis Wainwright was also stripped to her shift. Forty years had not ruined her figure. Miram might have smiled, but she didn't. Beyond Lis were younger girls. Miram knew them all—had taught them. The Carters and the Lanthorns. The Lanthorn girls were simpering. There wasn't usually a lot of simpering in the laundry.

A hundred nuns and novices generated a great deal of laundry. The addition of four hundred farmers, their families, and two hundred professional soldiers, forced the laundry to boil linen day and night. The drying lines were stretched at every hour, and even senior sisters like Sister Miram received their linens slightly damp and badly ironed. Or left them missing things like caps.

She looked around for Sister Mary, whose week it was to run the laundry, and heard a man's voice. It was a cultured voice, singing.

She listened intently. Singing a Gallish romance.

She couldn't see him, but she could see the four Lanthorn girls in their shifts, giggling, preening and showing a great deal of leg and shoulder.

Miram's eyes narrowed. The Lanthorn girls were what they were, but they didn't need some smooth-talking *gentleman* to encourage them on their road to hell. Miram strode across the damp floor and there he was, leaning in the laundry door. He had a lute, and he was not alone.

"Your name, messire?" she asked. She had pounced so swiftly that he was locked in indecision—keep playing, or flee?

"Lyliard, ma soeur," he said sweetly.

"You are a knight, messire?" she asked.

He bowed.

"None of these four unmarried maidens is of noble birth, messire. And while it may suit you to bed them, their pregnancies and their unwed lives will weigh heavily on my convent, my sisters, and your soul." She smiled. "I hope we understand each other."

Lyliard looked as if he'd been hit by a wyvern. "Ma soeur!"

"You look like a squire," Sister Miram said to the young man at Lyliard's elbow. He also had a lute and while he lacked Lyliard's dash and polish Miram's opinion was he'd get there in time. And he was handsome, in a raffish, muscular way.

"John of Reigate, sister." He was young enough to drop his eyes and look like a schoolboy caught out in a lark. Which he was. She had to remember that they killed for a living, but they were still people.

The third man was the handsomest. He had polish *and* good looks. And he blushed.

"And you are the captain's squire," she said.

He shrugged. "Unfair. My fame proceeds me."

"Don't ape your master," Miram said. "The three of you, gently born, should be ashamed of yourselves. Now go."

Lyliard looked abashed. "Listen, sister, we merely crave some female company. We are not bad men."

She sniffed. "Do you mean you would pay for what you take?" She looked at all three of them. "You seduce innocents instead of committing out and out rape? Is that supposed to impress me?"

The captain's squire sniffed. His left hand patted the bandage around his waist. "You really have no idea who or what we are. What we face."

Miram caught his eye and stepped very close, close as a lover. Almost nose to nose. His eyes were blue, and she had once been a woman to enjoy handsome men.

Hers were a deep, old green.

"I know, young squire," she said. *"I know exactly* what you face." She didn't blink and he couldn't tear his gaze away from her. "Save your posturing for whores, *boy.* Now go and say twenty Pater Nosters, mean them, and think about what it might mean to be a knight."

Michael would have liked to have stood his ground, but the moment her regard dropped away, he stumbled a step.

She smiled at the three of them, and they backed away from the door.

Sister Miram went back into the laundry, where the Lanthorn girls were huddling, terrified, and trying to cover their bare legs.

Sister Mary came in, carrying a huge basket. "Miram!" she called out. "What's amiss?"

"The usual," Miram said. And started searching for her missing cap.

North of Lissen Carak—Thorn

Thorn felt bitten by the old bear's disdain. His walk back was full of thoughts about how the men in the Rock had, apparently, inflicted two defeats on him. He had to face the hard truth; to the irks and boglins and even to the daemons, these little fiery pinpricks were defeats.

He didn't really think that either of his lieutenants would challenge him, and he reached out more and more to the east as he walked, until he could feel the intense *wrongness* of the invaders. They were not like the peasants, the nuns, and the shepherds in the fortress. They smelt of violence.

He had always hated their kind, even when he walked among them as a man.

Also in the fortress, surrounded by all that cold stone worked by man, the enchantments an aeon old and proof against all but his strongest enchantment, he could feel the Abbess, a sun of power, with her nuns a star field behind her.

He flinched away from her.

And the tendrils of his questing power saw another, darker sun—the beacon that the daemons had seen—that Thurkan, the sharpest of the daemons, had seen and avoided. The shielded one, who had resisted, however briefly, his workings on the battlefield.

The bears hadn't refused him, precisely. But nor were they helping him with any force but a few angry warriors bent on revenge. He drew deep breath of clean air and turned north, back into the mountains, and lengthened his stride until he was all but running, his giant body now moving faster than the fastest horse. He could get where he wanted to with a phantasm, but he was suddenly wary of using too much power. Power attracted other power, and in the Wild, that could spell a quick end—all too often, something bigger than you arrived unexpectedly. And ate you.

Even as he ran the forest highways, Thorn contemplated eating Turkan.

Lissen Carak—Kaitlin

The four Lanthorn girls were quick to recover from Sister Miram, and the afternoon found them coring winter apples behind the kitchens. There were no sisters and no novices.

The eldest Lanthorn girl was Elissa. She was dark haired, as tall as a man, thin, with long legs and very little figure and a nose like a hawk. Despite this men found her irresistible, mostly because she smiled a great deal and was selective in her use of the family's principle weapon: a sharp tongue.

Mary was the second daughter. She was the very opposite of her elder sister; short, but not squat, with a full figure, guinea gold hair, a narrow waist and a snub nose. She thought herself a great beauty and was always puzzled when boys preferred Elissa.

Fran was brown haired, full-lipped and full hipped. She had her mother's looks, her father's brains and sense of honesty, and she seldom cared whether boys noticed her or not.

And Kaitlin was the youngest: just fifteen. She was not as tall as Elissa, not as full-figured as Mary, nor yet as witty, or as cutting, as Fran. She had pale brown hair that framed a heart-shaped face, and she appeared to be the quietest and most respectable of the Lanthorns.

"Bitch," Fran said, tossing a core aside. "She thinks we're going to be good little girls with pig shit on our feet for the rest of our lives."

Elissa looked around carefully. "We have to play this right," she said thoughtfully. She ate a slice of apple, deftly taking a knife from beneath her kirtle, cutting a slice, wiping the knife on her apron and putting back in her sheath faster than most people could follow. She looked down her long nose at Fran. "I hearby convene a meeting of the 'Marry a Noble' club."

"Silly kids' nonsense," Mary scoffed. She was eighteen. "No one around here is going to marry any of us." She flicked her eyes around the circle. "Maybe Kaitlin," she admitted.

Fran tossed an apple core viciously into the sty behind them. "If *some people* would stop making the beast with two backs with every farm boy in every blessed hay stack—"

Elissa's smile didn't even thin. "Ahh, Fran, you'll go a virgin to your wedding, won't ya?" She snorted.

Fran's next apple core hit Elissa in the nose and she hissed.

Mary shrugged. "Scarcely matters if I bed 'em or don't," she said, "seeing they say I did, and folks believe 'em."

The others nodded.

Elissa shrugged. "Listen, the men-at-arms don't talk to the farmers. They don't know *shit* about our lives. And even the archers—" She shrugged. "The archers have more money than any *farm boy* in this place. The men-at-arms—"

"They ain't all gents," Mary said. "I wouldn't touch that Bad Tom if I had armour on."

Fran shrugged. "I rather like him."

"You're dumber than I thought then. Aren't you supposed to be the smartest, fastest one? He gives me the creeps." Mary shivered.

Elissa raised a hand for silence. "That's as may be. What I'm saying is that we—" She looked around. "We have something. Of value." She smiled. The smile lit her face and turned her from a square jawed young harridan into a very attractive woman. Mary turned and saw that Elissa's smile was for a middle-aged squire just walking past the kitchen with a pail of ash. Off to polish armour somewhere.

Elissa folded up her smile and put it away. "There's sixty men-at-arms," she said. "Sixty chances one of them might marry one of us."

Mary snorted.

But Fran leaned forward, the apple in her hand forgotten. "You might have something there," she said.

Elissa and Fran weren't usually allies. But Elissa met her look and both smiled.

"So we don't," Elissa said. "We just don't. That's all you have to do, girls. *Don't.* Let's see what we're offered."

Mary wasn't so sure. "So what. We don't bed them? What else do we do? You're planning to learn to shoot a bow? Go to Mag and take up fine sewing?"

Elissa shook her head.

"Lis won't stop opening her legs for any likely lad," Mary said.

"Lis can do as she likes. She's old and we're not." Fran looked around. "Captain's not bad looking."

Elissa made a crude noise. "He's doing one of the nuns."

"He ain't!" said Kaitlin. She'd been silent thus far, but some things couldn't be allowed to pass.

"Oh, you're an expert, are ya?" asked Mary.

"I clean his room," Kaitlin said. She blushed. "Sometimes."

Elissa looked at her. "You, young maiden, are a dark horse."

"I ain't!" Kaitlin said, prepared for their mockery.

"You go right in his room?" Elissa asked.

"Almost every day." Kaitlin looked around. "What?"

Elissa shrugged. "One of us could be in his bed."

Kaitlin put a hand to her mouth. Mary spat. Fran, frankly, looked as if she was considering it.

"Too desperate," Fran pronounced. "He's scary, too."

"Creepy," said Mary.

"His squire's pretty as a picture," Elissa said.

Kaitlin blushed. Luckily the rest weren't watching.

North-west of Lissen Carak—Thorn

Thorn needed to know more. He needed his friend in the Rock to be less coy. Thorn summoned birds from the air even as he ran through the woods in the failing light. Now he was climbing ridges. The descent on the north side was never as steep as the ascent had been, and he was going higher and higher into the mountains. The trees thinned, and he moved faster as the land opened up.

A pair of ravens descended to his fists as if they were hawks to a knight. He spoke to them, planted messages in their wise heads, and sent them to the fortress. No one ever suspected ravens. They rose above him and then soared away to the south-east, and he turned and saw how very high he had come.

He looked out over the wilderness. At his feet—far, far below—was the chain of beaver ponds like miniature lakes sparkling in the last of the sun. The stream that connected them was a thread of silver, visible here and there in the warp and weft of trees.

He turned and climbed higher. The trail was steeper now, and he was not so fast. He had to use his long, powerful arms to pull himself from tree to tree. The stream began to descend in a series of waterfalls at his side.

Finally, he pulled himself over a slick rock and raised himself by main force to the top, his arms spread wide, grunting with effort as they lifted the full weight of his giant body. At his feet was a pool, deep and black, and a waterfall dropped a hundred feet into it. The spray coated him in moments. He stooped and drank deep of the magic pool.

A head broke the surface, just an arm's length away, and he started.

Who drinks in my pool?

The words appeared in his mind without a sound being spoken.

"I am called Thorn," he said.

The creature rose from the pool, black water flowing from him. As he moved up the side of the pool he grew and grew. His skin was jet-black and shone like obsidian.

He moved fast yet appeared to be perfectly still; the transitions were difficult to catch, movement always seemed to happen at the corner of Thorn's eye. And when the creature fully emerged, he was a quarter taller than the sorcerer.

A shining black stone golem, with no face, no eyes, no mouth.

I do not know you.

"I know a little of you," Thorn said. "I know that I need allies. Your kind are said to be fearsome warriors."

I can feel your power. It is considerable.

"I can see your speed and strength. They, too, are considerable." Thorn nodded.

Enough talk. What do you WANT?

The mind shout almost brought Thorn to his knees. "I want a dozen of your kind as my guards. As soldiers."

The smooth monster threw back his head and laughed, and suddenly there was a mouth after all, with cruel teeth. The stone of his face—if it was stone—seemed to flow like water. *We serve no one.*

Thorn would have smiled if he still had the ability to. Instead, he simply cast his binding. Simultaneously, he shielded his mind from the shout that was sure to follow.

The troll stiffened. He screamed, and his teeth clashed like rocks in a flooded stream, and his smooth arms grew hands and talons that reached for Thorn.

The sorcerer didn't stir. The net of his will settled in sparkling green strands over the creature and tightened, and that quickly it was over.

I will slay you and all your kind in ways too horrible for your mind to encompass.

Thorn turned. "No you will not," he said. "Now, obey. We have more of your kind to find, and a long night ahead of us."

The troll thrashed in his binding like a wolf in a cage. He screamed, his bell-like voice ringing across the wilderness.

Thorn shook his head minutely. "Obey," he said again, and pushed a little more of his will into the binding.

The monster resisted, showing—or growing—wicked black in a black mouth. His whole body stretched for Thorn.

To Thorn, it was like arm wrestling with a child. A strong child—but a child nonetheless. He slammed his will down on the troll's, and it crumbled.

That was the way of the Wild.

The other trolls weren't hard to find, and the second was considerably easier to *press* than the first had been...but the seventh was much harder than the sixth, and by the time the sun had set he had a tail of mighty trolls and that sense a man gets when he has lifted so much weight that he can no longer lift his arms.

He sat in a narrow gully, and listened to the wind while his blank-faced trolls crouched all around him.

After some time, as the sun began to slip beneath the rim of the world and he felt better, he reached out a tendril of his power toward the dark sun in the distant fortress.

And he recoiled from what he found, because—

Lissen Carak—The Red Knight

The captain was leaning on the wall, the curtain wall that covered the outer gate. He'd walked here almost without volition, because the confines of the Commandery were suddenly too close and airless.

He'd written her a note. Because he was not fifteen he had written one, not ten of them, and he'd placed it in the crotch of the old apple tree. And then, after cursing himself for waiting and hoping she might appear by some sympathetic magic, he'd walked to the wall for some air.

The stars burned in the distant heavens, and there were fires in the Bridge Castle courtyard below him. The Lower Town at the foot of the ridge was empty—a skeleton guard held it and no more. And there was no light.

He looked out at the darkness—the Wild was as dark as the sea.

Something was looking for him. At first it was a prickle in his hair, and then a presentiment of doom, and then, suddenly, he'd never felt so vulnerable in all his life, and he crouched on the battlement fighting a particularly awful childhood memory.

When it didn't relent, didn't let up, he took a deep breath and forced himself to his feet. He turned and made himself walk, despite the crushing fear, up the steps set into the wall to the first tower. The second step was so hard he had to use his hands on the fourth and fifth—by the eighth he was crawling. He pushed, made a sword of his will, and pushed through. The feeling relaxed like the grip of an unwelcome suitor as soon as he entered the stone structure.

Bent leaped to his feet, a deck of painted cards in his hand. "Captain!" he shouted, and a dozen archers leaped to their feet and snapped their salutes.

The captain glanced around. "At ease," he said. "Who's on the walls?"

"Acrobat," Bent answered. "Half-Arse on the main curtain, Ser Guillam Longsword and Snot commanding the towers with the engines. Watch changes in a glass."

"Double up," the captain ordered. He wanted to apologise—*Sorry, boys, I have a creepy feeling, so I'm costing a lot of you a night's sleep.* But he'd learned not to apologise when he gave an unpopular order, much less over-explain it. And the successful raid had given him credit in the hard currency of leadership—no commander is ever much better than his last performance.

Bent grimaced, but he started lacing up his embroidered leather jack. Like many of the other veterans, Bent wore his fortune on his body—a subtle brag, a statement of his worth, a willingness to see that fortune taken by his killer. The dark-skinned man looked around, and like true soldiers his fellow gamblers avoided his eye.

"Hetty, Crank, Larkin, with me. Hetty, if you don't want the duty, don't be so obvious about sneaking to the jakes." Bent glared at the youngest man in the tower room and then turned back to the captain. "That sufficient, m'lord?"

The captain didn't know Bent very well—he was Ser Jehannes's man—but he was impressed that his most senior archer would take the trick on the wall himself. "Carry on," he said coldly, and walked across the room surveying the piles of coins on the tables, and the dice and cards, as he did. He was pretty sure Ser Hugo would never have allowed such overt gambling. So he scratched his beard and beckoned to Bent.

The archer came up like a dog expecting a kick.

The captain pointed at the money on the main table. He didn't say a thing.

Bent raised an eyebrow and opened his mouth.

"Save it," the captain said. "Remind me of the company rule on gambling."

Bent made a face. "Total value of the game not to exceed a day's pay for the lowest man," he recited.

Two rose nobles gleamed up at the captain, with more than a dozen silver leopards and a pile of copper cats by them. The captain put his hand over the pile. "Must be mine then," he said, "I'm the only man in the company who makes this kind of money every day."

Bent swallowed but his eyes narrowed in anger.

The captain lifted his hand, leaving the pile untouched. He locked eyes with the archer and smiled. "You get me, Bent?"

The archer all but sighed with relief. "Aye, Captain."

The captain nodded. "Good night, Bent," he said, and touched the man's shoulder, to say, *And over is over, unless you dick up.* He'd learned from experts, and he wanted to believe he was doing the captain thing well.

He walked out onto the wall, and there it was again—not the fear, but the feeling he was being watched. Scrutinized. He was ready for it this time, and he reached into the round room, and—

—there was Prudentia.

"He is looking for you," she said. "His name is Thorn. A Power of the Wild. Do you remember how to avoid being found?"

He stopped to kiss her hand.

"How do you know it is this Thorn?" he asked.

"He has a signature, and he has cast many times tonight, gathering allies. If you would pay attention to the Aethereal, instead of dabbling—"

He smiled. "I'm not interested. Too much like hard work."

The door was open a crack. He often left it that way to give himself fast access to power, and tonight he could feel that searching presence through the crack in the door—more powerfully, if anything, than he had felt it on the wall.

Of course.

He continued past Prudentia and pushed the door firmly shut. The heavy iron latch fell into place with a comforting click.

North-west of Lissen Carak—Thorn

—the dark sun went out like a torch thrown into a pool.

He was disoriented, at first. The dark sun had dimmed and strengthened, dimmed and strengthened, and years of patient growth of power had taught him not to read too much into the fluctuations in power wrought by distance, weather, old phantasms that lingered like ghosts of their former powers, or animals who used power the way bats used sound. There were thousands of natural factors that occluded power the way other factors might affect sound.

In fact, he thought that the use of power and the movement of sound might usefully be studied together. The thought pleased him, and he spun off a part of himself to contemplate the movement of sound over distance as an allegory—or even as a direct expression—of power. Meanwhile, he sat and breathed in the night air and maintained, almost without effort, the chains of power that bound the trolls, and a third part of him looked for the dark sun with increasing frustration.

A fourth aspect considered his next move.

The conflict at the Rock had now forced a gathering of resources and allies that involved risks and challenges he had not anticipated. If he continued gathering, he would soon reach a level that would at least appear to challenge his peers—already the mighty Wyrm of the Green Hills was awake to him, raising, as it were, a scaled green eyebrow at his speedy accumulation of power and lesser creatures, men and resources. The old bear in the mountains did not love him either. And at some future point the trolls, scarcely people and more like cruel animals as they were—would come to resent his chains and find a way to throw them off.

So might one feudal lord be alarmed—or at least deeply curious—when a neighbour called in his vassals and raised an army.

The allegory occurred to the fourth self, because the fourth self had once been a man—a man capable of raising armies.

Before he'd learned the truth.

And at another level, the fortress was obviously not going to crumple at his command. Albinkirk's outer wall had fallen so easily that he'd allowed himself to be seduced by the easy victory—but the citadel itself, full of terrified humans, was not yet under his claws and the easy conquests were over.

And whatever the dark sun was, it was powerful and dangerous, and the men of violence who surrounded it were deadly enemies who he would not underestimate again. Neither could he accept their pollution of his land, attack of his camp, or the preceeding endless cycle of challenge and counter challenge that had led him to grant a favour and confront the fortress more directly.

And where, exactly, was his professed friend in the Rock?

Enough.

He had made his choices, and they led to making war. Now he had to marshal his assets without affronting his peers, rip the fortress from the face of the world—a warning and a tale for all his foes—and grant the Rock to the Wild.

And all the while he contemplated this next move, that part of him which was enjoying the cool of night continued to avoid the golden light cast by the Abbess, as if the mere admission of her existence would be a defeat.

Twenty leagues to the south a hundred of his creatures stirred and rumbled and slept in the cold darkness, and two hundred men huddled close to their fires and posted too many sentries, and over the mountain to the north, hundreds of Sossag warriors woke and made their fires and prepared to come to his cause. And west, and north, creatures woke in their burrows, their caves, their holes and hides and homes—more irks, more boglins, and mightier creatures—a clan of daemons, a moiety of golden bears. And because power called to power, they were coming to him.

The trolls would counter the knights. The Sossag would give him more reliable scouts. The irks and boglins were his foot soldiers. By morning, he would have a force to deal with anything that humankind could offer. Then he would close his claws around the fortress.

Of course, there was irony in his trust of men, rather than creatures of the Wild, to fight other men.

With this decision his selves collapsed, one by one, back into the body under the tree, and that body stretched, sighed, and was almost like a man's.

Almost.

Kaitlin sighed, and half rolled against the figure beside her. She sighed again, and wondered why her sister had to take up so much of the bed...and then she suddenly knew where she was, and she made a noise in her throat. The man next to her turned and put a hand on her breast, and she smiled. And then moaned a little.

He licked her under her chin and kissed her, his tongue dabbing away at the corner of her mouth like a questing thing, and she laughed and threw her arms around him. She was not a slut like her sisters, and she'd never had a man in her bed before in her life, but she was not going to be bound by their sordid plans or their poor taste. She was in love.

Her lover ran his tongue across the base of her ear lobe while one lazy finger traced the line of her nipple. She laughed, and he laughed.

"I love you," Kaitlin Lanthorn said into the darkness. She had never said the words before, not even when he'd first had her maidenhead.

"And I love you, Kaitlin," Michael said, and put his mouth over hers.

Chapter Eight

North of Albinkirk—Peter

Peter the cook's first thought was *I am still a free man.*

He had walked for two days along the road east, and he hadn't seen another man. Yesterday noon he'd smelt smoke, and seen the fortress rising to the south—a fortress he had to assume was the town of Albinkirk, although his appreciation of the landscape of western Alba was virtually non-existent and he had only the comments of his captors and the mercenaries to go by.

The two traders must have travelled some way to the east, then. And he was virtually back where he'd begun.

Or he was walking in circles.

But the sight of Albinkirk, five leagues or so distant, oppressed him. It was, after all, the place they'd been taking him to be sold. So he turned up the first decent path leading north, into the mountains, and he followed it even though setting his feet to it required an act of courage and marked his first decision.

He was not going back.

He'd rid himself of his yoke. It was easier than he'd expected—given time and some large rocks, he'd simply bashed it to flinders.

Like all slaves, and many other men, he had heard that there were people who lived at peace with the Wild. Even at home, there were those who did more—

Best not to think of those people. Those who sold their souls.

He didn't want to think about it. But he went north, the axe over his shoulder, and he walked until darkness fell, passing a dozen abandoned farmsteads and stealing enough food that he couldn't easily carry more. He found a good bow, although it had no arrows and no quiver. It was odd, going into the abandoned cabins along the trail—in some, the steaders had carefully folded everything away; chests full of blankets, plate rails full of green glazed plates from over the eastern mountains, Morean plates and cups and a little pewter. He didn't bother to steal any of these, except a good horn cup he found on a chimney mantel.

In other houses, there was still food on the table, the meat rotting, the bread stale. The first time he found a meal on the table he ate it, and later he burped and burped until he threw it up.

By the twelfth cabin, he'd stopped being careful.

He went into the barn, and there was a sow. She'd been left because she was heavy, gravid, and the farmer was too soft hearted—or just too pragmatic—to try and drive her to Albinkirk in her condition.

He was wondering if he was hard-hearted enough to butcher her when he heard the barn's main door give a squeak.

He saw the Wild creature enter. It was naked, bright red, its parody of hair a shocking tongue of flame. It had an arrow on its bow, the iron tip winked with steel malevolence, and it was pointed at Peter's chest.

Peter nodded. His throat had closed. He fought down his gorge, and the shaking of his arms, and managed to say, "Hello."

The red thing wrinkled its lips as if he smelled something bad and Peter's perspective shifted. *It* was actually a man in red paint, with his hair full of some sort of red mud.

Peter turned slightly to face the man. He held up his empty hands. "I will *not* be a slave," he said.

The red man raised his head and literally looked down his nose at Peter, who shivered. The arrow, at full draw, didn't waver.

"Ti natack onah!" the red man said in a tone full of authority. A human voice.

"I don't understand," Peter said. His voice trembled. The red man was obviously a war-leader of some sort, which meant that there were others around. Whatever kind of men they were, they were not what Peter had expected. They raised his hopes, and dashed them.

"Ti natack onah!" the man said again, with increasing insistence. "TI NATACK ONAH."

Peter put his hands up in the air. "I surrender!" he said.

The red man loosed his arrow.

It passed Peter, missing him by the width of his arm, and Peter felt his bowels flip over. He crouched, his knees going out from under him, and he put his arms around himself, cursing his own weakness. *And so quickly I am a slave again.*

Behind him there was a scream.

The red man had put an arrow into the sow's head, and she twitched a few times and was dead.

Suddenly the barn was full of painted men—red, red and black, black with white handprints, black with a skull face. They were terrifying and they moved with a liquid, muscular grace that was worse than all his imaginings of the creatures of the Wild. As he watched, they butchered the sow and her unborn piglets, and he was pulled from the barn—roughly, but without malice—and the red man lit a torch from a very ordinary looking fire-kit and set fire to the shingles of the barn.

It lit off like an alchemical display, despite weeks of rain.

More of the warriors came, and then more—perhaps fifty arrived within the hour. They passed through the cabin, and when the roof fell into the raging inferno of the barn, they gathered half-burned boards into a smaller fire, and then another and another, until they had a fire that ran the length of the small cabin, and then staked the unborn piglets on green alder and some iron stakes they found in the cabin and roasted them. Other men found the underground storage cellar, and pushed dried corn into the coals, and apples—hundred of apples.

By now there were a hundred painted men and women, and darkness was falling. Most had a bow and arrows; a few had a long knife, or a sword, or even, in one case, a pair of swords. A few had long falls of hair in brilliant colours, but most had a single stripe of hair atop their heads, and another across their genitals. They looked odd to him, but it was only after his brain began to grow accustomed to them that he realised that they had no fat on their frames.

No fat.

Like slaves.

No one was watching him. He was no threat, but he was also no use. He had a dozen opportunities to run, and he went as far as the edge of the clearing, where the farmer had been hacking down trees older than his own grandfather to make room for his crops. Then he stopped, lay on the low branch of an apple tree, and watched.

Before the ruddy sun was gone from the sky, he stripped off his hose and his braes—cheap, dirty, torn cloth—and walked back among them in his shirt. A few of them had shirts of deerskin or linen, and he hoped that he was making a statement.

He still had the wallet hanging over his shoulder, and the axe.

And the bow.

He came and stood near the barn-fire, feeling the warmth, and his stomach did somersaults as he smelled the burning pig-flesh.

One of the painted people had set fire to the cabin, and there was laughter. Another painted man had burned himself stealing pinches of pig's flesh from the sow's carcass, and all the warriors around him were laughing like daemons.

If there was a signal he didn't hear it. But suddenly, they all fell on the piglets as if a dining bell had sounded, and ate. It was like watching animals eat. There were few sounds besides those of chewing, ripping flesh from bone, punctuated by the spitting out of burned bits and cartilage and the continuing sound of laughter.

If it hadn't been for the laughter, it might have been nightmarish. But the laughter was warm and human, and Peter found he had stepped closer and closer to the fires, drawn by the smell of food and the sound of laughter.

The red man was close to him. Suddenly, their eyes met, and the red man gave him the flash of a grin—almost a grimace—and waved a rib at him.

"Dodeck?" he asked. "Gaerleon?"

The other warriors close by turned and looked at Peter.

One man—taller than most, painted an oily black, with oily black hair and a single slash of red across his face—turned and grinned. "You want to eat?" he said. "Skadai asks you."

Peter took another step forward. He was intensely conscious of his legs and neck and face, naked and very different from theirs.

The red man—Skadai—waved to him. "Eat!" he said.

Another warrior laughed and said something in the alien tongue, and Skadai laughed. And the black warrior laughed too.

"Was it your pig?" the black warrior asked.

Peter shook his head. "No," he said. "I was just passing through."

The black warrior appeared to translate this to his friends, and handed him a portion of pig.

He ate it. He ate too fast, burning his hands on the skin and his tongue on the meat and fat.

The black warrior handed him a gourd that proved to be full of wine. Peter drank, sputtered and then handed it back. The burns on his hands suddenly hurt.

They were all watching him.

"I was a slave," he said suddenly. As if they could understand. "I won't be a slave again. I'd rather be dead. I won't be a slave for you." He took a deep breath. "But short of slavery, I'd like to join you."

The black warrior nodded. "I was a slave, too," he said. He smiled wryly. "Well—of sorts."

In the morning, they were up with the first tendrils of dawn, moving down the narrow road that Peter had climbed the day before. They moved in complete silence, their only communication via whistles and birdcalls. Peter attached himself to the black warrior, who called himself Ota Qwan. Ota Qwan followed Skadai, who seemed, as far as Peter could tell, to be the captain. Not that he issued any orders.

No one spoke to Peter, but then, no one spoke much anyway, so he focused on trying to move the way they did. He was not a noisy man in the woods, and no one cautioned him—he followed Ota Qwan as best he could, across an alder swamp, up a low ridge dotted with stands of birch, and then west along a deer trail through beech highlands, with a lake stretching away to the right of the long ridge and the great river stretched out to the left.

They moved across the face of the wilderness, sometimes following trails and sometimes following the flow of the terrain, and their paths gradually made sense to Peter—they were following a relatively straight course west, and avoiding the river. He had no sense of how many of them there were, even when they made camp, because that night, they simply stopped and lay down, all nestled tightly in a tangle of bodies and limbs. No one had a blanket, few had shirts, and the night was cold. Peter found he despised the touch of another against him, front and back, but his revulsion was quickly forgotten in sleep.

In the rainy grey of not-quite-morning, he offered some very stale bread from his sack to Ota Qwan, who accepted it with gratitude, took a small bite, and handed the crust on. Men watched it eagerly, but no one protested when the bread ran out before the mouths did. Peter hadn't even had a bite. He had expected it to be handed back. But he shrugged.

On his second night with the painted people he couldn't sleep at all. It rained softly, and the sensation of wet flesh—paint, grit, and a man's naked thigh against his own—made him get up shiver alone. Eventually he crept back into the pile of bodies, disgusted but almost frozen.

The next day was agony. The whole group moved faster, running the length of a grass meadow curiously criss-crossed by an arterial profusion of canals the width of a man's outstretched arm. The painted people leaped them with ease, but Peter fell into several, and always received a hand out and a belly laugh for his troubles.

The painted people wore supple, thin leather shoes, often the same colour as their paint so that he hadn't noticed them at first. His cheap slave shoes were falling to pieces, and the great meadow was littered with sharp sticks pointing up from the ground. He hurt his feet a dozen times, and again, he was helped along and laughed at.

He was limping badly, exhausted, utterly unaware of his surroundings, so when Ota Qwan stopped Peter all but walked over him.

Just the length of a horse in front of them stood a creature straight from nightmare—a beautiful monster as tall as a plough horse, and as heavy, with a crested head like a helmeted angel, a raptor's beak and blank eyes grey, the colour of new-wrought iron. It had wings—small, but heart-breakingly beautiful.

Peter couldn't even look at it, because for the third time in as many days he was terrified beyond his ability to think.

Ota Qwan put a reassuring hand on his shoulder.

Skadai raised a hand. "Lambo!" he said.

The monster grunted, and raised a taloned claw-hand.

Peter had time to note that its left claw was wrapped in linen, the way an injured man's hand would be wrapped in bandages.

Then the monster grunted again—if it spoke, the tones were too deep for Peter to understand—and then it was gone into the underbrush. Skadai turned and raised his bow. "Gots onah!" he shouted.

There was an answering roar from all around them, and Peter was staggered to discover that there were dozens—perhaps hundreds—of painted warriors around him.

He grabbed at Ota Qwan. "What—what was that?" he asked.

Ota Qwan gave him a wry smile. "That was what men call an adversarius," he said. "A warden of the Wild." He eyed Peter for a moment. "A daemon, little man. Still want to be one of us?"

Peter took a breath but it was hard. His throat was closed again.

Ota Qwan put an arm around his shoulder. "Tonight we'll be in a regular camp. Maybe we can talk. You must have questions. I know a little." He shrugged. "I love living with the Sossag. I am one. I would never go back, not even to be a belted earl." The black painted man shrugged. "But it ain't for everyone. And the Sossag are Free People. If you don't want to continue with them, well, just walk away. The Wild might kill you, but the Sossag won't."

"Free People?" Peter asked. He'd heard it said before.

"You have a lot to learn." Ota Qwan smacked his shoulder. "Move now. Talk later."

Dormling—Hector Lachlan

Hector Lachlan walked into the courtyard of the great inn at Dormling like a prince coming into his kingdom, and men came out to stare, even applaud. The Keeper came in person, and shook his hand.

"How many head?" he asked.

Lachlan grinned. "Two thousand, six hundred and eleven," he said. "Mind you, master, that includes the goats, and I'm not so very fond of goats."

The Keeper of Dormling—a title as noble and powerful as any in the south, for all it belonged to a big bald man in an apron—clapped Lachlan on the back. "We've expected you a ten-day. Your cousin's here to join you. He says it's bad to the south." He added, "We were afraid you might be broke, or dead."

Lachlan accepted the cup of wine that the Keeper's own daughter pressed into his hand. He raised it to her. "I drink to you, lass," he said.

She blushed.

Hector turned back to the Keeper. "The Hills are empty," he said, "which trouble in the south explains. How far south? Is it the king?"

The Keeper shook his head.

"Your cousin told me that Albinkirk was afire," he said. "But come in and sit, and bring your men. The pens are ready, even for twenty-six hundred and eleven beasts. And I'm eager to buy—if I serve you a steak tonight, Hector Lachlan, you'll have to sell me the cow first. I'm that short."

The staff of the Dormling Inn descended on the drovers like an avenging army, carrying trays of leather tankards of strong ale and mountains of soft bread and sharp cheese. By the time the youngest, dustiest drover far in the rear had been served his welcome cup and his bread, their lord was clean of the mud of the trail, sitting in a room as fine as most lord's halls, looking at a new tapestry from the East and smiling at the back of a local woman—a grown woman with a mind of her own, as he'd just discovered. He rubbed his bicep where she'd pinched him hard as a land crab and laughed.

"Cawnor tried to levy a toll on me," he went on.

The Keeper and the rest of the audience shook their heads.

The drover shrugged. "So we opened the road. I doubt there's enough of his men left alive to hold their fort, should someone decide to take it from them now." Drovers never sought to hold land. Drovers drove.

His cousin Ranald pushed through the crowd.

"You're taller!" Hector said, and crushed him in an embrace. Then he sank back into his chair and took a long draught of ale. "Albinkirk afire? That's ill news. What of the fair?"

Ranald shook his head. "I was moving fast. I kept moving. I was already on the east side when I reached Fifth Bridge, so I stayed there and rode cross country." He shrugged. "I didn't see a thing."

The Keeper shrugged. "If I'd thought you'd be here today, I'd have held the two bloody peddlers," he said. "They claimed they'd been part of a merchant convoy headed west from Theva. Lost all their goods and slaves."

Hector nodded. "Like enough." This was the time of year for the great convoys.

"A pair of Moreans. Said it was an ambush. Whole convoy destroyed." The Keeper shrugged. "My sons say there was a good sized Theva convoy a ten-day back as well, on the south road, so they didn't pass by here." He shrugged again. "I have no faith in Moreans, but they had no reason to lie either."

"Ambushed by what?" Hector asked.

"They couldn't agree," the landlord said.

"They said the Wild," said a bold young farmer, a frequent customer, and a suitor for one of the Keeper's daughters. "Or, leastways, the younger one said the Wild."

The Keeper shrugged again. "That's true. Some of them said it was the Wild."

Hector nodded slowly. "I certainly didn't see an animal bigger than a dog the whole trip here," he said. He shook his head in weary disgust. "The Wild is set against Albinkirk? Where's the *king*? His people eat my cattle too."

The Keeper sighed. "I don't know, and that's a fact," he said. "I've put two of my sons and a dozen men on fast horses out to get ye news. We'll see what they have. Folk have spied Outwallers in the woods. Sassogs. I think that if they were really there, they'd have been seen and et alive—but then I'm a suspicious bastard."

Hector took a deep breath. "So it's war then."

The Keeper looked away. "I hope not."

Hector took another pull of ale. "Hope in one hand and shit in the other and see which one smells most. How long until you hear from your fast horsemen?"

"Tomorrow," the Keeper said.

"Assuming the Outwallers don't eat them." Hector kicked his sword out in front of him to make room for his legs and sat back, tipping his chair against the wall. "By the five wounds of Christ, Keeper. This will be an adventure to remember then—taking the drove into an army of the Wild. Not even my da did the like."

"Waste of courage and arrows, though, if the fair ain't happening," the Keeper said. "Lissen Carak may be so many burned cots and splintered stones when you get there."

Hector thumped his chair back down. "Truth in what you say," he said. "And no use pondering it until I know more." He looked around at the dozen men in the room. "But I have a real harper and a dozen other players in my tail—and unless Dormling's fallen on hard times, I wager a golden noble to a copper cat we can have us some fine music and dancing to rival the fairies tonight. So enough talk of war. Let's have wine and music."

In the far doorway, the tall serving woman tapped her foot and nodded approvingly.

The Keeper's youngest daughter clapped her hands. "Now that's why you're the Prince of Drovers," she said approvingly. "To Hector, Prince of the Green Hills!"

Hector Lachlan frowned. "The Green Hills have no lord but the Wyrm of Erch," he said. "The dragon will have no rival, and can hear all that's said by men, so let's not be naming me to the lordship of any hills—eh, Keeper?"

The Keeper took a long pull of his own ale and put an arm around his daughter's shoulders, and said "Honey, you know never to speak so. The Wyrm is no friend of man—but he's no foe to us, as long as we stay clear of him and keep the sheepfolds where he commands. Eh?"

She burst into tears and fled the room with every eye on her, and then the moment passed and the woman in the doorway clapped her hands. "Bother the Wyrm!" she said boldly. "I want the harper!'

Desiderata lay back on the daybed in her solar, wearing only a long shift of sheer linen and silk hose with red leather garters. Her nurse clucked disapprovingly at her mistress's déshabillé and began the herculean task of gathering up her shoes.

Desiderata had a scroll, a day book, and a lead pencil encased in silver with her, and she was writing furiously. "Why don't they build all the cart wheels to the same size?" she asked.

Diota made a face. "Because wheelwrights don't share their measures, mistress."

Desiderata sat up. "Really?"

Diota clucked, looking for a second damask slipper. She found it under the daybed. "Every wheelwright builds to their own set of sizes—usually given 'em by their father or grandfather. Some build cartbeds to the width of the narrowest bridge—I grew up in the mountain country, and the Bridge of Orchids was the narrowest lane in the baillie. No carter would build a cart wider that that, and no wheelwright—"

Desiderata made an impatient noise. "I take your point. But military carts—" She shook her head. "There are no military carts. We have vassals who give cart service. They hold their cottages and farms in exchange for providing a cart and a driver. Can you imagine anything clumsier? And when their cart breaks down, it's the king's problem." She chewed on the silver pencil. "He needs a professional train. Carts built for war, with carters paid a wage." She scribbled furiously.

"I imagine it costs too much, my lady," Diota said.

Desiderata shook her head. "You know what it costs to repair the wheels on one cart? War does not need to be this expensive."

"You make me laugh, my lady," Diota said. She had found both of the red calfskin slippers—a miracle in itself—and she was putting the whole collection all on shoe forms to keep them stretched.

Desiderata gave her nurse the sort of smile that squires at court fought to gain. "I make you laugh, my sweet?"

"You are the Queen of Beauty, with your head full of romance and starshine, and now you're organising his supply train." Diota shook her head.

"Without forage and fodder, a knight and his horse are worthless," Desiderata said. "If we want them to win glory, they must be fed." She laughed. "You think my head is full of starshine, nurse—look inside a young man's head. I wager that half of the young louts who try to look down my dress and fight to kiss my hand will ride off to do great deeds without even a nose bag for their chargers. Without an oiled rag to touch up their sword blades. Without a sharpening stone or a fire kit." She tossed her head to move her mane of hair. "I've watched knights my *whole life*. Half of them are good fighters—fewer than a tenth make even marginally competent soldiers."

Diota made a face. "Men. What more need be said?"

Desiderata laughed. She picked up a second scroll. "I'm moving forward with the plans for the tournament. The king will have almost the full muster of knighthood together anyway, so I'll move the date by a month—the fourth Sunday in Pentecost isn't a bad time for a big show. The planting will be done and only the haying will be in."

"Fourth Sunday—Lorica Cattle Fair," said Diota.

Desiderata sighed. "Of course." She made a face. "Drat."

"Have your tournament at Lorica instead."

"Hmmm," Desiderata mused. "Very good for the town—good for our relations there, as they'll rake in a profit. And I understand my husband had to make some concession there."

"Because your perfect knight burned the Two Lions," Diota spat. "Foreign fuck!"

"Nurse!" Desiderata swung a pillow with great accuracy, catching her nurse in the back of the head with a soft tassel.

"He's a lout in armour."

"He's reputed to be the best knight in the world," breathed the Queen. "You cannot judge him by the standards—"

"By the Good Christ," Diota said. "If he's the best knight in the world, then he should *embody* the standards."

They glared at each other. But Diota knew her duty. She smiled. "I'm sure he is a great knight, my lady."

The Queen shook her head. "I confess he lacks something," she admitted.

Diota made a noise.

"Thank you, nurse. That will be quite enough. Despite your ill-mannered grumbling, I take your point—no doubt the king does need something nice done for Lorica. Holding the tournament there—if the timing is right, if the army is returning that road, and if the town fathers are in favour—yes, it would do very nicely. And I would get my tournament." She rang a silver bell, and the door to the solar opened to admit her secretary, Lady Almspend, one of the few university-taught women in Alba.

"Two letters, if you please, Becca."

Lady Almspend curtsied, sat at the writing table, and produced a silver pen and ink from her purse.

"To the Mayor and Sheriff of Lorica, the Queen of Alba sends greeting—"

She dictated quickly and fluently, pausing while her secretary filled in titles and appropriate courtesies with equal fluency. It was the habit of kings and queens to employ scholars of repute as secretaries, as most of the nobility couldn't be bothered to learn the task and employed others to do any actual writing. But Rebecca Almspend managed to write fine poetry and research the works of the troubadours of the last two centuries, and still found time to do her job thoroughly.

"To his Alban Majesty, from your devoted, loving wife—"

Lady Almspend gave her an arch look.

"Oh, say what I mean, not what I say," Desiderata pouted.

"You Grace will forgive me if I suggest that sometimes your performance as a wilful beauty overshadows your obvious intelligence," Lady Almspend said.

Desiderata let the nails of her right hand pass lightly down the back of her secretary's arm. "Let my letter be coy, and let him gather how very brilliant I am by looking at the design of his new war carts," she said. "Telling him how very clever I am will only cause him distress. Men, my dear Becca, are like that, and you will never attract a lover, not even a bespectacled merchant prince who adores your head for long columns of figures, if you wear wimples that hide your face and seek to prove to every lover that you are the smarter of the pair." The Queen knew perfectly well that her intellectual secretary had attracted the devotion of the strongest and most virile of the King's Guardsmen—it had been something of a wonder at the court. Even the Queen was curious how it had happened.

Lady Almspend was perfectly still, and the Queen knew she was biting back a hot remark.

The Queen kissed her. "Be at peace, Becca. In some ways, I am far more learned than you." She laughed. "And I am the Queen."

Even the staid Lady Almspend had to laugh at the truth of this. "You are the Queen."

Later, when giving justice, the Queen summoned two of the king's squires, and sent them with the letters—one was delighted to go to the army, if only for a day or two, and the other, rather more dejected, riding to a merchant town to deliver a letter to a retired knight.

The Queen allowed them both to kiss her hand.

North of Harndon—Harmodius

Harmodius was on his second night without sleep. He tried not to think about how easily he'd done such things forty years before. Tonight, riding very slowly down the road on an exhausted horse, he could only hope to keep his hands on the saddle, hope that the horse didn't stumble, throw a shoe, or simply collapse beneath him.

He'd drained every reserve of energy. He'd set wards, thrown bolts, and built phantasmal dissuasions with the abandon of a much younger man. All his carefully hoarded powers were gone.

In a way, it had been marvellous.

Young magi have energy and old ones have skill. Somewhere in the continuum between young and old lies a practitioner's greatest moment. Harmodius had assumed his had been twenty years ago, and yet last night he'd thrown a curtain of fire five furlongs long—and swept it ahead of his galloping horse like a daemonic plough blade.

"Heh," he said aloud.

An hour after he'd extinguished the fiery blade, he'd met a foreigner on an exhausted horse, who had watched him with wary eyes.

Harmodius had reined in. "What news?" he asked.

"Albinkirk," the man breathed. He had a Morean accent. "Only the castle holds. I must tell the king. The Wild has struck."

Harmodius had stroked his beard. "Dismount a moment, and allow me to send the king a message as well?" he said. "I'm the King's Magus," he added.

"Ser Alcaeus Comnena," the dark-visaged man replied. He swung his leg over the horse's rump.

Harmodius had given him some sweet wine. He was pleased to see the foreign knight attend his horse—rubbing the gelding down, checking his legs.

"How's the road?" asked the knight.

Harmodius permitted himself a moment of glowing satisfaction. "I think you'll find it clear," he said. "Alcaeus? You're the Emperor's cousin."

"I am," said the man.

"Strange meeting you here," Harmodius said. "I've read some of your letters."

"I'm blushing, and you can't see it. You must be Lord Harmodius, and I've read everything you written about birds." He laughed, a little wildly. "You're the only barba— only foreigner whose High Archaic is ever read aloud at court."

Harmodius had a werelight going, and was writing furiously. "Yes?" he asked absently.

"Although you haven't written a thing in five years, now? Ten?" The younger knight had shaken his head. "I am sorry, my lord. I had thought you dead."

"You weren't far wrong. Here—deliver this to the king. I'm going north. Tell me—did you see any Hermetics fighting against Albinkirk?"

Ser Alcaeus had nodded. "Something enormous came against the walls. It pulled the very stars from the sky, and threw them at the castle."

They had clasped hands.

"I long to meet you under more auspicious circumstances," Ser Alcaeus had said.

"And I you, ser."

And with that, each had ridden off—one north, and one south.

Who can pull stars from the sky and hurl them at castle walls? Harmodius asked himself, and worried that there was only one answer.

The last light of day had shown him smoke rising over Albinkirk, and if the town was gone then he was bereft of a plan.

His original impulse was all but gone. The evidence of the road, and Ser Alcaeus, was that a marauding army of the Wild had come down on the north of Alba, and he was afraid—to the core of his chilled and weary bones—that all the work of the old King Hawthor was undone. Worse, whatever had cast the ensorcellment on him was out there. With that army.

And yet he hadn't pointed his horse's head back south. When he came to the road that turned west, into the woods, and saw fresh wagon ruts on it he turned his horse's head that way and followed them.

Part of that was pragmatic. He'd fought three bands of the Wild to win through this much of the road to Albinkirk. He wasn't ready to fight a fourth.

Two hours later, somewhere in the darkness, a horse gave a long snort and then a soft whicker, and his horse answered.

Harmodius sat up.

He let his horse stumble forward. The horses would find each other quicker than he could, and they rode on for long minutes. He stared with unaided eyes at the darkness that pressed in on the road like a living thing.

The other horse whinnied.

His horse gave a call, almost a mule's bray, in return.

"Halt! You on the road—halt and dismount, or you'll have enough crossbow bolts in you to play a porcupine in a show." The voice was loud, shrill, and sounded very young, which made the speaker dangerous. Harmodius slid from his horse, knowing in his bones that he was unlikely to be able to remount. His knees hurt. His calves hurt. "I'm off," he said.

A bull's-eye lantern opened its baleful eye in front of him, the powerful oil lamp all but blinding him.

"Who are you, then?" asked the annoying young voice.

"I'm the fucking King of Alba," Harmodius snapped. "I'm an old man on a done horse and I'd love to share your fire, and if I was a horde of boglins you'd already be dead."

There were chortles from the darkness.

"There you are, Adrian. Put that weapon down, Henry. If he's riding a horse, he ain't a creature of the Wild. Eh? Did you think of that, boy? What's your name, old man?" The new voice was authoritative without being noble. The bland accent of court was completely absent.

"I'm Harmodius Silva, the King's Magus." He walked forward into the lantern light, and his horse followed him, as eager for rest and food as his rider. "And that's not a tall tale," he added.

"Sounds pretty tall," said the new voice. "Come to the fire and have a cup of wine. Adrian, back to your duty, boy. Young Henry, if you point that weapon at me again I'll break your nose."

The man was in armour and had a heavy axe across his arms, but he stripped off a chain mitten and clasped Harmodius's hand. "They call me Old Bob," he said. "Man-at-arms to the great and near great," he laughed. "You really Lord Silva?"

"I truly am," said Harmodius. "Do you really have a safe camp and wine? I'll pay a silver leopard to have a boy see to my horse."

The man-at-arms laughed. "Long night?"

"Three long nights. By the blood of Christ and his resurrection—I've been fighting for three days."

They emerged into the circle of light from a big fire, and over the fire towered a heavy trestle that held the chains of three heavy cauldrons—and a pair of lanterns hung from the cross bar. It was the strongest light he'd seen since sundown. By the candlelight he could see a dozen men crouched over something on the ground, and the tall wheel of a heavy wagon. And beyond that, another.

"You've reached Master Random's convoy," the man-at-arms said. "Fifty wagons, or near enough, all the guilds of Harndon represented."

Harmodius nodded. He'd never heard of Master Random, but then, as had become increasingly clear over the last three days, he'd been lost to the world for ten years or more.

"You're safe enough here," Old Bob said. "Boglins ambushed us today," he said, and shrugged, clearly unhappy about it.

"You took losses?" Harmodius was anxious to ask about the numbers and strength of the opposition, but his desire for information was at war with his fatigue.

"The young knight," Old Bob motioned with his great axe at the group of men gathered around something on the ground. "He was badly wounded fighting a daemon out of the Wild."

Harmodius sighed. "Make way," he said.

They had a candle, and the horse leech was cleaning the man's wounds with vinegar. The young knight had lost a great deal of blood and, stripped naked, he looked pale and vulnerable. The new spring flies were feasting on him.

Harmodius cast almost without thinking, putting a small banishment on the flies.

Fatigue, which had seemed like a coat of mail, suddenly clamped like a vice around his heart. But he knelt by the wounded man, and Old Bob held the lantern high.

Just for a moment the wounded knight looked like the king.

Harmodius bent closer, examining the wounds. Three punctures, some slashes—nothing so deadly as to kill a healthy man, until he saw the burns. In the ruddy candle light, the man's eye looked like a pit of red.

"Sweet Jesu," the Magus said.

The odd pieces of dirt he'd seen on the man's shoulder was no dirt at all—his chain links had burned right into his shoulder. The burns weren't even red, they were black.

"He faced down an adversarius," a man said. "A daemon of hell. Even when it threw fire at him."

Harmodius felt his eyes closing. He didn't have the power to save this brave soul which was frustrating, especially as he only needed a little organic power to stabilise the burns. It took much skill, much shaping of the phantasm, but little power.

The concept that the power needed was organic gave him a thought, though.

He touched his own reserves—the items he'd carefully enchanted over the years—drenched in sun power, imbued, impregnated, imprinted with the rich golden light of the Sacred Sun. All were cold and empty. And so was his greatest reservoir—his own skin. Empty, cold, tired.

And yet, by the logic of the experiment in his tower—

"Everyone stand away," he ordered. He lacked the energy to explain; either this was going to work, or it was not. "I'm exhausted," he said to the old soldier. "You know what that means?"

"Means ye can't heal. Eh?" said Old Bob.

"Just so. I'm going to try tapping a local source. If I fail, nothing will happen. If I succeed—" Harmodius rubbed his eyes. "By Hermes and all the saints, if I succeed, I think something will happen."

Old Bob snorted. "Are you always that clear?" He held out a beaker. "Drink first. Good red wine."

Harmodius waved it away. The other men backed away, or fled to the fire—no one fancied watching a wizard work except Old Bob, who looked on with a cat's wary curiosity.

Harmodius reached out into the darkness until he found a pool of the green power that he knew had to be there. It wasn't far away. He didn't enquire what it was. He simply seized its power—

—and the night exploded with shrieking.

One does not work with the ultimate powers of the universe for many years without developing a concentration bordering on utter ruthlessness. Harmodius focused on the power, which was difficult to lay hold of, difficult to *seize,* and it tasted wrong, somehow. That wrongness would instantly have repelled him, had he not the scientific assurance of his earlier experiment that a creature of the Wild could interact with the Hermetic. The reverse had to be true.

The shrieking went on, and the men around him moved in a disciplined kind of panic—seizing weapons, calming horses. Harmodius was aware of them, but not enough to break the iron chain of his connection to the distant green source of power, which he took like an infant sucking greedily at a breast.

Ruthlessly.

And then it was in him, filling him with its odd, bitter, wintergreen tang, and there was far, far more than he needed for his small enchantment. But he worked with it, first a complex binding, then two simultaneous phantasms run by dividing himself into two working halves, as his master had taught him so long ago. And there was so much power that he could divide himself once again, to leave an awareness to watch the darkness. Taking the green energy, as he had, seemed to have kicked a beehive.

A village witch could funnel power independently through each hand. Harmodius could use each finger as a channel, and could use other foci on his body—rings and the like—as reserves, or clamps.

He used many of them now.

His first use of it was to look into the burns. They were worse than he'd thought by the firelight—the blackened skin was charred, and in some cases the damage ran all the way through the skin layer to the fat and muscle.

These were lethal burns.

Indeed, the man was slipping away even as Harmodius worked to block the pain and heal the greatest wounds.

Healing burns was the most difficult of all forms of healing and Harmodius, for all his power, was no healer. He juggled tendrils of power for a dozen heartbeats, attempting to rebuild charred tissue and in the process only charring more. The control required was incredible and in his frustration and fatigue, he let slip a greater packet of the green power than he intended. It was rolling through him in waves and he passed it straight into the young man's shoulder.

Harmodius had heard of healing miracles, but he had never witnessed one before. Under his hand, a patch of skin the size of a bronze sequin healed. The angry marks that pulsed in Harmodius's enhanced vision simply faded and were gone.

It was incredible.

Harmodius had no idea what he had done, but he was an empirical magus and so he reached for more power, drew it from its source like a man trying to haul in a great ocean fish with a light rod, and then pumped it through his hands into the swaths of burned flesh...

...and they healed.

A section of the knight's neck the size of the palm of a hand closed over and healed.

He reached for more power, seized it, struggled with the source and overcame it by main force of will, and then hauled with all his trained might, ripping the green power into his soul and then passing it down his hands into the knight, whose eyes suddenly opened with a great cry.

Harmodius stumbled back.

The screams from the woodlands stopped.

"Why did you kill me?" the young knight asked plaintively. "I was so beautiful!"

He slumped and his eyes closed.

Harmodius reached out and touched him. He was asleep, and the skin on his neck, chest, back, and shoulders was flaking away, the blackness and scabs simply falling away from the new flesh underneath.

New, pale flesh.

With scales.

Harmodius flinched, trying to understand what he had done.

Lissen Carak—The Red Knight

The captain woke still tired. He got up, called for Toby, and stumbled to his wash basin.

Toby came in, chewing on a biscuit, and began to lay out his clothes. He moved warily, and the captain assumed from his averted head that something was wrong. Whatever it was, the captain would have to work it out for himself.

"What news, Toby?" the captain asked.

"Boglins in the fields," the boy said, and went back to chewing.

"Where's Michael?" the captain asked, when no one came to help him point his hose.

Toby looked away. "At chapel, I reckon."

"Only if Jesu came and visited Michael in person in the night," the captain said. Mornings made him nasty. Toby wasn't to blame, but the boy idolized the squire and he wasn't going to rat him out.

The captain pointed his own hose, and took an old arming doublet and began to lace it up. He didn't call for Michael until he was ready to lace the cuffs. When the young man still wasn't there, he nodded to Toby. "I'm going to go find him," he said.

Toby looked terrified. "I'll go, master!"

The captain felt annoyed. "We can go together," he said, and his long legs took him out of the solar and down the hall to the Commandery where Michael slept.

Toby tried to beat him to the door, but a combination of shorter legs and deference kept him a stride behind.

The captain flung the heavy oak door open.

Michael leaped from his bedroll, a long dagger in his right fist. He was naked. So was the beautiful young girl he put behind him.

"Michael?" the captain said to the dagger.

Michael blushed. The blush started just above his groin, ran in splotches over his chest and up his neck to his face. "Oh my God—my lord, I'm so sorry—"

The captain looked at the girl. Her blush was even brighter.

"That's my laundry maid, I believe," he said. He raised an eyebrow. "Perhaps maid is the wrong word, given the circumstances."

She hid her head.

"Get dressed. Michael. It's full light, and when that poor young woman walks down the steps to the courtyard, every person in the fortress will know where she's been; either with you, with me, or with Toby. Perhaps with all three. Toby at least has the virtue of being her own age."

Michael was trying to put his dagger away.

"I love her!" he said hotly.

"Wonderful. That love is about to bring down a mountain of consequences that may end in your no longer being in my employ." The captain was angry.

"At least she's not a nun!" Michael said.

That stopped the captain. And filled him with black rage; in a moment, he went from a distant, weary amusement to the flat desire to kill. He was struggling not to draw a weapon. Or use his fists. Or his power.

Michael took a step back and Toby placed himself between the captain and the squire.

Heavy, strong arms suddenly encircled the captain from behind. He thrashed, angry beyond sense, but he couldn't break the grip. He tried to plant his feet and headbutt his adversary, but the man lifted him straight off the floor.

"Whoa!" said Bad Tom. "Whoa there!"

"His eyes are glowing!" Michael said, and his voice was trembling, Kaitlin Lanthorn cowering in the corner.

Tom spun the captain and slapped him clear across the face.

There was a pause. The captain's power hung in the air—palpable even to non-talents. Kaitlin Lanthorn saw it as a cloud of golden green around his head.

"Let go of me, Tom," said the captain.

Tom put his feet on the ground. "What was that about?"

"My idiot squire deflowered a local virgin, for sport." The captain took a deep breath.

"I love her!" Michael shouted. Fear made his voice high and whiney.

"Like enough," Tom said. "I love all the women I fuck, too." He grinned. "She's just one of the Lanthorn sluts. No damage done."

Kaitlin burst into tears.

The captain shook his head. "The Abbess—" he began.

Tom nodded. "Aye. She won't take it well." He looked at Michael. "I won't ask you what you were thinkin', 'cause I can guess it well enough."

"Get him out of my sight," the captain said. "Toby, get the girl dressed and get her...I don't know. Can you get her out of here without everyone seeing?"

Toby nodded soberly. "Aye," he said, eager to help. Toby didn't like it when his heroes were angry, especially not with each other.

The captain had a splitting headache, and he wasn't even into the day yet.

"What are you doing here, anyway?" he asked Tom.

"Sauce has a patrol out and there's the remnants of a convoy in the Bridge Castle," Tom said. "Bad news."

Sauce reported an hour later, handing a child down off the saddlebow of her war horse and saluting her captain crisply.

"Twenty-three wagons. All burned. Sixty corpses found, not yet ripe, and not much of a fight." She shrugged. "Slightly chewed." She lowered her voice, as there were dozens of people in earshot, all looking for news. "Many eaten down to sinew and bone, Captain."

The captain fingered his beard, looked at the desperate people surrounding his horse, and knew that any morale won by his raids on the enemy camp was now dissipated in a fresh wave of terror.

"Back to your work," the captain called.

"We ain't got no work!" a man shouted, and the crowd in the courtyard rumbled angrily.

The captain had mounted in anticipation of taking out a patrol. He was restless and depressed himself, and craved action—anything to distract him.

But he was the captain. He nodded to Gelfred. "Go north, and move fast. You know what we want."

He swung one spurred foot over Grendel's back and slid from the saddle. "Wilful Murder, Sauce, on me. The rest of you—well done. Get some rest."

He led them inside. Michael dismounted too, looking as furious as the captain felt having lost an opportunity to substitute honest fear for nagging terror. He clearly knew that he now had no opportunity to expiate his sin. But he took his own destrier and the captain's and headed for the stable without untoward comment.

Sister Miram—the heaviest and thus most easily identified of the sisters—was passing through the courtyard with a basket of sweet bread for the children. The captain caught her eye, and waved.

"The Abbess will want to hear this," he said to her. She put a biscuit in his hand with a look that might have curdled milk—a look of blanket disapproval.

There was a slip of vellum underneath it.

Meet me tonight

A bolt of lightning shot through him.

The Abbess arrived while he was still standing in his solar. He'd just stripped off his gauntlets and placed them on the sideboard, his helmet was still on his head. Sauce took it from him, and he turned to find the Abbess, hands clasped loosely in front of her, wimple starched and perfect, eyes bright.

The captain had to smile, but she did not return it.

He sighed. "We've lost another convoy coming to the fair—six leagues to the west, on the Albinkirk road. More than sixty dead. The survivors are panicking your people, and they aren't helping mine much." He sighed. "In among them are refugees from Albinkirk, which, I am sorry to report, has fallen to the Wild."

To Sauce, he said, "In future, no matter how badly off they are, take new refugees to Ser Milus. Let him keep their ravings contained."

Sauce nodded. "I should have thought—" she said wearily.

The captain cut her off. "No, I should have thought of it, Sauce."

Wilful Murder shook his head. "It's worse than you think, Captain. You're not from around here, eh?"

The captain gave the archer a long look, and Wilful quailed.

"Sorry, ser," he said.

"It happens that I know the mountains to the north well enough," the captain said quietly.

Wilful was not so easily put down though. He produced something from his purse and put it on the table.

The Abbess turned as white as parchment when she saw it.

The captain raised an eyebrow.

"Abenacki," he said.

"Or Quost, or most likely Sassog." Wilful nodded respectfully. "So you *are* from around here."

"How many?" the captain asked.

Wilful shook his head. "At least one. What kind of question is that?" The feather he had placed on the table—a heron feather—was decorated with elaborate quillwork from a porcupine, the quills dyed bright red and carefully woven up the stem of the feather.

Wilful looked around, and then, like a conjuror, produced a second item, very like the first in look—a small pouch, decorated with complex leather braids. When his audience looked blank, he grinned his broken-toothed grin. "Irks. Five feet of muscle and all of it mean. They make amazing stuff. Fey folk, my mother used to call them." He looked at the Abbess. "They like to eat women."

"That's enough, Wilful."

"Just saying. And there was tracks." He shrugged.

"Nicely done, Wilful. Now give me some quiet." The captain pushed his chin towards the door.

Wilful might have been surly, but he found a silver leopard pushed across the table to him, too. He bit it, grinned and left.

The captain glanced at the Abbess as soon as they were alone. "What's going on here?" he asked in his pleasant but professional voice. "This isn't the random violence of the Wild, an isolated incident, a murder, a couple of creatures come over the wall on a rampage. This is a war. Daemons, wyverns, irks and now the Outwallers. All we seem to lack is a few boglins, a goblin or two, and then maybe the Dragon will enter the field too. Abbess, if you know anything, I think this is the time to tell me."

She met his gaze. "I can make some educated guesses," she said. Her lips curled down. "I gather that the youngest Lanthorn girl spent the night here?" she said archly.

"Yes she did. I raped her repeatedly and threw her naked into the court-yard in the morning," the captain said. His annoyance showed. "Damn it, this matters."

"And Kaitlin Lanthorn doesn't? My Jesu says she matters as much as you do, ser knight. As much as I do. Perhaps more. And spare me your posturing, boy. I know why you're so touchy. She spent the night with your squire. I know. I have just spent a few minutes with the girl. We spoke about this." She looked at him. "Will he marry her?"

"You can't be serious," the captain said. "He's the son of a great lord. He may be on the outs with his family just now, but they'll forgive him soon enough. His kind doesn't marry farm sluts."

"She was a virgin a few days ago," the Abbess said. "Calling her a whore doesn't make her one. Nor does it make you stand any better in my sight."

"Fine," said the captain. "She's a fine upstanding lass with impeccable morals and my nasty squire got her to bed. I'll see to it that he pays for it—both morally and financially. Now can we please talk about the true threat here?"

"Maybe we already are. So far, no creature of the Wild has done so much harm as your men have done," the Abbess said.

"Untrue, my lady. I swear on my word: I will see to it justice is done for this young woman. I confess that she looked quite unsluttish this morning, and very young. I am embarrassed my squire has acted in such a way."

"Like master, like man," the Abbess said.

The captain clenched his fists. He mastered himself, unclenched them, and steepled his hands instead.

"I think you are avoiding the topic. Sister Hawisia was murdered. Her murder was planned. Perhaps she was the target—perhaps you were. The daemon that did the killing had inside help. The men who helped the daemon then fell out among themselves and one killed the other, burying his body on the west road. Shortly after, we arrived. We found a wyvern and killed it. Gelfred and I found a pair of daemons; one died and the other escaped. We scouted and found an army forming under a powerful sorcerer. As of this morning, the woods around us are full of enemies and the road to Albinkirk is cut. Albinkirk has fallen to the Wild, and I put it to you, my lady, that you know more than you are telling me. What is really going on here?"

She turned her head away. "I know nothing," she said, in a tone that merely showed that she was a poor liar.

"You cut down the sacred grove? Your farmers are raping dryads? By all you hold holy, my lady Abbess, if you do not help me understand this, we're all going to die here. This is a full invasion, the first that has been seen since your youth. Where have they come from? Has the north fallen? Why has the Wild come here in such strength? I grew up with the Wall. I've been to Outwaller villages, eaten their food. There are far more than we admit —tens of thousands. If they have come to support the Wild directly, we will be swept away in the sea of foes. So what *exactly* is happening here?"

The Abbess took a breath as if to steady herself, succeeded, and raised an eyebrow. "Really, Captain, I have no more idea than you. The actions of the savages are beyond me. And the Wild is just a name we give to an amalgam of evil, is it not? Is it not sufficient that we are holy, and seek to preserve ourselves, our God, and our way of life? And they seek to take that from us?"

The captain met her gaze and shook his head. "You know more than that. The Wild is not so simple."

"It hates us," the Abbess said.

"That's no reason to mass against you now," replied the captain.

"There's burned trees and new fields out east toward Albinkirk," Sauce said.

The Abbess turned, as if to reprimand the woman, but shrugged. "We have to expand as our people expand. More peasants to feed required more fields."

The captain looked at Sauce. "How many burned trees? I don't remember them."

"They're not right along the road. I don't know—ask Gelfred."

"They go all the way to Albinkirk," the Abbess admitted. "We agreed to burn the forest between us and bring in more farmers. What of it? It was the old king's policy, and we need that land."

The captain nodded. "It was the old king's policy, and it led to the Battle of Chevin." He rubbed his beard. "I hope that one of my messengers made it to the king, because right now we're in a whole heap of shit."

Michael came in with cups of wine. He flushed very red when he saw the Abbess.

The captain glanced at him. "All officers, Michael. Get Ser Milus from the Bridge Castle too."

Michael sighed, served the wine, and left again.

The Abbess pursed her lips. "You wouldn't abandon us," she said, but it was more a question than a statement.

The captain was looking through his window to the west. "No, my lady, I wouldn't. But you must have known there would be a response."

She shook her head, anger warring with frustration. "By Saint Thomas and Saint Maurice, Captain, you task me too heavily! I did no more than was my right, even my duty. The Wild was beaten—or so I'm told by both the sheriff and the king. Why should I not expand my holdings at the cost of some old trees? And when the killing started—Captain, understand that I had no idea that the killings were connected, not until—"

The captain leaned forward. "Let me tell you what I think," he said. "Hawisia unmasked a traitor, and died for it."

The Abbess nodded. "It is possible. She asked to go to the outholdings when, ordinarily, I would have gone."

"She was your chancellor? The post Sister Miram holds now?" he asked.

She shook her head. "No. She had more power than the other sisters, but she was too young to hold an office."

"And she was widely disliked," Sauce said.

The Abbess flinched, but she didn't deny it.

The captain had his head in his hands. "Never mind. We're here now and so are they. It's my guess that the Jacks, or the daemons, or both, were going to kill *you* and seize the Abbey in a coup de main; Hawisia ruined it all somehow, either by confronting the traitor or by taking your place. We may never know." He shook his head.

The Abbess looked at her hands. "I loved her," she said.

The Red Knight knelt by her and put his hands on hers. "I swear I will do my best to hold this fortress and save you. But, my lady, I still feel you know something more. There is something personal about all this, and you still have a traitor within your walls." When she didn't answer him, he got up from his knee. She kissed his cheek, and he smiled. He handed her a cup of wine.

"Not your usual contract, ser knight," she said.

"Damn it, my lady, this *is* my usual contract: it's a war between rival barons, except that this time the rival baron can't be negotiated with or turned from his path or simply murdered, and they are all good ways of avoiding a knock-down fight. But in every other respect you and the Wild are feuding border lords. You've taken a piece of his land, and in turn he's raiding you and threatening your home."

As the captain spoke, his officers trickled in—Bad Tom, Ser Milus, Ser Jehannes, Wilful Murder, and Bent. The others were either asleep or on patrol.

The Abbess was brought a chair.

"Park wherever you can," the captain said. "I'll try and make this brief. I'd say we're almost surrounded, and our enemy hasn't bothered to build trench lines and trebuchets. Yet. But he's got enough force to close the woods and every road around us. He's got Outwallers—who are those men and women who live in the Wild, for you godless foreigners." The captain gave Ser Jehannes a mirthless smile. "I'm guessing he has a hundred or more Outwallers, a thousand irks, and perhaps fifty to a hundred other creatures of the types we've already seen—wyverns, daemons and the like." He shrugged. "I'm guessing our enemy is a potent magus."

Bad Tom whistled. "Lucky we didn't get ourselves killed trying for their camp then."

The captain nodded. "When you move fast and plan well, you deserve a little luck," he said. "But yes, I'd say that getting away with that raid seized our luck with both hands."

"So now what?" Sauce asked.

"First, Jehannes, you are now the constable. Ser Milus, you are now marshal. Tom, you are now first lance. Sauce, you are now a corporal. In one sweep, I'm short three knights. Milus, are there any likely lads in your refugees? The merchants?"

Milus scratched under his chin. "Archers? Hell, yes. Men-at-arms? Not a one. But I'll tell you what there is down in my little kingdom—there's two wagon loads of armour in barrels, and some nice swords, and a dozen heavy arbalests. All for sale at the fair, of course."

"Better than what we have?" the captain asked.

"White plate—the new hardened breastplates." Ser Milus licked his lips. "The swords are good, the spearheads better. The arbalests as heavy as anything we have."

The Abbess smiled. "Those were for me, anyway."

The captain nodded. "Take it all. Tell the owners we'll give them chits for it and settle up at the end if we're still alive. How heavy are these arbalests?"

"Bolts a forearm in length and thick as a child's wrist," Ser Milus said.

"Put them on frames. Two for you and the rest up here for me." The captain looked at the Abbess. "I want to build an outwork."

"Anything you like," she said.

"I want to put all your farmers and all the refugees to work and I want your help seeing that I get no insolence from them. I need them to work quickly and be quiet." The captain took out a scroll of parchment and unrolled it.

"My squire is a gifted young man, and he drew this," he said. Michael flushed uncontrollably. "We want a deep V-shape of walls on both sides and ditches outside the walls; built three hundred paces from Bridge Castle, where the road from the Lower Town starts up the hill. It will allow us to send soldiers and supplies freely back and forth from the Lower Town to Bridge Castle. Put boards all along the bottom so men can walk quickly, without being seen, and put three bridges over it, so our sorties can move easily about the fields. See this cutaway? A nice hollow space under the boards. Good place for a little surprise." He grinned and most of the soldiers grinned back.

"We'll *also* put a wall along the Gate Road, running all the way to the top. We should have done it in the first place, anyway. Towers here and here, on earth bastions." He rubbed his beard. "First, we put in covered positions for these new frame crossbows—here and here—so that if they attack while we're building, it's all a trap and they lose a couple of their own for nothing. Last, we improve the path from the postern gate to the Lower Town."

All the soldiers nodded.

Except Tom. Tom spat. "We don't have the fucking men to hold all that wall," he said. "Much less in both directions."

"No we don't. But building it will keep the peasants quiet and busy, and when our enemy attacks we're going to make him pay for it, and then let him have it."

Tom grinned. "Of course we are."

The captain turned to the others. "I'm assuming that our enemy doesn't have a lot of experience in fighting men," he said. "But even if he does, we won't have lost much with these distractions."

The Abbess looked pained. Her eyes had a hunted look, and she turned away. "He is a man. Or he was, once."

The captain winced. "We face a man?"

The Abbess nodded. "I have felt the brush of his thought. He has some small reason to—to fear me."

The captain looked at her, gazing as intently as a lover into her flecked brown and blue eyes, and she held his gaze as easily as he held hers.

"It is none of your affair," she said primly.

"You are not telling us things that would be of value to us," the captain said.

"You, on the other hand, are the very soul of openness," she replied.

"Get a room," Tom muttered under his breath.

The captain looked at Ser Milus. "We cut the patrols down to two a day, and we launch them at my whim. Our sole remaining interest is getting any more convoys in here safely, or in turning them away. Albinkirk is gone. Sauce—how far did you go today?"

She shrugged. "Eight leagues?"

The captain nodded. "Tomorrow—no, tomorrow we won't send anything. Not a man. Tomorrow we dig. The day after, we send four patrols, in all directions except west. The day after that, I'll take half the company west along the road, as fast as we can go. We'll aim for twenty leagues, pick up merchants or convoys we can, and get a look at Albinkirk. Then back here, all with enough force to kill whatever opposes us."

Tom nodded. "Aye, but against a hundred Outwallers, in an ambush, we'll just be dead. And that's without a couple of daemons and maybe a pair of wyverns and a hundred irks to eat our bodies afterwards. Eh?"

The captain wrinkled his lips. "If we surrender the initiative and hunker down here we're all dead too," he said. "Unless the king comes with his army to relieve us."

The Abbess agreed.

"For all I know the Wall fortresses have already fallen," the captain said. His eyes narrowed, as if the subject had particular interest to him.

"Whatever the case, we cannot count on any help from the outside, nor can we hope that this is an isolated incident. We have to behave as if we have an unending supply of men and materiel, and we have to try to keep the road east open. We need to lure our enemy into some battles of our choosing." He looked around at his officers. "Everyone understand?" He looked at the Abbess. "We have to be ready to destroy the bridge."

She nodded. "There's a phantasm to do it. I have it. It is regularly maintained: when a certain key is turned in the gate lock, the bridge will fall into the river."

The officers nodded their approval.

The captain stood. "Very well. Ser Milus, Ser Jehannes, you are in charge of my construction project. Tom, Sauce, you will lead the patrols. Bent, get the arbalest frames up, and placed in those four covered positions," he smiled, "where Michael marked them. Bent, take charge of running the rotations inside the fortress too. Don't worry about who is a man-at-arms, who's a valet, who's an archer. Just get the numbers right."

They all nodded.

"You planning to take a nap?" Bad Tom asked.

The captain smiled at the Abbess. "My lady and I are going to raise a nice fog," he said. "She is a very potent magus."

He had the pleasure of watching her eyes widen in surprise.

Jehannes paused. "And you? Captain?"

"I am a modestly talented magus." He nodded to his new constable. "Ah, Michael. Please don't go anywhere."

The other officers rattled out, Michael stood uncomfortably by the door, and after a moment it was just the three of them.

"What do you have to say for yourself?" the Abbess asked.

Michael writhed. "I love her," he said.

She smiled, to his shock.

"That is the best answer you could have given, under the circumstances. Will you wed her?" she asked.

The captain made a noise.

Michael stood straight. "Yes."

"What a dashing young fool you are, to be sure," said the Abbess. "Who's son are you?"

Michael's lips tightened, so the Abbess beckoned to him, and he came to her side. She leaned forward, touched his forehead, and there was a magnificent burst of colour and sparkling shards, as if a sunlit mirror had shattered.

"Towbray's son," she said, and laughed. "I knew your father. You have twice the looks and twice the grace he ever did. Is he still a weak man who changes sides with every twist of the wind?"

Michael stood his ground. "Yes, he is," he said.

The Abbess nodded. "Captain, I will take no action until our war is resolved. But what I say now, I say as a woman who has lived at court with the great. And as an astrologer. This boy could do much worse than Kaitlin Lanthorn."

Michael looked at his captain, whom he feared more than ten abbesses. "I love her, my lord," he said.

The captain thought of the note in his gauntlet, and of what the Abbess had just said—he'd felt the power of her words, which had bordered on prophecy.

"Very well," he said. "All the best romances bloom in the midst of a good siege. Michael, you are not so much forgiven as pardoned for this. Your pardon does not include further tumblings of said girl in my solar. Understood?"

The Abbess looked long and hard at the squire. "Will you marry her?" she asked.

"Yes," said the squire, defiantly, bowed and left the room.

The captain looked at the Abbess and grinned. "And the sisters will go with her? They'll liven up castle life, I have no doubt."

She shrugged. "He should marry her. I can feel it."

The captain sighed. And sighed again when he realised that there was no one to help him disarm.

"Shall we go and make fog?" he asked.

She extended her hand. "Nothing would please me more."

Lissen Carak—Bad Tom

Bad Tom stared at the captain's steel-clad back, slim as a blade, as he squired the Abbess down the corridor to the steps. Jehannes made as if to pass him, and Tom put his arm up and blocked him.

They glared at each other, but if they had had fangs they'd have been showing.

"Give it a rest," Tom said.

"I don't like taking orders from a boy," Jehannes said. "He's a boy. An inexperienced boy. He's hardly older than his squire. That *gifted young man.*" He spat.

"Give it a rest, I said." Tom spoke with the kind of finality that starts fights, or sometimes ends them. "You were never going to be captain. You haven't the brains, you haven't the hard currency, and most of all, you haven't the birth for it. He has all three."

"I hear the boy almost lost the castle because he can't keep his hands off some nun. He was off billing and cooing while you were out with the sortie. That's what I hear." Jehannes leaned back and crossed his arms.

"You know what makes me piss myself laughing when I watch you?" Tom leaned forward until his nose was almost touching the older man's nose.

"When he issues his orders, you just fucking obey like the trained dog you are. And that's why you hate him. Because he's born to it. He's not new at this, he's the bastard of some great man, he grew up in one of the big houses, with the best tutors, the best weapons masters, the best books, and five hundred servants. He gives orders better than I do, because it's never occurred to him that anyone would disobey. And you don't. You just *obey*. And later, you hate him for it."

"He's not one of us. When he has what he wants, he'll go." Jehannes looked around.

Tom leaned back, shifted until his shoulders fitted neatly along a line of stone. "That's where you are wrong, Jehan. He *is* one of us. He is a broken man, a lost soul, whatever crap you want to call us. He has everything to prove, and he values us. He—" Tom spat. "I like him," he said. And shrugged. "He's a loon. He'll fight anyone, anytime."

Jehannes rubbed his chin. "I hear you."

"All I ask," said Tom. He didn't do anything obvious, but a subtle shift of his hips cleared the corridor. Jehannes stood straight, and then, quick as thought, his rondel dagger was in his hand—poised at shoulder height.

"Not planning to use it," he said. "But don't threaten me, Tom Lachlan. Save it for the archers."

The knight turned and walked away, sheathing his dagger easily.

Tom watched him go with a slight smile on his lips.

"Catch all that, young Michael?" he said, levering his giant form upright. Michael blushed.

"Not for his ears—hear me? Men talk. Sometimes with their bodies, sometimes like old fishwives. Not his business." He looked at Michael, who was not quite cowering in the doorframe.

But Michael was afraid, yes, but also determined. "I'm his squire."

Tom rubbed his chin. "So you get to decide some things. If you hear two archers talking about stealing from a third, would you peach?"

Michael managed to meet his eyes. "Yes."

"Good. And talking about raping a nun?" he asked.

Michael held his eye. "Yes."

"Good. And talking about how much they hate him?"

Michael paused. "I see what you mean."

"He's not their friend, he's their captain. He's pretty good at it, and he's better every day. But what he don't know won't hurt him. Get me?" Tom leaned in close.

"Yes." Michael didn't back away. He tried to stand tall.

Tom nodded. "You've guts, young Michael. Try not to get dead. We might make a man-at-arms out of you yet." He grinned. "Nice, that little chit of yours. Best act quickly if you want to keep her for yourself."

Out in the yard, a dozen archers and a pair of squires were gathered around a girl, and they were all furiously peeling carrots.

Lissen Carak—Father Henry

The priest watched the sell-swords come out of their leader's room. The captain, the source of infection. *She* came out first, and the Bastard was holding her hand like they were lovers. Perhaps they were—if he was an imp of Satan then pleasuring an old whore would be just his mark. Aristocrats. Birds of a feather.

Bile flooded his throat, and his hands shook a little to think that he had—he had—

He ducked his head to avoid looking at them, and went back to his sermon. But it was a long time before his hands were steady enough to scrape the old parchment as clean and thin as he needed it to be.

And when the biggest of the sell-swords came down the steps, he caught the priest's eye and smiled.

Henry felt fear go through him like a wave of cold and dirty water. What did the man know?

He got up from his work table as soon as the giant walked off, and he slunk across the chapel to the prie-dieu in the chapel. Reached under the altar cloth to make sure it was still there. His war-bow. His arrows.

He sagged with relief, and hurried back to his work table, imagining one of his shafts in the giant's groin. Listening to him scream.

Dormling—Hector Lachlan

The fast horsemen hadn't learned enough to change Hector's mind. He looked at the rough sketch of the country and shook his head. "If I go east, I'd as well take my beasts over the mountains to Theva," he said. "And I don't intend to do that. I have customers in Harndon and Harnford waiting for their cattle. West of the mountains, there's no way to pass a few thousand head except the road."

The Keeper had spent the night dancing and drinking his own ale as well as some nasty foreign spirits and his head was pounding. "So wait here and send a message to the king," he said.

Lachlan shook his head. "Sod that. I'll be away in the first light. What can you give me, Keeper? How many men?"

The Keeper grimaced. "Perhaps twenty helmets."

"Twenty? You have a hundred swords here, wasting your money and standing about idle."

The Keeper shook his head in turn. "The Wild's coming," he said. "I can't just drift away like some. I have to hold this place."

"You can hold this place with thirty men. Give me the rest."

"Maybe thirty like you—thirty heroes. Normal men? I need sixty."

"So now you'll give me forty? That's better. Forty brings me near a century strong—enough to watch both ends of the herd and still leave a sting in my tail." Lachlan looked over his sketch. "When we come down out of the hills, it'll be worse—I'll want horses. So I'll take fifty of your swords and two hundred head of horses."

The Keeper laughed. "Will you now?" he asked.

"Yes. For a third of my total profit," Lachlan said.

The Keeper's eyes widened. "A *third?*"

"Of the profit. In silver, payable when I'm standing on your doorstep on my road home." Lachlan was smiling as if he knew the punch line to a secret joke.

"And nothing if you're dead," said the Keeper.

"I confess, paying my debts won't matter so much to me if I'm dead," Lachlan answered.

The Keeper pondered a while. The tall serving woman came in, and the Keeper was surprised to see that nothing but the blandest of smiles passed between them. He'd been *sure* the dark-haired woman was the drover's type.

"I need your trade, and you're a well-known man," the Keeper said. "But you're trying to take all my horses and half my fighting strength on a wild-haired adventure with little profit and a great deal of death." He rubbed his head. "Tell me why I should help you?"

Lachlan kicked his sword blade around his chair and sat back. "If I told you I was going to make the greatest profit in my family's history by getting this herd through to the south—" he said.

The Keeper nodded. "Sure, but—" The drover's cheerful arrogance annoyed him.

"If I said that success would leave the king in my debt, and open new markets for my beef," Lachlan said.

"Perhaps," the Keeper said.

"If I said I lay with your youngest in the night, and she carries my son in her womb, and that I'll do this for her bride price and be your family?" Lachlan said.

The Keeper sat up, rage crossing his face.

"Don't you lose your temper with me, Will Tollins. She came to me free, and I'll wed her and be happy on it." But Lachlan put his hand on the hilt of his sword just in case.

The Keeper held his eye. And they sat there, diamond cut diamond, for a long time.

And then the Keeper smiled. "Welcome to my family."

Lachlan held out a great hand, and the other man took it.

"Forty-five swords, and all the horses I can raise by tomorrow, and I get half your profits—a quarter for my own and quarter for Sarah's bride price. And you wed her today." He had the drover's rough hand in his own, and he felt no falsehood in it.

Hector Lachlan, the Prince of the Drovers, withdrew his hand, spat and held it out, and Will Tollins, the Keeper of Dormling, took it, and the Inn of Dormling rang to a second night of revelry.

On the next morning, Lachlan led his tail and all his herds out onto the road into the watery sunlight. Every man had a shirt of shining rings, every ring riveted closed on a forge, every hauberk fitted to its wearer over a heavy cote of elk hide quilted full of sheep's wool, and every man had a heavy bow or a crossbow, a sword at least four feet high to the cross, and some had axes as tall as they themselves were, over their shoulders. Every man had a tall helmet with a brim that kept the rain off your face and a sharp point at the top, and a cloak of furze, and long leather boots like leather hose that went to the hip. The Keeper's men wore hoods of scarlet with black lines woven in, so that they made a check of red and black, and Lachlan's men had a more complex weave of red and blue and grey that made a colour that seemed to change with the trees and the rain. And Sarah Lachlan stood in her father's door-yard with a wreath of spring jasmine in her hair, kissing her man again and again while the flame of her hair lit the morning like a second sun. Her former suitor, the farmer, stood in the watery sun with a great axe on his shoulder, determined to go and die rather than face life without her.

Lachlan put an arm around him. "There's other girls, lad," he said.

Hector Lachlan took his great green ivory horn and put it to his lips and blew, and the deep note sounded up the vale and down it to the Cohocton, over leagues of ground. Deer raised their heads to listen, and bears paused in their orgy of spring eating, and beavers, surveying the dams broken by the spring rains, looked up from calculations. And other things—scaled and taloned, chiton brown or green—raised their heads and wondered. The horn call rang from hillside to cliff edge.

"I am Hector Lachlan, Drover of the Green Hills, and today I set forth to drive my herd to Harndon!" Hector shouted. "Death to any who oppose me, and long life to those who aid me." He sounded the horn again, and kissed his new wife, and took a charm from around his neck and gave it to her.

"Wish me luck, love," he said.

She kissed him, and gave him not one tear. But she looked at her father defiantly and was shocked to find him smiling back.

Then Hector crushed her to his burnie, and then he was walking out the gate. "Let's go!" he shouted, and the drive lumbered into motion.

West of Albinkirk—Gerald Random

Gerald Random scratched his head for the tenth time that morning under his linen coif and wished that he could stop his convoy for long enough to wash his hair.

The Magus rode by his side, all but asleep in the saddle. Random couldn't help looking at him with the same proprietary air a man might look at a beautiful woman who's suddenly consented to sleep with him. Having the Magus by his side was incredible luck, like a tale of errantry come to life.

The convoy was down a wagon this morning—the farrier's cart had been parked badly, had sunk in the rain and both oxen's throats had to be slit. The farrier himself was dry eyed, as his tools had been distributed among forty other carts and he'd been promised a place on the return. Altogether it was a small loss, but the whole column was exhausted, and Random was, for the first time, seriously considering turning around and going back south. The total loss of the convoy was a risk he could not really afford—his financial losses if the convoy failed but the stock survived would merely set him back ten years. But if it was destroyed, he'd be ruined.

And dead, you fool, he thought to himself. *Dead men never become lord mayor, nor sheriff.*

Set against that, he'd brought them through an ambush and one straight-up fight and last night most of them had snatched a little sleep. He was reasonably sure that, with the Magus at his side, they could cut their way to the fair at Lissen Carack.

But what if they arrived to find no fair? The farther north-west they went, the less likely it seemed that there was a fair at Lissen Carack. Or even a convent.

On the other hand, going back seemed both craven *and* dangerous. And the old Magus had been very clear: he was going to Lissen Carack, not back down the river to the king.

He scratched his itching head again.

He was seven leagues west of Albinkirk, if his notions of the road were accurate. About two days travel to the fords of the Cohocton, and another full day at oxen speed up the north side to the Convent.

The sun rose fully and the sky was truly blue for the first time in three days. Men's clothes dried, they warmed up, and the chatter of a well-ordered company began to spread. Men ate stale bread and drank a little wine, or small beer if they had it fresh, or hard cider if not, and the column rolled briskly along.

The soldiers were twitchy—Old Bob had a dozen mounted men spread a hundred horse-lengths wide in the trees ahead of the wagons, and the rest covered the rear in a tight knot ready to charge in any direction under Guilbert.

They didn't stop to eat a noonday meal, but rolled on.

When the sun was well down in the sky, Old Bob rode back to report that they were coming to one of the turn fields, the cleared fields maintained specifically for the fair convoys to camp.

"Looks like hell," he said. "But it has fresh water and it's clear enough. In fact, raspberry prickers had grown up over most of the field, and while one small convoy seemed to have made camp there a few days before, they had stayed to the edge by the road and cut no brush.

Guilbert sent his men out into the raspberry canes in armour, to cut armloads of the stuff with their swords, and he had the archers lash them in bundles on the sturdy Xs of a pair of fascine horses, cradles made of heavy logs where armloads of brush and prickers could be wrapped tight. In the last three hours of daylight, while the boys cooked and brought in water and the older men saw to the animals and circled the wagons, the soldiers build a rampart of raspberry cane bundles.

And then, the evening being dry, they set fire to the rest of the field. The canes went up like dried wood, burning into the edge of the trees in a few minutes.

The Magus came awake to watch the sparks rise into the clear night air.

"That was extremely foolish," he said.

Random was eating a garlic sausage. "Why?" he asked. "Clear field for archery. No cover for the little boglins and spider irks."

"Fire calls strong as naming," the old Magus said. "Fire is the Wild's bane." He glared at the merchant, and his glare held weight.

Random had been glared at all his life. "Convoy's safer with a clear field around," he said, like an angry boy.

"Not if six wyverns come, you idiot. Not if a dozen golden bears decide you've intruded—not if even a pair of daemon wardens decide you've broken the Forest Law. Then your clear field will not save you." But he looked resigned. "And irks have nothing to do with spiders. Irks are Fae. Now—where's my patient?"

"The young knight? Sound asleep. He wakes up, talks to himself, and goes back to sleep."

"Best thing for him," Harmodius said. He walked around the circle of wagons, found his man, and looked him over.

Harmodius put the blanket back after a long look, and then the younger man's eyes opened.

"You might have just let me live," he said. He looked pained. "Sweet Jesu—I mean you might have let me die."

"No one *ever* thanks me," the Magus agreed.

"I'm Gawin Murien," he said. Groaned. "What have you done to me?"

"I know who you are," the Magus said. "Now they can call you Hard Neck."

Neither man laughed.

"I don't really know what I did to you. I'll work it out over the next few days. Don't worry about it."

"You mean, don't worry that I'm gradually turning into some loathsome God-cursed enemy of man who will try to slay and eat all my friends?" Gawin asked. His voice strove for calm, but there was panic in it.

"You have a vivid imagination," Harmodius said.

"So I've always been told." Gawin looked at his own upper left arm and recoiled in horror. "Good Christ, I have scales. It wasn't a dream!" His voice rose suddenly, and his eyes narrowed. "By Saint George—my lord, must I ask you to kill me?" His eyes went far away. *"I was so beautiful,"* he said, in another voice.

Harmodius made a face. "So very dramatic. I seized the power to heal you from something of the Wild." He shrugged. "I wasn't really fully in control of the power, but never mind that. Without it, you'd have died. And whatever you may feel about it right now, death is not better!"

The young knight rolled away, closing his eyes. "Like you would know. Go away and let me sleep. Oh, Blessed Virgin, am I doomed to be a monster?"

"I very much doubt it," Harmodius said, but he knew that his own slight doubt was not very reassuring.

"Please leave me alone," the knight said.

"Very well. But I'll be back to check on you." Harmodius reached out with a tendril of power and it was his turn to recoil at what he saw. Gawin saw his reaction.

"What's happening to me?"

Harmodius shook his head. "Nothing," he lied.

An hour after full dark, the enemy struck. There was a whistle of arrows from the darkness, and two of the guildsmen on guard fell—one silently, the other with the panicked screams of a man in pain.

Guilbert had the wagons manned and alert in a hundred heartbeats. Which was as well, because a wave of boglins, announced by a sinister rustling, exploded into the north face of the wagon-fort.

But Guilbert was an old campaigner, and his dozen archers shot fire-arrows into the piles of cane and brush left around the old clearing, and most of them caught. And then, by the flickering light of spring bonfires, the guildsmen and the soldiers killed. Having negotiated the raspberry cane walls, the boglins were almost incapable of climbing the tall wagons after, and they died in dozens trying.

But the red arrows arching like vicious dragonflies over the fires began to annoy the defenders. The arrows lacked the potency to penetrate good mail, and their flint heads shattered easily, but they sunk deep in exposed flesh, and men who took them, even as a scratch on the hand, became fevered in an hour.

Harmodius went from man to man, pulling the poison by grammerie. He'd had a day to gather power and rest, and he was full of sunlight, his aids charged and ready except for the two wands, whose charging required greater time, attention, and investment.

When the fires burned down, he cast a powerful phantasm of light on a tree way out at the edge of the raspberry thicket. He repeated the spell six times, all the way around the wagon-fort, to back-light their attackers and blind their archers. But the Hermetic cost was immense, and he was shouting his power to the world.

As his sixth light casting began to fade, and the deadly, wasp-like arrows began to come in again, Harmodius felt the presence of an enemy. A practitioner.

Another magus.

There was a moment's warning—possibly as the other one raised a defensive ward.

Harmodius raised his own. And then, like a man fighting with a sword and buckler, he pushed his ward across the open space between himself and the other source of power. If his ward was held close to his body, it could only cover *him*. Held close to the other magus, the ward could cover the whole convoy.

A simple exercise in mathematica that most practitioners never learned.

It cost a fraction more energy to maintain the ward over there than here.

Energy exploded against his ward and was deflected. Irks and boglins died under the onslaught of phantasms which should have been supporting them.

Harmodius smiled wickedly. Evidently whoever was out there had a great deal of raw power and very, very little training.

In his youth, Harmodius had been an accomplished swordsman. And the practice of hermetical combat had many close analogues in swordsmanship. Harmodius had always meant to write a treatise on the subject.

As his adversary prepared another attack, Harmodius dashed through the labyrinthine palace of his memory, stacking wards and gardes in a sequence he'd practised but never used.

His opponent's next attack came with more force—a titanic, angry upwelling of power that came as a lurid green stripe across the night.

His first ward was voided. The enemy had moved off line, realising the strength of his forward defence.

His second ward, however, caught the attack and subtly displaced it—and the third ward reflected it down yet another line—right back into the caster, who was struck squarely by his own phantasm.

His wards flared a deep blue-green—and Harmodius struck. In the tempo of the opponent's own attacks, he launched a line of bright, angelic white—a line like a lance that connected his index finger and the enemy's wards. It cost Harmodius almost no power, but the enemy, having over-committed to warding in the wrong place, now used his reserve ward to block...

...nothing. The light beam was just that. Light. There was no force behind it.

Like a fencing master going for an elegant, killing thrust, Harmodius drew power for his attack, and launched it, all in a tenth of a beat of a panicked guildsman's heart. And as the blow went in—over one ward, under a second, and through the weakened energies of the third—he felt his enemy collapse. Felt him experience the despair of defeat.

And without intending to, he reached out and seized something—just as he had taken power to save the young knight. But this time, he took the essence of the enemy sorcerer much faster and more thoroughly.

His opponent's power was extinguished like a candle.

Harmodius took a deep breath, and realised that he was now more powerful than he had been when he started the night.

He cast a seventh light without any opposition.

The irks faded into the brush, and the rest of the night passed as slowly as he'd ever known, but with no further attacks.

West of Albinkirk—Gerald Random

A horse length from the Magus, Random stood with Old Bob. The last exchange of phantasm happened incredibly quickly. Random had watched it.

In the distance, something screamed.

A cruel smile spread across Harmodius's lips.

Random glanced at Old Bob, who was looking at him. "That was—"

Old Bob shook his head. "Legendary," he said.

In the morning, the convoy confronted the truth—the broken bodies of a hundred boglins lay among the wagons. No man could deny what they had fought. Several vomited. Every man crossed himself and prayed.

Random approached the Magus who sat, cross-legged in the open, greeting the rising sun with his arms across his lap.

"May I interrupt?" he asked.

"I'd rather you didn't," grumbled the Magus.

"My apologies," Random said. "But I need some information."

The Magus snapped his eyes open. "If you do not let me do this, I will have fewer arrows to my bow when they come again," he said.

Random bowed. "I think we should turn and go back."

The Magus frowned. "Do as you must, merchant. Leave me be!"

Random shook his head. "Why shouldn't I turn back?"

Harmodius's voice was savage. "How do I know, you money-grubbing louse? Do as you like! Just *leave me alone!*"

Old Bob was already mounted and Guilbert stood by his horse with a short, oddly curved bow across his saddle. Today was his turn to ride point.

Old Bob gestured tp Messire Random. "Well?" he asked.

"We press on for Lissen Carak," Random said.

Old Bob rolled his eyes. "What the fuck for?"

Random looked back at the Magus. And shrugged. "He made me angry," Random said, with simple honesty.

Old Bob looked at the pile of dead boglins. "You fought 'em before?" he asked.

Random nodded.

"Take every man to the pile and make him look at them. Careful like. In daylight. Make every man touch one. Make every man see where they're weak." He shrugged. "It helps."

Random hadn't thought of any of those things. So he ordered it done, and stood there while Old Bob hauled a corpse off the pile.

The guildsmen flinched as he slammed the body down.

"Don't be afraid, lads," Old Bob said. "It's dead."

"Fucking *bug*," said one of the cutlers.

"Not bugs. More like—" Old Bob shrugged. "Get the Magus to tell you what they're like. But look. They have hard parts and soft parts. Hard on the chest. Soft as cheese here under the arms." To demonstrate, he took his arming dagger and thrust it into the muddy brown skin, which extended like membrane from the soft-hard chitinous armour of the torso, under the arm with no effort at all. Green-black ichor covered his blade, but none leaked out.

"A thrust is always deadly," Old Bob said. He struck, and his heavy dagger blade punched through the thing's tough shell, and a putrid odour filled the air. One of the salters vomited.

Old Bob walked over and kicked him. "Do that when you're fighting and you're fucking dead. Hear me? Look at it. *Look at it!*" He looked around at the startled apprentices. "Everyone touch it. Take one off the pile for yourself, and try it with your sword. *Do it.*"

As Guilbert rode to the head of the column, he muttered to Harold Redlegs—loud enough to be heard—"Because the old Magus made him mad? That makes all sorts of sense."

It didn't make any sense to Random, either.

But an hour down the road, Harmodius rode up next to the merchant and bowed in the saddle.

"My pardon if I was brusque," he said. "Sunrise is a very important moment."

Random laughed. "Brusque, is it?" he asked. But then he laughed. It was a beautiful day, the woods were green, and he was commanding the biggest convoy of his life.

Riding to war beside a living legend.

He laughed again, and the old Magus laughed, too.

Thirty wagons behind, Old Bob heard their laughter and rolled his eyes.

The Sossag People had gathered almost their full fighting strength and brought it south across the wall. Ota Qwan said so, ten times a day, and the second full day in camp, he saw the whole fighting strength of the Sossag gathered in one place, the great clearing a mile south of camp. He stopped counting men when he reached several hundred, but there had to be a thousand painted warriors and another few hundred unpainted men and women. He'd learned that to be painted was to declare a willingness to die. Unpainted men might fight—or not, if they had other immediate interests, like a new wife or new children.

Peter had also learned that the Sossag had little interest in cooking. He had tried to win a place through efforts with a copper pot and a skillet, but his beef stew with stolen wine was eaten noisily and quickly by the band with which he travelled, the Six River Sossag who also called themselves the "Assegatossag" or "Those who follow where the Squash Rots" as Ota Qwan explained.

They ate it, and went about their business. No one thanked him or told him what a fine meal it had been.

Ota Qwan laughed. "It's food!" he said. "The Sossag don't eat that well, and we all know what it is like to grow hungry. Your meal was excellent in that there was enough for everyone."

Peter shook his head.

Ota Qwan nodded. "Before I was Ota Qwan, I understood what it was like to cook, to eat well, to *dine*." He laughed. "Now, I understand many things, and none of them involve fine wines or crunchy bread."

Peter hung his head a little and Ota Qwan slapped his back.

"You will earn a place. Everyone says you work hard. That is all the People expect of a newcomer."

Peter nodded.

But that night he made a number of new friends. Dinner had been a simple soup with some seasonings and deer meat that Ota Qwan had contributed, and one of the reptilian monsters had come, sniffed the carcass of the deer, and made its strange crying noises until Skadai came at a run.

Peter had been afraid, but it had left them in peace, the deer meat had gone into the soup, and all was well.

When the soup was served, two of the boglins came out of the woods. They were slim without being tall—when they stood erect, they were only the height of a tall child, and their heads were more like insects than men, with the skin stretched tight over light bones perched on bodies with a bulbous armoured torso and four very mammalian appendages. Their legs were thin and heavily muscled, the arms whipcord-tight. They were hideous, and just watching one move was the stuff of nightmare. They didn't mix much with Sossag, although Peter had seen Skadai speak to a group of them.

They also seemed to come in three types—the commonest were red-brown and moved very quickly; the second type were clearly warriors, with a more heavily armoured carapace and paler, almost silver, skin. The warriors were almost as tall as a man, and every appendage had a spike. The Sossag used the Albin name for those ones—*wights*.

And finally, there was what seemed to be a leader class—long and thin, like great mantis creatures. The Sossag called them *priests*.

These two creatures were both lowly workers, each carrying a bow and a spear, naked except for a quiver and a canteen. Peter tried not to watch the liquid sliding of plate on plate in their lower abdomens. It was disturbing.

They stopped by his fire. Both rotated their heads in unison, their strange lobe-shaped eyes seeing the fire and the man together.

"Guk fud?" said the nearer of the two. His voice was scratchy, almost a screech.

Peter tried to get past his fear. "I don't understand," he said.

"U guk fud?" said the other one. "Gud fud?"

The first one shook its head and abdomen—an alien display, but Peter understood it was showing impatience. "Me try fud," he screeched.

Peter still didn't understand their shrieks, but the pointing claw-hands seemed to indicate his stew pot.

None of the Sossag were rising to help him. As usual, they had eaten to satiety and now lay on the ground, virtually unmoving, although every one of them was watching him. Ota Qwan was smiling—a hard, cruel smile.

Peter bent, turning his back on the creatures, and poured stew into a bowl. He added a little wild oregano and handed it to the nearer of the two monsters.

He took it, and Peter watched him sniff the bowl. He wished he hadn't. Watching the thing's not-entirely-inhuman nose split open to reveal a cavernous hole in the face with spiky hairs—

The thing made a loud scratching noise with two of its arms and poured the whole bowl straight into the hole in its face.

Threw back its head at an unnatural angle and screamed.

Then it held out the bowl for more.

Peter scooped two more bowls, put oregano on both, and handed one to each boglin.

The entire process was repeated.

The smaller of the two boglins opened and closed its beak-mouth three or four times, emitting a chemical reek that caught at the back of Peter's throat.

"Fud gud!" it chirped.

Long, agile tongues of a shocking pink-purple emerged from their mouths, and they licked the bowls clean.

They emitted a long scratching noise together, and raced off, running lightly on the ground, bent half over.

Peter stood by his fire with two empty food bowls. He was shaking a little.

Skadai came. "You have been honoured," he said. "They seldom notice us." He looked like a man with more to say, but then he pursed his lips, patted Peter on the shoulder, smiled and loped off, as he always did.

Peter was still trying to decide what to make of the incident when the woman came and put a hand on the small of his back.

That hand on his back was a palpable thing—another means of communication, a thing he hadn't expected, and it conveyed a wealth of information to him—so much, in fact, that an hour later he was between her legs...and moments after that another man kicked him in the head.

Such a blow might have killed, but the painted man was barefoot and Peter had a little warning. And despite being a former slave and a cook, Peter had been bred to war, so as the kick turned his head, as he ripped himself free of the dark-haired woman's embrace, he was already moving, calculating, reaching for the knife he wore around his neck.

The painted man expected him to be easy prey. He screamed, in rage or feigned rage, and attacked again. Peter had rolled on his back with the force of the kick, and he had the knife in his hand, and when the painted man—his red and black and white mixed in blotchy patches that looked like a skin sickness—jumped at him, Peter killed him as easily as such a thing could ever happen. He rammed his blade deep into the man's belly and then rolled him over as he screamed in shock and desperation, his wild eyes suddenly wide with the despair of agony leading inevitably to death.

Peter ripped the knife up his abdomen, spilling his guts and covering himself in the man's gore.

Then, full of his own terror, he plunged the knife into the man's eyes, one and two.

By then, the blotchy man was dead.

Peter lay there for a moment. Every one of the last hundred heartbeats was open to him like a long book, carefully read, and the remnants of his erection reminded him that he had passed from one extreme of life to the other in that time.

He tried to get to his feet but his knees were shaking and there were men all around him.

All Sossag men.

Skadai held out a hand and hauled him to his feet with a firmness that seemed threatening. But was not.

Then Ota Qwan was there, with a steadying hand.

"Open your mouth," he said.

Peter opened it, and Skadai stuck a bloody finger into his mouth and began to chant. Ota Qwan grabbed his arm tightly. "This is important,"

he said. "Listen: Skadai says, 'Take your foe, Gruntag, into your body.'"
Ota Qwan squeezed again. "Skadai says, 'Now you and Gruntag are one.
What you were, he is. What he was, you are.'"

Peter wanted to retch at the taste of coppery, warm blood inside his
mouth.

"I say, don't make a habit of killing Sossag," Ota Qwan said.

"He attacked me!" Peter squeaked.

"You were fucking his woman, who was only using you to be rid of an
inferior man. She avoided the shame of sending him from her blankets by
arranging for you to kill him. Understand?" Ota Qwan turned to a group
of painted men and said something, and they all laughed.

Peter spat. "What's so funny?"

Ota Qwan shook his head. "Our humour. Yours later, but not now, I
think."

"Tell me," Peter said.

"They asked how you were. I said you weren't sure whether the dick or
the knife went in more smoothly." Ota Qwan's eyes were a bright blue,
and the man was amused. "You are now a man, and a Sossag. Killing your
own should not be a habit, but you must know by now what the Wild is."

Peter spat again. "It's every hand raised against every other hand," he
said. He had trained to kill all his young life, and his first failure to kill
another man had made him a slave. But this sudden success felt more like
rape than victory. He was covered in blood and worse, and yet these men
were congratulating him. "There is no law."

Ota Qwan shook his head. "Don't be foolish," he said. "There are many
laws. But the greatest of them is that the strongest is the strongest. And
every creature, weak or strong, makes a good meal." He laughed. "It's no
different at the king's court. But here, it's fair and honest, at least in that
no one lies. Skadai is faster and deadlier than I will ever be. I will never
challenge him. But another man might—or a woman—and the matrons
would name a form of challenge, and the challenger would face Skadai. Or
perhaps simply attack him—but that sort of victory does not always result
in the killer gaining the power and prestige he seeks. Am I making sense?"

"Too much sense," Peter said. "I want to wash." Peter wanted free of this
alien man and his paint and his aura of violence.

"I tell you this because now other warriors see you as a man and you
may be challenged. Or simply killed. Up until now, I have protected you."
Ota Qwan shrugged.

"Why kill me?" Peter asked.

Ota Qwan shrugged. "To raise the number of men they've killed? Or to
claim Senegral, your woman?" He laughed. "Grundag died easily because he
thought you were a slave. He wasn't much of a man, but he was a fighter,
and his very stupidity made men afraid of him. They are not afraid of

you—although the way you opened him and cut out his eyes may make some men afraid. But many men want Senegral, and she doesn't like to say no."

Peter had made it to the stream, and despite the cold and the sharp rocks, he threw himself into the low pool where the men washed their cups, heedless of the layer of water-swollen grains where a hundred wooden bowls had been washed after dinner. Heedless of leeches. Wanting only to get the sticky blood and intestinal matter off his hands and his belly and his groin.

From the water, he said, "Perhaps I should just kill her."

Ota Qwan laughed. "An elegant solution, except that her brothers and sisters would then surely kill you."

The water woke his brain and froze his skin. He put his head under the water and come up floundering, feet aching from trying to balance on sharp rocks. "What can I do?" he asked.

"Paint!" Ota Qwan said. "As a warrior on a mission, you are exempt from such treatment. Unless you provoke it, of course. But men are not as swift as other animals, as deadly in a fight, as well-taloned, or as long limbed. Eh? But in a pack, we are the deadliest animals in the Wild, and when we paint, we are a pack. Do you understand?"

Peter shook his head. "No," he said. "But I will paint. And that commits me to make war against people I do not know to gain a little peace at home." He laughed. His laughter was strange and wild and a little crazed. "But they enslaved me, so they can take the consequences."

Ota Qwan nodded. "I knew you would make one of us from the moment I met you," he said. "Don't disdain us. We do as other people do, we just don't call it by pretty names. We make war now to support Thorn, but also so that all the other killers and all the other predators will see our strength and leave us in peace. Will fear us. So we can go home and grow squash. It is not all war and knives in the dark."

Peter sighed. "I hope not."

Ota Qwan made a noise. "You need to paint soon, I think. And have a name. But I will let someone else name you."

He gave Peter a hand out of the stream, and then took him to a fire, where he removed the horde of leeches stuck to the former cook. On another day, the leeches would have appalled him, but Peter bore their removal with hardly a glance, earning a respectful grunt from an older man.

Then Ota Qwan spoke, and all the men and several women stiffened, paid close attention, and went to their blanket rolls, returning with pretty round boxes of pottery and wood—some covered in remarkable designs made with coloured hair or quills, and some made of gold or silver.

Every little vessel held paint—red, black, white, yellow, or blue.

"May I paint you?" Ota Qwan asked.

Peter smiled. "Of course," he said. He was exhausted and almost asleep. Three men and a painted woman did the actual painting, under Ota

Qwan's direction. It took an hour, but when they were done Peter was black on one side of his body and red on the other.

But on his face they had painted something more intricate. He had felt the woman's fingers on his face, around his eyes, her own rapt expression and slightly open mouth oddly transfigured by the fish she wore painted across her eyes.

When they were done one of the men brought a small round mirror in a horn case, and he looked at the mask over his face, the divisions of white and red and black like herring bones, and he nodded. It spoke to him, although he wasn't sure what it meant.

He left them his shirt.

He walked though the firelit darkness, and the air was cool on his painted skin, and the fires burning at every camp were warm, even from a distance. Ota Qwan led him from fire to fire, and warriors murmured to him. He nodded and bowed his head.

"What are they saying?" he asked.

"Mostly hello. A few comment on how much taller you are now. The old man tells you to keep your paint clean and sharp, and not muddy it as you used to do." Ota Qwan laughed. "Because, of course, you used to be Grundag. Understand?"

"Christ," Peter said. And yet, the murmured welcomes straightened his spine. He had *triumphed*. He didn't need to wallow in the killing.

He was alive, and tall, and strong, and he rather liked the paint.

At his own fire, Senegral had made all of Grundag's belongings into a small display, and she gave him a cup of warm, spiced tea, and he drank it. Ota Qwan stood at the edge of the firelight and watched.

"She says, look at the good bow you have. Some of your arrows are very poor. You should make better, or trade for them. And she says that she will try not to inflame other men, if you will only keep her the way she wishes to be kept."

Peter went through the carefully laid out goods by the bark basket, holding each item up in the firelight. Two excellent knives and a good bow with no arrows to speak of; some furs, a pair of leggings and two pairs of unadorned moccasins. A horn container full of black paint, a glass jar with red paint. Two cups. A copper pot.

"I thought women made their men shoes?" Peter asked.

Ota Qwan laughed. "Woman who fancy their men make them magnificent moccasins," he said.

"I see," Peter said. He packed everything back into the basket. The woman came and stood next to him, and he put a hand under her skirt and ran it up her leg to her thigh, and then around her thigh, and she made a sound, and soon enough, they were back where they had been when the dead man kicked him in the head.

At some point she moaned, and later he laughed aloud at the absurdity of it all. He wanted Ota Qwan to translate his thoughts to her, but of course, the man was gone.

Why is he helping me? Peter thought, and then he was asleep.

And in the morning, all the painted men rose, took only the equipment they needed for violence, and followed Skadai. Peter took the bow and the best knife, and his paint and a single red wool blanket and strode naked, after Ota Qwan. He found it surprisingly easy to ask no questions, simply follow.

Later, he asked Ota Qwan how to get arrows, and the man silently gave him a dozen.

"Why?" Peter asked. "Is it not every man against every other man?"

Ota Qwan laughed. "You know nothing," he said. "Do you not follow me? Will you do my bidding when the arrows fly and the steel fills the air?"

Peter thought about it. "I suppose I will."

Ota Qwan laughed. "Come. Let's go find your name."

South of Albinkirk—de Vrailly

Jean de Vrailly clamped down on his impatience and it turned, as it always did, to anger. The blossoming of his rage always made him feel sinful, dirty, and less of a man and a knight, and so, while riding easily through the high ridges and spring flowers of Alba's fertile heartland, he reined up his second charger and dismounted, to the confusion of his brothers in arms, and knelt in the dirt beside the road to pray.

The mild pain of kneeling for prolonged periods always steadied him.

Images floated to the surface of his thoughts as he imagined the crucifix- ion of the Christ; as he pictured himself as a knight riding to the rescue of the Holy Sepulchre, or inserted himself in meditation into the adoration of the Magi, a lowly caravan guard sitting on his charger behind the princes who adored the newborn lamb.

Contempt broke through his reverie. He despised the King of Alba, who stopped in each town to play to his peasants, win their sighs and their raucous laughter, still their fears and give them law. It was done with too much drama and it took too much time, and it was obvious—obvious to a child—that something was happening in the north that required the instant application of the kingdom's mailed fist.

Disgust. The knights of Alba were slow, slothful, full of vice and barbarity. They drank, they ate too much, belched and farted at table, and never, ever exercised in arms. Jean de Vrailly and his retinue rode from town to town in full armour, cap à pied, with heavy quilted cotes under hauberks of ring mail surmounted by shining steel plate—three layers of protection, which every knight in the East wore every day of his life—to town, to church or to ride out with his lady.

The Wild had not made a major incursion in the East in a century, yet their knighthood stood ready to fight at every moment.

Here, where stands of unkempt trees stood on every ridge, and where an incursion of the Wild threatened a major city just over the horizon—the knights rode abroad in colourful tunics with fashionable, long trailing sleeves, pointed shoes and carefully wrapped hats like the turbans of the far East, with their armour stored in wicker baskets and oak barrels.

Right now, four days from Albinkirk, a party of the king's younger knights and squires were hawking, riding their palfreys along the ridge tops to the west, and he wanted to punish them for their light-hearted foolishness. These effete barbarians needed to be taught what war *was*. They needed to learn to take off their chamois gloves and feel the cold weight of steel on their soft hands.

He prayed, and praying made him better. He was able to smile to the king, and nod to a young squire who ill-manneredly galloped down the column raising a cloud of dust, mounted on a hot-blooded Eastern mare worth a hundred leopards as a racehorse and worthless in a fight.

But when the army, which grew every day as contingents of knights, men-at-arms, and archers joined from each town, each county, each manor, settled for the night, de Vrailly ordered his squires to set his pavilion as far from the rest of the army as could be managed—out in the horse lines, surrounded by beasts. He dined simply on soldiers' rations with his cousin, summoned his chaplain, Father Hugh, to hear Mass and confession of his sins of passion, and then, shriven and spiritually clean, he bathed in water from the Albin, the mighty river that rolled by the door of his tent, dismissed his squires and his slaves, and towelled himself dry, listening to the sound of three thousand horses cropping grass on a beautiful spring evening. The smell of the wildflowers overpowered even the smell of the horses.

Dry, he dressed in a white shirt and braes and a white jacket, a jupon of the very simplest style. He unrolled a small, precious carpet from far to the east, and opened a portable shrine—two paintings hinged face to face for travel—the Virgin and the Crucifixion. He knelt before their images and prayed, and when he felt empty and clean he opened himself.

And his archangel came.

Child of Light, I salute you.

As he did every time the angel came, de Vrailly burst into tears. Because he never quite believed a visitation was real, until the next one confirmed all of the past ones. His unbelief—his doubt—was its own punishment.

Through his tears, he bowed. "Bless me, Taxiarch, for I have failed you many times."

He tried never to look directly into its shining face which seemed in memory to be made of beaten gold, but in fact looked more like mobile, sparkling pearl. Looking too closely might break the spell—

It is not your error that the King of Alba did not do as we wished. It is not through you that this kingdom has been untimely assailed by the forces of Evil. But we will overcome.

"I succumb to rage, to contempt, to self-righteousness and anger."

None of these will help you to be the best knight in the world. Remember how you are when you fight, and be that man at all times.

No priest had ever put it to him so well. When he fought, he dismissed all worldly concerns and was only the point of his spear. The archangel's words rang through him like the meeting of blades between two strong men, like the clarion call of a stallion trumpeting.

"Thank you, lord."

Be of good cheer. A great test is coming. You must be ready.

"I am always ready."

The archangel placed a shining hand on his forehead, and just for a moment, de Vrailly looked up into the archangel's shining face, his outstretched, perfect hand, his golden hair, so much brighter than de Vrailly's own and yet somehow alike.

Bless and keep you, my child. When the standard falls, you will know what must be done. Do not hesitate.

De Vrailly frowned.

But the angel was gone.

He could smell the incense, and he felt at peace—his mind comforted, languorous, as he was after he had a woman, but without the sense of shame or dirt.

He smiled. Took a deep breath, and sang the opening notes of a Te Deum under his breath.

West of Albinkirk—Harmodious

Harmodius lay on a pack of furs, the pottery mug of warm wine balanced on his chest, and watched Random stir a hot poker into another beaker, adding honey and spices.

Behind the merchant, Gawin Murien sat quietly mending a shoe. He didn't speak, but he was going about the tasks of soldiering, and Harmodius was content to keep a watch on him. His left shoulder was now heavily scaled from the nipple to the neck, and down to the base of his bicep. The scales no longer seemed to be spreading, but they were growing larger and harder. The young man seemed curiously heedless of them—since the first night, he hadn't remarked on them at all.

Harmodius was old in guile, and had known many young men. This one was preparing for death, and so Harmodius watched him carefully. The second ring on his right hand held a phantasm that would drop the boy like a blow from a spiritual axe.

"I like it sweet. But I have a sweet tooth," Random said. He grinned. "My wife says that all my efforts to win riches and fame are merely to ensure my supply of biscuits and honey."

Harmodius drank from his cup again. It was far sweeter than he liked it but on this evening, under the curtain of stars with a dreadful enemy as close as the edge of the firelight, the hippocras was all he could have asked.

Immanence.

It was a mild shock, like seeing a former lover walk into a tavern. Somewhere not so very far away, something powerful was manifesting. It might be something supremely powerful, a very long way away, or something merely awesome and terrifying, in the next field.

"To arms!" Harmodius said, jumping to his feet. He gathered himself for a moment and extended his enhanced senses.

Gawin Morion was already in his leather jupon, and his helmet was going on his head.

Random had a breast- and backplate on over his travel clothes, and he produced a crossbow from the same wagon bed which had held the makings of their wine.

Other men repeated the alarm, but most were fully dressed, armed and armoured, and Harmodius ignored them all, reaching out—past the orange glow of firelight, past the fields of bracken and fern that surrounded them.

Nothing. Not a single boglin.

Harmodius knew the laws of identity in the use of Power. There were two ways to locate another user. He could sit silently, his attuned senses waiting to see if there was another pulse of *immanence*. Or he could send out a pulse of his own power to ring across the night, which would identify him to every creature of the Wild with the slightest sensitivity to such things. Which was most of them.

He settled for the quieter, more passive option, even though it was not in his nature and although he was all but bursting with power. He hadn't felt so *capable* in many years. He wanted to play with it, the way a man will swing a new sword about, cutting the heads off ferns and fennel stalks.

Harmodius bore down on his power. And his impatience.

Pushed his senses further.

Further.

Well to the north he found trolls—their large, misshapen forms as horrible in their lack of symmetry as they were in their black crystalline alienness. They were marching.

To the west, he found a user of much talent and little training. But he had no context for the discovery—a village witch, or a boglin shaman or one of the Wild's living trees. He had no idea, and he dismissed the entity as far too weak to have displayed the power he had sensed.

Whatever it was, it seemed to have left the world—departed by whatever path it had chosen. It manufactured a new *loci*, or jumped to one that had previously existed.

The display of power remained like a beacon, and Harmodius was unhappy to find that it was behind them, to the south and the east by many leagues. But he swooped on it like a raptor falling on a rabbit—and fled just as quickly when he sensed the order of magnitude it represented.

When he was a small boy in a fishing village Harmodius, who'd had a different name then, had rowed out on the deep in a small boat with two friends to fish for sea trout and salmon with hand lines. Porpoises and small whales shared the sport, and sometimes they caught good fish only to have them snatched away by their aquatic rivals. But late in the day, while pulling in a heavy fish, Harmodius had seen a seal—an enormous seal as long as his boat—flash into a turn and reach for their magnificent fish...

...just as a leviathan, as much larger than the seal as the seal was larger than the salmon, turned under the boat to take the seal.

The size of the creature beneath the boat—fifty times its length—and its great eye as it rolled, the froth of blood that reached the surface without a sound as it took the seal, the gentle swell it made, and then, perhaps the most terrifying of all, its mighty fluke breaking the surface a hundred yards away and flinging spray all the way over them—

In all his life, Harmodius had never seen anything that moved him so deeply, or so impressed on him his own insignificance. It was more than fear. It was the discovery that some things are so great that they would not notice you even if they destroyed you.

He'd brought in the salmon, which died unaware of the role it had played in the death of the mighty seal, and the lesson was not lost on the boy.

And all of that came to him as he fled the immensity of whatever creature had briefly been in the Valley of the Albin, fifty leagues to the south.

He came back into his own skin.

Random was looking at him with concern. "You screamed!" he said. "Where are they?"

"We are safe," Harmodius said. But his voice was more of a a sob than it should have been. *No one is safe. What was that?*

East of Albinkirk—Hector Lachlan

East of Albinkirk, the sun rose on the western slopes of Parnassus, the westernmost of the mountains of the Morea where the streams rushed down, heavy with the last of the snow and the spring rains to flood the upper waters of the Albin.

Hector Lachlan was drinking tea and watching the East Branch. It was high—far too high—and he was trying to figure out how he might get his herds over it.

Behind him, the men in his tail were breaking camp, packing the wagon, donning their hauberks and their weapons, and the youngest, or the least lucky, were already out with the herds.

While he watched, his tanist, Donald Redmane, stripped naked at the water's edge and plunged in, using the edge of a ruined beaver dam as a diving platform. He was high spirited and strong and only heartbeats later, he was pulled out by the rope around his waist, his shoulder and collarbone bruised against the rocks.

Lachlan winced.

That night, something killed a stallion in their herd, and Lachlan, who had never fought an irk in his life, had to assume that it was some such creature who was responsible—multiple punctures and slashes from something much smaller than the horse. But the *why* of it eluded him. He doubled his herd guards, aware of how futile such measures could be. In the Hills, he had stone fences and deep glens with natural fortifications to take herds and guard them, but here, on the road—he was in the country that the drovers held to be *safe*. And something was hunting him. He could feel it.

Chapter Nine

Lissen Carak—The Red Knight

The fog was thin and wispy, but it did its job. It forced whatever was watching them to be more aggressive with the animals it was using. Rabbits came out of the woods in broad daylight. Starlings flew over the new diggings, first in pairs and then in swift flocks.

Toward midday, when Ser Jehannes had the double outer ditch dug and when the merchant adventurers of Harndon, Lorica, Theva and Albin were cursing their luck and their temporary taskmaster as the blisters on their hands popped, the Abbess cast again, the fog grew thicker, and the animals grew more numerous still.

By the time the nearly mutinous merchants were allowed to end their day and go to Mass, the fog was so thick that the watchmen on the fortress towers couldn't see the base of their own wall. They could see the far horizon, though. The captain had no intention of letting his own fog put him at a disadvantage. Despite which precaution, wyverns overflew the fortress every hour or two, and the hearts of the defenders flinched each time the leathery wings passed. Out in the trees beyond the fields there was movement—the kind of movement a hunter sees when his quarry shakes a tree, or when a squirrel leaps to a branch too light to support the weight of the jump.

Michael opened a blank book of bound parchment, and wrote in his best hand:

The Siege of Lissen Carak. Day One. Or is it Day Eight?

Today the captain and the lady Abbess raised a fog with a powerful phantasm. The enemy are all around us, and many have commented that the air seems thick and difficult to breathe. Maddock the Archer was shot dead with a longbow arrow from the cover of a stand of trees when he ventured from the new trenches to retrieve a mallet. He must have left the cover of the lady's fog.

There is a wyvern in the air over us. I can hear it scream. And I can feel it, even through the roof—a pressure on the top of my head.

Michael put a line through that last, and then very carefully inked it over until not a word was legible.

The captain has a sortie mounted and ready to ride at all hours. Every armoured man has a turn in the Sortie. He also ordered heavy machines constructed in the towers. The fortress has two heavy towers, and one now holds a heavy ballista and the other, lower tower holds a trebuchet.

The people of the countryside and the merchants of the caravans have dug a trench from the Lower Town all the way to Bridge Castle. It is deeper than a man is tall, and wide enough to drive a small wagon along the bottom. We are lining it with boards. The captain has ordered bags placed along the bottom and no man knows what is in them.

At sunset Michael went on to the walls, and joined with every man and woman in the fortress in prayer. They sent their voices up to heaven, and then the lady cast again, a simple sending such as any village witch might make, but aided, Michael hoped, by the wishes and prayers of every man and woman. She worked an aversion—the sort of thing Wise Women did for granaries on farms, which kept the smaller animals from eating the grain. She simply did it on a larger scale, and with a great deal more power.

West of Albinkirk—Gerald Random

Master Random's convoy shook out early despite the adventures of the night, or perhaps because of them.

He was quite proud of them. Men were singing in the dawn—some shaved at mirrors hung from wagon sides, and other men sharpened blades, sharpened arrow heads and crossbow quarrels. Men were rolling their blankets tight against the damp. Others boiled water in copper pots, or heated up a cupful of last night's porridge. At his own fire, the old Magus was heating ale in a copper shoe.

"You seem content to help yourself," Random said.

Harmodius didn't even raise an eyebrow. "I pay you the compliment of assuming that you are a generous man. And I made some for you."

Random laughed. He was camping with a legend, who was heating him ale on a chilly spring morning.

Birds sang, and men sang, and Random could see young Adrian from the goldsmiths sitting on a wagon box and sketching.

Adrian was a pargeter—an artist in gold leaf. He was a likely lad, just about to leave apprenticeship for journeyman status, which would be a brief stop for him. His father was both talented and rich—one of the goldsmith's coming men. Adrian was medium height, thin and fit, in expensive arming clothes made by professionals. He was wearing his breast- and backplate, his arming hood, and his armoured gloves lay across his lap. More and more of the young men were starting to ape the manners of the sell-swords—wearing their harnesses all day, carefully tending to their weapons.

Random couldn't see what young Adrian was sketching—it was on the other side of one of the goldsmith's wagons. Warm ale in hand, he went to look.

He smelled the thing long before he saw it. It had a horrible, sulphurous smell, overlaid with a sickly sweet-shop smell, like sugared liver.

He smelled the smell, but it didn't warn him.

The dead thing had been a daemon.

Young Adrian looked up from his sketch. "Henry found it in the bush." The other goldsmith apprentice stood by the corpse with determined possessiveness, despite the horror of it.

Close up and dead, the daemon was deeply disconcerting. The size of a small horse, it had finely scaled skin, like a river bass or a blue-gill; and the scales varied from white to pale gray with veins of blue and black like fine marble—all surmounted by an opalescent sheen with all the colours of the rainbow. Its eyes were empty pits, the lids collapsed on them as if its death had robbed it of its eyes. It had a heavy, raptor-like head with a snout or a beak, and a crest like the plumage a man might wear on a tournament helm. It lay limp in death, like wilted flowers. It had two arms on its long trunk that were disturbingly like heavy human arms—the muscled arms of a blacksmith, perhaps—and heavy, powerful legs that seemed twice the size of the arms. Upright it must have stood as high as a man on a wagon.

The legs and torso were balanced by a heavy tail covered in sharp spines.

It was no animal. The beak and spines were inlaid in lead and gold in fantastic patterns; the bony ridge above the eyes held more inlay, and the dead daemon wore a cote of scarlet leather lined in fur—beautiful work. Random couldn't help himself—he knelt, despite the stink, and fingered the material. Deerskin—dyed brighter and better than any dye he knew of, and tightly sewn in sinew.

There wasn't a mark on the monster, and the most disconcerting part of it was that its alien face was strangely beautiful, and wore a look of terror.

The old Magus wandered over, drinking ale. He stopped and looked at the daemon.

"Ah," he said.

Random didn't know how to broach his thought. "I'd like the cote," he said.

Harmodius looked at him as if he was mad.

"You killed it. It's yours." Random shrugged. "Or that's how we did things when I was in the king's army."

Harmodius shook his head. "Heh," he said. "Take it then. My gift. For your hospitality."

Three more of the goldsmith apprentices helped him roll it over. It took him five minutes to get the cote off. It was the size of a horse blanket, or perhaps slightly smaller and was untouched by whatever wound had killed the monster, and clean. Random rolled it tightly, wrapped it in sacking, and put it in his own wagon.

The apprentices were eyeing the gold inlay.

"Leave it," Harmodius said. "Their bodies generally fade rather than rot. I wonder—" He bent over the corpse. Prodded it with a stick, and despite having just rolled it over, the apprentices stepped back, and Henry hurried to get a quarrel in his crossbow.

The Magus drew a short stick from his cote. It was like a twig—a crazy twig that looked like a lightning bolt—but it was beautifully maintained with an oil finish that most twigs couldn't hold. The ends had minute silver caps.

Harmodius ran it over the corpse—back and forth. Back and forth.

"Ah!" he said. He said a verse of Archaic to the delight of all present, who had never imagined being allowed to watch a famous magus work. It was different in daylight. Men who had hidden away when he cast at night now stared like churls.

Random could see the power gathering around the older man's hand. He didn't have the talent to cast power, but he'd always been able to see it.

Then the old man cast, flicking his fingers at the daemon.

It seemed to pulse with colour—every man let go a breath—and then it dissolved to sand.

And not very much sand, at that.

"Fae," Harmodius said. "Something interrupted its decomposition when it died."

Their incomprehension was evident. Harmodius shrugged. "Don't worry," he said. "I'm only talking to myself, anyway." He laughed. "Master Merchant, a word with you."

Random followed the old Magus away from the wagons. Behind them,

Old Bob, the mercenary, rode up fully armed. The pargeter was showing off his sketch and Old Bob was suddenly silent.

"I've killed two of them in three days," Harmodius said. "This is very bad. I ask your help, in the name of the king. But I warn you that this will be dangerous. Extremely dangerous."

"What sort of help?" Random asked. "And for what reward? Pardon me, my lord. I know that all the court think my kind lives only for gold. We don't. But par dieu, messire, I have several men's fortunes in these wagons. My own, first and foremost."

Harmodius nodded. "I know. But there is clearly an incursion—perhaps even an invasion—from the Wild. The daemons are the enemy's most valuable and most powerful asset. I thought it horrifying that I should encounter one. Two means we are watched, and there is a force in behind us. Three...three is unthinkable. Despite which, I ask you to send a messenger to the king. Immediately. One of your best men. And that we continue north."

Random nodded.

"I have no idea if the king will guarantee the value of your convoy," Harmodius said. "What's it worth?"

"Sixty thousand golden nobles," Random said.

Harmodius sucked in a breath, and then laughed.

"Then I can safely say that the king can't replace it for you. Good Christ, man, how can you take so much into the wilderness?" Harmodius laughed.

Random shrugged. "We go to buy a year's produce of grain from a thousand farms," he said. "And beef from the hillmen—maybe fifteen hundred animals, ready to be fattened for market. And beer, small wine, skins from deer, beaver, rabbit, otter, bear and wolf—a year's worth for every haberdasher and every furrier in Harndon. That's the business of the Northern Fair, and that's without their staple of wool."

Harmodius shook his head. "I've never thought of the value of all these things," he said. "Or if I have, I've forgotten."

Random nodded. "Half a million gold nobles. That's the value of the Northern Fair."

"I didn't know there was that much gold in the world," Harmodius laughed.

"Nor is there. That's why we have helmets and crossbows and fine wines and goldsmith work, and gaudy rings and bolts of every fabric under the sun—and raisins and dates and olive oil and sugar and every other product the north doesn't have. To *trade*. It's why my convoy must get through."

Harmodius looked at the mountains, just breaking the distant horizon. "I've never thought about it," he said. "Now that I do, it seems very— vulnerable." He looked around. "What happens if there is no fair?"

Random had had that very thought several times in the last two days.

"Then Harndon has no beef; it gets only the grain from the home counties; there are no furs for clothes or hats, no honey for bread, less beer and ale in every house. And the king is less by the tax he collects on the merchandise, and less again by the value of—hard to say, but let's call it half of the wool staple. Small folks would starve. In the East, merchants who buy our wool would break. Most of the money-men of Harndon would break, and hundreds of apprentices would go out of work." He shrugged. "And that's just this winter. It'd be worse in the spring."

Harmodius looked at the merchant as if he was being told a fairy tale. Then he shook his head. "This has been an eventful morning, Master Merchant. We should be on our way. If you'll agree to go."

Random nodded. "I'll go. Because if I turn this convoy back," he shrugged. "Well, I'll lose a great deal of money." *And I'll never be mayor.*

Lissen Carak—Michael

The Siege of Lissen Carak. Day Two

Michael licked his pen nib, absently painting the corner of his mouth in tree-gall and iron.

Today, all of the small folk dug at the trench. I append a small sketch of the work; it runs from the gate of the Lower Town to the out-wall of the Bridge Fort, a distance of four hundred and twenty-four paces. With just under a thousand working men and women, we dug the ditch in two days. The upcast of the ditch has been made into low walls on either side, and the captain has ordered us to plant stakes from our stores—the palisades we use when we encamp—along the edge of the ditch.

All the day a heavy fog stayed over the length of the ditch—today's phantasm cast by the Abbess and is maintained by the good sisters, who can be heard praying at all hours in their chapel.

The enemy has sought all day to search out our new work. The air is thick with birds—starlings and crows and doves, but they dare not enter the fog, and the area close in to the castle walls seems abhorrent to them.

The Enemy has wyverns, and they ride the air currents high above us all day. Even now, there is one above me.

In the woods to the west, we can hear the sound of axes. Twice today, large bands of men advanced from the wood's edge to within bowshot of the fog, and lofted arrows into it. We did not respond, except that our own archers crept close and retrieved the arrows.

Nigh on sunset, we released three sorties; one north, one west, and one westerly, but right along the river.

The captain rode west into the setting sun, his armour gathering what little light penetrated the sun. Grendel had a cote of barding today—two layers of heavy chain falling to the mighty horse's fetlocks.

It took four valets to lift the cote and get it over the big horse's back. Grendel hated it, but the captain was confident that the Jacks would rise to his raid.

He had a dozen men-at-arms, fully harnessed, and their archers behind him, and as soon as Grendel's hooves were clear of the Lower Town—empty and sullen but for the two archers on the stone gate towers—he put his spurs gently to the great horse's sides, and Grendel began a heavy canter over the spring fields. The fog hid the light, and the terrain. It was possible to be ambushed in the fog, as he was aware.

But this was his own fog, and it had some special properties.

He rode south along the trench, going slowly, looking down to see the work that had been accomplished. It was a broad, deep ditch with a wooden floor. He had hidden a surprise under the wooden floor, but in ground this wet, the floor had its own essential purpose.

The palisades were too few to stop a determined enemy but, given time, he'd have the workers weave brambles and vines among them, and make a stouter barrier.

He shook his head. It didn't matter a damn, because the whole thing was a ruse anyway.

There were five bridges across the trench, each wide enough for two fully armed horsemen to ride abreast without making their horses shy. Again, given more time, he'd arrange mechanisms to raise and lower them.

Given time, he'd make his opponent look like a complete fool. But he didn't think he was going to get any more time. He could feel—no better explanation that that—his opponent's frustration. He didn't have much experience fighting men. He was arrogant.

Me too. The captain grinned and turned Grendel to cross the last bridge before Bridge Castle. Grendel's hooves sounded hollowly, as if he were riding over a coffin.

Where'd that thought come from?

He'd walked down to the apple tree at sunset the night before. She hadn't come. He wondered why. He remembered the touch of her lips on his.

Best concentrate on the matter at hand, he reminded himself.

He'd left her a note at the tree. She hadn't answered it.

He was running out of fog. Beyond, the spring fields were green with new grass that would eventually be hay and fodder—or weeds—all tinged red as the sun set.

He reined Grendel in, and waited for his company to sort themselves out.

Tom was at his shoulder, and he raised a gauntleted hand. "Everyone look around. The fog makes it hard to see, but look at how the ground is clear from here all the way to the wood's edge—not a ditch, not a hedgerow, not a stone wall. Keep that in mind. It we make another sortie it'll be along this path."

Tom nodded.

Ser Jehannes shook his head. "Let's survive today before we borrow trouble for tomorrow."

The captain looked back at his senior officer. "On the contrary, messire. Let us plan today for tomorrow's triumph."

Anger touched the older knight's face.

"Peace!" the captain said. "We'll discuss this later." He kept his voice light, as if the issue were of no moment. "If we contact the enemy, we ride through them, rally on the trumpet, and retreat into the fog immediately. No more. If we find boats, we destroy them. Is that clear?"

He listened carefully. If he was nervous, it didn't show—he seemed merely attentive.

Horses fidgeted. Men spat and tried to appear as unconcerned as their captain.

The fog seemed too thin to cover so many men. But nothing happened.

And then, well to the north, there were the sounds of men cheering, and horses neighing, and the clash of steel on steel.

"*There* they are," muttered the captain; three words to express fifteen minutes of nervous impatience. Tom grinned. Jehannes reached up and hit the catch on his visor. The sound was repeated all along their line.

But now the captain seemed in no hurry.

The cries were redoubled.

And then there were coarse bugle calls behind them, and high-pitched horn calls to the north.

It was all happening as he'd expected, and there, on the edge of battle, he had a moment of panic. *What if this is a trap? How can I expect to predict what they'll do? I'm pretending to know what I'm doing but this can't be so simple.*

His tutor in the art of war had been Hywel Writhe, his father's master of arms. His *supposed* father's master of arms. A brilliant swordsman, a magnificent jouster. Madly in love with the Lady Prudentia, and to no avail.

A memory crept into place.

Right there, on the edge of battle, the captain realised that he'd been had. His two tutors had been lovers. Of course they had been lovers.

Why do I think of this sort of thing when I'm about to fight? he thought.

Laughed aloud.

Hywel Writhe used to say, *War is simple. That's why men prefer it to real life.*

And his lesson for all six of the boys who would grow to be great lords, masters of armies: *Never make a plan more complicated than your ability to communicate it.*

The captain reviewed his plans one more time.

"Let's go," he said.

They rode out of the fog at a canter. About half a league to the north, Sauce led the northern sortie out of the shower of arrows sent by the now fully alerted Jacks, boglins and the irks who were gathering like clouds before a storm around her small force.

The captain led his men west into the setting sun, out of the fog, and right along the river bank.

There was a unmanned barricade on the road and he rode around it, and up the bank above the road, and round the first bend, and there they were.

Boats.

Sixty boats, or more. Farmers' boats, dug-outs, canoes. Rafts of lashed branches. All pulled up out of the water.

Every archer threw a linen wrapped parcel into a boat. Some got none—some got two—and he heard horns, and trumpets, and some shrill calls to the north.

They were taking too long.

The archers down at the far end of the beach received some arrows and charged into the woods on their horses, scattering the enemy archers. Tom set off in pursuit with half the men-at-arms, and the captain suddenly feared he'd been trapped after all. He was over-extended and the size of the bank beneath the ancient trees dwarfed his paltry raid. And now half his men were getting too far—

More shouts behind him.

He turned to Michael. "Sound the recall," he said.

Michael's trumpet playing wasn't his strongest suit. He was on his third try when the trumpet rang out clearly, against the sound of screams and heavy crashes from the west of the bank. The captain sat on Grendel's back in a rage of indecision—desperate to get his men back, afraid to commit the rest to the sortie all the way down the bank.

Tom emerged from the lowering trees, his sword raised.

The captain began to breathe again.

More and more of the men-at-arms and archers emerged from beneath the trees, swords a ruddy green in the failing light.

"Let's get out of here," the captain said. He wheeled Grendel just as two arrows hit the horse's withers, and he reared and grunted and then they were around.

There were Jacks at the edge of the trees, just to the north, their dirty white cotes shining in the last light of day. The polished heads of their war arrows seemed to flicker as they loosed.

Bootlick, one of the foreign horn-bow archers, took a shaft in the neck, right through his aventail. He went down without a croak, and his horse, well trained, kept formation.

Bill Hook—Bootlick's man-at-arms—was off his charger in a flash of white armour, lifting the fallen archer onto his crupper. He was struck twice—both blows at long range, falling on his breastplate, and he didn't even stagger.

The captain pointed Grendel's armoured head at the edge of the wood. If someone didn't stop the Jacks from shooting, his column was going to be dead in heartbeats. Most of the archer's light horses weren't even armoured.

Grendel rose from a heavy canter to a flowing gallop, apparently unencumbered by a hundred pounds of double mail.

An arrow struck his visor, and two more struck his helmet. The steel heads screamed against his bascinet and were gone, but each blow rocked him in his high-backed saddle. Another heavy arrow struck the bow of his saddle and another whanged off his right knee cop and then it was like riding through hail, and he put his armoured head down and pressed his long spurs to Grendel's sides.

He had no way of knowing whether anyone was behind him, and his whole world was narrowed to what he could see from the two eye slits of his helm.

Not much. Mostly, Grendel's armoured neck.

Clang.

Clang-clang-clang-whang-ping.

All hits on his helmet and shoulders.

Thwak-tick-tock-clang!

He sat up in the saddle. Got a hand on the hilt of his war sword and drew, and an arrow caught the blade, shivering it in his hand.

He got his eyes up, and there they were.

Even as he watched, they broke and ran. There were only six of them—*All those arrows came from six men?* and they ran with a practised desperation in six different directions.

His sword took the nearest neatly, because killing fleeing infantryman was an essential part of knightly training, taken for granted, like courage. He let his arm fall, and the man died, and he used his spurs to guide Grendel after the second man, the smallest of the group. One of his mates stopped, drew, and shot.

Cursed when his arrow glanced harmlessly off the captain's right rerebrace, and died.

Grendel was slowing, and the captain turned him. If he exhausted the war horse he'd be stranded and dead. Besides, he loved Grendel. He felt he and the horse had a great deal in common.

A healthy desire to live, for example.

The four surviving Jacks didn't run much farther than they had to, as they heard the hooves pause.

Whang, came the first arrow off his helmet.

It was a matter of time before one of those shots found his underarm, his throat, or his eye-slits.

Ser Jehannes came out of the woods to the archer's left, at a full gallop. He rode around the great bole of an ancient tree, and the ruddy-haired Jack lost his head in one swing of the knight's great blade.

The other three ran west, into a thicket.

"Thanks!" the captain called.

Jehannes nodded.

He's never going to like me, let alone love me, the captain thought.

He gathered Grendel under him, turned his head, and started moving east.

The fields to the north of him seemed to ripple and flow—boglins running in their odd hunched posture, low to the ground, irks, their brown bodies like moving mud.

But they were too late, and the handful of boglins who paused to loft arrows were ineffective.

At the edge of his effective casting range, the captain reined Grendel in. He stripped the gauntlet off his right hand, and pulled a small patch of charred linen from the palm.

He *stepped into his palace.*

"He's waiting for you," Prudentia said.

"He doesn't know what I can do, yet," the boy said. He'd already aligned his symbols. He walked to the door, but instead of opening it, he merely raised the tiny iron plate that covered the keyhole, and a waft of fierce green shot through.

"He's waiting for you," Prudentia said again.

"He's going to have to keep waiting," the boy said. He was proud of his work, and his careful preparation. "Look, it's sympathetic Hermeticism. The wicks on the fire bundles are all made from the same piece of linen and soaked in oil. I have a scrap here, too, already charred."

The breath of green touched his symbols.

"You are the cleverest boy," Prudentia said.

"Were you and Hywel lovers, Prude?" the boy asked.

"None of your business," she shot back.

He rose in his stirrups, and his charred piece of linen caught and burned red hot.

On the bank, forty-four firebombs made of oiled tow and old rags and wax and birch bark burst into flame with one, simultaneous roar.

Harndon City—Edward

Edward cast the first of the master's tubes in the yard. He cast it in sand, and used the same mandril, polished to a mirror shine, as the model for the wax tongue he put in the mould to make it hollow. He cast the walls of the tube a finger's width thick, as the master requested.

When it was done it wasn't much to look at. Edward shrugged. "Master, I can do better. The hole would be better if I bored it, but that would require—" he shrugged "—a week to make the drills and other tools. I'd like to add decoration." He felt incompetent.

The master picked it up and held it in his hands for a long time. "Let's try," he said.

He bored a small hole in the base of the bronze with a hand drill, and Edward was fascinated to watch his careful patience, coaxing the fine steel drill through the heavy bronze. Then he took the tube out of the shop and into the yard, and packed it with his burning mixture—four scoops. He searched for something to put down atop the powder.

Silently, Edward handed him a one-inch hawk bell. It wasn't perfectly round, and it was hollow, but it fitted well enough for purpose.

The master tied it to the oak tree, put wick in the hole, and lit it. They both hid behind the brick wall of the stable.

Which was just as well.

The fizzing, burning mixture made a flash and a bang like—like something hermetical.

It stripped a handspan of bark from the tree.

The tube had torn loose from its bindings and had smashed through a horse trough—a solid wood horse trough—flooding the yard with dirty water...and it was a day before the apprentices found the hawk's bell. Even then, they didn't find the bell itself, just the neat round hole it had punched through the tile roof of the forge building.

Edward looked at the hole and whistled.

Lissen Carak—The Red Knight

The captain had six magnificent bruises from the archery. Other men had worse. Bootlick was dead, despite Bill Hook—known to the gentles as Ser Willem Greville—despite his best efforts at rescue. Francis Atcourt had a Jack's arrow right through the join in his cote of plates—through his gut. Wat Simple and Oak Pew both had arrows in their limbs and were screaming in pain and mortal afraid the heads were poisoned.

If they hadn't had the nuns, all of them might have died of their wounds.

As it was, the skill and power of the nuns seemed to mean that any man who wasn't killed outright would be healed. The captain, who was just coming to terms with the idea of a convent of women of power, was staggered by the healing power they poured into his men—Sauce had six badly wounded men, including Long Paw—one of their best men in every respect.

But the barrage of phantasm was more effective than the barrage of arrows had been.

The captain walked through the hospital ward in his arming clothes. The wounded were cheerful—as any man or woman might be, waking to find an ugly wound completely banished. Oak Pew, a woman whose dark wood-coloured skin and heavy muscles had given her the name, lay laughing helplessly at one of Wilful Murder's stories. Wat Simple was already gone, the captain had seen him playing at piquet. Long Paw lay watching Oak Pew laugh.

"Thought I was a goner," he admitted, when the captain sat on his counterpane. He showed the captain where a shaft had gone into his chest.

"I coughed up blood," he said. "I know what that means." He raised himself, coughed, and looked at the nun in the corner. "Pretty nun says if it'd been a finger's width lower, I'd ha' been dead." He shrugged. "I owe her."

The captain squeezed Long Paw's shoulder. "How do you feel?" he asked. He knew it was a stupid question, but it was part of the job of being captain.

Long Paw looked at him for a moment. "Well," he said, "I feel like I was dead, and now I'm not. It's not all bad—not all good." He smiled, but it wasn't one of the archer's usual smiles. "Ever ask yourself what we're here for, Captain?"

All the time, he thought, but he replied, "Sometimes."

"Never been that close to being dead before," Long Paw said. He lay back. "I reckon I'll be right as rain in a day," he said. He smiled, a little more like himself. "Or two."

The pretty novice was, of course, Amicia. She was slumped in a chair at the end of the lower ward. When he saw her, the captain realised he'd been hoping to find her in the hospital. He knew she had power—had felt it himself, but he'd finally made the connection to healing when he saw her go in and out of the hospital building that adjoined the dormitory.

Her closed eyes didn't invite conversation, so he walked softly past her, and up the steps, to see Messire Francis Atcourt. Atcourt was not a gently born man; not a knight. Rumour was he'd started life as a tailor. The captain found him propped up with pillows looking very pale. Reading. The parchment cover with its spidery writing didn't offer the captain a title, but closer to, he saw the man was reading psalms.

The captain shook his head.

"Nice to see you, m'lord," Atcourt said. "I'm malingering."

The captain smiled. Atcourt was forty—maybe older. He could start a fire, trim meat, make a leather pouch, repair horse harness. On the road, the captain had seen him teach a young girl to make a closed back-stitch. He was not the best man-at-arms in the company, but he was a vital man. The kind of man you trusted to get things done. If you asked him to make sure dinner got cooked, it got cooked.

He was not the sort of man who malingered.

"Me, too. You've lost a lot of blood." The captain sat on his counterpane. "Your nun—the pretty one—"

The captain felt himself blushing. "Not my nun—" he stammered.

Atcourt smiled like a schoolteacher. "As you say, of course."

It was odd—the captain had remarked it before. The commonly born men-at-arms—leaving aside Bad Tom, who was more like a force of nature than like a man, anyway—had prettier manners than the gently born. Atcourt had especially good manners.

"At any rate, the lovely young novice who gives orders so well," Atcourt smiled. "She healed me. I felt her—" He smiled again. "That is what goodness feels like, I reckon. And she brought me this to read, so I am reading." He made a face. "Perhaps I'll finish up a monk. 'Ello, Tom."

Bad Tom towered over them. He nodded to his friend. "If that arrow had struck you a hand's breadth lower, you could ha' *been* a nun." Then he leered at the captain. "The tall nun's awake, and stretching like a cat. I stopped to watch." He laughed his great laugh. "What a set o' necks she has, eh?"

The captain turned to glare, but it was nearly impossible to glare at Tom. Having sat, the captain could feel every tired muscle, every one of his six bruises.

"We all saw you charge those archers," Tom said, as he turned away.

The captain paused.

"You should a' died," Tom went on. "You got hit what—eight times? Ten? By war-bows?"

The captain paused.

"I'm just sayin'," lad. Don't be foolish. You ha' the de'il's own luck. What if it runs out?" he asked.

"Then I'll be dead," the captain said. He shrugged. "Someone had to do it."

"Jehannes did it, and he did it *right*," Tom said. "Next time, raise your sword and tell someone to ride at the archers. Someone *else*."

The captain shrugged again. For once, he looked every heartbeat of twenty years old—the shrug was a rebellious refusal to accept the reality of what an adult was trying to teach him, and in that moment the captain was a very young man caught out being a fool. And he knew it.

"Cap'n," Tom said, and suddenly he was a big, dangerous man. "If you die I much misdoubt we will ride through this. So here's my rede: don't die."

"Amen," said the captain.

"The pretty novice'll be far more compliant with a living man than a dead one," Tom said.

"That based on experience, Tom?" Atcourt said. "Leave the lad alone. Leave the *captain* alone. Sorry, m'lord."

The captain shook his head. On balance, it was difficult to be annoyed when you discover that men like you and desire your continued health.

Atcourt laughed aloud. Tom leaned over him, and whispered something, and Atcourt doubled up—first laughing, and then in obvious pain.

The captain paused to look back, and Tom was taking cards and dice out of his purse, and Atcourt was holding his side and grinning.

The captain ran down the steps, his leather soles slapping the stone stairs, but she wasn't there, and he cursed Tom's leer and ran out into the new darkness.

He wanted a cup of wine, but he was sure he'd go to sleep. Which he needed.

He smiled at his own foolishness and went to the apple tree instead.

And there she was, sitting in the new starlight, singing softly to herself.

"You didn't come last night," he said. The very last thing he wanted to say.

She shrugged. "I fell asleep," she said. "Which, it seems to me, might be a wise course for you. My lord."

Her tone was forbidding. There was nothing about her to suggest that they'd ever kissed, or had intimate conversation. Or even angry conversation.

"But you wanted to see me," he said. *I sound like a fool.*

"I wanted to tell you that you were perfectly correct. I plotted to meet you outside her door. And she used me, the old witch. I love her, but she's throwing me at you. I was blind to it. She's playing courtly love with you and substituting my body for hers. Or something." Amicia shrugged, and the motion was just visible in the starlight.

The silence stretched on. He didn't know what to say. It sounded quite likely to him, and he didn't see a way to make it seem better. And he found he had no desire to speak ill of the Abbess.

"I'm sorry that I spoke so brusquely, anyway," he said.

"Brusquely?" she asked, and laughed. "You mean, you are sorry that you crushed my excuses and made light of my vanity and my piety? That you showed me up as a sorry hypocrite?"

"I didn't mean to do any of those things," he said. Not for the first time, he felt vastly her inferior. Legions of willing servant girls hadn't prepared him for this.

"I do love Jesus," she went on. "Although I'm not always sure what loving God should mean. And it hurts me, like a physical pain, that you deny God."

"I don't deny God," he said. "I'm quite positive that the petty bastard exists."

Her face, pale in the new moonlight, set hard.

I'm really too tired to do this, he thought. "I love you," he heard himself say. He thought of Michael and winced.

She put her hand to her mouth. "You have a funny way of showing it," she said.

He sat down suddenly. Like saying *I love you*, it wasn't really a decision. His legs were done.

She reached out a hand to take his, and as their fingers met, she flinched. "Oh!" she said. "Gentle Jesu, messire, you are in pain."

She leaned over him, and she breathed on him. That's how it felt.

He opened his defences, running *into the tower*. Prudentia shook her head, but her disapproval could be taken for granted for any woman, and he opened the door, secure that the walls of the fortress would protect him from the green storm.

No sooner did the door open, then she was all around him.

But the green was right behind her.

She was very distinct, and she looked the way ignorant men supposed ghosts to look—a pale and colourless picture of herself.

He reached out and took her hand.

"You are letting me in?" she asked. She looked around, clearly amazed. She curtsied to Prudentia. "Gracious and Living God, my lord—is she alive?"

"She is alive in my memory," he said, with some dissimulation. He had some secrets too evil to share.

She twirled. "It's magnificent! How many sigils have you?"

"Sigils?" he asked.

"Signs. Workings. Phantasms."

He shrugged. "More than twenty," he said. It wasn't a lie. It was merely an encouragement to underestimation.

She chuckled. She was bigger here, her face slightly more elfin and slightly more feral. Her eyes glowed like a cat at night, and were just faintly almond-shaped. "I knew you when I first saw you," she said. "Wearing power like a cloak. The power of the Wild."

He smiled. "We are two of a kind," he said.

She had his hand, and now she took it and put it on her right breast—except that things here were not of the world. His hand didn't find her breast. Rather, he found himself standing on a bridge. Beneath him flowed a mountain stream, burbling a dark, clear brown, full of leaves. The trees on either bank were rich, verdant green, towering into the heavens. Now, instead of the grey raiment of her order, she wore a green kirtel and a green belt.

"My bridge risks being swept away by a spring flood," she said. "But your tower is too confining."

He watched the power flow under the bridge, and he was a little afraid of her. "You can cast all of this?"

She smiled. "I'm learning. I tire quickly, and I don't have your twenty workings."

He smiled. "You know, unless Prudentia has misled me, now that we have been to each other's places we are bonded."

"As long as that armoured door of yours is closed, I can't even find you," she said. She gave him a flirtatious frown. "I've tried."

He reached out for her.

As his hands closed on her shoulders, her concentration slipped, or his did, and they were sitting on the bench in the apple-scented darkness.

They kissed.

She laid her head on his arming cote and he opened his mouth.

"Please don't talk," she said. "I don't want to talk."

So he sat, perfectly happy, in the darkness. It was some time before he realised she'd magicked his bruises. By then she was asleep.

Later, he had to pee. And the stone bench was icy cold, despite the warm spring air. And the edge of the bench bit into the back of his thigh at a bad angle. Gradually cut off the flow of blood to his leg, which began to go all pins and needles.

He wondered if it was his duty to wake her up and send her to bed. Or if he was supposed to wake her up and attack her with kisses. It occurred to him that the loss of a night's sleep was not a wise move on his part.

Later still, he realised that her eyes were open.

She wriggled off his lap. He considered a dozen remarks—all variations on being warmer than her gentle Jesus, but then dismissed them all.

He was, after all, growing up.

He kissed her hand.

She smiled. "You pretend to be far worse than you are," she said.

He shrugged.

She reached into her sleeve, and put something in his hand. It was a plain square of linen.

"My vow of poverty isn't worth much, because I have nothing," she said. "I did a little to ease the tire-woman's joints, and she gave me this. But I've cried in it. Twice." She smiled.

He hoped that he wasn't seeing her in the first light of morning.

"I think that makes it mine," she said.

He crushed it to his heart, pushed it inside his arming cote, kissed her hand.

"What do *you* want?" she asked.

"You," he said.

She smiled. "Silly. What do you want out of life?"

"You first," he said.

She smiled. "I'm easy. I want people to be happy. To live free. And well. With enough to eat. In good health." She shrugged. "I like it when people are happy." She smiled at him. "And brave. And good."

He winced. "War must be very hard on you." Winced again. "Brave and good?"

"Yes," she said. She shook her head. "You don't know me very well, not yet. Now you. What do you want?"

He shook his head. He didn't dare tell the truth and didn't want to lie to her. So he tried to find a middle ground. "To defy God, and my mother." He shrugged, sure that her face had just hardened, set in automatic anger. "To be the best knight in the world."

She looked at him. The moon was up—that's all it was, not daylight—and her face shone. "You?"

"If you can be a nun, I can be the best knight," he said. "If you, the very queen of love, can deny your body to be a nun, then I—cursed by God to sin—can be a great knight." He laughed.

She laughed with him.

That's how he liked to remember her, ever after—laughing in the moonlight, without the shadow of reserve in her face. She held out her arms, they embraced, and she was gone on soft feet.

He didn't even stop to shiver. He ran up the steps to the commanderies, drank off a cold cup of hippocras that had once been hot. But before he let himself sleep, he woke Toby and sent him for Ser Adrian, his company secretary. The man came softly, in a heavy wool overrobe.

"I don't mean to whine," said the scribe, "But do you know what time it is?"

The captain drank another cup of wine. "I want you to ask around," he said. "I don't know what I'm looking for, but I'm hoping you can find it for me. I know I'm not making sense. But there's a traitor in this fortress. I have suspicions, but nothing like a shred of proof. Who here can communicate with the outside world? Who has a secret hatred of the Abbess? Or a secret love of the Wild?"

He almost choked on the last words.

The scribe shook his head. Yawned. "I'll ask around," he said. "Can I go back to bed?"

The captain felt foolish. "I may be wrong," he said.

The scribe rolled his eyes—but he waited until he was out of the captain's door to do it.

The captain finished his cup and threw himself, fully dressed, on his bed. When the chapel bell rang he tried not to count the rings, so he could pretend he'd had a full night's sleep.

The Siege of Lissen Carak, Day Three.

Michael could hear the captain snoring, and envied him. The archers said he'd "been busy" half the night with his pretty nun, and Michael was vaguely envious, vaguely jealous, and desperately admiring. And mad as hell, of course. It was *unfair.*

The third day had been so without event that Michael had begun to wonder whether the captain was wrong. He'd told them the enemy would attack.

All day, the wyverns flew back and forth.

Something monstrous belled and belled, a high, clear note made somehow huge and terrifying in the woods.

No action today. We watched the enemy assemble rafts to replace the boats we burned. The captain warned us that they will eventually assemble machines of war—that the men among the Enemy would traitorously teach the monsters to use them. The fog kept up all day, so that, while the sentries on the fortress walls can see many leagues, almost nothing can be seen of the fields immediately around the castle. The men say that the Abbess can see through the fog.

We heard cutting and chopping all day.

Towards sunset, a great force moved through the woods to the west. We could see the trees moving and the glitter of the late sun on weapons. And the roar of many monsters. The captain says a force is crossing the river. He ordered a sortie to form when another force, even larger, formed in the woods opposite our trench, but then dismissed us to dinner when there was no attack.

Michael sat back. He wasn't any good at keeping a journal, and he knew that he was leaving out important developments. Wilful Murder had shot a boglin almost three hundred paces away—shooting from a high tower, over the fog, on the dawn breeze. He was now drunk as a lord on the beer ration provided by his mates. But it didn't seem to change the siege. Or be a notable or noble event. Michael had only the histories from his father's library as his examples, and they never mentioned archers.

The captain came in. He had dark circles under his eyes.

"Go to bed," he said.

Michael needed no second urging. But he paused in the doorway.

"No attack?" he said.

"Your talent for stating the obvious must make you wildly popular," the captain said savagely.

Michael shrugged. "Sorry."

The captain rubbed his head. "I was *sure* he'd attack the trench today. Instead, he's sent something—and I worry it's a strong force—south across the river, despite our burning his boats. There's a convoy down there, he's going to destroy it, and I can't stop him—or even try—until I've bloodied his nose in my little trap, and my trap isn't catching anything." The captain drank some wine. "It's all fucking hubris. I can't actually predict what the enemy will do."

Michael was stung. "You've done all right so far."

The captain shrugged. "It's all luck. Go sleep. The fun part of this siege is over. If he doesn't go for my nice trench—"

"Why should he?" Michael asked.

"Is that the apprentice captain asking, or the squire?" the captain asked, pouring himself more wine. He spilled some.

"Just an interested bystander," Michael said, and casually, by mistake done-apurpose, knocked the captain's wine off the table. "Sorry, m'lord. I'll fetch more."

The captain stiffened, and then yawned. "Nah. I've had too much. He has to assume I've filled the trench with men and that with one good rush he can overrun it and kill half my force."

"But you have filled it with men," Michael said. "I saw you send them out."

The captain smiled.

Michael shook his head. "Where are they?"

"In the Bridge Castle," the captain said. "It was very clever, but either he saw through the whole thing or he's too much of a coward to try us." He looked in his wine cup and made a face. "Where's Miss Lanthorn?" he asked. Then he relented. "Why don't you go see her?"

Michael bowed. "Good night," he said. And he slipped out into the hallway and pulled his pallet across the captain's door.

He spent an eternity searching the torchlit darkness.

Elissa was sitting on a barrel entertaining half the garrison with a lewd story. But her youngest sister wasn't there.

Mary was drinking wine in the Western Tower with Lis the laundress, Sukey Oakshot, the seamstress's daughter, Bad Tom, Ser George Brewes, and Francis Atcourt. There were cards and dice on the table, and the women were laughing hard. All seven looked up when Michael leaned in.

"She's not here," Tom yelled, and guffawed. The other men-at-arms laughed indulgently, and Michael fled.

"Who's not here?" Lis asked.

"His leman. Boy's in love." Tom shook his head and his great hand, under the table, chanced against Sukey's ankle. She kicked him. "Which I'm a'married," she said, apparently unafraid of the largest man in the castle.

Tom shrugged. "Can't fault a man for trying," he said.

"Who's his leman, then?" Lis asked. "One o' your slatterns? He's too nice for an oyster, ain't he?"

"Oyster?" asked Mary.

"A lass as opens and shuts with the tide," Lis said, and drank more wine.

"Like you, eh?" said Mary.

Lis laughed. "Mary, you're a local girl. Boys think you are easy. That's a long chalk from what those girls do."

Francis Atcourt shrugged. "They're people like everyone else, Lis. An' they play cards and go to church." He shrugged. "Sorry. I got a deep draught of mortality today."

Tom nodded. "Drink more."

Mary looked at Lis, caught beween admiration and anger. "So what you do—" she said.

"What I do is live my life wi'out being ruled by a man," Lis said. "Men is good for play and not so good for anything else."

Tom laughed.

Ser George tossed his cards on the table, disgusted. "What is this, philosophy hour?"

"And it's your fucking sister the young squire's riding," Lis said. She wasn't sure just why she was angry.

Mary stood up, affronted. "That's just like Fran—make a rule and then break it herself."

Lis laughed. "Not Fran."

Mary stopped dead. "Kaitlin? She's not—she wouldn't! She's—"

Lis laughed.

Michael found her in the stable with three other girls, all younger. They were dancing. He went from horse to horse, looking them over. The girls stopped dancing, and one suddenly shouted that she was an evil monster and started shrieking, and the other two were laughing, or crying.

And then one of them was screaming, and Kaitlin was soothing her. Michael had been fooled by the screams, but he was over the stall and with them in a moment.

Kaitlin's eyes met his. She had the little girl pressed against her.

"We're going to be *eaten*," bawled the child.

Kaitlin rocked her back and forth. "No, we're not," she said firmly. She raised her face to Michael.

Michael knew she was asking something of him, but neither of them were sure exactly what it was. So he knelt with them. "I swear on my hope of being a knight and going to heaven, I will protect you," he said.

"He's not a knight, he's just a squire," said the other girl, with the dreadful truthfulness that afflicts the young. She looked at Michael with enormous eyes.

Kaitlin's eyes met his.

"I will protect you anyway," Michael said, keeping his voice light.

"I don't want to be eaten!" said the first girl. But the sobs were fading.

"I'll bet we're gooey and delicious!" said the second girl. She grinned at Michael. "And that's why they attack us!" she said, as if this solved a deep, difficult problem she'd been having.

Kaitlin hugged them both. "I think some people are silly," she said.

The third girl threw a clod of horse manure at Michael and he was caught in an odd dilemma. He wanted Kaitlin alone and yet, watching her with children, he wanted this moment to go on forever. And for the first time, he thought—*I could marry her.*

Amicia reached out. *His door was very slightly open and she slipped through, a wraith in the green light. The Warlock who laid siege to the fortress was*

so powerful that he shone like a green sun in her woods, and the green light
battered his tower door.
  He was there, standing by the statue of a woman.
  "I was just coming to look for you," he said happily. And yawned.
  She shook her head. "Go to sleep. You didn't even renew your powers this
morn."
  He shook his head. "One hour with you—"
  She backed away. "Good night," she said, and she shut the door. From outside.

He fell asleep so quickly he dreamed of her.

Michael leaned down and placed his mouth tenderly on hers, and her lips
opened under his.
  "I love you," he said.
  She laughed. "Silly."
  He grabbed her chin. "I'll marry you," he said.
  Her eyes grew huge.
  The door of the next stall flew open. "Kaitlin Lanthorn!" shrieked her
sister. "You little bitch!"
  Green light exploded in the sky outside the stables, and a thunderous
concussion shook the walls.
  "To arms!" shouted twenty voices on the walls.

The captain leapt from his bed without knowing what had awakened him,
and found himself standing by his armour rack with Michael, who had
never gone to bed, getting him into his hauberk. He wasn't even awake
and Michael was pulling the laces as tight as he could at the back, and
then he had his old shoes on over bare legs and was racing along the wall.
  "Bridge Castle," Bent shouted from the tower above them. Michael was
trying to get into his brigantine while simultaneously watching the starlit
sky and the walls.
  The fog was gone—it had been swept away in a mighty gust of wind.
The captain felt the wind, and knew it for what it was. He smiled into it.
  "Here we go," he said.
  Two beacon fires were alight, and there was a lot of shouting—the
distinctive sound of men in danger, or anger.
  "We need a way to communicate with the Bridge Castle." The captain
leaned on the wall as Michael, now secure in his brigantine and feeling
the pain from his ribs, knelt to buckle his knight's metal leg harnesses
on—a pair of valets were carrying the armour along behind them as the
captain moved. It might have been comical, if the situation hadn't been
so terrifying.
  Michael gradually got the captain into his harness as the infuriating
man moved from position to position throughout the fortress. He made

off-colour jokes to nursing sisters and he clasped hands with Bad Tom and he ordered Sauce to mount up in the new covered alley in the courtyard—covered, Michael assumed, to keep the wyverns off the horses. It was the same sortie he'd prepared the night before, and ordered to stand down.

An hour later, the west tower ballista loosed with a sharp *crack*. As far as Michael could see the bolt had no effect out in the dark.

Michael got the rest of his own armour on, paused to rest, and fell asleep standing up at the corner where the west wall intersected the west tower.

He awoke to a loud roar. A sea of fire stretched almost to his feet and screams pierced the full-throated bellow of war. The captain's hand closed on his vambrace. "Here they come!" he shouted. "On my mark!"

Michael looked up, and saw a man leaning far out over the west tower edge, and the sky was not light, but it was grey.

"Welcome back," the captain said cheerfully. "Have a good nap?"

"Sorry," Michael mumbled.

"Don't be. Real soldiers sleep every minute they can, in times like this. Our attackers are making an attempt on the Bridge Castle and the Lower Town, while, I assume, sending men to look at what we built yesterday. Or perhaps to burn it." He sounded quite happy about the prospect.

Michael took a deep breath. A valet put a cup of warm wine into his hand and he drank it off.

The captain leaned well out over the wall. "Loose!" he called.

The trebuchet in the western tower creaked, and the whole tower moved by the width of a finger.

"Hail shot. Watch this."

Michael had sometimes entertained his brothers and sisters by throwing handfuls of stones into water. This was like that, only multiplied many hundreds of times, with larger stones, and instead of striking water most of them hit the ground. The rest fell on chitinous hides and flesh and blood, having fallen several hundred feet.

"Again!" the captain called.

Down in the Bridge Castle, both of their heavy onagers loosed together, throwing baskets of stones the size of a man's heart out into the trenches built the day before.

Screams rose out of the churned ground.

"You seem very pleased with yourself," the Abbess said. She was fully dressed and looked exactly the same as she did in the height of a calm day. She had come around the corner by the west tower, attended by stretcher-bearers and a pair of nursing sisters.

"The enemy has just fallen into our little trap with both feet." He turned to Bent. "We'll get one more round off. Then raise both red flags. At that signal everyone—everyone in the garrison except you and the engine crews—attacks down the road. On me."

The captain then managed to combine a bow to the Abbess with a duck under the lintel of the West Tower door. The valets had Grendel saddled, and the captain took his place at the head of Sauce's column. Michael, still fuzzy headed and with his ribs burning in his chest, tried to keep up with him.

Jacques was standing by Michael's horse. "You looked like you needed your sleep," the man said, with a smile. "Don't get fancy, youngster. Those ribs will kill you." He leaned close. "So will kissing girls, if it costs you sleep."

Then Michael was up, Jacques's hand shoving his rump to get him into the saddle, and he was out of the low stable gateway and into the courtyard. Toby was holding the captain's helmet while eating a half-loaf of bread, and the captain was pinning something—a white linen handkerchief—on his cote armour. It was very white against the scarlet velvet.

Michael grinned. "What is that?" he began.

"*Honi soit qui mal y pense,*" said the captain. He winked, took his helmet from Toby, gave the boy a smile, and wheeled Grendel with his knees. "Listen up!" he called.

The sortie quieted.

"Once we're through that gate kill everything that comes under your sword," the captain said. "The trench edge will be marked in fire so remember your route. If you lose me, follow the route. When you hear Carlus sound the recall, you turn and come back. Understand me?"

And with that as a speech, they rode from the gate as the trebuchet sprayed another rain of death out over their heads.

The hour was on the knife edge between day and night, and the trebuchet's great baskets of stones had obliterated life over a swathe of ground that was roughly the shape of a great egg—creatures had been turned to a bloody or ichorous pulp, and the ground itself was littered with the stones—softer ground had deep pock-marks. Bushes and grass were pulverized. In the half-dark it was a vision of hell, and the sudden burst of balefire in the new-dug trenches added to the terrible aspect.

Especially when viewed through the slit of a closed visor.

There was no fight in the men or the monsters that struggled to win free of the beaten ground, or routed away from the hail of missiles still pelting them from the Bridge Castle. They were streaming for the woods, over a mile distant.

The captain led his sortie well to the south, right along the river, along the smooth ground, and then formed them up in a single rank and brought up his trumpeter and his great black banner with the lacs d'amour and the golden collars—his personal badge—and drew his sword.

"All the way to the edge of the wood, and then *form up on me.*" He had his visor up, and he looked around—Bad Tom was at his back, Sauce to one side, and Ser Jehannes was close.

"Kill everything that comes under your sword," he said again. Michael didn't think they'd lost a single man getting here. The war machines had utterly shattered the enemy attack. He took a deep breath, and the routed enemy flowed past them, running on exhausted feet—or talons or claws or paws—for the woods.

"Charge!" he roared, and the banner pointed at the enemy and the trumpets sounded.

Michael had never been in a charge before.

It was exhilarating, and nothing on the ground seemed to be able to touch them. They swept over the irks and the broken men and a single larger creature, something nightmarish that gleamed a sickening green hue in the first light of the sun, but Bad Tom put his lance tip precisely in the thing's ear-bole as it turned its talons on Grendel, and his lance tip—a spear point as long as a man's forearm and as wide as a big man's palm—ripped its brain pan from its lower jaw.

"Lachlan for Aa!" the big man roared.

The monster died, and the line of knights swept over the pitiful resistance and then into the running men—and things.

By the time the sun was above the horizon, they had reached the wood's edge, and the creatures and men of the Wild were a bloody mangle on the grass behind them—or rather, any they'd chanced on were a bloody mangle, while hundreds more ran around them to the north or south, or lay flat and prayed as the horses thundered over them.

And then the captain led them back to the gate by much the same road, crashing though a line of desperate irks trying vainly to defend themselves with spears which splintered on steel armour. Right through, and on to the edge of the fortress hill, where twenty valets waited with fresh horses.

Michael was mystified. His elation was ebbing quickly to be replaced by fatigue and the thumping pain of his ribs, jarred by the gallop and barely held together by his cote armour.

All of the men-at-arms and many of the archers were changing horses. The men on the walls were cheering them.

The captain rode up to him and opened his visor. "You're moving badly," the captain said bluntly. "In fact, you look like shit. Fall out."

"What? Where—" Michael spluttered.

Jacques took his reins. Michael noted that the valet was in armour— good armour—as Jacques got him out of his saddle and Michael wanted to cry—but at the same time, he couldn't imagine fighting again.

Then Jacques swung up on a heavy horse of his own—an ugly roan with a roman nose. "I'll keep him alive, lad," Jacques said.

So Michael stood there and watched as they changed horses and formed up, and then to his surprise they turned away from the beaten enemy and rode south, along the edge of the rising sun, moving at a canter. They rode straight for the Bridge Castle's gate, and it opened as if by magic letting them pass through, canter over the bridge, and vanish onto the southern road.

Even as he watched, Gelfred, the master of the hunt, left Bridge Castle with three men and a cart. The men each took a brace of dogs—beautiful dogs—and moved briskly off to the west with a dozen archers covering them.

Just as the first starlings and ravens began to appear, gyrfalcons began to soar into the heavens over Bridge Castle, one after another. Up on the walls, a great eagle leaped into the air with a scream that must have chilled every lesser bird for three leagues.

Gelfred had struck, and the Abbess with him.

Braces of hounds emerged from the cover of Bridge Castle, running flat out for the leverets and the coneys and any other animal that lurked at the edge of the woods, and the gyrfalcon, Parcival the eagle and the lesser birds—well-trained birds brought from Theva to sell at the fair—struck the starlings, the ravens, and the oversized doves, ripping through their flocks like a knight through a crowd of peasants, and feathers, wings, blood and whole dead birds fell like an avian rain.

It took Michael half an hour to climb back to the fortress gate. The valets ignored him, and he stumbled many times, until someone on the walls saw the trail of blood he was leaving and a pair of archers appeared to hold him up.

Amicia cut the sabatons off his feet, and found the flint javelin which had cut deeply into the muscle at the back of his leg. Blood was flowing out like beer from an open tap.

She was speaking rapidly and cheerfully, and he just had time to think how beautiful she was.

Lissen Carak—the Abbess

The Abbess watched the captain's sortie head east along the road, moving so fast that they were gone from sight before she recovered her eagle.

I have certainly given away my station to every gentleman here, she thought. She wondered if the siege would leave her any secrets at all.

Parcival, her magnificent Ferlander eagle, was killing his way through the flocks of wild birds like a tiger let loose in a sheepfold. But she could see the big old bird was tiring, and she began to cast her lure. Just to be sure.

She whirled it carefully over her head, and Parcival saw it, turned at the flash of Tyrian red, and abandoned his pursuit of his defeated enemies. He came to her like a unicorn to a maiden—shyly at first, and finally eager to be caught.

His weight was far too much for her, but young Theodora helped her, and got a faceful of wings for her trouble as the creature bated and bated again, unused to his mistress having a helper. But she got the jesses slipped over his talons, and Theodora put the hood on him, and he calmed, while the Abbess said, "There's my brave knight. There's my fine warrior—you poor old thing." The eagle was tired, grumpy and very pleased with himself, all at the same time.

Theodora stroked his back and wings and he straightened up.

"Give him a morsel of chicken, dear," the Abbess said. She smiled at the novice. "It's just like having a man, child. Never give him what he wants—only give him what *you* want. If he eats too much we'll never get him into the air again."

Theodora looked out from the height of the tower. The plain and the river were far below them, and the eagle's sudden stoop from this height had shattered the lesser birds.

Amicia appeared from the hospital with a message from Sister Miram. The Abbess looked at it and nodded. "Tell Miram to use anything she needs. No sense in hoarding."

Amicia's eyes were elsewhere. "They're gone," Amicia said. "The enemy's spies. Even the wyverns. I can feel it."

Theodora was startled that a novice would speak directly to the Abbess.

The Abbess seemed untroubled. "You are very perceptive," the Abbess said. "But there's something I don't like about this." She walked to the edge of the tower and looked down. Just below her, a pack of nuns stood on the broad platform of the gatehouse and watched the end of the rout below and the disappearing column of dust that marked the captain's sortie.

One nun left the wall, her skirts held in her hands as she ran. The Abbess wondered idly why Sister Bryanne was in such a hurry until she saw the priest. He was on the wall, alone, and praying loudly for the destruction of the enemy.

That was well enough, she supposed. Father Henry was a festering boil—his hatred for the captain and his attempts to *discipline* her nuns were heading them for a confrontation.

But the siege was pushing the routine away, and she worried that it would never return. And what if the captain went out and died?

"What do you say, my lady?" Amicia asked, and the Abbess smiled at her.

"Oh, my dear, we old people sometimes say aloud what we ought to keep inside."

Amicia, too, was looking out to the east where a touch of dust still hung over the road that ran south of the river. And she wondered, like every nun, every novice, every farmer and every child in the fortress, why they were riding away, and if they would return.

North of Albinkirk—Peter

Peter was learning to move through the woods. Home for him was grass savannah, dry brush and deep-cut rocky riverbeds, dry most of the year and impassable with fast brown water the rest. But here, with the soft ground, the sharp rock, the massive trees that stretched to the heavens, the odd marshes on hilltops and the endless streams and lakes, a different kind of stealth was required, a different speed, different muscles, different tools.

The Sossag flowed over the ground, following trails that appeared out of nowhere and seemed to vanish again as fast.

At mid-day, Ota Qwan stopped him and they stood, both of them breathing hard.

"Do you know where we are?" the older man asked.

Peter looked around. And laughed. "Headed for Albinkirk."

"Yes and no," Ota Qwan said. "But for a sailor on the sea of trees, you are fair enough." He reached into a bag of bark twine made into a net that he wore at his hip all the time, and drew forth an ear of cooked corn. He took a bite and passed it to Peter. Peter took a bite and passed it to the man behind him—Pal Kut, he thought the man called himself, a cheerful fellow with a red and green face and no hair.

Peter reached into his own bag and took out a small bark container of dried berries he'd found in Grundag's effects.

Ota Qwan ate a handful and grunted. "You give with both hands, Peter."

The man behind him took half a handful and held them to his forehead, a sign Peter had never seen before.

"He's telling you that he respects the labour of your work and the sacrifice you make in sharing. When we share pillaged food—well, it never really belonged to any of us to begin with, did it?" Ota Qwan laughed, and it was a cruel sound.

"What about the dinner I cooked?" Peter asked, ready to be indignant.

"You were a slave then!" Ota Qwan thumped his chest. "My slave."

"Where are we going?" Peter asked. He didn't like the way Ota Qwan claimed him.

Skadai appeared out of thin air to take the last handful of the dried berries, he, too, made the gesture of respect. "Good berries," he said. "We go to look at Albinkirk. Then we hunt on our own."

Peter shook his head as the war captain moved on. "Hunt on our own?"

"Yesterday, while you rutted like a stag—wait, do you know even who Thorn is?" Ota Qwan asked him, as if he were a child.

Peter wanted to rub his face in it, but in truth, he'd heard the name mentioned but didn't know who he was. And he was increasingly eager to know how his new world worked. "No," he said, pouting.

Ota Qwan ignored his tone. "Thorn wishes to be the lord of these woods." He made a face. "He is reputed a great sorcerer who was once a man. Now he seeks revenge on men. But yesterday he was defeated—not beaten, but bloodied. We did not follow him to battle because Skadai didn't like the plan he heard, so now we go east to fight our own battles."

"Defeated? By whom?" Peter looked around. "Where was this battle?"

"Six leagues from where you rutted with Senegral, two hundred men died and twice that number of creatures of the Wild." He shrugged. "Thorn has ten times that many creatures and men at his beck and call and he summons more. But the Sossag are not slaves, servants, bound men—only allies, and only then when it suits our need."

"Surely this Thorn is angry at us?" Peter asked.

"So angry that if he dared he would kill us all, or destroy our villages, or force Skadai to die in torment." Ota Qwan cackled. "But to do so would be to forfeit the alliance of every creature, every boglin, every man in his service. This is the *Wild*, my friend. If he had won we would look foolish and weak." Ota Qwan gave a wicked smile. "But he lost, so it is he who looks foolish and weak while we go to burn the lands around Albinkirk, which was built on our lands many years ago. We have long memories."

Peter looked at him. "I assume you were not born a Sossag."

"Hah!" Ota Qwan sighed. "I was born south of Albinkirk." He shrugged. "It boots nothing, friend. Now I am Sossag. And we will burn the farms of the city, or what Thorn has left of it. He wants the Castle of the Women, which interests us not at all." Ota Qwan gave a queer smile. "The Sossag have never been to war with the Castle of Women. And he has failed." Ota Qwan looked into the distance, where the mountains rolled like waves on the sea. "For now. And Skadai says, let Albinkirk see the colour of our steel."

The words thrilled Peter, who thought he should be too mature to fall for such things. But war had a simplicity that could be a relief. Sometimes, it is good merely to hate.

And then Peter thought that Ota Qwan was an injured soul who had fallen into the Sossag to heal himself. But the former slave shook his head and said to himself, "Be one of them. And you will never be another man's slave."

At nightfall on the second day they were in sight of the town. Peter sat on his haunches, eating a thin rabbit that he'd cooked with herbs, sharing it with his new band. Ota Qwan had complimented his cooking, and had admitted that their new band of war-brothers—Pal Kut, Brant, Skahas Gaho, Mullet and Barbface (the best Peter could do with his name) were gathered as much for Peter's food as for Ota Qwan's leadership.

Either way, it was good to belong. Good to be part of a group. Brant smiled when he took food. Skahas Gaho patted the ground on his blanket when Peter hovered by the fire, looking for a place to sit.

Two days, and these were his comrades.

Skadai came to their fire towards true dark, and sat on his haunches. He spoke quickly, smiled often, and then surprised Peter by patting him on the arm. He ate a bowl of rabbit soup with his fingers, grinned, and left them for the next fire.

Ota Qwan sighed. The other men took sharpening stones from their bags, and began to touch up their arrowheads, and then their knives, and Skahas Gaho, who had a sword, a short, heavy-bladed weapon like a Morean xiphos, made the steel sing as he passed his stone over it.

"Tomorrow, we fight," Ota Qwan said.

Peter nodded.

"Not Albinkirk," Ota Qwan said. "A richer target. Something to take home with us. Something to make our winter shorter." He licked his lips and Brant asked him a question and then guffawed at the answer.

Skahas Gaho kept sharpening his short sword, and men began to laugh. He was stroking it tenderly, with long, lingering strokes of the stone. And then shorter, faster ones.

Brant laughed, and then spat disgustedly and unrolled his furs.

Peter did the same. He had no trouble getting to sleep.

South and East of Lissen Carak—Gerald Random

Random had been ready for ambush for five days, and it didn't matter when it happened. His men almost won through.

Almost.

They were now riding through deep forest, and the western road was a double cart track with the trees sometimes arched right over the road. However, the old forest was open, the great boles of the trunks sixty feet apart or more with little enough underbrush so his flankers could ride alongside, his advance guard could clear the trail a hundred horse-lengths wide, and his wagons were moving well—it was the fifth straight day without rain, and the road was dry except in the deeper ruts and puddles and some deep holes like muddy ponds.

The woods were so deep that it was difficult to gauge the passage of time, and he had no idea how far they'd travelled on the narrow track until Old Bob rode back to say that he thought he could hear the river.

At that news, Random's heart rose. Even though what he was doing was suicidally foolish, to aid an old Magus, and his wife would never approve when she found out.

He was on the lead wagon, and he stood up to look—a natural thing to do, even when listening would have been more natural. But all he could hear was the wind in the trees overhead.

"Ambush!" shouted one of the vanguard. He pointed at a dozen boglins around a young troll, a monster the size of a plough horse with the antlers like a great elk's and a smooth stone face like the visor on a black helmet. It was covered in thick armour plates of obsidian.

The troll charged them, racing like a mad dog straight at the wagons. The horses panicked but his men did not, and quarrels flew thick as snow, and the troll screamed and slowed, seemed for a moment to be swimming through steel, and then suddenly fell with a crash.

The boglins vanished.

Random, standing on the wagon seat, took an arrow in the breastplate. It didn't bite, but it knocked him off the seat and it hurt when he got to his feet—his shoulder hurt and his neck hurt like fire.

Just ahead, the vanguard was abruptly locked up with more boglins.

Old Bob was racing for the melee.

Random watched as his soldiers crushed the smaller creatures with weight of horse and better weapons, better skill, and the boglins, as was inevitable, broke and ran.

Old Bob shouted something, but his words were lost in the triumph of the moment, and the troopers turned as one to harry the fleeing boglins...and suddenly the trolls were on them—a pair, smashing in from either flank. Blood came off the melee like smoke as they struck, and horses died faster than they could fall to the ground.

Random had never seen a troll before, but the Wild name for them—dhag—stuck in his mind, as did a picture in a Book of Hours he'd purchased in Harndon for the market—taller than a peasant's house, as black as night or expensive velvet, with plates of black stone like armour and no face, topped with antlers like clubs. A troll could crush an armoured man's breastplate in one blow and behead him in another, could move as fast as a horse and as quiet as a bear.

The vanguard was dead before Random could close his mouth. Six men gone in a breath.

Old Bob had a light lance, and he lowered the point—one of the monsters turned, almost falling as it skidded to a stop, feeling the vibration of the charging horse. It braced itself, head low, horn-clad feet still churning at the earth, and Random could see the great plate of stone that protected its skull.

And then Old Bob's horse was by and his lance, thrown, not couched, went into the beast's side—struck deep between two stone plates, and the meaty sound of the heavy spearhead going home in the flesh carried across the distance.

A dozen bolts hit the creature.

Gawin had the rearguard up, forming to the right and left, with companies of guildsmen coming up next to the wagons on either side—not the smoothest, and their faces were as white as snow, and their hands shook, but they were coming.

"Halt!" Gawin shouted, and Guilbert came from the other side of the wagons with another five of the wagon guards.

Guilbert took command with one glance. "Pick a target!" he called.

The woods were surprisingly silent.

Old Bob had his horse around, but he never saw the dozen boglins coming. One of them put a spear into his horse effortlessly, like a dancer, the squat thing pirouetting as its spear skewered the beast, and the horse stopped its turn and gave a shrill scream as the wounded troll attacked. Its first blow ripped Old Bob's lower jaw off his face under the brim of his open-faced helmet—then it crushed his breastplate so that a fountain of blood blew out of his open throat.

The wounded troll slumped. The second one stopped and bent down to feed off both of them, its visor opening and a set of fangs showing sharp against the black of its mouth.

The wave of boglins charged the line of bowmen and soldiers, and this time his men broke and ran.

Random watched them with complete understanding, terrified and virtually unable to move his limbs too, and the sight of the old knight being ripped asunder by the troll seemed to have numbed his mind. He tried to speak. He watched as the guildsmen shuffled, cursed, and turned too. The guards had horses, and they put their spurs to their mounts.

"Stand!" Guilbert shouted. "Stand or you are all dead men!"

They ignored him.

And then Ser Gawin laughed.

The sound of his laughter didn't stop the horrified men from running. It didn't stop the mounted men from raking their spurs into their panicked mounts...but it did make many men turn their heads.

His visor fell over his face with a click.

His destrier took its first steps, already moving quickly, as any horse trained to the joust knows to do.

His lance, erect in his hand, dipped, the pennon fluttering, and then he was moving like a streak of steel lightning across the ground between the wagons and the boglins. They, in turn, froze like animals hearing a hunter's call.

The feeding troll raised its head.

The chief of the boglins raised a horn and it blew a long, sweet note. Other horns echoed, and Random was suddenly freed from the vice of fear that ground against his heart. He got his sword clear of its scabbard.

"Hear me, Saint Christopher," he vowed, "if I live through this, I will build a church to you."

Gawin Murien settled the lance in its rest. The boglin chief was standing on the dead troll's chest, the one the crossbowmen had killed, and the knight's heavy lance passed through him so quickly that for a heartbeat Random thought the knight had missed, until the small monster was lifted from its feet, all limbs writhing in a horrible parody of an impaled insect, and a thin scream lifting from its throat, and then it was crushed against the stone wall of the remaining troll's head with a wet sound like a melon breaking, and the stone troll staggered under the impact.

It roared—a long belling sound that made the woods ring.

Gawin thundered away to the right. He kept his lance, passed through a thicket and emerged to the far right of the wagons. His horse was moving at a slow canter.

Guildsmen and soldiers began to gather again, their rout forgotten, and the boglins began to reach them in ones and twos, their desultory chase become a desperate melee in the turn of a card. A dozen guildsmen were cut down, but instead of spurring the others to run, the deaths of their comrades pulled more and more of the townsmen back to their duty.

Or perhaps it was Gawin's repeated war cry that did it, ringing as loud as the monsters roar. "God and Saint George!" he shouted, and even the wagons trembled.

The troll dipped its antlers, and spat something. Great clods of moss flew up, and a smell filled the air—a bitter reek of musk. Then it lifted its armoured head and charged, shoulders bunched from its first massive leap forward.

Random swung his sword, his right arm seeming to function independently of his mind, and smashed a boglin with the blow. He backed a step, suddenly aware of a dozen of the things around him, and he got his sword up, point in line, left hand gripping it halfway down the blade.

He charged them. He had the example of the knight before his eyes, and he only had a faint notion that there was more to a charge than bluster. He felt the pain of the first wound and the pressure of the blows on his shoulders and backplate, he also had the time to kill one boglin with the point, break a second with his pommel so that it seemed to burst, and then sweep the legs from a third in as many heartbeats. They had armour—whether it was their own chitinous skin or something made of leather and bone, he had no time to tell—but his heavy sword penetrated it with every thrust, and when it did, they died.

Light flashed, as if lightning had pulsed from the sky.

In a single heartbeat all of his opponents fell, and as they fell they turned to sand. His sword actually passed through one, and beyond his suddenly evaporated opponents, Ser Gawin rode directly at the troll. A horse length from collision his destrier danced to the right—and Ser Gawin's lance passed under its stone visor to strike it hard in the fanged mouth, plunging his lance the length of a man's arm into the thing's throat and crossing the massive monster's centre-line so that it snapped the lance and tripped the beast, which fell, unbalanced, its armoured head digging a massive furrow in the earth as Ser Gawin and his destrier danced clear.

Lightning pulsed again, and two dozen more boglins spattered to the ground.

"Rally!" Guilbert demanded.

The guildsmen were winning.

And every boglin they broke, skewered, or sliced reinforced their growing belief that they might win this battle.

Men were still falling.

But they were going to hold.

…until the horses and the oxen panicked, and shredded their column in ten breaths of a terrified man. A wagon plunged through the largest block of guildsmen, scattering them, and the boglins who had stopped, or slowed their charge, or simply balked at entering weapons range, suddenly surged forward. A dozen more guildsmen died at their hands, and the wall of wagons protecting the right of the column was gone.

Random got his back to Guilbert's. "Stand fast!" he yelled. "Stand fast!"

A few feet away, Harmodius pulled a riding whip from his belt.

"Fiat lux!" he commanded, and fire raged over the boglins. A guildsman in the process of having his throat ripped out was incinerated in the strike, but the sweet horns were sounding all around them.

Random estimated that the little knot he was with had perhaps twenty men, and at least one of them was on his knees, begging for mercy.

Harmodius drew his sword. He raised an eyebrow.

"Damn," Random said.

Harmodius nodded.

Guilbert shook his head. "Wagons punched us a hole," he said. "The mounted men are that way." He pointed back along the track. Back the way they'd come.

Random spat. *I'm going to lose everything,* he thought.

Harmodius nodded. "Might as well try," he said. "Ready to run, every-one?"

Random felt he ought to contribute something, but it was all happening too damned fast.

Harmodius raised his arms, and a ripple rolled from his hands like a flaw in glass, spreading outwards in a semi-circle like the ripple made by throwing a pebble in a pond, except that trees blackened and grass vanished and boglins fell like wheat under a sharp scythe before it.

Gawin, out beyond the edge of the bubble, charged his destrier straight at it. Random saw him put the animal into a jump, and they were up; down again in moments, having leaped the growing edge of the wave of destruction in a bound. And done it apparently unharmed.

"Oh, well done," Harmodius said. "That's a proper fellow."

And then they were running back down the trail.

They ran, and ran.

When Harmodius couldn't breathe, Gawin dismounted, put the Magus up on his destrier and ran along with them for a while.

And then, as if by common agreement, they all stopped running at a deep stream—the stream they'd crossed that morning at the break of day. There were a dozen wagons there, and all the mounted men on the far bank. One by one, the desperate men scrambled across, soaked to the waist, uncaring. Some stopped in mid-stream to drink from parched throats.

The mounted men began to weep, and Random ignored them.

But Gawin, alone of the panicked men crossing the stream, didn't throw himself down in the illusory safety. He sheathed his sword.

"I have run from terror, too," he said to the mounted men. "And it is three times as hard to regain your honour as it is to preserve it in the first place. But this is where we will all make ourselves whole. Dismount, messires. We will hold the river bank while these good men get to safety, and in so doing, we will find both honour and peace."

And such was the power of his voice that one by one they dismounted. Random watched with disbelief.

There were nine of them, all well armoured, and they filled the gap of the trail.

Guildsmen took their horses as more men came in—a dozen in one group, wild-eyed, and then in ones and twos, their jackets torn.

And then no more.

There were perhaps fifty survivors from the three hundred men who had awakened that morning.

They had a dozen wagons—mostly the horse drawn carts whose animals had stuck to the road, or followed the military horses. But as they waited for the next assault of the enemy, whose horns could clearly be heard—a boy appeared on the far bank, no more than fifteen years old.

"I reckon I need some help!" he called. "Can't get these here oxen through the ford on my own!"

The boy had saved four wagons. He didn't seem to know that he was supposed to be afraid.

"They're busy a-killin all the horses and cattle!" the boy said. He grinned like it was all a great prank. "So I'm just walking up and taking any wagon ain't got a bunch of 'em aboard!"

Random hugged him after they had the oxen across. Then he turned to Gawin. "I honour your willingness to fight here and get us clear," he said. "But I think we should all go together. It will be a long road back, and as dangerous as these woods—every step of the way."

Gawin shrugged. "These men can go—although I believe they owe you a great service." A daemon appeared across the river, and a troll belled. "But I will stand here, for as long as God grants my hands the power to hold this ford," he said. And very softly, he said, "I used to be so beautiful."

Harmodius nodded. "You, messire, are a true knight."

Gawin shrugged. "I am whatever I am, now. I hear that daemon across the stream—I think I understand him. He calls for his blood kin. I—" He shook his head.

"You saved us," said Harmodius. "Like a knight."

Gawin gave him a wounded smile. "It is an estate from which I have fallen," he said. "But to which I aspire."

Harmodius grinned. "All the good ones do." He raised his hat. He was still mounted on the destrier, and he seemed a bigger man than he had before.

Across the river, the trolls belled again, and Random felt bile rise in his mouth.

But then there was the sound of a horn beyond the sweet horns of the boglins. A bronze trumpet call sounded through the trees.

South of Lissen Carak—Amy's Hob

Amy's Hob lay still.

He lay so still that ants crawled over him.

When he had to piss, he did so without moving.

There were boglins at the base of the hill. They were feeding. He tried not to watch, but his eyes were drawn, again and again.

They went to a corpse, covered it, and when they left it, there was nothing but bone, hair, and some sinew. A few fed alone, but most fed in a pack.

Beyond them, a pair of great horned trolls walked slowly down the ridge. Ten horse lengths from the unmoving scout, the larger of the two raised its head and called.

A dozen boglin horns sounded their sweet, cheerful notes in return.

Gelfred appeared at his side, and his face was as white as chalk.

"How many?" he breathed.

Amy's Hob shook his head. "Thousands."

Gelfred was made of different stuff. He raised himself on his elbows and scanned carefully from right to left. "Blessed Saint Eustachios stand with us," he said.

One of the trolls' heads whipped round and saw him.

"Run!" he shouted.

Gelfred aimed his crossbow and the string rang like a bell and the nearest boglin folded. So did the one behind it.

"We're dead," Amy's Hob said bitterly.

"Don't be such an ass," Gelfred said. "Follow me." They ran down the reverse slope of the ridge. The troll was crashing along behind them, much faster in the undergrowth than they were.

At the base of the ridge they were just a few horse lengths ahead of the thing, but to Amy's Hob's amazement, there were a pair of horses waiting. Both men vaulted into the saddle, and the horses were away, as terrified as their riders.

As soon as they outdistanced pursuit, Gelfred slowed. "Go to the captain—he's on the road."

"I'll tell him to get back to the fortress!" Amy's Hob said, eyes still wild.

Gelfred shook his head. He was still pale and his fear was obvious, but he was the kind of man who was afraid and kept on functioning. "No. Absolutely not. Tell him it can be done. If he's quick."

Amy's Hob might have stayed to argue, but staying there was insane. He put his bare heels to the pony's sides, and he was gone, leaving Gelfred alone in the woods with a thousand boglins and a troll.

The man knelt by his pony, and began to pray, intent on his purpose.

There was a flare of light, and Gelfred vanished.

South and East of Lissen Carrack—Bad Tom

Victory can be as much luck as skill, or strength of arms.

Bad Tom led the vanguard. They'd heard the boglin horns for a league and had stopped on the trail, a long column of twos, the war horses snorting, the archer's ronceys trying to avoid being nipped by the bigger horses. There was new grass by the road and all the horses wanted it.

Amy's Hob cantered in from the east and he looked as if he'd seen hell come to earth.

Tom laughed at the sight of him. "Guess we've found 'em," he said, delighted.

Amy's Hob saluted the captain, who looked remarkably calm, a tall figure in scarlet and steel. "Gelfred says—" He shook his head. "There's a mort of 'em, but Gelfred says it's now or not."

"We're right on top of them," Tom said. He nodded to the scout. "Well done, lad. Must take balls of brass to be out there alone wi' 'em."

Amy's Hob shivered. "Gelfred's still out there."

The captain listened. Sounds can be read as easily as sights, sometimes. He could see the action ahead—the road ran east along the south bank of the river, then south between the hills. Before it turned south and began to climb, it crossed a stream.

"What's happening?" Michael asked.

"The enemy is attacking a convoy," the captain said. He and Tom exchanged a look.

Hywel Writhe used to say, war isn't sword cuts, it's decisions.

"They're all on this side of the stream?" he asked.

Amy's Hob nodded. "Aye."

"Clumped up?" he asked.

"Which Gelfred said to tell you *it is now.*" He shook his head. "There's' a thousand of 'em—"

The captain's eyes met Tom's. "Go," the captain said.

Bad Tom grinned like a madman. "On me!" he roared.

Around him, men checked one more thing. It was different for each one—here, an armour strap, there, the way a helmet sat on your head. Or the check to make sure your dagger was right there, at your hip.

But men were smiling.

They said things.

They were going to do that thing that they did. When they moved like lightning and struck like the hammer on the anvil. Soldiers know, feel, these things. And luck rose about them, as if they were magi casting words of power with the hooves of their horses.

They rode right for the sound of the horns. Tom only reined in when he saw his first boglin, and he looked back to see Grendel and his rider pounding up the road.

The captain flipped him a salute. His visor was up.

"There they are," Tom said. He couldn't keep the grin off his face.

The captain listened and scratched his beard.

Their eyes met again.

"Never met a Wild creature that could fight in two directions at once," Tom said. "They don't fight. They hunt. And when they pounce—why, that's all they have."

"You mean, the Wild doesn't keep a reserve," the captain said.

"What you say," Tom said. He could tell the captain was of one mind with him.

"Someday they will," the captain said.

"Not today," Tom said.

The captain hesitated another moment. Breathed deeply, listening. Then he turned back to Tom, and his grin was wide and feral.

"Let's do it," he said. He raised his lance, and pointed with it. Carlus, his trumpeter, raised his long, bronze instrument, and the captain gave him a nod.

Tom didn't bother to form up, because surprise was everything. He was sure he knew what was happening ahead, and he led his men forward, armoured in that assurance. And when his destrier leaped a low fallen tree and the track turned and he saw hundreds of the little fuckers plundering wagons, he just raised his sword.

"Lachlan for Aa!" he roared, and he began to kill.

South and East of Lissen Carrack—The Red Knight

There is a great deal of luck involved in catching an enemy, especially a victorious enemy who outnumbers you twenty to one, flat footed, glutted with spoil, unable to either fight or flee.

There's even more luck involved when you catch your enemy glutted with spoil and pinned against a roaring torrent of a stream, with only one ford, and that ford held by a desperate madman.

Because he was in command, and because he feared a trap, the captain was among the last men onto the field, leading half a dozen archers and two men-at-arms and Jacques with all the valets as a reserve. He came forward still full of doubt at his own decision, which seemed rash, and yet full of a sort of certainty—almost like religious faith—that he could feel the enemy's failure.

He came on the heels of the main battle's charge to cover Bad Tom's headlong rush, and Jacques was less than twenty horse lengths behind the last man of the main battle, and still, by the time he rode under the big oak trees, the fighting was over by the abandoned wagons. He rode by what he assumed had been the convoy's a last stand—a dozen guildsmen face down, some of them looking half eaten or worse.

He rode past the carcasses of not one, but three, dead dhags. He had only ever seen one, before today.

He passed down a line of carts, their draught animals dead and partially butchered in their traces. Other wagons had their oxen or their horses untouched, panicked in the traces but alive. There were human bodies among the dead boglins and other things—one corpse looked like a golden bear, cleanly beheaded.

He shook his head in disbelief.

He couldn't have planned it this way. Couldn't have coordinated such a victory, not with a pair of magi to handle communications and twice the number of men.

Farther on, they were still fighting. He could hear Tom's warcry.

He came up to two men holding a dozen fretting war horses and Jacques sent four valets to take their reins. The two men-at-arms grinned, loosened swords in their scabbards, and headed off down the trail toward the sound of belling. The captain took a breath, thinking of the kind of men and women he employed. The kind who smiled and hastened down the trail to battle. He led them. They made him happy.

He dismounted, handed his horse to Jacques, who gave him his spear. And dismounted himself.

"Not without me, you loon," Jacques said.

"I have to," the captain said. "You don't."

Jacques spat. "Can we get this over with?" He gestured, and Toby appeared, somehow taller and more dangerous looking in a breast and back and a pot helm.

They ran forward. There was fighting off to their left—the humdrum sound of blade on blade. And ahead, heavy movement and grunting, like a huge boar in a deep thicket.

"Don't let it fucking cross the river!" Tom roared, almost at his elbow.

The captain came around the great bole of an old elm, and there was the beast—twenty-five hands at the shoulder, with curling tusks.

A behemoth.

It turned.

Like every creature of the Wild, its eyes met the captain's, and it roared a challenge.

"Here we go," said Tom, with relish. "Captain's here. Now we can dance!"

Jacques hip-checked the captain. "Mind?" he said, and shot the thing, a clean shaft that leapt from his bowstring at full draw and plunged through its hide, vanishing to the fletchings. His war-bow was as long and heavy as Wilful Murder's, and most men couldn't draw it.

Somebody behind it plunged a sword deep into its side, and then a man-at-arms was sawing at its neck, and it was roaring in anger. But the flurry of blows let up, and suddenly it got its feet under it, tossed the man-at-arms free, and put its head down.

"Oh fuck," Jacques said.

A solid lance of fire crossed the stream and struck the behemoth in the head, splintering a tusk and setting fire to the stump. Despite the fear, every man turned to look. Most of them had never seen a phantasm used in combat.

The captain charged it, because that seemed better than it charging him. His horse had done all the work until now, and his legs were fresh, despite the weight of steel greaves and sabatons.

The fire was a nice distraction and he slammed his heavy spear into its face, near an eye. It was collapsing back—Jacques, also unaffected by the pyrotechnics, was walking forward, putting arrow after arrow into its unguarded belly.

It turned away, suddenly less fearsome and sensing the defeat of near death. It tried to burst free across the stream but the rocky bottom betrayed it and it stumbled; a dozen archers, guildsmen and mercenaries alike, poured shafts into it, and its blood swirled in the fast water. It gathered itself up and leaped—awesome in its might—scattered the archers, and killed two guildsmen, massive front feet pounding their bodies to fleshy mush in the spring mud. And still it got its head up when the captain came out of the trees behind it, and it turned at bay. It's great eyes met the captain's.

"Me again," the captain said.

It raised its head and bellowed, and the woods shook. One of Tom's men-at-arms—Walter La Tour—landed a hard blow with a pole-axe and got swiped by the whole force of its mighty head in reply, crushing his breastplate and breaking all his ribs. He fell without a sound. Francis Atcourt, one day out of the infirmary, struck it with a pole-axe too, and danced aside as it's splintered, burning tusk sought his life. He tripped and fell over a rotten stump, which saved his life as its tusks and fangs passed over his head.

The captain ran rock to rock across the stream, his sabatons flashing above the swollen water, charging his prey. It turned to finish Atcourt, caught sight of the captain's rush, and hesitated a fraction of a heartbeat.

Bad Tom watched his captain rush the monster and laughed. "I *love* him," he shouted, and leaped after.

The monster lurched forward, and stumbled, and the captain thrust, catching it in the mouth, cutting up so that ivory sprayed. The splintered tusk caught the back of his rerebrace hard enough to slam him into the stream. He went down, his helmet filled with water, but he got a rock under his backplate and sprang to his feet, stomach muscles screaming as he levered his own weight plus sixty pounds up on his hips, and then he had his feet planted, knee deep in water, and he was cutting—down to the Boar's Tooth guard, his heavy pole-arm cutting from the height of his shoulder all the way down to his hip—then back up the same path, ripping up through its trunk to the Guard of the Woman. He reversed the blade and thrust down into its eye as the creature fell.

Bad Tom slammed his fist into the thing before it was done moving. "I name you—meat!" he shouted.

The mercenaries laughed. Some of the men-at-arms were even applauding and the guildsmen began to realise they might live. They began to cheer.

A last arrow flew into the corpse.

There was nervous laughter and then the cheers swelled.

"Red Knight! Red Knight! Red Knight!"

The captain enjoyed it for three heavy breaths. Three deep, lung filling breaths to enjoy being alive, being victorious. Then—

"We're not out of this yet," the captain snapped.

At the sound of his voice the young knight who'd led the defence of the ford got up from where he'd knelt to pray—or fallen in exhaustion.

They looked at each other for a moment too long, the way only mortal foes and lovers look at each other.

And then the captain turned away. "Get the horses. Get everyone mounted. Get as many of these wagons as we can save. Move, move, move. Tom, collect wagons. Who's in charge here? You?" He was gesturing at one of the men of the convoy.

He turned to Jacques. "Find out who's in charge of the convoy, get a head count. The knight in front of you—"

"I know who he is—" Jacques said.

"He looks wounded," the captain replied.

The knight they were talking about rose and hobbled forward. His right leg was shiny and slick with blood.

"You. *Bastard!*" he said, and cocked back his sword to swing at the captain. He collapsed just as Jacques took his sword.

Tom laughed. "Someone who knows you?" he said. Chortled, and got to work. "All right, you lot! Archers on me! Listen up!"

But the captain, sometimes known as the Red Knight, stood by the young knight's body. For reasons none of them knew, except perhaps

Jacques, it was a deeply satisfying moment. A great victory. And a little personal revenge.

Rescuing Gawin Murien.

Killing a behemoth. This one, in death, didn't look any smaller. It was still fucking huge.

The captain threw back his head and laughed and the favour on his shoulder fluttered in the breeze.

Tom met his eye.

"Sometimes, this is the best life I could ever have imagined," the captain said.

"That's why we love you," Tom said.

Harndon—Desiderata

Lady Mary stood by the empty bedstead, and watched a pair of southern maids roll the feather mattress.

"We're taking too much," Desiderata said.

Diota laughed. "My sweet, you won't lie easy without a feather bed. All the knights have them."

"The Archaics slept on the ground, rolled in a cloak." Desiderata swirled, admiring the fall of her side-slit surcote and the way the slightest breeze caught the thing. Silk. She'd seen silk before—silk garters, silk floss for embroidery. This was more like something from the aether. It was magic.

"You cannot wear that without a gown," Diota said. "I can see your tits right through it, sweeting."

Lady Mary turned away and looked out the window. *I think that's what the Queen had in mind,* she thought to herself. She exchanged a look with Becca Almspend, who glanced up from her reading to smile her thin-lipped smile.

"Sleeping on the ground under a cloak doesn't sound any worse than being a maid in the Royal Barracks," Becca said. "In fact," she glared at Lady Mary, "perhaps in a military camp, your friends don't come and steal your blankets?"

The Queen smiled at Lady Mary. "Really, Mary?"

Mary shrugged. "I have seven sisters," she said. "I don't mean to take other people's blankets. It just happens." Her eyes twinkled.

The Queen stretched, rose on her toes like a dancer, and then settled, arms slightly outstretched, as if she was posing for a portrait. "I imagine we'll all sleep together," she said.

Almspend shook her head. "Pin your cloak to your bodice, that's my advice, my lady."

Diota snorted. "She won't sleep under a cloak. She'll have a feather bed in a tent the size of a palace."

The Queen shrugged, and the maids packed.

Lady Almspend worked her way down the day's list. The preparations of the king's baggage train—and then of the Queen's—had made Lady Almspend a much more important person.

"War horses for my lady's squires," she said.

The Queen nodded. "How goes that task?"

Almspend shrugged. "I asked young Roger Calverly to see to it. He has a head on his shoulders and he seems to be trustworthy with money. But he's come back to report that there are simply no war horses to be had. Not for anything."

The Queen stamped her foot. It didn't make much noise, small as it was and clad in a dance slipper, but the maids stopped moving and stood still. "This is not acceptable," she said.

Rebecca raised an eyebrow. "My lady, this is a matter of military reality. I asked questions this morning at first breakfast in the men's hall."

Diota made a spluttering sound of outrage, perhaps she did it too often, but it still effective. "You was in the men's hall for breakfast, you hussy? Wi'out an escort?"

Almspend sighed. "There aren't any *women* likely to know much about the price of war horses, now, are there, Diota?" She rolled her eyes with the effectiveness that only a woman of seventeen can muster. "Ranald has taken me to the men's hall as a guest. And—" She paused and cleared her throat a little awkwardly, "And I had an escort."

"Really?" Lady Mary asked. "Sir Ricar, I suppose?"

Lady Rebecca looked at the ground. "He hadn't left yet—he was eager enough to help me."

Diota sighed.

The Queen looked at her. "And?"

Almspend shrugged. "Alba doesn't breed enough horses for all its knights," she said. "We import them from Galle, Morea and the Empire." She looked at her friend defiantly. "Sir Ricar explained it to me."

The Queen stared at her secretary. "Gentle Jesu and Mary his mother. Does the king know?"

Almspend shrugged. "My lady, the past week has revealed that men conduct war without women with all the efficency and careful planning that they do anything else without us."

Diota let out a most unladylike snort.

Lady Mary laughed aloud. "Is there beer involved?" she asked.

The Queen shook her head. "You mean to say we don't have enough war horses to mount our own knights, and no one cares?"

Lady Almspend shrugged. "I won't say no one cares. I could guarantee that no one has taken any thought for it."

"What of remounts?" the Queen asked. "Horses die. Like flies. I'm sure I've heard that said."

Almspend shrugged.

Lady Mary nodded. "But Becca—you must have a plan." Somewhat cattily, she added, "You always do."

Lady Almspend smiled at her, immune to her sarcasm. "As it happens I do. If we can raise a thousand florins we can purchase a whole train of Morean horses. The owner is camped outside the ditch. I met with him this morning and offered for his whole string. Twenty-one destriers."

The Queen hugged her impulsively.

Diota shook her head. "We have no money, sweeting."

The Queen shrugged. "Sell our jewels."

Diota stepped up to the smaller woman. "Don't be an arse, sweet. Those jewels are all you have if he dies. You don't have a baby. If he goes down, no one will want you."

The Queen looked steadily at her nurse. "Diota—I allow you nearly unlimited liberties."

The older woman flinched.

"But you talk and talk, and sometimes your mouth runs away with you," the Queen continued, and Diota backed away.

The Queen spread her arms. "You have it precisely backwards, dear heart. If the king dies, *everyone* will want me."

The silence was punctuated only by the barking of dogs outside. Diota quailed. Lady Mary pretended to be somewhere else, and Becca opened her book.

But finally, Diota straightened her spine. "All I'm saying is let the king look to his own war horses. Tell the squires where they can buy them and let them squeeze their rich parents for the money. When you sell your jewels, sweeting, you will have *nothing.*"

The Queen stood very still. Then she smiled her invulnerable smile at her nurse. "I am what I am," she said. "Sell the jewels."

Chapter Ten

Otter Creek Valley, East of Albinkirk—Peter

Peter lay on the ground behind a tree as big as a small house, unable to see anything, and waited for battle.

More than anything, he wanted to piss. From a tiny irritant at the base of his penis, the feeling gradually grew to envelope his every thought. After the first of several eternities, the need to void himself overtook his fear and terror.

From time to time, he drifted off on other thoughts—the possibility of moving to a better hiding space; finding a view of the oncoming enemy; finding some actual cover. He had no experience of war in the west, and couldn't imagine what it might be like to face a man in steel armour.

He had a knife, a bow, and nine arrows.

And he had to piss.

It began to seem possible that he should just let go, and lie in his own urine for however long they lay there.

He wondered if he was the only one. He wondered if Ota Qwan had meant to tell him to relieve himself before the ambush was set. Or if he had not told him deliberately. The black painted man had some cruelty in him—Peter was already sensing that Ota Qwan had few followers because he enjoyed twisting the knife too much. And he thought that the honeymoon between them was ending—in the beginning, Ota Qwan had been as desperate for his company as Peter had been desperate for an ally amidst the alien Outwallers, but now, with a war-group forming around him, Ota Qwan was undergoing a subtle metamorphosis. And not a pretty one.

And he really had to piss.

There was no way to measure the time. An ant crawled the length of his body, from moccasined left foot to right shoulder. Something larger crossed one of his knees. A pair of hummingbirds came and visited a flower by his head, and he was so still in the agony of his need to relieve himself that the male, bright red in spring plumage, all but landed on his painted face.

There were three hundred men—more, perhaps five hundred—lying on either side of the road as it led downhill to a ford over a deep running stream. They were somewhere east of Albinkirk. No one made a noise.

He had to piss.

He heard the metallic scrape of an iron-shod hoof on stone, and a shriek—a cry, and then a scream that seemed to come from the other side of his tree.

No one was moving.

The scream was repeated and suddenly cut off, and its sudden removal left another sound—the sound of shod hooves galloping away.

Suddenly Skadai was on the trail, just a few arm's lengths away, calling softly. "Dodak-geer-lonh!" he said. "Gots onah!"

All around Peter, warriors rose from their ambush spots, rubbing themselves, or scraping bark off their skin. Half of them immediately began to relieve themselves. Peter followed suit, previously unaware that urination could be such a great pleasure.

But Skadai was moving. Ota Qwan swatted Peter on the shoulder. "Move!" he said, as if Peter was a child.

Peter gathered his bow and followed.

They ran east on the trail for twenty horse lengths, and there was a horse, dead, across the trail, and a man pinned beneath it with his face and hair cut away and his throat slit. His blood pooled between the rocks and ran in a sticky rivulet headed downhill to the stream.

After running for what seemed a long time, they began to spread out amid big trees. The stream was well behind them, and Peter was terrified—they were running at the enemy, or so it seemed.

Skahas Gaho must have felt the same, because when they stopped running he got in front of Ota Qwan and said something that was clearly remonstration.

Ota Qwan struck him—not a hard blow, but a fast one, and the younger warrior bent over with the pain.

Ota Qwan spoke quickly, spittle flying from his mouth.

Skadai ran up silently, listened to Ota Qwan, and nodded, running off down the loose line of warriors that extended as far as the eye could see into the great trees on either flank. The trees here—mostly Adnacrag maples and beeches, tall old trees with magnificent tops—were big enough that two men couldn't get their arms around them. But there was little undergrowth because of the high canopy, and despite the sun-dappled forest floor, little grew amidst the carpet of old leaves except the most magnificent irises that Peter had ever seen.

Skahas Gaho got to his feet, glared resentfully at Skadai and spat at Ota Qwan. He said something to the other warriors, and ran off down the line. Brant turned to follow him, and Ota Qwan raised his bow.

Peter acted without thought. He pushed Ota Qwan's bow arm, hard.

The warrior tried to hit him in the ear with the tip of the bow but Peter caught it and, in a single turn of his arm, he had Ota Qwan's right arm in an elbow lock that threatened to dislocate the man's shoulder.

"I wasn't *born* a slave," Peter said. "Don't fuck with me."

"They are deserting me!" Ota Qwan watched the two men running off.

"You hit Skahas Gaho when you needed to reason with him." Peter wanted to laugh to hear himself explaining basic leadership to Ota Qwan. But he had the arm lock, and he wasn't letting go.

The other man stiffened, and then went limp. "He was about to disobey. To disobey Skadai!"

Peter let the black painted man go. "I've only been Sossag for three days, but it seems to me that's Skadai's problem, not yours. I think you thought like an Alban, not a Sossag." Peter shrugged.

The other three—Pal Kut, Barbface, and Mullet, watched them warily.

"You will be loyal to me!" Ota Qwan hissed at Peter. "Will you?"

Peter nodded. "I will," he said, finding that the words made him feel queasy.

Pal Kut called something. The line, well-spread, was moving rapidly forward, almost at a run. Most men had an arrow on their bows.

Peter sprinted to make his place in the line, fumbled an arrow and dropped it, and turned back to get it—he had too few to lose one. He bent, and in that moment, the world exploded.

To the front of the line, off amidst the drover's herd, a bull gave a long, low growl. And suddenly the air was full of arrows flying both ways. And the Sossag gave a great cry, almost like a scream...

...and charged.

Peter had his arrow on his bow. He ran forward, saw Pal Kut take an arrow in the gut, an arrow so big and so powerful that it emerged from his back in a gout of blood, and the head was shaped like a swallow and gleamed with a horrible red-blue malevolence.

Peter ran forward, following Ota Qwan.

He saw his first enemy—a tall blond boy in ring mail who coolly rose from behind a bush and loosed an arrow into a warrior he didn't know— shot him from so close that the man was knocked off balance by the arrow and stumbled like a beheaded chicken before collapsing in death.

But Ota Qwan leaped at the man with a dire scream and loosed his own arrow at arm's length, and the barbed head drove through his ring mail at the shoulder. A dozen warriors converged on the wounded boy and he was dead and scalped in a few heartbeats.

Ota Qwan took the boy's sword—four feet of shining steel—and brandished it, and all of the warriors who had seen him attack gave a great cry, and then they were pelting forward again.

Otter Creek Valley, East of Albinkirk—Hector Lachlan

As soon as the scouts reported, Lachlan knew he was in serious trouble. North of the Inn, in the Hills, the Wyrm of Erch kept the Outwallers at bay. It cost him animals to keep the Wyrm happy, but that was the way of the Hills. For a thousand years or more, the Wyrm had kept the Wild out of the Hills, to the benefit of generations of clansmen and drovers.

Here in the south, the king was supposed to keep the Outwallers away. Otter Creek was taken by some to be the border between the Green Hills and the Kingdom of Alba. But for Lachlan, whoever's territory it was, Otter Creek was safe ground. Not battle ground. Otter Creek ran down into the Albin. Albinkirk itself would be visible from the height of the next ridge but one—even if there was still a long day to drive the beeves to get them to the ford at Southford.

But the point was that they were *almost there.*

But now—he had scouts, and they knew their business. The clansmen and drovers knew the Outwallers. Outwallers were fierce, savage, and expert in arms. And they'd set an ambush for his drove, which meant they had scouted his herds, knew his strength and felt that they could take him. That meant three to four hundred warriors.

Hector didn't hesitate. It was a situation he'd imagined many times, although he'd never had to face it.

He turned to his tanist, Donald Redmane. "Go back to the drag guard. Take every animal you can, turn them, and run for the Inn."

Donald was a good man—loyal, dogged. Not the smartest, but a wonderful man in a fight, with a beautiful voice and clever hands that made things. "You go, Lachlan. I can hold them here."

Lachlan shook his head. "With your bruised ribs and all? Go. Now."

Redmane shook out his hair. "By the Wyrm, Hector. We're just a day's march from Albinkirk. Let's stampede the cows at the bastards, and put the survivors to the sword."

Hector looked at the woods under his hand. "No. My word on it, Donald. They're two to one or more against us, and scattering the herd in these woods—" He held his peace, lest he lower spirits more than he had to.

He turned and looked at the scout. "Ride clear all the way to the Inn. Take two horses so that you can change. Ride like the wind, yunker—they may already be in the High Country. Don't come back unless you can bring a hundred swords with you."

The other men with him in the vanguard loosened their swords in their scabbards. A few checked bows, and one took off his arming cap, replaced it, and went to his mule for his helmet.

"Bad luck you boys are with me, this day, and not in the rear with the drag," Hector said. "None of us will be dining this evening, I fear."

Ian Cowpat, a big man with a muddy brown face, gave him a grin. "Bah. Never met a loon I couldn't kill."

"Outwallers," Hector said. "We'll meet them in the woods where they can't shoot us down. Make a fight of it as long as we can. When I sound the horn, every man to me, and we form a shield wall and make a song of it." He looked around. The duty changed every day, because working the back of the herds was so much worse than walking in front, and so he didn't have the oldest or the youngest, or all the best fighters, or even all men he knew. He had a scattering of his own and the Keeper's men; but they were well armed, fifty strong, and not a face betrayed the terror that every one of them must feel. Good men for making a song.

By which hillmen meant dying well.

He thought of his new bride, and hoped she had kindled with him because, while he had a few bastards, he didn't have a son to avenge him. He caught the stirrup of his messenger.

"Listen!" he said. "Tell my wife that if she has a son he is to grow tall and strong, and when he is rich and well-loved, he is to take an army north and cut a bloody swath through the Outlanders. I'll take five hundred corpses as my wergild. Tell him when he's old enough. And tell her that her lips were the sweetest thing I ever knew, and I'll die with the taste of them on my own."

The young man was pale. He'd watched a boyhood friend die, and now he was being sent to ride a hundred leagues alone, quite possibly the only survivor of the drove.

"I could stay with you," he said.

Hector grinned. "I'm sure you could, boyo. But you are my last message to my wife and kin. I need you to go."

The messenger changed horses. A bull was lowing, and the cows were turning, the rear of the column was already moving north, away from the line of enemy that was out there somewhere.

Then he turned back to his men, most of whom were helmed and mailed and ready to fight. The lone priest, his half-brother, lifted his cross in the air and all the men knelt, and Paul Mac Lachlan prayed for their souls. When they all said amen, the priest put the cross back into his mail cote and put an arrow on his bow.

His cousin Ranald had a great axe—a beautiful thing, and he was cutting the air with it. He also had steel gauntlets; having served the king in the south he had fine gear like a knight.

"Ranald takes command if I fall," Hector said. "We'll go forward into the woods—the youngest ahead as skirmishers. Don't get overrun. Shoot when you can and then retreat. When you hear my horn, retreat. We have to hold until the sun reaches noon, and then Donald will be away and we will have died for something."

Ranald nodded. "Thanks, cousin. You do me honour."

Hector shrugged. "You're the best man for it."

Ranald nodded. "I wish your other brother were here with us."

Hector looked out into the trees. He could all but feel the oncoming enemy. Perhaps—perhaps they would wait in ambush too long, or balk at a close fight.

But there was too much movement out at the edge of the meadow. The Outwallers were coming.

"Me, too," Hector said. He looked up and down the line. "Let's go. Spread well out."

They went forward into the woods, moving quickly. His greatest fear was that the enemy was already at the woods' edge—but they weren't, and he got his fifty into the deep woods where the irises bloomed like crosses in a graveyard.

He put two men at every tree, and his ten youngest and swiftest a spear's throw in advance of his very open line, and then the bull roared again in the distance and suddenly the arrows began to fly.

Hector almost died in the first moments. An arrow hit his bassinet, spinning him, and a second arrow hit the nose guard of his helmet and bent it in—a finger's width from an arrow in the eye and instant death.

His men did well, although the boys in front were overrun and killed— and it was his mistake. The Outwallers were faster, bolder, and more reckless than he had imagined—but they still took a fearful toll among the savages. When his loose line retreated, running from cover to cover in their heavy mail, the Outwallers hesitated for a moment too long before following them, allowing them a clean break and leaving another thin line of kicking, wounded and gutted corpses.

One lone Outwaller, painted red from head to toe, stood between two great trees and called, and then sprinted forward. He tackled Ian Cowpat, and Cowpat never rose again—but only a handful of the painted men followed the red one.

Thanks be to God, Hector thought.

His men had been forced back into the last cover before the meadow, and the sun was not yet halfway into the heavens.

Otter Creek Valley, East of Albinkirk—Peter

Peter was out of arrows, and he had a great cut across his right shin—he'd been caught by the very end of a wild cut from a fleeing man's sword, but it was enough to send him to the earth for several long minutes.

He had a dead man's big dagger, almost the size of a short sword, and he had a buckler from the same corpse. He was no longer close to Ota Qwan—the black painted warrior had vanished early—and now Peter was close behind Skadai, who moved with more grace than any warrior Peter had ever seen.

Whomever they were fighting, the men were brave, big, silent, and far too well-armed.

The Sossag were dying. There were fifty men down already, perhaps more. Peter thought perhaps it was time for the Sossag to admit defeat. But Skadai didn't agree, running right into the enemy line, tackling a huge warrior and slitting his throat with a knife.

Peter couldn't hang back when such daring was shown.

The next time the enemy turned to run, Peter joined his wild yell to Skadai's, and saw Ota Qwan, who suddenly appeared just an arm's length away, do the same. The three of them rose from their cover, where they had lain to avoid the arrows—and charged. To Ota Qwan's right, Skahas Gaho also rose to his feet, sword in hand, and others joined them—not many, but a dozen all told.

An arrow flicked out of the sunlight like a hornet and hit Skadai in the groin. He stumbled, tumbled, and lay still.

Peter kept running. The man who had loosed the arrow had lost a step on his companions, and Peter ran for him, his whole self concentrated on that man, a red-haired giant in a fine mail shirt that gleamed in the woodland shade. He had an iron collar, a gorget, and long leather gloves.

Peter opened his mouth and screamed. The man dropped his bow and drew his sword—an arrow stung the inside of Peter's thigh as the head cut his skin, before flitting away between his legs, and Peter reached out with the buckler and the man's sword slammed into it. Peter pushed forward, the buckler pinning the sword, and his own short blade cut hard into the man's face, teeth sprayed and an eye was cut before the man turned away but Peter's sword was past his head, and he grabbed the blade with his buckler hand, locked the blade against the man's throat and sawed back and forth until he crushed his windpipe through the mail and iron collar.

Arrows hit his dying opponent—a dozen shot by his friends. But they had loosed unthinking, Peter's rush had spun him around, and every arrow intended for him hit the red-haired man.

He fell through Peter's hands, dead before he hit the ground, and Peter dropped his long knife and stooped to pick up the great sword from the grass. Ota Qwan screamed in triumph, and the scream was taken up along their line.

Otter Creek Valley, East of Albinkirk—Hector Lachlan

The priest, Paul Mac Lachlan, died badly, because he'd never been much of a swordsman, and one of the painted devils was through his guard and into him, slicing his face, choking him, using his body as a shield.

It demoralized them to watch one of their own carls die so easily, in single combat against an essentially unarmoured man.

On the other hand, Hector thought, they'd inflicted an incredible number of casualties. All the stories said that Outwallers were averse to taking casualties, and his people had killed fifty, perhaps more.

And their red leader was down.

Give the priest that—he'd shot him.

Hector grinned at the men around him. "We all have to do better than that," he said.

"Fucking Paul," Ranald said. One of the savages paused to scalp the priest, and Ranald flicked a shaft into the painted bastard. He screamed.

Hector held his horn over his head, so all the men left were ready.

"We're going to charge through their line and make our shield wall over there," he said. Retreating any further, into the open ground, was foolish.

The Outwallers were gaining courage from the success of the last rush, and they were coming forward now. His men were loosing their last shafts. Even as Hector watched, all the Outwallers went to ground again. If he had more woods, he'd retreat again. But he didn't. The wildflowers of the long meadow were at his back.

He held his horn to his lips and sounded it.

Every man left to him turned and sprinted towards him. It only took heartbeats for them to join him, and in that time, only a bare handful of enemy shafts flew.

He didn't wait for the laggards. When he had enough carls to make a song, he started forward.

Otter Creek Valley, East of Albinkirk—Peter

Peter was running out of courage.

Ota Qwan was not. He rose to his feet and dashed forward even as one of their warriors bent over the corpse of the red-haired man, knife in hand, and died for it.

"Gots onah!" Ota Qwan roared.

But the warriors didn't follow him.

Peter could scarcely breathe. The lightning nightmare of the close fight with the red-haired man had taken all his breath, all his energy, all his courage. He wanted to lie down and go to sleep.

The wound in his leg ached, and worried how deep it went.

Ota Qwan went bounding forward as the mail-clad men sounded a horn.

Peter forced himself to follow the black-painted man. As he looked back, he saw Skahas Gaho and Brant rise from the grass as well.

They were following *him*, and there were ten more with them. They loped after him, and he ran as hard as he could after Ota Qwan.

To the right, the enemy shocked all of them by charging—not a handful of them, but a solid wedge, which ran right for the centre of their line.

Peter was so far to the right that the end man of the wedge wasn't even close enough to fight—the wedge ran by him in him moment of indecision and then there were cries deeper in the woods.

Ota Qwan continued to run forward. Peter didn't think he'd even seen the enemy charge, but he followed.

Skahas Gaho stooped and scalped the red-haired man.

Otter Creek Valley, East of Albinkirk—Hector

Hector was fresh and unblooded, and the first clump of Outwallers died on his sword point and edge as fast as he could roar his war-cry three times, and then they were down and his wedge was alone in the woodlands.

The essence of warfare is to force the pace and hope your enemy makes a mistake. That was his father's law of war, and his own. So he didn't stop and form a shieldwall.

"Follow me!" he roared, and continued on.

On, and on.

The Outwallers were faster but not fitter than the drovers, and tricks of terrain and bad luck—pulled muscles, wounds—left them at the mercy of the hard-faced armoured men, and their mercy had nothing of mercy in it. A dozen Outwallers died in a hundred paces.

Hector ran on, his sides heaving and his legs burning. Running any distance in mail was an effort.

Running five hundred paces was more than an effort. It was like a test.

Most of his men stayed with him. Those few who paused, died.

The Outwallers fled, but even in panicked flight they ran like a flock of swallows or a school of fish, and those ones unthreatened by the charge recovered first, and arrows started to lick through the trees.

"Keep going!" Hector cried, and his men gave him everything they had.

An Outlander boy tripped over a root and fell, and Ranald beheaded him with a flick of his wrists.

On and on.

And then Hector had to stop. He leaned on the hilt of his great sword, and his sides heaved.

Ranald put a hand on his armoured elbow. "Water," he said.

The length of a barn away they found young Clip, the farmer from the Inn, pinned under his dead horse with his throat slit. A bowshot farther on they came to the ford that they would have crossed. Outwaller arrows had begun to fill the air again, and Hector had perhaps thirty men left when he crossed the ford and won a respite. His men drank water, spread out in the trees, and caught their breaths. Those that had shafts left, or who had pulled them from the ground, began to pick their targets carefully—and it began again.

Ranald scratched his beard. He'd taken an arrow in the chest—it hadn't penetrated his fine mail, but it had cracked a rib, and breathing was hard. "That was worth a song, that run," he said.

Hector nodded. "It's noon and we've led them back a mile, anyway. When they come at us across the stream—well, Donald's away." Hector shrugged. "If I'd kept all the boys together, would we have beaten them?"

Ranald spat some blood. "Nah. They're too canny, and we didn't kill nearly enough of 'em. Hector Lachlan, it's been a pleasure and an honour knowing you, eh?" Ranald held out his hand, and Hector took it. "Don't fash yourself, man—I reckon there's five hundred of the loons out in the woods. This way, if you put a boy in that lass—well, he's got a fortune and fifty good men to start him off."

Hector shook his head. "Sorry I am I brought you here, cousin."

Ranald shrugged, despite fatigue and the weight of his chain mail. "I'm honoured to die with you." He smiled at the sunlit sky. "I'm sorry for a certain lass I love, but this is a good way to die."

Lachlan looked up at the sun. Arrows were flying thickly, and a few were starting to come from their own side of the stream—the savages had found a crossing too.

Despite it all the sky was blue, the sun was warm and golden, and the flowers of the forest were beautiful. He laughed, and held his sword in the air. "Let us make a song!" he roared.

Otter Creek Valley, East of Albinkirk—Peter

Peter followed Ota Qwan until his lungs were starved for air, and then he slowed. The black-painted man slowed, too, as if they were attached by a string. They had reached an open field, and there was a small herd of cattle, every head facing them—a single horse, and dozens of sheep.

And no men.

Ota Qwan leaped for joy, dancing on the grass. "We have beaten them! All their herds are ours!" He embraced Skahas Gaho.

The taller warrior didn't address Ota Qwan, but Peter. "Where?" he asked. He mimed swinging a two-handed axe or sword.

Peter pointed back the way they'd come. He was bone weary, the wound in his leg was now a cold ache, and all the fury of combat had ebbed away to leave nothing behind. But Peter, having started something, couldn't give it up.

Ota Qwan shook his head. "The cattle! We need to get the cattle, or this is for nothing."

Peter looked at the black-painted man wearily. "Have you not seen the numbers of our dead, Ota Qwan? This is already for nothing. Skadai's death means there is no one to tell the Sossag to stop attacking." He shrugged. "And this is only a tithe of their herds."

Ota Qwan looked at him. Understanding dawned slowly.

"We must stop it. We can shoot down anyone who still stands—take our time."

You can be war leader. Somehow Peter knew that this was Ota Qwan's only thought.

But together with their two hands of followers, they turned and began to walk back towards the distant screams that marked the current edge of the battle. No one, not even Ota Qwan, had the energy to sprint, so they ran and walked fitfully.

The sun was just past its height when they scrambled down the last part of the steep glen and crossed the water on rocks slick with blood.

There were still men fighting.

A dozen of the armoured giants stood in a ring, and some two hundred Sossag stood around them in a ring, and between the inner ring and the outer ring was a wall of corpses, some of which still moved. Even as they crossed the stream, a pair of bold youths leaped at the circle of steel and died, one beheaded by an axe, the other spitted on a four-foot sword.

Their bodies were cast on the growing barricade of the dead.

And then the blood-spattered daemons began to sing. They weren't very good, but their voices rose together, and the Sossag paused a moment in respect. A death song was a great thing—a magic not to be interrupted. Even Ota Qwan was silent.

Their song went on, many verses, and when it was done their faces, which had been lit with passion, seemed to slump.

Ota Qwan leaped up on a stump. "Shoot them! Back into the trees and shoot! My curse on any man who tries to rush that circle!"

Some men listened. Arrows began to fly, and when a Sossag arrow hit a mail cote, dust flew, at least, although few shots from their short bows were powerful enough to penetrate.

But there were many arrows.

Peter saw Sossag die from arrows shot from across the circle. The arrows flew faster and faster, striking hillmen and Sossag alike and the hillmen began to sing again, and they charged and the Sossags ran—again.

But not far.

Peter had no arrows. He picked up a spear decorated with feathers, and the next time the enemy charged the circle, he chose his moment and hurled the heavy spear into the back of the charging men. The shaft spun out of control, but the weapon hit the back of the man's armoured legs and he stumbled. Peter ran for him, a dozen Sossag with him, and they tore the hillman to bloody rags.

Again, the hillmen gathered in a circle, and again the Sossag shot them, creeping closer, emboldened by the hillmen's obvious exhaustion and despair. One more time, their leader rallied, whirled his sword and led them at the closest Sossag, bent not on escape but on slaying as many as they could—and again they caught the fringe of the circle, killing a dozen painted men and losing two more of their own. Ota Qwan was roaring for them to fall back and shoot, and Peter joined him.

The Sossag fell back to the trees and shot their last shafts.

Another giant fell screaming.

The Sossag yelled, but it was a tired, thin sound.

Ota Qwan looked around. "When they next charge, we must charge them in turn, and finish them," he said. "We cannot let any of them escape. We must be able to tell the matrons we killed them all."

Peter spat. His mouth was dry, and he had never, in all his life, slave or free, been so tired.

Otter Creek Valley, East of Albinkirk—Hector Lachlan

Alan Big Nose, Ranald Lachlan, Ewen the Sailor, Erik Blackheart and Hector. The last men left.

Hector was hit again with a shaft that tickled his ribs. He was ready to die. He had no wind left, no joy in battle, and he was in enough pain that simple cessation seemed like a victory.

Even as he thought it, Ewen took an arrow in the throat and went down.

He wracked his memory for a song to end with. He was no bard, but he knew some songs. Nothing came to him but drinking songs, but then he smiled—a free smile—to think of his young wife crooning. She'd sung to him, a lullaby.

He knew it well. Hill folk called it "The Lament," the song of their loss. *A fine song with which to end.*

Hector stood straight, took a deep breath, and began to sing. He swung his sword back onto his shoulder and cut an arrow from the air, and Ranald picked up the tune, and Alan Big Nose was there, his voice strong and true on the notes, and Erik Blackheart stepped over Ewen's corpse and roared into the chorus.

At some point the Sossag stopped loosing arrows.

Hector finished the song, raised his sword—a salute to his enemies, who had given him that gift of peace, right at the end.

A warrior, painted black head to toe, raised a sword—just a short bowshot away. And Hector could see that the Outwallers had gathered in tight while his men sang.

Good. It would be a clean end in a straight fight.

Ranald sighed. "Your brother will never forgive himself for missing this," he said, and they charged.

Otter Creek Valley, East of Albinkirk—Peter

When it was over, Peter sat on the ground and wept. He didn't know why he was crying—only that his body needed the release.

Skahas Gaho came and put a hand on his shoulder. Brant was meat for the ravens. Ota Qwan had a wound across his chest that would probably kill him, inflicted when the last giant had stumbled forward, dragging three Sossag warriors, shaken them off, and landed one final cut with his great axe before Ota Qwan and Peter had managed to put him down.

The woods were full of death.

But even after a day of vicious fighting—and Peter couldn't imagine worse fighting—there were still hundreds of Sossag unwounded, or capable of movement, and Ota Qwan had enough breath to send them to round up any cattle they could find and start them for home.

Peter sat by Ota Qwan and held his hand, watching the blood leak out of the man's chest.

Just at sunset, the faeries came.

Peter had never seen one before but he'd known men who believed in them. He was sitting with the dying Ota Qwan. There were a hundred wounded Sossag groaning or worse, and scavengers had begun to move in on the corpses.

Peter was too tired to care.

The first one he saw looked like a butterfly, except that it was ten times the size and glowed faintly, as if sun lit. Behind it were four more, in a formation.

Peter had time to wonder whether they were predators, scavengers, or pests, and then the first one alighted on Ota Qwan's chest.

What is he worth to you, man of iron?

Peter started, wondering if he had been dreaming.

A faerie is to a man as a hummingbird is to a bumblebee. Or so Peter thought, gazing at the jewel-like being.

What is he worth to you? A year of your life?

Peter didn't think. *Yes,* he thought.

The pink shape drifted along Ota Qwan's chest, and then reached out, oh, so gracefully, and touched Peter—and that touch was like every slaver's iron ever forged. Something was ripped from his chest, as if red-hot pincers had entered his heart and dragged it out past his ribs, and he vomited over his lap.

And the faeries laughed. Their laughter seemed to echo in his empty head like the shouts of revellers in a cave—

And Ota Qwan coughed, spat, and sat up.

"No!" he said suddenly, his usually too-calm voice alight with wonder. "No! You didn't!"

But Peter was crying, because now he had something to weep for— whatever it was he'd just lost.

And the faeries laughed.

So sweet, so sweet. So far away! So rare.

A bargain is a bargain.

Perhaps we'll give you another, you were so sweet and rare.

Their laughter sounded more like a curse.

Otter Creek Valley, East of Albinkirk—Ranald Lachlan

Ranald Lachlan rose from the black curse, through pain, and into the soft darkness of an April night. He sat up without a thought in his head, and the arrow that had penetrated his mail fell by his side, and he cut his hand on his own long sword lying in the bloodstained flowers by his side.

And then he knew where he was.

Never say we do not give everything we promise!

So sweet, so sweet!

Peter saved you. Peter saved you!

Fair folk. And Ranald knew that he had been dead, or close enough as made no matter, and someone named Peter had given them the usual trade. A piece of your soul for the life of a friend.

And the Outwallers were all around him in the moonlit dark. Just for a moment, he thought to steal away—but they were looking at him. A hundred of them.

Cursing, he dragged himself to his feet.

Black death was behind him, and in heartbeats would be his again, and he spat.

Ah, Rebecca, I tried. I love you, he thought. He lifted the axe that Master Pyle had made for him—well tested now—and put it on his shoulder.

At the base of the little knoll where he'd made his last stand, he saw the gleam of moonlight, and one of the dark figures got to its feet, lit by four of the fair folk like some kind of ethereal bodyguard.

The man was painted black. Ranald remembered him. He came up the knoll, and Ranald awaited him, hands crossed on the haft of his axe.

"Go," said the black man.

Ranald had to replay the word again. It was a shock to hear Gothic, and another to be told to go.

"We are the Sossag people," the man said. "What the faeries return, we do not touch." The man's eyes were brilliant in the darkness. "I am Ota Qwan of the Sossag. I offer you my hand in peace. I was dead. You were dead. Let us both walk away from here and live."

Ranald was a brave man, veteran of fifty fights, and yet the relief that flooded him was like a mother's kiss and the release of love, and never, ever had he felt he had so much to live for.

He looked down at the corpse of his cousin. "May I bargain with the faeries for him?" he asked.

Their laughter was derisive.

Two! We gave two! And we will dine for days!

So sweet and rare.

Ranald knew what men said of the fair folk. So he bowed. "My thanks, fair people."

Thank Peter!

Hee hee.

And they were gone.

Ranald reached down and took Lachlan's great sword from his cold, dead hand. He unbuckled the scabbard from the great gold belt, and left the belt for spoil.

"For his son," Ranald said to the black man, who shrugged.

"I would meet this Peter," Ranald said.

They walked down the knoll together, and the Sossag all moved back.

One warrior, reeking of vomit, was weeping uncontrollably.

Ranald pulled the man to his feet, and put his arms around him. He didn't know why himself. "Don't know why you saved me," he said. "But thank you."

"He saved me," Ota Qwan said, his voice thick with wonder. "Somehow, the fairies chose to bring you back, too." Ota Qwan leaned forward. "I think you killed me."

Ranald nodded. "I think I did."

Peter sobbed, and was still.

"I hurt," he said. "I'm cold."

Ranald knew the cold to which he referred. He shook the man's hand again, shouldered his dead cousin's sword, and walked away to the east, through a corridor of silent Sossag warriors.

A league from the convent, the captain began to relax and let the feeling of victory suffuse him.

They had almost thirty wagons, full of goods—many of them would be of no use, but he'd seen the armour in one, fine helmets, and weapons in another, and wine, oil, canvas cloth—

But it wasn't rescuing the wagons that lifted his heart. Nor the capture of the wounded knight, a moment that he had yet to allow his mind to savour.

It was the men. Ten professional soldiers, three dozen guildsmen with bows—almost fifty stout men. If he could make it back to the fortress, he'd have hurt his adversary cruelly and *gained* in strength.

Half a league from the fortress, when it was plain that Lissen Carak was not afire, had not fallen to assault of black sorcery, he found himself whistling.

Sauce rode by his side. "A word?" she asked.

"Anything you like," he said.

"Do you have to kill every single one of the monsters?" she asked, and she spat like Bad Tom.

Looking carefully, he could see she was literally spitting mad.

"I had that tusked thing," she said. "I don't need you stealing my kills. If another man had done it, I'd gut him. Even Tom."

The captain rode in silence for a few paces. "I can't help it," he said.

"Fuck you," she said.

"I don't mean that the way it sounds, Sauce," he said. "I can't help it. If they see me, they come straight at me. It has been that way for as long as I've faced the Wild."

Sauce didn't wrinkle her lip—she wrinkled her whole face. "What?" she asked, but her tone betrayed that she had noticed something of the sort.

He shrugged, but he was tired and wearing forty pounds of hauberk and armour, so it wasn't all that evident a movement.

"Why?" she asked.

"I don't know," he said, lying.

She narrowed her eyes.

He didn't offer any further information.

"Who's the knight?" she asked.

The captain realised he was entering a whole field of cowpats with her questions. "Ask him when he wakes," the captain said.

"He was going to kill you," she said. It was somewhere between a statement and a question.

"Haven't you ever been tempted yourself?" Jacques asked from behind them.

Sauce's clear, honest laugh rolled across the river and announced them to the Bridge Castle.

And the captain rode on, whistling.

In his head, he saw a beaten, angry adolescent, who said hot words—hot and true—to a man who was *not* his father, and rode away bent on death. He tried to reach out to that boy, across the years.

Whatever befalls us, he told the broken boy, *today we won a great victory, and men, if any survive, will speak our name for a century.*

Of course, the desperate, angry boy simply kept riding. He would ride his horse to death, and then he would walk, and then he would try to kill himself with a dagger, and he would find that he didn't have the stomach for it, and he would fall asleep, weeping. And wake to try again, and fail, hating himself for what he was, and hating himself again for his cowardice.

The captain knew it. He'd been there. He still had the two sloppy knife scars.

"Happily ever after," he said, with very little bitterness. He touched the white handkerchief at his shoulder and rode to the convent, still whistling.

Lissen Carak—Mag the Seamstress

Mag watched them return from her barrel by the main gate, where she sat with her back against the lead down pipe from the chapel gutters, sewing.

Like many of the farmers and folk in the fortress she had reason to fear the armoured men. But today, they were different. Today, they seemed less like a gang of thugs bent on violence and more like something from a song.

The young knight who led them was first through the gate, and he paused to call something back to the column—in fact, he shouted to them "Finish like you started!" And she saw them all sat up in their saddles, even the ones with blood showing.

The only difference she could see was that most of them were smiling. But there was something else—a pride to them—that she hadn't felt before.

The captain swung down from his charger and gave the reins to Toby, and the boy beamed at him, and the captain grinned and said something that made the servant boy grin even harder.

Defeated men wouldn't look like that, the seamstress was sure.

Ser Thomas rode in with the female knight by his side, and the two barely fitted through the gate, but neither would give way to the other.

The courtyard was filling with nuns and farmers and their folk, taking horses, talking—in moments, it was clear that a great victory had been won, and an air of festival filled the fortress.

Mag finished her line of stitches quickly, gathering the heady aura of victory against long odds with every stitch and pulling it into the cap.

The old Abbess came to the steps from the hall, and the young captain, resplendent in his bright red surcote and gilt-edged armour, climbed up, knelt on one knee in salute, and spoke to her.

She nodded, gave him her hand, and then raised her hands for silence.

"Good people!" she called. "The captain informs me that our little army has won a great victory through the grace of God. But we are to expect an immediate attack, and every one of you is to get under cover now."

The men-at-arms were already pushing people back into the nunnery, dormitory and the great hall. Mag saw the young knight turn, and catch the eye of the novice.

Oh aye, she thought. She smiled, mostly because they both smiled.

When the archers on the walls began to look at her pointedly, she gathered her basket and slipped into the dormitory herself.

But she'd just seen the priest do the oddest thing: he'd taken a dove from a cage and thrown it over the wall.

She might have said something, or reacted—but even as she watched, the Red Knight appeared and the priest departed. They didn't see each other. The Red Knight spoke to someone who was with him up on the wall—a leg appeared over the dormitory balcony, and suddenly the armoured man held someone in his arms. Someone in the plain garb of a novice.

The intensity that bound them was blinding. Mag could see it, feel it, the way she could feel the well of power under the dungeons and the Abbess working her spells. It was a magnificent thing.

It was also private and she turned her head away. Some things, people are not meant to see.

Albinkirk Citadel—Ser John Crayford

The Captain of Albinkirk sat at his glazed window, and watched the distant woods.

My Lord,

I must assume that my last messenger has reached you. The citadel of Albinkirk continues to hold. Indeed, it is some days since we have been assaulted, although we are still close-pressed and we can see creatures of the Wild moving about in the town and in the fields.

Yesterday I felt it was my duty to take a sortie beyond the citadel walls. We scattered the creatures in the main square and rode beyond the city walls, too. As soon as my small force appeared in the fields north of the river, we were joined by dozens of local families who had held one of the outworks and sought admission to the citadel. I had no choice but to let them in—they had no food. Among them were two guildsmen from Harndon, members of the Crossbowmen of the Order of Drapers. They say that a great battle was fought yesterday, south of the Fords, and that the

Red Knight prevailed, albeit with a small force, crushing a great ambush of the Wild, for which praise to God. But another pair of refugees from the east informed me that Sossag raiders have burned every town east of the Fords all the way to Otter Creek, and that the hills are crammed with refugees.

All of this may be rumour. If I can spare the men, I will send a scout west to cooperate with the Abbess and the Red Knight.

My lord, we face here the very worst of the enemy. I beg you for immediate aid.

Your servant,
John Crayford, Captain of Albinkirk

Chapter Eleven

East of Albinkirk—Thorn

Thorn sat cross-legged beneath the tree that bore his name and watched the world.

He couldn't pretend that he liked what he saw.

He had suffered a crushing defeat the day before—the little army that the sisterhood had hired, led by the dark sun that could extinguish itself—had combined with the last convoy coming upriver to crush his best mobile force.

Even now, he couldn't reach any of his chieftains among the irks. Boglins were coming back across the river. But the losses had been staggering.

And he could feel the waves of sheer power that still rolled across the sea of trees from the fight. Someone almost as great as him had loosed powers that were better left unloosed. That power sang through the Wild like a clarion call. And Thorn knew the taste of that power.

I should have been there, he thought. His stone mouth creased in a near smile. *My great apprentice, free from his tower and loose on the world at last.* He flexed the reins of his spell of ensorcellment, but the reins hung slack, severed at the far end, and he reeled them in. *I wonder how the boy worked it out?* He thought. But he didn't waste much thought on it. His apprentice had tricked him once and would never, ever best him again.

But his rebellious apprenctice wasn't the only problem. Someone had killed three of the dhags which men called trolls, the great cave giants armoured in stone of the high mountains. He had only bound a dozen to serve him, and now three were slain.

And perhaps the worst blow of all was the Sossag's defection. Their chiefs had deserted him, and gone east to fight their own battle. Had they been present with his force, none of this would ever have happened.

Thorn wheeled his starlings and doves in the sky, and looked down from their eyes, and knew that he had been misled by the powers in the old fortress. The assault of the birds of prey had pushed his little helpers away. And he had been blind. *For one scant hour.*

But in his hand was a precious jewel. His friend had, at last, sent him word. Detailed word.

Despite the defeat, he now had the true measure of his enemy, and his enemy was not as strong as Thorn had feared. He didn't like the taste of their power, but he didn't need to fear their soldiers. They were too few.

Thorn had not risen to power by ignoring the causes of defeat. He didn't accept false pride. He acknowledged that he had been fooled, and beaten, and immediately altered his plans.

First, the Sossag had won a victory that would serve his ends—and they were badly hurt and their leaders looked fools. This was the time to force them back to their allegiance to him. He needed them, and their ruthless human cleverness—so very different, and so much more cunning than the irks and bogglins.

He needed to consult with his allies among the Qwethnethog daemons, and he needed to convince them, with a show of force, that he was still the master of these woods. Lest they slip away too.

He savoured the irony. He was attacking the Rock for them, and yet they threatened to defect.

He sighed, because all these petty inter-plays of emotion and interest resembled the very politics that had driven him away from other men, when he was a man. The Wild had been his escape and now proved the same.

It was foolish that he needed a victory to convince the unwilling when he could take the lives of most of his allies merely by reaching into the essence of their Wildness and *pulling*—

He remembered one of his students admonishing him that you could not convince men by killing them, and he smiled at the memory. The boy had been both right and wrong. Thorn had never been very interested in convincing anyone.

But reminiscence would solve nothing. He withdrew his attention from the doves and the lynx and the fox, the hares were all dead, taken by dogs, and he moved his thinly distributed consciousness back to the body he had made for it.

A dozen irks stood guard over him, and he acknowledged them. "Summon my captains," he said in the harsh croak he now had as a voice, and they flinched and obeyed.

The army that now trailed north on the last stretch to Albinkirk, was many times larger than the elite force that had left Harndon a week before. And much, much slower.

Gaston sat his horse in the midst of a road blockage bigger than some towns in his home province and shook his head. He was watching four men who sat hunched under a bridge, eating a side of bacon.

"It's like the rout of a beaten army," he said in low Archaic. "Except that it is still headed towards the enemy."

The king was virtually unapproachable, now, as the entire knight-service of the country had reported in, and all of his great lords surrounded him. No longer could Jean de Vrailly pretend to threaten the king with his three hundred knights—his convoy was no longer the largest. The Count of the Borders, Gareth Montroy, came in with five hundred knights, hard men in lighter armour than the Galles but just as tall, and five hundred archers as well. The Lord of Bain's banner led another two hundred knights, with the popinjay Edward Despansay, Lord Bain, at their head. They were the great lords, with uniformed retinues of professional warriors who trained together, but there also were hundreds of individual knights from the counties under the King's Lieutenant's banner, and almost a hundred of the king's own Royal Knights, his elite bodyguard that also canvassed the countryside as justices and monster hunters under the king's trusted bastard brother, Ser Richard Fitzroy. There were another hundred knights of the military orders, priests and brothers and lay brothers of Saint George and Saint Maurice and Saint Thomas whose discipline was as good or better than any company Gaston had ever seen, riding silently in their black-robed armour under the Prior of Pynwrithe and his marshal.

All together the king had more than two thousand knights and as many again men-at-arms, plus three thousand infantry who varied in quality from the superb—the green clad Royal Huntsmen rode ahead of the column and covered its flanks, dashing silently through the increasingly dense brush on specially trained horses, although they fought on foot as archers—to the ridiculous: county levies with spears and no armour who served for twenty days or until their side of bacon was eaten.

The men at his feet were eating as quickly as they could.

His beautiful cousin was riding at the head of his convoy. He wore his full harness—all the Galles did—and rode a war horse. But the last few days, the Alban knights had begun to do the same—not all at once, but in fits and starts. And in the evenings, they had begun to practise with their lances and with their swords, with their horses formed in great long lines.

And de Vrailly went from group to group, praising some and challenging others. He praised the diligent and ignored the lazy, and men began to speak of him.

Knightly men. Not this sort.

Gaston watched the men under the bridge, and they watched him, chewing and swallowing as quickly as they could manage, forcing the cooked bacon down their gullets.

He gave his horse some rein and she picked her way down the grassy bank to the stream. The men under the bridge began to pick up their belongings, but he raised a hand to forestall them.

"We haven't done nothing," a sandy-haired yokel with a short beard said, raising two greasy hands.

Gaston shook his head. "Answer me the one thing," he said carefully. Speaking Alban always left him feeling muddled.

The sandy-haired one shrugged. Gaston noted that he hadn't said one word of polite greeting—neither saluted, nor bowed.

Albans. A nation of fools and outlaws.

"Why are you so anxious to eat your cooked ham and scurry home?" he asked. He walked his mare forward another few steps so that they could hear him better. He looked down at them.

All four of them looked at him as if he, not they, was the fool.

"Cause my wife needs me home?" said one.

"Cause it's going to be haying in another ten days, if the sun keeps on," said the second man. He had a fine linen shirt and a silver ring on his finger. By Galle standards, Alban farmers were rich, fat and very ill-mannered.

"Cause my duty says I can go home when this here bacon is et," said the third, a long-haired old man. His hair was mostly white and Gaston could see the outline of a crusading badge on his tunic, carefully removed.

"You have fought before, eh?" he asked.

The older man nodded, his face still. "Right enough, boyo," he said. Here under the bridge, their voices echoed.

"Where?" Gaston asked.

"In the East," the old man said, and took another bite of bacon. "And before that, under Ser Gilles de Laines, against the Paynim. With Lord Bain, too. And under the old king, at Chevin. Ever heard of it?"

Gaston smiled. "You are pleased to make game of me," he said pleasantly.

"Nah," said the old archer. "You foreigners don't really know much about war, and you haven't ever seen a big fight like Chevin. If you had, you wouldn't be asking us these tom-fool questions. We're eating our bacon so we can get home and not fight. Because it's going to be horrible, and I, for one, know just fucking how it's going to be. And my son-in-law and his two friends here will all come with me."

Gaston was shocked by the man's tone, and by the murderous gleam in

362

his eye. "But you—you have been a *homme armé*. You know what honour is—what glory is."

The man looked at him, finished his chunk of bacon, and spat. "Done. Time to go home." He wiped his greasy hands carefully on his leather quiver and the bow case on his six-foot bow.

"If we lose," Gaston said, looking for a way to reason with this arrogant peasant, "if we lose, your farms will be lost."

"Nah," said the younger man with the beard. "If you'n lose, they'll squash the north flat. We ain't northerners." He shrugged.

The old archer shrugged.

The other two grinned.

The old archer came over to the knight's stirrup. "Listen, ser knight. We stood our ground at Chevin, and a lot of folk died. The old king told us we was done, for our lifetimes. Well, I'm holding him to that promise. Right? Here's some advice from an old soldier. When the boglins scream and charge you, say a good prayer. Cause they won't stop coming, and there's a lot worse behind them. They eat you while you're still alive. There's creatures that're worse, and eat your *soul* while you're still alive. So it don't even matter if you heard Mass, does it?"

Gaston had considered killing all four of them for their insolence, but the old archer had touched on something, and instead, he found himself nodding.

"I will prevail. We will prevail," Gaston said. "You will be sorry you were not there, for our day of glory."

The old archer shook his head. "Nope. That's just what gowps like you never see. I won't be sorry, but I do wish you luck." He chuckled. "We had twenty thousand men when we went into battle at Chevin." He nodded again. "The king has what—four thousand?" He laughed, and it was a nasty laugh. "Can I offer you a bite of bacon?"

Talking to the peasants had caused Gaston to fall behind, and when he rode up the far bank, chewing on bacon, he found himself in the midst of the Borderers. He rode forward until he was among the liveried knights, the professionals, who rode around the Count of the Borders.

A herald spotted him and he was quickly passed from the herald to the captain of the bodyguard, and then on to the knot of men around the count himself. He was riding armed, in a good white harness made in the East, with mail and leather under it. A squire carried his helmet, and he had a green velvet cap on his head with an Eastern ostrich plume sprouting rakishly from a diamond brooch.

"Gareth Montroy," said the great lord, extending his hand even as he reined in his horse. "You're the Count of Eu?"

"I have that honour," Gaston said, bowing and clasping the man's hand. He was thirty-five, with dark hair and heavy eyebrows and the absolute air of command that came with great lordship. This was a man who commanded men every day.

"Your cousin has the big convoy—all Galles?" Lord Gareth grinned. "They look like bonny fighters. Big boys every one of 'em, like my lot." He jerked a thumb over his shoulder.

"Your men look like fighters," Gaston said.

"Pour us a cup of wine to cut the dust, eh, Gwillam?" Lord Gareth said over his shoulder. "My lads have seen a spot of fighting."

Every man in the count's escort had a facial scar.

Gaston felt more at home here than he had in days. "Where have you been fighting?" he asked.

Lord Gareth shrugged. "I hold the Westland borders, though there's some awkward bastards at court and elsewhere who don't give me my due," he said. A silver cup, beautifully made, with sloped sides and a carefully worked rim, was put in his hand, and another was passed to Gaston, who was delighted to find that it was lined in gold and full of chilled wine.

Chilled wine.

"Company magus," Lord Gareth said. "No reason he can't keep some wine chilled until we fight." He grinned. "And sometimes, we fight the Moreans. Bandits, the occasional boglin—we know what boglins look like, don't we, boys?"

They laughed.

"And you, my lord?" Lord Gareth turned to Gaston. "You've seen service before, I take it."

"Local wars," Gaston said dismissively.

"How big is a local war, in Galle?" Lord Gareth asked.

Gaston shrugged. "When my father marches on an enemy he takes a thousand knights," he said.

"Mary, Queen of Heaven!" Lord Gareth swore. "Christ on the Cross, my lord. Only the king has a thousand knights, and that only when he sends out Letters of Array." He raised an eyebrow. "I'd heard of such doing, but never from a witness."

"Ah," Gaston said.

"And what do you fight?" Lord Gareth asked. "Boglins? Irks? Daemons? Trolls?" he looked around. "How many creatures can the Enemy muster, that your father takes a thousand knights?"

Gaston shrugged. "I have never seen a boglin," he said. "In the East we fight men."

Lord Gareth winced. "Men?" he said. "That's a nasty business. I admit, I've faced the Moreans on a few fields—but mostly brigands. There's little joy in facing men, when the Enemy is to hand." He leaned close. "Who fights the Enemy in the East, then?"

Gaston shrugged. "In the north, the military orders. But no one has seen a creature of the Wild for—" He searched for the words. "Please do not take this ill—but if you Albans were not so very sure of the Wild, we'd doubt you. None of us has ever seen a creature of the Wild. We thought they were exaggerations."

To a man, the knights around Lord Gareth threw back their heads and laughed.

A tall, swarthy man in a harness of scale armour pushed his horse through the press to Gaston's side. "Ser Alcaeus Comnena of Mythymna, my lord."

"A Morean," Lord Gareth said. "But a friend."

"Perhaps your convoy needs to be taught about the creatures, yes?" he volunteered.

Gaston shook his head. "No, no. We'll do well enough. We train very hard."

All the knights around him looked at him as if he'd just sprouted wings, and Gaston had a moment's concern.

Alcaeus shook his head. "When the boglins get in among the horses, they will give their lives to gut your charger," he said. "A single troll loose in a column can kill ten belted knights as fast as I can tell you this. Yes? And wyverns—in the air—are incredibly dangerous in open ground. Only men with heavy crossbows threaten them, and the very bravest of knights. On foot, horses will not abide a wyvern. And no amount of tiltyard training will prepare you for their wave of fear."

Gaston shrugged, but now he was annoyed. "My knights will not succumb to fear," he said. The Morean looked at him as if he was a fool, which made him angry. "I resent your tone," he said.

Ser Alcaeus shrugged. "It is of no moment to me, Easterner. Resent me all you like. Do you want your knights to die like cattle, paralysed by fear, or would you like to strike a blow against the enemy?"

The Count of the Borders pushed his horse between the two men. His displeasure was evident. "I think that the good Lord of Eu is saying that we have nothing to teach him about war," he said. "But I do not tolerate private quarrels between my knights, Lord Gaston, so please do not taunt Ser Alcaeus."

Gaston was flabbergasted. He looked at the man. "What is it to your knight whether you tolerate his quarrel?" he asked. "Surely if a knight's honour is at stake, the least his lord can do is to stand behind him."

Lord Gareth's face became carefully neutral. "Are you challenging Ser Alcaeus on his honour, because he tried to tell you that your convoy needs training?"

His tone, and the point he made, caused Gaston to squirm in the saddle. "He suggested that my men would be *afraid.*"

Alcaeus nodded as though this were a forgone conclusion. All the other men-at-arms around them were silent, and for a long moment the only sound was the jingle of horse harness and the rattle of armour and weapon as the retinue knights walked their horses down the road.

"You do know that every creature of the Wild projects a wave of fear, and the greater the beast the stronger it is." Lord Gareth raised both eyebrows. It made the diamond on his cap twinkle.

Gaston shrugged. "I have heard this," he admitted. "I thought it might be... an excuse..." He stammered to silence in the face of the massed disapproval of a dozen scarred knights.

Ser Alcaeus shook his head. "You need us," he said quietly.

Gaston was trying to imagine how he might convince his cousin while he rode up the column.

North of Lissen Carak

They came, each with his own tail of followers, because that was the way of the Wild.

The man known as Jack, the leader of the Jacks, came from the west. His face was masked in ruddy leather, and he wore the same dirty off-white wool jupon and hose of his band. He wore no badge of rank, and carried no obvious symbol of it—no fancy sword, no magnificent bow. He was neither short nor tall, and a greying beard came out from under his mask to proclaim his age. With him were a dozen men with long yew bows, sheaves of arrows, long swords and bucklers.

Thurkan came from the south, where he had run the woods with his qwethnethog daemon kin, watching the Royal Army coming up the Albin River. A fifty-mile run through the woods had not winded him. The wave of fear that he projected made the hardened Jacks fold their arms; even Thorn felt his power. With him were just two of his mighty people—his brother Korghan, and his sister Mogan. Each was the size of war horse with jaggedly pointed beaks, inlaid brow ridges, beautiful eyes and long, heavy, muscular legs, long arms tipped with bone scythes, and elegant, scaled tails. With them came the greatest of the living abnethog wyverns in the north woods; Sylch. His people had borne the greatest losses, and his anger was betrayed in bright red spots that moved like flickering fire on the surface of his smooth grey skin.

From the east came a party of painted men; Akra Crom of the Abenacki led them. They had harried the suburbs of Albinkirk, taken a hundred prisoners, and were now ready to go home. Such was the way of the Outwallers—to raid and to slip away. Akra Crom was as old as a man could be and still lead Outwaller warriors—his skin betrayed his age. He was hairless, painted a metallic grey that gleamed like silver in the light. He was the rarest of Outwallers—a possessor of power. A shaman, warrior, and a great song-maker among his people, the old man was a living legend.

Exrech was the chief paramount of the gwyllch that men called bog-glins. His thorax gleamed white, and his arms and legs were a perfectly contrasting ebony black, as was his head. He was as tall as a man and power flickered around his mandibles, far more pronounced than a lower-caste gwyllch; his natural armour was better, and his chain mail, carefully crafted in the far East and taken in war, had been riveted carefully to his carapace to join the living armour. He carried a pair of man-made great swords in his two large hands and wore a horn at his waist.

Thorn was pleased they had come, and he offered wine and honey.

"We have taken heavy losses, and suffered costly victories and humiliating defeats," Thorn began. He left it there—the fact of defeat.

"The Sossag have won a great victory in the east," said the painted man. The other warriors with him grunted their approval.

"They have, at great cost," Thorn nodded. Overhead, the stars were rising—a spectacular display of light in the blue-black sky of late evening. But their meeting was not illuminated by fire. Few creatures of the Wild loved fire.

Thorn pointed at the heavens. "The Sossag and the Abenacki are not as numerous as the stars," he said. "And many Sossag fell at the Crossings of the Otter."

Exrech's jaws opened and closed with a firm click indicating *waste of valuable warrior stock; not easily replaced; no clearly defined target. Strong disapproval.*

Akra Crom shrugged. *When you rule the Outwallers, you may choose their wars.*

The black and white gwyllch lord gave an acrid spray of anger. *In deep woods, all soft-skins alike to we.*

Thorn grunted and both lords settled down.

Thurkan spoke, his daemon voice high and badly pitched—a shock from such a large and beautiful creature. "I blame you, Thorn."

Thorn had not expected a direct challenge and began to gather power.

Thurkan reached out a long forearm and pointed. "We each act under your order—but we do not mesh. We are not *together*. No gwyllch stand with the Sossag. No gwyllch climb with the Abnethog when we fly against the Rock. Abnethog and qwethnethog and gwyllch fight the same foe in the same woods, but no creature goes to the support of the other. The hastenoch died with gwyllch a few hands away."

Thorn considered this—full of power, ready for the challenge that criticism usually led to, he was not at his most rational.

"You have armed yourself against me," whined the great daemon. At least, his every utterance sounded like a whine. "Yet I challenge you not, Once Was Man."

Thorn let some of the power he had gathered dissipate.

Faeries had been attracted, as they always were by raw power, their slim and elegant shapes flitting suddenly through the air where his release of power glowed a virulent green.

Mogan plucked one from the air and ate it, and the faeries' death-curse filled the night as the little thing vanished down her gullet.

Exrech nodded. *Strong one. Well taken.*

Jack of Jacks shuddered. To most men, the killing of a faery was sacrilege. He spat. "Thorn, we are here for one reason only. You promised us you'd defeat the aristocrats. For that, we have gathered every bow from every farm. Our people suffer under our lords' hammers this summer so that we can defeat them. And yet, the king's army comes closer and closer." Jack scowled. "When will we fight?"

"You are a deadly secret, Jack of Jacks." Thorn nodded. "Your long shafts will be the death of many a belted knight, and your men—you said yourself they must stay hidden. They will emerge from decades in the shadows at the right moment, when we play for everything. I will face the king and his army on ground of my choosing. You will be there."

He turned to the qwethnethogs. "I am guilty of sending each of you to fight your own foes in your own way. This still seems wise to me. Between gwyllch and Outwaller there is no friendship. The Jacks have no love for any creature of the Wild. Every beast in the woods fears the qwethnethog and the abnethog." He ate a dollop of honeycomb. "We should have triumphed by now, and I feel the strong hand of fate on the rim of our shield. I command that you all take more care." He'd lowered his voice and imbued it with power from the air around him and the store he held for emergencies, and even so the daemons challenged him.

"Obey me, now. We will not fight the king at Albinkirk. We let our early victory spread us too far, dissipate our strength. Let Thurkan watch the king and eat his horses. No more. Let Exrech withdraw from Albinkirk. Offer no battle. Let the Sossag and the Abenacki fall back to their camps here. Let the Jacks sharpen their bodkins. Our day approaches, and the king will never reach Lissen Carak."

Thurkan nodded. "This is more to my liking," he hissed. "One mighty fight, and a rending of flesh."

Thorn forced a piece of a smile—it seemed to crack the flesh around his mouth—and all but the daemons quailed. "We will scarcely need to fight," he said. "But when they have fought among themselves, you may rend their flesh to your heart's content."

Thurkan nodded. "Such is always your way, Thorn. But when it comes to teeth and spears I do not like having the Cohocton at my back."

Thorn hated being questioned, and his anger rose. "You fear defeat before a single spear is cast?"

The great daemon stood his ground. "Yes," he said. "I have seen many defeats, and many empty victories; my hide bears the scars, and my nest is empty where it should be full. Both of my cousins have died in the last moon—one on the spear of the dark sun, and one with his soul ripped from him by their cruel sorceries." He looked around. "Who will come to my aid? You expect treason—and I agree that humans are born to betray each other. But many will fight, and fight bitterly. This is their way! So I say—who will come to my aid?"

"Have you finished whining?" Thorn bellowed.

Jack squared his shoulders. "If it is your unshared plan that the mighty daemons face the king then my comrades and I will be honoured to share the danger with our scaled allies."

. Thorn wanted to scream in frustration. *My plan is my plan is my plan. I will not share it with the likes of you.* But he narrowed his eyes, banished the bile from his great heart, and nodded.

"Then gather more boats, and prepare to cross the river. This time, protect them. For unless the king is a great fool, he will advance on the south side of the river, as my brother Thurkan fears. Yes? And if you are hard pressed, I will send gwyllch, at least the lighter kind, who can pass the river."

Exrech spat a clear fluid. *Waste of resources; conflict of interest.*

Thorn took a deep breath, and pushed power into his word.

"Obey," he said.

By the time the fireflies came out, the clearing in the woods was empty.

Lorica—Desiderata

Desiderata sat on her throne in the Great Hall of the castle of Lorica, still dressed for travelling. She had a dozen minor issues on which to pronounce justice, and all she wanted was dinner and bed. Taking a train from Harndon to Lorica in a day was harder work than she'd expected.

She worked her way through the cases—the murder of a draper by a woman, the theft of a herd that trailed off into accusations and counter-accusations by the monks of two rival abbeys—and then there was a messenger.

He wore the royal scarlet and midnight blue livery, and even covered in road dust it commanded instant attention.

He was young and not particularly handsome, and yet had an air about him. He knelt at her feet and presented a bag.

"The king sends to you, my lady," he said formally.

She didn't know him, but word of war had made the king increase every part of the household—an action that would affect the royal budget for ten years to come.

"Royer Le Hardi, my lady," the messenger said.

"The news?" she asked.

"All is well with the army," Royer replied.

The Queen took the pouch and opened it, cutting her husband's seal carefully and opening the lead wafers that secured the buckles with the small knife she always wore in her girdle.

There were four scroll tubes holding about a dozen folded and sealed letters—she saw letters to the Emperor of Morea and the King of Galle—and a thick packet with her name on it in his handwriting, which she snatched up.

She read a few lines and frowned. "My lords, ladies, and good men and women," she said formally, rising to her feet. "I will hold court in the morning, and all cases are held over until then. The seneschal and sheriff shall attend me, as will my own lords." She smiled, and many in the multitude at her feet smiled back, so personable was her smile.

The hall's chamberlain smacked the floor with his staff. "The Queen has dismissed the assembly," he said, in case there were those who didn't understand.

Before the last draper had cleared the portico the Royal Steward and the King's Treasurer—were at her side. "News?" asked Bishop Godwin. Lord Lessing—a banker promoted to the aristocracy by the old king—rubbed his beard.

She tapped the cover note against her teeth. "We will continue north to join the army," she said. "If we have a tournament at all, at this rate it will be in the face of the enemy, at Albinkirk or even Lissen Carak." Her thoughts were clearly elsewhere.

Her king's note sounded desperate, and he had ordered her not to come.

"Strip this town of carts," she said. "I will leave everything that I don't need—I'll take four maids. No state gowns, no frippery, no clothes. You, my lords, should stay here. You will form the government." She paused. "No. Go back down the river to Harndon."

The bishop breathed a sigh of relief.

"I might be gone a month," she said. "Or more. I may stay with the king until the emergency is past. Lord Lessing, I would take it as a kindness if you would organise the supply convoys as I have been doing."

Lessing pulled at his beard. He had gold wire in it, which somehow served only to make it look greyer. "I will do your will, Lady," he said gravely. "But some of those wagons need to start coming back. We have stripped the southern kingdom bare and I doubt that there is even a wheeled cart to be had in Harndon. If they are lost, the harvest will rot in the fields."

"Best they not be lost, then," she said lightly. "I'll see to it that the wagons I've sent north are turned around—either empty, or full of the northern harvest."

"Boats," Lessing said suddenly. "If he's aiming for Lissen Carak, you should go by boat. The docks here are full of empty hulls—Master Random of Harndon's boats. He's arrayed a mighty fleet of river boats to buy the grain harvest in the north. It's supposed to be a secret, I admit. But I had it from his wife, and you can go faster by oars and sail up the river. And it's safe as houses—never yet heard of a boglin as could swim. Eh?"

She loved her lords because they weren't going to try to stop her, and because both of them began immediately to plan for the practical details of her trip to join the army.

After they'd made a dozen lists and summoned half the prominent men of Lorica to witness deeds and to become commissioners of this and that, she collapsed at last into the best bed in the royal keep of Lorica.

Mary stripped off her silken cote hardie, her kirtle, her shift, and the man's hose she'd worn underneath so she could ride astride. "You will take me with you?" Mary asked.

"You and Emmota, Helena and Apollonasia," the Queen said languorously. "And Becca."

"Bath?" Mary asked.

"Perhaps the last for many days," the Queen said. "Oh, par dieu, Mary, we are about to break free of it all and have an *adventure*."

Lady Mary smiled at her mistress. But her eyes had no smile in them, as if she was looking far beyond their room.

"Do you still think of him?" the Queen asked her First Maid.

"Only when I'm awake," Hard Heart admitted. "And sometimes when I'm asleep."

"He is not with the army." Desiderata had received two missives from her husband that included the name of Gawin Murien, but in both his whereabouts was unknown.

"I will be closer to him," Mary said. She sighed. "I didn't know that I loved him until the king sent him away."

Desiderata held her Mary for a few tears, and thought of her husband's letters.

He was worried. That came through, either despite his foolish banter or because of it.

He needed her there. To remind him who he was.

She fell asleep thinking of Mary and Gawin, and awoke to find that she was the admiral of a fleet of forty river boats, twenty oared boats with sturdy masts and slab sides, capable of a turn of speed and a heavy cargo. By the time the sun was above the river banks, her flotilla was pulling north, and the townsmen were glad to see the backs of the rowers, who had made more trouble than a dozen companies of soldiers. Despite her plans she'd ended up with all of her ladies, a set of pavilions, and a cargo of armour and dried meat for the army. And a company of Lorican guildsmen in horrible purple and gold livery; crossbowmen who had, to the man, never been out of the town before. They were the only soldiers that the bishop could find.

"Give way, all!" called the timoneer.

She lay back under the bright sun, dressed in white, and let the sun turn her hair to gold.

Chapter Twelve

Lissen Carak—The Red Knight

The Siege of Lissen Carak—Day Six

The woods around us are silent. Do monsters mourn?

Day before yesterday, the captain won a great victory over the Enemy. He took most of the company across the Cohoctorn to the south, where Master Gelfred had located a convoy coming to us. It was hard hit, but the captain's sortie took the enemy in the rear, and destroyed them. The captain thinks we killed upwards of five hundred of the enemy, including four great monsters, to whit, three great Stone Trolls and a Behemoth.

The men say the captain killed the Behemoth himself, and that it was the greatest feat of arms they had ever seen.

Yesterday, the company stood to all day, waiting for attacks that never came. Men slept at their posts, fully armed.

Many of the farmers and as many nuns say this will be the end of the siege—that the enemy will slink away. The Abbess has called a great council of all the officers.

The Abbess had a table brought in, and the captain thought it might be the longest he'd ever seen—it filled the Great Hall from hearth to dais, space for thirty men to sit at table together.

But there were not thirty men at the table.

There were just six. And the Abbess.

The six were the captain himself, sitting in one chair with his feet on another, and Ser Jehannes, sitting upright in a third; Master Gerald Random, who by virtue of saving almost half his convoy had suddenly become the representative of all the merchants, taking another pair of chairs, and Ser Milus, as the commander of the Bridge Castle, sat with his head propped on his hands. Master Gelfred sat separately from the other men, a self-imposed social distance. And the priest, Father Henry, sat with a stylus and wax tablets, prepared to copy their decisions.

The Abbess sat to the captain's right, flanked by two sisters, who stood. The captain understood that the two silent figures were her Chancellor and Mistress of Novices, the two most powerful offices in the convent. Sister Miram and Sister Ann.

When all the men had settled the Abbess cleared her throat. "Captain?" she asked.

He took his booted feet off a chair and sat up. "Right," he said. "We are now, at long last, under siege. Our Enemy has finally realised how few we are, and has sealed the roads." He shrugged. "Frankly, this is a harsher defeat than any we have suffered in the field. He should have thought, after yesterday's incredible stroke of luck—"

"The work of God!" Master Random said.

"The Enemy should have assumed," the captain went on, "we had a big garrison and a lot of potent phantasm to pull off such a coup. Instead, he's used the night to push in all my outposts. I lost three good men last night, gentlemen and ladies." He looked around. The cunningly hidden heavy arbalest in the dead ground hadn't been cunning enough, and now Guillaume Longsword, one of his officers, as well as his page and archer were dead, and Young Will, as his squire was known, was weeping his guts out in the infirmary. "More men than we lost in yesterday's fight," he went on.

The other mercenaries nodded.

"On a more positive note, Master Random brought us a dozen men-at-arms and sixty archers." *Of very variable quality, and every one of them ran yesterday, at one point or another. Every one but one,* he remembered sourly. Ser Gawin had not yet condescended to open an eye.

"My guildsmen are not mere archers," Master Random said.

The captain sat back, assessing the man. "I know they are not," he said. "But for the duration of the siege, Master, we must treat them as soldiers."

Random nodded. "I, too, can swing a sword."

The captain had noticed that he was wearing one, and reports had it that the merchant had acquitted himself well.

"So," he went on, "we have forty men-at-arms well enough to wear harness, and our squires; call it sixty knights. We have almost triple that in archers, thanks to the better farmers and the guildsmen." He looked around.

"Our Enemy has at least five thousand, boglins, irks, allies and men taken together."

"Good Christ!" Ser Milus sat up.

Ser Jehannes looked as if he'd eaten something foul.

Master Gelfred nodded when the captain looked at him. "Can't be less, given what I saw this morning," he said. "The Enemy can cover every road and every path at the same time, and they rotate their forces every few hours." He shrugged. "You can watch the boglins digging trenches out beyond the range of our trebuchets. It's like watching termites. There are—" he shrugged, "a great many termites."

The captain looked around. "In addition, we have another hundred merchants and merchants' folk, and four hundred women and children." He smiled. "In the East, I'd be sending them out right now, to fill the besieger's lines with useless mouths." He looked around. "Here, they'd literally fill the enemy's bellies, instead." No one appreciated his humour.

"You can't be serious!" said the Abbess.

"I am not. I won't drive them out to die. But the merchants and their people must be put to work, and I'd like to assign a dozen archers and two men-at-arms to training them. If we cannot be rid of these useless mouths, we must make them useful. We have about forty days' food for a thousand mouths. Double that at half rations."

"And we have all that grain!" the Abbess said.

"Grain for two hundred and eighty days," he said.

"The king will be here long before then," the Abbess said firmly.

"Good day to you," said a voice from the door, and Harmodius, the Magus, came in. He smiled around, a little unsure of his welcome. "I received your invitation, but I was in the midst of a dissection. You, my lords, have a plentiful supply of candidates for dissection." He smiled. "I have learned some exciting things."

They all stared at him as if he was a leper newly arrived at a feast. He pulled out a chair and sat.

"There were rats in the grain, by the way," Harmodius said. "I've disposed of them. Do you know," he asked, his eyes on the Abbess, "who the captain of the Enemy is?"

She flinched.

"You do, I see. Hmm." The old Magus didn't look nearly so old, today. He looked closer to forty than seventy. "I remember you, of course, my lady."

The Abbess trembled—just for a moment—and then forced herself to look at the Magus. The captain saw the effort it took.

"And I you," the Abbess said.

"Well, three cheers for the air of dangerous mystery," the captain said. "I for one am delighted you both know each other."

The Magus looked at him. "This from you?" He leaned forward. "I know who you are too, lad."

Every head in the room snapped to look—first at the captain, and then at the Magus.

"Do you really?" asked the Abbess, and she clutched at the rosary around her neck. "Really?"

Harmodius was enjoying his moment of drama, the captain could see it. He wished he knew who the old charlatan was. As it was, he fingered his rondel dagger.

"If you reveal me, I swear before the altar of your God I will cut you down right here," the captain hissed.

Harmodius laughed, and rocked his chair back. "You, and all the rest of you together couldn't muss my hair," he said. He raised his hand.

The mercenaries were all on their feet, weapons in hand.

But then he shook his head. "Gentlemen!" he said. He raised his hands. "I beg your pardon, Captain. Truly. I like a little surprise. I thought, per-haps—but please, never mind me, a harmless old man."

"Who the hell are you?" asked the captain, across his bare blade.

The Abbess shook her head. "He is Harmodius di Silva, the King's Magus. He broke the enemy at Chevin. He bound the former King's Magus, when he betrayed us."

"Your lover," Harmodius muttered. "Well—one of your lovers."

"You were a foolish young man then, and you still are in your heart." The Abbess settled primly back into her seat.

"My lady, if I am, it is because he has glamoured me for years," Har-modius said. "I was not as victorious as I had thought. And he is still with us." Harmodius looked around the table. "The captain of the Enemy, my lords, is the former King's Magus. The most powerful of my order to arise in twenty generations." He shrugged. "Or so I suspect, and my guesswork is based on observation."

"You are too modest," the Abbess said bitterly.

"I tricked him, as you well know," Harmodius said. "I could never have even hoped to match him phantasm for phantasm. And less so now, when he has sold himself to the Wild and I have languished in a prison of his making for a decade, at least."

The soldiers and the merchant watched these exchanges—back and forth—like spectators at a joust. Even the captain, whose precious anonym-ity had teetered at the edge of extinction, was lost.

"Let me understand this," he said. "Our Enemy is really a man?"

"Not any more," Harmodius said. "Now he is an entity called Thorn. His powers are to mine as mine are to the lady Abbess's.

The priest at the end of the table had stopped writing. Now he looked at them all in horror. The captain almost felt sorry for the man. His aversion to those who possessed the power—Hermetic or natural—was like most men's aversion to coming in contact with disease.

The captain leaned forward. "Can we stop the flood of reminiscence and revelation and try to dwell on the siege?" he asked.

"He underestimated you, and you hurt him, and that's over now," Harmodius said. "Now he'll hurt us, in turn."

"Thanks for that," the captain said.

"Now that he's closed off our access to the outside world, there will be no more surprise sorties, no more victories." The Magus sat back. "Nor can you imagine that I can face him, because I can't. Although my presence here will make him hungrier to take this place."

"We can still make sorties with every prospect of success," the captain insisted. "With the addition of Messire Random's convoy, we have more men-at-arms and more archers than we had at the start."

Harmodius shook his head. "I don't doubt it. I mean no disrespect—you have done nobly. But the trick with the falcons and the dogs won't work again, and his intellect—pardon me, Captain—is staggering. He'll have traitors inside the walls and he'll be working to get traitors within the ranks of your companies and your merchants. He also has the power to reach out to any person among us who has power. How strong is your will, my lady?" he asked.

"Never very strong," she answered levelly, "but where he is concerned, it is like adamantine."

Harmodius smiled. "I imagine that's true, my lady," he admitted.

"Even if he has us locked in a box," the captain insisted, "even if he threw his allies at the walls every day—" He shrugged. "We can last."

"He won't," Harmodius said. He leaned forward, and it was as if he deflated, the change was so sudden. "What he will do is seek to undermine us, because that is how he works. He will use craft and misdirection—he prefers to use a traitor to open the gate, because that excuses his own betrayal. And because he likes to imagine his intellect is superior to any other."

The captain managed a smile. "My old sword master used to say that a good swordsman likes not just to win, but to do it his own way," he said.

"Very true," the Magus said. "Hubristical, but true."

The captain nodded. "Hubris—a common failing in your profession too, surely?"

Harmodius smiled bitterly.

The captain leaned forward. "I have two questions, and here you are to answer them," he said. "Can he attack the walls directly? With a phantasm?"

"Never," the Abbess said. "These walls have half a millennia of prayer and phantasm in them, and no power on earth—"

"Yes," Harmodius said. He shrugged at the Abbess. "He is not Richard Plangere, gentleman Magus, my lady, just dressed up in feathers and gone a bit bad. He is Thorn. He is a Power of the Wild. If he puts himself to it, he can assault the very walls of this ancient fortress with his powers, and he will, in time, break them." He turned to the captain. "But in my estimation, and I might be horribly wrong, he won't take that option unless all else fails, because the cost would be staggering."

The captain nodded. "Not very different from the answer I expected. Second question: you are the King's Magus. Do you have the power to distract him? Or to defeat him?"

Harmodius nodded. "I can distract him, I think. Once at little risk to myself, and once at great risk to myself." He laughed. "I can feel him all around us, my lords. He seeks to know our minds and, so far, the power in this convent and in the fortress walls has stopped him. He knows I am here, but as yet I do not think he knows who I am." Harmodius shook his head and seemed, once again, to shrink. "Yet until a few days ago, I didn't really know who I was myself. By God, the extent to which he cozened me."

The captain sat back, already thinking hard. "Can you imagine any circumstance under which he would abandon the siege?" he asked. "If the king comes, will he simply retire?"

Harmodius looked at all of them for a long time. "You really have no idea what you are dealing with, here," he said. "Do you seriously think the king will reach us?" he asked.

The captain made a face. "You are the all-knowing Magus, and I'm just the young pup commanding the mercenaries, but it seems to me—"

"Spare us your false humility," Harmodius snapped.

"Spare us your overweening arrogance, then! It seems to me this is not a carefully wrought plan, and with due respect, Magus, this Thorn is not as staggeringly intelligent as you seem to think." The captain looked around.

Ser Milus nodded. "I agree. He makes beginner mistakes. He knows nothing of war." He shrugged. "At least, not of the war of men."

Harmodius started to react and then pulled on his ample beard. There was a heavy silence. The men around the table realised they were prepared for the Magus to react.

But he shook his head. "That is—a very interesting point. And quite possibly a valid one."

Father Henry came out of the Great Hall with his shoulders slumped, and Mag watched him enter the chapel and sit on a carved chair near the door, his head in his hands.

He wasn't a bad priest—he had heard her confession and had passed her to God with an endurable penance. She wanted to like him for it, but there was something in his eyes she couldn't like—a quality to his moist hand on her brow that unsettled her.

She was considering all these things when the archers came by. There were two of them, younger archers she didn't know well. The taller one had bright red hair and a hollow smile. They had their brigantines off and were looking around the courtyard.

They looked like trouble.

The tall one with a beard like a Judas goat spotted Lis the laundress, but she didn't truck with men his age, and she turned her back so his attention passed to Amie, the Carters' eldest—a blonde girl with more chest than wit, as her mother herself had said, while her younger sister Kitty had all the wit as well as curly dark hair and slanted eyes.

The archers headed for the two girls who sat on stools by the convent kitchen, grinding barley for bread in hand mills. It was boring, exacting work that the nuns thought perfect for attractive young women.

They already had a court of admirers, and the young men—farmers' sons and apprentices—were, naturally enough, doing the work. This was, Mag thought, probably not a common problem among the nuns, but if they didn't wise up to it soon they were going to spoil the Carter girls and the Lanthorns and every other single woman in the fortress who wasn't a nun. And perhaps a few nuns too, Mag thought to herself.

Mag had started to get to know some of the senior nuns—

She never heard what the archer said, but every one of the farm boys and apprentices was on his feet in a heartbeat.

The archers laughed and sat, and began using tow and ash to polish their helmets and elbow cops to the uniform dark gleam that seemed to mark the men of the company.

Mag walked closer. She saw trouble coming, and while the archers didn't seem to be provoking it, they were.

"Any clod can follow a plough," Judas Beard said. He smiled. "I did, once."

"Who are you, then?" said an apprentice.

"I'm a soldier," Judas Beard said. Just from his intonation, Mag, who had known some boys, knew that every word he said was aimed at the Carter girls.

Amie looked up from her mill. She'd taken the pestle back from the Smith boy because Mag was there and might tell. "Did you—fight? Yesterday?"

"I killed a dozen boglins," Judas Beard said. He laughed. "It's easy, if you know how."

"If you know how," said the other archer, who until now had been silent. He wasn't doing much polishing.

"Then it ain't any different from any other trade," said a shoemaker's apprentice.

"Except that I'll die rich while you're still be up to your neck in your master's piss," Judas Beard said.

Kitty put her hands on her hips. "Mind your language," she said.

The archers exchanged a glance. "Anything for a pretty lady," the quiet one said with a smile. He got up and bowed, a courtly bow, better than any of the farm boys, Mag knew. "I'm sure you hear too much of that already, eh, lass?"

"Don't you lass me!" Kitty said.

Amie was smiling at the red-bearded archer.

Mag didn't know what she felt was wrong here—the tone of it? The anger of the local boys seemed to fuel the archers.

"If'n you put some tallow on that flax, it'd hold the grit better," said another boy—really, a young man. "Less you're just doing it for show." The lad grinned. He was tall, broad in the shoulders, and no more a local than the archers.

Silent gave him a mocking look. "If I need a yokel to tell me how to polish my armour, I'll ask," he said.

The big lad grinned again. "Yokel yourself, farm boy. I'm from Harndon, and I can smell the shit on your shoes from here."

Kitty giggled.

It was the wrong sound—feminine derision at a critical moment—and Silent turned on her. "Shut up, slut."

And suddenly everything changed, like cream turning to butter in the churn.

Kitty turned red, but she put a hand on the nearest farm boy. "No need to do ought," she said. "No need to defend me."

Mag was proud of the girl.

But Judas Beard stood up and dusted his lap of tufts of tow. "That's right," he said. "Be reasonable." He smiled. "Learn to spread your legs like she does, when there's a man about."

Every farm boy was back on his feet, and both archers suddenly had knives—long knives. They took up practised, professional stances. "Anyone here got balls?" Judas Beard said. "Heh. You're just sheep who pay us to guard you. And if I feel like fucking one of your ewes, I will."

The big Harndon boy stepped out of the knot of locals. "I'll take you both," he said. "And I'll see to it you are taken to law." He spat on his hands, apparently in no hurry—but as he spat on his left hand, his left leg shot out. He was in close with Silent, his left knee behind the archer's knee, and suddenly the knife hand was rotating and the knife wielder was face down in the dust, his knife hand behind his back.

"Christ!" he screamed.

The Harndon boy had his knee in the archer's back. He turned to the other. "Drop your whittle or I'll shatter his shoulder. And I'll still come and break your skull."

Judas Beard growled, and a heavy staff hit him in the back of the head—hit him so hard that he dropped like a sack of rocks.

Mag was all but nose-to-nose with the mercenaries' commander, who had appeared—apparently out of thin air—and hit the red-haired archer with his staff of office. She squeaked.

He was standing over the big Harndonner and the smaller archer, who was still locked face down in the bigger boy's grip. "Let him go," said the captain quietly. "I'll see he's punished, but I need his bow arm working."

The big youth looked up and nodded, and in one fluid motion he rose to his feet and let the archer drop to the cobbled pavement. "I could have taken your other man," he said.

"I'm know you could," the captain said. "You're a wagoner, aren't you?"

"Daniel Favor, of Harndon. My pater is Dick Favor, and he has ten carts on the roads." He nodded.

"How old are you, Daniel?" the captain asked, as he leaned down and seized Silent's ear.

"Fifteen," the Harndonner said.

The captain nodded. "Can you pull a bow, lad?"

The big youth grinned. "And fight with a sword. But a bow—aye. Any kind, any weight."

"Ever thought about the life of a soldier?" the captain asked.

Daniel nodded solemnly.

"Why don't you come along and see this miscreant punished," the captain said. "There won't be any carting for some weeks, if I'm any judge, and a boy who can pull a bow can help save his friends. Save some fair maidens, too," the captain said, with a pretty bow to the two girls and then to Mag.

Will Carter stepped forward. "I can pull a bow too, Captain," he said. His voice trembled.

The captain smiled. "Can you, now?" he asked. He looked at Mag. "A word with you, goodwife?"

She nodded. The captain took her aside, with the silent archer stumbling after as he kept his grip on the archer's ear.

"How bad was this?" he asked.

She met his eyes. They were very handsome eyes. He was younger than he seemed at a distance. His linens were terrible—the collar of his shirt was ruined and threadbare, and his cuffs were brown-black with grime and a long linen thread dangled from his arming cote. "Bad," she said. She found she was shaken, and her knees were weak. His eyes were not normal eyes.

"War does not make boys nice," he said, giving his man's ear a shake.

"But you're going to teach it to these young 'uns, anyway," she said, while thinking *what's got into you, girl?* "My lord," she added hastily.

He considered what she said. The archer tried to move, and the captain twisted his ear viciously. "I take your point, but the alternative is being eaten alive by the Wild," he said. He said it ruefully, as if he understood her point all too well.

"What will happen to him?" she said.

"Sym?" the captain said, turning the silent archer by means of his ear so that he cried out. "Sym will have forty lashes on his back—ten a day at two-day intervals, giving him something to look forward to. Unless my marshal thinks it is worth making an example of him."

Sym cried out.

"In which case, we'll tie him to a wagon wheel and cut open his back—" the captain went on, and Sym whimpered.

Mag swayed.

The captain grinned at her. "It may sound awful, but it is better than rape, and once it starts it will not stop. Sorry—I am too blunt." He looked at her, as if seeing her for the first time. "You are the seamstress—yes?" he asked.

She made a curtsy. "I am, my lord."

"Could you be kind enough to make the time to visit me, Mistress? I need...everything." He smiled.

She nodded. "So I can see," she said. Business straightened her back. "Shirts? Braes? Caps?"

"Three of each?" he asked. He sounded wistful.

"I'll wait on you this afternoon, my lord," she said with a quick bend of her knee.

"Well, then," he said, towing his archer away by the ear. He walked back to the locals—boys were competing to comfort the Carter girls. Curiously, the Harndon boy was standing uncertainly by, taking no part. Mag flashed him a smile and went about her business.

Lissen Carak—Bad Tom

Tom Lachlan was sitting at his table in the garrison tower. It had become his office—his and Bent's, because Bent was becoming his right hand.

He looked over his cards, and his ears picked up the unmistakable sound of spurred boots on the stairs.

He was on his feet, cards in a bag, and looking out an arrow slit at a party of boglins digging in the sun before the captain crested the stairs.

Low Sym was all but thrown across the table. He gave a long squeal as the captain released his hold on the man's ear.

Tom sighed. "What's the useless fuck done now?" Low Sym was one of the company's leading lights—in crime.

There were a dozen boys coming up the steps behind the captain.

The captain indicated them with a shift of his eyes. "New recruits. Archers."

Tom nodded. They were likely boys—he'd been eyeing them himself— yeomen's sons, all big, well-fed lads with good shoulders and muscles. At their head was a boy who looked as if he might, in time, be as tall as Tom himself.

Tom nodded again, and as he rounded the table to greet the recruits he slammed his fist into Low Sym's head. "Don't move," he said.

"I'll be in my Commandery," the captain said.

Tom bowed, and turned to the boys. "Who here can shoot a bow?" he asked.

"There's one other," the captain said. "Red Beve is lying in the courtyard with a busted noggin. Captain's court tomorrow for both. Nice and public, Tom."

Captain's court was official—not a casual ten lashes and no questions asked situation, but for a crime for which the captain might have a man broken, or executed.

The captain nodded at the boys. "Tell the truth and do your best. We don't take everyone, and your parents have to agree," he said.

Tom all but choked on laughter, but the Red Knight was good at this— he was a fine recruiter, while Tom had never been able to recruit anyone for anything unless he had a club in one hand and a whip in the other. *We don't take everyone.* He allowed a laugh to escape his gut.

"Let's go down to the archery butts and see what you boys are made of," he said in what he thought was his kindliest voice. Then he leaned down to Sym. "Best lie still, laddy. Captain means to have your guts on a stick."

Then he followed the boys down the steps to the courtyard.

The captain leaned on the railing of the hoardings that had been assembled outside his Commandery—in effect, giving him a covered and armoured porch that jutted from the walls four hundred feet above the plain. He was watching a party of men—captives? They had to be captives—under the direction of something horrible. They were digging trenches.

As far as his eyes could see, men and monsters were digging trenches. It was a maze—a pattern that he suspected was deliberate, and the scope of it was inhuman and both grotesque and awe-inspiring. The trenches were not in concentric rings, like those a professional soldier would have built—they clung to the ground, marking the edges of every contour like a tight fitting kirtle on a curvaceous woman.

Someone had planned it, and now drove it to execution. In one day.

He wanted Amicia. He wanted to talk to her, but he was too tired and the fortress was too full to find her. But he knew another way—if she was on her bridge. All it required was that he open his door a little. He reached to—

Enter the room. He waved at his tutor, Prudentia, and walked to the iron-bound door.

"Don't," she said.

She'd been telling him not to do things his entire life and, mostly, he ignored her.

"You can't trust her," Prudentia said. "And Thorn is right outside that door. He is waiting for you."

"He has to sleep sometime."

"Stop!"

He put his whole weight against the door—his whole dream weight—and turned the handle until the tumbler clicked—

And the door slammed back against its hinges and a solid green fog roared into his chamber, enough power to light a city—ten cities—

North of Lissen Carak—Thorn

Thorn grinned as he felt the dark sun—felt him surface to the world of power—and he sent all his power along the contact lines to bind him. No more hesitation. Men of power always tried a direct challenge. Thorn was ready.

Lissen Carak—The Abbess

The Abbess felt the rising tide of Wild power and stopped—she was feeding bits of chicken to her bird, and the plate of raw chicken fell to the marble floor. There couldn't be *this* much power in her fortress—she reached out and felt *him*—

North of Lissen Carak—Thorn

Thorn felt her golden brilliance and he paused, licking at it to taste her, amazed at her potency. Delighted, saddened, angered, guilt-ridden—

Utterly distracted.

The Memory Palace—The Red Knight

He lay on the floor, and Prudentia was trying to reach him, her marble hand inches from his own—her hand and the black and white parquetry tiles were the only things he could see in the roiling, choking cloud of green, the green of trees in high summer. He was pinned to the floor—he could see the shape of the cage closing over him, a phantasm so potent that he could only breathe his wonder as it crushed him—it hesitated. He strained, but it was too powerful, even as it seemed to lose its focus, and he pushed against it his mind screaming "Fool, fool, fool—"

The door slammed shut leaving him lying crumpled in the corner of his armoured balcony.

The old Magus stood over him, his staff still glowing, and wisps of fae-fire played along its length. "Well, well," the old man said. "That would be your mother in you, I suspect."

The captain tried to get to his feet and found himself boneless and almost unable to move his arms. "You have the advantage of me," he said softly.

The old Magus offered him a hand. "So I do. I am Harmodius, Royal Magus, and you are Lord Gabriel Moderatus Murien—Anna's son." He smiled grimly. "The Viscount Murien. Don't try and deny it, you little imp. Your mother thinks you're dead, but I knew who you were the moment I saw you." He got the captain to his feet, and led him across the room to a chair.

Jacques came in with a cocked and loaded arbalest. It was smoothly done—Harmodius had no chance to react.

"Say the word, my lord, and he's dead," Jacques said.

"You heard," the captain said. He felt as if he had the worst hangover of his life.

"I heard," Jacques said. The bolt-head on the trough of the crossbow didn't waver.

The captain took in a shaky breath. "Why shouldn't I have you killed?" he asked the Magus.

"Is your petty secret worth the lives of everyone in the castle?" the Magus asked. "None of you will live through this without me. Even with me the odds are long. In the name of the Trinity, boy, you just felt his power."

The captain wished he could think. The Magus's use of his name—Gabriel—had hit him as hard as the green cage had. He didn't even allow *himself* to think the name Gabriel. "I have killed, and allowed men to die, to protect my secret," he said.

"Time to stop doing that, then," said the Magus.

Jacques didn't move, and his voice was calm. "Why don't you just shut up about it?" He shrugged, but the shrug never reached the crossbow bolt's tip. "You being the mighty King's Magus, and all. You stop talking about some dead boy's name, and we can all go on together?"

"Three in a secret," the captain muttered.

The Magus pursed his lips. "I'll give my word not to disclose what I know—if you give me yours to talk to me about it. When and if this is over."

The captain felt as if the floor had dropped from under his feet, and all he wanted to do was jump into the hole and hide. "Fine," he said. He remembered that Gawin Murien was lying in the hospital, almost exactly over his head. *Four in a secret, and one my enemy,* he thought. *My lovely brother.*

"I so swear, by my power," the Magus said.

The captain forced himself to raise his head. "At ease, Jacques," he said. "He's just sworn an oath that binds—if he breaks it, his own power will be crippled." He turned back to the Magus. "You saved my life," he said.

"Ah—some shred of courtesy survives in you. Yes, boy, I saved you from a grisly death—he wanted your power for his own." The horrible old man grinned. "He was going to eat your soul."

The captain nodded. "I feel as if he did. Or perhaps he didn't like the taste?" he tried to grin and gave it up. "A cup of water, Jacques."

Jacques backed up a step, took the bolt from the action and used the goat's foot at his belt to slowly unlever the string. "Loons," he muttered, as he left the room.

When he was gone, the Magus leaned forward. "How powerful are you, boy? Your mother never said a word."

The captain's heart beat faster at the word mother, and flashed on his beautiful mother, drunk and violent and hitting him—

"Don't mention my mother again." He sounded childish, even to himself.

Harmodius hooked a stool over with his staff and sat. "All right, boy, sod your mother. She was never any friend of mine. How powerful are you?"

The captain sat back, trying to recover his—his sense of himself. His poise. His *captainness*.

"I have a good deal of raw power, and I had a good tutor until—" He paused.

"Until you ran away and faked your death," the Magus concluded. "Which of course you did with a phantasm. Of course you did." He shook his head.

"I didn't mean to fake it," the captain said.

The Magus smiled. "I was young and angry and hurt once, too, lad," he said. "Despite appearances. Never mind—cold comfort. I glimpsed your memory palace—magnificent. The entity within it—who is she?"

"My tutor," the captain said.

There was a long pause. Harmodius cleared his throat. "You— ?"

The captain shrugged. "No I didn't kill her. She was dying—my mother and my brothers, they...never mind. I saved what I could."

The Magus narrowed his eyes. "That's a human woman bound to a statue in a memory palace?" he asked. "*Inside your head.*"

The captain sighed. "Yes."

"Heresy, thaumaturgy, necromancy, gross impiety, and perhaps kidnapping too," Harmodius said. "I don't know whether to arrest you or ask how you did it."

"She helped me. She still does," the captain said.

"How many of the hundred workings do you know?" the Magus asked.

"The hundred workings, of which there are at least a hundred and forty-four, and perhaps as many as four hundred?" the captain asked.

Jacques came in with a tray—apple cider, water, wine.

"No one comes in," the captain said.

Jacques made a face that suggested that he was no fool—but perhaps his master was—and left.

The Magus fingered his beard. "Hmmm," he said noncommittally.

"I can work more than a hundred and fifty of them," the captain said. He shrugged.

"It was a splendid memory machine," the Magus replied. "Why—if I may ask—aren't you the shining light of Hermeticism?"

The captain picked up his cup of water and drained it. "It is not what I want."

The Magus shocked him by nodding.

The captain leaned forward. "That's it? You nod?"

The Magus spread his hands. "I'm keep saying I'm no fool, lad. So your mother trained you all your life to be a magus, I'll guess. Brilliant tutor, special powers. It all but drips off you—you know that?"

The captain laughed. It was a laugh full of anger, self-pity, brutal pain. A very young, horrible laugh he'd hoped he'd left behind him. "She—" He paused. "Fuck it, I'm not in a revealing mood, old man."

The old Magus sat still. Then he took the wine flagon, poured a cup, and drank it off. "The thing is," he began carefully, "the thing is, you are like a vault full of grain, or armour, or naphtha—waiting to be used in the defence of this fortress, and I'm not sure I can let you stay locked." He shrugged. "I've discovered something. Something so very important that I'm afraid I'm not very interested in what men call *morality* right now. So I'm sorry for the hurt your bitch mother caused you—but your wallowing in self-pity is not going to save lives, especially mine."

Their eyes locked.

"A vault full of naphtha," the captain said, dreamily. "I *have* a vault full of naphtha."

"She taught you well, this tutor of yours," Harmodius said. "Now listen, *Captain*. The mind that opposes us is not some boglin chief from the hills—nor even an adversarius, nor even a draconis singularis. This is the shell of a man who was the greatest of our order, who has given himself to the Wild for power and mastery and as a result is, quite frankly, godlike. I don't know why he wants this place—or rather, I can guess at some surface reasons, but I can't guess what he really wants. Do you understand me, boy?"

The captain nodded. "I have a thought or two in my head, thanks. I have to help you, if we're going to make it."

"Even in the moment of his treason, he was too smart for me," Harmodius said, "although, for my sins, I've only had to face my own failure in the last week." He shrugged and sat back. He seemed suddenly smaller.

The captain downed the soft cider in four long gulps.

"I'd like to survive this, too," he said. He sighed. "I'm not *against* the use of power. I use it."

Harmodius looked up. "Can you channel?" he asked.

The captain frowned. "I know what you mean," he said. "But I've never done it. And besides, my strength is poor. Prudentia taught that we grow in strength by the ceaseless exertion of muscle, and that the exercise of power is no different."

The Magus nodded. "True. Mostly true. You have a unique access to the power of the Wild." He shrugged.

"Mother raised me to be the Antichrist," said the captain bitterly. "What do you expect?"

Harmodius shrugged. "You can wallow or you can grow. I doubt you can do both." He leaned forward. "So listen. So far, everything he has done is foreplay. He has thousands of fresh-minted boglins; he has all the spectrum of fearsome boogiemen of the northern Wild—trolls, wyverns, daemons; Outwallers; irks. He has the power to cast a cage on you—on you who can tap directly into the Power of the Wild. When he comes against us in full measure he will destroy us utterly."

The captain shrugged and drank some wine. "Best surrender then," he said with a sneer.

"Wake up, boy! This is serious!" The old man slapped the table.

They glowered at each other.

"I need your powers to be deployed for us," Harmodius said. "Can you take instruction?"

The captain looked away. "Yes," he muttered. He sat back and was suddenly serious. He raised his eyes. "Yes, Harmodius. I will take your instruction and stop rebelling against your obvious authority for no better reason than that you remind me of my not-father."

Harmodius shrugged. "I don't drink enough to remind you of your odious not-father," he said.

"You left out the Jacks," the captain put in. "When you were listing his overwhelming strength. We caught some of them in camp, in our first sortie. Now he's moved them elsewhere and I've lost them."

"Jacks?" Harmodius asked. "Rebels?"

"Like enough," the captain said. "More than rebels. Men who want change."

"You sound sympathetic," Harmodius said.

"If I'd been born in a crofter's hut, I'd be a Jack." The captain looked at his armour on its rack as if contemplating the social divide.

Harmodius shrugged. "How very Archaic of you." He chuckled.

"Things are worse for the commons than they were in my boyhood," the captain asserted.

Harmodius stroked his beard and poured a cup of wine. "Lad, surely you have recognised that things are worse for everyone? Things are falling apart. The Wild is winning—not by great victories, but by simple entropy. We have fewer farms and fewer men. I saw it riding here. Alba is failing. And this fight—this little fight for an obscure castle that holds a river crossing vital to an agricultural fair—is turning into the fight of your generation. The odds are *always* long for us. We are never wise—when we are rich, we squander our riches fighting each other and building churches. When we are poor, we fight among ourselves for scraps—and always, the Wild is there to take the unploughed fields."

"I will not fail here," the captain said.

"Because if you are victorious here, you will have finally turned your back on the fate that was appointed to you?" said the Magus.

"Everyone has to strive for something," the captain replied.

Albinkirk—Gaston

There was no battle at Albinkirk.

The royal army formed up for battle just south of the town, on the west bank of the great river, with the smaller Cohocton guarding their northern flank. Royal Huntsmen had been killing boglins for two days, and the squires and archers of the army were learning to take their guard duty seriously after something took almost a hundred war horses in the dark of the night. Six squires and a belted knight died in the dark, facing something fast and well armoured—bigger than a pony, faster than a cat. They drove it off eventually.

The army had risen four hours before dawn, formed their battles lines in the dark, and moved carefully forward towards the smoking town. But after all that work, the mouse still escaped the cat.

Or perhaps the lion escaped the mouse. Gaston couldn't be sure which they were.

The king had almost three thousand knights and men-at-arms, and half again as many infantry, even without the levies who had been left to guard the camp. On the one hand, the force was the largest and best armed that Gaston had ever seen—the Albans had armour for every peasant, and while their mounted knights might seem a trifle antiquated, with too much boiled leather in garish colours over double maille, and not enough plate—the Alban king's force was now larger than any Gallish lord's and well mounted and well-served. His cousin had ceased commenting on them. This close to the enemy, the Royal Host had become slimmer, fitter, and altogether more competent, with well-conducted sentries and pickets. Young men no longer rode abroad without armour.

But his father King Hawthor had, by all reports, had at least five times as many men when he rode forth against the Wild, perhaps even ten times as many. And the signs were all around them—the lack of plate armour was not just a penchant for the old-fashioned. All along the road, he had seen abandoned farms and shops—once a whole town with the roofs falling in.

It gave him pause.

But on this day, as the sun rose behind them and gilded their lance tips and pennons, the enemy melted away before them, abandoning the siege—as if Albinkirk had never truly been under siege after the assault.

The army halted at the edge of the great river and the Royal Huntsmen finished off any boglins too slow to get down the great earth cliff to the beach below. Heralds counted the dead and debated whether to count the destruction of the small enemy force as a battle or not.

Gaston answered his cousin's summons, and saluted, his visor open and his sword loose in the sheath. It seemed possible that there would be an immediate pursuit across the river, even though it seemed odd that the enemy would retreat to the east.

But Jean de Vrailly handed his great bassinet to his squire and shook his head. "A royal council," he snapped. He was angry. It seemed his mad cousin was *always* angry these days.

Followed only by a handful of retinue knights and a herald, they rode across the field, covered in summer flowers, towards the king.

"We are letting the enemy escape," de Vrailly said. "There was to be a great battle. *Today.*" He spat. "My soul is in peril, because I begin to doubt my angel. When will we fight? By the five wounds of Christ, I hate this place. Too hot—too many trees, ugly people, bestial peasants—" He suddenly reined in his horse, dismounted, and knelt to pray.

Gaston, for once, joined him. In truth, he agreed with all of his cousin's pronouncements. He wanted to go home too.

A herald rode up—a king's messenger, Gaston saw. He went back to his prayers. Only when his joints ached and his knees could no longer bear the pain did Gaston raise his eyes to the king's messenger who had been patiently waiting for them.

"The king requests your company," he said.

Gaston sighed, and he and his cousin rode the rest of the way to the royal council.

It was held on horseback, and all the great lords were present—every officer or lord with fifty knights or more. The Earl of Towbray, the Count of the Border, the Prior of Harndon, who commanded the military orders, and a dozen midlands lords whom Gaston didn't know. Edward, Bishop of Lorica, armed cap à pied, and the king's captain of the guard, Ser Richard Fitzroy, the old king's bastard, or so men said.

The king was conferring with a small man with a grizzled beard, who rode a small palfrey and looked like a dwarf when every other man present was mounted on a charger. He was sixty years old and wore a plain harness of munition armour—the kind that armourers made for their poorer customers.

He had dark circles under his eyes, but his eyes still had fire in them.

"They were over the outwalls and into the suburbs after three assaults," he said. "They could run *up the walls.*" He looked at Ser Alcaeus. "But you must know the story from this good knight."

"You tell it," said the king.

"The mayor wouldn't send the women to the castle. So I sent out my best men to force them in." He shrugged. "And they did. And by the grace of the good Christ, I took twenty men-at-arms and held the gate to the castle." He shook his head. "We held it for an hour or so." He looked at Ser Alcaeus. "Didn't we?"

The Morean knight nodded. "We did, Ser John."

"How many died?" the king asked gently.

"Townspeople? Or my people?" the old man asked. "The town itself died, my lord. We saved mostly women and children—a few hundred of them. The men died fighting, or were taken." He grimaced as he said it. "We kept two posterns open the next night—a dozen pole-axes by each—and we got another fifty refugees, but they burned the town to the ground, my lord." He bowed his head, slipped from his nag and knelt before his king. "I beg your pardon, my lord. I held my castle, but I lost your town. Do with me as you will."

Gaston looked around. The Albans were in shock.

His cousin pushed forward. "All the more reason to pursue the enemy now," he said strongly.

The old captain shook his head. "No, my lord. It's a trap. This morning, we saw a big force—Outwallers, with Sossags or Abenacki, going into the woods to the east. It's an ambush. They want you to pursue them."

De Vrailly coughed. "Am I to be afeared of a few broken men?" he asked. No one answered him.

"Where is the main force of the enemy?" the king asked.

The old man shrugged. "We've had messengers from convoys headed west, and from the Abbess," he said. "If I had to guess, I'd say that Lissen Carak is besieged." He took the king's stirrup. "They say it's the Fallen Magus," he said suddenly. "Men claim they saw him while the walls were being stormed, smashing breeches in the wall with lightning."

Again, the Albans muttered, and their mounts started to grow restless.

The king made a clucking sound, as if thinking aloud.

The Prior of Harndon pushed his horse forward. He wasn't a big man and he was as old as the Captain of Albinkirk, but something shone from him—power of a sort, based on piety, humility. His black mantle contrasted sharply with the blaze of gold and colour on the other warriors, even the bishop.

"I would like to take my knights and outriders west, my lord, to see to Lissen Carak," he said. "It is our responsibility."

The Count of the Borders was at Gaston's elbow. Despite the frostiness of their last meeting, he leaned over. "The Sisters of Saint Thomas are his people—at least at a remove or two," he whispered.

The Captal de Ruth stood in his stirrups. "I would like to accompany them," he declared.

390

The Prior regarded him with a smile. It was a weary smile, and it probably wasn't intended to convey insult. "This is a matter for the knights of my order," he said. "We are trained for it."

The captal touched his sword hilt. "No man tells me my men are not trained," he said.

The Prior shrugged. "I will not take you, no matter how bad your manners."

Gaston put a hand on his cousin's steel clad forearm. In Alba, as in Galle, a man did *not* threaten or challenge a knight of God. It wasn't done.

Or perhaps his mad cousin thought himself above that law, too.

Lissen Carak—The Red Knight

A commander is seldom alone.

For the captain there was paperwork, often done with Ser Adrian. Drills to supervise, general inspections, particular inspections, and an endless host of small social duties—the expectations of a band of people bonded by ties forged in fire. A band of people who, in many cases, are rejects from other communities because they lack even the most basic social skills.

The captain needed to be alone, and his usual expedient was to ride out over the fields of whatever countryside his little army occupied, find himself a copse of trees, and sit amongst them. But the enemy occupied the countryside, and the fortress itself was full to bursting with people—people everywhere.

Harmodius had left him with a set of complex instructions—in effect, a new set of phantasms to learn, all in aid of defending himself against direct workings from their current enemy. And there was a plan, too—a careful plan—reckless in risk, but cunning in scope.

He needed time and privacy to practise. And he was never alone.

Michael came, served him chicken, and was dismissed.

Bent came to pass a request from some of the farmers that they be allowed to visit their sheep in the pens under the Lower Town walls. The captain rubbed his eyes. "Yes," he said.

Sauce came in with an idea for a sortie.

"No," he said.

And went somewhere else to find himself some privacy to practise thaumaturgy.

The hospital seemed like the best bet.

He climbed the stairs without meeting anyone—evening was falling outside, and he felt as if he'd fought a battle. He had to force his legs to push him up the winding stairs.

He passed the sister at the head of the stairs with a muttered word—let her assume that he was on his way to visit the wounded.

In fact, he *did* visit his wounded first. John Daleman, archer, lay on the bed nearest the far wall with a line of sutures from his collarbone to his waist, but by a miracle, or perhaps by the arts of the sisters, he was not infected and was now expected to live. He was also in a deeply drugged sleep, and the captain merely sat by him for a moment.

Seth Pennyman, Valet, had just come from the surgery, where they had set his broken arm and broken leg. He'd been brushed from the wall by a wyvern's tail. Nothing had set properly, and the sisters had just reset the breaks. He was full of some drug, and muttered curses in his sleep.

Walter La Tour, gentleman man-at-arms, sat reading slowly from a beautifully illustrated psalter. Fifty-seven years old, he wore new glass spectacles on his nose. He'd received a crushing blow from the behemoth in the fight by the brook.

The captain sat down and clasped his right hand. "I thought I'd lost you when that thing put you down."

Walter grinned. "Me too," he said. "Don't make me laugh, my lord. Hurts too much."

The captain looked more closely. "Are those things new?" he asked, reaching for the glass spectacles.

"Ground by the apothocary right here," Walter said. "Hurt the nose like anything, but damn me, I haven't been able to read this well in years."

The captain put them on his own nose. They wouldn't really stay, the heavy horn frames merely pinching. There was a fine steel rivet holding the two lenses together so that they pivoted—the captain knew the principle, but had never seen them in action.

"I...that is, we—" La Tour looked wistful. "I might stay here, Captain."

The captain nodded. "You'd be well suited," he said. "Although I doubt me that you are too old to chase nuns."

"As to that," Walter said, and turned crimson. "I am considering taking orders."

The things you don't know. The captain smiled and clasped the man's free hand again. "Glad to see you better," he said.

"I owe God," Walter said, by way of explanation. "They saved me, here. I was dead. That behemoth crushed me like an insect, and these holy women brought me back. For a reason."

The smile was wiped from the captain's face. "Yes," he said. "I, too, owe something to God."

He moved on down the line of cots. Low Sym lay with his face to the wall, his back carefully bandaged. Justice tended to be instant, in the company. He moaned.

"You are an idiot," the captain said with professional affection.

Sym didn't roll over. He moaned.

The captain was merciless, because next to La Tour and the others, Sym's pain was like the sting of a fly. "You picked the fight because you wanted the girl. The girl didn't want you, and beating up her brothers and her fellow farm-hands wasn't going to ever make her like you. Eh?"

Moan.

"Not that you care, because you are not above a spot of forced love, eh, Sym? This is not Galle. I didn't approve of your way in Galle, my lad, but this is our country and we are all holed up in the fortress together, and if you so much as breathe garlic on a farm girl, with or without her permission, I'll hang you with my own hands. In fact, Sym, let's be straight about this. You are the single most useless fuck in my whole command, and I'd prefer to hang you, because the message that I mean business would cost me nothing. You get me?" He leaned forward.

Sym moaned again. He was crying.

The captain hadn't been aware that Low Sym was capable of crying. It opened up a whole new vista.

"You want to be the hero and not the villain, Sym?" he asked very quietly.

Sym turned his head away.

"Listen up, then. Evil is a choice. *It is a choice.* Doing the wicked thing is the easy way out, and it is habit forming. I've done it. Any criminal can use force. Any wicked person can steal. Some people don't steal because they are afraid of being caught. Others don't steal because it is wrong. Because stealing is the destruction of another person's work. Rape is a violence against another person. Using violence to solve every quarrel—" The captain paused in his moralizing lecture, because, of course, as a company of mercenaries, they tended to use violence to solve every quarrel—he laughed aloud. "It's our work, but it doesn't have to define us."

Sym moaned.

He captain leaned close. "Not a bad time to decide to be a hero and not a villain, Sym. Your current line will end on a gallows. Better to end in a story than a noose." He thought of Tom. The man was a hillman—easy to forget, but his notions of word fame lingered. "Finish in a song."

The small man wouldn't look at him. The captain shook his head, tired and not very happy with his job.

He got up from the nursing stool by the archer and stretched.

Amicia was right behind him. Of course. There he was, the prince of hypocrites.

She looked down at Sym, and then back at the captain.

He shrugged at her.

She furrowed her brow, and shook her head, and waved him on his way.

He stumbled away, cast down.

He made an exasperated sound, and stepped out into the corridor that ran from the recovery beds to the serious patients' ward. He walked a few paces and turned the corner only to find himself standing by Gawin Murien's bed. The younger man had one leg bandaged from the crotch to the knee.

He sat by Ser Gawin's bed. "No one will look for me here," he said in bitter self-mockery.

Gawin's eyes opened.

This is not my day, the captain thought.

There was a pause long enough for vast conversations. For debate, argument, rage. Instead, they stared into each other's eyes like lovers.

"Well, brother," Gawin said. "So it seems you are alive, after all."

The captain made himself breathe in and out. "Yes," he said, very quietly.

Gawin nodded. "And no one knows who you are," he said.

"You do," the captain said. "And the old wizard, Harmodius."

Gawin nodded. "I gave him a wide birth," he said. "Would you help me sit up?"

The captain found himself obligingly raising his brother on his pillows—even fluffing one of them. His brother, who had killed Prudentia at his mother's orders.

"Mother said she was corrupting you," Gawin said, suddenly, as if reading his mind. But even as he got those words out, his voice broke. "She wasn't, was she? We murdered her."

The captain sat back down before his knees could give way. He wanted to flee. To have this conversation another day. Another year.

The truth was that the truth was too horrible to share. Shameful, horrible, and deeply wounding to everyone it could possibly touch. The captain sat and looked at Gawin, who still believed that they were brothers. That lie, at least, was intact.

"Prudentia knew something she shouldn't have," the captain found himself saying. He sounded remarkably calm. He was quite proud of himself, just for a moment.

Gawin made a choked noise. "So Mater got us to kill her," he said, after another mammoth pause.

"Just as she egged you on every day to torment me," the captain said bitterly.

Gawin shrugged. "I realised that, even before you left. Richard never saw it, but I did." He looked out the arrow slit by his head. "I did something terrible, down in Lorica. I got some good men killed and I did something despicable."

Suddenly the captain found Gawin's eyes locked on his again. "When I was kneeling in the mud, acting the craven, I realised that I had to avenge myself or go mad. And—and let me fucking say this, *brother*—I realised in one flash that I had been the instrument of your destruction, as surely as if I'd killed you myself. You think it didn't touch me? When we found your body, and how did you pull that off?—when we found your body, I rode away into the Wild. I was gone—off my head. I knew who killed Lord Gabriel. I did. Dickon and I did, together. We hated you into death, didn't we?" He shook his head. "Except now you are not dead, and I'm not sure where that leaves us. You are a magus?" he asked.

The captain sighed. "Mater had me trained as a magus," he said. "By Prudentia. Even while telling you two how effeminate I was, and what a poor knight I made. I had sworn never to reveal my studies—to her, to God, to all the saints." He laughed bitterly.

"Oh, my God," Gawin groaned. "Prudentia was a magus. So…oh, my God. Mater provided the arrow."

"Of Witch Bane," the captain said.

Gawin was whiter, if anything, than when the captain had first seen him. "I'm sorry," he said. "We both knew you loved her."

The captain shrugged.

"Gabriel—"

"Gabriel, Viscount Murien is dead," the captain said. "I am the captain. Some men call me the Red Knight."

"Red Knight? Like some nameless bastard?" Gawin said. "You're my brother, Gabriel Moderatus Murien, the heir of the Duke of the North, son of the king's sister."

"Oh, I'm the son of the king's sister all right," the captain said, and then clamped down, before any more came out.

Gawin choked. He sat up, and cursed. A slow thread of scarlet worked its way across his groin. "No!" he muttered.

The captain nodded. "Yes. If it makes you feel any better, we're only half brothers," he said.

"Sweet Christ and his five wounds," Gawin said.

The captain came to a decision—the kind of decision he made, where he threw out one set of options and adopted another, like life on the battlefield. He moved his chair closer to his half-brother. "Tell me this terrible fucking thing you did in Lorica," he said. He took Gawin's hand. "Tell me, and I'll forgive you for killing Prudentia. She already forgives you. I'll explain sometime. Tell me what happened in Lorica, and let's start again, from age nine, when we were friends."

Gawin lay back, so that their eyes broke contact. "The price of your forgiveness is steep, brother." He was suddenly red as blood. Then he hung his head. "I am deeply ashamed. I would not confess this to a priest."

"I'm no priest, and I have plenty of which to be ashamed. Some day I, too, will explain. Now tell me."

"Why?" Gawin asked. "Why? You'll only hate me more—add contempt to the list of your grievances. I played the caitiff, I was craven and I grovelled under another man's sword." Tears came down his face. "I failed and lost. I was nothing. For my sins, Satan sent this," and he pulled down his shirt to show the scales that had grown from his waist to his neck on the right side.

The captain looked at his brother—still so proud, even after such a thing happened, and all unknowing of his own pride. *So easy to understand others* the captain thought with wry amusement. And surprising sorrow. He couldn't keep his emotional distance with Gawin.

"Losing is not, in and of itself, a sin." The captain rubbed his beard. "It took me years to learn that, but I did. Failure is not sin. Wallowing in failure—" he hung his own head "—is something at which I can excel, if I allow it to myself, but that's more like the sin."

"You sound like a man of God," Gawin said.

"Fuck God," the captain said.

"Gabriel!"

"Seriously, Gawin, what has God ever done for me?" the captain laughed. "If I awaken after a sword thrust with the eternal flames burning my sorry arse, I'll spit in the maker's face, because that's all I was ever offered in a rigged game, and I will have played it *anyway*."

That blasphemy ended all conversation for a long time. The sun was setting.

Gawin rolled his hips a little. "My groin is bleeding again. Can you re-wrap it? I can't stomach the nursing sisters wrapping my groin."

"Crap," the captain said. What had been a thread of scarlet was now a rapidly spreading stain—a pool of blood. "Jesus wept! No, I'm getting expert help." He laughed. "We'll both likely die of the family curse—overweening pride—but I don't have to actively help you die." He scraped his chair back. "Amicia?" he called. "Amicia?"

She came so quickly that he knew—knew from her face, as well—that she'd heard every word they had said.

And she had a length of boiled linen in one hand and a pair of sharp scissors in the other. "Hold him down and this will go faster," she said, all business.

Gawin turned his face away.

"Really," the captain said, when the bandage was off, "you should enjoy having such a beauty work on your groin."

Amicia paused. He looked into her eyes for the first time in days and felt like a fool. "Sorry," he muttered weakly.

But she held his gaze. And then he saw her wink at Gawin. "A secret for a secret," she said, with that not-a-smile in the corner of her mouth. She bent over the long wound on the young knight's leg, and when her lips were a finger's width from his thigh, she breathed out—a long breath—and as she breathed, the wound closed. The captain saw the power flow through her, a great pulse of power, as great as anything he'd ever handled.

In his sight, it was bright green.

She looked up from her work and just a flicker of her eyes, and in them was a charge and a promise and in that flicker of a heartbeat he accepted both.

"What did she do?" Gawin asked. The captain's broad torso was blocking his ability to see. "It's all numb."

"A poultice," the captain said cheerfully. The room suddenly smelled of summer flowers. She was wrapping fresh linen around the wound, sponging off the fresh blood and the older dried blood.

Gawin tried to sit up, and the captain held him down. Under his left hand, something felt very wrong with his half-brother's shoulder, and he rolled the edge of his shirt collar back.

Gawin's shoulder was finely scaled, like a fish, or a wyvern. The captain ran his hand over it, and behind him, Amicia's breath came in a sharp gasp.

Gawin groaned. "And you think you are cursed by God?"

Amicia ran her hand over the young knight's scales, and the captain found himself instantly jealous.

"I have seen this before," she said.

Gawin brightened perceptively. "You have?" he asked.

"Yes," she said.

"Can it be cured?" he asked.

She bit her lip. "I really don't know, but it was not uncommon among...among..." she stammered.

The captain thought that an astrologer would have said it was a day for secrets, and their revelation.

"I will look into it," she said with the assurance of the medico, and she swept from the room, the pale grey of her over-gown fluttering behind her.

Gawin watched her, and the captain watched her. "She used power," Gawin said quietly.

"Yes," the captain said.

"She is—" Gawin let his head fall back. "I was headed north," he began. "The king had dismissed me from court for shooting my big mouth off. I fell in love—oh, I am telling this badly. I was trying to impress the Queen's Maid-of-Honour. She...never mind. I said something I shouldn't have said to the king and he sent me off to the Wild to *gain glory*." Gawin shook his head. "I have a great name as a bane of the Wild. You know why? Because after we killed you—well, we thought we did—I rode away to die in the Wild. Alone." He laughed. "A daemon attacked me, and I killed it." His laugh was a little wild. "Hand to hand. I lost my dagger in the fight, and I battered it to death, and so men call me Hard Hands."

"Pater must have been very proud," the captain muttered.

"Oh, he was," Gawin answered. "So proud he sent me to court so the king could send me away. I rode north to Lorica, and put up in an inn." He turned his head away. "I'm not sure I can tell this while I look at you. I took rooms. A foreign knight came with a retinue—I don't know how many, but it was a hundred knights, at least. Jean de Vrailly, God curse his name. He called me out into the courtyard, challenged me to combat, and attacked me." Gawin fell silent.

"So? You were always a better swordsman than I," the captain said.

Gawin shook his head. "No. No, you were the better swordsman. Ser Hywel told me after you died; you'd pretended to be inept."

The captain shrugged. "Fine. You were, and are, a fine man-at-arms."

"Ser Jean imagines himself to be the very best knight in all of the world," Gawin said.

"Really?" the captain said. "How very dangerous."

Gawin snorted. "You really haven't changed."

"I have, you know," the captain said.

"I never thought I'd be able to chuckle while I told this. He was in armour—I was not."

The captain nodded. "He would be, being a Galle. I was just fighting there. They take themselves very seriously."

"I only had a riding sword—by Saint George, I make too many excuses. I held him—took a wound, and he punched my sword into one of my squires. My own sword killed my sworn man." Now all the humour was gone, and Gawin was somewhere between toneless and sobbing. "I lost all sense of the fight, and he mastered me—pushed me down into the dirt. Made me admit myself bested."

How that must have tasted, the captain thought. Because he had imagined doing exactly that to this man a thousand times. He sat by the very man's bedside and tried to think what had changed in a few minutes, that now, it seemed impossible that he had imagined his half-brother's humiliation. Desired it. Tasted and savoured it, just two days ago.

"Then he went into the inn and killed my senior squire," Gawin said. He shrugged. "I have vowed to kill him."

The captain had a restless urge to go follow Amicia. He felt the need to extract a vow of silence. Or was that just an excuse? And the pain—raw, like a visible bruise—in Gawin's voice—he'd only just forced himself to decide in favour of the younger man, and now he was his confessor.

It was like being the captain.

"Your enemy is my enemy," he said simply, and leaned down, and put his arms around his brother's neck. Amongst the Muriens, a good expression of hate was a way of showing love. Sometimes, the only way.

"Oh, Gabriel!" Gawin said, and burst into tears.

"Gabriel died, Gawin," the captain said.

Gawin dried his eyes. "You have problems of your own, no doubt." He managed a smile.

"Where would you like me to begin?" the captain said. "I'm engaged in a siege with an enemy who can deploy any kind of creature, who outnumbers me ten or fifteen or twenty to one, and who is led by a ruthless genius."

Gawin managed another smile. "My brother is a ruthless genius."

The captain grinned.

Gawin nodded. "You're about to try something insane. I can taste it. Remember the chicken coup? Remember your alchemical *experiment*?"

The captain looked around, as if he feared an eavesdropper. "He's going to hit us hard, tonight. He has to. Up until now, to all intents and purposes, he's been losing the siege. The way the Wild works, eventually, some one of his own will see him as weak and take him down."

Gawin shrugged. "They're the enemy. Who knows what they think?"

The captain returned a grim smile. "I do. All too well."

"So?" Gawin asked, after a difficult moment. "Why do you know? What they think?"

The captain drew a long breath.

Why do you curse God every morning?

Because—

"Maybe sometime I'll tell you," the captain said.

Gawin absorbed that. "The man of secrets. Very well. What are you about to do?"

The captain shrugged. "I'm going to try for him. Try to drag him down. The old Magus is in on it."

Gawin sat up. "You're going for Tho—"

"Don't speak his name," the captain said. "Naming calls."

Gawin bit his lip. "I wish I were fit to ride."

"You will be, soon enough." The captain leaned forward and embraced his half-brother. "I'd rather be your friend than your foe. Foe was merely a habit."

Gawin patted the captain's back gently. "Gabriel! I'm sorry!"

The captain held the young knight until he slept. It didn't take long.

"I'm not Gabriel," he said to his sleeping half-brother. And then he went to find the woman. But he didn't have to go far. She was sitting on a chair in the corridor.

Their eyes met. Hers said, *Don't come too close—I'm vulnerable just now.*

He wasn't sure what his own said, but he stopped at arm's length. "You heard," he said, far more harshly than he intended.

"Everything," she said. "Don't offend me by requiring my silence. I hear the confessions of dying men. I care nothing for the secrets of the mighty."

In his head, he knew that her anger was a kind of armour to keep him farther away. But it hurt, anyway. "Sometimes, secrets are secret for a reason," he said.

"You curse God because your mother was unfaithful to your father and you grew to manhood with the torments of your brothers?" She spat. "I thought you were braver than that." She shrugged. "Or do you mean that you intend to sortie out into the night and die?"

He took a deep breath. Counted carefully to fifty in High Archaic, and let the breath go. "You have been in the Wild," he said softly.

She looked away. "Begone."

"Amicia—" He almost called her *Love*, and he stammered. "I have been in your palace. On your bridge. I'm not making judgment."

"I know, you idiot," she spat at him.

He was stunned by her venom. "I will protect you!" he said.

"I don't want your protection!" she said, the anger all but forming frost on her lips. "I am not a suffering princess in a tower! I am a woman of God, and my God is the only protection I require, and I do not know why my power does not come from the sun! I have enough weight of sin on my head without you adding to my burdens!" She got to her feet and gave him a sharp push. "I am an Outwaller chit, a slut, a woman lower than a serf. You, it turns out, are some lost prince. You can, I have no doubt, cozen any woman you like, looks, money and *power!*" She pushed him again. "I AM NOT FOR YOU."

He was not a blushing youth of sixteen. He caught her arm as she pushed him, and pulled. He thought she would fall into his arms.

She almost did. But she caught herself, and his kiss was deflected. His arms pinned her, and she said, with all the ice a woman can muster: "Shall I tell Sym you forced me? Captain?"

He let her go. Just in that moment, he hated her.

Just in that moment, the feeling was probably mutual.

She walked away to the main hospital room, and he had nowhere to which he could retreat except the dispensary behind him.

On the other hand, it was empty, and just then what he needed, perhaps more than ever before in his life, was to be alone.

He collapsed into the heavy wooden chair in the darkened room, and before he knew it, he was crying.

Lissen Carak—Sauce

Sauce had the duty. She was fresh enough to her promotion that she still enjoyed the responsibility—made a special effort to be clean, neat, her armour well-polished, her square-topped cap neat as a pin. She knew that a lot of the older men resented taking orders from a woman, and she knew that a perfect turn-out helped.

She set the guards on the main gate, and marched the duty detachment to the posterns, relieving each post in turn—challenge, password, posting by the numbers, and accepting the salutes—she loved the ceremony. And she loved to see the effect on the farmers and their families. Farmers clean and oil their tools, tour their livestock, morning and night. Farmers know a patient craftsman when they see one, even when the craft is war.

She relieved the last post and marched the off-going detachment through the courtyard to the base of the West Tower, where she dismissed them. Two slow-moving archers were detailed to wash the heavy wood piling driven into the ground for sword practice—Low Sym had been tied to it for his punishment, and it had various substances on it that needed cleaning off.

Then she climbed the steps to the tower, listening to the off-going soldiers. She was listening for criticism; she expected it. She wasn't really good enough to be a corporal. She wanted to be—but there was so much to learn.

And she knew that this was going to be a tough night. All across the garrison tower men were polishing, sharpening, trimming a belt end, checking the stuffing on a gambeson sleeve. A thousand rituals to conjure safety and luck in battle. And they were all tired.

At the head of the stairs stood Bad Tom, her nemesis, with his cronies. She straightened her back, noticed that even though he was supposedly off-duty he was still fully armed, wearing full harness but for the gauntlets and the bassinet, which sat together on the plank table. She noted that his armour was as carefully polished as her own.

He was talking to Bent, and they were smiling.

She met their looks and glared. "What?"

"Your people look good enough for the Royal Guard," Tom said with a rich chuckle.

"What the fuck does that mean?" she spat. She looked past him, over the walled balcony that let light and air into the tower from the courtyard. She could see the priest from here, climbing out on the wall. She wondered what he was doing there.

Bent slapped his thigh and roared. "Told you!" he shouted, and went back to his game, and she forgot Father Henry. "Can't even take a fucking compliment."

She glared at both of them and went to the roof to watch her posts. "Where are all the men-at-arms? Captain left a note—"

Tom nodded to her. "I've got it, Corporal. I'm preparing the sortie."

Sauce felt a keen disappointment edged with anger. "A sortie? But—"

"You have the duty," Tom said. "It's my turn."

"It's always your turn," she shot back.

He nodded, unrepentant. "I'm *primus pilus*, Sauce. I can take the sortie out until Christ returns to earth—maybe after. Wait your turn. Sweeting."

She drew herself up. But Bad Tom shook his head. "Nay—never mind me, Sauce. That was ill-said. But I want the sorties. The lads need to see me fight."

"And you love it," Sauce said. She put her nose very close to his. "I love it too, you bastard."

Tom laughed. "Point taken, *Corporal.*"

She backed off. "I want my turn. Anyway—where is everyone?"

"The boys are all off confessing to the priest. Don't worry, Sauce. We probably won't go. But there's going to be a sortie ready all night, every night, in the covered way."

Sauce shook her head and went up the steps to the roof-top feeling left out.

Full darkness had almost fallen, and the sounds made by the various species of besiegers would have been chilling if she'd let herself think of them that way, but she didn't. Instead she stood with the crew on the great ballista—as of today, re-mounted on a complex set of gimbals designed by the old Magus. She tried it herself. Now it moved like a living thing. No Head, the man responsible for the machine, patted it affectionately. "The old fuck magicked it, that's what he did. It's alive. Going to get us a wyvern, next time one comes."

She swung it back and forth. It was physically pleasant to move—like playing some sort of game.

"Sometimes a machine is just a machine," said a strong voice, and the old man himself emerged from the darkness. She had never been so close to a real magus, and she started.

"It's our good luck that we have fifty skilled craftsmen suddenly among us. A pargeter, who can draw precisely. Blade smiths who can make springs. A joiner who can do fine carpentry." He shrugged. "In truth, it is an Archaic mechanism I found in a book. It was the craftsmen who made it." Nonetheless, the old man seemed very satisfied with it, and he gave it an affectionate pat. "Although I confess I gave it a touch of spirit."

"Which he magicked it, and now it's alive!" said No Head happily. "Going to bag us a wyvern."

Harmodius shrugged as if mocking the ignorance of men—while accepting their plaudits.

His eyes lingered on her.

Christ—did the old Magus find her attractive? That was a chilling thought. She wriggled involuntarily.

He caught her movement and laughed. Then stopped laughing. "Something is moving down between the forts," he said.

She leaned over the tower. "Wait a little," she said. Then, "How did you know?"

His eyes glowed a little in the dark. "I know," he said. "I can make the sky bright for a moment."

"No need," she said.

Sure enough, there was a low clash, as if of cymbals, and then another.

"Captain put lines of tin bangles across the fields," she said as the ballista spun, No Head pulled its lever and a bolt crashed out into the darkness.

On the next tower, the onager released a bucket of gravel, and suddenly the night was full of screams.

A retaliatory bolt of purple-green lightning shot out of the darkness and struck the tower on which the onager rested. Sparks flew as if a smith was pounding red-hot metal.

"Christ, what *the* fuck was that?" Sauce asked the darkness. Her night-sight was ruined by the green bolt; all she could see was a pattern on her retinas.

Old Harmodius leaned over the tower, and a bolt of fire sprayed from his hand—it passed almost exactly down the line of the green lightning, as far as the dancing images on her retinas could discern.

"Damn, damn, damn," he said. Over and over.

His target caught fire in the distance—a giant of a man, or an oddly misshapen tree. Perhaps two trees.

"Dear God," Harmodius muttered. "Again!" he called.

No Head needed no urging. Sauce watched his crew as they danced through their drill—two men wound the winch, slipped the cocking mechanism into place, removed the winch again, a third carried the twenty-pound bolt as easily as if it was made of straw, dropped it into the charge-trough and pushed it back until the huge nock engaged the heavy string. No Head spun his machine with one hand, gave the burning tree-man a hint of windage, and pulled the release.

Another line of lightning, this one levin-bright—flashed onto the north tower and rock exploded. Men screamed. Her men.

She turned and ran for the stairs. And then paused. She couldn't be in both towers at the same time.

Behind her the two valets winding the bow sweated to do it as fast as they could, but No Head didn't look at them or at Simkin, a giant, who dropped the next bolt into the trough with perfect timing, so that just as the string clicked into place on the latch, the nock slid back and engaged the string, and No Head had the weapon aimed.

Harmodius grunted something, and cast fire on the earth. His fire was caught as if by a basket of green light, and cast straight back at them; quicker than thought, his own basket of blue lightning caught it and he threw it back—

No Head pulled the release.

The bolt hit the man-tree squarely in the torso-trunk. There was a roar and a burst of ball lightning like a summer night, and the tower trembled. The ball struck the curtain wall over the main gate and there was a cataclysmic explosion—like pouring water on a hot rock, expanded a thousand times. The curtain wall groaned, buckled and collapsed outward, and the new covered way behind the gate started to take hits.

Someone was alert and still moving on the onager tower, though, because a basket of red-hot gravel—another of the Magus's innovations—flew from the onager, the pebbles flashing through the air like meteorites.

All the lights went out together, and then there was quiet, punctuated by screams from the plain far below. And moans.

"Again!" Harmodius called. "Same target. Hit him again! Before he can—"

And then there was a wall of green light across the sky, and the onager tower exploded in sparks and a shower of stars. One long scream rang out across the night—and then the top of the tower leaned out, and out, and fell into the night, taking the onager and four men of the company with it. It crashed to the floor of the valley four hundred feet below, a long rumble like an avalanche.

And then there was only silence.

Sauce had made it to the courtyard when the green fire hit, and she was standing close enough to the gate to be hit by stone chips from the curtain wall. A stone slammed into her shoulder from the broken tower. Up on the main donjon, she could see Harmodius as he leaned out over the wall, with eldritch blue fire coursing over his hands.

The gate had taken a glancing hit and whole chunks of the crenellations had fallen on the covered way, crushing part of the roof. Inside, men and horses of Bad Tom's sortie were trapped in the pitch black, and there were horse screams of anguish and human shouts.

"Get torches! Lanterns! On me!" Sauce shouted.

Just under the back end of the covered way, Ser John Poultney was lying under the ruin of his charger, and his leg was broken. Sauce went with a pair of archers—One Lug and Skinch—to get the horse off him. The archers used spears to raise the carcass and Ser John worked not to scream.

The roof of the covered way had taken most of the gate's collapse, and it hung askew, and the beams were creaking ominously. It was pitch black under the roof, and men with lanterns appeared at last as the first man-at-arms emerged leading a bucking war horse whose off left foot almost killed the just-rescued Ser John. The horse was wild, and more archers grabbed for his reins to hold his head, and then off-duty valets were pouring out of the main tower.

"Where's Tom?" she asked. She plunged deeper into the gloom, and Skinch, usually not a man with any balls whatsoever, followed her. The lantern lit a dozen horsemen fighting their mounts for control in the enclosed space. All of them were dismounted, hauling at their horse's heads, and the horses would calm for a moment and then go off again as another horse continued to panic in the darkness and the noise. Ser John's dead horse was not helping—it smelled of blood and fear...

"Get them out!" Tom roared.

Hooves were flying. The men were in full armour, but the horses were not calming, and soon enough they'd kill their riders, armour or no.

With a *whoosh* the gate behind Tom exploded in flame. It illuminated the narrow space and the plunging horses, the men's armour, like a foretaste of hell.

Almost as one, the horses turned and ran from the fire. Most of the men-at-arms were knocked from their feet.

Skinch flattened himself against the wooden wall and Sauce, still in her harness, tried to cover him as the great brutes pounded past, leaping the corpse of the dead horse.

Out in the courtyard the valets were ready, and they lunged for reins, threw sacks over the horses' heads and spoke to them calmly and authoritatively, like lords speaking to their serfs. They took control of the horses quickly, kindly, and ruthlessly.

The men-at-arms began to get to their feet.

Sauce realised that the fire at the gate wasn't generating any heat about the same moment that the captain stepped out of the darkness and raised his hands.

The flames went out like a candle in the wind.

"Tom? Let's get a head count. Anyone missing?" he shouted, walking past her. It was dark again, but he seemed to know she was there—he turned unerringly to her. "We lost a dozen men in the Onager tower. Go and see if anyone can be saved."

His eyes glowed in the dark.

"M'lord," she nodded in the pitch black and went back into the relative light of the courtyard, past a dozen angry war horses and the men trying to calm them. Farmers and their wives and daughters were crowding the door yards and windows.

The onager tower looked like a broken tooth. About a third of the upper floor was gone, and Sauce thought the only blessing was that it had fallen out—away from the courtyard—and not in.

The second floor roof had collapsed inward though, showering stones and roof beams on sleeping soldiers. Geslin—the youngest archer in the company—lay dead, crushed under a beam, his broken body horrible in the flickering fire of the fallen floor. Dook—a useless sod at the best of time—was trying to get the beam off him, and was crying.

Sauce put on her best command voice, walled off her panic, and shouted, "I need some help up here!"

Archers poured up the ladders to her. Men she knew—Flarch, her own archer, and Cuddy, perhaps the best archer in the company, and Rust, perhaps the worst; Long Paw, moving like a dancer, and Duggin, who was as big as a house. They got the beam up off the dead boy, and discovered Kanny pinned under it, unconscious and with a lot of blood under him. And behind him, wedged into a safe space made by a window ledge, was Kessin, the fattest man in the company.

More and more men came—the Lanthorn men, the Carters from the courtyard, and the other farmers—at unbelievable speed they cleared the heavy timbers and the floor. One of Master Random's men, who had been working with the Magus, rigged a sling mechanism, and before the sun began to rise, the heavy stones that could be saved from the wreckage were being raised over the lip of the ruined tower and laid in the courtyard.

The captain stood there looking tired, hands on hips above his golden belt, watching the work. He didn't turn his head. "Well done, Sauce. Go to bed."

She shrugged. "Lots left to do," she said wearily.

He turned to her with a smile. Very quietly, like a lover, he leaned in to her ear. "This is the first bad night of a hundred to come," he whispered. "Save your strength. Go to bed."

She sighed and looked at him, struggling to hide her adoration. "I can do it," she said fiercely.

"I know you can do it," he said, rolling his eyes. "Save it for when we need it. I'm going to bed. You go to bed. Yes?"

She shrugged, avoiding his eyes. Walked away...

...and realised that her bed had been in the onager tower. She sighed.

Lissen Carak—Michael

The Siege of Lissen Carak. Day Eight

Last night the Fallen Magus attacked us in person. The captain said his powers are greater even than those that weave the walls together, and despite our efforts he toppled the south-west tower, where the onager engine was, and killed four men and several boys.

No Head, an archer, hit the Fallen Magus with a ballista bolt. Many men saw the bolt go home.

We now have the help of Lord Harmodius, the King's Magus, who duelled with the Fallen Magus with fire. Men hid their heads in terror. The Fallen Magus brought down the curtain wall by the postern gate, but Sauce saved many men and horses with her quick response.

Under the manuscript page, *No Head* and *Sauce* were crossed out. In their place were the names *Thomas Harding* and *Alison Grave*.

Lissen Carak—The Red Knight

In the end, they lost six archers and one man-at-arms. It was a hard blow. The captain looked at their names, crossed them off the list, and grunted.

On the other hand, he had the Carter boys, the Lanthorn boys, and Daniel Favor. And a likely goldsmith's apprentice named Adrian who was a painter and a lanky youngster called Allan.

He handed the list to Tom. "Fix the watchbill. Messire Thomas Durrem—"

"Dead as a nail," Tom said. He shrugged. "Gone with the tower. Didn't even find his body."

The captain winced. "We're down another lance, then."

Tom nodded, and chewed on a lead. "I'll find you a man-at-arms," he said.

The Bridge Castle—Ser Milus

Ser Milus stood with the seven new men-at-arms. They were, in his professional opinion, good men who needed a swift kick in the arse.

He had a pell in the courtyard; Master Random's apprentices had levered a huge stone out of the flagging, dug a hole as deep as a man's was tall, and put in a post—it was handy to have so many willing hands.

He walked around the pell, hefting his own favoured weapon. The pole-axe. The hammer head was crenellated like a castle with four miniature spikes projecting from it. On the other side, a long, slightly curved spike protruded, and from the top, a small, wickedly sharp spearhead. A foot of solid steel extended from the butt, pointed like a chisel.

Ser Milus spun it between his hands. "I don't expect we'll fight mounted, from here on out," he said conversationally.

Gwillam, the sergeant, nodded.

"Let's see you, then," Ser Milus said. He nodded to Gwillam, who stepped forward. By the Company's standard, his armour was poor. He had an old cote of plates, mail chausses, and a shirt of good mail with heavy leather gauntlets covered in iron plates. It was, to Ser Milus's eyes, very old-fashioned.

Gwillam had a heavy spear. He stepped up to the pell, chose his distance, and thrust. The spearhead went an inch into the oak. He shrugged, and tugged it clear with a heavy pull.

Dirk Throatlash, the next of the convoy's men-at-arms, strode up and took a negligent swipe at it with his heavy double-bladed axe. He embedded his axe head deeply in the post.

Archers were gathering in the towers, and merchants had emerged to watch from their wagons.

John Lee, former shipman, also had a double-bitted axe. He swung hard and precisely—matching Dirk's cut and carving a heavy chip out of the post.

Ser Milus watched them all.

"That's what you do at the pell?" he asked Gwillam.

The sergeant shrugged. "I haven't done much at a pell since I was a boy," he admitted.

Ser Milus nodded. "Want to kill a monster?" he said to the men. "Or a man?" he asked.

"Not really," Dirk said. His mates laughed.

Ser Milus didn't even turn his head. There was no warning. One moment, he was leaning on his war-hammer, and the next, he had tossed Dirk Throatlash into the mud, face first, and still had one arm behind his back.

"Wrong," he said.

"Jesus *Christ*!" Dirk wailed.

Ser Milus let him up. He smiled, because now he had their attention.

"We're all going to practise at the pell, every day we don't fight on the wall," he said, conversationally. "Like it was real. I'll teach you how. And if you can cut through it—good!" He grinned. "And then you can demonstrate your zeal by helping put in the next pell." He pointed to John Lee. "You have an accurate cut."

Lee shrugged. "I cut a lot of wood."

"Try again. But this time, cut as if you were fighting a man." Ser Milus waved at the pell.

The shipman stepped up and lifted his axe, like a man preparing to hit a ball.

Ser Milus nodded approvingly. "Good guard."

The former shipman cut at the pell, and a chip of wood flew. He got the axe back to his shoulder and cut again.

Ser Milus let him go on for ten cuts. He was breathing hard, and his tenth cut wasn't nearly as strong as the ninth.

Milus twirled his grey moustache with his left hand. "Leave off. Breathe." He nodded. "Watch."

He stepped up to the pell, his pole-axe held under hand.

He cut up with the back-spike, and it just touched the post. He danced to the right on his toes, despite his armour, and his cut finished with the pole-axe head behind his shoulder—a very similar position to that of the shipman's axe. Then he cut down, again stepping lightly, and the hammer-head slammed into the post, leaving four deep gouges. The knight stepped like a cat, back and then forward, powering the spearhead in an underhanded thrust—stepped wide, as if avoiding a blow, and reversed the pole-axe. The spike slammed sideways into the post, bounced, and Ser Milus was close into the pole and shortened his grip for another strike.

Lee nodded. "I could almost see the man you was fighting," he admitted.

Gwillam prided himself as a good man of arms, and he sprang forward. "Let me try," he said. His own weapon was a heavy spear with a head as long as his arm and as wide as the palm of his hand. He sprang forward on the balls of his feet, cut the pell—twice from one side, once from the other, and backed away.

"But use your hips," Ser Milus said. "More power in your hips than in your arms. Save your arms; they get tired the fastest." He nodded to them. "It's just work, friends. The smith practises his art every day—the pargeter daubs, the farmer ploughs, the shipman works his ship. Bad soldiers lie on their backs. Good soldiers do this. All day, every day."

Throatlash shook his head. "My arms are tired already," he said.

Ser Milus nodded. "The irks ain't tired."

Southford by Albinkirk—Prior Ser Mark Wishart

The king sent two messengers with the knights when the Prior took his men north-west from Albinkirk's souther suburb, Southford. The Prior moved his men carefully over the ground, their black surcotes somehow blending into the undergrowth. His men rode easily through the densest stands of woods, through thickets of spring briars.

They halted frequently. Men would dismount and creep forward, usually over the brow of a steep hill, and wave them forward.

Despite the halts, they made good progress. Individual knights would ride away—sometimes at right angles to the line of march—and unerringly find them again.

The thing the two king's messengers found hardest to understand was the silence. The Knights of St. Thomas never spoke. They rode in silence, and their horses were equally silent. They had no pages, no valets, no servants and no squires. Forty spare horses—a fortune in war horses—followed the main body, packed with forage bags and spares, but otherwise without bridle or lead. Yet the spares followed briskly enough.

It was, as the older messenger said, uncanny.

Still, it was a bold thing, to be riding through the North Country with the Knights of St. Thomas. Galahad Acon had been named for the saint's church in London, and felt he was almost one of them. His partner, Diccon Alweather, had been a professional messenger in the old king's day, a weathered man with more scars than a badly tanned hide, as he liked to say himself.

The messengers were used to a hard day riding and no company but their horses, but it was a hard day, even for them—fifteen leagues over broken country that challenged their horsemanship every hour. The knights didn't seem to tire. Many of them were older than Alweather.

Towards evening, one of the youngest of the knights rode back to the main body, and led them off to the right, north, and then up to a steep hill.

Without a word, every knight dismounted. They drew their long swords from their saddle scabbards, split into four groups of fifteen, and walked off.

The Prior waited a moment, looking at the two messengers. "Wait here," he said, aloud. The first words Galahad had heard from any of them since they left the Royal Camp.

The black-clad knights vanished into the woods.

An hour passed. It was cold—the spring evenings were longer, but not much warmer, and Galahad couldn't decide whether he was cold enough to take his great cloak out of the bundle behind his crupper or not. He didn't want to be caught dismounted at the wrong moment. He cursed the Prior and his silence.

He kept looking at the older messenger, Alweather, who waited, apparently calm, without fidgeting, for the whole hour.

"Here they come," Galahad said suddenly.

The Prior walked up to his horse and sheathed his sword on the saddle. "Come," he said. He was smiling.

He walked off up the steep hill, and all the horses followed him.

"Uncanny," Alweather said. He spat, and made an avert sign.

They wound around the hill, widdershins, climbing as they went around. It seemed a tedious way of getting to the top, but in the very last light, Galahad could see that the crown of the hill was steep and girt in rock.

The horse ahead of him shied, and then was quiet. Galahad looked down and saw a corpse. And then another. And another and another.

They were not human. He wasn't sure what they were—small and brown, with big heads, and cords of muscle, beautifully worked leather clothes and huge wounds made by two-handed swords.

"Good Christ," Alweather said aloud.

There was the smell of fire, and then they came over a crest.

The top of the hill was hollow. It was like a giant cup, and the knights had three fires going, and food cooking. Galahad Acon's stomach, outraged by the inhuman corpses and their red-green blood, now seized on the smell of food. Pea soup.

"Unsaddle your horse, and curry him," the Prior said. "After that, he'll see to himself."

Alweather frowned, but Galahad refused to be moved by the older man's caution. Galahad was suffused with joy. He was living one of his secret dreams.

Alweather, clearly wanted to go back to the king.

"They fought a battle," Galahad said, his eyes sparkling in the firelight. "And we didn't *even hear them.*"

The Prior smiled at Galahad. "Not really a battle," he said. "More of a massacre. The irks didn't see us coming." He shrugged. "Have some soup. Tomorrow will be harder."

Lissen Carak

It was a quiet night. The besieged collapsed into sleep. Sauce cried out in her dreams, and Tom lay and snored like a hog. Michael muttered into his outstretched arm, sleeping alone. The Abbess wept softly in the dark, and rose to kneel, praying at the triptych that sat on a low podium in the corner of her cell. Sister Miram lay on her stomach to sleep, exhausted from healing so many wounded men. Low Sym woke himself up repeatedly as he shouted, and then lay with his own arms wrapped around him staring at horrors in the dark until the pretty novice came and sat with him.

But however long and dark the night was, the enemy was quiet, and the besieged slept.

In the first light of morning, they struck.

The Siege of Lissen Carak. Day Nine

Today, the enemy burned all the country around the fortress, as far as the woods. The men—the traitor Jacks—burned all the farms, all the steadings and barns—even the patches of woods.

The farmers stood on the walls and watched. Some wept. We were cursed for being poor soldiers, for allowing the fields to be burned.

The Abbess came out and watched, and then promised that it would all be rebuilt.

But many hearts turned. And before noon, the creatures of the enemy were in the air over the fortress, and we could feel them again.

Lissen Carak—Mag the Seamstress

It was a simple, unstoppable act that changed the nature of the siege, and that cut at the farmers and the simple people of the fortress more effectively than all the military victories that could be scored.

The first fires were visible to the north-east. Hawkshead, the furthest east of the fortress's communities was put to the torch before morning creased the sky, and the last watch saw the town burn, just two leagues from the walls.

Just as the sun began to cast forth a ruddy light, Kentmere went up to the west. By then, the walls of the fortress were lined in farm folk. Then Abbington.

Mag watched her town burn. From this high, she could count roofs and she knew when her own cottage burned. She watched it with a desperate anger until she could no longer see which house was hers. They were all afire—every cottage, every house, every stone barn, every chicken coop. The fields around the fortress ridge were suddenly full of the enemy—all the creatures who hadn't shown themselves in the first days. There were boglins, and irks; daemons and trolls, great things like giants with smooth heads and tusks which the soldiers told her were behemoths. And, of course, men.

How she hated the men.

The enemy was now girdling every tree. Orchards of apple trees and pears, of peaches and persimmons, were being destroyed. Vines that had grown for generations were gone in an hour, their roots destroyed or seared by fire, and every structure was burning. As far as the eye could see, in every direction, there was a sea of fire and Lissen Carak a dark island in it.

Mag couldn't take her eyes away from the death of her world.

"Sausage without mustard, eh?" said a heavy voice at her elbow.

She started, turned to find the giant black-headed hillman, the company's savage, sitting on the other barrel beside her, watching over the wall.

"War without fire is like sausage without mustard," he said.

She found herself angry at him. "That's—my village. My *house*!"

The big man nodded. He seemed not to know she was crying. "Stands to reason. I'd hae' done the same, in his place."

She turned on him. "War! In his place? This isn't a game! We *live* here! This is *our land*. We farm here. We bury our dead here. My husband lies out there—my daughter—" The tears became too much for her, but in that moment, she hated him more than she hated the boglins and their horrible faces and their willingness to burn her life away.

Tom looked hard at her. "Not yours unless you can hold it," he said. "Way I hear it, your people took it from them. Eh? Melike, their dead are buried there too. And right now, I'd say it was theirs. I'm sorry, goodwife, but war is my business. And war involves a lot of fire. He's showing us that we only hold what we stand on—that he can win without taking the fortress. We hurt him last night and now he strikes back. That's war. If you don't want to have your farm burned, you had better be strong—stronger than you were."

She struck him, then—a glancing blow, pure anger without force.

He let her do it.

"Not many folk can say they've struck Bad Tom and lived to tell the tale," he said. He flashed a crooked smile in the early morning light, and she turned and fled.

Lissen Carak—Thorn

Thorn watched the farms burn with no great satisfaction. It was a cheap victory, but it would help break the will of the farmers to resist him.

He shrugged inwardly. Or it would harden their resolve to fight to the end. Now they had nothing to save but themselves, and even when he'd been a man, he'd had trouble understanding men. And, increasingly, he felt this contest was too complex for even his intellect. He had made himself the Captain of the Wild, and yet his own interests were scarcely engaged, here. He was far more interested in the puzzle that was the dark sun, and in *her*, then he was in the prosecution of the siege.

He wondered, not for the first time, what he was doing here, and how he'd ended up so committed to this action that he was willing to risk himself in combat. Last night he'd taken his invincible new form out onto the field, and the fortress had hurt him. None of the blows he had taken were deadly, but he felt the pain of his exertions and their blows. The pain had angered him, and in anger he had unleashed some of his carefully hoarded power—enough to damage the fabric of the fortress. It had impressed his allies, but the cost—

Again, he rustled his leaves in what would have been a shrug, in a man.

Last night, he had felt the breath of mortality for the first time in twenty years. He didn't like the smell of it. Or the pain.

But as the siege continued it was becoming a rallying point for the Wild in the North Country, and despite minor set-backs, more and more creatures were coming in. His prestige was increasing, and that prestige would directly affect a rise in his power.

None of which would matter if he were dead.

He thought of *her*.

He could no longer shake his head—it was now a continuous armoured growth from his neck, and he had to pivot around the waist to look to the left and right. But he made an odd clucking sound as he considered her. She had attempted to hurt him directly, last night.

And finally, he considered the third presence in the fortress besides the dark sun. Power—cold, blue power—had struck him. Pure power, untrammelled by doubt or youth. Trained and honed, like fine steel.

It was his apprentice, of course. Had Thorn been able to smile, he would have.

Harmodius.

There was a solvable problem.

Lissen Carak—Amicia

Amicia stood on the wall watching the world burn. She didn't notice him until he was at her shoulder.

"It was a matter of time," he said, as if they had been in conversation all morning.

She wasn't sure, in truth, if she wanted to say anything. She didn't want to look at him—didn't want him to see how committed she was, or how angry.

"He has to show his allies that he is making progress." The captain leaned on the crenellation and pointed to the western edge of the woods. "His men are building a pair of trebuchets. Before the end of the day, we'll be feeling their power. Not because it will actually help him win, but because it will make his allies see him as—"

If she kept listening to him she would...

She turned on her heel and walked away.

He hurried to catch up to her.

413

"People are watching," she hissed. "I am a novice in this convent. I am *not* your lover. Let me go, please."

"Why?" he asked. He seized her arm in a steel grip. He was hurting her.

"Let me go," she said. "Or you are no knight."

"Then I am no knight. Why? Why change your mind so suddenly?" He leaned towards her. "I have not changed mine."

She hadn't meant to have a conversation. She bit her lip, and looked around for a miracle. Sister Miram. The Abbess. "Don't you have to do something? Save somebody? Give orders?" she asked. "Why not go and save the farms?"

"That's unfair!" he said, and let go of her arm. "No one is watching us. I would know." He shrugged. "I cannot save the farms. And I'd rather be here, with you."

"You want me to have that on my soul, as well? That in addition to breaking my vows, I am endangering the fortress?"

He smiled his wicked smile. "It's worked on other girls," he said.

"I imagine it works all the time." She put her chin as high as she could manage. "I do not choose to be your whore, Captain. I don't even know your name. Girls like me don't get to know the names of the great lords who try to put their knees between our legs, do we? But I am choosing to say no. You are not afraid of Jesus, and you are not afraid of the Abbess. So I cannot appeal to you along those lines. But by God, messire, I can protect myself. If you lay a hand on me again, I will hit you hard."

He looked at her.

He had tears in his eyes, and she hesitated. But she'd made her decision, and she carried it through. She walked away, and didn't look back.

It was difficult for her to decide *why* she was so angry. It was difficult for her to say—even to herself—*why* she was choosing to walk away. But he was not for her, despite the feeling that her very soul was screaming as she walked down the steps.

Despite the look, like agony, on his face.

Lissen Carak—Harmodius

Harmodius

He couldn't shut it out. Once two entities of power are linked, the link is forever. He couldn't shut Thorn out, but he could wall him off.

Harmodius

That is, he could mostly wall him off.

Harmodius was sitting cross-legged under an ancient apple tree that stood alone on the battlements, in a stone circle. It was a beautiful thing, in full flower, and it was redolent with power. The seat under it was placed to absorb the power that flowed, as if from a well or a spring, around the place. Somewhere just under his feet, was the well spring. It appeared neither green nor golden. It merely *was*.

Harmodius drank as deeply as he dared.

Harmodius

Would it really hurt to talk to his former master?

It was dangerous. If he opened the link, Thorn might try to overwhelm him with raw power.

But sitting here, on the bench by the apple tree, he didn't think Thorn could take him before he could close the link. He wasn't like the boy. The boy—

To hell with it.

Hello Richard.

I knew you would respond.

It must be satisfying to be right all the time.

Don't be snide, Harmodius. You hurt me, last night. You have grown very powerful.

I killed your mortal body at Chevin, old man.

Yes. But I knew how to deal with that. And I out-subtled myself, of course. There was a suggestion of smugness. *How was my world of mirrors, boy?*

Harmodius thought for a moment. *Very subtle, you bastard. How did you bind the spirits to the cats?*

So nice to discourse with someone intelligent. You learned to leave your body then? Ahh! I see you have not. Interesting.

Harmodius didn't think he could damage his cause by honesty. No more than by having any contact with Thorn. *Why are you fighting here?* he asked. *Must it be war?*

Harmodius! How unlike you! You wish to negotiate with the power of evil? I thought that you had chosen a different path.

I have come to realise that there is nothing intrinsically evil about the Wild. Or good about the Sun.

Ahh. Thorn gave a suggestion of great pleasure. *You have learned much, then.*

I am still struggling with the concept Harmodius admitted.

The Wild is far more powerful. Men are doomed. They have no role to play in the future. Too fragmented. Too weak.

That's not how I see it Harmodius shot back. *From where I sit, it is the Wild who is losing.*

You delude yourself.

Not as effectively as you deluded me.

Let me make it up to you with knowledge. Look. This is how you can possess anybody you choose. And here—this is how to build your own body. See? I give you this knowledge freely. Come. Be a god. You are worthy. And I'm bored—

Harmodius laughed aloud. *Bored of monsters and pining for decent company? You betrayed your king and all of humanity, you piece of shit. As* swiftly as he could, with all the borrowed power of the well, he slammed the link closed.

He sat back against the bole of the tree and examined the conversation. "I think that went well," he said aloud.

But Thorn had planted something in him, a seed in damp soil. It was like finding a beautifully wrapped package on your doorstep.

He put the packages in a room in his memory palace, and he carefully walled that room off from his consciousness. He twinned off a second self to remain in the room.

The second self opened the first package. A third self stood ready with an axe.

The phantasm was heartbreakingly beautiful. Thorn had been a great magus, of course.

Harmodius allowed his second self to subsume himself in the complexities of the working.

He shut down the room, withdrew his second self, and sat in another created room in his memory palace, a comfortable room with a circle of armchairs. His second self sat in another, wrote the phantasms out in longhand, and they discussed them in detail. His third self stood behind the second with an axe.

Suddenly he understood how the cats had been used.

He understood how his former master was using animals to watch the fortress.

He understood how he could possess the body of any creature he wanted, unless they had the power to resist him. How he could subsume their essence—in effect, eat that part of a mortal that Harmodius thought of as the soul.

For power.

And take the mortal body for his own, or make one.

Harmodius let the knowledge roll around inside his head for a little.

And found himself watching a mongrel dog—one of the mercenaries had brought the animal into Lissen Carak—rooting in the midden heap that was beginning to fill the courtyard. Eventually, the dog would be eaten, if the siege went on.

I could just try it on the dog.

The dog is going to die, anyway.

The dog turned and looked at Harmodius. She tilted her head to one side, watching to see if the man had anything interesting to offer.

Power poured out around him. *No wonder the creatures of the Wild want this place back*, Harmodius thought. He reached out to the power, took a taste, and ran it through the phantasm—

And made a motion of negation with his hands, cancelling the working and draining the power into the walls of the fortress.

He got to his feet and grinned at the dog. "You've got to draw the line somewhere," he said aloud.

He did that on purpose, the subtle bastard. He's inviting me to fall.

Harmodius could smell breakfast, and he decided he needed to be with people.

East of Albinkirk– Ranald

Ranald was tired, and he wept a great deal. He wasted an afternoon trying to catch a horse. At every step, he expected to find the drag, the rear guard, or another survivor. But he saw no one.

He wasted more time at the edge of the battlefield, trying to find his pack.

Eventually he gave up and walked, wet when it rained, scorched when the sun shone. He had nothing to cook with, nothing to eat, and no means of acquiring food.

On the evening of the fourth day after the fight, he walked up the lane to the great Inn. Men shouted when they saw him.

Every man and woman in the dale came running, when they knew whom he was. And because he was his cousin's tanist, they thought, at first, that his appearance must bode well.

But when they came closer, they saw the tracks of his tears, and the sword. And they knew.

By the time he walked the last few paces to the porch of the great Inn, the Keeper alone barred his way, and he was grim-faced. "Greetings, Ranald Lachlan," he said. "Tell me how many were lost?"

Ranald had no trouble meeting the Keeper's eye. Death made you less careful of such things.

"They're all dead," he said. "Every man of us. I, too, was dead."

They gasped, the folk of the Dale, and then the tears began, and the wail of loss, the roar of rage.

Ranald Lachlan told his story quickly, and without embellishment. And then he turned to the weeping woman who stood by her father. "Here's his sword," Ranald said. "If you bear him a son, he says the boy is to avenge him."

"That's a heavy load to lay on an unborn bairn's shoulders," the Keeper said.

Ranald shrugged. "It's not my choice," he said wearily.

Later, he sat in the Keeper's own rooms, and told the story of the last fight. Hector's wife listened through her tears. And when he was done, she looked at him long, and mean.

"Why'd they send you back, then?" she spat. "When they might have sent my love?"

Ranald shrugged.

The Keeper shook his head. "Too many men lost, along with the whole herd." He put his chin in his hand. "I'll be hard pressed if they turn on the Dale."

Ranald didn't even pretend to be interested. And the Keeper let him go.

He was not interested when the men in the Inn offered him ale.

He wasn't interested when the woman of the Inn offered themselves, nor when a travelling player offered to make a song of the battle.

He slept, and the next day he was just as numb as he had been the day before, and the day before that. But he went down from his room to the common room at dawn, and there he faced the Keeper and asked for a horse and gear.

"You can't mean to go fight the Outwallers all by yourself," the Keeper said, gruffly.

"No," Ranald said.

"You mean to just ride home?" the Keeper asked, incredulous.

"I'm a drover," Ranald said. "I have no home."

The Keeper drank some small beer and wiped his moustache. "Where, then?" he asked.

Ranald sat back. "I'm going to find the Wyrm of Erch," he said. "I mean to ask why he allowed us to be attacked by the Wild." The drover shrugged. "We pay a tithe to the Wyrm in exchange for protection from the Wild. It's the Law of Erch. Eh? Ancient as the oaks and all."

The Keeper put his beer down slowly. "You mean to *speak* to the Wyrm?"

"Someone has to," Ranald said. "I might as well; I'm already dead."

The Keeper shook his head. "I have just a dozen horses left. Your cousin took my herd."

Ranald nodded. "I mean to remedy that first, before I go to the Wyrm. Give me twenty men and I'll bring in the herd. There's a lot of it left. A thousand head at least."

"You are like your cousin," the Keeper said. "Always a sting in the tail."

Ranald shrugged. "I wouldn't bother, but Sarah's boy will need those beasts, if he means to be a drover." He didn't say the other thing that was on his mind. That he was a King's Man, and he owed the king a warning of the Wild.

That afternoon, with twenty wary men, he rode south.

They rode quickly, spread in pairs over a mile of ground, scouting every hummock and every stand of trees.

They made a cold camp and Ranald ate the oatcakes that Sarah had given him, and when the sun was a red disc on the edge of the world they rode on.

By noon they found the first beasts. The Dalemen were spooked, terrified of the Sossag, and afraid, too, to find corpses grinning at death in the woods, but they were still, by Ranald's reckoning, miles north of the battleground. The herd had turned and headed home, as animals will do.

Ranald swept south along the road, and before darkness he found the boy that Hector had sent back as a messenger. He was dead, and he'd either been lost or he'd ridden a long way west to get around something. He lay on his face, a cloud of flies around his bloated corpse, and his horse was still standing nearby. The boy had four arrows in him, and it was clear he'd died trying to fulfil his mission. The Dalemen buried him with love and honour and his cousins, two tall, grey-eyed boys, wept for him.

But the next day held the greatest shock.

They were well west of the fight, collecting animals hard against the great Swamp, and Ranald scented a fire and went to scout it himself. It was a foolish risk to take, but he couldn't bear to be the cause of any more Dalemen's deaths.

What he found was the drag—twenty of Hector's men, alive, with a third of the herd. Donald Redmane had led them west, and they had fought three times against scattered Outwaller bands, but they had lived and kept a great deal of the herd together.

Ranald had to tell the story all over again, and Donald Redmane wept. But the rest of the men in the drag swore a great oath to avenge Hector Lachlan.

Donald took Ranald aside. "You fought in the south," he said. "You think Tom is still alive?"

"Hector's brother Tom?" Ranald said. "Aye. Unless the red hand of war has taken him, he'll be alive. On the Continent or in the East, I reckon. Why?"

Donald Redmane's eyes were red. "Because he's the Drover, now," the older man said.

"He won't want it," Ranald said.

"He will if it means he can make war," Donald pointed out.

The next morning, scouts killed a strange creature—shaped like a man, short like a tall child, with heavily muscled arms and legs like thick ropes and a misshapen head like a man's but heavier. Ranald had to assume the beast was an irk, a creature somewhere between myth and reality to the men of the hills. Legend said irks, like boglins, came from the deep woods far to the west.

Ranald made camp with the whole band—forty-four men. They had more than twelve hundred head of cattle, and all of the goats. Seventy-five head of horses. Sarah Lachlan would not be a pauper, and the clan was not dead.

Hector Lachlan was gone.

But Lachlan was for Aa.

The Queen watched the banks go by and she smiled at a young guildsman with a crossbow who crouched behind the boat's high sides, watching the banks. In truth, he wasn't really watching them. He was of an age where he was conscious of nothing but Desiderata a few feet away. His eyes flicked to her over and over.

She watched the banks and smiled inwardly. The rowers chanted, on and on, and the mosquitoes descended on them in swarms unless a breeze rose upriver.

Lady Almspend lay next to her in the bow, a wax tablet open across her lap and a stylus ready to hand. "Another letter?" she asked somewhat languorously.

The Queen shook her head. "It's too hot."

"Pity the poor rowers," Lady Almspend answered. She turned her head. Most of them rowed naked to the waist—a few more naked even then that. Their work left them, to a man, with magnificent physiques, and Lady Almspend considered them carefully. "They are like the Archaics," she said. "I withdraw my former statement. I don't think they are to be pitied, but rather admired." She smiled at one in particular, and he smiled back even as he brought his sixteen-foot oar through the end of its sweep and brought it back to the top of its arc.

The Queen smiled. "Do have a care, my dear," she said.

"I will only admire from afar," Lady Almspend said. "Do you think the sentries really saw a boglin in the night?"

The Queen nodded. "Indeed, I'm quite sure of it." She was not going to enlighten her secretary any further, but the banks were already dangerous, and the boats were now using islands in the river for camps.

"Could we not arm the rowers?" Lady Almspend asked.

"They have weapons; javelins and swords," the Queen answered. "But against a sudden onslaught in the dark, we're safest behind a wall of water."

Lady Almspend shook her head. "I cannot imagine what has happened, for the North to be so utterly over run. The king must have his work cut out for him. When will we be at Albinkirk?"

"Tomorrow mid-day, at this pace," said Almspend. "If the Queen could wear even less, the rowers might row even harder."

Desiderata grinned at her friend. "I aim to row through the night," she said. "The river remains broad, and we are late."

Lady Mary looked at her oddly. "Have you had a message?" she asked.

The Queen shook her head. "I have a feeling," she admitted, "nothing more. If the king has made any pace at all, he'll already be gone west, towards Lissen Carak." The Queen lay back, feeling the summer sun on her shoulders. The bugs never troubled her. "Send a message to the king,

Becca. Tell him how close we are," She batted her eyelashes at the rowers closest to her. "Tell him we can be with him in three days."

Royer Le Hardi volunteered, and they put him ashore with his horse and a spare. He received a kiss from the Queen, and he was still red as a beet when he rode west.

Albinkirk—Gaston

Gaston watched the Royal Army break camp and turn west with something very like trepidation. None of the military orders knights had returned, despite Lissen Carak being only two days' march west of Albinkirk. Each night, light rippled in the western sky.

Whatever they were fighting was utterly alien. The boglins had startled him at Albinkirk—even a few of them, they were so ugly and so very *wrong*. He wanted to call them *unnatural*, except that they were spawned by the Wild.

His cousin was ecstatic—the flashes of light in the west guaranteed that the castle there still held, and that meant that battle was at last imminent. For Jean de Vrailly, that battle had become the guiding force—the lodestone on which his life turned.

Gaston inspected his company and reminded them, for the tenth day in a row, of the lessons they'd learned from the Count of the Borders. To always have scouts—front, flanks, and rear. To ride with the knights inside a strong box of spearmen and bowmen, so that, in case of an ambush, the knights could react instantly, from safety. To put the wagons at the very centre of that box.

All good sense. But it required a reliance on the low-born men by the knights.

His scouts rode off into the pre-dawn and he mounted his charger. His squire handed him his weapons and then he sat quietly watching the column form, and waiting for the sound—the shouts, the trumpets—that would signal a fight.

Once again, he felt homesick. He wanted no part of this strange warfare against fabulous beasts and monsters. At home, he fought men. He understood men.

When his company was formed with his cousin's he rode west along the column to the king, who sat mounted amidst a circle of his lords. He had a scroll in his hand, as he did most mornings—the Kings of Alba had a fine express service, and its riders continued to reach him despite the increasingly dangerous roads.

"She's ignored me," the king said happily. He looked up, and greeted the captal with a nod. "My wife has ignored my advice and is on her way here," he said.

The captal, as usual, mistook his meaning. "Then I suppose your Majesty must punish her," he said.

The king chose not to take exception, and instead, smiled. "I think we would be most ungrateful," he said, "to be rude to a lady who brings us a great supply of food."

The Count of the Borders smiled. "When do you expect her?"

The king looked out over the woods that stretched like a sea of green to the west. "She's three days' march to the south of Albinkirk," he said. He shrugged. "But she's commandeered a flotilla of boats—she's moving much faster than we are."

"But she has to follow the snake of the river," said the Count of the Borders.

Sir Ricar Fitzroy fingered his beard. "You Grace, she's got a head on her shoulders. She'll still be faster, and she'll carry a great deal more food and fodder than a wagon convoy."

The constable sat back on his charger and put a fist in the small of his back. "Am I the only man who thinks he's too old for all this?" he said. "Your Grace, I propose that we fall back along the line of the river until we link with the Queen. We only have five days' rations—we're short on meat already, and the woods are scoured of animals. The Royal Huntsmen—begging your Grace's pardon—aren't bringing in enough game to feed the Royal Household."

The Count of the Borders agreed. "No need to rush to a fight," he said. "Not with the Wild."

The Earl of Towbray shook his head. "The fortress could fall," he said.

"Lissen Carak will stand or fall," the constable said. He looked around, and lowered his voice. "My lords, we carry the weight of the kingdom on our shoulders. If we lose this army there is no new army to replace it."

"Albinkirk is all but in cinders," the king answered. "I will not lose the Fortress of the North, as well."

"We need food," the constable argued. "We planned to resupply from the magazine at Albinkirk. Or to find the drove coming south from the Hills and buy their beef."

"Can we last five days?" the king said. "And how long can the fortress last?"

Jean de Vrailly rose in his stirrups. "Bah," he said. "The men can last without food. Let us find the enemy," he said.

The Albins looked at him wearily.

"Let us finally face these creatures!" the captal insisted.

The Lord of Bain didn't comment. He merely raised an eyebrow.

The king's friend, Ser Driant, scowled. "I'm not the hardiest warrior, and I'm well known to these gentlemen as a lover of my dram." He leaned forward towards the captal. "But we are not going to risk the king's host on a battle where we have unfed horses."

Jean de Vrailly sneered. "Of course, you must be *cautious*," he said.

The constable narrowed his eyes. "Yes, my lord. That is exactly what we must be. We must be cautious. We must fight on ground of our choosing, with a well-ordered host in tight array, with secure flanks and a defensible camp to which we can retreat if it all goes awry. We must take every possible advantage over our foes. This is not a game, nor a tournament, my lord. This is war."

"You lecture me?" Jean de Vrailly allowed his charger to take two heavy-footed steps toward the constable.

The constable raised an eyebrow. "I do, my lord. You seem to need it."

The king nodded. "The captal's willingness to go forward is noted, but I sense my constable would rather dig in here and wait for the Queen. Is that your thought?"

The constable nodded. "It is. I expect to hear from the Prior in the next day. It would be foolish to move forward without word from our most trusted knights."

Jean de Vrailly's anger was palpable.

Gaston put a hand on his arm and his head snapped around like a falcon's.

Gaston met his wild gaze.

"And let us at least travel south of the river. Our best information places the enemy on the north bank." The constable was openly begging the king to take these measures, and Gaston felt for him.

The captal made a grunt of contempt for such precautions. "If the enemy is on the north bank," he said with patronising and deliberate offence, "surely it is our duty as knights to be on the north bank to contend with them?"

But there were quite a few nods of agreement in favour of the south bank, so the king smiled gracefully at the Galle and turned to his knights. "We cross back to the south bank," he said. "It is my will. We will encamp and dig a fortification on the south bank of the Cohocton, and throw out a heavy screen of prickers and pedites."

"So cautious," de Vrailly spat.

"It is my will," the king said. He didn't lose his smile.

Gaston had a bad feeling in the pit of his stomach.

Lissen Carak—Michael

Michael sat and wrote by strong afternoon light.

The Siege of Lissen Carak. Day Ten

Yesterday the enemy destroyed all the villages west of Albinkirk by fire and sword. We were forced to watch. Today, the enemy fills his siege lines with monsters and overhead his foul creatures fill the air with their cries. When more than two of them are over the fortress, it is as if they darken the sky. And it has disheartened many of the people to see how many our enemies really are. They are literally uncountable. All our efforts to kill them now seem like the efforts of a man with a shovel to move a mountain.

The captain was tireless today, moving from point to point around the fortress. Our people began to build an artillery platform in the ruins of the Onager Tower. He and Lord Harmodius helped the workmen lay stones in new cement and then worked the cement so that it dried faster—a great miracle, and one that did much to encourage the people.

Now it is the middle of the afternoon. The enemy had set engines of war to work, but their stones could not even reach the fortress, and we watched them sail uselessly through the air and land well short of our walls—indeed, one killed a creature of the Wild out in the fields. The captain says that the spirit of resistance can be fuelled by things as small as this.

But an hour ago, using his thousands of slaves, the enemy rebuilt his engines closer to us.

Lissen Carak—The Red Knight

"He's going to have a go at the Lower Town," Jehannes said.

The captain was staring out, watching the distant engines as they were cranked back. The enemy had two trebuchets built about four hundred paces from the Lower Town's walls, on a timber and earth mound almost forty feet tall. The speed with which they had built the siege mound had been, for the captain, the most horrifying moment of the siege.

Perhaps not quite the most horrifying. *I am not your lover.*

It was ironic that Harmodius was training him to divide himself, to rule himself, to wall off dangerous elements of spells and counter-spells. He had issued his new apprentice an absolute injunction.

"Never use this power on your emotions, boy. Our humanity is all we have." The old man had told him that this morning, as if it was a matter of great moment.

The captain had used his new talent to wall off his emotions almost the moment Harmodius left. The Mage wasn't attempting to prosecute a siege while feeling as if his leg had been ripped off by daemons.

Why?

Clearly his control needed work.

He settled back into the crenellations as a rock struck one of the Lower Town gate-towers squarely. The tower shrugged off the hit.

The captain breathed.

"We have men down there," Jehannes said. "We can't hold it."

"We have to," the captain said. "If we lose the Lower Town, he's cut us off from the Bridge Castle. Then he shifts his batteries south. It's like chess, Jehannes. He is playing for the ground just there," the captain pointed at a set of sheepfolds to the south and to the west. "If he can build a siege mound there, and put his engines there, he can destroy the Bridge Castle one tower at a time."

Jehannes shook his head. He was a veteran of twenty sieges, and he clearly hated it when the captain talked down to him. "He can build there any time he likes," Jehannes snarled.

The captain sighed. "No, Jehannes. He cannot. Because he fears our sorties. Despite his immense power and force, we've stung him. If he places engines there without killing the Lower Town, we can sortie out and burn his engines."

"He can build more. In a day." Jehannes was dismissive.

The captain considered this.

Jehannes bored in. "He has limitless muscle power and wood. Probably metal, as well. He can build a hundred engines, in ten different places."

The captain nodded. "Yes he can, but not if his creatures desert him," he said. "He doesn't want us to win any more victories."

"Why should he care?" Jehannes said bitterly.

The captain was watching a party of novices going into the hospital, to take their turn at duty.

"Why, Jehannes!" the captain said. His eyes flashed, and his bitterness was evident. "I thought that you believed that God was on our side."

She hadn't so much as glanced at him as she passed.

Jehannes made a fist. "Your blasphemy is an offence," he said quietly.

The captain whirled at his marshal. "Make of it what you will," he said.

They were standing, their eyes locked, when a third trebuchet went into action, and they heard the sound of the northern gate tower in the Lower Town collapsing.

"You need to pull those men out of the Lower Town," Jehannes said.

"No. I will reinforce them. And I'll lead them myself. Who has the Lower Town today? Atcourt?"

"Atcourt is still injured. It's Ser George Brewes." Jehannes looked out over the walls. "We're losing too many men," he said.

"We're stronger than when we started the siege." The captain was bottling his anger and storing it out of reach.

"It's time you looked around," Jehannes said. "We have bitten off far more than we can chew. We cannot win this."

The captain turned back to his senior marshal. "Yes, we can."

Jehannes shook his head. "This isn't a time for boyish enthusiasm—"

The captain nodded. "You overstep yourself, Ser Jehannes. Go to your duty."

Jehannes continued "—or chivalric daring-do. There are two realistic options—"

"And when you are captain, you can act that way," the captain went on. "But let me be as blunt as you seem to be, messire. You can't see the simplest tactical consequence. You play favourites among the archers and the knights. You lack the birth to command men who prize such things. Most of all you don't have power, and I do. So I'm bored with explaining everything to you, messire. Obey. That is all I ask of you. If you cannot, then I will dismiss you."

Jehannes crossed his arms. "In the middle of a desperate siege."

The captain's mouth formed a hard line. "Yes."

They stared at each other.

By nightfall, the enemy had six engines throwing rocks into the Lower Town.

The captain collected the relief watch and headed down the slope towards it. There were two routes—the road, which wound in multiple cutbacks down the face of the ridge, and the path, which went straight down the spine of the ridge and had two sets of stairs. Several portions of the path were walled and covered to protect parties going to the Lower Town but, of course, you couldn't take a horse down the path.

The watch took the path anyway, their feet wrapped in rags to be as noiseless as possible. Given the enemy's dominance of the plain below them, the captain put out scouts to either side of their route—Daud the Red and Amy's Hob were moving carefully down the bare rock.

It took them an hour to make their way down the ridge. All the while, great rocks fell from the sky on the Lower Town, destroying houses and cracking the cobbles. Sparks flew as each mass of flint struck the town. The heavy *thump-snap* of the trebuchets sounded every few heartbeats, so clear in the smoky air that the engines seemed near at hand.

The air was acrid and heavy. Burning barns and roofs on a damp day had saturated the air with smoke.

An archer coughed.

They crept on. No stars showed and the darkness had become a palpable thing, an immortal enemy. The choking smoke was far worse down on the plain, and the rocks were raising dust and stone grit with every strike to add to the difficulties.

Far out on the plain, one of the engines loosed its burden. As it rose in a graceful arc, it could be seen dully—it was burning. Its misty appearance showed just how dense the smoke was.

The burning mass seemed to come right at them.

"Come on," the captain said, ignoring it. "Follow me."

The fire crashed to earth out in the fields.

Another engine loosed.

Even the vague light of the burning missiles was enough to help the relief watch move down the path.

The captain launched into a stumbling run. His sabatons rang on the stone steps as he came to the postern gate.

Link, Blade, Snot, and Hetty caught him up.

"Relief watch!" he called softly.

There was no answer.

"Fuck," the captain said softly. "RELIEF WATCH!" he called.

"Dead," said Kanny, softly. "We should go—"

"Shut up," Blade said. "Cap'n, you want me to climb the wall?"

The captain was reaching into the postern with his power.

It was unmanned.

"Help him up the wall. Kanny, make a bucket. Then onto my shoulders. Stand on my helmet if you have to." The captain stood next to Kanny, who grumbled but made a stirrup with his gauntleted hands.

Blade stepped up into Kanny's hands, and then onto the captain's shoulders. The captain felt a shift of weight, and then the man jumped.

Above him, the archer grunted, swinging from his arms. But on the third swing, he pulled powerfully and got one leg over the lowest part of the wall. And then he was in.

"Garn, that was too easy," Kanny said.

Snot blew his nose quietly. "You are a useless fuck," he said. "We used to take towns in Galle this way."

Blade opened the postern. "No one here," he said.

A rock crashed into the wall, far too close, and all of them had to clamber back to their feet.

"In," the captain said. He rolled in through the low postern gate, and drew his sword. Daud the Red appeared at the wall with Amy's Hob and No Head. "Get in here. Daud—you and Hob take the postern in case we have to come back through."

The two huntsmen nodded.

Moving across the Lower Town was a new nightmare. Rocks hit the wall—once, an overcast hit a house less than a street away. The streets were already full of rubble, and all of them closed their visors against the rock chips and wood splinters. They fell frequently and cursed too loudly when the did.

The sky was lightening when the relief watch made it to the northern gate tower. It had taken several direct hits, but the massive fortification was fifteen feet thick at the base and had so far survived.

The captain hammered at the lower door with the pommel of his sword.

It took time for a terrified pair of eyes to appear at the grille.

"Watch!" the captain hissed. "We've come to relieve you."

They heard the bar lifted.

A big stone hit, somewhere to their right, and they all cringed. Stone chips rang off the captain's helmet.

Blade began to pant.

The captain looked back at him—then reached to catch him as he slumped to the ground, a four-inch wood splinter in his neck. Before the captain could lower him to the ground, he was dead.

"Get the door open," the captain roared.

The door opened outward a handspan and stopped. It was jammed by rubble.

Two more rocks struck nearby, and then a ball of fire struck fifty paces away, illuminating the smoky air.

No Head got enough of the rubble off the doorsill to get it open and they piled into the tower, dragging Blade.

Scrant, just inside the doorway, flinched at the look in the captain's eye.

The captain pushed the archer out of the way and stalked along the low corridor. Outside, another rock struck, and the tower gave a low vibration—torches moved in their brackets, and plaster came off the walls.

Ser George Brewes was sitting in a chair in the donjon. He had a cup of wine in his hand. He looked blearily at the captain.

"Are you drunk? Why wasn't the postern manned?" The captain turned to No Head. "Round up the off-going watch. Ser George will be staying."

Kanny lingered in the doorway of the donjon, clearly interested in listening, and No Head grabbed him by the shoulder. "Move your arse," he said.

Kanny could be heard grumbling all the way up the stairs.

Ser George waited until the archers were gone. "This can't be held," he said. The effect of his statement was largely ruined by a belch. "It's not tenable," he said, as if his careful pronouncement would settle everything.

"So you thought you'd leave the oncoming watch hanging out to dry?" the captain said.

"Fuck you and your righteousness," Ser George said. "I've had a bellyful. It's time someone told you what a posturing arse you are. I pulled my men into the tower to keep them alive. You got here anyway. I was sure someone would. I haven't lost a fucking man, and if I'm drunk, that's no one's business but mine." He snorted. "You were outside. It's hell out there."

The captain leaned over. "If we abandon the Lower Town, he'll take the Bridge Castle in a day."

Ser George shook his head. "You just don't get it, do you? You're playing at being a knight errant—is that because you're doing a nun?" he guffawed.

The captain could smell the liquor on the man's breath. The sweet cloying smell of wine and hate. Just for a moment, he thought of his mother.

"We're mercenaries, not heroes. It's time to find whoever is behind this siege and cut him a deal. Take your girlfriend with us, if that's what it takes. We're done here. And there's no money in the world that would make it worth dying here." Ser George hawked and spat. "Now get out of my way, Captain. I've done my twelve hours in hell and I'm going back up to the fortress."

The captain stood up straight. "No. You're going to stay right here, with me."

"Like hell I am," Ser George said.

"If you try to leave this room. I'll kill you," the captain said.

Ser George made a plunge for the door.

He wasn't in his full harness and he had a good deal of wine in his belly. In a moment, he was kneeling at the captain's feet, with his arm in a lock that threatened to dislocate his shoulder.

"I don't want to kill you," the captain said. "But to be honest, Ser George, I'd really like to kill someone, and you are the likeliest candidate right now."

Ser George grunted.

The captain let go his hold, a little at a time.

Ser George backed away. "You're mad as a hatter."

The captain shrugged. "I am going to hold this fortress to the bitter end," he said. "I'm going to hold it if I have to do it by myself. When we march away from Lissen Carak—and by my power, Ser George, we *will* march away—we won't be a nameless company of broken men on the edge of banditry. We will be the most famous company of soldiers in the North Country, and men will bid to have us."

Ser George rubbed his shoulder. "We're going to die here, and that's not what we do, boy. We live. Let the other bastard do the dying." He looked at the captain. "You have a very persuasive way with an arm lock."

Two rocks struck close together. *Slam—slam*, and plaster rained down on their heads.

The Lower Town, Lissen Carak—The Red Knight

An hour later, as the light began to grow outside, the off-going watch started up the path with two heavy beams—the rooftrees from collapsed cots—carried high on their shoulders.

The enemy's machines launched a flurry of stones but the off-going watch was already out of range. They scurried up the ridge, and men came out of the fortress's main gate to help.

And then there was silence.

Hours passed.

The captain had been sleeping in his armour, his head down on the table in the donjon. He woke to the silence, and he was up the ladder in

429

a twinkling, his sabatons ringing, his hip armour scraping on the hatch to the first floor of the tower.

No Head was already on the battlements. He pointed to the enemy machines—just three hundred paces further west. Close enough to touch, or so it seemed.

"Cuddy could reach 'em with an arrow. Or Wilful Murder." No Head grinned. "I'm tempted to try, myself."

"Even if you caught one or two," the captain said, "there are many, many more of them." He was much more exposed here—his Hermetic defences weren't buttressed by the power of the fortress. He could feel Thorn.

He looked around.

The Lower Town's curtain wall was breached in four places.

Harmodius he called.

He felt the old man stir.

Well sent. I understand you.

The captain concentrated. *There will be an attack on the Lower Town. I need men. Please tell Ser Thomas.*

You are stronger.

I am practising sent the captain.

He went back to watching.

Sauce watched the beams come through the gate. Skant came over to her—hollow eyed, rubbing his arms—and handed her a note.

She looked it over and nodded. She had the day watch formed in the courtyard for inspection, and she found Wilful Murder easily. "Wilful," she said. "On me."

He stepped out of the ranks.

"Find Bent. And any artificers you can rustle up. Master Random's man is in the dormitory—I think that the pargeter boy is in the Great Hall. These beams are to form the pivot arm of a trebuchet—mounted where the onager was."

Wilful Murder digested this. Nodded. Chewed on his moustache.

While he was looking at the tower and Cuddy was inspecting the duty archers, Bad Tom appeared in his armour. He didn't look like a man who'd been up all night.

"Captain needs the quarter guard. At the double." He nodded.

Ser Jehannes came along the wall and down the curtain steps. "Hold hard, Tom."

Tom's eyes met Sauce's. "Now," he said.

He turned to face Ser Jehannes.

The quarter guard was the watch reserve—half the able men, usually the very best men, but today simply half the available troops. Sauce had more than a dozen men-at-arms in the day watch—most of the rest were kept ready for the sortie—led by Ser John Ansley, a big, cheerful, ruddy-faced young man. "Ser John, you have the watch," she said. "I'm taking the quarter guard. On me!" she called, and the quarter guard came; sixteen archers and eight men-at-arms. Most of the archers were guildsmen she didn't know—with all five of the new recruits—the local boys. Ben should have been her master archer, but he was already standing with Wilful Murder.

"Cuddy—you're the senior," she said.

"Like enough," he said.

Jehannes raised his voice. "You are insane!" he roared at Tom.

Tom laughed.

Her senior man-at-arms was Chrys Foliak—one of her own tent-mates. He had the others ready to move.

Cuddy made a motion with his hand and Long Paw stepped out of the ranks and joined him.

They went out the postern. It was obvious to them all that Ser Jehannes disagreed with the order to send them. But then the courtyard was behind them, and they were out in the light.

Below, on the fields, hundreds—perhaps thousands—of creatures were moving toward the Lower Town. The fields themselves seemed to be moving.

"Good Christ!" Chrys Foliack muttered. "Good Christ."

Long Paw spat thoughtfully.

He paused in the postern, leaned back, and shouted "Toby! Michael!"

He couldn't see the captain's valet or his squire. "JACQUES!" he roared.

A nun—tall and pretty despite her hollow eyes—came to the postern. "May I help?" she asked.

"Captain's in trouble. Tell Bad—tell Ser Thomas we'll need relays of arrows and all the men in harness."

She nodded. "I'll tell him."

"See you do, lass," Long Paw spat carefully to one side, flashed her his best smile, turned, and ran down the long path to catch up with the others.

Lissen Carak—Harmodious

Harmodius watched the bustle in the courtyard as he climbed past the two men-at-arms arguing—reached the wall—

It was worse than he had thought.

He ran, barefoot, along the wall to the apple tree.

Summoned power, and raised his staff...

Lissen Carak—The Abbess

The Abbess watched the day watch form under her window. There was something particularly well-ordered about the company. Their scarlet jupons, their bright polished armour. They made her feel safe even when she knew that she was anything but.

Even as she watched—looking for the captain, and missing him, and assigning herself a penance for looking, all in one thought—the woman who wore men's armour shouted an order, and all of the men on the right of the formation turned and followed her.

There was suddenly an air of crisis—men moved in many directions.

She reached out—

He was preparing an attack.

She felt well-slept and immensely strong. She walked across her solar to the windows on the outer wall, three hundred feet above the fields below, and looked out.

Her fields seethed as if covered in maggots.

Her feeling of revulsion was more than physical.

A pair of her novices, alerted by her movements, appeared with a cup of warm wine and a fur-lined robe. She drank the one and shrugged on the other while the older novice brushed her hair.

"Hurry," she said.

She put light shoes on her feet, pulled the mantle of her profession over her fur robe and was off while the creatures in the fields below were still merely a tide lapping at the foundations, and not a mighty wave.

She collected the crozier—the crooked staff that the Abbess bore by tradition, with a curious green stone head.

And then she ran, like a much younger woman, for her bower—her apple tree.

She was shocked to find another there. Not just there, but swimming in her power.

"Master Magus," she said, coming to a stop.

"Lady Abbess," he said. "I'm working."

Even as she paused, he raised his staff. His power was visible. His whole form gave off tendrils of power.

The Lower Town, Lissen Carak—The Red Knight

The captain watched the enemy's creatures gather. They were well within bowshot, and No Head and his fellows began to pink them. The two youngest archers carried sheaves of fresh shafts from the second floor, and the older men began to loose.

The captain had seen archers in action before, had watched his men practise at the butts, but he'd never watched a dozen professionals at full stretch.

He'd fussed at No Head while the older man felt the breeze, and carefully arranged his sheaves in brackets for the purpose set into the wall—little iron buckets.

The two senior men—No Head and Kanny—raised their bows, loosed, discussed their aiming points, and watched the fall of their shafts.

"Over," said Kanny. It was a different tone of voice from his usual hectoring, barracks-lawyer voice.

"Over," No Head said. "Ready, lads?"

He raised his bow, and every man on the tower raised his in emulation, and they all loosed together. Their arrows rose and rose, and before they had begun to fall the next flight was on its way.

Down on the plain, the distant irks screamed their defiance, showed their hooked teeth, patted their backsides and hefted their spears.

There were a thousand of them—more, most likely. In their homespun greens and their leathers and brown skin, they looked as if they'd been grown from the earth under their feet.

The first flight of arrows struck. They all struck together, and tore a small whole in the great patchwork of brown-green irks.

The phalanx of spears moved a step closer.

The second flight struck.

And the third.

And the fourth.

The regiment of irks started to look like a piece of leather on a shoemaker's bench punched with an awl. And again, and again. The punches only made small holes. But it made a great many of them.

The irks screamed, their handsome elfin faces contorted into masks of rage, and they charged.

"Fast as you can, boys," No Head called.

His arms became a blur of motion. He drew and loosed, took a shaft from his bracket, nocked, drew, and loosed so quickly that the captain had difficulty sorting his actions.

Brat, the youngest archer, opened a linen sack and dumped the shafts, points first, into No Head's bracket, and ran to load the next archer.

Kanny was grunting with every draw. The sound was so frequent and rhythmic it was obscene.

The irks had little or no armour, and no shields. As they crossed the three hundred paces to the breaches in the northern wall, they left a trail of wounded and dead creatures behind them. It was as if the whole phalanx was a wounded animal, bleeding little corpses.

They reached the first breach.

Kanny ran dry of arrows, and had to pause to get his own bundle. Brat couldn't keep up. One by one, the bows stopped twanging.

"They're not going anywhere," No Head said calmly. "Don't rush. Everyone get their quivers full again. Brat, you get one more load up here and join us on the wall."

The captain felt superfluous.

Lissen Carak—Sauce

Cuddy watched the first charge out of the slits of one of the covered ways halfway up the ridge. Then he ran down the steps to Sauce.

"They're going to need help," he said.

She glared at him.

"We can hit them from down there," he said, pointing to the lower path. "With arrows," he continued. The men-at-arms tended to forget the power of the bows.

Sauce paused. "Yes," she said. "Let's go!"

They pounded down the track—over a streambed, down steep steps, around a long curve, and then they were right above the Lower Town. The wall had a fine low parapet, and the Gate Tower was just a hundred paces away and almost at eye level.

Cuddy admired No Head's archery for three long breaths. The shooting was continuous, now, and the flow of shafts like a waterfall crashing down on the irks in the field. The creatures died and died.

It was clear to Cuddy that the irks were defeated. Archery combat had a ruthless logic of its own. Cuddy was an expert in it.

"Five shafts," he said to the men around him. "Right in the midst of them. Fast as you can." Two of his guildsmen had crossbows—not really worth a thing in a fight like this.

Oh, well.

"Ready?" he called. Every longbowman had five arrows in the ground, ready to hand, and another on the bow. Long Paw had one on his bow, one in his bow hand, and four in the ground.

Cuddy raised his bow.

Lissen Carak—The Red Knight

The irks broke.

The new arrows came from behind, plunging down and killing them. In a minute a tenth of their numbers were pinned to the ground, screaming their thin screams.

Lissen Carak—Sauce

"Save your shafts," Cuddy said. He had only fifteen more. High above, on the ridge, he could see valets starting down with bundles of arrows, but it would be ten minutes before those arrows reached them.

He pointed to the town. "Some of them got in," he called to Sauce.

"Are you happy to stay here?" she asked.

Cuddy nodded.

"Men-at-arms—on me." She waved to Cuddy and started for the postern gate.

Long Paw winked at Cuddy as he followed her.

Lissen Carak, The Lower Town—The Red Knight

The captain went to open the tower's lower door himself. He and Ser George were the only men without bows.

Sauce was outside, with a crowd of armoured men. "Town's full of irks," she said. Her sword was in her hand, and behind her, men were cleaning the dark blood from their blades.

He nodded. "We have to keep the street clear for sorties," he said.

She nodded. "That's going to suck," she said in a matter-of-fact voice. And took her party to move stones and fallen roof tiles.

The captain went with them.

It was brutal work. As the spring sun rose it burned, distant and orange, through the smoke-filled air. It was growing warm, and inside forty pounds of chain and plate, and a heavy quilted arming cote, it was hot.

Just bending to lift a stone was hard enough in armour.

It took five of them to lift a fallen roof beam.

When they began to complain, he pointed out that it was their horses who would come through here in the dark.

They went on, picking up rubble, pushing obstructions aside.

After an hour, the captain was soaked through. He collapsed on a low stone wall and Toby handed him a flagon of water.

Thump-snack.

"Son of a bitch," the captain cursed, and the stone slammed into a church fifty paces distant, blowing a hole through the tile roof and vanishing inside.

He began to stand up, and the irks attacked.

There were only a dozen of them; desperate, and brave, and ferocious.

When the rush was cleared, the captain found that the armoured man at his back was Ser George Brewes.

The flagon of water was still unbroken by a miracle. He took a swig, spat, and handed the jug to Ser George.

Ser George leaned on his sword. "Feg," he said, shaking his head. "Irks. I've heard of them."

The captain just panted.

"Like killing children," Ser George said.

The whole sky was a pink-red. Another rock crashed to earth off to their left.

"You really think we can hold?" Ser George asked.

"Yes," the captain wheezed. He'd taken a cut on the back of his shoulder. He could feel the blood mixing with his sweat. *I need to learn to heal myself.* It was trickling down his side—warm, instead of cold.

Why? Why did she turn her back on me?

He made a face.

"It would be something," Ser George admitted.

"Yes," the captain managed.

Toby—unarmoured and unarmed—had survived the rush from the irks. He'd simply run away. Now he was back.

"I've food," he said.

His scrip was packed with beef, bread and good round cheeses and Sauce's men-at-arms fell on him like scavengers on a carcass. His head was patted a dozen times. He had a meat pie for himself. But he always seemed to.

Sauce moved among them. "Drink water," she said, as if they were children and turned to the captain. "Think they'll try again?" she asked.

The captain shrugged, and the weight of his armour and the pain in his shoulder defeated the motion completely. So he bobbed his head. "No idea." He took a deep breath. His breastplate seemed to be too small, and he couldn't catch his breath. The smoke in the air was burning the inside of his lungs.

It was a very small working, an insidious thing. He saw it as soon as he made the effort.

The air was *full* of a poison. He couldn't even see how it was done.

Sauce started to cough.

Harmodius! He called.

I see it, lad.

Do something! the captain shouted in his head.

Lissen Carak—Amicia

His shout came to her as clearly as his anguish.

She was working on Sym's back, running her hands along the weels left

436

by the lash, and trying to fix some of the deeper issues, as well. The captain's thoughts were not helping her concentration.

She reached out instinctively. It was in the air. Poison. She read it from his thoughts.

She tasted the air through his mouth, and felt it through his lungs.

She was in him.

Then he slammed his gate shut.

She was standing over Sym, with her hands clenched into fists. Shaking.

Captain! She sent.

He responded.

It's an unhealing. A curse.

Tell me.

You cannot banish it. You can only heal it.

Another voice. The Magus. *I see! Well thought, mistress.*

Now it was her turn to raise her defences. *Get out!* She said it aloud too.

Sym looked at her.

"Not you, silly," she muttered.

Lissen Carak, The Lower Town—The Red Knight

The captain could feel the poison thickening in the air and he didn't know how to heal. Although now that she showed him, he could see it.

A curse.

The physical manifestation of a curse.

He *went into his tower*. *"I need help,"* he said to his tutor.

She smiled. "Ask me anything," she said.

"A curse. A physical curse—a poison in the air." He went to the door to his tower.

"He's waiting for you to open it," she said.

"I think he's busy, and a lot of people are going to die if I don't act." He reached to door.

"If it is physical, perhaps we can move it physically," Prudentia said. She smiled sadly. *"I don't know healing, either."*

"That's a fine thought." He looked up at his symbols. *"Wind,"* he said.

"Yes," Prudentia agreed.

He spoke the names. "St. George, Zephyr, Capricorn," he said, *and the great ranges of symbols rotated silently.*

He touched the door.

He could feel the enemy, and he opened it anyway.

And slammed it back shut.

Lissen Carak—Sauce

The wind came up without warning—first a heavy gust that cooled them, and then a mighty rush of air from the east.

Sauce drew a shuddering breath.

"Get a scarf over your face," the captain shouted. "Anything."

The wind moved the poison—but he could still smell it.

And then he felt the sending. It was gentle as snow, and just for a heartbeat the air seemed to sparkle all around them, as if the world was made of magic.

Lissen Carak—Harmodius

Harmodius watched the Abbess's working and he could only think of Thorn's statement that men were too divided.

It was beautiful. The sort of mathematical Hermeticism that moved him the most deeply. In it were the rotations of the planets and the paths of the stars across the heavens. And many other things, thought and unthought...

"You are far more powerful than I had imagined," Harmodius said.

She smiled. Just for a moment, it was the Queen's smile.

"Who are you?" he asked.

"You know who I am," she said it playfully. She rose from her seat. "I think Thorn will find it very hard to use that trick again."

Harmodius raised an eyebrow. "Trick?" he asked. "It wasn't Hermeticism. It wasn't a working. Not as I understand them."

"There are more things on heaven and earth than are in your philosophy," she said. "He uses the deaths of the irks to fuel his curse. It is a very, very ancient way to power magic."

Harmodius nodded in sudden understanding. "But you—"

"I stand for life," the Abbess said. "Me, and my God, as well." She smiled sweetly. "He will not be back for some time. I need to speak to a novice. Pray excuse me."

Harmodius bowed. As she swept past him, he said, "Lady—"

"Yes? Magus?" She paused. Her attendants paused, and she waved them on.

"If we linked, lady—" he said.

She made a moue. "Then you would know all my innermost thoughts. And I yours," she said.

"We would be more powerful," he insisted.

"I am already linked to my novices. And to all my sisters," she said. "We are a choir."

"Of course you are," Harmodius said. "Gads, of course you are. I'm a fool." It was obvious, when she said it. Forty weak magi would still be very powerful indeed, together. But it would require incredible discipline.

Like monks.

Or nuns.

"I will think on it," she said. She smiled.

He watched her go, and then sat beneath the apple tree.

Chapter Thirteen

Lissen Carak—Michael

The Siege of Lissen Carak. Day Eleven

The captain took the watch to support our garrison in the Lower Town—a small fortified bastion at the base of the ridge. The Enemy has constructed siege engines—catapults and trebuchets—to attack. Because of the rage of our engines atop the fortress, and because we can launch sorties from the fortress through the streets of the Lower Town, the captain says that the Enemy must take the Lower Town first.

He made two attempts, but both resulted in heavy losses of creatures of the Wild. We lost not a single man or woman yesterday. The Abbess called on the Power of God and defeated the Enemy's poison air. Many men felt lighter at heart after she prayed.

But the Enemy's engines now throw heavy stones all the time. The air is full of smoke, and many of the farm folk have become angry and downcast.

During the night boglins assaulted Bridge Castle, but their surprise failed and they were driven off.

Michael put his quill down and shook his head at the ink stain on his forefinger.

Kaitlin had not come out to meet him last night, even though he was on his way to the Lower Town. The farmers were angry—he could feel it.

Old Seth Lanthorn, an oily bastard in the early days of the siege, was now surly and silent. Farmers muttered when he walked by.

They resented their boys being taken to be archers. And perhaps resented—

I will marry her, he said to himself. But he couldn't keep his eyes open…

Lissen Carak—The Red Knight

The curtain wall around the Lower Town was gradually pounded to rubble.

Before the sun rose, the stars were obscured, and clouds rolled in. The rain that started wasn't hard, but it was soaking, and cold.

"Attack coming," Toby said, rubbing his cheek. The boy's breath was sweet with apple cider.

The captain rose blearily, feeling as if he'd been kicked repeatedly. It was an effort of will to run through his Hermetical exercises and it was torture to arm. Toby had to put his harness on him—Michael was down in the Lower Town. Every man and woman had to do their duty, now.

When he went out on the wall, the fields were moving again, lines of irks marching to form up opposite the northern flank of the town. Now they had shields—great pavises of heavy bark stripped from downed trees in the deep woods.

They formed in six deep columns, glistening in the light rain.

Bad Tom had twenty men-at-arms and as many squires and valets waiting for them, and twenty archers on the tower. The breaches in the town wall glittered damply with men in harness.

The enemy's engines were silent.

Wilful Murder stepped up on the wall with his captain. "It's done," he said. He pointed to the squat remnants of the former southern tower. Now it was an engine platform, two storeys tall, crowned with a trebuchet whose launching arm was as tall as the spire on the chapel.

The captain gave him a tired smile.

"Let's see if we can give Master Thorn another surprise," he said. "Let's go."

The first stone was loaded with some trepidation. The arm of the trebuchet would throw a man in armour five hundred paces. A war horse three hundred paces.

Wilful fussed like a mother sending her child to church the first time.

No Head, who was supposed to be off duty but whose love of engines outweighed his good sense, pushed the loader out of the way and muscled the stone into the great hemp-rope web.

"Care to do the honours?" Wilful asked the captain.

"Everyone off the tower," the captain said.

Every one of the farmers was in the courtyard. They'd worked like draught animals to get the machine built and in place—to level the stump of the tower. Their grumbling was loud and aggressive, and the captain ignored them.

But he needed them to wind the arm into place. The trebuchet depended on farm women for its motive power.

When they were all clear, the captain pulled the lever.

The trebuchet's arm moved slowly, at first, then rotating faster and faster until the great sling at the end was lifted clear of the deck—the arm and its massive weight passed the centre of rotation and the weight crashed down onto a massive pile of old hordles—*thump*—and the sling opened—*crack*, and a stone the weight of a man flew free—rising for what seemed an incredibly long time.

And of course, the heavy stone started three hundred feet above the fields below.

It rose and rose, passing over the irks, who had just started to move forward, clearly unsure of the efficacy of their new shields, and then it began to fall. It came down at a steep angle, it passed over the irks, over the deep trench the boglins had dug, over the enemy's artillery platform, the mound on which his engines sat, and vanished into the trees of the woods at the western edge of the cleared ground.

It did no damage to anyone, or anything.

But the farmers cheered, and the archers cheered and the captain grinned to see it.

Wilful Murder ran back up the ladder and pounded his captain on the back.

The captain smiled. "Nice work." He turned to No Head. "Get the engines."

No Head grinned.

The first assault was retreating by the time the great engine was wound again. Bad Tom's men-at-arms had mangled it, and the great bark shields hadn't done as much to stop the archer's shafts as the irks might have wished.

The captain gathered a sortie under Ser Jehannes in the courtyard. "Tom's going to be hard pressed," he said to Jehannes. "A dozen men ahorse will make short work of their next assault."

Jehannes nodded. "Yes, ser," he said coldly. "I know my business."

The captain noted that Francis Atcourt was in harness and mounted. He pressed the man's gauntleted hand. "Good to see you about," he said.

"Good to be here," Atcourt said. "Although, it seems to me another day abed—" He laughed. "I'd be strong enough to swim a mountain or climb a river."

The trebuchet released.

The captain wasn't the only man who ran to the walls to watch the fall of the shot.

No Head's first round landed out of sight beyond the enemy's engines. The captain watched the next assault. It was halfhearted. The irks stayed away from the worst of the archery by bunching up in the front of the central breach, and very few of them went forward all the way to the men-at-arms.

Then one of the enemy's engines released.

The rock fell like a lightning bolt, into the breach, crushing men-at-arms and goblins alike.

"Damn," the captain said. "I should have expected that."

A creature gave a long, bone-chilling cry—like a trumpet, but louder and more hideous—and irks crept from houses and cellars in the Lower Town. They had crept in during the night, or made it past the archers in the first assaults, and now they struck the rear of Bad Tom's line.

A great armoured troll sprinted from behind the engine platform and pointed its antlered head at the breaches in the curtain wall.

The irks got out of its way.

Another rock plunged from the heavens to strike in the central breach. The stone seemed to explode as it hit, spraying attackers and defenders alike with lethal stone chips.

The men on the walls watched the men in the breach like spectators at a joust.

Ser Philip le Beause died when a stone chip caved in the side of his helmet.

Robert Beele fell, stunned, and an irk got its dagger in his eye slit.

Ser John Poultney died trying to get his back to the wall, swinging his sword in wide arcs. He stumbled when a stone hit his backplate, and was on his knees; in a heartbeat, a wave of the little monsters were on him. He crushed one with his gauntleted left fist, swung his sword one handed through another pair, and then two were hauling his head back.

"Release the sortie," the captain ordered.

No Head loosed the trebuchet. The stone flew high, and vanished into the forest of upright machine arms atop the enemy's artillery mound.

Wood chips flew, visible even from the fortress.

A half-loaded trebuchet in the enemy's battery was loosed by a panicked boglin and his loader was caught in the casting net and flung a hundred paces to fall wetly to earth.

Jehannes galloped down the road from the fortress followed by a dozen knights.

They flew down the switchbacks, and the troll raced for the breach, and a swarm of irks pushed the defenders of the breach into a knot.

"Damn," the captain said.

He'd never cast power at this distance, but he had to try.

Bad Tom was a pebble in a crumbling sand castle.

He threw back his helmeted head and bellowed.

The irks quailed.

He killed them.

His sword was everywhere, and he was faster than they, taller, longer, stronger.

They went where he wasn't, but the other men-at-arms knew what Tom was like, and they stuck to him like glue. Francis Atcourt stood at his shoulder, advancing when Tom advanced, retiring when the big man spun away. He had a short spear, and he used it sparingly. He let Tom kill the irks. He only killed those who could threaten Tom.

They began to retreat off the breach. They couldn't hold it—too many of the men-at-arms were down.

Atcourt saw movement above him on the ridge. "Sortie," he called.

Tom was frozen.

"Troll coming," he said. "Francis, clear what's behind us and open a lane to the tower."

Atcourt didn't need to be urged. He tapped the captain's squire and three other men on the helmet as he passes them. "On me!" he called.

An irk appeared in his range of vision—paused, surprised, perhaps to find men in the town, and not on the wall, and died with Atcourt's short spear in its forehead.

"Michael!" he called. "Get to the tower. Tell Cuddy and Long Paw to cover us."

The squire had excellent armour, lighter and better than any of the professionals. Besides, he was the youngest.

The great troll ran through the irks. At the base of the rubble-strewn slope up into the breach, it paused, glaring around like some eyeless worm seeking daylight or warmth—or human blood. Then it picked its way to the top of the breach, clearly unwilling to move quickly in the bad footing. When it reached the top it paused again, caught sight of the men-at-arms and threw back its head and roared its challenge, its grotesque mouth, back-hooked fangs and black gullet on display as it sounded its challenge.

The sound rang through the woods, and echoed off the ridge and the walls of the fortress high above. The Abbess heard it at her prayers, and Amicia heard it in the hospital. Thorn heard it and clenched a mighty fist. The captain didn't hear it at all. He was preparing to work.

Bad Tom stood his ground, threw back his head, and roared back.

The sound crashed back and forth—from the fortress walls to the woods, and back.

They charged each other.

A stride from contact, Tom side-stepped—the monster hesitated, and Tom's sword swept through. The troll's antlers caught him and slammed him to the ground.

The troll's momentum carried it a dozen steps, and it turned.

Tom got a leg under him. He put the point into the ground and used his great sword as a lever to get to his feet.

The troll completed its turn, and put its armoured head down.

Tom laughed.

Cuddy leaned out over the tower wall. The troll turned, and he let it turn, reasoning that its arse couldn't be as well armoured as its front. He raised a chisel point above the wall, leaned into his draw, and loosed.

The arrow struck with a sound like a butcher's blade into a leg of mutton.

The troll stumbled. The arrow had struck from behind, between its shoulder blades, and sunk in all the way to the fletchings. The troll gave a moan and raised its head.

Tom stepped forward.

The monster flinched, and then punched for Tom's throat with both stone-shod hands.

Tom cut.

Struck, and was struck to earth in turn.

Ser George Brewes leaped over Tom's body to face the troll in his place. "Go!" he roared at the rest of the men-at-arms. "Run!"

But Francis Atcourt came and joined him, and Robert Lyliard too.

The troll eyed them, pawed at the earth once, twice, and then slumped slowly to it and lay still.

"Son of a bitch," Lyliard said. He stepped forward and slammed his hammer into the thing's head.

"Get Tom!" Atcourt called. The irks had the breach, and the troll's death didn't seem to make any difference to them.

They all got a hand on him. He weighed as much as a war horse, or so they swore later.

And then they ran for the tower, the irks hard on their heels.

The archers shot right into them, Cuddy and Long Paw assuming that their armour would hold.

Mostly, it did.

The irks fell back—flooding the Lower Town, but letting the men have a path to the tower—and the postern opened. Long Paw loosed a shaft right down the line of men-at-arms and then drew his hanger and his buckler, flinging his bow through the door behind him. He stepped out, and the men-at-arms carried Tom past him.

There was a brief flood of irks. They were all armoured in scale mail and carrying round shields—warriors.

Long Paw's sword and buckler swept up, bound as if they were one weapon—his buckler slammed into the face of one irk's shield, and then, in the same tempo, his sword beheaded another. In the same flow, he swept his sword back into guard, fell back a step, and parried not one but two spear thrusts with a single sweep of his blade. He stepped in, passed his buckler under the spear-wielding irk's arms, wrapped them, slammed his pommel into the irk's unarmoured face, and used his advantage to throw the lighter creature into his mates.

Stepped back again, and the postern crashed shut.

Lissen Carak—The Red Knight

Ser Jehannes had halted the sortie two-thirds of the way down the ridge, when it became clear that the breach had fallen. Now the sortie turned and rode silently back up the road.

The captain was waiting in the gate.

"Right," he said to Jehannes. "Good call."

Jehannes dismounted, gave his reins to a farmer—the valets were all in harness—and started to turn away. "The Lower Town is lost," he said.

"No," the captain said. "Not yet."

Over their heads, the trebuchet lashed out again.

"You are risking everything on the hope that we will be relieved. By the king." Jehannes was obviously restraining himself. The words were very carefully enunciated.

The captain put a hand on his shoulder. "Yes," he said.

"Christ be with us," Jehannes said.

West of Albinkirk, South Bank of the Cohocton—Gaston

Gaston had done his exercises of arms, and had prayed. And now he had little to do. He'd had enough of his cousin, and enough of the army in every way.

He mounted his riding horse, left his valet at his tent door, and went for a ride.

The camp was enormous—a sprawling thing as big as a market fair or a small town, with more than two thousand tents, hundreds of wagons drawn up like a wall, and a ditch all the way around it, dug to the height of a man and with the upcast flung back to form a low rampart.

No man was allowed outside the ditch on pain of punishment. Gaston understood—better than his cousin—that he needed to set an example, so he rode slowly around the perimeter, nodding to the Alban knights he knew, and their lords.

He saw a pair of younger men with hawks on their wrists, and he was envious.

He thought of home. Of sun-drenched valleys. Of riding out with his sister's friends, for a day of wit and wine and frolic, chasing birds, climbing trees, watching a well-formed body on a horse, or by a stream…

He shook his head, but the image of Constance d'Eveaux looking back over her naked shoulder before leaping into the lake haunted him.

There had been nothing between them. Until that moment, he hadn't even noticed her except as a pretty face among his sister's friends.

Why am I here? Gaston asked himself.

"See something what you like?" said a familiar voice.

Gaston reined in, his reverie exploded.

It was the old archer. Gaston was surprised to find that he was happy to see the low-born man.

"You were going home," Gaston said.

The old man laughed. "Heh," he said. "Lord Edward asked me to stay. I'm a fool—I stayed. I sent my useless brother-in-law home." He shrugged. "Of the two of us, my daughter probably needs him the more."

"The Lord of Bain?" Gaston asked.

"The very same. I was his archer on the crusade, oh, ten years back." He shrugged. "Those were some hairy times."

Gaston nodded. "I knew you were an man-at-arms."

The old archer grinned. "Aye. Well. I meant what I said. It's all foolishness. Why are we at war with the Wild? When I lie out at night hunting I love to have a chat with the faeries. I've traded with the irks more than once. They like a nice piece of cloth, and mirrors—hehe, they'd trade their mothers for a bit o'mirror." He nodded. "Admit I can't stand boglins, but they probably feel the same about me."

Gaston couldn't imagine such a life. He covered his confusion by dismounting. He was surprised to find the archer holding his horse's head.

"Habit," the old man said.

Gaston held out his hand. "I'm Gaston d'Eu."

"I know," the old man said. "I'm called Killjoy. Make of it what you will. Harold Redmede, it says in the christening book."

Gaston surprised himself by clasping the man's arm, as if they were both knights.

"Surely it is a crime against both the King and Church to trade mirrors to the irks."

The old archer grinned. "It's a crime to shoot Lord Edward's deer. It's a crime to take rabbits in his warrens. It's a crime to leave my steading without his leave." The archer shrugged. "I live a life of crime, m'lord. Most low-born do."

447

Gaston found himself smiling. The man was really very likeable. "But your immortal soul," he began softly.

The old man pursed his lips and blew out a puff of air. "You're easy to talk to, foreigner. But I don't need to debate my mortal soul with the likes of ye."

"But you are willing to speak with evil." Gaston shook his head.

The archer gave him a wry smile. "Are all the men you know so very good, m'lord?"

Gaston winced.

"Stands to reason all the irks ain't bad, don't it?" he went on. "What if none of 'em is bad? Eh? What if there's no power on earth as bad as a bad lord?"

Gaston shook his head. "What bad lord? This is rebel talk."

"Rest easy, m'lord, I'm no Jack." The old man sneered. "Boys playing at causes. And broken men and traitors." He nodded. "Some good archers, though."

"Let's say I'm coming around a little to your way of thinking," he said carefully. "I would like to confess that I want to go home."

"Knew you was a man of sense." Redmede laughed. He looked under his hand and shook his head. Pointed at an archer, asleep. "Swarthy, you useless sack of shit, get off your arse and work."

Gaston turned and saw the young archer trying to hide in the ditch. He was all huddled up, as if by being very small, he could avoid the old man's wrath.

"Now I'm the master-archer, and I wear myself out riding these boys." He laughed.

Gaston didn't think he looked worn out.

Redmede stepped closer to the ditch and bellowed, "Swarthy!" at the young man.

He paused and in a moment Gaston saw what he saw.

The boy was eviscerated. And very, very dead.

"Damn," the old archer said.

West of Albinkirk—Galahad Acon

Galahad Acon had never been so cold for so long, and he lay as still as he could lie, watching…

Well, watching nothing at all. Watching the woods. A breath of breeze stirred, moving the new leaves, and the light rain fell and fell. Despite a wool jupon and a wool cote over it, with a heavy wool cloak over all, he was soaked to his linen shirt and colder than he was when riding through heavy snow in December.

The Prior had left him to watch at the first grey light of dawn. Had said he'd be back.

He'd taken Diccon with him.

As time went by, his fancies grew darker and darker. Why would they ride off and leave him?

He had a fire kit. But the Prior had been very forceful on the subject of fires.

I'm going to freeze to death.

For the thousandth time, a twig cracked in front of him.

Galahad wondered how twigs could just crack, in the woods.

A bird fluttered in the wet leaves, and made a low thrumming sound— and then burst out of the leaves and leaped into the air.

Something had just moved.

Galahad felt his blood still in his veins.

He scanned his eyes frantically back and forth.

Oh good sweet Virgin Mary now and in the hour of my death amen.

They were almost silent—filing along the streambed at the base of the low hill.

But there were hundreds of them.

Oh my god dear god ohmygod

In the lead was a willowy daemon, all black, which moved like an embodiment of shadow, flitting rather than walking. Behind him, came the hosts of hell, walking, strutting, shambling—

Galahad found he could neither watch nor turn his head away. That when he closed his eyes, he couldn't picture exactly what they looked like.

He couldn't make his mind work. Run? Stay?

He was fear.

They moved along the watercourse, and they scarcely moved the leaves. They travelled quickly, passing from left to right before him.

Eventually, he realised they weren't going to turn and rend him limb from limb. But that didn't stop his breath from coming in low pants, nor the deep cold from settling into his bones.

And then they were gone, away to the north, towards the river.

It was a long time before his breathing returned to normal.

When the Prior found him, at sunset, still lying there, he burst into tears.

The Prior embraced him. "I'm sorry," the mailed knight said. "You did well."

Galahad was ashamed of his tears, but he couldn't stop them.

"They got between us and you," the Prior went on. "I couldn't risk my knights for you. That—that is how it is, out here." He patted Galahad. "You did very well."

They moved camp, in the same silence that the knights did everything. They went north, and Galahad saw that the tracks made by the daemons had the shape of human feet. He looked very closely, and he couldn't see anything but bare feet and soft shoes.

A young Thomasine nodded to him. He cleared his throat quietly and leaned close. "Sossag," he said.

Galahad knew enough to knew that the knight was honouring him by speaking.

"I thought they were daemons." He looked at the knight.

The young man shook his head. Put a finger to his lips, and rode on.

That night, Diccon put an arm around him. "Sorry, lad. It should hae' been me left with the baggage. I don't even know why we're here."

The Prior came and offered each of them a cup of warm mead. He sat on his heels, still armed from head to toe in plate and chain.

"You are here to take my news to the king—when I have news." He looked back and forth. "Tomorrow."

Diccon drank his mead. "What did you learn today?"

"The fortress still holds," the Prior said. "And holds the bridge, as well. The Abbess has done far better than I expected of her, and I owe her an apology." He smiled at Galahad. "The trouble with a vow of silence is that it leaves you vulnerable to talk," he said.

Diccon nodded. "I'll ride at first light."

The Prior shook his head. "The woods this side of the river are full of the enemy. Sossag, Abenacki, irks, boglins and worse." He shook his head. "Tomorrow night we'll make a demonstration. A loud demonstration. We will draw every creature of darkness like—" he smiled "—like moths to a flame." He nodded. "Then you'll ride."

Lissen Carak—The Red Knight

Just a few leagues north of the hillock where the Prior camped, the captain stood in the castle gateway with the Abbess. Behind him were most of the men-at-arms, led by Jehannes, and twenty squires and valets led by Jacques. Every man wore a nun's habit over his harness.

He gathered them in a circle.

"What a very scary passel of nuns we make," he said. "The order of Saint Thomas will need to be a little more careful in their selection process."

The Abbess laughed. The men going on the sortie managed a sort of nervous titter.

"This needs to be fast, so listen up. It's like taking a town in Galle. Sneak to the wall. Ladders up on the whistle. That's all there is. When you are in, head for the towers at the gate. We get the lads there and back we come. Don't leave your wounded behind. You know all this." He grinned. Turned to Ser Michael, the sergeant of the original garrison. "You must keep the gate open until the sortie returns. But don't leave it open for a few men.

You hear me? When the sortie is in, close the gate." He turned to No Head. "When you see my blue fire pound the town. Everything you have."

No Head nodded. "The Bridge Castle has the word, too."

Beside him, Harmodius crossed his arms. And winked.

The captain nodded. "You all know Tom would come to get you. Let's go get Tom."

A murmur.

He jumped down from his barrel, and led the way—not to the gate, but to the dispensary stairs, and the Abbess walked with him.

She led them through the lower dispensary, and then down steep steps to a basement, and then down another set to a well—a spring in the deep hillside, a cleft off to the right with lights burning.

The captain could feel an immense welling of power. Raw power. Neither gold nor green.

He reached into the well and filled himself.

You are much stronger, Prudentia said. *But not as strong as he is.*

I know.

You don't. You are arrogant. You are outmatched.

Fine. Yes, I know.

Fool! she spat.

He dropped back into the cleft and came to a long storage room, packed to the rafters with wagon sides and barrels of pork.

It took long minutes for men to shift the wagon beds.

There was a door behind them.

The Abbess drew a key from her girdle. Their eyes met.

"Now you know all my secrets," she whispered.

"I doubt it," he said, and kissed her hand.

"I am quite sure I should not give you this," she said. She smiled bitterly and handed him a small scrap of curled parchment, hard as an old leaf in his hand. Smooth as a woman's skin.

"I could disapprove, as her spiritual mother," the Abbess went on. "I could just be a jealous woman." She shrugged. "Sister Miram brought this note to me and confessed that she had passed another." She met his eyes. "Amicia is not for you, Captain. She is greater—far greater—than we."

He smiled. "That is not what I expected you to say." He bowed. "I beg your indulgence." He turned aside, and held the scrap up to a torch on the wall in a clamp. He read, and he couldn't control the smile that crossed his face.

Your gate is closed.
Meet me.

He turned back to the Abbess.

She shook her head. "You are glowing."

"How is she greater?" the captain asked.

The column had begun to move. The door was open, and the lower door, too.

He kissed her hand again. "Thank you," he said.

She smiled. "You have brought me no peace, young man." She waved her hand. "Go—kill our enemies. Triumph." She sounded tired.

He turned and all but leaped down the steps. On his way he stopped to touch the favour he wore on his shoulder.

Amicia felt him, like a touch on her cheek.

She smiled, and went back to tearing linen into strips.

I'm a fool, she thought.

The company went down through the Abbess's passage and entered a maze of stone corridors.

To those who knew what to look for, it was obvious that men had not made these curving corridors.

But they were empty, although, to the captain, every yard of them reeked of the power that had been used in storming them. More than a hundred years ago. More than two hundred years.

And still the power lingered, like the smell of smoke after a fire.

Eventually, the Abbess's will-o-wisp led them to a double door of oak, bound with iron, copper, and silver. To the captain's eye, it was covered in sigils—powerful wards drawn Hermetically.

He'd never seen anything like it.

She'd given him the key.

He held it with renewed respect.

Some of the lads were very much on edge. An hour in silent, haunted corridors deep under the earth isn't the best preparation for combat. The sounds behind him were of men on the edge of panic.

He turned, and cast a soft light.

"Ready, friends?" he asked softly.

More and more men stumbled into the antechamber in front of the great doors.

"We'll come out into the chapel of the Lower Town," he said. "The roof is collapsed. Don't run. Out here a rolled ankle is a death sentence and we're not coming back this way. So don't linger." He couldn't explain why.

He was about to open the fortress's Hermetic defences, for a moment.

He imbued his voice with calm. Humour. Normalcy.

"Let's go get Tom," he said. He smiled at Jehannes, who, praise be, smiled back.

And he turned the key.

North of Lissen Carak—Thorn

Thorn felt the change. He was busy resighting his battery, wishing again that he had a mathematician or an engineer—some reliable human calculator who could command the tedious business of putting the great rocks on target. Exrech had proven uninterested. And far too slow. Unwilling to *build* anything.

He watched the boglins dig, raising a new mound out of range of the new machine on the fortress. He knew this new battery represented a heavy defeat in time and effort.

He was trying not to acknowledge that he had to go into the debatable ground and destroy the fortress's new machine with his own power. He had no other weapon available with the necessary reach. And he would have to squander power like an angry boy to breach the fortress's millennium-old defences.

That would leave him weak.

And then he felt the shift. He tasted the air—wasted valuable time sending a raven stooping over the walls, and he saw the nimbus of fire on his former apprentice's hands, saw the great engine cranked all the way back, saw—

—nothing.

His raven was struck by an arrow, and tumbled out of the air.

He cursed, disoriented by the loss of his connection. Reached for another—

The fortress's defences were down.

He stepped out from behind his new siege mound. Raised an arm, and let fly a bolt of pure green lightning.

And he laughed.

Lissen Carak—Harmodius

Harmodius threw a shield in front of the lightning, like a knight making a parry in the tiltyard, and the two castings extinguished each other with a flash of light.

Harmodius stumbled and had to reach for the well of power at his feet. "Sweet Lord have mercy," he mumbled.

One blow. Thorn could empty him of power in a single blow.

Lissen Carak, The Lower Town—The Red Knight

The captain was first out the gate, and Jehannes was on his heels, leading his party of men-at-arms to the right and out of the chapel.

The nave was full of sleeping boglins.

The killing began.

He counted the armoured shapes coursing past him, lost count in the middle, and had to guess.

But Sauce was true to her promise. She was last.

"Last out!" she called, and danced off to the right around the gate.

The captain slammed the great doors shut, with the key inside.

As the two doors met, their power meshed, and the gate vanished, leaving a black stone wall behind the altar, only the shape of the two doors burned onto his retinas remaining.

Bent and the archers were clearing the nave.

Jehannes was already gone over the broken wall.

The captain began to cut his way to the front of the church.

Thorn cast his second levin bolt, and then, without pausing to gather power, he cast a third.

Lissen Carak—Harmodius

Harmodius's second defence was more refined than his first—a working of his own, weaker than Thorn's but deflective rather than resisting. Thorn's strike bent like a beam of light in a prism and blew a piece of slate the size of a small barn off the side of the ridge.

His third cover was not quite fast enough—he intended to cast a single line of power like a sword parry—but Thorn's speed left him too late, and he tried to widen his cast, with too little power.

He still stopped most of it.

The rest fell on the curtain wall to his left. A section of wooden hoardings twenty paces long burned in a flash, and a section of the wall cracked and fell outward, killing two archers instantly and crushing the two older Lanthorn men to pulp.

Harmodius felt them die.

His failure made him angry, and anger made him lash out. His riposte was pitiful, small, weak, too late.

It was also entirely unexpected. Like a slow attack in a sword fight, his flare of anger sailed out into the dark and caught Thorn unprepared.

Pain enraged Thorn. It always had.

He struck back.

The Lower Town square was carpeted in corpses. The captain passed in the chapel doorway looking for his men-at-arms. The archers were spreading out, right and left.

"On me," he said. "Let's go!" He ran across the square, and they pounded along behind him.

Parties with ladders broke off and headed east, through the rubble.

He could hear fighting to this left, and more straight ahead. Angelo di Laternum materialized out of the darkness.

"Ser Jehannes prays your aid," he said formally.

"On me," the captain said, and followed the squire. The captain had no time to comment that Jehannes was off course.

A vast burst of light lit the sky, like all the summer lightning ever seen combined in one single burst. The levin flash showed the captain that Squire Angelo was bleeding from the shoulders of his harness; the archers were splashed in red and black and, ahead of him, Jehannes's men-at-arms were caught in the flash, illuminated like a manuscript illustration of knights fighting monsters.

"Ware!" the captain shouted. "Daemons!"

The terror struck him like a heavy mall. He set his teeth and pushed himself forward through the terror, and one of the things turned on him with its supernatural speed.

The captain had supernatural speed, too.

The daemon's blade met his, so hard that sparks flew from his blade, and he yielded before the creature's awesome strength, rotated his blade around the fulcrum of his armoured wrist, stepped inside its terror and pushed his point into its brain.

It fell away off his sword, and he was on the next. It turned its head—its beautiful eyes catching his.

The daemon's taloned hand came up, too fast to block.

His sword came down.

The daemon stumbled away, spraying fear the way a skunk sprays scent, and the captain found himself retching. There was blood in his eyes.

My faceplate is open.

It got me.

A different fear, colder and heavier, settled on his gut.

But the daemons were not immortal; their ichor was mixed with the blood of men on the ground and they were retreating. As they began to put distance between them and their foes, the fear abated.

The captain saw there were fewer than a dozen of the things.

The archers—frozen in place—suddenly burst into action. The last daemon—the one the captain had wounded—sprouted shafts like a field growing grass.

The thing turned, its fear welled, and it fell.

Jehannes was shouting for his men.

"Stand!" called the captain. It sounded like a squeal. But Wilful Murder roared it from behind him. "Stand!" he called.

Jehannes paused.

"The tower!" the captain insisted.

Lissen Carak—Thorn

Thorn's burst of rage fell like a hammer.

Harmodius watched the strike come in, helpless to stop it, a whole heartbeat to see his death wash at him in sickly green radiance.

He felt the fortress's Hermetic defences go back up, and knew it would never be enough.

The great works that powered the defence were brilliantly designed—they funnelled what they could, channelled some more, reflected yet more. They were so well artificed that they almost seemed *intelligent*. New practitioners attempted to meet force with force—skilled practitioners knew to meet force with guile, deflecting the opponent's energy like a skilled swordsman. Most static sigils were easily overcome, but this…

In the moment of his annihilation, Harmodius thought *Who built this?*

The wards caught, turned, and covered. But there was only so much the ancient sigils could do.

And the rest burst through the great wards like a river in flood bursting through a levy.

He raised a hand.

The Abbess reached past him, and stopped the overflow of the great spell of wrath just short of their place on the wall. She flung it back down the path of the casting.

She reached out and put her left hand on his shoulder.

I know nothing of this sort of war she said. *Let me in.*

Through her, he could feel her sisters, singing plainchant in the chapel. Their power did not fuel the Abbess directly. It was far subtler than that.

Despite the situation, he had to pause to admire the magnificence of the structure. The fortress. The sigils. The sisters, who could maintain the power of the sigils indefinitely, regardless of their individual weakness.

He wondered, yet again, who made this?

Then he gripped her spiritual hand in his own and led her through the great bronze doors of his palace, like a bridegroom leading a bride. "Welcome," he said.

She was a much younger and less spiritual woman, in the Aethereal. Suddenly

456

he had a frisson of memory. Of this same woman dressed for hunting, standing in his master's chamber, tapping her whip on her hand. Trying to get his master to go out riding.

He dismissed the memory, although here it took on a visible aspect, so that she saw it and smiled. "He was the worst lover imaginable," she said with a sad smile. "He didn't hunt, didn't ride, wouldn't dance. He was always late, and made many promises he couldn't keep." She shrugged. "I wanted him. And look at the consequences. Some sins do not wash away." She spread her arms. "It is very nice here."

He flushed with her praise, as if he was a much younger man. Time in the Aethereal had virtually no meaning so he had no sense of urgency. "Did you ever suspect?" he asked carefully. "When he turned?"

The Abbess sat in one of his great leather armchairs. She had riding boots under her voluminous riding skirts, which she crossed over the arm of the chair. "You know, don't you, that in old age, one doesn't easily adopt positions like this," she said happily. "Ah, to be young." She leaned back. "You must have asked yourself, many times."

"I've been largely trapped in his phantasm for many years," Harmodius said. "But yes. I think of it now. All the time."

"I only know that in the months before Chevin he discovered something. Something terrible. I badgered him to tell me, and he would smile and tell me that I wasn't ready to understand it."

Harmodius grimaced. "He never said as much to me."

The Abbess nodded. "But now you know what he knew. I know it too, now."

There aren't many secrets in the Aethereal.

"Yes," he said.

The Abbess shook her head. "Any servant of the Order of Saint Thomas knows that the green and the gold are the same," she said. "Richard was a fool who saw the world entirely in shades of black and white. He still is. A staggering intellect, a tower of puissance, and no common sense whatsoever." She shrugged. "Enough chatter. My home is being blown to bits. Show me how to use our power to stop him."

"Like this," he said. "But it will be more efficient if you pass me power and I cast."

In a heartbeat—in no time at all, because in the Aethereal, time had so little meaning—they stood on a balcony of his great palace, looking out over the world of solidity.

In his vision, Thorn stood out like a beacon tagged in green. Harmodius pointed her hand at the thing that had been her lover.

She flooded Harmodius with power.

He made fire.

Lissen Carak—Thorn

For the first time, Thorn paused to raise a shield. His burst of temper was over, and Harmodius's response had been respectable. No more, but no less.

And the fortress's defences were back. He had landed some good blows. But now he was risking himself for nothing. He raised a second shield.

Harmodius's mighty blow rolled away like a child's stick on a knight's armour.

Thorn grunted.

It might have been a laugh.

Lissen Carak, The Lower Town—The Red Knight

Tom's unconscious body took six men to carry and the captain was unwilling to lose the horses that had been left for the Lower Town garrison, so a party of archers cleared the town's upper gate and opened it. The garrison escaped behind the horses, and the sortie went over the walls via ladders.

It was all going very well, until the daemons struck back.

His rearguard was slow in forming—understandable, in the conditions—and suddenly three of them were down, dead, and a gleaming monster stood over them with a pair of wickedly curved axes gleaming in the soft spring moonlight. Marcus—Jehannes's valet—and Ser Willem Greville, his armour opened as if he was wearing leather. A third man was face down beside them.

The fear was like a waft of foul air.

There were more daemons behind it—fluid and horrible, arresting and beautiful in their movements. And below them, a legion of boglins, irks and men poured into the town they were leaving.

Just like that, the captain was alone.

"Run, little man," the daemon whispered.

The captain reached *inside and found Prudentia.*

The working was already aligned.

He opened the door before she could protest—he was so much faster than he had been.

The green whistled through the crack, a tempest—

"*He can reach you!*"

"He's otherwise engaged," the captain told his tutor.

"*I need to tell you so many things,*" she said.

He smiled and was back in the dark.

His sword arm was bathed in silver.

The daemon rotated its two axes, one over each wrist and golden-green light joined the two.

"You!" said the daemon. "Ahh, how I have longed to meet you."

The captain got his blade up into guard, and cast.

The beam of silver-white light rose into the night like a beacon. And then fell to earth in the centre of the town.

"Missed," hissed the daemon.

The captain backed away, rapidly.

Above him on the trail, a crossbow loosed with a snap.

The daemon grunted as the bolt struck.

Let loose his own spell.

The captain caught it—marvelling at the ease with which he fielded the blow. In *the Aethereal, his adversary's blow was like the cut of a sword, and he caught it and parried it with a sword of his own power, flicking it away.* And he was back in the solid, because the daemon followed his phantasm immediately with a heavy cut from his right axe.

He could remember the first time he'd stopped such an attack by Hywel. Had been hit in the next instant because of the sheer pleasure of having accomplished it. Now, as then, he almost died through admiring his own cleverness.

He passed forward into the attack, his sword at eye level, the Guard of the Window, and the axe fell away harmlessly like rain off a roof.

He began to cut overhand, his left foot powering forward, and he caught the growth of his opponent's power and he *turned the blow even as it was rising from his adversary's talons.*

In the *solid* the attack came in, and he drove the power into the stones of the road between them.

The road exploded, knocking him flat.

With a high scream the daemon leaped the crater and swung both axes at once.

He saw Michael step over him and he caught both blows—one on his buckler, one on his long sword. The squire staggered, but the blows fell away.

The captain was backpedalling from between his squire's knees; using his elbows, steel sabatons scraping the road, he got himself back.

He rolled to the left, almost falling off the elevated road. The daemon captain was pounding Michael with blow after blow, and the lad was standing his ground, pushing his sword and his buckler up into the blows, deflecting them, using the daemon's strength against it as best he could.

The other daemons were trying to get around the fight.

The captain got his feet under him and he cut at the daemon from the side—but the thing parried his blow high with an axe blade—a horrifying display of skill—and flicked his weapon forward. It was all the captain could do to bat the blow aside.

Both men fell back as the daemon hammered blow after blow, one axe then the other, in an endless rhythm. It might have been predictable, except that it was so *fast.*

And then, during the moment that the captain had one axe turned on his long sword, and Michael had the other—just for a heartbeat—safely on his buckler—

Jehannes punched his pole-axe between them.

The daemon fell away, folding over the blow. But its armour—or its eldritch skin, or its sigils of power—held.

The captain stumbled back, and he felt Michael at his shoulder.

"Let me in," Jehannes shouted.

Michael slumped and Jehannes stepped past him.

Two daemons leaped past their leader, who was just gaining his feet.

Far above them on the fortress, the trebuchet loosed.

Thump-snack

The ballista on the north tower loosed.

Whack.

The war engines on the towers of the Bridge Castle loosed.

Crack!

Crack!

High above them, Harmodius leaned out over the wall, hand in hand with the Abbess like lovers, and spread his fingers.

"Fiat lux," he said.

The Lower Town seemed to explode as a hail of fire fell, a hand of fate that struck buildings flat.

The daemons were silhouetted in fire. At the back of their company, daemons turned to see what had happened.

The captain had to fight the vainglorious urge to charge them. He backed another step.

The two things came at them, and their fear...

Wasn't as strong as it had been. Somewhere deep inside, or perhaps above, the fight, the captain had time to smile at the irony. He had lived his entire childhood in fear. He was afraid of so many things.

Familiarity breeds contempt. He was *used* to acting while he was afraid.

The terror projected by the daemons wasn't having any effect on him.

Despite which, it was all he could do to stand his ground, because they remained big, fast and dangerous.

Jehannes had a pole-axe. He cut two handed into a blade attack, and his axe-hammer broke the daemon's sword arm. It stumbled back, and he got his haft between the other's legs, and as it stumbled, the captain had all the time he needed to step forward and cut overhand from the garde of the long tail, the sword flashing up, powered by his hips, his arms, his shoulders as he levelled the blow, right to left.

His blow went under its weapon. Beheaded it.

Beside him Jehannes stepped forward again and rammed pole-axe's spike into the supine daemon, so that it screamed.

There was a sound very like applause.

460

The captain wondered who was watching.

They were most of the way up the ridge, under the main gate. And still bathed in the silver-white light of his casting. He was breathing hard. His helmet was like a trap over his face, constricting him, the visor was like a hand over his mouth, and he was bathed in sweat.

The daemons came on again. There were boglins trying to get around them on the left and right, and his archers were shooting with methodical regularity, but he couldn't stop to think about that. They were on him.

The daemon in front of him swung its axe two handed, and he cut at its hands—its blow turned to a defence, and it's left claw shot out and slammed into his shoulder and he stumbled back in a flash of pain.

He'd been hit.

Again.

Jehannes threw three fast jabs with his spear point, reversed his pole-arm to bat his opponent's axe out of the way and planted his spike in the daemon—it screamed and fell back, taking the haft with it, planted in its breastbone. Jehannes struggled too long to keep it.

The captain's adversary swung on Jehannes from the side, catching the knight in the side of the helmet and Jehannes fell.

He came back for me, the captain thought.

He lunged, his long sword held only by its pommel in his right hand, and raked the point across his opponent's beaked face—an attack of desperation. But the blow landed, and the daemon stumbled off balance. He recovered forward, grabbing the blade near the point, which he rammed into the daemon's scaled thigh, and with that as leverage, he hurled it from the road. It fell away into the darkness.

He stepped forward again, past Jehannes.

The one that had spoken jumped forward, shouldering past two of its own kind.

"I am Thurkan of the Qwethenog," it said.

She hadn't intended to come out onto the wall.

Her place was in the infirmary and wounded men were coming through the gate.

She told herself that she would only look. Only a moment. People were cheering.

She ran barefoot through the infirmary's second floor balcony doors, and leaped lightly from the stone balustrade, between a pair of gargoyles that decorated the lower gable ends, and skinned her thigh on the slates as she slid down to the curtain wall. She'd taken this path a thousand times to go out after the nuns blew out the last lights.

She was a level above the gatehouse. She skidded to a stop when she saw that a section of curtain wall was simply gone, and her left foot hovered over empty space.

Below her the hillside was bathed in a cruel white light.

When she was young, her Outwaller family had called them guardians and worshipped them. North of the wall she had thought they were angels.

Now a mighty one stood on the cobbled road, facing the Red Knight.

How she hated that substitute for a name. *The Red Knight.*

He looked tired. And heroic.

She couldn't watch.

She couldn't look away.

The guardian struck with two axes, cutting with both at the same time—something a mere man could never hope to do.

He stepped forward and to the right, and smashed an axe to the ground; the guardian stepped back. She saw it draw power. Guardians were not like men in any way except for their love of beauty. It took in power as if breathing—a natural movement—and then it snapped its working at the knight.

Who turned it. Then he stepped forward, and raised his sword slowly, an elaborate gesture like a salute.

Achieved his guard.

And froze.

The guardian raised its axes.

And froze.

Time stopped.

She couldn't breathe.

When one of them moved, it would be over.

The Ings of the Albin—Ranald Lachlan

Donald came and sat on a rock by Ranald's tiny fire. Half their force was out on picket—the men cooking breakfast spoke in low tones.

"I've a notion," Donald said.

Ranald ate a piece of bacon, and raised an eyebrow. He was feeling better. More alive. Ian the Old had made him angry, pissing in the stream where they got drinking water.

Yesterday nothing had made him angry, so he savoured that anger as a sign he was alive.

All those thoughts flitted through his head while he chewed, and then he nodded. "I thought I smelled smoke," he said, and managed a smile—another triumph.

Donald leaned back. "None of yer sass, now. And you half my age." He grinned. "I think we should push the herd for Albinkirk. It is only twelve leagues, or like enough as makes no difference."

Ranald was alive enough, and enough of a hillman, to be taken with the boldness of it. "Right over the same terrain where we fought the Sossag?" he said. He shrugged.

"They're gone, Ranald. Nobody's seen dick of them for three days. Not a feather, not a scout, not a bare buttock. It's their way. They don't hold ground." Donald leaned forward. "What's the herd worth at the Inn? A silver penny a head or less? And it's a far longer walk to the Inn than it is to Albinkirk."

Ranald stared into the flames of his small birch bark fire. He added leaves from a pouch at his belt to his copper cup full of water, stirred honey in, drank it, and gave a quiet thanks to God. His belief in God had suffered—or maybe not. He wasn't entirely sure.

I was dead.

Hard to take. Better not to think of it. Except that, in some horrible way, he could remember the *deadness*. He didn't want to be dead again.

He sighed. "Daring," he said. But from Albinkirk he could send a messenger to the king. He owed the king that much. More. He sighed.

Donald's eyes sparkled. "Let's do it."

Ranald knew that the older man needed to perform a deed of arms if only to justify the fact that he had lived and Hector had died.

But deep inside, he shared the feeling. And if they could get the herd through—why, then Sarah Lachlan would be rich, and all the little crofters and herders in the Hills would get their shares, and the Death of Hector Lachlan would be a song with a happy ending.

He drank off the last of his scalding tea, and watched the stream. "We're loons. And some of the boys may 'decline to accompany us.'" He gave the last words a distinctive Alban accent.

Donald chortled. "Good to see you coming back to yourself. Faeries brought my Godmother back from dead—did you know that? Took her months to laugh again, but then she was dead a whole day." He shrugged.

Ranald gave a little shudder. "Ouch," he muttered.

"Oh, no. She said that having been dead, life was always sweet." He nodded.

Ranald was still thinking of that when the herd lumbered into motion, headed west. The boys had muttered about it but none of them turned for home.

Four hours they moved west, down the old drove road through increasingly wooded country. The west slope of the Morean Mountains had been farmed once—grape vines still grew over the new trees, and they passed a dozen farmsteads standing open-roofed and abandoned. None were burned. Men had simply left, one day, and not returned.

Ranald had seen it all before. But now he noticed it more.

That evening, they made camp under the Ings of the Albin. They'd pressed the herd hard and come twenty leagues or better, and the young men were exhausted enough that Donald made up a new duty list, writing slowly and carefully on his wax tablet, making signs for some men and writing the names of others in the old way.

Kenneth Holiot was not a bard, but they all knew the boy could play, and that night he sang a few lines to his father's old lyre, and shook his head, and laid down a few more. He was writing the song of the Death of Hector. He knew the death of another Hector, in Archaic, and he had the bit in his teeth—he was going to write the song.

After an hour he cursed and went off into the darkness.

Ranald cried.

The other men just let him cry, and when he was cried out, Donald came and put a hand on his shoulder, and then he rolled up in his cloak and went to sleep.

Lissen Carak—The Red Knight

He watched his adversary, and waited to die.

His shoulder was bleeding. His face was bleeding. Jehannes was somewhere half a pace behind him, he didn't dare try to retreat, and for some reason his people seemed to think he wanted this to be a single combat.

Warm blood ran down his side.

The effort of holding his sword above his head in the Guard of the Window would eventually be too much. He would have to strike, and that would be the end.

It was faster and stronger than he was. He'd tried attacking, tried thrusting, tried most of his tricks. They all required some advantage—reach, perhaps—that he just didn't have.

The daemon just stood there, two axes above its head.

And then, as sudden as its attack had come, its eyes slipped past him and with a shrug it was *gone*. The air popped as it displaced itself.

He was damned if he was going to fall over. He stood there looking at an empty road down the hill, and the fires of hell raging in the Lower Town.

He turned around, and Michael had Jehannes under the armpits and was dragging the knight up the path.

Cuddy stood just behind him, with his bow at full draw. Very slowly, the archer let the tension out of the limbs, and the great bow returned to shape. He dropped the arrow back into the quiver at his belt.

"Sorry, Cap'n," he said. "You wasn't going to win that one."

The captain laughed. He laughed and laughed as they pulled him through the gate and slammed it shut, and Ser Michael lowered the great iron portcullis.

He slapped Cuddy weakly on the backplate. "Nor was I," he said.

Then Michael had his helmet off his head, and he was sucking in great gouts of fresh, cool air. A dozen men were pulling at his armour.

He saw the Abbess. Saw Harmodius, who grinned at him.

Red Knight! Red Knight! Red Knight! Red Knight!

He drank it all in for a moment, and then, as his breast and backplate came off, he got to his feet. The men stripping him grinned and backed away, but their grins faltered when they saw how much blood was running down his side.

He nodded, waved, and ran, unarmed, unaware of his wounds, into the crowd and seemed to vanish. He didn't see Amicia. But he'd felt her there.

He went to find her.

She was waiting for him under the apple tree.

She bit her lip.

"I won't talk," he said cheerfully. "I—"

She pushed him down on the bench with a strong arm, and bent—he hoped, to kiss him. But his hope was cheated. He felt her breath, hot, moist, fraught with magic, on his face and felt his wound heel. She raised her hands like a priest invoking the deity and he saw the power all around her, the well below the tree, the tendrils that connected her to her sisters in the choir and to the Abbess.

She reached a hand under his arming doublet and her touch was cold as ice. Her hand passed over his chest and his back arched in agony as she touched the edge of his wound—one he hadn't felt.

"Silly," she said. He felt the power go out of her, into his shoulder. For a moment, briefer than a single heartbeat, the pain was infinite. And for that moment, he was her. She was him.

He lay back. To his shame, a whimper escaped his lips.

She leaned over him, her hair covering his face. Her lips brushed his. "Men will die if I stay with you," she said.

And she was gone.

Lissen Carak—Michael

The Siege of Lissen Carak. Day Twelve

Last night the watch came and relieved the garrison of the Lower Town. The Red Knight led the watch in person. All the garrison were rescued, but brave knights and men-at-arms were killed and wounded, and the Lower Town, in the end, was lost. The Enemy has limitless creatures.

Michael looked at the parchment and tried to think what he could write. Shook his head, and went to find Kaitlin, who's father had died when the curtain wall fell.

*

In the first light, three wyverns came out of the rising sun carrying rocks the size of a man's head in their claws.

They came in high, and dived almost straight on the trebuchet.

The watch was just changing and the soldiers were completely unready. The ongoing watch was already tired, the offgoing watch was exhausted, and no one reacted in time.

Before No Head could even rotate the ballista the first monster's claws opened, and his rock fell—struck the stump of the tower a few paces from the engine, and bounced away with a crack like lightning to fall harmlessly to the hillside below.

The second wyvern dropped lower, wings folded against his back, but he opened his wings too early, bobbed, and his rock went sailing away to kill one of the hundreds of sheep who were still penned on the ridge.

The third wyvern was the oldest and the canniest. It swooped off the target Thorn had intended and laid its rock almost gently on the ballista, smashing the engine and throwing No Head off the tower.

The archer shrieked and grabbed at the gargoyles of the hospital balcony as he fell.

The wyverns swept away.

Lissen Carak—The Red Knight

An hour later the wyverns were back. This time all three imitated the eldest, coming lower along the ridge and rising on the last thermal before the walls of the fortress to unleash their missiles at point blank range.

This time they were met by a hail of darts, bolts and arrows, loosed from every corner of the courtyard, the towers, and even the hospital balcony.

All three were hit, and flew away, angry and unsuccessful.

Their stones knocked a hole in the captain's Commandery, killed two nuns in the hospital, and crushed a war horse and a squire in the stable.

The captain slept through it.

Lissen Carak—The Red Knight

He didn't wake until late afternoon. He awoke in the comfort of his own room, although it felt odd. Air was moving around him.

Someone had fixed blankets and an old tapestry over a hole the size of a cart. A hole in the wall that went right through to the outside air.

His little porch was gone, too.

He got his feet on the floor, and Toby Pardieu had his clothes laid out on the press, and long leather boots over his arm, clean and black.

His knight's belt was polished, shining like something hermetical.

"Which the Abbess has invited ye ta' dinner," Toby said. "Master Michael is at his exercises."

The captain groaned as his weight came on his thighs and hips, and just for a moment he had a flash of what old age might be like.

"Ta semptress ha gi'in me these linens," Toby said. He pointed to a basket. "New, clean, an' pressed. Shirts. Caps. Braes. Two pair black cloth hose." Toby pointed at the basket.

The captain ran his hands over a shirt. The stitches were neat, very small, almost perfectly even but not quite, almost a pattern. The seamstress had used an undyed thread on the glorious new white of the linen—so confident in her skills that the very slight contrast was itself a decoration. A very subtle declaration of skill. Subtle, like the power with which she'd imbued the garments.

He picked up the shirt. The power was golden—a bright, white gold, the colour of purity. The Sun.

The shirt didn't burn him, nor did he expect it to. He'd found that out, years ago.

Toby interrupted his reverie. "Wine? Hot cider?" he asked. He looked at the floor. "Cider is good," he mumbled.

"Cider. And I'll wear these new things, but with my scarlet cote, Toby. Black is for—" He sighed. "Black is for other occasions."

"Sorry, my lord." Toby blushed.

"How could you know? Any word on the wounded? How's Bad Tom?" He felt the crisp cleanness of the new white shirt. "I'll have a bath before I dress, if you can arrange it."

Toby nodded at the challenge. "Twa shakes of a lamb's tail." He vanished. Reappeared. "Ser Thomas is up and about. An' Ser Jehannes, as well."

The captain heard the boy's footsteps, running. The boy made him smile. Made him feel old.

He stripped out of his arming clothes. He had had them on for—hmm. Two days now, without rest?

The shirt was damp and warm and smelled bad. Not like sweat, but like old blood. There was a lot of blood in it. It had a tear, too, all the way down one side.

He had a mirror, somewhere in his kit. Michael had unpacked his malle and his scrip and the portmanteau he stored in the wagons—he rooted around, vaguely aware that evening was coming, and he wasn't armed.

He found his bronze mirror in its travelling case, found his razor, and unfolded it from its fancy bronze handle. Looked in the mirror.

He'd forgotten the wound he'd taken last night. He had a long crease down the left side of his face which was still sweating a little blood. As soon as he looked at it, it started to hurt. It didn't look bad. It merely hurt.

He shook his head. Felt fuzzy with post-combat shock, and the shock of what he'd just seen in the mirror.

He tried to look at the wound in his right shoulder. It was a dull ache, and he couldn't locate it, despite the fact that his arming clothes were soaked in blood.

A bit more of a shock, that.

Stiff with blood would be more accurate.

He peeled his braes off. They were stuck to his crotch with blood and sweat, and where his leg met his groin, he had sweat sores. He *stank*.

Toby reappeared. "Which the bath is on its way, m'lord. I told Master Michael and Master Jacques you was awake."

Jacques came through the door and sniffed.

Even naked, the captain still had authority. "Toby, take my arming cote out and air it. Give my linens to the laundress and ask her respectfully if they can be saved."

Jacques was holding one of the new arming caps. "This is *fine* work. As good as court." He looked at Toby.

"The tire woman. Mag." Toby shrugged. "She tol' me what the captain had ordered of her. Did I do aught wrong?"

The captain shook his head. Jacques smiled. "I'll go and pay her. And order my own," he said. "You are commanded to dinner with the Abbess," Jacques went on. "As are a number of other worthies. Best dress well and try to behave yourself."

The captain rolled his eyes. After a pause, he said, "How bad is the wound on my back?"

Jacques looked at the back of his shoulder. "Healed," he said with professional finality.

Toby had the arming jacket over his arm.

The captain snatched at it and held it up.

The right arm had a slash that ran from just above the underarm voider of chain all the way down to the top of the underarm seam.

Jacques gave a sharp noise like a dog's bark.

"One of the daemons tagged me." The captain shrugged. "I slept...what a sleep!" Suddenly he picked up the goblet by his bedside.

"The pretty novice gave me a cordial I was to give you," Toby said. He cowered a little.

The captain found his wallet, a small miracle all by itself, and extracted a silver leopard. He snapped it across the room to young Toby, who scooped it out of the air.

"I think I owe you a debt of thanks, young Toby," he said. "Now—*bath.*" He scratched himself.

Out in the yard he could see that there were men with swords and bucklers, practising. He walked across the room, and peeled back a corner of the tapestry to gaze out over the fields, the sheepfolds, and the smoking ruin of Lower Town.

"Wyverns?" he asked. He was still unbelievably tired.

"Been pounding us with rocks all day," Jacques said cheerfully. "Gave No Head the fright of his life. Ballista is gone."

"He's moving his engines again," the captain said. "No—he's having boglins dig a new mound, but the engines are still safely out of range." The captain found he was scratching things that could not publicly be scratched, not even in front of servants.

"I need to see Tom, if he's up to it. With the day's reports."

Then he squeaked and ripped the coverlet off the bed as two farm girls appeared in the doorway with a tub of steaming water.

"Coo!" said the dark-haired one. "Nothing I ain't seen before." She giggled, though, and the other girl blushed, and then they were gone.

But the water wasn't gone.

"I'll wash myself, if you don't mind," he told Jacques.

Jacques nodded. "You're too old to be bathed." He counted the linens in the basket. "I'll just go pay the lady, eh? And fetch Tom."

"Thanks, Jacques," said the captain. The water was hot—nearly boiling hot.

He got in anyway, hoping to scald some of the dirt and worse away. The captain was sure there was something crawling over him.

He had just immersed his torso—slowly—when there was a stir behind him.

"Tom?" he called.

"No," replied Harmodius.

The captain wriggled. The water seemed to burn where he had abrasions, and where he had cuts, and where he had sores.

So pretty much everywhere.

He realised that his soap—his lovely almond scented soap from Galle—was in his leather portmanteau.

Harmodius came across the room. "You are stronger," he said without preamble. "I saw you last night. Fast and strong."

"I do your exercises every day," the captain admitted. "And as you said—I try to do everything I can by the arts." He shrugged, and the water was delicious. "When he lets me."

"Our adversary?" Harmodius nodded.

"He's camped outside my place of power." The captain reached all the way to the well, a long way for him. Thirty paces through rock. But he could feel the power there, now. He reached out, touched it, took a sip, and cast.

The soap rose, crossed the room, and fell into the bath with a splash.

"Damn," said the captain. Not his soap. The sharpening hones for his razor.

Harmodius grinned. "Soap? Is it pink?"

"Yes," said the captain.

"Still, you are much improved. I know you were well trained, you just have to be less secretive." He shrugged. "An easy thing for me to say." He picked up the soap and then held it out of reach.

"I'd be able to do more if he weren't right outside my door, waiting to come in and rip my soul out," said the captain, scratching. "Soap please?"

Harmodius looked out from the tapestry. "Nice new window," he said. "Get your power elsewhere. You know how."

"From the well?" the captain asked.

"How about the sun?" Harmodius asked.

"I'm a child of the Wild," the captain said. "My mother made me that way."

Harmodius wasn't looking at him. He was looking out over the fields. "Do you trust me, boy?"

The captain looked at the tall, proud figure. "Not really," he said. "Not to give me my soap, anyway."

Harmodius barked a laugh. "Fair enough. Fair enough. Do you trust me as a mentor in Hermeticism?"

The captain thought for a long few heartbeats. "I think so," he said.

The old Magus nodded and ripped the tapestry off its hooks, so that the afternoon sun fell right on the tub. "Take the soap. With the sun. Do it." He held the soap where it could be seen.

The captain felt the sun against his bare skin like a faint weight. He held up a wet hand, and let the sun lick it.

He had always liked the sun. Especially in spring.

...scent of flowers...

For a fraction of a heartbeat he'd had it, and then revulsion set in. It was like a gag reflex.

The soap didn't move.

"Try harder," Harmodius said.

"You could just give me the soap, and we could do this when I'm dressed." The captain felt very much at a disadvantage, naked, wet, hurt and vulnerable.

Harmodius narrowed his eyes. "Cast."

The captain tried again. He let the sun kiss him. He drank in—

And spat up, narrowly avoiding his bath. "No," he said.

"Better," Harmodius said. "Very good indeed. May I tell you what I admire in you, Captain?"

"You're going to try flattery now?" asked the captain.

"It's not that you are not afraid of anything, because, as far as I can see, you are afraid of everything." Harmodius crossed his arms. "It's that you overcome that fear every time." He nodded. "Now seize the power of the sun and *cast.*"

He let the sun caress him. He felt the power of it, which was rich, like good cheese—thicker than the power of the Wild, and more intense.

And then something in his mind slammed shut.

"Damn it," Harmodius said. "Again."

The captain took a deep breath, and tried again. He could *feel* the power. And he wanted it. To touch the sun—

To touch the sun was to be clean.

I am the child of incest and hate. I was made to be the destroyer. I can never harness the power of the sun.

The bathwater was warm, and the sun was warm. He pushed his revulsion down, and he reached for it. He thought of riding in the sun. Of horses in the sun. Of Amicia standing in the sun—

Just for a moment, he connected again. The sun falling on his hand was a conductor, and his skin drank in raw power like a sponge.

And then he gagged on it again. He coughed, physically, and the soap, halfway across the room, fell to the floor.

"Ah-HA!" roared the Magus.

"I can't do it," said the captain.

"You just did it," Harmodius said. He picked up the soap and handed it to the man in the bath. "There is no limit, boy. There are no rules. You can tap the sun. For a long time, you will resist it—something in you will resist. But by God, boy, you just reached out and tapped the sun in its purist form. I know men who take the sun from water, from the air. Damn few take power straight from the source."

His water was cooling, and the captain began to soap himself.

It grew cooler, too fast.

"You bastard," the captain said to the Magus.

"Best do something about it," Harmodius said.

The captain reached out to the well.

Harmodius was there, a tower of blue fire.

He *went into his palace.*

Don't, said Prudentia. He's waiting.

"So he is, said the captain after touching the key hole.

He could feel the bath getting colder. "You bastard," he repeated.

The sun was all around him, and he reached for it.

And nothing much happened.

He thought of a summer day. But he thought too much and all he saw was sweat and bugs.

Autumn. The colour of pumpkins and standing corn and wheat ready for harvest—so many things golden and orange and ruddy in the setting sun—

Prudentia laughed aloud. "Well done, young master!" she cried.

"Pru!" he said. He was alight with a ruddy gold.

Without intending it, the windows—the stained glass windows, in the clerestory above the rotating panels—flared to brilliant life. Coloured light fell across the floor.

"Son of a bitch," he said.

He pointed to a statue, a panel, a symbol. "Saint Mary, Herikleitus, Cancer," he said.

The wheels turned. And stopped, with a click.

Prudentia smiled a solid marble smile. "Here," she said. "Watch."

She held up a prism. It took the coloured light, bent it, and sent it as one coherent beam to strike the central panel of cancer.

Ah!

The water was warm. Then warmer. Verging on hot.

Harmodius laughed aloud. "Well done!" he said.

The captain lay back in the bath, tired. Amazed. "I had help," he said, to cover his confusion. "Magus, that shouldn't have been possible. How is it possible?"

Harmodius shook his head. "I have theories. No proof." He rubbed his neck. "I didn't plan to ride out on errantry, two weeks ago. I planned to find some quiet, far from a trap Thorn had set for me. I wanted to perform some experiments."

"Instead, you got the siege." The captain was soaping himself shamelessly.

"I managed a few of my experiments," Harmodius said.

"Like what?" asked the captain.

"I got a Wild caster to use sunlight instead," Harmodius said smugly. "I *knew* you could do it."

The captain shook his head. He ought to be angry. But he felt—

He felt very powerful, indeed. "What if you were wrong?"

Harmodius shrugged. "It was unlikely. I had reason for my theory in the first place. Besides, I no sooner got here than I found a woman who cast in both colours. Wild and sun. Every time I watch her heal, it is like a miracle." He rubbed his hands together in glee. "Last night I linked with the Abbess," he said.

"You sound like a boy bragging about his first kiss," the captain said.

Harmodius laughed. "You *are* quick. She used to come around to our rooms—oh, in those days she was the very embodiment of what a woman should be." He shook his head. "It's funny, how you are never too old to be young. But I'm not here to bandy tales of lust and love, lad. The lady has proven what I already suspected. This is going to change the world."

"I like the world fine as it is," Tom said from the doorway. "When you two man-witches are done having your bloody rites, sacrificing babes and eating them or whatever heathen thing you do, I'm ready with the day's muster."

The captain was still lying in the hot water, unmoving. "Did you come to find me just to experiment on me? Or did you have another motive, Magus?"

"Thorn is planning to attack us. Directly." The Magus was trying to put the tapestry back over the opening. For a man of such power, he was curiously inept at the task. "Last night he learned he could overcome our defences. Now he'll come."

Tom came over, shkk'd him out of the way, and reached the corners out to tug them over heavy iron spikes driven into the end beams of the floor above.

"Really?" The captain asked. "How do you know?"

Harmodius shrugged and poured himself some wine. "We are linked to each other, for good or ill. I can feel his fear. And his anger, and his gloating. As can the Abbess."

"Fear?" Tom asked. "Fear? Yon mighty godling is afraid o' we?" He laughed. But the captain understood. "He must be afraid," he said. "I would be."

"He has a great deal to lose," Harmodius said. "But he knows he can destroy our trebuchet with one shot if he gets close enough. Of course, he has to risk himself on the plain to get it, hence his attempt to get it done with the wyverns. But they've failed."

Tom shook his head. "You make him sound like he's but an engine himself."

Harmodius bobbed his head. "Not bad, Tom. In a way, the magi aren't much more than siege engines, on a battlefield. Except we move much faster and we are much deadlier. But I agree, the effect is the same."

The captain made a face. "Why must he get the trebuchet? So he can move his engines against the Bridge Castle?"

Harmodius nodded. "I suppose so. That's not my department." He put his wine cup down. "I'll leave you to get ready. The Abbess asked us for sunset." He paused in the doorway. "Don't stop practising, young man. We need you."

Tom watched him go. "He's an odd one and no mistake."

The captain smiled. "This from you?" He summoned a linen towel from the door. It flew to his hand. He grinned and rose, dripping.

Tom rocked back in his seat. "Don't do that again," he said. He had his heavy knife half out of its sheath. "I'll thank ye to keep that sort o' thing private, where it belongs."

The captain felt himself blush. "I can cast magic, Tom," he said. "You know I can."

Tom grunted. "Knowing and watching is different beasts." He shrugged and looked uncomfortable. "We lost five men-at-arms yesterday and three archers." He looked at a wax tablet. "Nine men-at-arms and nineteen archers since the siege began. "Twenty-eight, and two valets is thirty." He shrugged. "One man in four."

The captain got his shirt over his head.

"I'm not saying we should quit," Tom said. "But it may be time to see if we can make a deal."

"You, too, Tom?" The captain got into his braes. They felt clean and crisp. He felt clean and crisp too. And very tired.

"We're losing 'em faster every day," Tom said. "Listen. I'm your man. You're a fine captain, and even Jehannes is coming around to that." He shrugged. "But this ain't what we do, lad. One monster; sure. An army of of them?" He frowned.

The captain sat on his cot and reached for his new hose. They were rich black wool—a trifle coarse and itchy, but heavy, warm, and stretchy. He took one and pulled it carefully up his right leg.

"We're not losing," he said.

"As to that..." Tom said.

"We're going to hold here until the king comes." He grabbed the second leg.

"What if he's not coming?" Tom leaned forward. "What if your messengers didn't get through?"

"What if pigs fly?" the captain said. "I know the owners of this fortress were notified. I saw it, Tom. The Knights of Saint Thomas will not let this convent—the base of their wealth, the sacred trust of the old king—they will not let it fall. Nor will the king."

Tom shrugged. "We could all die here."

The captain started rooting through his clothes for a clean doublet, or at least one without a noticeable smell.

The one he found was made of fustian and two layers of heavy linen, rumpled but completely clean. He began to lace his hose to it.

"We may all die here," the captain admitted. "But damn it, Tom, this is worth doing. This isn't some petty border squabble in Galle. This is the North Land of Alba. You're from the Hills. I'm from the Adnacrags." He raised his arms. "These people need us."

Tom nodded, obviously unmoved by the needs of the peoples of the north. "You really think the king will come, eh?"

"One day's time. Perhaps two," the captain said.

Tom chewed his moustache. "Can I tell the lads that? It will help their morale...only once I tell them, that's all the time you get. M'lord."

"Is this an ultimatum, Ser Thomas?" the captain stood up straight, as if that would make it better. "Are you telling me that in two days, my troops will demand that I look for another solution?"

Bad Tom sneered. "Like enough there's some as would. And more every day after that. Yes." He stood. Six feet and six inches of muscle. "Don't you go and mistake me, Captain. I like a fight. I don't really care who brings it. I could fight here forever." He shrugged. "But there's some as can't."

"And they might want to quit," the captain said, with a feeling of relief.

"They might," Tom said. He grinned. "I swear, there's something in the air, like a poison today. Lads are touchy. Every comment has an edge."

The Red Knight took his scarlet cote off the stool and began to lace it. "I've felt it."

Tom shook his head. "I hate your magery. Takes all the sport out of a

474

fight." He shrugged his great shoulders. "I don't so much mind dying, so long as I go down my way. I like a good fight. An' if it's to be my last, well, all I ask is it be good." He nodded. "Good enough for a song."

The captain nodded. "I'll see what I can do," he said.

"I'll tell the lads," Tom said.

As soon as he passed the door, Michael and Toby came back. His scarlet jupon was brushed, and he saw that the embroidered lacs d'or on the front were repaired.

Michael helped him into it. They each laced a wrist while he stood, thinking.

He thought more while he pulled on his long boots. Toby did his garters and Michael held his cote.

Toby brushed his hair and got the water out of his beard. Michael brought out his riding sword.

"War sword," said the captain. "Just in case."

Michael shortened the belt and buckled it at his waist, and then stood back while the captain drew it three times, testing the hang of the belt. Toby buckled his spurs on. Michael held the heavy gold belt with a questioning air.

The Red Knight smiled. "Why not?" he asked.

Michael buckled it around his waist, handed him his hat, gloves, and baton. "You'll be early," he said, "but not by much."

The captain walked down the steps to the courtyard. Men and women looked at him—clean, and, although he couldn't see it, glowing.

He walked across the yard, nodding to all. He stopped to compliment young Daniel on his swordplay; to share a jibe with Ben Carter, and to tell the younger Lanthorn girl that he was sorry for her loss, as both of her parents had died in the night. She rose to give him a curtsy, and he smiled when he saw her eyes slide off him to Michael, who was following him.

He heard the tale of No Head's near death experience told by a circle of archers who slapped their booted thighs in merriment, and he listened to a complaint that someone was stealing grain from Ser Adrian, who also handed him a piece of parchment rolled very tight.

"As you asked," the clerk said. "I've spoken to a dozen sisters and some of the farmers." He shrugged. "If you want my opinion, Captain—" He let the words trail off.

The captain shook his head. "I don't," he said. He smiled to take the sting out. Tucked the scroll into his cote sleeve and bowed. "I have an appointment with a lady," he said.

Ser Adrian returned his bow. "Count your fingers after you eat," he said softly.

There was a long table, set for thirteen. In the centre was the Abbess's throne, and he sat on her right hand. The table was empty as he was the first to arrive. He went and exchanged glares with Parcival, on his perch and was suffered, with incredible grumpiness, to stroke the bird's head.

A sister came in, saw him, and gave an undignified squeak. He turned, bowed, and smiled. "Your pardon, sister. A glass of wine, if I might?"

She departed.

He walked over to the *Lives of the Saints*. Now that he knew its secret, he was far more interested and only lack of time had kept him from it. It was so obvious now—a Hermetical Grimmoire. He turned the pages, deciphering them roughly. *Know this one. Know this one. Hmm. Never even heard of this one.*

It was, quite literally, an awe-inspiring tome. Which was sitting in the open, under a window, in a fortress.

He scratched under his beard.

Say that every woman here is like Amicia, he thought. *And the Order sends them here. To be safe? And to keep them out of common knowledge. Why else—*

She was standing at his side. He could smell her—her warmth. And he could feel the golden power on her skin.

"You," she said.

He turned. He wanted to take her in his arms. It was like hunger.

"You have come to God!" she said.

He felt a flare of anger. "No," he said. "Nothing like."

"I can feel it!" she said. "Why would you deny it? You have felt the power of the sun!"

"I tell you again, Amicia," he insisted. "I don't deny God. I merely defy Him."

"Must we argue?" she asked. She looked at his face. "Did I heal you?"

"You did," he said, far more rudely than he meant.

"You were bleeding out," she said, finally moved to anger. "You scared me. I didn't have time to think about it."

Oh. He raised a hand. "I thank you, mistress. Why must we always spar? Of course. Is it the cut on my face you worry about? I scarcely feel it."

She licked her thumb, like a mother removing dirt from her child. "Don't flinch," she said, and wiped her thumb down the wound. There was a flare of intense pain, and then—

"You should pray when you cast, Amicia," said the Abbess from the doorway.

The captain took a step back from the novice. They had been very close indeed.

"We are none of us without sin, without need of guidance. A prayer concentrates the mind and spirit. And sometimes His hand is on our shoulders, and His breath stirs our hearts." The Abbess advanced on them.

"Although, in the main, God seems to help those who help themselves," said the Red Knight.

"So easy to mock, Captain. I gather you have tasted the sun. And yet you feel nothing?" The Abbess tapped the floor with her staff, and two novices helped her onto her throne.

"It is, after all, just power," Harmodius said from the doorway.

The Abbess nodded at the Magus in greeting. "There are more things on heaven and earth, Magus."

"So easy to mock," Harmodius said. "And yet—as a seeker after *sophia*, I confess that when I look inside you, lady, I see something greater than myself. In you and in the Queen." He nodded. "Perhaps, in this novice too." He shrugged. "And in Thorn."

"Name him not!" said the Abbess, striking the floor.

Ser Jehannes came in. With him came Ser Thomas, and the Bailli, Johne, and Mag the seamstress, of all people.

Sister Miram sat quietly and with immense dignity, next to Ser Thomas. He grinned at her. Father Henry sat the far right of the table.

Ser Milus arrived late, with Master Random and Gelfred from the Bridge Castle.

"You took a risk," the captain said, looking at the Abbess.

She met his gaze mildly enough. "They came through your trench, Captain, and through the tunnels. This hill has many rooms and many doors."

"Like your father's house?" asked the captain.

The Abbess's look suggested that he wasn't as witty as he wanted to be.

"And many secrets," Harmodius said. "We are thirteen."

"The number of Hermeticism," said the Abbess.

"Jesus and his disciples," Harmodius added.

The captain gave a lopsided smile. "Which of us, I wonder, is Judas?"

The men at the table gave a nervous laugh. None of the women laughed at all.

The Abbess looked up and down the table, and they fell silent. "We are here for a council of war," she said. "Captain?"

He rose and stretched a little, still feeling strong. A curious feeling, for him. "I didn't summon a council of war," he said. "So what do you wish of me?"

"A report," she snapped. "How are we doing?"

He was being told to mind his manners. Amicia was glaring at him, and Jehannes, too. He thought of Jacques's admonition to be on his best behaviour. Jacques seldom said such things by chance.

"We're not losing." He shrugged. "In this case, that constitutes winning." Jehannes looked away and looked back.

"Your own men disagree with you, Captain," the Abbess said.

"That's an internal matter," the captain said.

"No, Captain. It is not." The Abbess tapped the floor with her staff.

The captain took a deep breath, looking around to pick up social cues from the audience as he had been taught.

Amicia was very tense. The Abbess gave nothing away, nor did

Harmodius, although their blankness contrasted—his a studied indifference, hers an apparently angry attentiveness. Father Henry was nervous and upset. Mag was *willing* him to do well. To deliver good news. Johne the Bailli was too tired to listen well.

Tom was trying to look down Amicia's dress; Jehannes was on the edge of his seat; Master Random was sitting back with his arms crossed, but his whole attention was on the captain.

Ser Milus was trying not to go to sleep.

The captain nodded.

"Very well, lady. Here it is." He took a steadying breath. "This fortress is ancient, and contains a powerful Hermetic source that is of equal value to magisters of all species. This fortress and the people in it are an affront to the Wild. Events—a slow progression of events that recently reached a crescendo, and include the advent of this company—forced the hand of certain powers of the Wild. And now, the Wild has come to take the fortress." He paused.

"Take it back," he said, slowly, for dramatic effect.

Even the Abbess was startled.

"It was theirs," the captain said, in a quiet, reasonable voice. "They built the well. They carved the tunnels." He looked around. "We took it in a night of fire and sorcery," he picked up his wine cup, "two hundred years ago, I'll guess. And now the Wild is back, because the lines are shifting and things fall apart, and now we're weaker than we were."

"Alba?" asked Jehannes.

"Humanity," the captain said. "That's all just background. But it is important, because I have puzzled again and again over why the enemy is taking casualties and engaging us here. It *is* costing them. Jehannes, how many of the enemy have we killed?"

Jehannes shook his head. "Many," he said.

"So many that I can only wish I'd signed the Abbess to a per-creature contract," the captain said. "In fact, I was suckered into this contract. My youth was taken advantage of." He smiled. "But never mind that. The enemy has lost several dozen irreplaceable minor powers, as well as hundreds—perhaps even thousands—of the small inhabitants of the High Wilderness. We have lost twenty-seven local people, seven sisters, three novices, and thirty of my soldiers. We have lost all the farms, and all of the animals not penned within the fortress. We have lost the Lower Town." He spread his hands and leaned onto the table. "But we have not lost the fortress. Nor the bridge. Most important of all, we have not *lost.*"

"Lost what?" asked the Abbess.

The captain shrugged. "It's spiritual. A matter of faith, if you like. Our enemy depends on success as much as on displays of power to hold his place. It is the way of the Wild. Red in tooth and claw. Wolf eat wolf. Every tiny defeat we hand him, every bee sting, causes his allies to wonder—is he as strong as he seems?"

The Abbess nodded. "Can we win?" she asked.

He nodded decisively. "We can."

"How?" she asked.

The captain crossed his arms and leaned against the mantelpiece. "By hurting him so badly that his allies think he is weak."

Harmodius shook his head. "None of us can take him, lad."

"He's not that bright," the captain said. "I think that all of us, working together, can take him."

Harmodius rose. "You're out of your depth," he said. "He's more powerful than you can imagine. And even if you hurt him—" He paused, obviously a man on the verge of saying too much.

The captain sipped wine. "I've seen him retreat twice now."

Harmodius spread his arms. "I admit he's cautious."

"If his people see him run from us, surely that's enough." The captain looked at the Magus. "Isn't it?"

The Abbess slammed her stick on the floor. "Captain. Magus. Surely you don't believe that we have to raise the siege ourselves?" She looked at the captain. "Don't you believe that the Prior is coming? The king?"

Harmodius didn't turn to face her. "The king—" he said. He shrugged.

The captain smiled at her. "Lady, I believe the king is a day or two away. But I believe that the essence of a good defence—whether my opponent is a tribe of barbarians, a feudal lord, or a legendary mage, is a good offence planned to keep my opponent off balance. Let me tell you of the next two days." He grimaced—for the first time, the others saw the fatigue under his banter. "Let me guess at the next two days," he said.

"Tonight, the enemy will cross the fields in force, and endeavour to cut us off from Bridge Castle in two ways. He'll try to occupy the trench we built, and he'll seek to destroy our engines." He looked at Harmodius. "He'll try it directly. With powerful workings overloading the Hermetical defences of the walls."

Harmodius nodded emphatically.

"His purpose is so that he can storm Bridge Castle. He is only interested in taking it now because the king is on the south bank of the Cohocton. As long as we hold the Bridge, we have the ability to end the siege in an afternoon."

"You don't know that," Jehannes said.

"Sometimes," the captain said, looking at the Magus, "You know a thing to be true, whatever the evidence. Our enemy is not that good at war. In fact, he's learning to lay a siege *from* us, as we hurt him. He learned, perhaps three days ago, that the king was coming along the south bank. I'm guessing based on the tempo of his attacks." He shrugged.

Jehannes shook his head. "If you are wrong—"

The captain slammed his fist on the table. "When, exactly, have I been wrong? I've done a pretty damn good job here, and we've gone from victory to victory—even when we stumble. We're still standing, at odds of twenty to one." He looked around. "Our magazines are full. Our casualties are acceptable. At this rate, if the worst happens," he realised he was growing too angry to sway them but his words were tumbling out, "then we'll lose the siege engines tonight, but it will be four more days before he storms the Bridge Castle, it will cost him a thousand creatures to take it. And he *still won't have a chance to take this fortress!*"

Ser Milus snorted. "I think you just condemned my garrison to death."

The captain shrugged. "I'll go and command the Bridge Castle and you can command here. This is war. We are not losing. Why are any of you considering surrender?"

Jehannes swallowed heavily.

"Speak!" the captain insisted. "Why are you all so silent?"

Amicia said quietly, "Your eyes are glowing red."

The Abbess snorted. "Every young man would have glowing red eyes, if they only could." She got up. "But I agree with you, wholeheartedly, Captain. We will have no more talk of truce, surrender, or accommodation. The Wild will kill us if they penetrate these walls." She raised her staff. She appeared to grow. Not taller, nor more beautiful, nor younger, and yet, in that moment, she was greater than any of them.

"Do not be weak, my friends." She smiled, and her smile had the warmth of the sun. "We are strongest, we mere humans, when we unite. Together we can resist. As individuals—we are no stronger than our weakest."

She diminished, and sat.

Harmodius sat silent.

Ser Milus leaned forward. "Captain," he said.

"Aye, messire?"

"I agree. He'll go for us next. Bolster the garrison. Give me fresh troops and more men-at-arms and I'll hold it a week." He nodded.

The captain subsided into his seat. "Excellent thought. Take them tonight, when you go back—as soon as ever you can."

Harmodius shook his head. "I still think he is too intelligent for all of us, even if we could all cast in concert." He rolled his shoulders like a North Country wrestler preparing for a match. "But I'm game. And I admit that the captain has a point. We don't have to defeat him, only make it look as if he can be beaten."

The Abbess smiled. "Well said. This is the kind of company I love. Let dinner be served."

The dinner was not rich. There was no roast swan, no peacocks with gilded beaks, no larks' tongues. Duels between torsion engines had killed a dozen sheep on the ridge so every mess in the fortress was eating mutton, and they were no exception.

The venison sausage was superb, though, and the wines were as ancient as human possession of the fortress.

The conversation was slow to start but by the second cup of wine, Mag was amused by Tom's ribald story, and Johne the Bailli roared with laughter at the tale of the student and the hornsmith's wife. He told one of his own, about a bad priest who disgraced his vows, and Father Henry glared.

The Abbess passed wine. She had the captain on her right, and Amicia on her left. When the talk had become general, she turned to the captain. "You have my permission to engage her in conversation," she said.

The captain tried to smile. "I'm not sure my eyes aren't still glowing," he said.

"Anger and lust are different sins," said the Abbess. "Amicia is going to take holy orders, Captain. You should congratulate her."

"She has my fullest congratulations. She will make a remarkable nun, and in time, I expect she will make a remarkable Abbess." He sipped his wine.

"She is not for you," the Abbess said, but without rancour.

"So you keep telling me, while dangling her like a tourney prize." He took a bite of meat. His tension was only visible in the force he used to cut the mutton.

"I'm right here," Amicia said.

He smiled at her.

"Once again, you bite her with your eyes." The Abbess shook her head.

After dinner, the Abbess held the magi back. Mag was surprised to be invited. "My working is very slow," she said. "I never even know—" She shrugged.

Amicia put a hand on the seamstress's shoulder. "I can feel every stitch you sew," she said.

Harmodius snorted. "You share a mixing of gold and green," he said. "I should have come to this place years ago to have all my notions of Hermetics shattered."

The Abbess said, "It is my will that we should stand in a circle, and link."

Harmodius winced. "I'm granting my secrets to every woman in the room!"

"You have little time for mere women," Amicia snapped at him. "We're too patient in our castings, are we not?"

"Women are all very well for healing," Harmodius said.

Amicia raised her head, and a sphere of golden green sat in it. She projected it to a point roughly halfway between herself and Harmodius.

"Try me," she said.

The captain was surprised by her vehemence.

The Abbess, on the other hand, merely smiled a cat's smile.

Harmodius shrugged and slapped at the sphere with a fist of phantasm. It moved the width of a finger.

Then it shot across the room at Harmodius. He caught it, struggled with it, and it began to move—slowly, but without pause—back.

"Of course he is stronger than you," the Abbess said, and she extinguished the globe with a snap of her fingers. "But not as much stronger as he would have expected. Eh, Magus?"

Harmodius took a deep breath. "You are most powerful, sister."

The captain grinned. "Let us link. I reserve some memories. But my tutor taught me to hold some walls while opening other doors."

"I give a great deal for very little gain," Harmodius said. "Bah—and yet, the Abbess is right. I am not an island." He extended his hand to Amicia.

She took it graciously. They took hands around the circle, like children in a game.

"Captain, I intend to pray. Try not to vanish in a puff of smoke," said the Abbess.

She began the Lord's Prayer.

Prudentia was standing at the door. "If you were having guests, you might have asked me to sweep up," she said.

The Abbess appeared in his hall. She was young, voluptuous in a tall, thin way, with an earthy power to her face that belied her spirit.

Amicia was elfin and green.

Harmodius was young and strong, hale—a knight on errantry, with a halo of gold.

Miram was shining like a statue of polished bronze.

Mag looked just like herself.

He was at once in his place of power, and simultaneously in Amicia's, standing on her beautiful bridge. He sat in a comfortable leather armchair in a great tiled room—that had to be Harmodius—surrounded by chess boards and wheels with wheels. He stood in a chapel surrounded by statues of knights and their ladies—or, as he realised, ladies and their knights, each with a golden chain attaching them. A chapel of courtly love—surely the lady's place of power. He knelt before a plain stone altar with a cup of red blood on it. Miram's place of power.

He stood in the Abbess's hall, and there was a needle in his hand. Mag's place of power was external—in that moment, he understood how very powerful her making was, because where the rest of them worked the aether, she worked the solid.

There was a glow or health, of vitality, of goodness, of power. And no time at all.

He knew many things, and many things of his were learned.

They made their plan.

And then, like the end of a kiss, he was himself.

He sagged away from them, tired from the length of the link. Other perspectives were haunting, exhausting—he could see, as quickly as Harmodius had, how a sisterhood of dedicated nuns was the ideal basis for a choir of Hermeticists, because they learned and practised discipline—*together.*

Harmodius was stroking his beard. "You are taking all the risk, lad," he said aloud.

The captain gave them all a lop-sided grin. "A single, perfect sacrifice," he said.

The Abbess rolled her eyes. "Sometimes your blasphemy is just banal," she said. "Try not to die. We're all quite fond of you."

Amicia met his eye and smiled at him, and he returned her smile.

"I have many things to prepare," he said. He bowed to the company, and went out into the night.

First he walked to the northern tower and climbed the steps to the second floor. He climbed softly, his black leather boots and smooth leather soles giving nothing away. The card players were attuned to the sound of sabatons.

Bad Tom was playing piquet.

"A word," he said.

Tom raised his head, pursed his lips, and put his cards face down with a start. "I can leave cards like this any time," he said, a little too carefully.

Bent was hiding something under his hand.

Given the circumstances, the captain didn't think he needed to care.

Bent shrugged. "They'll be the same when you come back," he said.

"Better be," Tom said. He followed the captain out onto the garrison room's balcony over the courtyard. "My lord?" the big man asked, formally.

"I'm going for a ride tonight, Tom," the captain said quietly. "Out into the enemy. I'd like you to come."

"I'm your man," Tom said cheerfully.

"We're going to try and take him," the captain said. He made a sign with his fingers, like antlers or branches growing from his head.

Tom eyes widened—just a hair. Then he laughed. "That's a mad jest," he said. "Oh, the pleasure of it!"

"Forget the watch bill. I want the best. Pick me twenty men-at-arms," the captain said.

"'Bout all we have on their feet," Tom said. "I'll get it done."

"Full dark. You will have to cover me when I— Tom, you know that I will have to use power?" the captain said.

Tom grinned. "I guess." He turned his head away. "Everyone says you used power against the daemons."

The captain nodded. "True. If I have to cast, I need you to cover me. I can't fight and cast." Then he grinned. "Well. I can't fight and cast well."

Tom nodded. "I'm your man. But—in the dark? After yon horned loon? We need to bring a minstrel."

The captain was lost by the change of subject. "A minstrel?"

"Someone to record it all, Captain." Bad Tom looked off into the dark. "Because we're going to make a song."

The captain didn't quite know what to make of that. So he slapped the big man on the shoulder.

Tom caught his arm. "You can't be thinkin' we can take him with steel."

The captain lowered his voice. "No, Tom. I don't think so, but I'm going to try, anyway."

Tom nodded. "So we're the bait, then?"

The captain looked grim. "You are a little too quick, my friend."

Tom nodded. "When there's death in the air, I can see through a brick wall."

Near Lissen Carak—Thorn

Thorn had everything he needed to proceed. He'd built his two most powerful phantasms in advance, storing them carefully in living things he'd designed just to store such things—pale limpets that clung like naked slugs to his mossy stone carapace.

He didn't bother to curse the wyverns who had failed him. It had been, at best, a long shot.

But now it was down to him, and he didn't want to do it.

He didn't want to weaken himself by taking on the fortress directly.

He didn't want to expose himself to direct assaults from his apprentice and the dark sun. However puny, they were not unskilled or incapable.

He didn't want to fight with *her*. Although his reason told him that when he killed her, he would be much stronger for it. His link to her was a link to his past life. A weakness.

He didn't want to do this at all. Because win or lose, he'd engaged forces that forced his hand. Made him grow in power. In *visibility*.

Damn them all, the useless daemons most of all. It was *their* fortress, and they were all busy watching him to see if they could bring him down, instead of helping.

And Thurkan had failed to take the dark sun.

Thorn was not without doubt. In fact, he was full of doubt, and again, for the hundredth time since the siege began, he considered taking his great staff and walking off into the Wild.

But without him the Wild might fail. And that would be catastrophic. At best it would be fatal for his long term plans.

He extended his hands, and power flowed smoothly. A cloud of faeries began to gather, so great was the power concentrated in a few yards of air.

He tried to imagine what it would be like when she was dead. He would miss her. She had once been the standard by which he measured himself. But that self was largely gone, and it was time he did without her.

And the apprentice. *It is a weakness, to miss the company of men.*

The Wild had to win. Men were like lice, undermining the health of the Wild.

It was time to act, and he could imagine all of his actions, a fugue of them extending back to his earliest conscious thoughts, culminating here.

He surfaced from the tide of his thoughts and looked around, unhampered by the darkness. He looked at Exrech. "Your people must storm the trench," he said. "And hold it. By holding it, we separate the fortress from the Bridge Castle."

"And then we dig," Exrech said.

Thorn bowed assent. To Thurkan he said, "The dark sun will come for me."

"We will lay in ambush for him," the daemon promised.

Thorn looked at the trolls—mighty creatures which he suspected had been created in the distant past by magi. As bodyguards. He had now acquired two dozen of them, as was the way when one became a power. He was like a beacon, and so they came. He no longer saw them as horrible. Instead, he saw them as beautiful, the way a craftsman views his perfect chisel, the one that fits his hand as if made for it.

Thorn tapped his great staff on the ground. "Go," he told his captains.

Lissen Carak—The Abbess

The Abbess felt the spells he cast. She had lain down to rest, but it was happening sooner that she expected and she sat up, her mind reaching for the threads of power that bound her to her stone.

She felt him, in the darkness out there, planning the ruin of her home, and she narrowed her eyes and reached down the link they would always share.

Traitor! she said. She flung the word with a woman's contempt.

Sophia! He cried into the Aether.

She hurled her defiance at him and she felt her venom strike home, and in the moment of his startlement she read him, and saw that he had a trap prepared—that she had a traitor in her midst, as she had long suspected.

Then she was running, her bare feet slapping the stone floor, her unbound hair trailing behind her like the tail of a comet, running for the courtyard.

She felt him respond, and she had her defences up. She felt his come up—slowly, but when raised, as strong as a wall of iron. She couldn't even sense him through them, merely that he must be behind that veil. She prayed as she ran—prayed for his ruin.

The young captain was standing by his destrier in the courtyard, with twenty knights behind him.

"You cannot go out there!" she screamed. "He is waiting for you! It is a trap!"

The captain gave her an odd smile, and waved to Michael, who had his bascinet. "He's coming already, is he?" he said to her. He turned to his knights. "Mount!" he shouted.

She grabbed his bridle, and his great war horse—quick as lightning—bit at her hand, and only his instant reaction saved her. The Red Knight slapped his hand at Grendel's neck, and the war horse took one step, and tossed his head, as if to say "could have, if I really wanted."

"He is coming *now*—"

His squire placed his helmet on his head, and pulled the chain of his aventail down over his cote armour. The captain flexed his shoulders and arms—left, right. All through the courtyard, squires held up gauntlets—slid them onto their master's hands, and then reached for the great lances, as tall as small trees and as thick, tipped in long heads of steel.

His face appeared from under the brow of the helmet. He was smiling. "Yes," the captain said. "I feel him. Through you." He laughed. "What did you do?"

"I told him what I think of him," she said. "A woman scorned—for power?" She threw back her head and laughed. It sounded mad.

"I imagine," the captain said, even as Michael moved the helmet back and forth, seating it securely on his brow, "that must have been a shrewd blow."

She shook her head. "His amour propre will shed it soon enough. But I saw into him. He has a traitor in the fortress."

"I know," said the captain. "I told you," he gave a nasty smile, "and that traitor has been giving our foe a somewhat incorrect version of events for some time now. It is now or never. He can lay all the traps he likes. Sometimes, it all comes down to speed, and audacity. He is cautious. He is sure." The captain seemed to glow with the power he'd prepared. "He wants this fight," the captain said. "So do I. One of us is wrong. We can only try our best, so guard yourself, my lady."

The main gate slid open.

"Follow me!" ordered the captain.

She stood out of the way, and watched him ride out. The hooves rattled with finality, and the knights began to move. Knights reached out to her—Francis Atcourt accepted her blessing and she reached up to pray for Robert Lyliard, who accepted her benison with a salute. Tomas Durrem bowed to her from the saddle and swept by.

The Red Knight paused in the gateway.

Above her, on the balcony of the hospital, she saw Amicia. She saw him touch the favour on his shoulder, saw her bow her head.

Grendel reared a little, and plunged through the gate, and he was gone.

She turned to Bent, who was standing by her. "Everyone is to go to the basements and lie down," she said. "Everyone!"

She ran into the courtyard, shouting orders.

The alarm bell was ringing, and the archers were pouring out of their barracks, to their battle positions. All of them were in armour. They knew the score.

The Abbess stopped in the courtyard, and looked around once—the last doors were slamming closed. She nodded in satisfaction, wished she had time to hunt for Father Henry, and ran for the chapel.

Lissen Carak—Father Henry

Father Henry saw the Abbess talk to her boy—his revulsion showed raw on his face. They were all creatures of Satan—the Abbess, the mercenary, the sisters. He was surrounded with witches and man-witches. It was like hell.

He was done with inaction. He had the power to destroy them. He had all the tools a normal man had to use against evil.

He knew he would not survive it—but all his life, he had endured pain and mistreatment for what he knew was right. His only regret was that he could not act directly against the mercenary. That man was like Satan incarnate.

Father Henry went into the chapel, where a dozen sisters were already gathered—not real sisters, he knew it now, but a coven of witches. All gathered to sing their damnable mockery of praise to God.

He made himself smile at Miram. She was too busy to pay him any heed. Just for a moment, he considered striking with his knife—right here. Taking Miram and a dozen witches—

He hid his eyes lest they read his mind, and slipped past them to the altar. He reached behind it. Seized the long staff of heavy wood, and his hand unerringly found the one arrow he needed.

Black as her heart.

It was a most remarkable arrow. Behind the head and the first three fingers of the shaft, all white bone, the rest of the arrow was of Witch Bane.

Lissen Carak, The Lower Town—The Red Knight

In a plan dependent on preparation and planning and Hermetic mastery, it was ironic that the first part required twenty brave men and one middle-aged woman to risk their lives to sweep the road clean. And he didn't even know if they'd succeeded.

But Thorn couldn't possibly expect him to come on horseback, through the Lower Town. In fact, the captain had seen to it that Thorn would expect him on the covered footpath instead.

Out in the darkness, where the Lower Town had been, a line of lights sprang up. It was a small casting—hardly a ripple on a sea full of heavy waves.

But when the blue lights sprang up, the captain gave Grendel his head. They marked a sure way through the rubble of the Lower Town.

He found that the lights heartened him. He wouldn't fail because of a detail. Now, it was a fight.

He grinned inside the raven-face of his visor, and reached for *Prudentia. He was in the room, and he didn't want anything to do with the door. He merely touched his tutor, and she smiled.*

"Find me Harmodius," he said. "Open the link."

She frowned. "But I have things I must say to you—"

He grinned. "Later," he said.

He drew power—just a trickle—stored from the sun and placed it in a ring given him by the Abbess. It had come with power; now he used it in the Aether to ignite his darksight.

Back in reality, and his sense of the night altered. The outline of the trap was clear now, and he smiled like a wolf when the prey begins to tire.

Thorn had sent creatures into the ditch beyond the remnants of the Lower Town wall—the ditch his own men had dug to communicate with the Bridge Castle. It was now full of boglins, which suited him just fine.

Off to the south, at the entry to the defended path which the archers had taken and retaken every day of the siege, waited a company of daemons. At least forty of them, enough to exterminate his company of knights.

He grinned. *I didn't go that way,* he thought, smugly. The creatures of the Wild were not as clever as men at hiding themselves in the Aether. It occurred to him as he cantered down the steep road that they didn't think of hiding in what—to them—was their natural element. Or something.

And out on the plain, moving steadily forward towards the town, was Thorn.

The great figure towered over his allies. Even at this distance he stood head and shoulders above the trolls who surrounded him, at least twenty feet tall with antlers like a great hart's spreading away on either side of his stone-slab face. He towered, but he was not particularly fearsome from five hundred paces. He was a beacon in darksight, though, and his power wound away in a hundred threads—to the skies, to the creatures around him, to the woods behind him—

Two-dozen trolls guarded the horned figure, reflecting his power.

Even as the Red Knight watched the horned man he raised his staff.

Thorn raised his staff. He could see the dark sun. For a moment he was tempted to lay his great working on the mysterious, twisted creature, but a plan is, after all, a plan. He reached into the slug on his left shoulder, and green fire washed up his right arm, pulsed once on his staff—and it was like joy; like the ultimate release of love.

The light was like that of the deep woods on a perfect summer day. It was not a pinpoint, a line, a bolt, a ball. It was everywhere.

The Abbess was in her choir, and she felt the assault on the wards—felt them stumble. She raised her voice with those of her sisters. She could hear them, feel them in the Aethereal, feel Harmodius and Amicia.

The light was everywhere. Its green radiance was seductive, the siren call of summer to the young, to run away from work and play, instead. The Abbess remembered summer—summer days by the river, her body wet from a swim, her horse cropping grass . . .

Far, far away, the sigils that defended her house were—

Harmodius read the working, and its immense subtlety, and just as he was about to throw his counter, he saw the trap.

Thorn wanted him to swat the working aside.

The summer light was an insidious working that struck directly at the sigils from all sides and drained their strength into the Wild itself. The craftsmanship was magnificent.

The power involved was majestic.

And any counter—any reinforcement—would drain away with the sigils themselves, into the hungry maw that awaited.

If I survive this, I'm going to learn that working, *Harmodius thought.*

He took his narrow sword of bright blue power, and severed the Abbess's connection to the fortress sigils.

The fortress sigils fell. Thorn gave a grunt of satisfaction, tempered by knowing that Harmodius had done the only thing he could have to avoid being sucked down with them.

The faerie folk danced around Thorn's head, in the sudden accession of power—this ancient power, the very life-blood of wards that had stood for centuries. It was bleeding into the ground at his feet, and they bathed in it, their winged forms like tiny angels flitting in a rainbow of light.

The final collapse was like the opening of a window. There—and then nothing.

He didn't pause. His staff swept up, and he released his second working— a simple hammer.

One Leg and Three Legs and the trebuchet and the top third of the great North Tower vanished in a flash of light. The explosion that followed destroyed every window in the fortress—the stained glass of the saints became a hurricane of coloured shrapnel.

Father Henry, head down behind the altar below the great window, had his back flayed bloody. His robes were all but ripped from his body although his head and arms were covered. He screamed.

The captain reached into his *palace and drew power through the ring.*

He had the charred cloth in his gauntlet, where he couldn't lose it in the dark, and he funnelled the power through it.

Four feet beneath the duck boards at the base of his trench, beneath the boglin horde, ten fuses sprang alight.

Above him, in the fortress, a single massive pulse of power ripped through the night air—the concatenation almost cost him his seat on Grendel.

But the fuses were lit, and now—

Now it was a hundred long heartbeats to Armageddon.

He had reached the base of the slope and now he followed the path between the first of the blue lights across the rubble to the town's back gate. Grendel couldn't move quickly here, and this was the weakest part of the whole plan. If he could see Thorn then Thorn would see him. Indeed, the whole *point* was that Thorn should see him. And yet even now, the daemons were starting to shift. They must already know that their trap was in the wrong place. And the huge shapes around the enemy were new.

Thorn had already struck the trebuchet, and destroyed it.

We're too late.

He was halfway across the town, Grendel was moving at a trot, and one bad step on rubble and he would be down. The risk was insane.

Fifty heartbeats.

He turned in the saddle and looked back. Tom was right behind him, and the sound of the column of knights filled the darkness robbed of other sound by the force of the explosion.

He rose in his stirrups as Grendel stepped over a downed roof beam—the blue lights seemed to ripple—and then he was over the outer wall and in the field. Bad Tom passed the wall right behind him, and they reined in together.

He turned Grendel and pointed his muzzle at the horned figure, now at eye level, just two hundred paces away across the plain. Behind him, his sortie shook out into a wedge as they got free of the tumble of rocks and roof tiles that had been a town. In the dark.

The captain thought, *Damn, we're good.*

He raised his right arm, lance and all. He used a little power to light the tip of his lancehead—not just light it, but make it burn like a star.

He swept his lance down.

Grendel gave a little start, and went from a stand to a gallop in three strides, as if they were in a tiltyard.

Thirty heartbeats.

Lissen Carak—Thorn

Thorn watched the dark sun come at him, and he waited with a curious mixture of elation and loathing for the misshapen thing. It was like a man, but it was not like a man. He was some odd fusion of man and Wild. He might have pitied it, but he hated it, as well—because its fusion was different from his.

It was coming, just as his secret friend said it would. But not by the path it had said it would take. That meant the secret friend was compromised.

And that meant...

The dark sun held a power that shouted itself to every Wild creature on the battlefield.

This was his first clear look at the thing, and Thorn felt a tingle—not of fear, precisely. But in that creature was something that bellowed a challenge to him. Like a vast predator roaring defiance across the swamps of the Wild. And every Wild creature felt that call. Some flinched from it. Some were attracted to it.

That was the Way of the Wild.

...and so the dark sun must be a creature of the Wild, and that meant—

It was too fast. Thorn's discovery came very, very late. He had allowed himself to ponder the thing's creation for long *thuds* of his great, slow heart, and in that time the man had crossed the ruins of the Lower Town like a dhag—so fast that even as his hidden ambush of daemons sprang from their concealment and raced to save him they were already too late to strike a blow. The wedge of knights was past them.

Something was slowing him!

Bitch he roared in his head. *She was working her will on him—*

He shook himself free of her enchantment, even as—

Lissen Carak—The Red Knight

He put his spurs to Grendel—just a pressure of the pricks to the sides, so that the great horse knew not to stint. This was the great effort.

Thorn was standing facing the fortress, and his bodyguard of misshapen horrors were shoulder to shoulder holding massive bill hooks and spiked clubs, wearing armour of wood and leather. They glowed, not with the healthy summer green of Thorn's workings but with a sickly putrescent colour.

The captain had hoped to save his lance for Thorn with a tiltyard trick, so he gave Grendel the sign to put its head down. He flicked his lance down, and the troll followed the lance tip, cutting up—

Grendel struck the troll as it parried the lance, so that the spike on his great horse's head drove into the monster's stone-armoured chest. It was six inches long, sharp as a needle on its tip and as broad as a man's hand at the base, and the horse weighed more than the troll by several times. The horn broke the stone plate in two and punched through its hide, to shatter the bones of its chest. Grendel crushed the troll flat, and planted a great steel-shod hoof precisely on its hips, the horse's charge virtually unimpeded by the collision.

With the practise of a hundred jousts, the captain let his lance come down again. Thorn was ten paces beyond his bodyguard, just turning to ward himself.

He leaned forward, adding the power of his body and hips to the weight of the horse. By luck, or a last second intuition, his lance struck home within a hand's span of where the ballista bolt had struck Thorn hours before and he rocked his enemy back. Thorn tottered, reached out with his staff—

Fell backwards and crashed to earth.

The captain struggled after the impact—it felt much like slamming a lance into a castle, but he kept his seat and swept on, leaving his lance, and the next two men in the wedge—Bad Tom and Ser Tancred—each put their lances into the thing after him; or so he had to hope, because he was riding past, and the rest of the bodyguard were on him. The trolls were as tall as he was, and one blow from one of their weapons would crush his armour and kill him. But he rode as if inspired—he leaned, Grendel danced, and no blow fell fully on him.

Grendel put his spiked head into the next one. The unicorn's horn of twisted steel bit deep again, and again the captain almost lost his seat in the shock—the great horse went from a gallop to a stand, screamed his anger and struck the thing with his hooves—one, two, each landing with greater force than ten belted knights could muster, yet precise as a boxer.

The Wild monster's sickly green glow was extinguished between the first and second blow to its great stone head, and the horse reared in triumph.

The captain drew his great sword.

Another troll screamed from his left, rose to its full height, and was struck in the chest by a lance that knocked it flat.

Bad Tom roared, "Eat me, you son of a bitch!" at his side and was gone into the green-tinged darkness. Tom was a legend for temper, for ill manners, for lechery and crime. But to see him on a fire-lit battlefield was to see war brought to earth in a single avatar, and as his knights swept past him, the captain watched as Tom's lance, unshivered, swept through the trolls.

"Lachlan for Aa!" he roared.

When his lance broke in his third victim, he ripped his five-foot blade from its scabbard and the blade rose and fell, catching the fires of the plain on its burnished blade at the top of every cut so that it seemed to be a living line of fire—rose and fell with the smooth and ruthless precision of a farmer scything grain at the turn of autumn.

By himself, Bad Tom cut a hole through the company of monsters.

The captain nudged Grendel back into motion. On his sword side, a smooth stone head rose out of the darkness and he swung down with all his might, rising in the stirrups to get the most out of his cut—the sword rebounded from the stone, but the head cracked and dropped away, it's roar changed to the caw of a giant crow as it fell.

And then he was through the enemy line. His sword was wet and green with acrid blood, and behind him, the trolls who survived the charge were already gathering to cut him off from the fortress. The crisp spring air was suddenly full of arrows, announced only by their whickering flight—almost unnoticed against the ringing of his ears—but then they began to strike him. And Grendel.

Whang!

Ting-whang WHANG.

There were irks behind the trolls, and they were loosing into the melee—unconcerned about their own, or perhaps Thorn was too fully armoured to fear an irk arrow.

More creatures charged at his knot of knights from either side, and he rode for the long trench he had ordered dug. A trench full of boglins.

Ready? he asked into the Aether, and looked back.

Bad Tom had already made his turn. At least a dozen knights were with him.

They all knew the score, and the plan. He'd lost count of the time. But it had to be close.

He rode right for the trench, wondering if—hoping that—he had put Thorn down. He had to hope. It had been a mighty blow.

The trench was only a few strides away. A handful of darts rose to greet him, but the boglins were as stunned as their master by the speed of it, and then Grendel rose, and for a moment, they flew.

He landed with a thunderclap of strained armour straps and saddlery, a clank and a rattle, his teeth rattled, his jaw hurt, and his helmet slammed into his forehead despite arming cap and padding, and he was blind for a critical moment—

—and Grendel shuddered and stumbled, and all around the two of them, his knights were jumping the trench and the boglins were turning—too slowly.

The last knight—Tom—cleared the trench. Landed, and passed Grendel, who was slowing under his master's hand.

The boglins, fooled for a moment by the speed of their passage, came over the lip of the trench in a flood.

The captain just had time to think *Now would be good.*

The naphtha charge buried under the boards in the trench ignited. It didn't explode. It went with a great *whoosh* as if God himself had willed it, and then there was only a wall of fire behind them.

The captain might have laughed in his triumph, but in that moment Grendel died under him. The horse had given his life to get his master over the trench with a dozen well-thrown javelins in him, and he crashed to the earth, and all the lights went out.

Lissen Carak—Harmodius

A third of the choir was dead.

Harmodius found the Abbess, and got a hand under her elbow, but she levered herself to her feet with dancer's muscles and *reached in the Aether –*

He was wounded. The boy had hurt him.

Harmodius had Miram steady on her feet, and the chorus began again—shaky, trembling, but lifting once again. Amicia's voice was clear above them all—for a long minute, she had carried the choir by herself.

The power was still there—the immense power of the well, wrapped in the working of the choir.

Harmodius spread his arms, and raised his staff, and began to cast.

Lissen Carak—Father Henry

Father Henry lay in a pool of his own blood, ears ringing.

The pain on his back and shoulders was incredible.

He shrieked.

But Christ had born pain. Pain was like the Enemy—it could be vanquished.

Father Henry rose to his knees.

By a miracle, his bowstring had not been cut by the glass that was all around him.

He nocked his arrow with shaking hands.

Lissen Carak—Thorn

Thorn felt the pain of his wounds, but not as much as he felt the mockery of the attack. The dark sun was taunting him—had ridden through his trap with deliberate mockery.

Hatred suffused him.

He rose to his feet. Tested his strength and grunted.

He was struck by a crossbow bolt, which didn't even distract him. He spread his fingers, flame crackled and a dome of green power sprang over his head, another flashed into being on his left hand like a verdant buckler, and in his right hand he raised his staff.

He took a stride toward the trench, and his guards followed him.

Look, I am an epic hero, he thought with bitter irony. *And I have to do everything myself.*

He didn't run. He took long strides to his boglins, surging out of the trench the men had cut like an obscene wound on the earth.

And then alchemical fire exploded in front of him. It wasn't a manifestation of power, or he'd have sensed and quenched it. In fact, he tried. It took him wasted seconds to realise that his enemy had filled the ground under the trench with naphtha—they had poured poison into the very veins of earth.

Men must die.

Lissen Carak—The Red Knight

He never quite lost consciousness, although he hit the ground very hard. But he rose before the pain could fill him, and nothing was broken. His sword was lying under Grendel's body, but he got a hand on the pommel and dragged it clear.

He looked around but the hoofbeats said that it had all worked better than he might have hoped. He hadn't wanted Tom to stay and die. On the other hand, somehow he hadn't ever thought he would lose Grendel.

He didn't take up his sword because he expected to live, so much as because it seemed appropriate.

For the first time since the sortie began he had time to breathe. Beyond the confines of his faceplate it was a big, dark, violent night. Many of the boglins in the trench had made it out, and some had started to follow the knights before the naphtha charge went off, and of course he was an infernal beacon to creatures of the Wild. They were coming for him.

So was Thorn.

The captain couldn't manage a smile inside his Raven's beak. But he wasn't shaking too badly, and he had control of his head.

His job now was to hold Thorn's attention as long as ever he could.

Best do a proper job of it.

He reached out, and summoned the nearest creatures of the Wild to serve him, the way his witch of a mother had taught him to. He'd sworn never to do it. But this was his last stand. Now, for everything, the oaths of an angry boy were thrust aside...

Lissen Carak—Thorn

The dark sun's challenge was contemptuous.

He was forcing the boglins to his will, on the other side of the trench.

Thorn shrieked with rage, as if he'd been struck. He threw caution to the wind, and leaped the trench of fire.

Lissen Carak—The Red Knight

The captain was surrounded by boglins—a crush of them, and their acrid scent filled his helmet.

He had never been so close to the creatures, and despite his revulsion for them, he found it impossible *not* to notice things about them—how their soft shells seemed to be formed like armour, their human arms emerging from breastplates.

He waited for the coup de grâce... But he was holding them, and all their thoughts were his.

This was what he had been made to do. Created. Honed. Polished for it. And he began to work on them.

He was in the room of his palace, and Prudentia was off her pedestal, standing by the iron-bound door. She had her stone arms locked against it, and it trembled on its hinges despite her efforts.

"He is coming for you," Prudentia said.

"Open the door," he said, trying to master his terror.

"He wants you to face him in the Aetherial! He will eat your power, you arrogant child!"

Prudentia said. "Can't you hear him?"

The captain could hear his bellows of victory, all through the Aether. "I could use some advice here," he said.

"Don't stand against the powers of the world until you are much, much more powerful," Prudentia said in a matter of fact tone. She shrugged. "But when brute force will not suffice, consider artifice. Recall, dear boy, that he will not know the limits of your power. He calls you the dark sun."

Good advice. But he couldn't think of anything he could do with it. He reached for Harmodius and opened the door.

Thorn was there.

He had crossed the trench of fire, and now he stood, smouldering, the acrid smoke of his wounds rising in wisps, and he was backlit by the fire in the trench.

The captain coughed.

Thorn towered over him and even from a horse length away, the captain could see that the sudden shock of lances had hurt him. Something dark and watery oozed form a deep pit in his breast.

You thought yourself my peer, you little thing.

The captain was fighting the wave of nausea that came with the fear. Whatever Thorn was, his coming brought terror, revulsion, a deep, sick feeling of oppression and violation. The captain struggled with it. For a long, long moment, all he saw was his mother, promising him—

You dared to oppose me. Do you know who I am?

Deep in the grip of the horror, the captain writhed. His conscious, rational mind registered that only the most unstable beings asked such questions.

And he had a lifetime's experience of pretending courage when all he wanted to do was roll in a ball and weep. It was like arguing with his mother.

He cast—not an attack, but a subtle reinforcement of his armour.

He raised his sword. "Well," he said. His attempt at a drawl actually sounded somewhat hysterical. "Well," he said again, and his voice was better. He used to goad his mother this way. "I understand you used to be the King's Magus."

Thorn leaned down and one giant, hot hand slapped the captain to the ground. He saw the blow coming, his wrists answered his will, his sword swept up, and the blade shattered as it touched the sorcerer's skeletal hand. The power of Thorn's blow hurt the captain right through the steel harness he wore. Even through the power supporting it.

I am infinitely greater than the mere man who was the King's Magus.

The captain couldn't muster a laugh, or even a cackle. But he got back to his feet, as he had when his brothers beat him.

Thorn raised his hand.

One finger fell away.

The captain felt a wild, foolish joy. He tossed the shards of his sword away and drew his rondel dagger instead. "You are just one of the many Powers of the Wild, Thorn." He took a deep breath against the pain in his ribs. "Don't get above yourself, or someone will eat you."

Good shot, muttered Harmodius, inside his memory palace. *Almost ready.*

There was a pause, as if the earth stood still. The captain tried to see Amicia's face—to think any worthy, noble, or merely human last thought that was not born of fear and would not leave him to die the slave of this creature.

But he couldn't.

Hold on, said Harmodius.

You are challenging me?!

The Red Knight stiffened his spine, stood as tall as he could, and said, "My mother made me to be the greatest Power of the Wild," He managed another breath. And delivered his sentence, like a sword cut. He said,

"You are just some parvenu merchant's son trying to ape the manners of his betters."

He ordered the boglins to *Kill Thorn* and the crowd of boglins turned their weapons on their former master.

Stung—even though none of them could penetrate his glowing green armour—he clenched one gnarled fist.

Boglins died.

The sorcerer's rage was automatic rage, unthinking rage at being challenged, at insult piled on insult. Thorn bellowed. ***You are nothing!*** Faster than the captain could parry, strike—react at all—Thorn's fist slammed into him and knocked him to the ground again, except this time he felt bones break. Collarbone? Ribs, for sure.

Suddenly he was *in his palace, and Prudentia stood with a handsome young man in black velvet embroidered with stars. So great was his fear and his confusion that he took long heartbeats to see that the stranger was Harmodius.*

But he couldn't hold the palace in his mind. He was too afraid, and even as Harmodius opened his mouth he was on his back and the pain was remarkable. His armour had probably saved him from death. But not from pain.

That was a laugh.

He used his stomach muscles to roll over, to get to his feet.

There was Thorn.

Why are you not dead? Thorn asked.

"Good armour," the Red Knight said.

Aah! I can see your power. I will take it for my own. It is wasted on you. Who are you? You are no different from me.

"I made different choices," the captain answered. He had trouble breathing but, just there, he started to be proud. He was *holding his own.*

Thorn threw a working; bright as a summer day, fast as a levin bolt.

The Red Knight parried it to the ground with a flash of silver white.

I see, now. You were made. You were constructed. Bred. Ahh. Fascinating. You are not an ugly mockery after all, dark sun. You are a clever hybrid.

"Cursed by God. Hated by all right thinking men." The captain was gaining strength from sheer despair. With nothing left, he was going to beat his fear, the way he'd beaten it a thousand other times.

The time of men is over. Can you not see it? Men have failed. The Wild is going to crush men, and before ten thousand suns set, the young fawn and the bear cub will ask their mothers who wrought the stone roads, and the faerie will weep for their lost playthings. Even now, men are but a pale shadow of what they once were.

But then, you are scarcely a man. Why do you cleave to them?

Breathing was difficult, but he was achieving calm. Calm meant mastery of the Aethereal.

Hope gave rise only to more fear. But fear was the ocean in which he swam, and he reached through the fear—he used the fear.

He was in the palace of memory. He reached out to Amicia, who took his hand and Harmodius's, and the Abbess's, and Miram's. And Mag's. And that of every surviving nun singing in the chapel.

He mastered his thoughts.

Cast his very favourite phantasm.

"Holy Saint Barbara, Despoina Athena, Herakleitus," he said, pointing at each statue as he spoke the name, and the great room began to spin.

Prudentia reached down from the plinth and put a hand on his shoulder. She smiled at him. It was a sad smile. And she reached out and took his hand free hand. "Goodbye, my lovely boy. I had so many things to say. O Philae pais—"

He was flooded with power—power like pain, when it rises beyond any possible point of pleasure—like victory. Like defeat, like hopelessness and hope. And he stayed there, for an eternity, balanced between all and nothing.

Like love when love is too much to bear.

What did she mean, goodbye?

He was back in the acrid night air.

He wondered if the calm that suffused him was artificial.

Thorn leaned over him, blocking the stars.

You are ours. Not theirs.

The captain laughed, a laugh he treasured. "There is no *us*, Thorn. In the Wild, there is only the law of the forest and the rule of the strongest. And if I join you, I will subsume *you* to my needs."

Just to make his point, the captain projected, as his mother had taught him, the imperative. **Kneel.**

More than two thirds of the surviving boglins feel immediately to their knees.

He was deeply gratified to see Thorn twitch so that his singed branches shook as if a strong wind had passed through a forest.

And even as he exchanged words with the Enemy, buying precious heartbeats, an agony of power rose inside him—the greatest power he had ever felt, as if love personified drove his phantasm. Between two heartbeats, the captain knew what she had done.

Prudentia had not opened the door, which would have invited Thorn to take him from inside.

She had ended herself, and as a phantasmal construct, she had poured her own power and the power of her making into his work. It explained the love.

Oh, the love.

I make fire, he said in the purest High Archaic.

Lissen Carak—Thorn

Thorn felt the swelling of power—such a sweet power, with a taste he had forgotten. He lost a thousandth of a heartbeat trying to identify it. Only then did he reach for his shield of adamantine will.

You don't remember that taste, my sweet? That taste is love, and once, you were capable of it.

The lady was in his head—in his place of power—naked, exposed, and rendering him the same.

Confused—a storm of rage and hate—he struck at her.

In striking, he did *not* raise his shield.

Lissen Carak—The Abbess

The Abbess took her stand in the ruined chapel, in near darkness, her hair unbound, her feet bare in the shattered glass. Her nuns stood in close array behind her, and their voices rose in sacred music.

Harmodius stood beside her, his staff in his hand, riding the song of power into the darkness, into the labyrinthine mind of the young man on the field below, facing a monster—

She, too, faced a monster. A variety of monsters, many of them of her own making. That she had loved this thing which now sought the ruin of all she loved—

She hit him with her frustration and her love, her years of loss. She poured her love of her God into his wounds, and she added her contempt—that he had abandoned her to turn traitor to humanity. That he had taken her gift and made this depravity with it.

She *hurt* him.

And he struck back. But he was hampered, and still—*still*—he hesitated to hurt her.

She hit him again. She'd had years to expunge her hesitations.

Lissen Carak—Mag the Seamstress

Mag, standing in the former street of the Lower Town, nonetheless felt the old Abbess struggle with the Enemy. It was terrifying, but she felt the Abbess's power and she raised her own hands in sympathy. Unknowing, untrained, the seamstress nonetheless poured her carefully hoarded power into the Abbess.

The Abbess smiled in triumph.

*

Father Henry rose from behind the altar, and drew his arrow to his mouth, and loosed.

And from the darkness, a cry of rage.

The Abbess screamed like a soul in torment, and was knocked flat on her face—dead before her head hit the stone floor.

Blood welled from her eyes and she lay still, a vicious black arrow in her back.

Fire—a pure fire of crystalline blue—Prudentia's favourite colour—enveloped Thorn's mortal shell. The heat of it was stupendous.

And from the fire, smoke—a rich, bright smoke, luminescent and alive, more than white, more than smoke, and the captain could feel Harmodius sending the smoke through him, through his place of power and down his arm and into the air about him. A subtle working—insidious, clever, a fog of a million mirrors.

She had hurt him—hurt him so much. And the dark sun had hurt him, and now he was screaming in agony. A moment's remorse—and the cost had been cataclysmic.

But he was saved—she was dead, her light extinguished, and not by him. Some other power had struck her down and he was innocent of that crime, and he turned—strong enough to finish this pretender.

But he writhed inwardly in the knowledge that she was dead.

It had to be done.

It should not have been done.

And then—too late! He felt his apprentice's working, the complex, layered phantasm that was that boy's trademark—a coloured smoke, so quiet, so harmless, so complex—

He lunged back up the line of Harmodius's casting, as he had attacked along the line of his lover's.

Harmodius felt his former master's power coming.

His counter-strike was so tiny, so very subtle, that it cost him almost no power. It relied on his enemy's hubris and his sense of his own power.

Lissen Carak—Thorn

Thorn killed the apprentice effortlessly, although he couldn't, for some reason, take the man's not inconsiderable power for his own. Typical of the man—to squander his power rather than let his master have it. His former apprentice fell back amidst a choir of nuns. If he'd had time, Thorn might have exterminated the nest, but the dark sun was still pounding him with his strange blue fire.

If Thorn had been a man he might have laughed. Or cried.

Instead, his consciousness raced back to the plain below, where his shell faced being consumed by fire.

Another slow heartbeat while he poured power into the problem and extinguished the blue fire.

He was surprised—and concerned—to see how badly hurt he was. Again—yet again, he would appear weak.

He had no time to take stock. Even now he was so badly hurt that any of the lesser powers could take him.

He raised his staff and was *gone*.

Lissen Carak—The Red Knight

Run, boy! cried Harmodius.

The captain tried to run.

He crawled through the prostrate boglins. He forced himself to his feet, and he ran, a broken, stumbling run while waiting for the levin bolt in the back that would end him. *He stood in the palace, and the plinth was empty, and Prudentia's statue lay cold and still on the ground.*

Damn.

Time to mourn later, if he lived.

He leapt onto the plinth, and called his names.

Honorius! Hermes! Demosthenes!

Desperation, luck, and a strong will.

Goodbye, Prudentia! You deserved better than I ever gave you!

He ran to the door, and pulled it open.

The flicker of a casting—Thorn reached out, trying to find its source. The dark sun was still on the battlefield. Still casting?

I am badly hurt, he conceded. He summoned his guards to withdraw.

Lissen Carak—The Red Knight

—*powered his phantasm and slammed the door shut again.*

His body rose in a leap, sailed through the heated air, and fell to earth again—a hand's breadth clear of the wall of the trench.

The captain turned away from the fire, and saw a wedge of knights, their mirror-bright harnesses like liquid fire in the smoky darkness. Off to the north, boglins hovered, uncertain.

A daemon raised his axes in challenge.

But the knights did not pause to fight. Even as the captain ran, strong arms grabbed him, an arm under each shoulder, and he was swept away as cleanly as if he'd been snatched by a great bird.

Chapter Fourteen

Valley of the Cohocton—Peter

Peter didn't recover so much as grow used to what was gone, like a man who has lost a hand, or an arm. And it took days, not hours.

Ota Qwan scarcely paid him any heed at all—indeed, now that he was paramount war leader, Ota Qwan was loud and definite and far, far too important to waste time on one new warrior. Peter walked all the way back from the Ford Fight, as the Sossag came to call it, to their camp in a haze of fatigue and a darkness that he'd never known, even as a slave.

Three nights in a row, he sat by a dead fire, staring at the cold coals and considering ending his own life.

And then he would hear Ota Qwan—instructing, ordering, leading, demanding.

And that would give him the strength to go on.

On the fourth night on the trail back, Skahas Gaho came and sat with him, and offered him some rabbit, and he ate of it, and then together the two of them drank some of the dead men's mead—honey sweet. The Sossag warrior was quickly drunk, and he sang songs, and Peter sang his own people's songs and in the morning his head hurt, and he was alive.

It was just as well, because they were moving easily along trails as soon as the sun was up, and suddenly, every warrior fell flat on his face, so that—just for a moment—Peter was the only man standing. Then he threw himself flat. He'd been so deep in his pain that he had missed the signal.

Scouts wormed their way into the bush and came back to Ota Qwan with reports, and the rumour swept the column that there was a great army on the road. Far too large and well-prepared for the Sossag people to challenge alone.

They had won the Ford Fight. But they had lost many warriors. Too many warriors. Too much experience, too many skills.

So they rose as they had fallen to the ground, almost as if a single spirit inhabited many bodies—and they loped off to the north, and they climbed well into the foothills of the Adnacrags, avoiding the enemy by many miles. It was only after three days of gruelling travel over the most difficult terrain that Peter had ever known when they climbed over a low ridge, and saw their camps spread across the woods and green fields of the Lissen where it ran into the Cohocton. From the top of the long ridge, Peter could see thousands of points of light—like the stars in the sky, but every one of them was a fire, and around that fire stood a dozen men, or boglins, or other creatures—such creatures as served Thorn and yet loved fire. And more creatures slept cold in the woods, or slept in streams, or mud.

Peter let Skahas Gaho pass him on the trail and he stood in the deepening twilight at the top of the ridge, and looked down. Almost at his feet rose the great fortress of the lady, which the Sossag called the Rock, and its towers looked like broken teeth, and its arrow slits glowed with fire like a Jack-o'-lantern.

And away to the east, at the edge of his vision, he could see another host of fires burning. The army around which the Sossag had slipped. The King of Alba.

The armies were gathered, and in the last light, Peter watched a tall column of ravens and vultures riding the drafts over the Valley of the Cohocton.

Waiting.

He sat and watched the play of light—massive pulses of power, flashing back and forth like a summer storm.

Lissen Carak—Thurkan

Thurkan watched the dark sun slip away. He had seen the Enemy captain face down Thorn, pounding him with blue fire until the Wild sorcerer fled. And unlike Thorn, the dark sun's bodyguard came and rescued him, their ranks closing tight around him.

The daemon had learned much about the skills of the knights.

He turned to his sister. "Thorn is beaten."

She spat. "Thorn is not beaten, any more than you were last night. Thorn said he would kill the great *machine-that-throws-rocks* and he has done so. Stop your foolish preening."

Thurkan shivered with suppressed need to fight.

"I will challenge Thorn," Thurkan said.

"You will *not!*" Mogan replied.

Lissen Carak—Michael

The Siege of Lissen Carak—Day Thirteen

Last night the enemy came with all his might to storm the fortress. The King's Magus and the Abbess and the Red Knight duelled with him and drove him back, but the Abbess died defending her place, shot in the back by a foul traitor.

Michael sat with his head propped on one hand, looking at the hastily scrawled words. He sipped the wine next to him and tried not to go to sleep over the journal.

The captain was in the hospital. His breastplate had a dent in it the size of a man's fist. They'd lost five men-at-arms.

The archers were openly saying that it was time to ask for terms.

He turned on the wooden stool he was using. Kaitlin Lanthorn lay, fully dressed, on his bedroll. She'd come in after the sortie returned, kissed him, and stayed by his side while he saw to little things—like having the armourer get the dent out of the captain's breastplate.

"You shouldn't be here," he said.

She lay, open eyed. "I'm pregnant," she said. She sat up. "Oh, I might be wrong, but Amicia says I am. She'd know." Kaitlin shrugged. "I'm pregnant, and the sorcerer is going to kill us all, anyway. So what's it matter if I spend the night with you?"

Michael tried to think like the captain. To balance it all out. But he couldn't, so he put the quill down, and took her face in his hands. "I love you," he said.

She smiled. "That's good," she said. "Cause I love you, too, and we're going to have a baby."

"If we live through the next few days." He lay down next to her.

She turned to him. "You'll protect me, I think."

Michael stared into the dark.

Mag stood with her daughter Sukey and a dozen other nuns and local women, laying out the dead.

This time there was no feeling of triumph. The cost was high—the Abbess was dead, and there was a line of figures wrapped in white linen to show the losses of her community and the losses of the captain's company, intermingled.

And the Red Knight was gone, carried into the hospital.

The Abbess had been killed by an arrow. And no one seemed to be looking into her murder.

Mary Lanthorn smoothed a sheet over Ser Tomas Durren. "He was bonny," she said.

Fran shook her head. Sukey sobbed, and Mag pulled her daughter's head against her chest. Sukey's husband was dead too. Third winding sheet from the right. She held Sukey for a long time, and then went back to wrapping Third Leg. His body had been crushed—his face almost erased—and yet Mag was gentle in wrapping the fresh white linen tight. Details mattered to Mag.

God, let these boys come to you swiftly despite the lives they led.

"I hear the Red Knight's on the verge of death," Mary said.

Amy Carter looked up. "That novice will save him. Amicia."

Kitty looked at her sister. "The men are saying she's a witch." She looked at Sukey and Mag for a moment, and then back at her sister. "Ben says she killed the Abbess."

Amy's eyes grew wide.

Mag put a hand on the girl's shoulder. "Best not be spreading that kind o' talk, girls."

"It's all around in the stables," Kitty said. "All the boys is saying that some of the sisters is witches."

Sister Miram was shaking out a winding sheet. Her hearing must have been unnaturally sharp. She turned.

"Who says we are witches?" she asked.

Kitty blanched.

Miram frowned. "Child. Who is spreading this poison?"

Kitty looked around, uncertain. "My brother Ben says the priest said it."

Sukey looked at her mother. "Bill Fuller too." She spat the words. "Fuller's been talking crap all night."

Miram looked around. She went and touched the first body in the row—smaller then the others. The Abbess.

"I have been remiss," Sister Miram said. "I let loss cloud my vision of earthly iniquity."

Kitty Carter looked at her sister. "I didn't really think Amicia killed the Abbess."

Amy rolled her eyes.

Lissen Carak—The Red Knight

It wasn't yet morning when he came to. Noise in the corridor had awakened him. He heard armour—and he was in the wrong bed.

There was no sword by his bed.

The door opened, and Sister Miram entered his cell, in the full robes of the order; Ser Jehannes in harness, and Michael; Johne, the Bailli of one of the towns, and Master Random.

He pulled the linen sheet up over his chest.

"The Abbess died in the enemy attack," Sister Miram said. Her face had aged.

The captain had scarcely heard her speak. What she had said took a moment to register, so that his mind explored the fact of Sister Miram's speaking for heartbeats before he realised the import of what she said.

"I'm sorry," he said. Useless, empty words.

"There's open talk of negotiation. Of surrendering the fortress for free passage away," Ser Jehannes said. The others flinched at his tone.

"No," The captain said. "There will be neither surrender nor negotiation." He was noticing that he'd been bandaged around the ribs, and that all the hair had been shaved away—well. Lots of hair. He winced. The Abbess was dead and he realised that he had, in his way, loved her.

Always looking for a better mother, he thought. "If you all will leave Michael to dress me," he said quietly.

"Dress quickly," Ser Jehannes said. "It's happening right now." He was quiet. "All the local people. Some of the men."

Sister Miram withdrew to the door. "She would never have surrendered," she said quietly. "The men in the courtyard are saying Amicia did it," she added.

The captain winced and met her eye. "I'll see to it."

The nun closed the door.

The captain got himself out of bed, despite a touch of vertigo. He had a feeling he knew from childhood—the feeling of having tapped his Hermetical powers utterly. An emptiness, but also a good feeling, like a well-exercised body.

Prudentia is dead.

It was not the first time that good people had died to keep him alive.

Toby appeared with his old black doublet and his old black hose and his fine gold belt. He looked terrified.

Hose took time to get on—he tried to quiet his own pulse. To think about something besides the Abbess and his tutor.

"She was murdered," Ser Jehannes said. "Someone shot the Abbess in the back." He lowered his voice. "Gelfred says it was Witch Bane."

The thought of it made him physically sick.

"And no one saw this?" he asked wearily.

"Everyone was watching the fight outside the walls," Ser Jehannes said.

The captain sighed. "Secure the gates and all the passages. There is a passage under the main donjon which leads out of the fortress. Right now, it's blocked by our wagon-bodies, but put a pair of archers—good archers—on the stairs. Give me a nod when this is done."

"When you say I should secure—" Jehannes paused.

"As if we were taking the fortress for ourselves," the captain said harshly. "As if we were in Galle. Trust no one who is not one of ours. Use force if you have to. *Secure the exits, Jehannes!*"

The old knight saluted. "Yes, my lord."

Michael had his boots. He buckled them around the ankles, laced the tops to the captain's pourpoint.

"Full armour, gloves, war sword," the captain said.

Michael began to arm him. It wasn't a quick process and some parts hurt a great deal. But wearing armour was itself a statement.

The arming doublet and mail haubergon weighed on him like a shirt of lead and a hairshirt all together. Many knights believed that the very pain of wearing armour was a penance before God.

Well.

Leg harness, starting with the cuisses, and then the greaves and the steel sabatons that buckled so neatly over his boots, right to the shaped and pointed toes. Michael pointed the cuisses into his arming doublet at an amazing speed, while Toby supported him.

He stood, flexed his legs, and Michael, aided now by Jacques, fitted his breast and back over his head and latched it shut.

"Had a dent in it like you wouldn't believe," Michael said.

"Oh, I would," the captain said.

Michael snorted. "Carlus says taking the dent out took more strength than he's ever had to use," he said. "Like the steel was magicked."

Each of them took an arm harness—vambrace, elbow cop and rerebrace in a single unit on sliding rivets, a miracle of craftsmanship in gilded bronze and hardened steel—and clipped them on, buckling them to his upper arms and then to his shoulders with straps, and then his pauldrons went on, and the circular plates that strapped to the pauldrons and guarded his under arms.

The golden belt at his waist.

Golden spurs at his heels.

Gloves, and a sword, and the baton of his office.

"There you are, my lord," Michael said.

The captain smiled—it was done as fast and as painlessly as it could have been done by anyone. "You are a fine squire," he said.

He walked out of the recovery ward, looked down the main corridor, and saw his brother.

Gawin had his feet over the edge of the bed.

"Stay where you are," the captain said gently. "Michael, stay here with this man."

Michael nodded. And saluted. He recognised his captain's tone.

"But—" Gawin began.

The captain shook his head. "Not now, messire."

He walked down the corridor to the other ward. Ser Jehannes had already passed. Low Sym was dressing in his gambeson.

"Have a sword, Sym?" the captain said.

Sym nodded wordlessly.

The captain pointed at Amicia's elegant back, standing at the dry sink across the room. "She is not to leave this ward until I return," he said. "If you harm her you are a dead man. But she is not to leave this room. Understand?"

Amicia whirled on him. "What?"

"For your own protection, sister," he said, his voice quiet. "Father Henry has killed the Abbess. But he will seek to blame you."

"Father Henry?" she came towards him, a hand at her chest. "The priest?"

He was at the top of the stairs. "Obey. On your life." He ignored her outcry, and went down the steps, past the commanderies, to the courtyard. At the door, Bad Tom waited, armoured cap à pied, a pole-axe in his left hand.

"It's bad," he said.

The captain nodded. He pulled on his gloves, and took the staff of his command from his belt. "On me," he said, and Tom opened the door.

The sound hit him. Anger first—then fear.

Every farmer and tenant was in the courtyard—four hundred men and women packed into four hundred square ells. The noise was like a living thing.

The dispensary had a wooden step, and two of his men-at-arms were keeping it clear.

On the other side of the courtyard, a dozen big farmers stood together. With them were some of the merchants.

The captain turned to Carlus, and he blew his trumpet. It was loud, and shrill.

Every head turned.

The captain waved the staff over the assembly. "Disperse!" he said into the sudden silence. "There will be no negotiation, and no surrender," he went on.

A dangerous murmur began.

"Kindly disperse to your stations and your beds, and let's have no more of this," the captain kept his voice level and kind.

One of the merchants raised his head. "Who are you, messire, to decide for us?"

The captain took a deep breath and struggled with the spark of rage that hit him. Why did good men always make him feel like this? "I will not debate this with you," he said. "If you wish to leave, the gate will be opened for you."

Another farmer shouted "Fuck you! That's just death! It's our land that's destroyed. Our farms that are burned, you sell-sword. Get out of the way, or we'll put you out."

Jehannes was waving to him from the portcullis winch. He had a key in his hand.

"This fortress is under the protection of my company," the captain said loudly. "The lady Abbess charged me with its defence, and I will hold it until I am dead. The power that invests us will not hesitate to lie, deceive, or betray us to our doom—but it will not let anyone here escape alive. The only hope any of you have is to join us in resisting to the last drop of our blood. Or better yet, to the last drop of theirs." He looked around. "The king," he almost choked on the title, but he got it out. "The king is on his way. Do not give way to despair. Now, please disperse."

"You can't fight all of us!" shouted the farmer.

The captain sighed. "In fact, we can kill every one of you." He spoke out. "Look around you. Would the Abbess ever have given in? She isn't even buried yet and look at you. Ready to surrender?" He pushed his way into the courtyard, ignoring Tom's protests. He pushed his way through the crowd until he was nose to nose with the big farmer.

"Priest says she was a witch," the farmer said.

People were shuffling away from him.

"Priest says all these so-called nuns is witches!" the farmer insisted. "Souls black as night."

A few men nodded. None of the women did.

The captain passed his arm through the farmer's arm. "Come with me," he said.

"I don't have to—argh!" the farmer stumbled. He was unable to resist the armoured man, and was pulled along through the crowd to the great gate.

The gate was open, and the sun was shining beyond the walls of the fortress.

"Look out there," the captain said. "Look out there at what Thorn has done. *He* betrayed his king. *He* betrayed his people. *He* has made himself a construct of the Wild, a sorcerer without compare, unlimited by laws or even friends. *And you think that is better than your Abbess? Because a priest told you that black is white, and white is black?"* The captain spat the words.

"And I should trust you?" the farmer growled.

"Since you are so obviously a fool—yes. You'd do better trusting me, the man who fights to defend you, than trusting to the God-damned priest, *who killed your Abbess."*

The crowd was backing away from him, and he had to assume his eyes were burning.

The farmer stood his ground, but his jaw was trembling. "You're one of them too. And the priest says the other witch killed the Abbess. For her power."

The crowd muttered again. "You're one of them!" shouted a man at the front.

"I am whatever I choose to be," said the captain. "So are you. What do you choose?"

Tom and Jehannes stepped up behind him. And with them, a dozen other men-at-arms in plate armour, and most of the archers. There were archers on the walls, on the stumps of the towers.

"Don't make me do this," the captain said to the crowd.

Sister Miram walked out of the wreckage of the chapel with Mag, the seamstress. Miram raised her arms.

Mag spat. "Look at you, Bill Fuller." She put her hands on her hips. "Playing with fire. Going to stand here and get shot?" She looked over the crowd. "Go to your beds. Let go. We've lost the Abbess. Let's not spill any more blood here."

"We can take 'em," Fuller said. But his tone suggested he knew he was lying.

Mag walked over and slapped his face. "You always were a weak fool, Bill Fuller," she said. "They'll kill every one of us, if they have to. We wouldn't even hurt them to do it. And for what? The enemy is *out there*."

Johne the Bailli came out of the chapel. "Well said, Maggie." He went and stood with Bad Tom. "I stand for the Abbess. We will not surrender."

Maggie's daughter Sukey came and stood with her. She was shaking.

The Carters started to burrow through the crowd.

Dan Favor went and stood with Ser Jehannes.

Amie Carter grabbed her sister's wrist and towed her across the open space. She turned and faced the crowd. "Don't be a pack of tom-fools," she said. "You been sorcelled. Can't you feel it? Don't be so stupid and pig-ignorant you can't face it."

Liz the laundress came and stood by Tom. Kaitlin Lanthorn walked across the open space.

"Sluts and harlots," said a voice.

The heads of the crowd turned, as one.

Father Henry looked as if he'd been on the cross. His face was streaked in old, dried blood. His robe was flayed and fell around his waist, showing his ascetic body, lacerated with further cuts.

The people parted for him. He walked between them like a king.

"Sluts and harlots. Are these your allies, Satan?" He stopped at the edge of the crowd.

"Not all of us are sluts, priest," said Master Random, and he burrowed into the crowd. "Adrian! Allan Pargeter! What are you doing with this man? Fomenting mischief?" Master Random walked into the crowd, looking for other apprentices he knew.

"You killed the Abbess," the captain said.

Father Henry drew himself up, and the captain knew he had his man. He was too proud to deny the crime.

Fool.

"She was a witch, a creature of Satan who chose to put her own appetites against—"

The stone hit the priest in the head. He snapped around, eyes blazing, and just for a moment, he didn't look like a gentle and crucified Jesus. He looked like a madman. His eyes raged.

"Take that man," the Red Knight said. He pointed his baton.

Bad Tom reached out with his pole-axe, caught the priest's foot with the head, and pulled, and the priest fell. Tom kicked him viciously, his armoured foot making a distinctive meaty sound as it connected with the priest's gut.

The priest retched.

Two archers grabbed him and hoisted him. He tried to speak, and he got the butt of Tom's pole-axe in the arch of his foot. He screeched.

And suddenly, there was no crowd. Just frightened people, looking for salvation.

And most of them asked—*Where is the king?*

Chapter Fifteen

Albinkirk (Southford)—Ranald Lachlan

When Ranald Lachlan led his scouts down to the edge of the Albin River, he could scarcely believe his eyes.

Fifty great boats, like galleys, lay in the river opposite the landing. The river fleet covered the river in four long files of boats, and their oars went back and forth like the legs of water-running insects.

At his back, the Royal Standard of Alba fluttered in the breeze over the gate-towers of Albinkirk, and the fields by the great bridge were empty of foes. It was like a dream, because the familiar ground was so empty.

Ranald sat his horse, watching the big river craft row, and even as he watched, they turned, all together, at a flash of a great bronze shield, and suddenly the whole fleet went from four columns advancing west to four lines heading toward the north shore. His shore.

He walked his horse out onto the landing stage where the ferry had run, in better times, and waved.

A woman in the bow of the largest galley waved back. An awe-inspiringly beautiful woman in a flowing white overkirtle. It took an effort of will to tear his eyes away from her, and he knew her well, from his years in the south.

Queen Desiderata.

Unbidden, a smile came to his face, and he laughed.

Who is that?" Desiderata said to her maidens teasingly. She was standing in the bow, waving. "I feel I know him."

Lady Almspend stood and waved. "Ranald the barbarous hillman, my lady," she said brightly.

Desiderata smiled at her secretary. "You seem happy enough to see him," the Queen said.

Lady Almspend sat a little too suddenly. "He—gave me the most wonderful book," she said haltingly.

The other ladies laughed, but not unkindly.

"Was it a big book?" one asked.

"Very old?" asked another.

"Perhaps more like a nice, thick scroll?" suggested Lady Mary.

"Ladies," the Queen said. The oarsmen were losing the stroke, laughing so hard. But the bank was rushing at them, despite the current.

As they rowed into the landing, the Queen stepped lightly up on the gunwale and leaped onto the pier.

Ranald Lachlan, who she remembered perfectly well, bowed deeply and then knelt.

She gave him her hand. "It is a long way, since you were in my bridal guard."

He smiled at her. "A pleasure, my lady."

She looked past him, up the tall bank, where Donald Redmane had the lads dismounted. "You have a small army of your people here. Come to aid the king?"

He shrugged. "My cousin lost a small army, my lady. We've already fought the Outwallers. But I have a thousand head of beeves and some sheep, and I'm looking to sell them to the Royal Army."

She nodded. "I will buy them all. What's your asking price?"

If he was surprised by her tone or manner, he hid it well. "Three silver marks a head," he said.

She laughed. "You drive a hard bargain," she said. "Is it chivalrous for a knight to bargain with his Queen?"

Ranald shrugged, but he couldn't stop looking into her eyes. "Lady, I could say I'm no knight, but a drover. And I could say I'm a hillman, and not in any way your subject." He grinned, and knelt. "But he'd be a rude bastard and no kind of a man, who ever failed to acknowledge you as his Queen."

She clapped her hands delightedly. "You are the very spirit of the north, Ser Ranald. One mark per beeve."

"You, my lady, are the living embodiment of beauty, but for a mark a head, I could have sold them to the Keeper of Dorling. Two silver marks a head." His eyes flicked to something behind her, and his smile intensified. "You remember my secretary, the very learned Lady Almspend?" she asked. "One and a half."

"One and a half, right here, on this side of the river?" he asked. He made another deep bow, this time to her secretary, who was standing on the gunwale, beaming. "Two if I have to drive them over the river."

"What's a kiss worth," sang Lady Almspend. She blushed, shocked at her own boldness.

"Everything!" he shouted back. "But these aren't my beeves, so I can't trade them for a kiss, my sweet." He relented. "Your Grace, my price is two, but I'll drive them where you like, and pledge my lads to serve your Grace."

The Queen nodded. "Sold. Fetch me my navarch. I have a thousand head of cattle to ferry over the river." She turned back to the hillman. "So despite your sordid money, you'll do a deed of arms with me?"

She put extra effort into her voice. She saw a coldness in him—something absent, some terror recently passed—and her voice caressed it like liquid gold.

The hillman looked cautious. "What kind of deed?"

"What knight asks what deed is required of him? Really, Ser Ranald," she said, and put her arm through his.

"I'm no knight," he said. "Except perhaps in my heart," he added.

She smiled at Lady Almspend. "We must do something to rectify that."

On the bank above them Donald Redmane watched his cousin with the Queen.

"What's happening?" asked one of the boys.

"We just sold the herd to the Queen," Donald said. "What's an Alban mark worth?" he asked, and then shrugged. "And now we have to live to spend it."

Lissen Carak—Harmodius

Harmodius listened to the angry crowd and kept his head down. He was almost drained of power—needed more recovery time, and the last thing he needed was a confrontation with ignorant witch-hunters.

Let the boy handle all that.

He dressed carefully. The old Abbess had never been a friend of his—but now, in death, he had to admire her. She had disclosed power of a level she had never had in youth—and had deployed her power brilliantly. She'd held the Enemy for long moments, while he prepared his masterstroke.

Sadly, his masterstroke hadn't quite come off. But she hadn't died in vain. The fortress still stood. And the Enemy's beard had been badly singed.

Again.

Harmodius imagined himself standing at the Podium at Harnford, staff in hand, lecturing on Hermeticism. *I learned the underpinnings of the nature of reality in the middle of one war,* he would say, *and I learned to manipulate them myself in the middle of another.* Or perhaps he would say, *I saved the world for mankind, yes, but I only stood on the shoulders of giants.* That was better. Quite good, in fact.

And now all of her secrets would go to her grave with her, and her soul would fly to her maker.

Harmodius ran his fingers through his beard.

What if—

What if all the power in the world came from a single source?

That's what it was, wasn't it? It was, in a way, a commonplace.

Green or gold, white or red? Power. It's just *power*

And that meant—

No good. No evil. No Satan. No—no God?

Did it mean that, in fact? Were there really any fewer angels on the head of a pin, if all power came from a single source?

His head spun.

What if Aristotle was wrong?

He could hardly breathe. One thing to think it. Another to know it to be true.

He stumbled down the tight staircase to the common room of the dormitory, and then he forced one foot in front of the other as he walked toward the chapel.

Bad Tom appeared at the captain's side. The captain was doing his damnedest to appear to be a member of the congregation. He had just sung a hymn. He had himself well in order.

She had wanted him to understand.

He knelt when the other attendees knelt. Sister Miram led the service in the absence of the priest, a matter that seemed to excite no comment.

I swear on my name and my sword that I will avenge you, my lady.

"My lord?" asked Tom, at his elbow.

"Not now."

"Now, my lord," Tom said.

Glaring at his corporal, the captain stood, walked to the aisle and genuflected to the crucified figure that towered over him, and then backed down the aisle to the doors. Every head turned.

Too bad.

"What?" he barked, when he was outside. The nuns were singing her to rest—every voice it the woven fabric of music a thread of power. It was incredibly beautiful.

Tom looked at the door to the cellars. "I hae' the priest, God rot his false soul to hell. I put him i' the darkest room wi' a lock." Anger made his voice thick.

The captain nodded. "You valued her too."

Tom shrugged. "She blessed me." He looked away. "That priest, he's going to die hard."

The captain nodded. "We'll try him for treason, first," he said.

Tom had his back to the door. "Why try him? You're the captain of a fortress under siege. Law of War."

Lissen Carak—Gerald Random

Gerald Random picked his way fastidiously along the captain's trench, following Ser Milus—clambering over the cooked bodies of a hundred boglins, their charred remnants a testimony to the power of fire. They smelled like cooked meat, and when he lost his balance and stepped on one, it crunched as if he'd stepped on charcoal. He paused.

His skin prickled.

Gelfred the huntsman strode past him, eyes wary, moving faster. The mercenary didn't seem to mind stepping on the cremated boglins.

Random wondered how long he'd have to do this before he was like Gelfred, or Milus.

Behind him, forty men moved carefully along the trench—company archers, new recruits, farm boys. The reinforcements.

They came out of the trench under the wall of the Bridge Castle and hollered to the watch to open the postern. Random had answered the call from the fortress before mains, and he wasn't in armour. He grabbed a bite of bread and a sound apple, and one of the young whores who'd come with the convoy handed him some good cheese. He smiled. "What's a nice girl like you doing in a place like this?" he asked Dora. She was Dora Candlesomething. Young Nick Draper fancied her, and Allan Pargeter had drawn her naked, which was still a nine-day wonder among the wagons, despite the flying monsters and magic. That made Random laugh.

She smiled back at him. "Money," she said. "Same as you."

He shook his head and laughed again. "If we get back to Harndon, come and ask me for a job," he said.

She looked at him. "You mean that?" she asked.

He made a face. "Of course."

She rolled her eyes. "Just when we're all going to die."

Lissen Carak—The Red Knight

The captain looked out through the hole in his wall and watched the fires burning in a swathe across the enemy's camp. The enemy's men, at least, cooked supper.

The rest of the camps were dark.

His back hurt. But then, his side hurt too, he now had cracked ribs on both sides of his ribcage—his shoulders were wrenched from the stress of being plucked off the ground by his knights, and his right hand had odd, numb spots in it and he had no idea why.

He was supposed to be in bed.

Toby stood uncertainly by the door.

"You want to be in bed, I suppose," he said.

Toby shrugged. "I'm hungry."

The Red Knight went to the table in the middle of the room and tossed his valet a biscuit.

Then he looked at the lute on the table. He hadn't played it in—

He couldn't remember when he played it last.

He picked it up, suddenly decisive, and walked out the door into the hallway. Toby tried to cut him off.

"Oh, Toby," he said. "I don't give a fuck." He knocked on the door to his Commandery.

In three heartbeats, Michael was there.

"Grab your lute," he said. "Good evening, Miss Lanthorn. Michael, these people need some music. Not a grim silence. Let's light a fire."

Michael sometimes forgot that his master was only a few years older than he was. He grinned. "Give me—us—a moment."

Lissen Carak—Mag the Seamstress

Mag looked out into the darkness because she'd heard music.

There it was again, the sound of a southern lute. A wild, joyous sound.

And then another, lower lute played back.

There was a bonfire burning on the cobbles.

An archer, Cuddy, came and peered out of the North Tower. He shouted something.

Amy Carter peered out of the stable door and saw Kaitlin Lanthorn dancing by firelight, her legs flashing.

She ran back inside and rubbed her sister's cheek. "They're dancing!" she said.

Kitty sat up, fully awake.

Low Sym heard music playing below the windows at the end of the hospital room. He threw his feet over the end of the bed and walked softly across the floor and opened one casement, and the sound of the notes raced in like a spell. He leaned out, listening.

The nun appeared by his side. "What is it?" she asked.

Sym giggled. "Capt'n likes to play. Fast." He shook his head. "Leastways, he used to play. On the Continent. Ain't heard him in an age."

She smiled. Leaned out. "You like him," she said.

Sym thought about that for so long she thought he wouldn't answer.

From their vantage point, they saw the music do its work. Men came out of the stable and down the steps from the towers and the stumps of the towers. Women emerged from the stables and from the nun's dormitory.

Suddenly, there were as many people in the courtyard to dance as had been there for the priest.

The two instruments were joined by pipes and a drum.

The dancers began to move in a circle.

"I don't hate him," Sym admitted.

Amicia turned. "You are not lost, Sym," she said. "You are more hero than villain, even now."

He stepped back as if she'd struck him. But then he grinned.

Then he stiffened. "Where you going?"

She smiled. "You can come guard me. I'm going to dance. Or at least to watch."

In the courtyard, Sister Miram stretched her arms and smiled wearily at the Red Knight, who stood with his back to the fire playing his lute like a madman. She turned to Sister Anne and ordered a cask of ale opened.

Bad Tom put a man-at-arms on the door to the cellars and another on the barracks. He and Jehannes whispered for a moment in the darkness beyond the fire, and Jehannes doubled the watch and forced some unwilling soldiers onto the walls where the farmers could see them.

When Jehannes looked down, Tom was dancing with the seamstress's daughter.

Mag, Lis, and Sister Mary Rose hauled a great cauldron of beef soup to the door of the dormitory. Cheering archers and farmers hauled it together into the firelight.

Long Paw appeared with a brace of wine jars, and handed them to the first men he saw. They toasted him, and the bottles passed around, soldier to farmer, and farmer to soldier, until they were empty.

A farmer went and burrowed in his belongings in the stable, and returned with a jug that proved to contain apple jack.

And the lutes played on.

Lissen Carak—Michael

At some point, Michael knew he had never played so well, and he also knew that his fingers were going to hurt all the next day. Kaitlin whirled by, leaped in the air and was caught by Daniel Favor; Bad Tom caught Mag's Sukey around the waist and she, a widow of twenty-four hours, squealed like a girl; Low Sym turned with the eight-year-old daughter of the Wackets, and Sister Miram and Sister Mary turned a somewhat statelier pavane together when Long Paw bowed, very Continental, and took Sister Miram's hand and led her around the yard. Francis Atcourt bowed over Sister Mary's hand and she laughed, and curtsied. Amicia danced with Ser Jehannes, Harmodius whirled Lis like a much younger man, and her feet spun her skirts out around her like a king's cloak. and then Amicia spun by again with Ser George Brewes, and the Red Knight drank off his fourth glass of the Abbess's red wine and played on. Cuddy tilted the apple jack back and back...and rolled off the barrel on which he was perched, and landed flat on his back, and didn't move, and the farmers laughed. Wilful Murder had an arm around Johne the Bailli and a leather flagon in the other hand, and was singing at the top of his voice, his face lit like a daemon's in the firelight.

The Carter girls began to dance, a fast, flashy dance of their own creation, and the Lanthorn girls, not to be beaten, leaped into the circle, and the music ran away with them. More pipes joined in, and Ben Carter produced bagpipes, and his drunkenness seemed to fall away as he played for his sisters. Fran Lanthorn leaned out of the turning circle and kissed him hard on the cheek as she swept by, and he blushed furiously and his tune tumbled, but he caught it and launched it anew.

Lissen Carak—Michael

Michael and his master allowed their fingers to fall still. The lutes dropped out of the busy music, which swept on.

Michael felt his captain's arms go around his shoulders. He was afraid he'd cry. The captain had never hugged him before. Or anyone else that he knew of. He'd never seen the man's face so open. So—defenceless.

And then he was gone into the swirling darkness and firelight.

Lissen Carak—Thorn

Thorn could hear the music. It drew him the way a candleflame will draw insects and frogs on a still summer night in the deep woods. He walked heavily to the edge of the woods, and listened with his keen senses to the sounds of people laughing and dancing, to the sounds of as many as ten instruments.

He listened, and listened. And hated.

Lissen Carak—The Red Knight

The Red Knight lay with his head in Amicia's lap. She was looking at the firelit scene at their feet, inside the walls of the courtyard, and he was looking at the line of her throat and jaw. She was thinking about how simple happiness could be, and he felt the current of her thoughts through their joined hands.

Gradually—glacially slowly—she lowered her mouth over his.

Playfully, at the last moment, he licked her nose, and they both dissolved into laughter, and he shifted, grabbed her under the arms and began to tickle her and she shrieked and tried to hit him.

He put her in his lap and bent to kiss her. She arched her back to reach him more quickly, and their tongues touched, their lips touched—

He drank her, and she drank him. Each of them could feel the contact, real, aethereal, spiritual.

He had pulled her robes above her hips, and she had not stopped him. The feeling of her naked flank inflamed him, and he pressed on.

She broke the kiss. "Stop," she said.

He stopped.

She smiled. Licked her lips. And then rolled out from under him, as swift as a dancer. Or a warrior.

"Marry me," the Red Knight said.

Amicia stopped. She froze. "What?"

"Marry me. Be my wife. Live with me until we die, old and surrounded by children and grandchildren." He grinned.

"You'd say that to any girl who keeps her legs closed," she said.

"Yes, but this time I mean it," he said, and she swatted him.

"Amicia," said Sister Miram. She was standing by the apple tree. She smiled. "I missed you at the fire." She looked at the captain, who felt like a schoolboy. "She may choose for herself whether to marry a mercenary or be the bride of Christ," Miram said. "But she can choose in daylight, and not on an apple-scented night."

Amicia nodded, but her half-hooded eyes concealed a spark that the Red Knight saw, and rejoiced at. He sprang to his feet. And bowed low. "Then I bid you good night, ladies."

Miram stood her ground. "It was well thought," she said. "They needed to rejoice. And the lady would have wanted a better wake than we were providing."

The captain nodded. "It *was* good. I didn't—" He shrugged. "I just wanted some music. And maybe to lure this lady into my lair." He smiled. "But it was good."

"There is more heart in us tonight than last night, despite everything." Miram looked at Amicia. "Will you wed her?"

The captain leaned very close to the nun. "Oh, yes," he said.

Miram put a hand on the girl's shoulder. "Then tell us your name," she said.

"I know his name," Amicia said. "He's—"

There was a sudden cheer from the courtyard, and then a roar of voices. The captain saw that Ser Jehannes was standing at the edge of the firelight, and behind him were three men in full plate, the fire lighting them like moving mirrors. They had black surcotes with white crosses.

The Red Knight turned away from the two nuns. He waved to Ser Jehannes and leaned out into the courtyard. "What's happened?"

"Now someone's come *into* the secret passage," Ser Jehannes said. "From outside. From the king." At the word *king* the courtyard burst into cheers again. Jehannes pointed to the trio of armoured figures standing in the ruin of the covered way. "Knights of the Order."

The music stopped.

One of the three knights raised his visor. He was an old man, but his smile was quite young.

The relief that flooded the captain was palpable, solid. He felt giddy. He felt weak. He said, "Splendid."

The captain clasped hands with the first man in the long black cloak that marked the Knights of the Order of Saint Thomas of Acon.

"I'm the captain," he said. "The Red Knight."

"Mark, Prior of Pyrwrithe," said the man whose right hand was clasped in his own. "May we offer you our compliments on a brilliant defence? Although I understand from Ser Jehannes that the lady Abbess is dead."

"She died last night, my lords. In battle." Suddenly the captain was hesitant. He had no idea how the fighting orders felt about Hermeticism or any other form of phantasm.

The Prior nodded. "She was a great lady," he said. "I will go and pay my respects. But first—the king is across the river, moving carefully. But he should be opposite the Bridge Castle by late tomorrow. The next day at the latest."

The captain grinned with pure joy. "That is welcome news." He looked at the three men, all in full armour. "You three must be tired."

The prior shrugged. "The armour of faith is such that we feel little fatigue, my son. But a glass of wine is never amiss."

"Let us go to chapel," murmured the central figure. He wore a black tabard with the eight pointed cross of the order.

"If I may: I'd rather you stood where the people could see you just a little longer," said the captain. "There have been doubts."

The Prior shook his head. "We're late and no mistake, Captain."

The captain raised his hand for silence. In the courtyard, they cheered and cheered. But after a a few resurgences of spirit, they fell quiet, with Mag shouting "Shut up, you fools" and a titter of laughter.

"Friends!" the captain said. His voice carried. "Our prayers have been answered. The king is here, and these three knights of the order are the vanguard." There were cheers, but he went on. "We've had a sip or two and a dance tonight. But when the king comes, we'll have to break this siege. The enemy is still out there. Let's have some sleep while we can. Aye?"

Men who had cursed him as Satan a few hours before raised wooden jacks now.

"Red Knight!" they shouted. And others shouted "St. Thomas!"

And then, as if by magic, they tottered off to bed. Sym and Long Paw put Cuddy over their shoulders and carried him to bed in the hospital. Ben Carter found himself carried by Wilful Murder and Fran Lanthorn to his pile of straw in the stable.

Together the four men walked to the chapel.

The Red Knight didn't say anything. The Abbess lay on her bier, and the three knights knelt around her. After some time, they rose, in unison. The captain led them to his Commandry, which, as he expected, was empty, without a sign of Michael's sleeping gear.

"This is my office," the captain said. "If you wish to disarm, I can send you a couple of archers."

Ser John smiled. "I've been sleeping in harness since I was fifteen," he said.

"Are you three alone?" the captain asked.

The prior shook his head. "I have sixty knights in the woods east of the ford," he said. "Short of direct intervention by the enemy, they won't be found."

The tallest knight nodded and pulled his helmet over his head. He gave a sigh of pure pleasure. "It's what we do," he said. He pulled a cushion off one of the chairs, put it under his head, and went to sleep.

Lissen Carak—Gerald Random

The Siege of Lissen Carak. Day Fourteen

Yesterday the folk of the towns talked rebellion—but it was all shock at the death of the Abbess, and the captain restored order and none were injured. The priest, Henry, was taken into custody. The Enemy's engines pounded the Bridge Castle, but the enemy was hesitant and careful in their movements, and we saw a large force crossing the river to the west. We had heavy rain in the afternoon, and at nightfall the captain (crossed out) the people celebrated the Feast of Saint George. After dark a party of Knights of St. Thomas entered and told us we were to be relieved by the king.

It was a lovely late-spring morning. There was a low fog, and Master Random looked out at it for a moment, enjoying his small beer. He waved to Gelfred, who was fussing with his falcons, and found young Adrian to get armed.

While he was still getting his arm harnesses on, the alarm sounded.

Before the bell had stopped ringing, he was on the curtain wall of the Bridge Castle with the master huntsman. The bridge was still down, and although the bridge gates were closed and heavily barred, it was still the hope of every merchant in the lower fortress that more survivors would stumble in from the Wild—despite all evidence to the contrary.

Gelfred had a trio of big hawks with him, and from time to time he flew one away into the morning light. He wasn't much of a conversationalist—mostly he spoke to the hawks, murmuring to them in much the same language that Random's daughters spoke to their dolls.

Two archers assisted him.

Random watched the open ground out to the line of trees. Plenty of movement this morning—boglins crawling through the deep grass. They continued to believe that they were invisible in the grass, and Random, for one, hoped they continued to believe it.

He motioned to one of the small boys who had survived the caravans. "Tell Ser Milus that there is a boglin attack coming on the curtain wall," he said. And was proud that his voice remained steady and professional. He refused to let his mind dwell on how he had seen a line of boglin take his men apart.

The boy ran along the wall.

The bell rang again. The new company formed. It was a hodge-podge of men; a dozen goldsmiths with crossbows, with a dozen spearmen, all farmers sons or young merchants in borrowed armour; but the front rank was all men-at-arms, and Ser Milus led them in person.

When they were well-formed and he'd inspected their armour, he led them up the ladders onto the curtain wall.

"Good morning, Master Random," he said, as he got to the top of his ladder.

"Good morning, Ser Milus," Random answered. "Nice of them to announce themselves."

"I've doubled the watch in the towers," Ser Milus said. "Look sharp!" he said, loud and clear, and the men on the wall stopped their conversations and looked through the crenellations. "You—Lusty Luke, or whatever your name is. Where's your gorget? Get it *fastened*."

Out in the deep grass, irks and boglins began to loose arrows.

One, lucky or perfectly aimed, struck one of the third rank spearmen and killed him instantly, and he fell bonelessly from the wall into the courtyard behind them.

The other farmer-spearmen shuffled nervously.

"And did he have his gorget properly fastened?" Ser Milus roared. "And did I *just speak to him about it?*" he bellowed.

Gelfred finished lashing his birds to their perches and putting on their jesses and hoods. He went into the north tower followed by his two archers. His calm, unhurried movements contrasted with the spearmen.

Their shuffling stopped.

The boglins made their run at the wall. There were enough of them that they covered the ground—it was like a charge by a nest of ants. The grass seemed to come alive, and there they were—hundreds of them, scurrying to the wall, the elfin irks bounding ahead in great leaps.

Like most fortress walls at the edge of the Wild, this one had a slope at the base and then rose sheer for the last few metres. The design had an immediate function beyond stability—as Random had seen in the last four attacks. Boglins misjudged the wall because of the initial slope and attempted to run straight up it—over and over. Apparently, they couldn't help themselves, and they ran at the wall, harder and harder, and very few ever made it to the top.

Random had come to believe that this, too, was by design, as the success of a few egged the rest on to continue their mostly-fruitless runs.

The men-at-arms with pole-axes and heavy swords began the slaughter of the soft-bodied things.

The crossbowmen cleared any that managed to alight on the crenellations, their heavy bolts plucking the creatures off the wall to a body-crushing fall.

The spearmen were there to catch any who got through the defence.

Random appointed himself to the third rank. He was much better armoured than the farm kids, and yet—he was more one of them than he was a knight. Or a man-at-arms.

The fight went very well for two long minutes. The armoured professionals massacred the boglins, and the crossbowmen covered their backs, and one big, fast boglin who knocked Ser Stefan to the ground got a farmer's spear between his limbs and writhed—literally like a bug pinned to paper—until a half-dozen axes finished it. Ser Stefan got back to his feet, unharmed.

Random was unengaged—almost bored, despite the tide of monsters lapping at the wall. But his boredom saved them, because he was the one who heard the screams of the sentries in the north tower.

Random whirled and saw boglins on the tower top.

He turned and went into the tower through the open curtain wall door, drawing his heavy sword as he ran. He had a buckler on his hip and he got that into his left hand.

"Boglins on the tower!" he shouted at a huddle of men—Gelfred and his huntsmen.

Then he ran up the ladder to the tower top.

"Ring the alarm," shouted Gelfred—a better response than Random's one-man fire brigade.

Random threw back the roof-trap and immediately received a blow to his head. It fell on his bassinet and glanced away and he was up another step, buckler over his head—two fast blows to the small shield, and he was atop the ladder and cutting low with his sword, and he felt it cut into the firewood-hard flesh of a boglin's leg and then he pushed with his legs and got clear of the trap door.

A blow to his back plate.

Random punched with his buckler, the steel rim cracking a boglin's head with the same feeling of a lobster's shell giving under a hard blow, and then he pivoted on his hips—a new move, learned from Ser Milus—and cut with his sword—one, two. The second blow was wasted—his first went home, splitting a head, and the back cut plucked the head off the body and blood spewed from the thing.

But they were all around him, stabbing with spears. One spear skidded across his back plate and went in under his buckler arm, stopped only by his chain voiders, and another spear-blow hit the side of his head hard enough to make him see stars. He stumbled forward and tangled with yet another of the things, who tried to pin him by wrapping all four limbs around his legs, but he put the pommel of his sword into the centre of the boglin's face and—it's nose seemed to open into a horrible parody of a gullet, lined in spikes—it shrieked in pain, and all four limbs began to scrabble at a tremendous rate.

Random swept his buckler in a desperate arc, let go his sword, and whipped his dagger from his belt. He rammed it into the leathery parts of the boglin's six-segmented chest, stabbing more times than he cared to count, and the thing almost literally fell to pieces under his hands.

Then he saw a flash of dark green, and Gelfred was there, swinging a short-hafted boar spear with practised efficiency—cut, thrust, cut, thrust, like a weapon's master demonstrating for a class.

And then they were done.

Random was covered in blood—but he felt like a god.

He leaned over the wall to call down to Ser Milus and saw that the courtyard was full of boglins.

White boglins. In armour. *Wights.*

"Gelfred!" he screamed.

The Red Knight woke from a dream of Amicia with a smile on his face and Bad Tom's hand on his shoulder.

"You look like hell," the captain said.

"Bridge Castle is under assault," Tom said. "It looks bad, and they've stopped signalling."

"Right," said the captain. He took a deep breath. Of course the Enemy knew the king was a half-day's march away. Hence their assault. An all-or-nothing assault. And the trebuchet was gone. But—Bent had spent yesterday with the farmers erecting a trebuchet that filled the stump of the old tower. The captain rolled off his bed. He was fully dressed.

"Bent!" he called.

The senior archer came from under the scaffolding. "My lord?"

"Start laying buckets of gravel across the trenchline," he said. "Commence as soon as you can get loaded."

Bent saluted.

The captain turned to Tom. "Tell the archers to start loosing into the field between here and the Bridge Castle. Everything we have. Don't spare shafts now. Someone heat rocks for the trebuchet. Michael! Get me Harmodius."

His squire had, apparently, spent the night in his room.

"And then armour, helmet and gauntlets," he called out.

Tom licked his lips.

"Sortie?" he asked.

"Not much choice. Tom, the three gentlemen in my Commandery are knights of the order—see to it they get a cup of wine—"

"And horses," said the Prior, appearing in the doorway. "If you will allow me, my lord, I will have my knights meet us in the field below. Which may be a dolorous surprise to our foes, by the grace of God."

He raised a hand and made a sign and spoke a word—a single word that the captain did not know—in Archaic.

Something definitely happened. But the captain didn't know what it was.

It did become clear, though, that the military orders used Hermeticism.

"Wine and war horses, then," the captain said. *The king is coming. Let's not get rash.*

Overhead, the trebuchet slammed into its supports, and the whole scaffolding creaked.

Several hundredweight of gravel flew out into the early morning.

Above him, on the remnants of the south tower, the heavy arbalests began to *thwack* away at the creatures in the fields below.

"You called?" asked Harmodius.

"I need to save the Bridge Castle. He's throwing everything at it—and he's waiting for us to respond. I'm hoping that we can pound his attack flat with artillery but I can't count on it. The Prior, here, has offered us another trick up our sleeves, but I need more. What can you do?"

"It's the King's Magus!" the Prior said. "The king has never ceased to look for you."

Harmodius shrugged. "I was never lost." He fingered his beard. "I think this is a case for misdirection," he said. He smiled, and it was particularly nasty smile. "He thinks I'm dead."

Lissen Carak—Gerald Random

Random led the valets and the spearmen against the wights. There were fifty of them, and they were bigger and far better armoured than the boglins who had climbed the tower walls.

By the time Gelfred reached the courtyard many of the merchants who had come in the first convoys were dead. They were no match for the boglins, who were faster and better armoured and whose every limb had a killing scythe or a spike. The merchants did not live in their armour like the mercenaries; they fought unarmoured, and they died.

But in the light of the sun Gelfred and his archers, high above in the tower, began to slaughter them like rats in a trap.

The heavy longbow arrows went through their iron armour with a wet slapping sound, and the big boglins shrieked as they died and tried to crawl over each other to reach the tower steps. They were already flowing up the ladders to the curtain wall—up the top and the underside of the ladders. They jammed the open doorway of the tower, and Gerald Random set his feet and fought to hold the door.

"Fortress is signalling!" called Nick Draper. *"On the way."*

Random set his teeth, and slammed his visor shut.

The arrows flying from the towers were answered by flights of arrows from the ground outside, from the courtyard—the hole there was a yawning maw vomiting monsters.

There were massive irks, nothing like the slim elfin creatures he'd seen before, but as big as a big man, armoured in ring mail with shields and long swords. There were more boglins as white as the moon, with hooked spears and iron plate. They came at him in one gout.

The farm-boys slammed spears past him—sometimes they fouled his sword arm, and one pinked him in the buttock, but he was their shield and they were his weapon, their nine-foot spears pinning the armoured things so that Random cut pieces off them—and just past the door, the hail of shafts continued to reap the enemy.

But there were more and more of the things out in the courtyard.

*

To all appearances, the sortie emerged after a concerted volley from all the engines in the fortress—a veritable rain of projectiles from fist-sized rubble to twenty-pound rocks; crossbow shafts two feet long and weighing two pounds.

The sortie rode down the fortress ridge at top speed, a blur of motion at the edge of the dark, and halted at the foot of the ridge to form its wedge. But they took too long. Men and horses were too far behind—other men had over-ridden the assembly point and had to turn back—and a hundred heartbeats were consumed achieving their formation.

Thorn watched the enemy sortie emerge. He watched them ride down the cliff face and he tasted the power of the phantasm that surrounded them. And spat at the taste.

Thorn sent the signal to his ambush, and triggered the massive spell he had spent the day preparing. Power leapt across the late morning light, raw and green, and coalesced—

Thorn choked.

That was *not* the sortie. It was an illusion. The spectre of a sortie.

The Fallen Magus roared his rage. But it was too late, and the carefully prepared power of his magic fist slammed to empty earth.

Lissen Carak—Harmodius

"He didn't used to be this easy," Harmodius said, looking up to the captain, who sat on a borrowed destrier. The Magus grinned like a small boy. "The Wild has sapped his imagination."

The shattering thunderclap of the outpouring of the Enemy's power rang in their ears and the massive flash still burned across the captain's retinas. "Can he do that again?" the captain asked.

"Perhaps, Harmodius admitted. "I doubt it, though."

The captain exchanged a glance with Sauce, who rode by his side. It was Tom's turn to have the duty, and the big man was fretting about missing the sortie.

"No heroics," the captain called. "Right across the plain to the castle, then around the walls. Kill anything that comes under our hooves."

The Wild—Peter

Peter had just finished making breakfast when the two boglins came to his fire. They had a pair of rabbits, already skinned, in each arm—eight rabbits in all. They also had a large animal carcass—also field dressed—carried between them on a pole.

"U kuk fr us?" said the larger one.

Peter realised with a shock that the larger mammal was a woman—beheaded and skinned. Gutted. *Cleaned.*

"Kuk?" said the larger boglin.

Peter took a deep breath, pointed at the dead woman, and shook his head. "I will not cook a person," he said.

He had his fire going, and he had already fed his friends. So he handed the remains of his squash and squirrel stew with oregano to the larger boglin. "Eat," he said.

The boglin looked at its partner. They touched their heads together for a moment, and a flood of acrid, complex smells filled the air.

The smaller boglin opened its gullet and swallowed half, and then passed the small copper pot to the larger boglin, who consumed the rest.

Peter didn't watch.

Ota Qwan came and stood by him. "Aren't you two supposed to be in the big attack?" he asked.

They remained perfectly still. Animal still. As if they couldn't hear him.

"Kuk?" asked the larger.

"I—will—cook—the—rabbits." Peter spoke slowly.

"Gud." The larger boglin bobbed. "Go kill. Back to eat." He made a chittering noise, his partner joined him, and they bent forward and loped off into the gathering night.

Ota Qwan looked at Peter. "Do you have the power, laddy?" he asked.

Peter shook his head.

Ota Qwan shrugged. "Among the Sossag people it is mostly shamans who can talk to the Wild," he said. "I would like to have boglins to follow me," he said. "If they offer to join us, accept."

Peter swallowed. "You would have them in camp?"

Ota Qwan shook his head in mock anger. "Boglins are big medicine, you know that?"

"Where do they come from?" Peter asked. "I had never seen one before—I came here."

Ota Qwan sat by the corpse of the gutted woman. He didn't seem to notice her, or care. "I don't know, but I can tell you what men say. The word is that they grow in great colonies like giant termite hills in the deep Wild—way out west. All the creatures of the Wild fear them. The great Powers of the Wild cultivate them, recruit whole colonies, and send them to their deaths." Ota Qwan sighed. "I've heard said they were made—they were created—by a great Power. To fight an ancient war."

Peter shook his head. "That's just a way of saying you don't know."

"Don't I?" Ota Qwan laughed. "You have so much to learn about the Wild. Because the Powers pretend that they fear nothing, but they fear the little boglins. A thousand boglins are a fearful sight. A million boglins—" He shrugged. "If they could be fed, they could conquer the world."

Peter swallowed bile.

"Maybe you could cook for them, eh?" Ota Qwan said. "You know the matrons have given you a name?"

Peter nodded expectantly.

"Nita Qwan." Ota Qwan nodded expectantly. "A very potent name. Well done."

Peer sounded it out in his head. "Gives—something."

"He gives life," Ota Qwan said.

"Like your name," Peter said.

"Yes. They see us together. I like that." He nodded.

"What is Ota?" Peter asked.

"Take. Like *ota nere!*" he paused.

"Take water. When we are on the march." Peter nodded. And then turned. "You are *Take Life* and I am *Give Life.*"

Ota Qwan laughed. "Got it in one. You were Grundag. Now you are Nita Qwan. My brother. And my symbolic opposite." He nodded again. "Now—recruit me those boglins. This siege is almost over; we'll go home as soon as the dead are eaten."

Peter shook his head. "I lack your experience of war," he said. "But the Alban Royal Army is just coming up the Vale of the Cohocton."

Ota Qwan rubbed his chin. "That," he said, "is a very good point. But Thorn says we will triumph tonight."

"How?" Nita Qwan asked.

"Pick up your bow and spear and come with me," Ota Qwan said.

Nita Qwan put the rabbits on green stick spits and left his woman to turn them. He took up his bow and his new spear, tipped with the fine blued-steel head that had come to him as a share of his spoils from the Fight at the Ford. He had many new things, and his woman was impressed.

And it had only cost him a year of his life. But he spat and followed Ota Qwan, because it was easier to follow than to think. He ran, and caught Ota Qwan by the elbow. The war leader stopped.

"One thing," Nita Qwan said.

"Be quick, laddy," Ota Qwan said.

"I'm not anyone's lad. Not yours, not anyone's. Got me?" Nita Qwan's eyes bored straight into the war leader's.

He didn't flinch. But after several breaths, his nostrils flared, and he smiled. "I hear you, Nita Qwan."

He turned and ran, and Nita Qwan followed, better satisfied.

At the edge of the woods, many of the surviving Sossag warriors were waiting—almost five hundred of them. Beyond them, painted fiery red in the sun were Abenacki, and even a few Mohak, in their characteristic skeleton paint.

The Abenacki war chief, Akra Crom, walked to the centre, between the groups. He raised an axe from his belt and held it over his head.

Ota Qwan smiled. "If he falls today," Ota Qwan said, "I will be war chief of the Sossag, and perhaps the Abenacki, too."

Nita Qwan felt as if he'd been punched in the gut.

"Don't be so naïve," the older man said. "This is the Wild."

Nita Qwan took a deep breath. "What does he say?"

"He says that if we ever want to get home, we must fight well tonight for Thorn, and kill the armoured horsemen as we have so many times. We have a thousand warriors. We have bows, and axes. La di da." Ota Qwan looked around. "In truth, this Thorn doesn't seem to have a serious plan for us—as if he thinks that by ordering us out of the woods and into the fields, we will kill all the knights." He shrugged.

Nita Qwan shuddered.

Ota Qwan put an arm around him. "We will go and lie in ambush by the enemy back gate," he said. He barely waited for the Abenacki man to stop his oration before he rose to his feet, shook his spear, and the Sossag gave a scream of power and followed Ota Qwan into the green of the woods.

Lissen Carak—The Red Knight

The horses were all tired, and many of them bore light wounds, muscle strains, scars—and so did their riders.

There were twenty-five men-at-arms—a pitiful number against a sea of foes.

And at the base of the ridge, a perfect circle of cooling glass marked the best efforts of their foe.

The captain was operating in a haze of fatigue and minor pains that all but subsumed emotion. He knew—at a remove—that the Abbess was gone. That Grendel, almost a friend, was dead and probably eaten down on the plain. That his beloved tutor was cold marble—no longer even a simulacrum of life.

But at another level, he walled all that away.

Can you fight every day?

He knew he could. Every day, until the sun died.

The place in his head where his friends were dying was like a bad tooth, and by an effort of will, he didn't run his tongue over it.

Nor did he think, *If we win today, we're saved.*

He didn't think that, because he didn't really think much beyond his next stratagem, and he was now pretty much out of tricks.

All of this went through his head between one leap of his new mount and the next.

He hurt.

They all did.

And then the sortie was down onto the plain, and forming their wedge.

Random was more tired than he had ever been, and had he not been wearing first-rate armour, he'd long since have been dead. As it was, blows slammed into him more and more often as the monsters in the courtyard crawled over their own dead to reach him.

Twice, shouts behind him told him that more of the cursed things had made it onto the tower or the wall—apparently using their vestigial wings, or perhaps they were a new and horrible breed—but the spearmen at his back held their ground.

Twice he had a respite from the attacks on the door, but he had no idea why the white things stopped coming. He would pant, someone would hand him water, and then they'd come again. The white boglins were bad. The big irks were worse.

A farmer tried to help him in the doorway—braver or stupider than the rest—and died almost as soon as he took his place, while one of his mates begged him not to go.

"Ye have no armour!" a bigger, Harndon accented man called.

He didn't have armour on his arms and legs, and the wicked scythes on their limbs sliced him to pieces, dragged him down and carved him up. And they ate him—even the dying ones took a bite.

Random couldn't lift the buckler high any more. He knew it was just a matter of time before he was struck in the visor or the groin—only luck and the efforts of the spearmen kept him at it.

More irks came. They took their time coming over the low mound of dead, and they all came at him together. A shield caught his outstretched arm—the vambrace held the blow, but he was unbalanced, and the boglins dragged him to his knees—a blow struck the back of his helmet and he was *down.*

He could feel a sharp pain across his instep—something was hacking at his armoured shin—and then, to his horror, he began to be dragged out of the doorway, into the pile of corpses.

He couldn't help it. He screamed.

And then he wasn't being dragged, and a heavy weight crushed him. Only the strength of his breastplate and his backplate and their hinges kept the crushing weight from taking the breath out of him.

There was a sharper pain in his right foot.

He tried to call out, and suddenly his helmet was full of liquid—he spat. It was hell—dark—bitter. He choked and spat and realised that he was drowning.

In boglin blood.

He tried to scream.

More pain.

Christ, I am being eaten alive.

Christ, save me in my hour of need.

The Wild—Peter

Nita Qwan loped through the woods. The circle of the sun was high overhead. It was a poor time to set a trap, and he wanted to wait for night, but
it was late spring, and darkness—true darkness—was still a long way away.

A brilliant emerald flash lit the sky to the south. A titanic concussion
rocked the earth.

Ota Qwan grinned. "Our signal. He is mighty, our chief. Let's go! Gots
onah!" The acting war chief ran ahead of the band, and they began to
sprint over the grass, angling east, and the summer light threw shadows
under them.

They had almost a mile to go. Nita Qwan was a strong man, and had
lived with the Sossag for weeks, but running a mile to fight was the most
exhausting work—especially after a morning of food gathering and cooking.
He put his head down and tried to seal off his mind from his thighs and
his lungs, and he ran.

It took many long minutes to run all the way to the east of the great
ridge, but finally, Ota Qwan raised a hand. "Down!" he called, and the
People fell to the earth in the tall grass. He turned to Skahas Gaho and
another warrior and sent them off farther to the east, and then he lay down
by Nita Qwan.

"Not long now," he said. "We are in the right place. Now we see if Thorn
knows what he is doing."

Lissen Carak—Thorn

Thorn watched the action develop from the utter safety of the western edge
of the woods. He was not strong enough to risk himself today—because
he'd thrown too much in a single casting. It rankled. But he had thousands
of servants to aid him, and today he was spending them like water, his
usual caution forgotten.

Many of his servants would have been disturbed to note that he had
already decided to use them all, if he had to. He knew where more creatures
of the Wild could be raised. He himself was irreplaceable.

And she was dead.

He had made mistakes, but the end game was going to play out with
the inevitability of one of those ancient plays he had once so enjoyed, and
now could no longer remember.

The king would come, and be defeated. That trap was already laid.

And then it would all be his.

He could no longer set his tent away from the army. Tonight, the army was camped hard by a small stream that ran down to the Cohocton; the carcass of a great beast of the Wild lay in sodden and hideous majesty, the bones picked redly clean in mid-stream. A litter of corpses and the screams and quarrels of the animals that fed on the recent dead marked the scene of a recent battle.

The king ordered the wagons pulled in, trace to axle tree, a fortress of tall, wheeled carts chained at the hubs, and even de Vrailly couldn't fault him for his caution. They were in the very midst of the Wild, and the enemy was palpable, all around them. Many of the footsoldiers and not a few of the knights were afraid—scared, or even terrified. De Vrailly could hear their womanish laughter in the firelit dark, but he himself knew nothing but a fierce joy that at last—*at last*—he would be tested, and found worthy. The much-discussed fortress of Lissen Carak was three leagues away to the north, the Queen's flotilla was, by all reports, already lying in mid-stream, ready to support their attack in the morning. Even the cautious old women of the king's council were forced to admit that there would be a battle.

He was kneeling before his prie-dieu when the angel came. He came with a small thunderclap and a burst of myrrh.

De Vrailly cried out.

The angel hovered, and then sank to the earth, his great spear touching the cross-beam of the great tent.

"My lord de Vrailly," the angel said. "The greatest knight in the world."

"You mock me," de Vrailly said.

"Tomorrow will see you acknowledged as such by every man," said the angel.

Jean de Vrailly was struggling with his doubt. He felt as a man does who knows he should *not* mention a certain fact to his wife, but does so, anyway—precipitating an avoidable argument. "You said we would fight a battle," he said, hating the whine of doubt in his voice. "At Albinkirk."

The angel nodded. "I am not God," he said. "I am merely a servant. The battle will be here. It *should* have been at Albinkirk, but forces—circumstances—forced my hand."

The angel's hesitation froze de Vrailly.

"What forces, my lord?" asked Jean de Vrailly.

"Mind your own role, and leave me to mine," said the angel. His voice sounded like a whip-crack. Like de Vrailly's own. Beautiful and terrible. Imbued with power.

De Vrailly sighed. "I await your orders," he said.

The angel nodded. "Tomorrow, at dawn, the king will attack. The Enemy has a blocking force on the road between here and the bridge. Let the king lead the attack on that force, and when he falls—" The angel paused.

De Vrailly felt his heart stop.

"When he falls, seize command. Cut your way free, save the king's army, and you will save the day." The angel's voice was pure and precise. "His day is done. He has failed. But he will die well, and you, my lord, will take the woman and be king. She is the kingdom. Her father was the greatest lord of Alba next to the king. With the woman, you will rule. Without her—you will not. Am I making myself clear to you?"

De Vrailly's eyes narrowed. "And what of the north?" he asked. "If I am to save the army, am I to let this mighty fortress fall?"

"You can retake it," the angel said reasonably. "When you bring an army from Galle."

De Vrailly bent his proud head, shading his eyes from the brightness of the angel. "Pardon me, my lord," he said aloud. "I have doubted, and been misled by false images."

The angel touched his head. "God forgives you, my son. Remember—when the king falls, take command, and cut your way clear."

De Vrailly nodded, eyes downcast. "I understand very well. My lord."

Lissen Carak—The Red Knight

The captain pointed his wedge south and raised his hand. He could feel the heat coming off the hot glass circle to their right—it went right through his steel gauntlet and his glove.

Ouch, he thought. And thanked Harmodius with a silent nod.

"Let's ride," he called, and they trotted forward, formed tightly. A perfect target for another burst of power.

His back tingled as he rode *away* from where he felt his enemy to be, towards the near corner of the Bridge Castle, just two hundred horse-lengths away or less.

The wedge negotiated the trench—last night it had been an inferno—crossing it carefully and wasting precious time. Some men had to dismount.

It was still better than riding the other way around the walls.

Some men jumped it, but most men were less flashy and more cautious. They reformed on the far side, unopposed.

The captain rose in his stirrups. He pointed across the darkening grass toward the near corner of the Bridge Castle.

"It's a trap. If it wasn't, those boglins—" the captain pointed at a hundred or more boglins who were watching them from a hastily erected earthen assault ramp that rose to the top of the wall of the Bridge Castle "—those boglins would have tried to hold the trench against us. Instead of watching like spectators."

"Has the Bridge Castle fallen?" Sauce asked.

The captain watched it for ten heartbeats. "No," he said.

The Prior of Harndon came up on his left side. "If you let me send my signal, my knights will ride to meet us," he said. "They are just there, in the woods closest to the river."

The captain looked a little longer. "Catching their ambush between two hammers," he said. "Yes." He turned to his valet. "Sound—single rank, full interval."

Lissen Carak—Peter

Ota Qwan was on his knees in the high grass. The enemy—a small party of knights in highly polished armour—had hesitated at the edge of the Trench of Fire, as the Sossag called it now, though it was black and cold in the sun.

"That lordling knows his business," Ota Qwan said. "I don't know him—lacs d'amour? Whose banner is that?" He spat. "He's spreading his knights."

"So?" Nika Qwan asked.

"So in a tight bunch, his men kill a few unlucky warriors and we massacre them from all sides. In a long line, every one of them kills a warrior—or maybe five. It is a lucky warrior who gets an arrow into one of them."

The knights began to come forward in the strong light, and the blue sky was mirrored in their harness. They looked like monsters from the Aether—like mythical beasts. The overhead sun sparkled from their harness and stung men's eyes.

Skahas Gaho appeared as if by magic from the grass. "More tin-men behind us," he said. "Forming by the woods closest to the river." He shrugged. "Their horses are wet. They swam the river."

Ota Qwan made a grunt. Nita Qwan could see he'd made his decision, just in that moment. The war leader stood, put a horn to his lips, and sounded a long call.

The Sossag stood and ran like songbirds before an eagle. They ran north, even as the two long lines of knights closed on them.

Lissen Carak—The Red Knight

The captain watched the painted man rise from the grass just a hundred horse lengths in front of him, sound his horn, and begin to sprint north, out of the closing jaws of the counter-trap. He watched with a sense of failure and the vaguest professional admiration. He knew the Outwallers.

He ordered his valet to sound "Charge—ahead!"

His line caught a handful of stragglers but, obedient to his orders, the line swept east and south, and didn't deviate to pursue the Sossag. Arrows flew as the Sossag rearguard gave their lives for their fellows, and one man-at-arms went down in a tangle of armour plate and dead horse, and then the black-clad knights from the riverside swept over the rearguard, killing every one of them in an instant, no quarter given.

The Prior moved past him, raised his hand, and summoned the military order knights to him without a word being spoken. It was a magnificent display of power.

The captain shook his head. "I thought we were good," he said.

Sauce had blood on her lance tip, and she reined in. Jacques was sounding the rally, and a wounded knight—Ser Tancred—was being hauled bodily onto Ser Jehannes's horse. She leaned over. "We are good," she said.

To their left front the whole squadron of black- and red-clad knights went from a galloping charge to a dead stop in a few hoofbeats—then wheeled right around as if performing some gypsy horse trick and halted facing the Bridge Castle in a neat wedge.

Sauce shook her head—not a big motion in an aventail and bassinet. "Sweet Jesu. They are good," she admitted reluctantly.

The Prior cantered to the centre of the new line. "Well, Captain?" he asked. "Shall we relieve the castle?"

The captain raised his hand. "At your command, Prior."

Seventy mailed knights made the earth tremble.

The boglins scattered.

Lissen Carak—Thorn

Thorn watched in weary anger as his useless allies ran rather than face the knights. So many claims—so many boasts that they could fight anything, that they could conquer the maille-clad riders.

He watched them run, and knew—with the pain of intimate and exact intellect—that his entire plan for the day would come apart.

A burst of power from the field alerted him. The power itself was very low in intensity, but also very tightly controlled. Only someone as imbued with mastery as he himself would detect it.

And immediately recognise the wielder.

Prior Mark.

Thorn watched as the Prior used his power to pass signals to his knights—to turn them into finely crafted weapons, responsive to his will. Another man who loved power.

For a moment, he considered using all of his remaining puissance in a single spell to kill the Prior.

But that was foolish. He needed that power. He reminded himself that there was no hurry. That the king's army would never reach the river.

But the fall of the Bridge Castle would have made all that unnecessary.

Thorn rarely spoke aloud. He had no peers to whom he could speak his mind—voice his indecision, his secret fears.

But he turned to his startled guards. The shamans who worshipped him. The cloud of midge-like followers who attended his every need. His voice came out as a harsh croak, like the voice of a raven.

"Thirty days ago, a daemon sought to take this place from an old woman with no soldiers," he said. "Fate and bad luck have left *me* to contest it with the King of Alba and whole armies of knights, with a dozen able magi and now with the best warriors in the world." He laughed, and his wicked croak startled the birds in the trees. "And yet I will still conquer."

Lissen Carak—The Red Knight

Nothing withstood their charge, and the strong band of knights scoured the ground around the Bridge Castle. They rode all the way around it, close against the walls, killing every creature of the Wild that didn't scuttle clear of their path. The lesser boglins rose in brief bursts of flight or lay flat in the tall grass where they were difficult to find, and the greater boglins and irks, those with armour, struggled into their hastily dug tunnels to emerge in one last spurt of violence to the burning hell of the Bridge Castle courtyard.

The captain raised his hand for his company to halt when they returned to the base of the soft earth ramp that the worker-Boglins had run up to the curtain wall on the north side of the Bridge Castle.

"Dismount!" he called. The sun was past noon, but still high. There were streaks of cloud in the west, but hours of daylight remained. Still, experience told him that if he didn't clear the courtyard before full dark he would lose the Bridge Castle.

And thus lose his connection to the king.

If the king was coming at all.

Every fifth valet took ten horses in his fist.

"Spears!" the captain called, and his men formed a tight line at the base of the ramp; men-at-arms in front, valets and squires in the middle, and archers in the rear rank.

The Prior rode up and saluted. "We'll cover you!"

The captain saluted as Michael handed him his heavy spear. "If we aren't out before full dark," the captain said, "Assume the bridge is lost."

The Prior crossed himself. "God go with you, Ser Knight."

"God doesn't give a shit," the captain said. "But it's the thought that counts. On me!" he called, and started up the slope of new turned earth. It was damp and hard—hardened with something excreted by the boglins, to judge from the smell. Acrid, like naphtha.

There were fifty boglins on the wall, and they died when the men-at-arms ripped through them.

The captain looked down into the inferno of the courtyard. All the merchant wagons were afire, and the courtyard crawled with figures like the damned in hell—men stripped of their skin, shrieking their lungs out; armoured boglins in glowing, fire-lit white. Most of them crowded to the door of the nearest tower, but more poured from a gaping wound in the earth where a dozen flagstones had been hurled aside, like maggots in a bloated corpse when it is opened. More boglins on the walls—but on the east wall, a small, disciplined company fought back to back, holding the opposite curtain against assault from both directions.

"Files from the right!" the captain called, and led his men down off the curtain wall—down the ramp intended for siege engines to be hauled up to the curtain, and there were a pair of pale boglins gleaming there, each with a pole-axe.

He had no time for finesse. He raised his spear, point low and butt high and caught the first creature's heavy cut on his haft—wrapped its arm with his own in the high key that men practised when wrestling in armour—and then ripped its arm from its body like a man ripping a crab leg from a new-cooked crab.

The thing's other arm came at him—he rammed his spear point into its head, let go of the shaft with his armoured left hand and punched into the boglin's throat. It's great maw opened, mandibles flashing at his visor—overhand, he rammed the spearhead down its gullet and acrid ichor blew out of the top of it like lava from a new volcano.

"Form your front!" he roared, even as Sauce beheaded the second armoured boglin with her axe.

Ser Jehannes came up on his left, and Sauce cleared her weapon and fell in next, tapping her axe-haft against the breastplates of Ser Jehannes and Ser Tancred, and the line was formed.

The armoured creatures were trying to overrun the defenders of the north tower, and the captain pointed with his spear. "Charge!" he called.

Twenty paces into the rear of the things.

His sabatons rang on the pavement—he stumbled on a corpse.

And then—a storm of iron. Skittering screeches and staccato clicks like the beat of an insane drummer as the mass by the North Tower turned and charged him.

In the first meeting he was head to head with an armoured monster the size of Bad Tom—the complex interlacing of its front armour over the interstices of its six armour plates was like an obscene mouth as the thing reared back, its whole strength bent on a single, crushing blow from its great hammer, its body bent like a bow with the effort.

He set his feet and took the blow on his haft, rotated the weapon on the pivot of his opponent's blow, and slammed a spike into the middle of its helmeted head. His spike penetrated the thing's face plate, and it spasmed.

Behind his dying opponent towered another, wielding two long swords, and even as he watched, the thing beheaded Ser Jehannes's new squire, the two weapons coming together like a tailor's shears. Jehannes leaped to avenge his squire and took a pommel to the helmet that staggered him, and two lightning fast blows followed it, literally beating him to the ground.

The captain's command sense shrieked in panic. The boglins had stopped his men-at-arms. It shouldn't have been possible. There was nothing in the Wild that could stop twenty fully armoured men.

Not many things.

The captain paused and locked eyes with the thing standing over Jehannes, and it *knew* him. He leaped at the double-sworded thing, but his spear remained lodged in his last kill, and he had to leave it.

Double Sword turned from his prey—Jehannes—and faced him. It was yet another kind of boglin—sleek, taller than Bad Tom and heavily muscled, with man-made chainmail covering all its joints and feral, organic plate armour that might have been grown, or very finely forged. A wight.

At the edge of his peripheral vision, Sauce rammed a spike through the carapace of another armoured monster and screamed her war cry.

Ser Tancred was locked with another, his arms straining against it as his squire stabbed his long sword into its armpit—rapid, professional stabs that made its limbs thrash.

Double Sword tapped its blades together and leaped at him with animal rapidity.

The captain snatched his rondel dagger from his belt and trusted his armour. He entered between the blades, arms high, dagger in both fists, and the longsword blows crashed into his shoulder plates. The hardened steel bent and split—only to cut into the rings of the mail haubergeon underneath, and the blades were held, though the force drove through the thickly padded jupon under the mail, and still managed to bruise his shoulders...

But he swung the dagger overhand, two handed through the boglin's mail aventail and into its neck.

Six times.

It's limbs spasmed, but it's forearms tightened like a band of steel around the captain's shoulders. And it lit up with power, eyes glowing cool blue as it prepared—

He drove his armoured knee in between its legs—nothing there to hurt, but his blow took it off balance, and he pushed his left foot forward and threw the thing over his outstretched right leg. Its wing cases snarled in his knee armour's flanges and ripped free. Its own weight accelerated its fall, but its limbs clasped him fast, and he fell atop it, his rondel dagger a projection from his fists.

His steel carapace held.

The monster's didn't. The triangular blade punched cleanly though it, and ichor jetted out.

542

He didn't stop, but pulled the foot-long steel dagger clear of the wound and drove it up under the thing's mandibles that were opening and closing with terrific force on the slick metal of his helmet. They ripped his visor off his face, forcing his head around in a painful arc, and he was eye to eye with the thing—its eyes glowing with unfocused power.

He countered with a lightning blow to its nearer eye-patch. He raked the point through the oblong eye—and again, and again, as a scythed foreleg reached for his face.

It was not going to die before it cast its phantasm.

He got his left gauntlet under its head and slammed the dagger into its left eye—through the eye patch, through the skin and bone. He reached for his memory palace to fight its power, even as he stirred its brains with the blade...

And a wave of power entered him—a sickly blue wave of chilling intensity, and he writhed—

Its eyes went out.

He took its force into him, subsuming the alien thing as creatures of the Wild do. He had never done it before, and hadn't known how. He thought it was probably best that Prudentia hadn't been there to watch.

He bounced to his feet, suddenly awash in concentrated calculations as to the survivability of his host under the conditions of the current combat, and for a fleeting instant, the captain was able to see and calculate as *both sides* in the courtyard.

But the balance had shifted.

A third of his men-at-arms were down—dead, wounded, or merely tripped, he had no way of knowing, but the back of the enemy resistance was broken and already the fringes of the melee had become more like a hunt than a fight.

His archers began to clear the walls, their shafts joined by the dozen archers loosing from the towers, and the pace of victory accelerated. A dozen of the white boglins scuttled down a hole. A man, half the skin ripped from his flesh and trailing down his back, screamed again, and an archer put a shaft into his throat with rough mercy, and stopped his screams—and all through the courtyard, armoured figures opened their visors and heaved air into desperate lungs.

The captain walked up a ramp of dead bodies to the door of the north tower where a young giant, drenched in acrid boglin-blood, stood leaning on a six-foot bill with a heavy steel head, coated in gore.

"Well fought, young Daniel," the captain said.

The former carter shrugged. "'Twas Master Random held the door, Cap'n. For most part of an hour, seems to me."

"Dead?" the captain asked.

Daniel shrugged again. "They drug him into the pile," he said. "We fought 'em for the corpse but lost him when you charged their rear." He stood straighter. "Deserves finding, I think." He seemed to shake off his fatigue, and then he reached out, spiked an armoured boglin on the back-spike of his bill, and flung it from the pile like a farmer moving hay with a pitchfork.

The captain grabbed another. Dead, the boglins were curiously harmless—disgusting, but less insectoid, and more animal. He tossed one aside, and then another. His hands shook. His knees were weak.

He was *insanely* full of power.

Sauce joined him. "What are we doing? Killing the wounded?" she asked, her voice a little too sharp and bright. This was a fight that men—and women—would relive too many times.

"Looking for a body," the captain said. He was down to waist level, now.

"I've got his leg!" Daniel called.

Michael joined them, and suddenly there was Ser Milus, and Ser Jehannes, blood still leaking from the joints of his shoulder, and they hauled, and the corpse of the merchant stiffened, and he screamed.

His armour was slick with boglin blood, and human, and he popped out of the pile of corpses. The flesh of his left foot was gone at the ankle, and blood was leaking too slowly out of the wound where sharp mandibles had flensed the flesh from his foot.

"Tourniquet! Cut his greave off!" the captain shouted.

Daniel already had a small knife in his great paw of a hand, and he slit the straps holding the greave—Sauce opened the catch and the greave came loose with a gout of fresh blood.

The captain grabbed the stump of his leg. Sauce got her sword belt around the small of the ankle, got it through the buckle, and pulled with all her strength.

The blood stopped.

"Tie it off," the captain said unnecessarily. Every soldier in his company could be a leach in an emergency.

Then he took a weary breath and ran for the wall.

Lissen Carak—Thorn

Thorn felt the dark sun take Exrech and he cursed. Cursed that he had been fooled again, cursed that every encounter seemed to go against him.

The accession of power by the dark sun made him far more dangerous than he had been.

Thorn reached out to the two Sossag shamans attending him and subsumed them, stripping their essences and their power, feeding on it. Their empty corpses collapsed to the earth. It wasn't much power, but sufficient for him to *see* and *send*.

The coming darkness was not his friend. He needed light, where he could deploy his superior numbers and his massed archery.

And then he sent his powerful senses questing for Clackak. Found him deep in the earth under the stone fort by the water, with a hundred more of his kin.

Break off, he demanded.

The sun had begun to slide toward evening. There were long hours until night.

Thorn shook his massive head and torso. "Tomorrow," he said.

Lissen Carak—The Red Knight

The archers opened the gate and the knights rode in, their black hooded surcotes hiding the gleam of armour, their black horses like nightmare creatures in the full dark.

The Prior rode to the captain, who was sitting on a folding stool, scraping crap out of his sabatons to make the plates work properly. His whole body felt like a badly maintained machine.

"With God's help, you have conquered," the Prior said.

"If you like," the captain said. "We have conquered, for the moment. But only by the skin of our teeth, as old wives say. And where are the wyverns? Where are the daemons? The Jacks?" He gazed out into the last light. Killing off the last of the boglins had taken another hour, and now the enemy machines were throwing stones again.

The valets were stacking corpses outside the gate. The courtyard of the Bridge Castle stank of burned wood, dead boglin and ordure—horses killed in their traces, oxen butchered, men and boglins dead. The rotting meat smell rose like an evil sacrifice in the too-warm evening air, and midges were settling on the working men like an evil plague.

The Prior dismounted, his own sabatons ringing on the stones of the courtyard. "Where indeed? I haven't seen so many evil creatures in many years."

"We saw them every day. Now they are gone," the Red Knight said. "Next wave, perhaps?" he added. "That's my guess. Wear us out with the boglins. Then break us with the bigger creatures." He tested his foot on the ground. "Then—"

"It's what I'd do. Bleed us with the easily replaced critters and save the others. He needs them to fight the king. This was all just to fix us in place."

"We can hold until the king comes," the Prior said. He was pulling his sodden arming cap off his head and paused to slap a mosquito.

"Despite wyverns and daemons? I hope so," said the captain. He got to his feet. "Michael—tell the valets to serve beer and maple sugar." He smiled at the Prior. "It's going to be a long night." He looked around. "Gelfred?"

"My lord?" Gelfred said.

"I need you to do something insanely brave," he said.

Gelfred shrugged.

"Can you get a message to the king?" the captain asked.

"In the dark? Through a host of enemies?" Gelfred smiled. "I can with God's help. And by my faith, messire, if you make a crack about God not caring, you can take your cursed message yourself."

The captain got to his feet and gave the huntsman his hand. "I am rebuked, Gelfred."

Gelfred shrugged. "Join me in prayer," he said.

"Let's not get carried away," the captain replied.

Gelfred laughed. "Why do I like you so much?" he asked.

The captain shrugged. "The feeling is mutual."

Half an hour later, Gelfred went straight into the river from the docks.

He swam for fifteen minutes in the dark, and then went with the current for a while to rest. He heard, or felt, a wyvern in the dark air overhead, and he went under the water and stayed down as long as he could. When he surfaced, his heart was beating so fast that he had to head for shore.

"There goes the bravest man in all my company," the Red Knight said to the Prior.

"Because he faces his fears?" the Prior asked. "He has God's aid."

The captain shook his head but said nothing. Only watched the darkness, and wished he was in the castle. He touched the soiled handkerchief pinned to his arming cote. It was no longer white, indeed, it held the blood and ichor of several foes, and it was cut almost in two.

Lissen Carak—Amicia

Amicia tried *not* to go to the gate. She tried not to look out the window. When a party of men-at-arms clattered in on exhausted horses, she forced herself to wait until the wounded came in.

Ser Tancred told her that the Red Knight was spending the night in the Bridge Castle.

When the last wounded were healed, she knelt in the chapel by the Abbess's bier and prayed. She opened herself, as the nuns had taught her, to God. And she made God a hard, heartfelt promise.

Somewhere—Gelfred

He was tired and cold and very, very scared when he heard the sound of men's voices on the other bank, and he struck out for them. He swam quietly, as well as he could.

They had boats.

After some time, he swam to the boats, and a sentry saw him.

"Halt! Alarm! Man in the water!" A crossbow loosed, and the bolt passed somewhere near him.

"Friend!" he spluttered. He was short of breath. "From the fortress!"

They were too alert, but they weren't great marksmen. He swam in, shouting that he was a friend. Eventually, they stopped loosing their bolts at him, and strong arms pulled him into a big barge.

"Take me to the king!" he said.

A big man with a hillman's accent pulled him over the side and put him on a bench. "Drink this, laddy," he said. "You've found the Queen, not the king."

Chapter Sixteen

Lissen Carak—Michael

Michael watched the captain sleep. It was dawn, or near enough, and he cursed that he was awake. He rose, pissed in a pot, drank half a glass of stale wine and spat it out into the courtyard.

The place stank like a charnel house, and most of the soldiers had slept in rows in the tower. In their harness.

He walked to the table, opened his wallet, and took out a pair of wax tablets, withdrew his stylus, and wrote:

The Siege of Lissen Carak. Day Fifteen

Yesterday the enemy tried to storm Bridge Castle and, despite putting monsters inside, was repelled. We lost more than forty men, women, and children of the convoys, and three men-at-arms and two archers, as well as four men of the militia. These are our worst losses so far.

But the king is coming. Knights of the Holy Order of Saint Thomas came at nightfall on the thirteenth day to tell us we were saved. And yet we fought all day and the king did not come.

Where is the king?

Michael looked at the last line. He took the butt of the stylus to rub that line out. Then he shook his head, and went to wake the captain.

Near Lissen Carak—The King

The sun was an arc of fire in the east.

The king's magnificent golden armour and brilliant red and blue heraldry caught the first rays of the sun so that he seemed to catch fire.

Behind him stood three hundred of the most heavily armoured knights Alba had ever seen, their heavy horses left in camp.

The golden helmet moved to the right and left, examining the dressing of the long line of chivalric warriors that vanished into the woods on either flank, each with his heavily armoured squire at his back.

His golden gauntlet was raised high, and fell, and the line of the vanguard advanced along the line of the old Bridge Road. The three hundred knights were each a man's height apart, their line was a half-mile long, and the men at either end had hunter's horns—noted horns, which they played back and forth like huntsmen.

The figure of the king seemed to dance forward joyfully.

He pressed through the woods, and the woods parted before him. There is nothing in the woods that can impede a man in full harness—no branch, no trailing vine, no bank of thickset canes, no matter how thorny, will stop a man in armour. Or slow him.

The line ground forward at a walking pace.

Half a mile.

A mile.

He raised his hand and his own horn bearer played a long note and the line stopped.

Men-at-arms raised their visors and drank water, but the morning was still early and it was cool in the dark woods.

Men pulled the branches out of their knee-armour, out of their elbow cops, out of the joints in their faulds.

And then, with the sounding of two horn calls, the line swept forward again, like a great boar hunt.

A mile behind them, the rest of the army lurched into motion.

The van pressed forward into the woods. Led by the king, in person.

Bill Redmede—Jack of the Jacks—saw the armoured figures coming on foot, armoured cap à pied, and the bitterness in his heart was enough to melt steel.

So much for Thorn and his contempt for men.

Jack turned to his lieutenant—Nat Tyler, the Jack of the Albin Plain. "Bastard aristos have a spy, brother."

Tyler watched the inexorable approach of the armoured men. "And we're in deep brush."

"Thorn said they'd be mounted on the road," Jack said. "Fuck!"

"Let's loose and get gone," Tyler said.

"This is our day!" Jack argued. "Today we kill the king!"

Seventy yards away, the king stood virtually alone. He stood in a shaft of light in the deep forest, and he raised his arms—he had a four-foot sword in one hand and a sparkling buckler in the other.

Redmede drew his great bow and, suiting thought to deed, loosed.

Beside him, Nat Tyler's bow twanged deep, the harp of death.

All along the line, Jacks rose from ambush and loosed at the king.

The king's figure twinkled as he pivoted on his back heel and spun, his buckler sweeping over his head, his sword scything through the first fall of arrows.

All around him, men-at-arms broke into a dead run, charging the line of archers.

The king stood his ground—stepped and swung, stepped, cut, and then ran forward.

"Good Christ," Jack muttered. Not a single arrow had gone home. "Too far—too damned far!"

But the Jacks were robbers and partisans, not battlefield men, and they turned and ran.

A hundred paces to the rear, the line of Jacks steadied. Nat Tyler got them into a line at the edge of a meadow of flowers a third of a mile long and two hundred yards deep—an ancient beaver meadow, crisscrossed by a stream. Bill led them over the stream, emerging wet to the waist, and they formed a new line on the far side.

"Better," Nat Tyler said with a grim smile.

The men-at-arms must have paused to drink water and rest. The sun was much higher when they came—and they came all together. Forward in a line. This time the captain yelled at them to pick their targets and leave the king to the master archers, and the shafts flew thick and heavy over open ground.

He could no longer cut every arrow in the air, and heavy shafts rang off his buckler, his helmet—he was leaning forward like a man walking into a storm, but his heart was singing, because this was a great deed of arms. He laughed, and ran faster.

The stream opened under his feet and he fell—straight down the banks and into a thigh deep pool.

Two peasants stepped to the edge of the pool and loosed arrows at him from a few feet away.

Gaston saw the charge falter and blew his horn. Men were falling into something—a line of pits, a hidden trench—

An arrow rang from his breastplate, denting it deeply, and then he had an armoured fist on the king, and he pulled him straight out of the muddy pool in one long pull. By his side his squire, angered, threw his short spear across the stream and it struck—more by luck than skill—in the torso of a peasant, who folded over it and screamed. And the king got his feet under him and ran straight at the beaver dam—the only clear bridge over the stream.

Gaston followed him, and every man-at-arms nearby followed, too. The dam was half in and half out the water—far from solid, just an animal's hasty assemblage of downed branches and rotten wood. But the king seemed to skim across it, even as Gaston's right leg went into water as cold as ice—and he lost his balance, flailed, almost lost his sword and an arrow slammed into his helmet.

The king ran on, across the uneven top of the dam. The first half ran to a rocky island, and then the dam was even worse, the centre of its span under water, and yet the king ran across it, his feet kicking up spray in a brilliant display of balance—straight across the dam into the archers pouring shafts at him, and one got past his buckler to bury itself in his shoulder by the pauldron, and another rang off his helmet, and then he was among them, and his sword moved faster than a dragonfly on a summer's evening. Gaston was struggling to catch him, breathing like a horse at the end of a long run, soaked, his left leg trapped in mud for a moment and then Gaston was with the king, through the line of archers, and the horns were playing the *avaunt* and the *mort*.

He followed the king up the rise to the ridge that dominated the meadow, and more and more men-at-arms crossed behind them—and far off to the left, more men-at-arms had crossed the narrow footbridge on the road, and now the whole line of peasant archers was compromised, and they ran again.

But even as they turned to run, the wyverns struck.

Gaston saw the first one—saw the flicker of its shadow, and looked up in stunned unbelief, even as the wave of its terror struck him and the Alban knights with him. The Albans flowed through the palpable fear—and he refused to let himself pause, although for a moment it was so intense he couldn't breathe—they surged forward even as the carthorse-sized monster killed a dozen of their number in a single flurry of talons and beak.

There were three of the things.

That was all Gaston could comprehend—that, and that the king was like a fiend, leaping forward at the first wyvern, and his sword sliced a wing through at the root and his back cut flayed a sword's length of scales from the thing's neck, and it whirled to face him but he was gone, under the flailing neck and his blade went up into its belly—ripped the thing open from anus to breastbone, and was gone again as its intestines fell free.

Gaston followed him to the second one, where it crushed the Bishop of Lorica to the ground with one blow and ripped his squire's head from his trunk with its beaked head. Gaston got his spear up, and spiked the head—lost his balance on the uneven ground, broken with the spiked branches the beavers had left—stumbled, and lost his spear, whirled and drew his sword as the head, trailing his spear, went for him.

He cut into its snout with every muscle in his body.

Its head knocked him flat.

The head reared above him, with his spear *and* his sword stuck in it, and the king straddled him. Blood leaked from the arrow in his left shoulder, and the man cut one handed at the monster's neck and severed its head.

The surviving knights roared their approval and Gaston got slowly to his feet, drenched by the hot blood of the thing, and dug in its jaw for his sword—he had to kick it off his blade.

The third wyvern was already airborne, leaving a trail of broken knights behind it, but after leaping into the air, he pivoted and collapsed on the king, bearing him to the ground.

Every knight still alive in the meadow fell on the wyvern, and blows rained on it like a steel hail—pieces of meat flew free like dust rises from the first fall of rain.

The wyvern hunched and tried to rise again into the air, but Gaston slammed his spearhead into its neck, and a few feet away, Ser Alcaeus hit the thing with a maul and staggered it. The king struggled from beneath it, staggered to his feet, and rammed his sword to the hilt in its guts before falling to his knees.

The wyvern screamed.

The king fell to the ground, his golden armour all besmirched with the blood of three mighty foes.

Ser Alcaeus swung his maul up over his head, screamed his defiance, and slammed the lead head into the wyvern's skull, and the beast crumpled atop the king.

A dozen gauntleted hands scrambled to pull the dead thing off the king, even as trumpets sounded behind them and the mounted chivalry emerged from the tree line.

Gaston ran to the king. He got the king's head on his knee and opened his faceplate.

His mad cousin's eyes met his.

"Am I not the greatest knight in the world!" he roared. "And no craven, to basely let my liege be slain!"

His eyes flickered. "Get the arrow out of my chest and bandage me tight," he said. "This is my battle!" And then the light went out of his eyes.

Gaston held his cousin tight while a pair of squires tried to staunch the flow of blood, stripping his breastplate and his haubergeon. The remnants of the vanguard pressed on.

"He demanded it, this morning," said a voice behind Gaston, and suddenly the squires were bowing.

The King of Alba stood there, in Jean de Vrailly's cote armour.

"He said he knew of a plot to kill me, in an ambush—and he wished the honour of taking my place." The king shook his head. "He is truly a great knight."

Gaston swallowed his thoughts, and wondered what his mad cousin had done. And why. But the mad eyes were closed forever.

Near Lissen Carak—Thurkan

Thurkan watched the king fall. His eyesight was tremendous and from two ridges away he and his clan watched the abnethog fling themselves on the knights.

Of course, he had told them that he would support their attack.

He'd told the Jacks much the same.

But Thorn was doomed, and Thurkan had no intention of letting his people suffer any more.

He turned to his sister. "If the men begin fighting among themselves, well and good—we will feast."

"I see nothing of the sort," Mogan said.

"Nor I," Korghan said.

Behind them stood forty of their kind—enough Qwethnethog to turn the battle. "Go tell the Sossag and the Abenacki that the battle is lost," Thurkan said to his sister.

"It isn't lost unless we flee," his sister insisted. "By rock and flowing water—is that your will?"

Thurkan frowned, deep creases appearing in his jaw. "Thorn must die—now, while he is weak. Otherwise he will hunt us down."

Mogan poked her snout close to her brother's. "Do not let me believe that this is all the rivalry of two Powers," she spat. "I have lost kin—you have lost kin. We were promised a feast, and—"

"We had a feast at Albinkirk and another on the road." Thurkan shook his head. "I do not do what I do lightly. Thorn must go. We are being—" he flexed the talons on his forefoot, moving each digit in an intricate arc, "—manipulated. By something. I can feel it."

Mogan snorted. "Very well," she said. "I obey. Under protest." And ran off into the trees, as fleet as a deer.

"West," Thurkan told his brother.

"I can help you," his brother insisted.

"Perhaps. But Mogan cannot lead our clan or fertilize new eggs. And you can." The great head turned. "Obey, brother."

Korghan flicked his tongue in anger. "Very well, *brother.*"

The two clan companies started west, even as the Royal Household Knights began to climb the ridge towards them.

*

Bill Redmede ran, loosed an arrow from his dwindling store, and ran again. His bodkin points were all but gone, and he had only hunting arrows.

The *God-damned* aristocrats had more plate armour than he'd ever seen. And the monsters—he'd been a fool to ever trust them and no doubt imperiled his soul, as well. He was bitter—tired, angry, and defeated.

But he'd seen the king fall. It was some consolation, but it didn't seem to slow the rest of the aristos any, and like all his kind, he faced an ugly death if he was caught, so he waited a heartbeat, stepped from behind his tree and put a shaft under the arm of somebody's fucking *lord* and turned, and ran again.

He made it up the second ridge, where they had started the morning, where the big daemon lord had issued its orders.

All the daemons were gone. Sod them, too. Oligarchs. Bad allies for free men.

The river was close now.

There were knights in red surcotes at the base of the ridge, and he could see them coming up the hill—most of them had dismounted, and a flurry of arrows told him that his boys were still fighting back. Fighting the Royal Guard.

He was damned if he was going to lose any more Jacks.

He turned and ran diagonally across the face of the ridge.

He came up behind Nat Tyler as the man loosed his last arrow. "Come on, Nat—the boats!"

Tyler turned like a wild thing—but he got a hold of his wits, paused, and winded his horn and whistles sounded in response.

"Follow me!" Bill called, and ran back up the hill—legs labouring, lungs searching for breath.

Behind him, the Jacks loosed a last arrow and ran—the *sauve qui peut* had been blown.

Bill ran, and the Jacks ran behind him. He paused when he saw three of his own trying to face a knight with drawn swords and bucklers, and he put a shaft to his bow—another knight burst from the trees and crossed the crest of the ridge—raised his visor—

Too good a shot to miss.

Hawthor Veney made it to the top of the ridge on pride alone. It was his first fight, and he was a King's Guardsman. His red surcote shouted his allegiance, and the Jacks were his enemies, and he pursued them ruthlessly. He caught one and hewed him from behind, a clumsy stroke that buried his point in the man's neck, but the man fell hard, blood burst from the wound, and he ran on, wrenching the sword from the man's corpse.

The next one he caught fell to his knees and begged for mercy. He was perhaps fourteen years old.

Hawthor paused, and an older guardsman beheaded the boy. "Nits make lice," he said, as he swept by, and Hawthor hardened his heart and ran on. Running in armour was hard. Running up a ridge with soft footing and tangled spring undergrowth was worse. His lungs began to labour and, as the Jacks rallied and rallied again, whipping deadly shafts at the guardsmen, Hawthor had to fight the temptation to open his visor.

He began to pass men when he could see the light through the trees that meant the crest of the ridge was coming. There was shouting to the right—he turned to look, and he heard the sound of steel on steel. He looked back and forth—it was closer, and with his faceplate closed, he couldn't see where. There was a flicker of motion to the front—he looked, ran a few steps, stopped, and looked again.

Heard the scrape of blades. A voice called "Sauve Qui Peut!"

He was breathing like a horse after a race. He was afraid—he was afraid they were behind him. He popped his visor, turned his head—

And died.

Near Lissen Carak—Bill Redmede

Bill got another shaft on his bow after putting one through the knight's face—felt better for doing it—but two more of his men were down and he knew better than to join the hand to hand fight. He ran.

They crossed the ridge, and started down the far side towards their boats. A handful of knights from the vanguard tried to stop them, and the Jacks just ran around them—exhausted men without armour have an advantage over exhausted men in armour.

Bill saw the Count of the Borders, close enough to touch, and he cursed his fate, that he should be so close to a mortal foe and be able to do nothing.

But he ran past the man, down the steep berm, into a broad field— ploughed, until recently. Nat Tyler came out of the trees to his left, and dozens more—a handful, compared to their numbers three weeks ago. But enough to start again.

Up the last dyke, and there were the boats. Fifty light bark boats—it had taken them three careful trips to get everyone over, night before last, and now...

Now they'd all fit in one go.

He tossed his bow into the bottom of the light boat, pushed it into the water, and stepped in, running lightly down the length of the boat to kneel in the bow. Then he rocked the stern off the muddy beach, and held his position in the current with his paddle until a young blond man in dirty white tossed his own bow into the boat and stepped clumsily into the stern. He almost swamped the light boat, and they were away into the current.

Twenty other boats were putting off behind him—the better boatmen got the boats moving. The less competent men started to die, as the Royal Guard began to close on them.

A few last Jacks dived into the water, abandoning packs and bows, quivers of invaluable arrows, but a few men had had the presence of mind to drag the rest of the boats off the mud and tow them and, safe in the current, they got the swimmers into boats.

More than a hundred Jacks had been saved from the disaster.

They began to paddle out into the centre. It was obvious from here that Bridge Castle was still in the hands of the sell-swords—an arbalest bolt skipped across the water to put a hole in one boat.

Tyler waved, pointed downstream, waved again, and paddled frantically to turn his boat.

Jack looked into the rising sun and it's brilliant reflection on the broad river—and saw flashes. Rhythmic flashes—banks of oars on heavy bateaux, rowing upstream. He counted twenty—counted a second twenty—

Disaster. Disaster after disaster.

He turned his head. "Less power and more finesse, comrade. We have to turn this boat and paddle upstream—all your power will serve us well, then."

A pair of crossbow bolts, like swallows feeding on insects, skipped by, passing within an arm's length of their boat before sinking out of sight.

The man in the stern shook his head. "I'm no boatsman, brother," he admitted.

"Never mind, lad. Drag your paddle on the left—just there. And we're around." Bill hadn't risen to leadership for nothing; he was patient, even when everything was at stake.

Then they were around, and his young companion's strong arms were pushing the boat forward like a leaping deer. It was a waste of the man's energy to spend so much but Jack let him tire himself, steering from the bow. Another volley of crossbow bolts from the distant bateaux and he lost a trio of Jacks—they were broadside on to the enemy and all three of them caught bolts.

Bill Redmede was an old boatman. And a master archer. He stowed his paddle, took his bow from the bottom of the light boat, wiped the stave and the string—good wax, not too much moisture. He was glad he'd left it strung, and he rose to his feet, the boat tipping—leaped lightly onto the ash gunwales, one foot on each.

"Good Christ!" shouted his stern paddle in dismay.

He drew and loosed in one motion, tipping the boat from side to side, loosing high—a hunting point. Then he knelt as he watched the fall of his arrow.

He lost it in the sun-dazzle. But he felt better for the shot, and he took up his paddle and gave way with a will.

Desiderata was in a borrowed chain shirt—worn with a man's hose, a heavy wool kirtle laced as tightly as her maids could manage, and a man's arming cap. The effect should have been ludicrous, but was instead both martial and quite attractive, to judge from the reactions of the guildsmen and the hillmen all around her on the foredeck of the lead row-galley.

Lady Almspend stood by her side, also in a shirt of mail, with a sallet on her head and a sword at her waist. She was more ridiculous, but beaming at Ranald Lachlan, whose attention was torn between his lady-love and the approach of combat. The herd was penned in camp, with twenty of his brother's men as guards. He stood in hauberk and leg armour, his open-faced bascinet and leather cote almost barbaric in comparison to the crossbowmen of the guilds of Lorica, most of whom had fancy cotes of plates and visored helmets, the latest fashion from the Continent. His hands rested on the great axe he carried.

The Queen looked at him. He was quieter than she had known him in year's past. According to her secretary, he had actually been *dead*. The Queen suspected this might be a sobering experience.

"Boglins on the bank," Ranald said, pointing a gauntleted hand.

"Got them," said one of the guild officers. "Boglins to starboard. Pick your targets. Loose!"

A dozen bolts flew.

"The king must have been victorious," Lady Almspend said. "Those aren't our men fleeing across the river in front of us."

Ranald turned so fast the chain aventail at his neck slapped his helmet. "Good eyes, my lady." He flashed her a smile—pleased to have her company in his favourite pursuit. He looked under his gauntleted hand for a long time. "They're men—they're in a sort of uniform. Now they turned their boats away—"

The guild officer had scrambled up into the bows past the Queen. "Jacks, by God. Rebels! Traitors! Heretics!" He raised his arbalest, took careful aim, and loosed a bolt.

The boglins on the north bank began to flick arrows at them.

The Queen started. The back of her throat was scratchy. For the first time, she was afraid.

"We have come too far west," Ranald said. "There are enemies on both banks, and the king won't yet know that we are here."

The Queen had received a message from the king late in the afternoon, and she had ordered the boats to row all night. She'd picked up the messenger at midnight, and his information had been exact. Today was to be the day—she intended to see it.

She stood on the foredeck and shaded her eyes with her hand—to the front, and to the right, and to the left. To the left, she saw a flash of red, and then another—and then half a dozen Royal Guardsmen appeared on the bank. She waved, and her ladies cheered.

"Anchor here," she ordered.

A half-dozen boglin arrows fell onto the lead galley—most were deflected by the leather curtains that protected the rowers, but one struck home, and the man's oar fell from his hands as he screamed. The arrow was deep in his shoulder.

Boglins poisoned their arrows, and his screams froze her blood. He had laughed and joked with her maids when they lay on the banks of the Alba, eating sausage.

It was as much of a shock as the sight of a boglin.

An arrow plummeted from the heavens like a stooping hawk, struck her helm, ripped down her back and knocked her flat.

She lay on the deck—suddenly the day was darker, and her back was wet.

"Ware the Queen!" Ranald called.

She reached for the golden light of the sun—it was all about her, such a glorious day—

"She'll bleed out. It is in her back." Ranald was doing something.

"Is it poisoned?" Lady Almspend asked.

"I don't think so—give me your pen knife. Wicked bastard—a swallowtail point." Lachlan sounded afraid.

She was floating above them, able to see the hillman digging in the flesh of her back with a knife. He had the mail shirt hiked over her hips having cut the shaft of the arrow. She'd seldom seen herself look less elegant.

"It's in her kidneys," Lachlan said, and sat back on his haunches, suddenly defeated. "Sweet Jesu!"

The captain had slept in his harness like everyone else, his helmeted head in the corner of the curtain wall where the west wall met the north tower. Four assaults had failed to re-take the wall, but he was so tired—

"Boats on the river, Captain." Jack Kaves, senior archer, stood over him. "I brought you a cup of beer. Young Michael tried to wake you and went off to find more wine."

The captain took the beer, rinsed his mouth and spat onto the mound of dead boglins outside the wall, and then took a long pull. Half of the mound of boglin bodies was still moving, so that the whole pile seemed to writhe—and they made mewling sounds like a pile of kittens, somehow more horrible than the screams of men.

No more men were screaming. The wounded had been sent up the hill to the fortress during a lull between attacks—the Knights of Saint Thomas, like their sisters, were doctors as well as fighters, and they gave basic care and rigged stretchers between horses. And the enemy killed every wounded man they could.

He got slowly to his feet. The weight of his armour and his own fatigue combined to make the process of rising painful—his neck hurt like he had been kicked by a horse. "Michael?" he asked, confused and looking around.

"In the store rooms," Kaves said.

"Jack, help me get my helmet off," the captain said. He unbuckled his chinstrap, and Jack lifted the helmet clear of his head. The aventail was clotted with gore, which dragged across his face. The visor was gone.

He unlaced his arming cap. It was one of Mag's, and with the intense interest of total exhaustion, he noted that she had embroidered his lacs d'amour across the crown—lovely work.

The cap was full of power. He hadn't seen it before—perhaps hadn't been *able* to see it. He held it closer and saw that every stitch held a tiny rainbow of light—the whole, with the lines of embroidery, was not unlike a set of tiny fish scales.

Jack Kaves whistled.

The captain turned and looked at his helmet, which had a great gouge in it where some weapon had punched right through it. Indeed, with all too little effort, the captain could remember the boglin chief's scythes, slicing at his unvisored face and never quite reaching it.

"Well, well," he said. He leaned forward, and Jack upended a pot of river-water over his head.

The old archer handed him a rag and he dried his hair, face and beard. While he used the rag, he walked along the wall, feeling the damp spread down inside his breastplate. He could all but hear it rusting. Michael was going to be—

There were, indeed, boats on the river. Fifty row galleys—obviously crewed by men.

He stood and watched them for several long minutes.

Jack Kaves stood beside him, holding out a sausage. "What's it mean, Cap'n?" he asked.

The captain gave a wry smile. "It means we win," he said. "Unless we screw it up really badly, we win."

Albinkirk—Desiderata

Lady Almspend shook her head. She was tying the points of her sleeves back. "Don't be a ninny. That's fat. You there—get my kit-bag up from the hold. The barbs—I have a tool for them."

"You do?" Lachlan asked.

Almspend took the Queen's hand. "I know you can hear me, my lady.

Stay with us. Take power from the sun—take strength. I can get this out, with a little luck."

Lachlan grunted.

An oarsman came up the foredeck ladder with her leather bag.

"Dump it on the deck," she ordered. He did, breaking an ink bottle and putting black ink on every shift she owned.

She snatched the item she sought—a pair of matching halves, like a mould for an arrow.

"Hold on, my lady," she said. "This will hurt."

She pushed the mould over the arrow—in and in, along the path of the original wound, and the Queen moaned, and a long line of saliva mixed with blood came out of her mouth.

Lachlan spat. "She'll—"

"Shut up," said Lady Almspend. She gave her moulds a twist and they snapped over the arrowhead—covering the wicked barbs.

"Pull it out," she said to Lachlan.

He tugged and looked at her.

"Pull it out, or she dies," Lady Almspend insisted.

Lachlan set his shoulders, hesitated, and then pulled. The arrow—moulds and all—popped free with a horrible sucking noise.

Blood spurted after it.

Lissen Carak—Peter

Nita Qwan knew that the great battle had started. But he was cooking. He had built a small oven of river clay, fired it himself, and now he was making a pie.

A third of the Sossag warriors were watching him. Sometimes they clapped. It made him laugh.

The pair of boglins were back, too. If you didn't look too closely at their bodies they looked like a pair of rough-hewn, slightly misshapen back-country men.

They lay full length in the grass, beyond the circle of men, so that their wing-cases were atop them like upturned boats. When they approved of his cooking, they rubbed their back legs together.

His pie was the size of a mill wheel.

His fire was even larger—a carefully dug pit that he had filled with coals from patient burning of hardwoods.

There was no reason that the project should work, but it kept him busy, and it entertained the other warriors.

Nita Qwan wondered what Ota Qwan intended. The man had touched up his paint, polished his bronze gorget, sharpened his sword and his spear and all his arrows, and now he lay watching Peter cook with the other warriors.

Waiting.

The problem with a pie was that you never really knew if it was done.

Battle seemed to have some of the same qualities.

Nita Qwan went and sat with the pie for a while, and then he went over and squatted on his heels by Ota Qwan.

The war chief raised his head off his arms. "Is it done yet?" he asked.

Nita Qwan shrugged. "No," he said. "Or yes."

Ota Qwan nodded seriously.

Skahas Gaho laughed.

"Why are we not on the field?" Nita Qwan asked.

"Pie isn't done yet," Ota Qwan said, and all the senior warriors laughed. There was a unanimity to their laughter that told Peter that Ota Qwan had passed some important test of leadership. He was the war leader, and they did not contest it. A subtle change but a real one.

Ota Qwan rolled over, carefully brushing bits of fern from the grease that carried his paint. "Thorn is going to fight the knights in the fields," he said. "Fields from which every scrap of cover has been burned."

The older warriors nodded, like a chorus.

Ota Qwan shrugged. "We almost lost a lot of warriors last night," he said. "I won't risk the people on such foolishness again. This time, we will go when it is right for us to go. Or not. And the pie is as good a sign as any."

Off by the edge of the clearing, a woman—Ojig—sat up quickly, and her sister, Small Hands, stiffened like a dog at the scent of a wolf, and took up her bow, and suddenly all the people were moving—weaponed, alert—

"Qwethnethog!" shouted Small Hands.

Nita Qwan never heard an order given but in heartbeats, the clearing was empty, save only his fire, his pie, and the six eldest warriors standing around Ota Qwan.

The Qwethnethog emerged from the underbrush moving as fast as a racehorse, and she took several long strides to slow. She looked back and forth at the line of men, and at the fire.

"Skadai," she said in her shrill voice.

"Dead," said one of the aged warriors.

"Ahh," she keened. Made an alien gesture with her taloned paws, and turned. "Who leads the Sossag people?"

Ota Qwan stood forth. "I lead them in war," he said.

The Qwethnethog looked at him, turning her head from side to side. Nita Qwan noted that her helmet crest was a deep scarlet, and the colour came well down her forehead. But the crest was smaller than on a male. It amused him—even through the terror she broadcast—that he'd become so well-versed in the ways of the Wild as to know male from female, clan from clan. She was of their own clan—the western Qwethnethog, who lived in the steep hills above the Sossag lakes.

"My brother speaks for all the Qwethnethog of the Mountains," she said in her shrill voice. "We are leaving the field, and will fight no more for Thorn."

Ota Qwan looked at the men to the right and left. "We thank you," he said. "Go in peace."

The great monster turned and sniffed. "Smells delicious," she said, to no one in particular.

"Stay and have a piece," Nita Qwan found himself saying.

She coughed—he assumed that was her simulation of laughter. "You are bold, little man," she said. "Come and cook for me another time." And with a flick of her talons, faster than a deer, she was gone into the woods again.

No sooner was she gone then a dozen women came out of the woods—matrons, every one. They spoke so rapidly in Sossag that Nita Qwan couldn't understand even single words.

So instead, he went and opened his temporary oven.

It was burned all down one side, but the rest had steamed well and the crust was a nice colour—a rich golden brown, shot with darker brown. Perhaps the oven had cracked—he had no idea why part of the outer rim was so singed.

Nor did he care, for the people came forward like an avenging army and seized the pie as fast as he could cut slices off it. He had made enough, and it wasn't the way of the people to complain.

Ota Qwan took a piece—a burned piece. "Well done. Now we are fed, and well-fed. We will run all night."

He ate his piece in four bites and drank a cup of water. Nita Qwan emulated him, and noted that his wife had packed his baskets. He took one on his back. She smiled shyly at him.

He smiled back.

He shouldered his quiver and his sword, and then—with no further discussion—they were off into the trees.

Albinkirk—Desiderata

The row galley landed against the Bridge Fort's dock; the garrison was alert and manned the walls. The captain was waiting on the dock.

The row galley was full of women, each one more beautiful than the last. It wasn't what he'd expected.

One woman—short, blonde, and harried—stood on the foredeck. "I need a healer," she said. "A good one."

The captain turned to Michael. "Get me a Knight of the Order," he said.

Then he turned back. "They are superb healers," he said. Unfortunately, they had gone on a sortie to clear the trench at dawn, and they hadn't returned.

"I know," she spat. "How long?"

"A few minutes," he said, hopefully.

"She doesn't have a few minutes," the woman said, her face cracking. She seemed to clamp down on a sob. "She's lost a great deal of blood."

"Who has?" he asked as he tried to get a leg over the gunwale. A dozen oarsmen reached to pull him into the boat.

"The Queen," she said. "I'm Lady Almspend. Her secretary. This is Lady Mary, chief among her ladies."

The Queen.

The Red Knight ignored the people gathered around the figure on the deck. The woman lying on the deck was losing blood at a tremendous rate. He could feel it.

And he had very little strength, at least in terms of power. What he had he'd squandered, fighting boglins. And to heal her here, now, would give himself away—at least as a Hermeticist.

So much blood.

She was young—imbued with power, herself.

In that moment, he realised that if she died, he could *take* her. As he had taken the boglin chief. She was defenceless—wide open, trying to use her power to strengthen herself. She drank in the sun's rays—the pure power of Helios. She was very potent.

He put a hand on her back.

"Well?" Lady Almspend asked, impatient. "Can you help?"

Vade Retro, Satanus, the captain thought. He took his arming cap off his head, and pushed it into the wound. Put one finger on the cap as it turned from dirty white to brilliant scarlet.

He almost grinned. He was linked to a legion of healers. It was easy to forget that.

The palace seemed empty without Prudentia. He knew the basic phantasms of healing now—he wondered if he could release the power of Mag's bindings to power them. And keep the power—and funnel it through workings he knew mostly from long ago lessons.

"Amicia?" he asked.

She was there. "Hello!" she said. She took his hand, smiled—and let his hand drop.

"I need to heal someone." He wished—

"Show me," Amicia said briskly.

He took a moment to kneel by the fallen statue, and brush a hand across Prudentia's marble back. "I miss you," he said. "Help me, if you can."

Then he took Amicia's hand and laid it on the Queen.

She pointed to workings he now knew—through her—in a mind-wrenching moment, he was on her bridge using her memory palace even as he stood on Prudentia's pedestal and collected what was left of his power.

It wasn't enough.

Amicia shook her head. "I have nothing to give," she said. He looked up at her, and even in the aethereal her exhaustion was obvious. "So many wounded," she said.

Sighing for the loss, he tested the binding of power on Mag's cap. He cast, as Harmodius had taught him, guided by Amicia's sure hand on his—three workings, each contingent on the other, like nested equations on the chalkboard. The loosing, the binding for power, the healing. He used what was left of the life force he had taken from the boglin chief.

"Saint Barbara, Taurus, Thales. Demetrios, Pisces, Herakleitus. Ionnes the Baptist, Leo, Socrates!" he invoked, pointed, pivoted, and the room moved—the gears of his imagined rooms turning at the speed of a man's muscles, so that the room spun like a top.

It was the most complex conjuring he had ever attempted—and the power that flared from it astounded him, a backlash of released power that rose in the room around him.

The arming cap immolated itself in a paroxysm of power—a brief flare, and all that power vanished into her.

A red mist crossed her back from her spine to the top of one tanned leg and around to her hip, right across the kidney. A flake of grey-white ash fell away from it.

The captain fell back away from her.

The Queen gave a squeak, and then sighed, as if stroked by her lover. And then gave a low moan.

Lady Almspend clasped her hands together. "Oh, by the power of God, ser! That was brilliant!"

The captain shook his head. "That wasn't me," he admitted. "Or not just me." His voice was a croak.

The wound began to bleed again. They bandaged it tightly, being careful of the wound which still seemed to be open.

The captain shook his head. "But I *felt* the power flow," he said in frustration.

"I feel the pain less," the Queen said bravely. "It was well done, Ser Knight."

A red-haired giant threw his cloak over the Queen. "We need to get her ashore."

The captain shook his head. "I wouldn't. That castle is the lynch pin of the battle, and I've been holding it all night. I wouldn't risk the Queen of Alba in it."

But other boats were pulling up against the pilings of the bridge, anchoring or tying up, their crossbowmen engaging the boglins on the north bank.

The bolder boatmen were pulling under the bridge, through the narrows, to further outflank the enemy in the meadows north of the river.

"I have twenty brave men to add to your garrison," Red Beard said.

"I'd rather have all those nice crossbowmen," the captain said. He smiled to take any apparent sting from his remark. "Very well. Land the Queen. Don't mind the boglin guts—we haven't had time to tidy up."

He rose from the deck, almost unable to walk. He clambered back over the side to the dock, and managed to give the required orders.

He collapsed onto a bollard. He was aware that Red Beard was standing with him, talking, but he hadn't slept, hadn't recovered any power, and he'd just cast—he was phantasm sick, something about which Prudentia had warned him, over and over.

He reached out into the wan sunlight. Pulled the gauntlets off his hands and raised them to the sun.

What would mother think of this? He wondered. Because as soon as the sun licked his hands, he felt a trickle of power through his arms. The headache receded. The depression—

Amicia?

Captain? she asked tartly.

The sun. Reach out and take power from the sun.

I cannot. It is not given to me.

Crap, my lady. To paraphrase Harmodius, power is just power. Take it.

Did I hear my name?

Show her what you showed me. Show her the way to the sun.

With pleasure, as soon as I have a moment in which I am not fighting for my life. Harmodius's image in the Aethereal was looking tattered.

Use the well, then, countered the captain.

Without intending, he was on her bridge over her stream. The stream was a trickle, the rocks dry, the foliage wilted.

He took her hand and she sighed.

"We're going to win," he said. "It is close, but we are going to win." He wasn't sure just how the well would manifest in her place of power. He conjured a well cover, and a hand pump, just at the end of her wooden bridge. "Hold out your hands," he said.

She smiled. "The sun is not for me, but I can use the well."

He shook his head. "It's just there. Power is power. Take what you need." He pumped the handle and a surge of power shot from the nozzle like water under pressure and soaked her through her green kirtle.

She laughed. Power sprayed around them—into the pool under the bridge, into the trees.

The light became richer, the stream began to sing.

"Oh!" she said, and reached out to the well—

The well-cover and the pump-handle vanished, and the stream beneath their feet roared to life.

"Oh!" she said. Her eyes were tightly closed. "Oh, my God!"

He sighed. It was not the denouement he had hoped for.

But outside the palaces of the Aethereal, men were calling his name.

He leaned over and kissed her, all the sweeter for being there.

"I must go," he said.

"Those are Royal Guardsmen," Red Beard shouted, pointing to the south across the river, and back east of the bridge. "I know them."

"Horses," the captain said to Michael. "War horse for you, another for me, a mount for the red giant. Ser Milus, you are in command until I return. Send to the fortress for a healer. Tell them that the Queen of Alba is dying." He was hard put to leave her. It wasn't his way to turn his back on a project. He had a new reserve of power—but she needed a fine, trained hand. And he needed to have something left for the fight.

They carried her past him.

"Fuck it," he muttered to himself. He reached out and put a hand on her naked shoulder. He gave her all the power he had—everything that he had taken through Amicia at the well, and all he had taken from the sun.

He sagged away from her. Spat the taste of bile into the water, and fell to his knees.

She made a sound and her eyes rolled up.

Michael caught his shoulder, and put a canteen in his fist. He drank. There was wine in the canteen, mixed with the water, and he spat it out, then drank more.

"Get me up," he said.

Red Beard got under his other shoulder. "You're a warlock?" he asked brusquely.

The captain had to laugh. "I'll forgive you your imprecise terminology."

The wine was good.

Michael handed him a chunk of honey cake. "Eat."

He ate.

He let the sun fall on his face and hands, and he ate.

Fifteen feet away, Ser Milus was trying to find the bottom of a leather jack of water. He nodded, sputtered. "Is the fight over?"

The captain shrugged. "It ought to be," he muttered. He could hear them fetching horses—could hear the heavy clop-clop of the hooves on the cobblestones of the Bridge Castle's yard, and the rattle-slap of the tack going on.

"Jacques has him," Michael said.

"I hate that horse," the captain said. He finished his honey cake, swallowed more wine and water, and made himself run up the ladders to the top of the Bridge Castle's north tower.

Sixty feet above the flood plain many mysteries were explained.

He couldn't see beyond the ridges south of the river, but the brilliant sparkle of armour told him that the men-at-arms pouring over the last ridge had to be the Royal Army.

To the west the trees were full of boglins, and north, almost a mile away, a trio of creatures—each larger than war horses—emerged from the woods with a long line of infantry on either hand.

The new trebuchet mounted in the ruins of the north tower of the fortress loosed—*thump-crack*—and the hail of stones fell short of the Wild creatures, but they shied away anyway.

But as far as he could see, along the woods' edge, the undergrowth boiled with motion.

"Why are you still here? Even if you win you won't take the fortress. You've lost, you fool," the captain muttered. "Let it go. Live to fight another day." He shook his head.

For a mad moment, he thought of reaching out to Thorn. Because if Thorn stayed to fight, some of his men were going to die, and he'd come to love them. Even Sym.

I'm tired and maudlin.

He scrambled down the ladder and found Jacques holding his new charger. Michael was at the postern gate. Jack Kaves waved.

The captain got a leg over his saddle and groaned. The big stallion shied and tossed his head.

"I hate this horse." He looked down at Jacques. "Go straight for Jehannes, now."

"Ser Jehannes is wounded," he said.

"Tom, then."

"Tom's the man, aye," Jacques said.

"Get every man-at-arms of the company mounted, and by the foot of the ridge," he said. "All the farmers and all the guildsmen along the trench and to the fort, here."

Jacques nodded. "Just for the sake of conversation," he said, "we could keep the fortress." His smile was transparently empty of guile, like a boy who has just thrown a rock at a hornets nest and remains unrepentant.

The captain nodded. "We could. Hold it for ransom. Sell it to the highest bidder." He sounded wistful. "We could be the baddest. The Knights of Ill-Repute. Rich. Feared." He shrugged. "Sometime in the last month we became paladins, Jacques."

Jacques nodded. "'Bout time, my prince."

"Stow that, Jacques," the captain said. He turned his horse's head, backed his charger a few steps, and saluted Smoke, the archer commanding the gate. "Open it," he called. "And the Bridge Gate." He turned back to Jacques. "Don't forget to bring healers," he said.

Red Beard joined them, mounted on an old roncey that had seen better days.

"Sorry about the horse," the captain said. "I'm the captain."

"That's your name?" asked the red giant. "I'm Ranald. Ranald Lachlan."

"You know the Royal Guard?" the captain asked. Then he paused. "Lachlan? Tom Lachlan's brother?"

"Cousin," the other man said. "You know Bad Tom?"

"Doesn't everyone?" the captain said. "Let's go find the king." His voice was a little shaky.

"Amen," the hillman answered. "Do you know him? The king?"

"What a very interesting question," the captain answered. "No. Not exactly."

Michael followed them, and their horses' hooves rang as they crossed the bridge. At the middle the captain reached into the purse on his sword belt and produced a key—intricate, beautiful and apparently solid gold. He leaned out—groaning at the pressure on the muscles of his back and neck—*how long ago did I fight the God-damned wyvern in the woods?* He fitted the key into the great gate, turned it, and the gate vanished.

"Nice trick," muttered Ranald.

Near Lissen Carak—The King

The king was collecting his guardsmen and the knights of his vanguard— the vanguard had lost fifty men-at-arms and as many squires, the men were exhausted already, and the morning was young. Two of his leading noblemen were dead—both the Bishop of Lorica and the constable had both gone down in the first fighting. The Captal de Ruth had taken a mortal wound defending the king, and was dying.

But the valets were coming up with the horses and the machines of war were grinding along—surgeons were searching among the wounded for those who could be saved, and his huntsmen, who had swept east to guard the flank of the onslaught of the vanguard, were trickling in. They, too, had lost men fighting monsters in the woods by the river—nor had they been victorious, by all accounts. The Wild creatures had burst through them and run off east. They had lost sixty men. Good men. Trained men.

It was hardly the great victory he sought. He had been ambushed and his column had survived. That was all.

"Messengers, Sire. From across the river," called a herald.

The king looked north-west, and saw them—three men crossing the bridge at a fast canter.

"Sound the rally," the king said.

More and more of his Royal Huntsmen were merging from the west, moving warily.

The Count of the Borders rode up and saluted. "The flower of our chivalry is half an hour behind me with the main battle," he reported. The

568

man slumped. "By Saint George, my lord, that was the hardest fighting I ever need to see."

"The guardsmen say there are boglins across the river," the king noted.

"Boglins?" The count shook his head. "I struck a blow at a wyvern this morning, sire. This is the Wild, my lord, fighting for its life."

"I thought the Wild was beaten," said the king.

The Count of the Borders shook his head. "Where is Murien? What has happened to the Wall Castles?"

The king's master huntsman, Febus de Lorn, bowed respectfully. "This isn't from north, my lords. This is from west. I see Gwyllch—boglins—across the river, and Bothere has huntsmen who claim to have faced trolls in the low ground west of the road. Dhag's come from the west, my lords."

The king looked back at the approaching messengers. They weren't messengers—all three in were armour, two cap à pied on war horses, and the third—

"Par Dieu, gentlemen—that's Ranald Lachlan, or I'm a minstrel's son." The king turned his horse and rode towards the approaching trio.

Lachlan waved. The king had eyes only for him, and they rode together and embraced.

"By all the saints, Ranald—I never expected to greet you on a stricken field!" The king laughed. "How fares your fortune?"

Ranald looked away. "Aweel," he said, and a shadow touched his face. "I'll tell ye, when we've time, my lord. These gentlemen, now, they seek to parley with you. This is the captain of the company yonder, that holds Lissen Carack for the nuns. And his squire, Michael."

The king extended a hand to the knight—a man of middling height with a black beard and blacker circles under his eyes—absurdly young to be any kind of commander, but wearing superb armour.

"Messire?" he said.

The man was staring at him. Then, as if remembering his manners, the man touched his hand and bowed in the saddle. "My lord," he said.

"You hold the fortress?" the king asked eagerly.

"The fortress and the Bridge Castle," the captain replied.

The king thought there was something familiar about the young man's face, but he couldn't quite place it. Something—

"My lord, if you would bring your forces across I believe we can relieve the fortress and evacuate the villagers—and leave the Enemy facing a newly victualled and garrisoned fortress they cannot hope to take, without the loss of another man." The captain was speaking quickly, and his eyes were on the far wood line. "The Enemy—your father's magus, or so they say—has made a number of errors. Not the least of which has been his consistent underestimation of our side's intelligence. I believe he intends one more all-out attack, to attempt to restore his fortunes through the heroic exertions of his allies." The young man smiled crookedly. "I built a trench line twenty days ago for just this moment, my lord. If you would place your archers in that trench, and gather your chivalry behind the Bridge Castle, I believe we can hand this arrogant Magus a heavy defeat."

"Might I have your name and style, messire?" the king asked. The plan was solid—the lad had a head on his shoulders, and his pure Alban speech made him one of the king's subjects, mercenary or no.

The dark-headed man drew himself up straight in his saddle. "Men call me the Red Knight," he said.

"I thought you to be a Galle, and a good deal older," the king said. He turned to the Count of the Borders. "My lord—will you take the constable's place? Command the Royal Guard? And where is the Count d'Eu? He must have the command of the vanguard now, eh?"

The Count of the Borders turned to the young knight. His banner bore a dozen lacs d'amour. "How many lances do you have, my lord?"

"Twenty-six, my lord Count—and the Knights of Saint Thomas. And several hundred very able militiamen, in the form of a contingent of Harndonner merchants. And I have the pleasure of having the aid of the king's own Magus—Harmodius." The young fellow bowed in his saddle again.

"Harmodius is here?" the king asked. Suddenly, his day looked considerably brighter.

The young man looked away. "He has been a pillar of our defence," he said. "With my lord's leave, I must prepare to receive you."

The king smiled—such an odd young man. "We're right behind you. Go!"

The man bowed, as did his squire, and together they rode back across the bridge.

The king turned to the Count of the Borders. "He seems odd but able. Wouldn't you say?"

The count shrugged. "He's held this place for twenty days against Richard Plangere and his legions of Hell. Do you really care if he's odd?"

"He reminded me of someone," the king said. He glanced at Lachlan, who had stayed with the command group. "You have something to say about our young sell-sword?"

Lachlan shrugged. "No, my lord. About the Queen. She was struck—in the back—by an arrow. She is resting and doing well, in part thanks to the young fellow there. He used power. I saw it."

"The Queen? The Queen is hurt!?" asked the king.

"She's now resting quietly—in the Bridge Castle. The young captain sent for healers."

The king rose in his stirrups. "Attend me, guards. Let's go!"

The Count of the Borders was left with the Royal Staff, sitting on their horses in the dust stirred by the king's rapid departure.

He shook his head. "A great knight," he said, watching his king. He sighed. "Very well—messires, attend me. The Royal Guards will cross the river first, followed by the Huntsmen and the Household. In the second line of battle, the Chivalry—"

Near Lissen Carak—Gaston

Gaston, Count D'Eu, was as tired as he had ever been, and something was wrong with his left hip—it didn't seem to move as freely as it ought—but he managed to get his leg over his destrier's broad back and he rode forward under his own banner, with his cousin's men arrayed behind them—two hundred knights and men-at-arms. Fully a hundred gentlemen lay dead or wounded in the woods and meadows along the road—an absurdly steep price for his cousin's reckless desire to be the man who broke the ambush his angel had told him awaited the king's army.

His cousin, who lay in the arms of death. Who only wanted to be the greatest knight in the world.

Gaston wanted to go home to Galle, sit in the chair of judgment of his castle, and pontificate on which wine was the best at harvest time. He thought back to the peasants under the bridge, his heart now full of understanding. He vowed—would God accept such a vow?—to go home and beg Constance for her hand in marriage.

At the top of the last ridge, the king's friend, the Count of the Borders, was sitting with a number of other gentlemen under the flapping folds of the Royal Banner. The Count d'Eu rose in his stirrups—damn it, that left hip hurt—and looked down to the river where the red-surcoted Royal Guard were just marching for the great three span bridge. On the other side, two companies of men-at-arms were formed in neat wedges at the base of the great ridge on which the fortress sat—half a league north of the river. From the Fortress of Lissen Carack to the bridge ran a trench, black, as if it had been burned.

At the western edge of the meadows and burned-out farms that had marked the demesne of the Abbess, thousands—perhaps tens of thousands—of creatures swarmed like ants from a recently kicked hive.

As he watched, the long arm of a trebuchet mounted high in the fortress swung. It appeared to swing slowly, but its payload—invisible at this distance—flew at the sudden whip-crack release of the counterweight. The count looked for the fall of the shot, but he couldn't see it.

The Count of the Borders waved. "My lord," he said. "You command the vanguard?"

"I do. My cousin is wounded," Gaston said. "I have fewer than two hundred lances, and many of my younger knights are spent."

"Despite which, the king begs that you will use every effort to get your men across the river—dismount and occupy the line of works prepared for you." The count pointed at the black slash that ran from the fortress's ridge to the bridge.

"I see it," Gaston said. "But I lack the force to occupy that length."

"You shall be with the Royal Guard and all our archers," the Count of the Borders added. "All dispatch, my lord!"

Gaston could see creatures from the swarm now venturing farther and farther into the fields beyond the wood's edge.

"A moi!" he ordered. "En avant!"

Lissen Carak—Thorn

Thorn watched the Royal Army begin to deploy across the river. His blow was ready—a single hammer strike to win Alba.

The Royal Army appeared singularly unharmed by a morning-long ambush. That was unexpected. The Qwethenethogs alone should have done great damage amongst their ranks.

He felt a ripple of power—identified it, and cursed again. Both the dark sun and his former apprentice had survived. He acknowledged his own hubris in imagining them dealt with. It was the very curse of his existence. Why did he constantly think things would go his way?

Because they should.

He felt another use of power—closer to him, and it smelled like Qwethnethog. Like Thurkan.

He nodded and drew power to himself. The Qwethenethogs' presence on this side of the river was very revealing.

The great daemon was coming for a trial of power. Thorn rocked his stone head.

Idiot. Traitor. I undertook this for **you**.

Turquoise fire began to play along the edges of his stick-like tree limbs and his beard of grey-green moss oozed power, and the faeries flitting through the clearing, excited by the overflow of his vast resources, he now drained of power in a single sip, leaving their fragile bodies to flutter to the ground.

The magnificent daemon entered the clearing from the south. His hide was still wet from swimming the river, but green and brown lightning played along the sides of his head, down to his long, scythed arms and over his richly inlaid beak and armour.

Thorn let him come.

When they were a few horse lengths apart, Thorn raised one hoary arm. "Stop," he said. "If you mean me harm, save it for the defeat of our enemies."

Thurkan stopped but he shook his mighty head. "Greater Powers than you or I contend here today," he said. "You are a pawn in the plans of a greater Power."

Those were not the words Thorn expected, and they stung—stung with the peculiar power of words that carry their own truth.

"It cannot be," Thorn said.

"Why else do the humans have every advantage when we have none? That thing you call fortune; we have none. Every turn we make favours the enemy. Let us withdraw from this field." Thurkan held up an axe. "Or we must be rid of you."

Thorn needed time to test the hypothesis that he had been used. He was the one who used others—the enmity of the Outwallers for the Albans, the needs of the boglins for new ground to live, the hunting instincts of the wyverns and the trolls.

He was not, in turn, used.

"We have been used!" Thurkan insisted. "Order the retreat, and we will fight another day!"

Thorn considered it.

And he considered the great mass of his infantry—the wights in their magnificent armour, the five thousand irk archers, the squadrons of trolls ready to engage the enemy's knights. The Outwallers and the wyverns and the other daemons.

"Even if what you say is true," Thorn said, "we are about to win a great victory. We will scour the kingdom of Alba from the face of the continent. We will *rule* here."

Thurkan shook his great head. "You delude yourself," he said. "There is no number of boglins who can match this number of armoured men in combat. And Thorn—I call you by name—I call you three times to attend my words. A battle, says my grandsire, is the result of a situation wherein both sides imagine they can win a conclusive fight with one throw of the knucklebones. *And only one side is right.* Today, the King of Alba believes he can defeat us. You believe that you can defeat him, despite everything. I say we will lose on this field. Withdraw and I am your loyal ally. Order this attack and I will fall on you with fire and talon."

Thorn chewed on Thurkan's words for many heartbeats, and not a breeze stirred the torpid late spring heat in the woods. Insect noises stopped. Not a gwyllch chattered, as if all of nature waited on Thorn's decisions.

"Not for nothing do men call you The Orator, Thurkan," Thorn allowed. "You speak brilliantly. But I doubt your motives. You want this army for your own. The only good you know is the good of the Qwethnethog." He took a breath and let it out slowly, to still his rage. And then he threw a single phantasm, a long prepared blow, like a single punch.

The daemon reacted instantly, raising all of its not-inconsiderable power in a wall of walls to stop the blow.

Quick as a mountain lion Thorn cast again.

The single gout of green lightning blasted through his walls like a siege ram through the walls of the wattle and daub house, and the tall daemon crumpled to the ground without a sound. He lay still but for the thumping of his left leg under the command of his hindbrain, still battering the ground in rage and frustration at his own death.

"Attack," Thorn ordered his other captains. To the corpse, he said, "One of us was wrong, Thurkan." He reached out and subsumed the daemon's power. And rose from it more powerful than he had ever been.

I should have done that a year ago, he thought, and smiled. And walked out onto the field at the head of his armies.

Near Lissen Carak—de Vrailly

Jean de Vrailly lay dying, content in knowing that he had performed a marvellous feat of arms—one of which men would speak for hundreds of years. His cousin had left him; a correct action, as the battle continued and the king's standard was advancing, and he lay pillowed on the legs of his squire, Jehan, who had also taken a terrible wound.

The pain was so great that de Vrailly could barely register thoughts—and yet, he was in an ecstasy of relief to be atoning for sin with every waning beat of his heart. The massive damage to his side—the great puncture wounds that sucked air and spat blood and bile with every breath—were living penance, the very stuff of chivalric legend. He would go pure to his Saviour.

His only regret was that there was so much more he might have done—and in his darker moments of dying, he reviewed how he might have swayed his hips a little farther, evaded the wyvern's blow, and carried on unhurt. So very close.

The archangel's manifestation took him by surprise—first, because he had refused the angel's orders, and second, because the archangel had always insisted on coming to him in private.

Now he appeared, glorious in armour, cap à pied in dazzling white plate, with the red cross emblazoned on a white surcote so utterly devoid of shadow as to seem to repel death.

All over the beaver meadow wounded men stopped screaming. Servants fell on their faces. Men rose on an elbow, despite the pain, or rolled themselves over despite trailing intestines or deep gouges—because this was the *heaven* come to life.

"You fool," the archangel said softly—and with considerable affection. "Proud, vain, arrogant fool."

Jean de Vrailly looked into that flawless face in the knowledge that his own had deep grooves of pain carved into it. And that he was going to his death. But he raised his head. "Yes!" he said.

"You were quite, perfectly brilliant." The archangel bent and touched his brow. "You were worthy," he said.

Just for a moment, Jean de Vrailly wondered if the archangel were a man. The touch was so tender.

The words cheered him. "Too proud to betray the King of Alba," he said.

"There is a subtle philosophical difference between killing and letting die," the archangel said softly. "And thanks to you, all my plan is in ashes, and I must build a new edifice to make certain things come to pass." He smiled tenderly at the dying knight. "You will regret this. My way was better."

Jean de Vrailly managed a smile. "Bah!" he said. "I was a great knight, and I die in great pain. God will take me to his own."

The archangel shook his head. "Perhaps," he said. "But I think you should live a while longer, and perhaps learn to listen to me next time." He bent low, and stripped the bright steel gauntlet off his hand—a slim, ungendered hand—and ran it along the knight's body. That touch struck de Vrailly like the shock of taking his first wound—and lo, he was healed.

He took a deep and shuddering breath, and found no pain at the bottom of it.

"You cannot just heal me," de Vrailly snapped. "It would be unchivalrous of me to walk away healed when my brave people lie at the edge of cruel death."

The archangel turned his head, brushed the long hair back from his forehead, and he stood. "You are the most demanding mortal I have ever met," he said.

De Vrailly shrugged. "I will beg and pray, if that's what you require, Taxiarch."

The angel smiled. "I grant you their healing—those who have not already passed around the curve of life into death. And I grant to you great glory this day—for why would an angel of the Lord visit you except to bring you great power in battle? Go and conquer, arrogant little mortal. But I tell you that if you ever choose to match yourself against the greatest Power that the Wild has ever bred, he will defeat you. This is not my will, but Fate's. Do you hear me?"

"Craven fate would never keep me from a fight," de Vrailly said.

"Ah," said the angel. "How I love you!" The angel waved his spear over the beaver meadow.

A hundred knights and as many squires, men-at-arms, servants and valets were cured, their pain washed away, their bodies made whole. In many cases they were better than they had begun the battle. A peasant-born man-at-arms, a Galle, had the permanent injury to his lower left leg healed and made straight—a valet missing one eye had his sight returned.

All in the wave of a spear.

Several dozen wounded Jacks were cured, as well.

"Go and save the king," the archangel said. "If that is your will."

Every man in the meadow knelt and prayed until, in a puff of incense-laden displaced air, the armoured angel vanished.

Lissen Carak—Desiderata

Desiderata lay in a patch of bright sunlight. Her power was dimmed—she herself felt like a candle under a shade. Flickering.

So unjust! That single arrow, plummeting from heaven, and she was done. She had desired to be her husband's support, perhaps to win herself a share of glory. And instead—this.

The strange young man had put the pain at a distance. That was a blessing. She could feel *his* worthiness like a bright flame. A knight and a healer—what a superb combination—and she longed to know him better.

Around her, her ladies were silent.

"Someone sing," she said.

Lady Mary started, and the others slowly joined her.

Desiderata lay back on the cloaks of a dozen soldiers.

And then old Harmodius came. He came unannounced, walked into the castle courtyard and knelt beside her.

She was pleased to see the look in his eye. Even mortally wounded, he found her pleasing. "There you are, you old fool," she said happily.

"Fool enough to leave the battle and save you, my dear," he said.

Carefully, painfully, with Lady Almspend and Lady Mary, he rolled her over and stripped the linen from her back. "It's really quite a nice back," he said conversationally.

She breathed in and out, content at last.

Lissen Carak—The Red Knight

The captain could see the king riding for the bridge at the head of his household, and he could see the king's battles—each with more men-at-arms than he had ever commanded—coming down the ridge.

He rode along the trench—a trench currently occupied by two hundred archers and valets of his own company, and all the farmers from all the out-villages.

His sanguine surety that the Enemy had made a tactical error was gone, blown away on the wind, and now he watched an endless line of boglins crossing the open ground toward the trench with something akin to panic. It was hard to breathe.

The Prior was sitting on his destrier with Bad Tom, in the non-shade of a burned oak tree.

The captain rode his horse over to them, and then wasted his strength controlling his young war horse as the stallion sought to make trouble with the Prior's stallion. Finally, he curbed the big horse mercilessly.

"I miss Grendel," he said to Tom.

"Bet Jacques doesn't," Tom said. He looked back over the sunlit fields. "They're coming."

The captain nodded. Overhead, the trebuchet disgorged another load of small stones. Cast from a height, it smashed into the oncoming tide and ripped a hole in the enemy line.

The hole closed almost at once.

"It's so *stupid*, the captain said petulantly. "When he burned the farms, he did all the damage he needed to do." He turned his head to where the king's Royal Guard was pouring into the trench, led by two hundred purple- and yellow-clad crossbowman from Lorica. "And his attack—whether it carries this trench or not—won't take the fortress."

The endless wave of boglins, and larger, worse things, swept across the burned plain towards the black line of his trench.

The reinforcements were not going to make the near end of the trench in time.

The farmers and the guildsmen were spread too thin, and they knew it. And the inexperienced purple and gold Loricans were halting, only a third of the way along the trench, and loosing bolts. Like militia.

Of course, they *were* militia.

"The farmers will hold," Tom said. He was chewing on the stem of a flower. It was an oddly disconcerting sight. "The guildsmen will break. They've broken before."

The captain looked at the Prior. "Messire, you are so much my senior—in years, in experience, and in this place—guide me. Or command me."

The Prior let his horse put his head down to munch grass around the heavy bit. "Oh, no, you don't. You have led this force to this point—you think I'm going to change commanders now?"

The captain shrugged. "I wish you would," he said.

Tom was watching the oncoming line. "You know we have to charge that line," he said. "If we charge the line, we should buy—hmm—ten minutes or so." He was wearing a grin that made him look like a small boy. "A hundred knights—ten thousand boglins—and trolls, and daemons, irks…" He looked at his captain. "You *know* we have to."

The Prior looked at Tom, and then back at the captain. "Is he always like this?" he asked.

"Pretty much," the captain said to the older man. "Will you come? I'm not at all sure any of us will come back."

The Prior shrugged. "You are lucky," he said. "And luck is better than any amount of skill or genius. I can feel the power in you, young man. And I think your presence here is God's will, and God is telling me to go where you go."

The captain rolled his eyes. "You're making this up," he said.

"Did you speak so to the Abbess?" the Prior said.

For once abashed, the captain looked away.

"We will follow you," the Prior continued. "If this fortress falls our order will have lost everything."

The captain nodded. "Have it your way, then. Tom; we'll file across the trench on the two bridges and form line on the far side in open order." He looked around—to see Sauce, Michael, Francis Atcourt, Lyliard all looking pale with exhaustion.

"Kill whatever comes under your sword," the captain said with an edge of sarcasm. "Follow me."

The king entered the Bridge Castle's courtyard to find his Magus, Harmodius, kneeling by the Queen. He was examining a wound in her back, and Lady Almspend put a hand on the king's shoulder and kept him from approaching any closer.

"Give him a moment, my lord," she breathed quietly.

"Here they come!" called a voice on the walls.

Crossbows began to release in a series of flat snaps.

The king didn't know what to do. "I must see her!" he said to Lady Almspend.

Lady Mary came up. "Please, my lord. A moment!"

"The battle is about to be won or lost," the king moaned.

"Fast as you can, lads! The captain is depending on us!" called the voice on the walls.

"My love?" Desiderata called.

Harmodius stepped back, face pale, and the king came forwards.

Desiderata reached out and took his hand. "You must go and win this battle," she said.

"I love you. You make me a better king—a better man. A better knight. I can't lose you," the king said.

She smiled. "I know. Now go and win this battle for me."

He bent and kissed her, mindless of the thread of blood that ran from the corner of her lip.

As he pulled himself away, Harmodius followed him.

"I might ask you what you are doing here, but we're in haste," the king said.

Harmodius narrowed his eye. "This battle is a closer run thing than I would ever have imagined, and even now, our enemy has increased his power to a degree I could never match," he said. "If I work to heal her he will know me, and he will assail me here. And I will be destroyed. This is as much a fact as the rising of the sun."

The king paused. "What can we do?" he asked.

Harmodius shook his head. "There are protections in the fortress—especially in the chapel." He shrugged. "But even if I could get her there, my saving her would deprive the army of my protection, and when he starts to kill, he will devastate us."

The king frowned. "Save her," he commanded. "Save her. I will form up my knights and guard her to the fortress on a litter, and you can take her to the chapel, though all the enemies in the world stand between us and them."

Harmodius considered his king, who was willing to sacrifice the army for the love of his queen.

But his feelings were very much engaged as well. "Very well," he said.

Lissen Carak—Father Henry

He didn't like what he had to do. He didn't like that they all hated him, now, and he wanted to argue with them. To show them what they were going to become.

Like her. Like the witches.

Gnawing the ropes was easy. But the archers had hurt him, and his back was flayed raw. It took time, and pain. He paused and rested. Paused and slept.

Awoke when he heard voices coming into the cellars. *From below.*

He gnawd his bonds again, mad with fury like a trapped animal. When he exhausted his muscles, he made himself pray. He overcame the pain.

He was good at pain.

After hours and more hours, he had the ropes off. And then he got through the scuttle—a trap door to the next cellar room. He moved carefully, and he only passed out once and woke again minutes or hours later.

He made it to the base of the main cellar ramp—where he could hear a pair of archers on duty.

He prayed...and God showed him the way. Whoever had come up into the cellar had left a door open. He dragged himself to the portal, and looked down.

Scrambled and found a lantern with a candle and a tinderbox. It was God's will.

He dragged himself down the steps into the dark.

The mercenaries, efficient as always, had left arrows painted on the rock. He began to follow them.

Lissen Carak—Thorn

Thorn watched his great assault sally forth from the edge of the woods, and knew fear.

He had lost many, many creatures in the weeks of siege and now he feared he lacked the resources to survive.

His fear hadn't started there, though.

As his assault began, something whose level of manifested power was to Thorn as Thorn was to a boglin shaman, had appeared on the other side of the river. It had cast a single phantasm of such complexity and power that it beggared the very strongest sending Thorn had ever cast. And then it had vanished.

A Power. A great Power of the Wild.

Thorn stood at the edge of the burned fields, watching his massive assault leap towards the hated enemy; seeing the fruition of his revenge on the king and his useless nobles, watching as his boglins finally seized the empty Lower Town and boiled through its streets.

And all he could think was—*Damn the daemon. He was right. I've been had.*

Lissen Carak—The Red Knight

The captain led his men in single file across the boards laid across the burned, vitrified trench. As he crossed, two farm boys with halberds waved. They gave a cheer.

Why not? They weren't riding into a horde of boglins.

He laughed. Turned to find Jacques behind him, Carlus the armourer with his trumpet on his hip, and Michael carrying his banner.

"Form your front," he called.

The line of boglins was about six hundred paces distant.

He looked back at Bridge Castle, hoping to see the king.

He looked across the river, but the main battle was just straggling down the ridge. Two thousand knights.

The king was just a little late.

He could see a handful of knights crossing the bridge. The banner was from Galle, and not one he knew.

Move! he thought.

He looked back.

His men-at-arms, with the addition of all the military orders knights, formed in two ranks, and took up two hundred yards of front—leaving as much again on either flank.

Empty air.

He was the centre man in the line.

The boglin line was four hundred paces away, give or take.

"Advance! Walk!" he called, and Carlus repeated it by trumpet.

"Remember this, boys!" Bad Tom called from his place in the ranks.

The big horses made the earth shake, even at a walk. Their tack rattled and clinked, and the sound of their riders' armour added to it. The sound of a company of knights.

Two hundred and fifty paces.

"Trot!"

Even a hundred and fifty armoured men on destriers make the ground rumble like an earthquake.

One last time, the enemy had underestimated them. They had more than a dozen of the great trolls, belling and ranting several hundred paces to the rear of the infantry line. They were coming on now—coming quickly. But like the king, they were going to be much too late for the moment of impact.

The captain had a feeling, though, that the trolls were not at their best in the open, and that they wouldn't be particularly manoeuvrable. Or was that his own hubris?

But that was all passing away. Strategy and tactics were over, now.

He turned his head at the cost of some pain, and saw the Gallish knights pushing along the trench. The Lorican crossbowmen were moving too—Ser Milus was visible, roaring orders at them.

There would be no gap in their line when the Enemy struck.

The two lines were approaching each other at the combined speed of a galloping horse. The boglins were not going to flinch but they were spread out over the ground, all cohesion lost, like a swarm of insects pouring over the ground.

"Charge," he shouted. Carlus and Jacques might not have heard him over the drumming hooves, but he swept his lance down to point at his first target—locked it into the hook-shaped rest under his arm, and Jacques sounded the charge.

The captain leaned forward into his lance.

For a few glorious heartbeats, it was the way he had imagined, when he was a small boy dreaming of glory.

He was the wind, and the roar of the hooves, and the tip of the spear.

The slight bodies of the boglins were like straw dolls set in a field, and the lances ripped through them so smoothly that creatures died without dragging the lances down, and the stronger men were able to engage three, four even five of the creatures before their lances broke, or their points touched the ground, dug in and shattered or had to be dropped.

The horses were spread widely enough to allow horse and rider to thread the enemy line, to take advantage of spaces between boglins, to weave their path.

For a few deadly heartbeats, the knights destroyed the boglins, and there was nothing the boglins could do to retaliate.

But like mud clogging a harrow, the very density and sheer numbers of the boglins began to slow the knights' charge and even their heavy horses had to shy—or simply could no longer trust their hooves to ground that was so thickly littered with boglins. The charge slowed, and slowed.

And then the boglins began to fight back.

Lissen Carak—Father Henry

Father Henry paused at the base of the steps to gather his courage. His hate. He was deep underground, and his candle was guttering, and he had no idea how far it was to the outside. And he *hurt*.

He prayed, and then he walked. Walked and prayed.

And, of course, it wasn't much farther than walking down the castle road, outside.

He finally found a pair of double doors, as high as two men, and as wide as a church. He expected them to be locked with all the power of Hell. But the sigils lay cold and empty. He reached for the two great handles. There was a key between them.

Lissen Carak—The King

The king had his queen on a litter between four horses, and he and his household knights got out the main Bridge Castle gate even as the garrison shot bolt after bolt over their heads into the oncoming line of creatures.

Even as he watched he saw the Prior and the sell-sword knight lead their men-at-arms over a pair of narrow wooden bridges and onto the plain.

He looked to the right and left, trying to imagine why they were charging the enemy.

But it was *glorious* to see.

The knights took their time, formed up neatly, and the endless horde of enemies ran at them silently—perhaps the most horrible aspect of the boglin was its silence. He could hear the mercenary captain calling orders, and his trumpeter repeated them.

"Ready," Ser Alan said.

The king gestured across the front of the trench. "Since our friends have been kind enough to clear us a path," he said, and touched his spurs to his mount.

As he rode, he watched the charge go home.

It was superb, and he was annoyed that he wasn't a part of it. He leaned back to Ser Alan. "As soon as we have the Queen to the fortress, we will join them," he said, pointing to charge which was cutting through the enemy like an irresistible scythe.

Ser Ricar shook his head. "My lord," he protested. "We have only sixty knights."

The king watched the charge even as his household trotted across the front of the trench. "He hasn't much more than that."

"But you are the *king*!" Ser Alan protested.

The king began to feel the onset of the indecision that infected him on every battlefield. A lifetime of training in arms as a knight demanded that he lead his knights in that wonderful charge—a charge that even now was beginning to lose its impetus, three hundred paces from the trench at his feet.

He was also aware—as a man is aware of a distant call—that it was not his duty as king to perform feats of arms.

But Desiderata had said—

The fighting was so close.

And his queen didn't need him. She had a clear path all the way to the gate of the fortress.

"Knights!" roared the king. "On me!"

Lissen Carak—Father Henry

The priest had the secret doors open, and he stood back and watched the boglins flood through the great opening, squirming in a very inhuman way, to vanish onto the steps which ran up and up into the ridge. He watched for a moment, and then something slammed into his head.

He started to fall. Out of the corner of his eye he could see some sort of spike.

In a moment of vertigo, he realised it had to be *through* his head.

He tried to move, and couldn't.

Something hurt more than his back.

Slowly, like a tree falling, he went to the ground. He tried to pray, but he could not, because they pressed all around him and he screamed, trying—

Trying to die before they began to eat him.

Lissen Carak—Ser Gawin

Ser Gawin had risen with the dawn and managed to get himself to the chapel to pray. He remained on his knees for a long time in the morning light, unaware of anything except the pain in his side and the crushing sense of his own failure.

But, eventually, he roused himself when he heard the soldiers bellowing for every man-at-arms to get mounted. He rose and crossed himself, and then walked as steadily as he could manage out the door of the chapel, and hauled himself in front of Ser Jehannes.

"I can ride," he said.

Jehannes shook his head. "He didn't say the wounded," Jehannes said. "I'm not riding, myself, lad. Stay here."

Gawin was minded to disobey. The longer he was on his feet, the better he felt. "I can ride," he said again.

"Ride tomorrow, then," Jehannes said. "Tom's got all the men-at-arms already. If you want to be a help, arm yourself as much as you can and walk around looking confident. It's bad out there." Ser Jehannes pointed into the courtyard of the fortress, where the farmwomen and the nuns stood in knots, silent. Most of them were watching the plains below. "We've perhaps forty men to hold the fortress, and yon ladies feel they've been abandoned."

"Sweet and gentle Jesu," Gawin swore. "Forty men?"

"Captain's trying to win the day," Jehannes said. "Stupid bastard. All we had to do was sit tight in the fortress and let the king do as he would. But the little bourc always has to be the fucking hero."

Gawin gave the older man a lopsided smile. "Family affliction," he said, and went to do his share.

It took him long minutes to find his armour, left unpolished in a heap and not in the hospital but in a closet off the apothecary.

But he couldn't seem to get into it.

He managed, in the end, to get into his arming cote, and to get his breast and back closed by lying full length on the floor and closing it around him like a clamshell. But then the pain in his side kept him from buckling it.

"I'll do your buckles, if you'll let me," said a voice.

It was the novice. The one whose appearance made his brother squirm. The one who had used power to heal him.

"You are—"

"Amicia," she said. She nodded at an archer, who stood quietly across the room. He looked tired and unhappy. "He was left to guard me, but he's bored, and I haven't turned into a boglin or a dragon yet. Stop moving."

Her hands were curiously confident. And strong.

"You are using power," he said.

"I'm giving you some strength," she said. "Something evil is coming—I can feel it. Something of the Wild. We're going to go and stop it." She sounded fey, terrified, and overly bright. Brittle.

Gawin took her assertion at face value. He looked at the archer. "What's your name?" he asked.

The boy wouldn't meet his eye. "Sym, my lord," he said sullenly.

"Sym, can you fight?" Gawin asked.

"Anything," Sym said assertively. Looked away. "Only thing I'm any good at, and look at me—left to guard the captain's nun."

The fingers on Gawin's shoulder harness stiffened.

Sym looked at the two of them from under his eyebrows. "Sorry. Know you ain't. But I'd rather be with my mates." He shrugged. "This is the big fight. I never been in one. All the oldsters talk big about this fight and that fight, but this is the biggest the company was ever in, and I want my part of it by fucking God." He looked away. "Want to be a hero."

Gawin laughed. He surprised himself with the purity, the unforcedness, of his laugh. "Me, too," he said. He slapped his shoulders. He couldn't bear the weight of his arm harness, but he had a breast and back, and she put the gauntlets on his hands, and then, with Sym's help, they put his bascinet on his head, slipping the aventail over his hair.

He considered saying something flirtatious—*Best looking squire I've ever had.* But at the thought of *squire* he choked.

While Sym pulled his aventail down over his back plate, she did something—something that started as a word, and rose in pale yellow fire, and ended like the pop of a soap bubble.

"Mater Mary," she said, and crossed herself. "They are here. Right here. In the fortress. Follow me!" she called and ran for the door.

Sym followed her, leaving Gawin to find his long sword resting in a corner, pick up Sym's buckler, and follow.

Lissen Carak—The Red Knight

Whatever his other failings, the captain's borrowed young destrier had a great heart, and he loved to fight.

The horse swung back and forth—pivoted on his forefeet and kicked with his iron-shod back hooves, half-reared and pivoted on his back feet, punching with his front, keeping the captain in the centre of a carefully cleared circle devoid of standing foes. Boglins who tried to get under the horse to hamstring him or worse were trampled to sticky ruin or simply kicked clear.

The captain had long since lost track of how many of the creatures he'd killed. His arm was tired—but then, he'd *started* the action almost too tired to lift his weapon.

But, as they had practised, the companions were drawing together—horse to horse, man to man.

The captain swung from the shoulder, nipped both arms off an enemy on the foreswing like a farmer pruning vines, leaned well forward using his stirrups for balance, and cut back into another creature's head, clearing his front, and George—somewhere in the combat, the captain had named his horse George—backed a few paces.

And tucked in behind Bad Tom, who was like a millwheel of destruction.

He let Tom do it. Thumbed his visor, and raised his face plate, and drank in great gouts of fresh air.

George wanted to be back at it.

The captain stood in his stirrups and looked over the battle line. His people had formed up well and although there were gaps, there were not many.

His people going to get buried.

He had no sense of time—no one did, in a hand-to-hand fight. But at his back, the purple and yellow tabards had flowed all the way down the trench to Master Random's guildsmen, and a sturdy line of scarlet was filling in behind them. And beyond them, just crossing the bridge, was solid green. Archers of the Royal Hunt.

"Jacques!" he roared.

His valet was two horse lengths away, fighting for his life.

"Carlus!" he roared.

The trumpeter didn't even look around.

"Damn," the captain said. It was a game of seconds and hard-fought inches, and he was losing time. They needed to ride clear.

He gave George his head and sent the war horse crashing into one of Jacques's adversaries. A ton of war horse versus a hundred pounds of irk was no contest at all.

His sword took another, and then Jacques went down as his horse fell—killed by one of the dozen creatures under its hooves. That quickly, Jacques was gone. The captain turned, cut at the irk under George's feet and watched a spear catch Carlus under the jaw, killing him instantly. Down he went, with his trumpet, and with it, their chance to cut their way free. The captain cut down, his sword beheading a boglin even as the hideous thing bit into Jacques's throat—and he roared and looked for help, but there was none.

Lissen Carak—Desiderata

Guarded by Ser Driant and five knights, the Queen's litter started up the long and twisting road to the great gate of the fortress.

The king had ordered his knights to form a compact company behind him.

"Once more, my lord," Ser Alan said, "I'd like to remind the king that if Lord Glendower were alive, he would never allow this."

At the word *allow* all sense left the king's head. "I'm the king," he said. "Follow me!"

Most of the mercenary knights and their retainers had formed in a thick knot, almost dead centre in the field. The king aimed his horse's spiked head at the banner with the lacs d'amour. "Follow me!"

Lissen Carak—Harmodius

Harmodius spat with rage, turned his horse, and followed the king, who was throwing himself into the arms of his enemy when almost any other action would have saved him.

The Queen would die. And he, Harmodius, loved her in a way the king never could—she was the perfect child of Hermeticism. An angel, come to earth.

But like an artist with a favourite painting, Harmodius could not bear to see the king die either. Not here—not so close to triumph, or at least to survival.

We are all making the wrong decisions, Harmodius thought. And he realised that if he died here, his new-found knowledge would die with him.

It was like some ancient tragedy, in which man is granted knowledge only to be destroyed.

But he didn't have to waste much more time on such thoughts.

Lissen Carak—Thorn

Thorn watched, almost unbelieving, as the target of his campaign threw himself forward, unprotected. He couldn't have manipulated the king into such a foolish move.

The king.

He had made a dash for the fortress and Thorn had suddenly seen his defeat—for in the fortress the king would be unassailable.

But no.

The fool was now leading his knights forward into the very maw of Thorn's monsters.

And his boglins were *in the fortress.*

Just for a moment, he was balanced on an exquisite knife-blade of doubt as to whether to kill the king himself, by means of power, or to send his choicest creatures to do his work.

But in that moment, he decided that, regardless of the campaign, if he killed the king, he had won. No matter which power was using him, killing the King of Alba would place him in the front rank. It would cause civil war. Would weaken the human hold on Alba.

He gathered power to him.

Lissen Carak—The Red Knight

The company was dying around him.

The anonymity of armour kept him from knowing who—he could never spare more than a glance—but as the boglins surrounded them and hemmed them tighter and tighter, armoured figures went down—either hamstrung horses, spear thrusts, or lucky arrows.

Tom continued to be like a hammer at his side, Sauce was like an avenging angel, and the military order knights fought like the legions of Heaven.

Even as he raised and lowered his sword yet again, he would have chuckled at the pointlessness of it all, if he had not been occupied. They had bought the time, and the battle should now be safely won. And the bitterness—had Carlus not gone down with the trumpet, had Jacques lived fifty more heartbeats—

He slew two more boglins before he saw the troll.

It reared, its blank stone face smooth and black, and it belled, it's shrill trumpet ringing out above the ring of weapons and the silent intensity of the boglins.

Not just one of them.

Six of them.

And the wave front of their fear made the boglins beneath his horse's hooves quail and void their attacks. George rose, kicked out, and then plunged forward.

The wave of terror passed over them.

The captain got his sword in a good two-handed grip, and George leaped for the nearest troll as he brought it up high above his head on the left. *You are supposed to use a lance on these things,* he thought.

The troll saw him, turned, and put its antlered head down, low, so its antlers covered its neck, and charged, seeking to get its antlers under the Red Knight's sword and unhorse him.

George turned mid-stride.

Faster than human thought, the animals struck.

Like a cat, George pivoted his weight and one hoof licked out and caught the monster a staggering blow in the centre of the forehead, so hard that it cracked its stone face.

The troll screamed, turned its head, whipping its antlers through a spray of motion and leaped, turning, caught the armoured horse in the right rear haunch. George got his back feet off the ground with a caper and the blow slewed the horse around on his forefeet—

The line of attack opened like a curtain as the two creatures turned into each other. The captain felt as if he had all the time in the world—as if this moment had been predicted since the dawn of the world. The troll's turn—his destrier's turn—the open line at the back of the monster's neck…

His sword struck, two handed, like the fall of the shooting star to earth, and cut along the line where two great plates of hardened flesh met; sliced through the troll's spine, and in, down, out and free in a gout of ichor—

George leapt free, stumbled, and the captain was thrown from the saddle.

He got a shoulder down, landed on something squishy and rolled, the plates of his shoulder harness clanking like a tinker's wagon and the muscles in his neck, injured and re-injured since early spring, wrenched again.

But he ended his shoulder roll on his knees, and pushed immediately to his feet.

Off to the right, Tom and Sauce were pouring blows into another troll, but behind them the thick knot of companions had begun to dissolve as the remaining trolls ripped into their horses. Armour crumpled; men died.

Lissen Carak—Ser Gawin

Gawin followed Sym as the archer followed the novice—down the stairs, across the courtyard to the entrance to the cellars where the stores were kept.

There were two archers guarding the heavy oak door to the cellars.

"The Wild is coming up the escape!" Amicia yelled, fear and frustration powering her words.

Every farm wife and nun in the courtyard heard her.

The two archers looked at each other.

Sym came up next to her. "Captain's orders!" he yelled, his thin voice shrill and not very heroic.

The bigger of the two archers fumbled with his keys.

Gawin ran across the yard to join them.

The women were frozen, and he had a moment to consider the looks on their faces—panic, determination, and a sullen kind of anger that it should come to this when they had already lost so much.

Yes, he understood those looks of loss. Of failure.

"Arm yourselves!" he called to them.

The bigger archer opened the iron-bound oak door and Sym ran down the steps into the darkness.

Gawin pushed past the novice.

The first cellar was gloomy but well-enough lit. A stack of spears leaned against one of the company's great wagons. Gawin caught one up as he went by.

There was another door, ahead, which was just opening.

Sym was too late to stop it, so he spitted the creature that opened it—ripped his sword out of the boglin's armoured thorax and kicked it so hard that it folded backwards—

Gawin caught a glimpse of steps going down and a seething knot of the creatures filling the stairwell.

"Hold the door!" Gawin called. He thrust with his spear, and felt the steel head crunch through the soft hide around the boglin's neck and head—just like digging a knife into a lobster. Something popped, it fell off his spear, and he pushed.

Sym cut, and cut again, and again, desperation and terror lending wings to his sword arm.

The stairwell was crawling with them.

He killed another one.

And another one.

And the novice turned, raised her hands, and spoke a single word in Archaic, and golden-green light filled the cellar.

Lissen Carak—Desiderata

Desiderata could scarcely breathe for the immanence of power. And the pain, which was returning. But she could feel the enemy—the centre of the power of the Wild, its emerald intensity shot full of black—gathering force. She could feel it as surely as she could feel the power of the sun on her arms.

"What's happening here?" Ser Alan asked. He bent to carefully place her litter on the doorsill of the chapel.

The woman was older—dressed plainly, like a servant or a farmwife. She had a spear in her hands. "If it please you, Ser Knight—there's boglins got into the cellars, and all the garrison is trying to hold the doors."

"Good Christ!" Ser Alan cursed. The other knights of the escort drew their swords.

Lissen Carak—Thorn

Thorn watched as the king and his knights obligingly fought their way into the centre of his range.

Sometimes plans did work out.

His trolls—the magnificent *dhags*—were cutting the knights to pieces. They were also dying, but he had more. Or he could obtain more. The Wild was fecund beyond human imagining.

He let the king fight on—on and on—until his reckless charge broke through the ring of bone and hide around the mercenaries. Around the dark sun.

The king and the dark sun together.

He took his gathered power, summoning every tendril that he could muster—the might that had been Thurkan, the souls of the fair folk, the convoluted essence of the Sossag shamans—

He savoured it, for a moment.

There was nothing to interrupt him, no distractions as he placed his power almost lovingly on a spot just between his two foes.

The edifice of his memory was no palace but a twisted yarn of ropes and webs, and he braided them in his mind with the mastery of an aeon.

Laid his hand to the completed cord, and cast.

Harmodius felt it, saw it, and cast his counter: a mirror. Even his counter had tails and vestiges—traps within traps. As he had learned.

Lissen Carak—The Red Knight

The captain felt the moment the great phantasms were loosed as a single instant. It was as if fire or lightning had flashed through every inch of the air between the two casters.

He was *Harmodius. As, for a moment, he had been Amicia.*

There was no time.

He had so little left—but he gave it, straight into Harmodius's arms. He reached and took from Amicia, who was herself fighting for her life—from Miram and her choir. And from the very sunlight around him.

And it wasn't going to be enough.

The captain reached out to the great iron-bound door, and threw it open, and green light flooded into him.

He threw it through Harmodius to strengthen the counter work.

There was a thunderclap—a gout of white-green fire that shot into the heavens. A ripple in the curtain of reality so that, just for a moment, the veil of the world was wrenched aside. The captain saw black night pierced with white stars, and the dawn of chaos, and the rising plume of power that was the coming of the world.

Lissen Carak—Desiderata

Desiderata felt Harmodius's power rise to meet the emerald giant—and she saw the deep subtlety of his mind in his casting.

But the emerald's might was twenty times greater than that of the court Magus, and the tide of green rolled over him—dissipated, mirrored, channelled—but overpowering, like a rising river facing a plain full of channels and damns, yet eventually overcoming all of them to spill in one unstoppable flood—

But vast quantities of the emerald power hung in the air, cast aside by Harmodius's counter spell. Or part of it.

The ripple of power passed the king, who watched, horrified, as Ser Alan was burned at his side, his armour straps charring, his face a livid red as he screamed—and man and horse collapsed. Beyond him, Harmodius frowned—his hand withered and blew away to ash and then, in a few heartbeats, the Magus was subsumed. He turned to ash, crumpled and was borne away on the wind.

Thorn was struck by the mirror in the very moment of completion of his phantasm, and some of his own carefully hoarded power struck right back down the channel of his casting, burning him.

He screamed. Flinched. But far across the battlefield, Harmodius's essence flickered and went out.

Lissen Carak—The Red Knight

The captain struck, the sword descending more from the force of gravity than from any power of his shoulders.

In the Aether he had Harmodius by the hand.

Take me, boy.

In one moment, the captain had to understand, and to act. He opened *his way into his palace, seized the spirit of the dead Magus with one Aethereal hand and cast his own phantasm with the other. The air outside was heavy with discarded power, green and ripe for plucking, and he took it, aided by the meticulous ordering of last night's foe, aided by the thaumaturgical knowledge of his tutor—of Amicia's Wild casting—*

And there he was. Standing on the plinth, where she had always stood.

"Better the slave of a bad master," the Magus muttered.

Suddenly the captain was unsure whether he should have allowed this— entity—refuge to his palace.

"Any port in a storm, lad," the dead Magus said. "Go fight monsters, or you'll be as dead as I am."

And he lifted his sword again. The air was still redolent with power.

George was behind him, and on his feet.

Amplify my voice, he told the dead Magus.

"Wedge! On me! Michael—the banner to me!" His voice rang out like some antique god's.

In a moment out of time, the captain wondered if this was *exactly* how the antique gods came about.

No time like the present.

Kneel! He commanded the creatures of the Wild.

Hermes Thrice-sainted, boy! You are challenging his control! Stop!

A third of the creatures around him stopped fighting, fell back or stood, stunned.

Lissen Carak—de Vrailly

Ser Jean de Vrailly led the main battle of the king's host down the last ridge, and their hooves clattered like a fall of hail as they crossed the bridge. He had more than a thousand belted knights, and no one—not even the Count of the Borders—questioned him. An archangel had given him great glory, and every man in the main battle knew it.

Jean could see the Royal Standard trapped, far out in a sea of foes, with another standard he didn't know—lacs d'amour in gold on a field of black. A foppish banner.

But he laughed to see the battle, and led the first files to cross the bridge off to the left, west towards the setting sun.

The soldiers in the long trench were rising from it, either in loyal determination to save the king, or in eagerness to join his attack.

Good for them. For once, there was to be enough glory for all.

He continued to ride west, and the long file of knights followed him—gradually enveloping the southern flank of the enemy.

Behind him, the Count d'Eu rose to his feet, and pointed his cut-down lance at the knot around the Royal Standard. "A moi!" he roared.

Daniel Favor, former wagoner, climbed over the edge of the trench, to stand on the grass in the wind. Around him, farmers from the villages around Lissen Carack looked at him, and knew they could not let him be a better man.

Adrian Pargeter climbed out of the safe trench, and put his crossbow on the ground to draw his sword. Older guildsmen looked at each other. A draper with a grey beard asked his lifelong business rival—*we really doing this?*—and then they were up the vitrified earth too, drawing their swords.

Ranald Lachlan leaped up the side of the trench, waved his axe at his comrades, and pointed it at the enemy. "Come on, then!" he said.

The trench emptied in moments, and they came.

Lachlan threw his axe in the air, and it spun in a great wheel of light over his head and fell back into his hand.

And the thin line of men charged.

Lissen Carak—Ser Gawin

Gawin saw Sym stumble, and a pair of the armoured things took him—dragged him down. Sym's dagger licked out, gutted another boglin which fell atop him... and then the archer was gone, and Gawin was alone in the doorway.

A bright green light flashed, and Gawin was able to see far too much in the illumination. The crawling things beneath him on the stairs turned brown, their eyes burned away and dozens of them sank to the ground, all vitality leaching away as their bodies crumbled.

Gawin heaved a breath.

There were a dozen of the things left—all in a clump, a crawling, rolling mass of legs—he cut and cut at them like a madman, and then forced the door with sheer weight and determination, and he stumbled back...

A swarm of armoured men fell on the knot of boglins, hacking with axes, stabbing with spears—six knights he knew all too well. Ser Driant—the King's Companion—other men of the household.

Gawin found himself pulled to the floor. He'd lost a moment's attention and two of the things had him—

But he was Hard Hands, and he closed his left hand and slammed it into a lobe-shaped eye, keyed his hand around his adversary's arm, and ripped it off the boglin with a tearing like ripping old leather, and then he swung the taloned arm like a club beating the bleeding thing to the ground. Ripped his rondel from its place at his hip, drove his knee into the soft place at the centre of the second boglin's breast, and as its arms closed on him, slammed the dagger home, breaking its back. Spears slammed into the thing from all sides.

He got to his feet with his dagger clenched like a mantis's claw. But the only figures standing in the green-lit cellar were armoured men.

Gawin sagged.

Ser Driant reached out an ichor-spattered hand. "Ser Gawin?" he said.

Gawin was looking for the novice.

She was slumped against the wall. At her feet were the remnants of Sym the archer—the skin of his face flensed away where they'd swarmed atop him. She was pouring her power into him.

"You cannot help him," Gawin said. "However great your talent, you cannot help him."

She ignored him.

Ser Driant seized his shoulder. "Is she a healer?" he asked.

Lissen Carak—Thorn

Thorn felt the challenge as a blow in his gut.

The dark sun.

The young Power glowed with fresh vitality. He had taken new prey, and he was stronger for it.

Thorn gathered his wits.

I am hurt. He is not. And I have been duped.

What if he can best me?

The air between them was thick with the misspent green power of his last phantasm, only partially expended. He had only to reach forth and take that power...

But if he was caught while doing it, it would be the end of him.

What if this was a Power's plan all along? To lead me to over-extend, so that I might be destroyed?

Oh, Thurkan, it may be I owe you an apology.

Carefully, he began to wrap sigils of concealment about himself, even as he roared with false defiance.

Attack! he commanded his creatures.

High above him, in the fortress of his enemies, someone seized the power of the Wild—raw—and shaped a mighty phantasm with it.

So!

He wasn't waiting for the trap to close. He fled.

Lissen Carak—de Vrailly

Jean de Vrailly judged his moment well. He had led the chivalry of Alba off to the west almost a league along the river. A handful of boglins had tried to oppose him, his sword was wet with their hellish ichor, and it was as easy as taking the heads off fennel plants in his mother's garden.

And now—

Oh, the glory.

He raised his arm, closing his fist—turned his horse. "Halt!" he ordered. "Now turn to face the enemy!" Not a military command, but he had never led so many knights, and he didn't know their commands in their language. So he turned out of the line, and cantered along the column. "Face me!" he called. "Come! Turn your horses!"

As soon as half a dozen knights understood him, they all understood. And the great column, a thousand horses long, turned into a line a thousand horses wide as he cantered down the front, his lance held above his head, the royal arms of Alba sparkling on his chest.

I will be king.

He didn't know where the thought came from, but suddenly it was there—he grinned and turned his horse to face the enemy. He was in the centre of this mighty line. To his right front, his own dismounted knights, led by his cousin, and the men of the King's Guard had just slammed into the enemy fighting line. They were outnumbered badly.

But it didn't matter.

Because he lay across the enemy's line, like the crossing of a T, and the enemy had committed all of his reserves. And there was no force on earth, in the Wild or out of it, that could stop a thousand of his kind charging in a line.

He raised his lance high, feeling the astonishing, angelic vitality that filled him. "For God and honour!" he roared.

"Deus veult!" cried the knights. Men closed their faceplates.

And then the line started forward.

The battle was over long before the first lance struck home. The enemy's whole right wing had begun to melt back into the forest as soon as the knights emerged over the bridge—and now, as their charge rumbled forward, the wyverns, the trolls, and the handful of daemons edged back too. Some simply turned and ran for the woods. They didn't have the bad judgment of men. Like any animal in the Wild faced with a larger predator, they turned and fled. Wyverns leapt into the air; the remaining trolls ran with stone-footed grace, and the daemons ran at the speed of racehorses—untouchable.

Only the boglins and irks stood and fought.

And in the centre, held by Thorn's will, a dozen mighty creatures and a horde of boglins continued to try to kill the king and the dark sun.

Lissen Carak—The Red Knight

The captain could no longer raise his sword to cut. He had the weapon in both hands—his left gauntlet held the blade halfway down, and he used it as a short spear, slamming the point into faces and armoured chests.

Moments of terror blended together—a scythe talon that came inside his visor, luck or skill directing the razor-sharp claw to curve up into his scalp and hair, leaving him alive instead of blind or dead.

A trio of irk warriors dragged him down with their sheer weight, their thin, strong limbs racketing against the steel of his armour in a killing frenzy. As slowly as honey poured on snow, or so it seemed, his right hand burrowed past the hideous strength of their limbs to the rondel dagger at his hip, and then he was on one knee, and they were gone, and his dagger dripped gore.

The comfort of steel armour rasping against his own—back to back. He didn't know who it was, he was just thankful for steel not chitin.

And then, a daemon.

This lord of the Wild was taller than a war horse. The captain hadn't remarked on their absence from the battlefield, but now that he faced one some part of his brain registered that he hadn't faced one before.

The crest on its head was a livid blue—utterly different from the one he'd faced in the woods to the west, or in the dark.

It watched him intently, but it didn't attack.

He watched it and wished he had his spear—currently leaning against his armour rack inside the fortress—and a horse, and a ballista, and twenty fresh friends.

The thing had a pole-axe the size of a wagon's axle-tree. The head was flint. It was crusted with blood.

It turned its head.

Had he been fresh he'd have sprung forward with a mighty attack while it was distracted, but instead he merely breathed again.

It looked back at him.

"You are the dark sun," it said at last. "I can take you, but if you hurt me, I will die here. So instead—" It saluted him with a flourish of the great pole-axe. "Live long, enemy of my enemy."

It turned and ran.

The captain watched it go, throwing boglins from its path, with no idea who or what it was. Or why it had left him alive.

But he was trembling.

He fought more boglins. He cut some sort of tentacled thing from the Prior, who flicked him a salute and went back to work. Later, he saw the king go down, and he managed to get a foot on either side of the king's head, and then all the monsters in the Wild came for him.

Some time passed, and he was standing between Sauce and Bad Tom, and the King of Alba's body lay between his feet. The last rush of the monsters had been so ferocious as to rob the word of all meaning—an endless rain of blows, which only fine armour could repel, because sheer fatigue had robbed muscles of the ability to parry.

Tom was still killing.

Sauce was still killing.

Michael was still standing…

…so the captain kept standing too, because that's what he did.

They came for him, and he survived them.

There finally came a point when the blows stopped. When there was nothing to push against, no fresh foe to withstand.

Before he could think about it, the captain slapped his visor open and drank in the air. And then bent down to check the king.

The man was still alive.

The captain had had a leather bottle, just an hour ago. He started to search his person for it with the slow incompetence of the utterly exhausted.

Not there.

He felt an armoured back against his, and turned to find the Captain of the King's Guard—Sir Richard Fitzroy. The man managed a smile.

"I will build a church," Michael chanted. "I will burn a thousand candles to the Virgin," he went on.

"Get the crap off your blade," Tom said. He had a scrap of linen out of his wallet, and he was suiting action to words.

Sauce didn't grin. She took a handkerchief from her breastplate and wiped her face. Then she took in what her captain was doing and handed him a wooden canteen of water, pulling it over her shoulder on a strap.

He knelt and gave water to the King of Alba.

Who smiled.

The knight who reined in above him provided some shade. His giant war horse had a hard time standing securely on the shifting pile of dead boglins, and his rider curbed him savagely and swore in Gallish. He looked around, as if expecting something.

The king grunted something, and the captain bent over further, his shoulder screaming at the effort, the helmet and the aventail on his head and neck feeling like the weight of a lifetime of penance.

The king had a horny talon between the plates of his fauld, buried deep in his thigh, and his blood soaked the ground.

"I have saved you," said the knight who towered over them. "You may take your ease—you are saved." Indeed, as far as the eye could see, a wave of knights were dispatching the last creatures too foolish or too bound by Thorn's will to flee. "We have won a mighty victory today. Where is the king, please?"

The captain was able for the first time in hours—it felt like hours, and later it would prove to be only a few minutes—to look around.

His company—

His men-at-arms were gone. They lay in a ring, their white steel armour, even matted with gore, brilliant when surrounded by the green, grey, white and brown of their adversaries.

But their red tabards were very like those worn by the king's knights.

The king's household knights were intermixed with them, and the Knights of Saint Thomas in their black. Many of the latter were still standing—more than a dozen.

"The king is right here," Fitzroy said.

"Dead?" the foreign knight asked.

The captain shook his head. He could easily come to dislike this foreigner. Galles were superb knights but very difficult people.

His mind was wandering.

Don't give him the king, said Harmodius.

The captain stiffened in shock. *How did you do that? Prudentia never spoke to me outside the memory palace.*

Do I look like Prudentia? Harmodius muttered. *Do not give this man the king. Take him to the fortress, yourself. Take him to Amicia, with your own hands.*

"Give him to me," said the foreign knight. "I will see he is well guarded."

"He's well-guarded right here," said Sir Richard.

Bad Tom leaned forward. "Sod off, son."

The captain reached out a hand to steady Tom.

"You need manners," said the mounted knight. "But for my charge, you would all be dead."

Tom laughed. "All you did was to lower my body count, pipkin," he said.

They glared at each other.

The Prior waded over to them. "Ser Jean? Captal?"

De Vrailly backed his horse. "Messire."

"A litter for the king." He waved.

Other knights rode forward—there was the banner of the Earl of Towbray, and there was the Count of the Borders. They came in a rush, now that the king had been discovered. Towbray found the king's squires and the Royal Standard, and raised it, covered in ichor.

There was a low cheer.

A long line of infantrymen came over the field of the dead. They had to pick their footing, and they weren't quick about it. As they came, the captain and Michael got the king's breast and back off, and got his hauberk up. Bad luck had slit a dozen rings—worse luck to receive a second blow that bent the fauld and penetrated the leg. There really was a lot of blood.

Do I have anything left?

You can stop the blood flow. But I've been squandering your power, keeping you alive, for a long time now. Amicia?

I'm right here.

The captain smiled, knelt, placed his hand on the king's bare thigh when Michael peeled back his braes and his hose, and with no conscious effort he released Amicia's power.

Harmodius did the actual casting.

It made the captain feel a little sick, as if he was three people.

You feel sick? The dead Magus laughed in his head.

And then the footmen of the Royal Guard were there—everywhere around them—and the king was lifted high, placed on a cloak across two spears...and he held onto the captain's hand. So they walked, hand in hand, across the stricken field. It was the longest walk the captain had ever taken—the sun was beating down like a new foe, the insects descended like a plague, and the footing was impossible.

But eventually, they were free of the corpses and were climbing the long road to the fortress.

Soldiers stopped and bowed, or knelt. Men in the field had begun to sing the Te Deum, and its strains rose like the casting of a mighty phantasm from the fields below. The captain felt the king's hot hand in his own, and tried not to think too much about it.

The Queen lay in the chapel—on the altar. She raised her head, and smiled.

The king released a sigh, as if he had been holding his breath.

The captain saw Amicia. She stood in the light of the window behind the altar. She appeared inhuman, a goddess of light and colour, and she was, to his sight, sparkling with power.

Christ. Look at her, boy.

The captain ignored the dead man.

He couldn't take his eyes off her anyway.

She was healing each injured person brought to her. The power went into her as easily as breathing—she was drinking the unspent green from Thorn's hammer blow, and from the sun streaming through the broken chapel window, and the well—taking all three streams of power and releasing it in a cloud of rainbow light so that soldier after soldier approached her, knelt, and arose healed. Most stumbled away and went to sleep in the arms of their comrades.

She passed her hands over the king as if he were any other soldier, any of the women wounded in the desperate defence of the courtyard, any of the children injured in the collapse of the West Tower—and he was healed.

And then she turned, and her eyes looked into his.

He couldn't breathe.

He had the foolish impulse to kiss her.

She touched him. "You must open your powers, or I cannot heal you," she said. She gave him a smile. "You were not this powerful, a few days ago."

He sighed. "Nor were you," he said.

The room was the same. He was almost afraid to enter it, but it looked better. The moss was gone from the floor, and Prudentia's statue was repaired, and now occupied a niche that hadn't existed before.

The Magus stood on the plinth in the centre of the room.

The captain by-passed him, and walked to the door.

"Think on what you do, boy," said the dead Magus. "She is a Power, neither more nor less than you."

The captain ignored him, and opened the iron-bound door.

And she was there.

And he was healed.

She looked at the plinth and her eyes widened in horror. "My God," she said. "What have you done?"

And she was gone.

North of Lissen Carak—Peter

They stopped in a clearing in the woods. The ground had been rising steadily to the north, and they were running almost due north, and that was all Nita Qwan knew except that, as usual, he had never been so tired in all his life.

They all lay down in a muddle and slept.

In the morning, Ota Qwan stood up first, and they ran again. The sun was high in the sky before they straggled over a ridge, and young warriors were sent back without their baskets to fetch the matrons and mothers of newborns who had lagged behind.

And when the last of the women was over the ridge, fires were lit carefully and the people made food, and ate.

And when Nita Qwan felt as if life might be worth living, Ota Qwan came to the centre of the ring of fires with a spear. And Little Hands, the senior woman, came and faced him.

He handed her the spear. "Our war is over," he said. "I give you the spear of war."

Little Hands took it. "The matrons have it, ready for any enemy. Our thanks, Ota Qwan. You have surprised us, and done well."

No one said anything more—there was neither applause nor censure.

An hour later, they were running north again.

Chapter Seventeen

Lissen Carak—The Red Knight

Days passed.

Wounded men were healed, and slept.

Dead men and women were mourned, and buried.

The creatures of the Wild were burned, and their ashes spread over the fields.

The company was not entirely dead. A few men-at-arms were found wounded, and healed. Ser Jehannes and Ser Milus had not been part of the charge; Bad Tom and Sauce were untouched, although they each slept for more than thirty hours after their armour was stripped. But the archers were still alive, many of the valets and a few squires.

The captain was very difficult to find. Some said he was drunk, and some said he was with his pretty novice, and some said he was taking service of the king, or of the Knights of Saint Thomas.

None of these things were true.

The captain spent a great deal of time weeping, and when he buried his company dead, he invited no others. They lay in neat rows, sewn in white linen by Mag and her friends, who now stood silent in a light rain. Dora Candleswain stood with Kaitlin Lanthorn, and the Carter sisters stood watching their surviving brother who, with Daniel Favor, was in the ranks of the company.

And the knights of Saint Thomas appeared from the rain. The Prior came out at their head, and said the service for the dead. Bad Tom, Sauce, Ranald and the captain himself lowered the bodies. There was Carlus the Smith, smaller in death but no lighter; there was Lyliard, no longer the company's handsomest man. They went into marked graves with headstones, each of them marked with the eight-pointed cross of the Order. It made a great difference to many of the man and women—better, in fact, than most mercenaries ever imagined.

One corpse absorbed the captain, and he wept. He wept for all of them, and he wept for his own errors, and the ill-judgement of others, and a thousand other things—but Jacques was his last tie to childhood, and was gone.

Your mother's still alive, lad. Doesn't she count? said the old Magus in his mind.

"*Could you shut up?*" muttered the captain to the interloper in his head.

Sauce looked at him, because he muttered to himself a great deal, lately, and because Sauce helped Dora Candleswain to stop screaming every night. She was sensitive to the other men and women in the company who were near the breaking point, or past it. Not all wounds bled.

They all stood there in the light rain—the survivors. Atcourt, and Brewes and Long Paw. Ser Alcaeus, who wore the red tabbard and stood with the knights; Johne the Bailli. Bent. No Head. Knights and squires and archers and valets, men and women, soldiers and prostitutes and laundresses and farm girls and servants. And to a man and woman, they looked at the captain and waited for him to speak.

Like a fool, he hadn't planned anything. But their need was palpable—like a spell.

"We won," he said, his young voice as harsh as the croaking of a raven. "We held the fortress against a Power of the Wild. But none of these men or women died to hold the fortress—did they?"

He looked at Jehannes. The older man met his glance. And gave him a small nod of agreement.

"They died for us. We die for each other. Out there in the world, they lie, and cheat each other, and betray, and we, here, don't do that." He was all too aware that sometimes, they did. But funerals are the time to speak high words. He knew that, too. "We do our level best to hold the line, so that the man next to us can live. We—we who are alive—we owe our lives to these, who are dead. It could have been us. It was them." He managed a smile. "No one can do more than to give his life for his friends. Every drink of wine you ever taste, every time you get laid, every time you wake and breathe the spring air, you owe that to these—who lie here in the ground." His eye caught the smallest bundle—Low Sym. "They died heroes—no matter how they lived." He shrugged and looked at the Prior. "I suspect it's bad theology." He had more to say, but he was crying too hard, and he found that he was kneeling by the mound of damp earth that was Jacques.

Who had saved his life so many times.

"Jesus said, I am the way, and the life," said the Prior in a calm, low voice.

The captain shut out the sound of his company praying.

And eventually, there was a hand on his shoulder. It was a light hand. But he didn't have to open his eyes to know to whom it belonged.

He rose, and she stepped back. She smiled at the ground. "I thought you'd just hurt your back again, with all that kneeling," she said.

"Marry me?" he asked. His whole face ached from crying—and he knew she didn't care how he looked, or sounded. It was the most remarkable thought.

She smiled. "I'll tell you tomorrow," she said lightly. "Open to me?" she asked, and he thought he heard an immense strain in her voice. He put it down to fatigue, and he opened his *door, and she entered in. She kept her distance from Harmodius, and instead she pulled him out his own door and into the green wonder of her bridge—but it was no longer a simple green. Overhead, the sky was a golden blue, and the sun shone in splendour in heaven and the water that rushed under her bridge was clear as diamonds and the spray was as white as the brightest cloud. The leaves of the trees were green and gold, and every tree was in flower. The smell was of clean water and brilliant air and every flower scent he'd ever imagined or smelled.*

"God," he said, involuntarily.

She smiled at him with her slightly tilted eyes, and she passed her hands over him, and a dozen small knots were eased, and the lump at the back of his throat passed away.

"I'm not so arrogant as to heal your sorrow," she said.

He caught her hands. "You will heal my sorrow," he said.

She smiled, and put her lips on his, her eyes closed.

And after a time, she pulled away. "Goodbye," she said.

"Until tomorrow," he said. "I—I love you."

She smiled. "Of course you do," she said with a little of her old tone. Then she softened. "I love you, too," she said.

She walked away into the rain, and he watched her until the grey of her cloak merged with the sky and the stone and the hillside.

And the captain found his services very much in demand. He accepted a contract in the east, serving among the Moreans with Ser Alcaeus. They concluded the contract just a week after the day of the battle, after an hour of loud and apparently angry bargaining that had featured several cups of wine and a warm embrace at the end.

Then he picked up the staff of his command and walked out of his tent—the company were back in their tents on the plain, so that the Royal Household could occupy the fortress—and mounted a pretty Eastern mare that had belonged to Master Random. No amount of miraculous healing could fix his partially-eaten leg, so the merchant would be bed-ridden for some time. He'd been delighted to sell the mare for a profit.

The captain rode up the familiar road to the main gate. Royal Guardsmen held the post, and he saluted them. They returned the salute.

He gave his horse to a newly minted Royal Squire—somebody's younger son—and climbed the steps to the Commandery. No longer his office.

The Prior was at prayer.

The captain waited patiently.

Eventually, the Prior rose and put his rosary back around his waist. He smiled.

"Your servant, Captain."

The captain smiled back, reached into his wallet and fetched forth a pair of heavy gilt-bronze keys. "The keys to the fortress and the river bridge," he said. "They were placed in my keeping by the Abbess. I relinquish them to you in peace and triumph," he said formally. And then added, with a smile, "You owe me a sizeable sum of money."

The Prior took the keys and settled into a seat. He waved the captain into another, and the captain had the oddest feeling—one of having lived this moment before, perhaps from the other side of the desk.

The Prior took a writing set, checked the pen for sharpness, used a little ink and began to write.

"You would not consider turning to God, my son? Become a knight of my order?" he asked, raising his eyes briefly.

"No," the captain said.

The Prior smiled. "So proud. Amicia tells me that you see God as your enemy." He shook his head.

"Amicia has misinterpreted the information with which she was provided," the captain said. Then he shrugged. "Or maybe not. Your God and I are not friends."

"Ahh," said the Prior. He shook sand over the paper, shook it, and blew on it. Then, after struggling with a candle, he managed to drip heavy black wax on the document and he affixed the great seal from the ring on his thumb. "Your defence here will never be forgotten by my knights." He shrugged. "Even if outside these walls men say the king won the battle, and defeated the Wild." He handed over the parchment. "My God loves you, and every other living thing, Captain. My God loves the sick, the blind, the leper, the unclean—the irk, the boglin, and the witch."

The captain glanced at the sum, drawn on the Church—a draft redeemable at any bank, anywhere—and nodded. He even smiled.

"This is more than I contracted for," he said.

"I supposed that you contracted for the loss of men and horses, and for the usual victory bonus," the Prior said.

The captain shook his head. "No," he said. "I had no idea what I was getting into."

The Prior nodded. "I don't know what your problems are with my God," he said. "But I won't let you add ingratitude to your list of His inadequacies. Without you and the sacrifice of your company, this place would have been lost and all humanity would have suffered for it."

The captain rose and bowed. "You do me too much honour. For my company—" He found himself unable to speak. When he was master of himself, he said, "I will recruit more."

"Easily, I predict," the Prior said. "Listen, young man. You have interests beyond the mundane. You will not turn to God. So be it. But you have a brain, and it's a keen one. Did we win here?"

The captain hadn't expected this turn of conversation. He stood in the doorway with his payment in his hand.

The Prior rose and poured two cups of wine. "Sit."

He sat and drank. "No?"

The Prior shook his head. "Of course we did. Had we lost the king would be dead, the Alban border would be south of Albinkirk and the Royal Host would be shattered." He crossed himself. "But of course, we didn't win either, did we?"

"Thorn burned every house and barn from here to Albinkirk," the captain said. "And hit the population hard."

The Prior nodded.

"Most of the survivors will leave. Move south." The captain sipped some more wine. "That's why—I'm guessing—there was no fight at the wall first. Thorn never intended to fight there. He went deep—"

"Stop saying his name," the prior said. "He still lives, licking his wounds."

"He still lives, and nothing died out there but this year's crop of bog-lins," the captain said bitterly. "Sixteen trolls, a dozen wyverns and some daemons." He rubbed his beard. "We're losing the exchange."

"We're losing, period," said the Prior. "In our order we have records that go back six hundred years. We are not winning this war." He shrugged. "If the Wild were not so utterly divided against itself, they'd have swept over us a thousand years ago."

In his head, Harmodius said, *Exactly. Who knew the Prior was a kindred spirit?*

"What can we do?" the captain asked.

The Prior bent forward. "Well, at least you are interested. Where is your next contract?"

The captain leaned back. "Morea. A rebellion and a magus gone bad." He looked out the window. "What will you do with this place?"

"Put a garrison into it, for a while. I don't quit easily—I'll offer a sizeable benefit and a total remission of tithes to any family who will stay here and rebuild. And I, too, will recruit—there must be younger sons south of the river looking for farms. I'll find them."

"That will cost a fortune," the captain said.

"I have a fortune," said the Prior. He leaned forward. "You have power."

The captain shrugged.

The Prior shook his head. "Your power comes from the Wild. I've seen it."

Again, the captain shrugged.

The Prior nodded. "Very well. But if you ever choose to talk about it there are many knights of the order who channel the Wild. We know more about it than you might think."

The captain finished his wine, rose, accepted the Prior's embrace and even stayed still while the man blessed him.

"Will you not tell me why you turn your back on God?" the Prior asked.

The captain looked at him, smiled and shook his head. "When you offered to make me a knight of the order, just now—" he said.

"The offer remains open," said the Prior.

"—I'll treasure that," he finished.

"Your brother turned me down, as well," the Prior said.

The captain nodded. "Gawin is riding east with me," he said.

He walked out of the Commandery, and down the stone steps. A valet in de Vrailly's arms stood by the steps up to the Hall, holding a beautiful destrier—tall and grey as steel. The captain didn't feel the slightest need to take leave of the king. Or the Queen. Or, for that matter, their new favourite the Captal de Ruth, already known as the Victor of Lissen.

Instead, he walked to the hospital, up the steps, and to Master Random's bedside. A trio of local farmers stood by his bed, with Master Johne the Bailli.

"A moment, good sirs!" cried Master Random. "This worthy knight must always have first call on my time. Damn my foot," he said, trying to twist in the bed. "How can it hurt so much when it isn't there?"

The captain embraced the merchant. "You look better."

"I am better, my friend. That wonderful young lady poured her spirit into me, and I feel twenty years younger for it." His eyes sparkled. "Though if I was home, I daresay the goodwife might tell you that the deal just struck with these worthies was part to my joy. Eh?"

The captain looked around. Master Johne had acquitted himself very well against the enemy, every farmer present had carried a spear or an axe. The captain knew them by name—Raimond, Jaques, Ben Carter and young Bartholemew Lanthorn, a rogue, a scoundrel, and despite that, a very successful farmer.

"He's bought the whole grain crop," Johne the Bailli said. He smiled.

The captain glanced around. "Of course—it's all in the cellars."

"A little messed about," Random noted. "But grain's grain, and the need downriver—the price, when they hear of the battle and the burning of farms!"

"How will you ship it?" the captain asked, to be polite.

"Boats!" Random said. "All those boats which brought the Queen? Mine."

The captain shook his head. "A coup, my friend. You will be rich."

"I'll break even or a little better," Master Random said with a smile. "Drink with me," he said.

The captain nodded. "May I broach a small item of business, myself?" he asked.

Random nodded. "Always open."

The captain took the Prior's note from the breast of his jupon. "You are a bank, are you not?"

Random sniffed. "Not of the size of the Etruscan banks, perhaps. But I do my—Gracious God!" he said. His eyes snapped to the captain's.

"I'm investing in you," the captain said. "I may have to make some pay outs, and buy some horses, but three-quarters of this sum is at your service for at least a year."

The captain had a cup of wine, embraced all concerned, and met the Bailli's eye. The man nodded.

He went back through the ward, to the bed where his brother lay reading. He had his feet up, but he was fully dressed and his kit was neatly packed in wicker hampers. "She's not here," he said. "Don't even pretend you are here to see me."

"I won't, then," the captain said. "Where is she?"

Gawin shrugged. "I need out of here, Gabriel. I'll kill the foreigner if I stay."

"I'll have another cot put in my pavilion. We ride tomorrow." He turned to go. "Where is she, Gawin?"

Gawin met his brother's eye. "I'd tell you if I knew," he said.

Their eyes locked, and Gawin motioned with a finger. A woman's form was outlined in the curtain of the courtyard window.

The captain raised an eyebrow.

"He's not the enemy, Mary," Gawin said, and the Queen's Lady in Waiting emerged. She was blushing.

"You have other things to take up your time," the captain said.

Gawin laughed. "I really don't know where she is," he admitted.

The captain turned with a wave, and headed out. He peeked into the dispensary and the apothecary, and he climbed the steps in the dormitory. No one had seen her. The smiles he left in his wake pained him.

Finally, in the courtyard, he met Sister Miram. She smiled at him, and took him by the hand to her cell in the chapel. "You are going," she said, pouring him wine.

He tried to refuse the wine but she was a forceful woman, and a pleasant one, and her silence intimidated him. She waited him out. Finally, he drank it. "Tomorrow."

"We will celebrate the feast of Mary Magdalene tomorrow," she said. She smiled. "We will inter the old Abbess." Sister Miram looked at her hands. "I will be ordained Abbess in her place."

"Congratulations," the captain said.

"There is talk that the whole convent is to be moved south to Harndon," Sister Miram said. She looked the captain firmly in the eye. "I won't have it."

The captain nodded.

"We will also accept the vows of novices advancing to the sisterhood of Christ tomorrow," she said.

Ice formed in the captain's stomach.

"She is performing her vigil at the moment," the sister said. "Drink your wine, Captain. No one is forcing her to."

The captain took a breath.

"We owe you so much," Sister Miram said. "Do you think we do not know it? But she is not for you, Captain. She is to be the bride of Christ; it's what she wishes." She rose, went to her prie-dieu, and opened the triptych. From it she drew a folded piece of parchment. "She left this for you. If you should come."

The captain took it with a bow. "Your servant, ma soeur. May I express my congratulations on your elevation, and my—" He stopped. Swallowed. "I will make a donation to the convent. Please give Sister Amicia my congratulations and my kindest regards."

Somehow, he reached the courtyard.

Toby was holding his horse.

The captain took the reins, and vaulted into the saddle, aware, in that cursed part of him that was always awake, that he was on the stage of chivalry, and that half of the knights of Alba were watching him.

Then he rode down the hill to his camp. He paused at the guard fire.

Don't be a fool. Read it.

The Red Knight took the parchment from his breast, and threw it in the fire unread.

You idiot.

Michael was sitting in his tent. He leaped to his feet, obviously guilty about something. "Master Ranald is waiting for you," he said. "I was entertaining him!"

Ranald Lachlan sat with a mug of beer, and his cousin Tom sat across the captain's camp table with another. They had dice on the table, and cards.

"It'd be a pity to stop him playing," Tom said. "Especially as I'm taking all his money," he added.

"I'm so pleased you two feel free to make use of my tent and table," the captain spat.

Tom raised an eyebrow. "Brother's got something to say," he said.

Ranald rose. "I—need to make a great deal of money," he said. "I wonder if you'll have me as a man-at-arms." He looked embarrassed to ask.

"I'd have thought the king would've knighted you," the captain said.

Ranald shrugged.

"All right," said the captain, sitting and pouring wine for himself. "Now deal me a hand."

"But first," Ranald said, "I have to pay a visit to the Wyrm of Erch."

The captain gagged on his wine. "The Wyrm?"

"Our liege lord in the hills, or so we call him," Ranald said, and Tom nodded.

The captain shook his head. "I don't understand." He frowned. "Possibly because I'm drunk."

Tom shrugged. "The ways of the hills are easier on a man with drink in him. Tis like this, my lord: the Wyrm guarantees us peace for a tithe of the flocks. Tis been that way for twenty generations of men or more. These Outwallers that killed Hector—the Sossag—they were serving a Power of the Wild called Thorn. Aye?"

"Naming calls. But yes." The captain drank.

"So I call him and he comes and I gut him," said Tom. "So?"

"Excellent point," the captain said. "Go on."

"The Wyrm owes us for our loss," Ranald said.

The captain sat back. "I'm not drunk enough to believe that," he said.

Tom and Ranald sat with set faces.

The captain finished his cup. Michael poured him more, and he didn't say no. And then he said, "She's taking orders as a nun, Tom."

Tom shrugged as if all women were one and the same. "Best find another one then," he said. And then, as if the collapse of the captain's hopes was not the most important thing in the world, he said, "So we want leave to go to the Wyrm."

The captain shook his head. "I have a better idea," he said. "Let's all go."

Ranald looked at him and raised an eyebrow at his brother.

"I love him," Tom said to his brother. "He's mad as an adder."

Ranald smiled. "So we all go? The company?"

Yes. This is important.

The captain suddenly had a piercing pain between his eyes.

Be quiet. You're a guest.

You are getting drunk because you've been spurned by a woman. How romantic of you. Of course, that note might have confessed her undying love for you and her willingness to elope tonight to face the future as a mercenary captain's whore. Hmm? But you burned it, so you'll never know. Youth is wasted on the young.

Shut up. Fuck off.

Listen, young man. The Prior is right—humanity is losing. But he is also wrong—as I will endeavour to prove. The world is not as I thought it was, and your going to see the Wyrm is the very best idea I have ever heard. You must go to the Wyrm. The stakes of this game are immense. The consequences of failure are extermination—the death of our race. Your dalliance with some novice—albeit one imbued with power of the very highest order—is not quite in the same league.

The captain put his head in his hands.

Tom grinned at him. "You're drunk, my lord."

The captain looked around for Jacques, but of course he was dead. The last piece of his old life—the last man to connect him with—

I'm conveniently dead, too. Prince Gabriel.

The captain took a deep breath. "I have a headache," he said. "I find it unfair that I have the hangover before I'm done with the drunk."

Michael leaned forward and poured more wine.

Ser Jehannes came in with Ser Milus, both of them drunk too. They were singing "Green Grow the Rushes" with their arms around Sauce, who seemed to be carrying them.

> *Three, three, the lily white boys, clothed all in green, oh,*
> *Two, two the rivals.*
> *And one is one and all alone, and ever more shall be, oh.*

Their attempt at harmony was almost as horrible as a charge of boglins.

Tom started to laugh.

Jehannes poured a cup of wine, sat on a stool, and raised his cup. "Absent friends," he said.

Tom's laughter stopped. He rose to his feet, and so did the rest. "Victory and defeat are for amateurs," Tom said. "For us, there is only life and death."

They all raised their cups, and drank. "Absent friends," they chanted, one by one.

The captain put his cup down on the table carefully, because it seemed to be a long way away and it moved slightly, and he leaned on the table to make sure he could stay on his feet. "They will bury the old Abbess tomorrow," he said. "I'd like every man and woman at that service in their best kit. But with the camp struck first, ready to march."

His corporals nodded.

"The Prior paid me today," he said. "With a success bonus and a tallage for the horses we lost. A pretty sum. I invested it. But none of you needs to fight for a living. Your shares will be a hundred gold nobles or more. Enough to buy a knight's fee."

Jehannes shrugged.

Tom sneered.

Sauce looked away.

Michael laughed.

Ranald smiled. "Wish it was mine," he said.

"It will be," the captain said. "We have a new contract, and I mean to wrap it up quickly." He felt a little better. "Sauce, come here."

She was dressed in old hose and a well-cut man's doublet—something of a brag, since it flattered her figure as much as any kirtle. She leered at him. "Any time, Captain," she said, with a spark of her old sauce.

"Kneel," the captain said. He held out his hand to Michael.

Michael handed him his war sword.

Sauce paused and knelt. On the edge of a double entendre, she stopped.

Tom nodded. "Do it."

The captain raised his sword. "By the virtue of knighthood and my birth, I dub thee knight," he said. He didn't slur the words. His sword pressed down hard on each of her shoulders.

She burst into tears.

Tom smacked her, quite hard, on the shoulder. "Let that be the last blow you ever accept without reprisal," he said. He grinned.

"Michael, kneel," the captain said.

Michael knelt.

"By the virtue of knighthood and my birth, I dub thee knight," the captain said.

Michael accepted the slap from Tom, rocked back on his heels, and smiled.

The captain took his wine cup. "I meant to do it on the battlefield," he said. And shrugged. "We were busy."

Michael stood up. "I'm a knight?" he laughed. "A man-at-arms and not a squire?" He laughed again.

"I'll need a new squire," the captain said.

Sauce was still crying. "Is it real?" she asked.

Tom put an arm around her shoulder. "Of course it is, lass. He wouldn't mock you with such."

The captain sat back down. "We need twenty new men-at-arms. We need as many squires and a dozen valets and some archers." He shrugged. "My brother Gawin is one. Johne the Bailli is another. Both have their own harness, and they'll ride away with us. Ser Alcaeus himself, despite negotiating our contract, will be joining us. Any other prospects?"

Jehannes nodded. "I have half a dozen younger sons ready to sign articles—all with harness and horses."

Ranald shrugged. "All my lads, too," he said. "We have no other means of employment, at least for the balance of the year."

Tom leaned forward. "Daniel Favor. Likeliest man-at-arms I've ever seen. He signed with me. And two of the Lanthorn boys—dangerous boys. Murderous." He grinned. "Archers."

Jehannes nodded. "I made out a watchbill," he said. "If we go to one man-at-arms, one squire, one valet and two archers to a lance, we have a company." He looked at the captain. "Gelfred should start arming as a man-at-arms too."

The captain nodded. "We could use twenty more lances," he said. "I wrote a contract for forty, and we only have what—twenty?" He sat up, decided that was a mistake, and shuffled to his feet. "Tomorrow night we'll be on the road. Less wine." He raised his cup. "To the company," he said.

They all drank.

"Now, since it's my tent I'm going to bed," he said. And motioned to the door.

One by one they ducked under the awning and left, until it was Michael and Sauce—each seeming to want the other gone first. Finally Michael spoke.

"Can I help you, my lord? I'm not above myself yet." He laughed.

"I'm guessing you already have a nice pair of solid gold spurs to go on those heels, and you'll have them on your boots in the morning," the captain said, slapping his shoulder. "Just send me young Toby."

Michael smiled. "Thanks," he said. "I—"

The captain waved his thanks away, and Michael bowed low.

That left Sauce.

"Good night, Sauce," the captain said. He avoided her embrace. "Good night."

She stood with her hands on her hips. "You need me."

He shook his head.

"I won't go all soppy on you, Captain." She shrugged and then smiled engagingly.

"Good night, Sauce."

She grunted.

"I just made you a knight," he said. "Don't play the woman scorned part." Even drunk he could see his refusal hurt her. He raised a heavy hand. "Wait," he said, and stumbled through the curtain to his bed, reached into his trousseau and found his other spurs. The solid gold ones his mother had given him, which he never wore.

He came back out. "Take these."

She reached out and took them. Realised they were solid gold. "Oh, my lord—"

"Out!" he said.

She sighed, and walked out of the tent, swaying her hips to brush by Toby, who came in, and silently relieved him of his clothes and accoutrements.

"How old are you, Toby?" he asked.

"Rising twelve, my lord. Or perhaps thirteen?" he said.

The captain lay his body down on clean linen sheets. "Would you care to be a squire, Toby?" he asked.

He survived the protestations of joy and eternal loyalty, and waved the boy away. When he put his head down, though, the tent spun. So he put a foot on the ground. Gave sleep up as a bad job, sat up, and drank some water.

The headache was back.

He stood by his water basin for a full watch. Staring into the dark.

It was, as such things went, pretty dark.

You make them love you, and then you tire of the energy they demand, the voice said.

He sighed, lay down, and went to sleep.

The chapel was magnificent, with all the decoration that could be managed for an occasion that featured the King, the Queen, the Prior, and a thousand noblemen—virtually the whole peerage of Alba.

But there wasn't room for all of them. The chapel had been built for sixty nuns, as many novices, and perhaps another hundred worshipers.

In the end the service was held in the chapel, but only a select few were there. The rest waited in the courtyard and were served communion there. It was well-managed, and had a festive air despite the great solemnity of the occasion. The courtyard was full to bursting, and velvet clad gentlemen stood shoulder to shoulder with farmers and farm wives.

The Prior and the new Abbess had been very mindful of the future in their assignment of places. Only the greatest lords were in the chapel. The King and Queen sat enthroned. By the king's right hand stood the Captal de Ruth; by the Queen stood Lady Almspend and Lady Mary. The Count of the Borders stood with the Count D'Eu; the Earl of Towbray stood with Ser Alcaeus, as the ambassador of the Emperor Basileus. And next to him stood the captain.

The Prior said the mass, and a thousand beeswax candles burned.

It was brutally hot.

Out in the courtyard, the company stood in full armour, four ranks deep. With them, by a curious choice of the Prior's, stood the surviving knights of the military orders in their black. Mag stood nearby, with the women of the company. Her home was gone, and Johne the Bailli had made her a proposal.

The Prior preached about Mary Magdalene. He spoke about sin, and forgiveness. About faith, hope, and charity, and the nuns brought forth the bier on which the Abbess lay. When her corpse entered the chapel, the air temperature dropped, and a smell, like lilacs, wafted in through the doors.

The captain looked at her and wept.

The Captal de Ruth looked at him and raised an eyebrow.

The Queen placed a hand on the captal's arm.

The captain looked up—he'd surprised himself—and found that he was eye to eye with Amicia. She was standing by the rightmost choir stall, near the altar screen, with six other women in sparkling white-grey. She had, no doubt, been watching him weep.

And now, her eyes remained fixed on his.

She was knocking at the door.

He left it closed.

One is one, and all alone, and ever more shall be so.

The service went on for too long.

When the novices had been elevated; when the new Abbess had been formally invested—when the last words had been spoken over the old Abbess—then the whole congregation rose from their knees and walked in procession from the chapel, through the gate, and down onto the plain. The company acted as guards to the bier with the knights. It was a signal honour, subtly granted by the Prior.

She was lowered slowly into the newly turned earth by six knights.

The Prior threw a shovel of earth onto her.

The captain found that he had wandered away into a world of his own, when the king—the king himself—materialized in front of him.

"I owe you a debt of gratitude," the king said. "You are not an easy man to find."

The captain shrugged. "Your servant, my lord," he said dismissively.

The king was shocked by the mercenary's rudeness, but he mastered himself. "The Queen has requested that she meet your company. We know what sacrifices they made for our kingdom."

"Oh, as to that," the captain said, "We were well paid." But he turned, and led the king and Queen and a small host of their courtiers through the ranks of the company.

The first man on the right was Bad Tom, and next to him, his brother. The king smiled. "Ranald!" he said. "I thought that you had returned to my guard?" He laughed. "I note the colour of your tabard remains the same."

Ranald looked straight ahead. "Business," he said, seriously. "My lord."

"But this is a woman, surely?" asked the Queen, who had taken a few more steps.

"Ser Alison," the captain said. "Her friends call her Sauce."

"A woman knight?" the Queen asked. "How delightful."

By her elbow, the captal laughed. "Knighted by whose hand?" he asked.

"My own," the captain said.

Conversation stopped.

"By what right do you make knights?" demanded the captal. "That is reserved for the very highest nobility, members of the greatest orders, and knights of great renown."

"Yes," the captain said. "Yes, I agree."

The king cleared his throat. "I doubt any knight in this gathering would doubt the captain's renown, Captal."

The captal laughed. "He is a bastard—a bourc. Everyone says so. He cannot be noble, and he cannot make a knight—most especially not make a knight out of a woman."

The captain felt the tension in his chest—not fear, but something like anticipation.

In a low voice, he said, "My lord, you requested to see my company. If you are done, we will take our leave."

"Unsay it," the captal insisted. "Unsay that this woman is a knight. Make her take that golden belt off her hips. It is unseemly."

"Captal!" said the king. "Control yourself."

The captal shrugged. "You are too easy, my liege." He looked at the captain and sneered. "I say you are a bastard, a caitiff, a low-born poseur, and I say before all these gentlemen that you cannot make a knight, that no knighting of yours—"

The captain turned to the king. Leaned over, and whispered in his ear.

The king whirled, looked at the mercenary, and the blood left his face like a tide slipping away from a white sand beach. In three beats of a man's heart, the king aged—he looked as white as parchment. His upper lip trembled. The Queen, who had not been able to hear the words, felt his hand close on her arm like a vice and gave a little grunt of pain.

On the other side of the grave, Sister Amicia gave a start, and went as pale as the king.

The silence went on for so long that wasps could be heard droning, and the grunt of the men filling the Abbess" grave.

The king looked at the captain, and the captain looked back at the king, and then the king inclined his head—the sort of civil motion that a gentlemen makes to a lady about to proceed him through a door.

In a hoarse voice, the king said, "This gentleman has the power to make a knight anywhere within the kingdom of Alba, of anyone, no matter how ignoble their birth or station. Such is my word."

The captain bowed deeply and the captal was silent.

The king acknowledged the captain's bow, and he took the Queen and led her on, up the hill to the fortress.

The captain caught the captal's eye. Jean de Vrailly was afraid of nothing—so he stopped.

"I take it I have managed to offend you?" he said. "It is difficult for me to understand how a whore like you can take offence. You fight only for money."

The captain had control of himself. He took his time. Composed his answer while the captal was pinned in place by convention like a butterfly to parchment.

"Sometimes I fight for free," he said. "But only when it interests me." He paused, holding the captal with his eyes. "But I imagine that in the end, someone will pay me to put you down like the mad dog you are."

Jean de Vrailly smiled—a beautiful smile that filled his face. "So," he said. And laughed. "I look forward to see you try."

"I imagine you do," the captain muttered. He wasn't sure that he'd had the better of the exchange, but he walked away without falling over his feet.

Lissen Carak—Michael

The Earl of Towbray left his tail of men-at-arms and all but ran down the steps behind the Commandery to catch the captain's squire. Former squire.

"You are a knight!" he said.

Michael turned. "Pater. So are you, I find."

Towbray couldn't be angry. "I gather you won your spurs and then some," he said. "Can you come home now?"

Michael shook his head. "No, Pater." He looked up, and found it easier to meet his father's eye than he had expected. "I was glad to see our banner. With the king." He looked around. "Surprised. But glad."

Towbray shrugged. "I can't love the king. But—damn it, boy! Who are you to tell me how to play the game of court?"

Michael shook his head and then bowed. "A new-minted knight, who makes twenty-eight florins a month in a company of mercenaries. "He stepped back. "I must go."

Towbray reached out a hand. "I admire you."

"You won't admire me as much when I tell you that I'm planning to marry a farm girl from Abbington." Michael grinned, feeling, for once, that he was master of a conversation with his father.

His father started, but with grim determination, extended his hand. "So be it," said his father, although his face showed distaste.

Michael took the hand. "Then may I have my allowance back?"

Lissen Carak—The Red Knight

An hour later, the company was mounted and ready. All week the wagons had been swayed out of the cellars and re-built, rolled down the hill, and loaded. The company's stock had been safe in the fortress, and they were hitched with the company's usual efficiency. The valets mounted the wagons, the archers collected the spare mounts, and the camp followers got their nags and donkeys. At the head of the column, the captain mounted a strange new war horse, just given him by the Prior, and looked back to see Michael—Ser Michael—attending to the banner.

One by one, the corporals reported in, ready to march. A small crowd formed—mostly Lanthorns and Carters and a dozen guildsmen from Harndon, come to see their boys off as they marched away. And their girls. Amy and Kitty Carter, Lis the laundress, Old Mag—who hadn't looked as young in twenty years. Her daughter Sukey, whose husband had died in the siege. The captain had noted Sukey with Bad Tom. Twice. He made a note to himself to look into that.

The captain looked repeatedly for a single face in the crowd, but it refused to be there. Many women looked—for an instant—like her. Too many women.

So when all his people were ready, and the sun was so high in the sky that it made a mockery of his intention to march away, he raised a hand. "March!" he said.

Whips cracked, men shouted, and wagons rolled.

Gerald Random waved from the walls, and Jean de Vrailly watched silently. The Prior saluted and women cried.

The king stood alone in the north tower, watching the convoy begin to roll east. His hands shook. And the Queen watched him from the courtyard and wondered what was amiss.

A young nun knelt, her back straight, at the high altar of the chapel.

A mile from the fortress, the captain came upon his huntsman, sitting his horse silently at a bend in the road. It took him a long moment to recognise where they were.

"We still never caught the man who killed that nun," Gelfred said. "It sticks in my craw. I want justice."

"It was the priest," the captain said. "Sister Amicia and I figured it out—far too late to punish him for it. He's off to the Wild, I suspect."

Gelfred crossed himself. "He will go to Hell!" Gelfred said. "God will punish him."

He captain shrugged. "God doesn't give a fuck, Gelfred," he said. He touched his heels to his magnificent new charger. "But I do, Gelfred, and I promise you, the priest will die."

And with that, he put his horse's head to the east, and rode away.

Far to the west, Thorn paused at the top of a ridge. He could see fifty leagues in the clear air, and he breathed deep. He had twenty wounds, and his powers—greater than they had ever been—were nonetheless spent.

He looked east.

That was foolish, he thought. The further he got from the rock, the more it was like a bad dream.

I could have been killed. For ever.

But I wasn't, and when I return—

The great creature that was Thorn could not smile, but something passed over the heavy bark and stone of his face.

On the downslope of the ridge, he thought, *Or perhaps I'll do something else. Unify the boglins, perhaps.*

Chapter Eighteen

The North Road—The Red Knight

The column rolled east at a good pace and within hours, the captain's precautions were justified by huntsmen flushing creatures of the Wild—a pair of boglins, and a lone irk.

They made camp early, dug a trench, and stood watches.

The captain lay awake most of the night.

In the morning they moved with the dawn, and his heart began to lift. The process of camping, of moving camp, and the sounds of the horses and the wagons—the sounds of people and animals—it all raised his spirits.

It took them three days to come to the Southford of the Albin. Albinkirk still smouldered, on its hill. The Royal Standard still flew from the castle, and the captain and his officers rode to the town gate, were admitted, and dined with Ser John Crayford.

Ser Alcaeus, who was falling into the company as if he had always been there, walked them around the walls. "This is where we held their first rush," he said at the ruined west wall. "Here's where a dozen of us held the gate." And again, with a wry look, "Here's where we almost lost the wall."

Crayford shook his head. "You're the very King of Sell-Swords, now, I reckon," he said. He leered at the captain. "My squire's older than you, boy! How'd you do it?"

The captain raised an eyebrow. "Clean living."

Crayford shook his head. "Good on you, lad. I'm a jealous old man. If I had another battle in me, I'd follow you."

The captain smiled. "Even though two of your men are leaving you for my company?" he asked.

The old man managed to nod with a good grace. "Even then, you scapegrace."

He let them go with a fine meal and a hogshead of wine.

"No one left here to drink it," he muttered.

People were trickling back into the town. The captain bought bread for the whole company from a young woman with haunted eyes. Haunted, but practical.

"Burned the house," she said, eyes on the west. "Couldn't burn the ovens, though, could they? Little fucks."

They rode north on the east side of the Albin in the morning, and Ranald told them of having met the Queen at the ford as her boats rowed past.

Past Albinkirk the huntsmen ranged wider, over the hills on either side. Summer was coming and the abandoned farms seemed sinister in their wrappings of verdant life. Grains stood tall and ripe and there wasn't going to be a soul to harvest it.

The captain watched it go by.

Ser Alcaeus rode by his side. "There were men and women in these farms when I came through in late winter."

The captain shook his head. "I wonder if men will ever farm here again," he said.

Two days north of Albinkirk, they came to the crossroads and made camp. The East Road ran up over the passes and down into the Vale of Delf, and on into the Morea.

The North Road ran into the Hills, past the Inn of Dorling and eventually to the Lakes and the Wall.

That night, over dinner in his tent, the captain put a map on the table. "Jehannes, you'll take the company east to Morea. Find us a secure camp. I'll join you in a ten-day."

Jehannes made a face. He looked at Tom Lachlan. "If this is so important, why don't we all go?"

Tom laughed. "We're going to see the Wyrm, Jehannes. Not pay a call on a lady, nor smoke out a company of brigands."

The captain leaned over the table. "The Wyrm is a creature of the Wild. A Power like Thorn. And the company won't impress it. Him."

Not like Thorn, Harmodius said in the captain's head.

Jehannes shook his head. "I mislike it."

"Reservation noted," the captain said.

Tom sat back, his booted feet on one of the captain's stools. "Ahh. I can smell the hills already."

Ranald nodded. "At some point," he said, "we need to talk about the drove."

Tom nodded.

The captain looked at Ser Alcaeus. "We won't be gone long," he said. "And Jehannes can deal with any emergency."

The Morean knight raised an eyebrow. "I never thought otherwise, messire," he said. "But I will be with you."

Ranald shook his head. "No offence. But why?"

The Morean shrugged. Twirled his moustaches. "It is a Deed," he said. "I wish to see a dragon."

The captain smiled.

When the company's wagons rolled, the captain sat his elegant riding horse under the shade of a great oak tree and watched them go by. Men saluted him. It made him want to cry.

There was Bent, riding with Long Paw; behind him rode No Head and Jack Kaves and Cuddy. They were laughing as they passed, but they all gave him a smile and a nod. Behind them were younger men—Tippit arguing with Ben Carter and Kanny about something. They stopped when they saw him, and saluted—Ben Carter drew his sword to salute, and then looked sheepish about it.

Dan Favor rode by with Ser Milus and Francis Atcourt, who was explaining a jousting technique using a walking-stick tucked under his arm.

And more, and more. Men-at-arms, valets, squires, archers. Wagoners and tailors, prostitutes and seamstresses.

Sauce—Ser Alison Graves, now—made her horse rear a little, and flicked him a showy salute. And near the back of the column, Mag the seamstress hugged her man and rode her donkey clear of the column's dust to join the captain. "If it please m'lord," she said.

"Your downcast eyes are wasted on me," he said.

"I would like to accompany you," she said.

He rolled his eyes. "Why?" he asked. "A few days of sleeping on the ground and bad food?"

In his mind Harmodius said, *Excellent.*

So when the column was gone, headed up the long ridge to the east, Ranald turned his horse's head north. "I don't know where you are sleeping tonight, Captain," he said. "But I'm for the Inn of Dorling." To Mag, he said, "It's a little more comfortable than the cold, hard ground."

The Inn of Dorling—The Red Knight

The Keeper came into the yard with eyes as wide as new-minted pennies. His people were on the walls, and the gate was open to receive them.

His eyes went right past Ranald—wearing armour like a knight, and a red tabard. He nodded to the captain. "You are welcome here, messire. The best of everything, the most reasonable prices."

"Don't you know your own kin?" Ranald drawled.

Tom kicked free of his stirrups and dismounted in a clash of plate and mail. "I hear my brother married your Sarah," he said.

The Keeper looked back and forth. "By God!" he said.

Tom took him in a bear hug.

"We all thought you were dead," said the Keeper.

Tom growled. "Not yet, ye bastard."

He looked past the Keeper at the young woman on the porch. "Hello, spark. You'll be Sarah. Last I saw you, you was smaller than a pig."

"Now I'm big enough to carry your brother's seed," she said.

He left the Keeper's embrace and gave her a hug.

The captain hadn't seen Bad Tom as a man who embraced people. It shook him a little.

"Hillmen," Ser Alcaeus said. "I'm quite fond of them."

"You sound like you are talking about dogs," Mag said.

Alcaeus snorted. "Touché, madame. But they are more like us than you Albans. They burn hot."

Ranald dismounted and kissed Sarah first. Then hugged the Keeper. He went to his malle, slung across the back of his horse, and took out a slim leather envelope, the size of a letter.

He tossed it to the Keeper.

The Keeper looked at it, frowning.

"Six hundred silver leopards," Ranald said. "In a note of hand on a bank in Etrusca. That's yours. And another twelve hundred for Sarah." He gave the girl a lop-sided grin. "I sold the herd."

She clapped her hands together.

Men in the courtyard grinned. There were two dozen hillmen—local herdsmen, small farmers, and the like—and every one of them knew in that instant that his money wasn't lost.

They grinned. Embraced. Gathered round Ranald and slapped his back, shook his hand.

The Red Knight laughed, to find himself so far from the centre of attention.

But the Keeper disentangled himself from the celebrations shaping in his courtyard and came forward. "I'm the Keeper," he said. "I'm guessing you're the Red Knight."

The captain nodded. "Men call me the captain," he said. "Friends do, anyway."

The Keeper nodded. "Ay—Red Knight's a heavy handle to carry and no mistake. Come off your horses, now, and my people will see to you. Leave your cares here, and come and be easy."

Easy it was. The captain shucked off his riding armour and left it in a heap for Toby and went down the steps to the common room, where he found his brother and Ser Alcaeus sampling the ale.

Mag came and sat by herself, but the captain wasn't having any of it. He walked to her table, and offered his hand. "Ma dame," he said. "Come and sit with us."

"Mag the seamstress with three belted knights?" she asked. There was a wicked gleam in her eyes, but the words seemed sincere.

"Play piquet, mistress?" asked Gawin.

She let her eyes drop. "I know the rules," she said, ill-at-ease.

"We'll play for small stakes," Ser Gawin said.

"Couldn't we play for love?" she asked.

Gawin gave her an odd look. "I haven't felt cards in my hands for a month," he said. "They need a little fire."

Mag looked down. "If he takes all my money—"

"Then I'll order a dozen more of your caps," the captain said.

Looking at the seamstress, the captain smiled inwardly. *How powerful is she, Magus?*

Hard to say, young man. Untrained talent. She had to learn everything for herself, from first principles.

Ah.

Possibly the greatest of us all, though. She was never trained. She has no chains.

The captain sat watching Gawin deal the cards. Something about the hawkish expression on Mag's face gave her away.

But a very limited repertoire . . .

Harmodius spluttered in the captain's palace. *Drink some wine, so I can taste it. She may have had a limited grimmoire, but not any more—eh, young man? She has your phantasms, and mine, and all of the Abbess's. And Amicia's, too*

As do I. As does—

Yes.

Mag sorted her cards. A boy brought an armload of sawn oak and started to lay a fire. The smell of lamb filled the common room.

Gawin sat back. "Captain? I need to borrow some money."

The captain looked at him.

Mag was grinning.

"Doubled and rebated," Maggie said.

"I'll never be wed at this rate," Gawin said.

"Wed?" asked the captain.

Ser Alcaeus smiled politely into his ale. "To the Queen's Lady Mary, if I'm not mistaken," he said politely.

The captain laughed and laughed, remembering her. "A most beautiful lady," he said.

"Eldest daughter of Lord Bain." Gawin looked off into the distance.

"She loves me," he said suddenly. He choked on the words. "I—I'm not worthy of her regard."

The captain reached out to his brother tentatively but Gawin didn't seem to notice.

Youth. It's wasted on the young.

Alcaeus barked a laugh. "Listen, messire. I have known a few knights. You cede worthiness to none."

Gawin said nothing. He drank off the rest of his jack, and raised his cup to the tap-boy. "Wine, boy. And in truth—" He rose. "I need to piss."

Alcaeus cleared his throat when Gawin was gone. "I can't help but note," he said with some diffidence, and paused. "He calls you brother."

The captain laughed. "He does me that honour." *Here we go.*

"I had thought—pardon me, messire—" Ser Alcaeus sat back.

"You thought I was some man's bastard. And here's the great Duke of Strathnith's son, calling me brother." The captain leaned forward.

Alcaeus met his eye steadily. "Yes."

The captain nodded. "I had thought—pardon *me*, messire—I had thought that you were a free lance, a knight on errantry, joining my company. And yet—" He smiled. "Sometimes, I might be tempted to a thought. And that thought..." He sat back.

Mag looked back and forth. "Men," she said quietly.

"What thought would that be?" Ser Alcaeus whispered.

The captain drank some excellent ale. "Sometimes it seems anything I say to you will go straight to the Emperor." He shrugged. "I mean no insult. You are his liege man."

"Yes," Ser Alcaeus admitted.

"And his cousin," the captain went on.

"Ah? You know this?" Ser Alcaeus sighed.

"I guessed. So as to my own parentage—"

Ser Alcaeus leaned forward. "Yes?"

"It is not your business, messire. Am I clear?" he said leaning forward.

Ser Alcaeus didn't flinch. "Men will speculate," he said.

"Let them," the captain said.

Mag put a hand on the table and picked up the cards—large squares, beautifully painted. "People are watching you, my lords. You look like two men about to draw daggers."

Alcaeus finished his ale. "Beer makes men melancholy, " he said. "Let's have wine, and I'll think no more about it."

The captain nodded. "I don't mean to be a touchy bastard. But I am."

Alcaeus nodded and extended his hand. "For what it is worth, so am I. A bastard."

The captain's eyes widened. He reached out and took the hand. "Thanks for that."

Alcaeus laughed. "No one has ever thanked me for being a by-blow before." He turned to Mag. "Would you like me to shuffle?" he asked.

She shook her head. "You rich boys," she said. "You think bastardy matters? Look at yourselves—gold rings, fine swords, wool cotes worth fifty leopards. Fine horses. By the Gentle Jesu, m'lords. Do you know what a poor man has?"

"Parents?" Ser Alcaeus said.

"Hunger," Mag answered.

"God's blessing," the captain said.

Gawin came back. He had a glow on, a brittle humour. His eyes sparkled. "A fine inn. Maybe the best I've ever seen. Look at that lass—red hair. Red! I've never seen so much red hair in all my life." He looked around. "Their fires burn hotter, or so men say."

Maggie smiled, reached under her cap and teased out the end of her braids. Her hair was bright red. "Really, ser knight?" she said.

Gawin sat back and laughed. The captain laughed harder, and Alcaeus caught it too. It was infectious.

As if his laughter was a signal, the Inn burst into life. Tom and Ranald came in, and joined their table, and men and women came pouring in. Local farmers and shepherds from the hills arrived as the word spread, and the mercenaries who served the Keeper, and a tinker and his apprentices—the smith, and his apprentices too.

The common room could hold them all, well enough.

Men called for music, and Tom sang surprisingly well. Gawin turned to the captain amidst the uproar. "You used to play the harp," he said.

The captain frowned. "Not in years. And not here."

But the Keeper had heard him. He took a harp down from the wall and put it in the captain's arms. He shushed the room—something he did as easily as a magus might cast a spell.

"There's a man here as may be a harper," said the Keeper.

The captain cursed Gawin under his breath.

"Give me some time," he said, when it was clear to him they wouldn't let him off. He took the harp and his second cup of wine and walked out into the summer night of the yard.

It was quiet out there.

Sheep baaed, and cattle lowed, and the sounds of men in the Inn were muted, like the babble of a distant brook.

He started to tune the harp. There was a plectrum in the base-board, just where he would have expected it, and a clever mechanical key for the strings.

Let me, said Harmodius. *It's just mathematica.*

He drew power, and cast—and his power manifested in the strings.

The rule of eight, rendered in sinew, said the dead Magus.

Thanks, said the captain. *I always hated tuning.*

He walked about the yard, plucked out a simple tune—the first he'd learned—and walked back into the Inn.

They fell quiet when he appeared, and he sat down with Gawin and played some simple stuff. He played *There Was a Squire of Great Renown* and everyone sang, and he played *Green Sleeves* and *Lovely On the Water.* He made mistakes, but the audience was forgiving.

"Play for dancing!" the young widow called.

The captain was about to admit he didn't know any dances, but Harmodius forestalled him.

Allow me.

His fingers plucked the strings slowly, and a jig peeled out—slowly at first, and then faster and faster, and then it was a reel and then it was a hillman dance tune, sad and wild and high—

The captain watched his fingers fly over the strings, and wasn't altogether pleased. But the music swept on, higher and higher, and the men fell out of the dance, and the women danced, skirts kirtled up, legs flashing, heads turning and Mag jumped up and leapt into the circle.

The harp grew warm under his hands.

Sarah Lachlan leaped and flashed like a salmon. Mag gave a turn and one of the Inn's servants twirled in billow of skirts. The men applauded wildly as the hands on the harp fell still, and the captain seized control again.

Ahh, said Harmodius. *I had forgotten.*

Please don't do that again, old man. The captain went to steady his own breathing. People were crowding around him, slapping his back.

"I swear," said the Keeper. "You play like a man possessed."

Later when men and women had paired off, when Mag had gone, bright eyed, to her room, and Ranald had been congratulated by every man and woman there, and when Ser Alcaeus had the Inn's prettiest serving girl in his lap—he went back outside.

He stood under the stars, and listened to the cattle.

He played *Green Grow the Rushes* to them.

Harmodius snorted.

In the morning, they mounted for the ride north. None of the captain's companions seemed to have a hard head and he was surprised to see the Keeper mount a fine riding horse, as eastern in its blood as the captain's own.

The Keeper nodded to the captain. "You're a fair harper and no mistake, m'lord. And a good sport."

The captain bowed. "Your house is one of the finest I've ever visited," he said. "I could live here."

"You'd need to learn some more tunes first," Gawin said.

"Coming to see the Wyrm?" Ranald asked the Keeper.

He nodded. "This is my business as well as yours an' Tom's.

They rode.

There was a good path, the width of two horsemen, and it ran like a snake between the hills, and the bottoms of valleys were damp and the heights were rocky. They didn't go fast.

Crossing the Irkill River took half a day, because the bridge was out. The Keeper begged a favour of the captain and sent Toby back to the Inn with the news.

"This is my business," he said. "And I don't like it." The bridge looked as if a battering ram had struck it—it was beaten to flinders, heavy oak beams now splinters.

That night they slept in a cot by a quiet burn. The farmer and his family moved out into a stone barn so that the gentles could use the beds.

In the morning, the captain left a silver penny and they were away with the sun, full to bursting with fresh yogurt and honey and walnuts.

They rode higher and higher into the hills, and passed a pair of heavy wagons loaded to the tall seat with whole, straight trees—oak, maple, and walnuts, trunks bigger around than a tall man might reach, and straight as giant arrow-shafts. The wagoners allowed as there were lumbermen working in the vales.

Gawin sneered. "It must be all they can do to move these monsters."

The wagoners shrugged. "Maybe. Maybe not."

Ser Alcaeus waited until they were past. "They float the larger logs on the water."

The Keeper nodded grimly. "That's what happened to my bridge." He led them down into the dale and they found the foresters hard at work—not local men, but easterners.

They had cut a swath through the dale, and a dam on the big stream that fed the Irkill. The leader of the woodsman stood in the new clearing, obvious in his long cloak. He had a heavy axe in his hand, gull winged and long hafted, and his wood-cutters were tall and strong, with long beards.

The Keeper rode up to him. "Good day to you," he said.

The man nodded. His eyes were wary. He watched the troop of horsemen—more armoured power than anyone liked to see, especially far from home.

"What can I do for you?" he said. His accent was thick.

The Keeper smiled pleasantly enough. "Pack and leave. Let the water off your dam slowly."

The woodsman's eyes widened and then narrowed. "Who are you, then?"

His men were gathering, and horns were blowing.

The Keeper didn't touch his weapons. "I'm the Keeper of Dorling," he said. "You owe me the cost of a bridge, and more. No one logs these dales without my leave—and the time to cut was early spring, when the last snow lies on the ground."

The captain swatted a black fly.

The woodsman frowned. "The woods are any man's, or no man's. This is Wild Land."

"No. These Hills are in the Circle of the Wyrm," the Keeper said.

The woodsmen began to gather. Many had spears, and every man had an axe. They were forming.

Gawin dismounted and, as fast as a dancer, remounted on his war horse. He drew his great sword.

The Keeper raised his hand. "Peace, ser knight." He looked back at them. "No need for arms."

"You have wisdom, old man," called the leader of the woodsmen.

"You have been warned," said the Keeper.

The woodsman spat. "I laugh at your warning. What business is it of yours? And if one of your bridges is swept away by my logs—" He shrugged. "There is wood everywhere. Build another."

The Keeper looked around at the crowd of woodsmen. "If you remain here, every one of you will die," he said.

They looked unimpressed.

The Keeper wheeled his horse. "Let's ride," he said.

The Keeper led the way, and they rode at a trot until they were out of the dale and up the next green ridge.

"I feel as if I just ran away," Gawin said.

The captain grimaced. "Me, too."

The Keeper turned in the saddle. "If the Wyrm is of a mind, he'll kill them all for this, and us, too, by association."

That night, for the first time, they camped. There was little grass for the horses, and they had to put nosebags on them and use the oats that the pack animals carried. Mag watched Gawin start dinner and then pushed him out of the way.

"By the good and sweet Christ," she said. "At least use a clean knife."

Alcaeus laughed and took the cook knives to the stream and washed them, scouring them with sand.

The Keeper rode out with the hillmen and came back with two big turkeys.

Gawin greeted them with a pair of big trout. "I take it there's not much in the way of angling in these parts," he said. "Glad I brought a line."

Mag looked at the birds and the fish. "What you catch, you clean," she said. "I'm a cook, not a servant."

That made the captain laugh. He'd spent the late afternoon building a shelter and digging her a fire pit and now he helped clean the fish with a good grace. They drank the last of the wine by firelight.

"Tomorrow," said the Keeper.

They rode with the dawn.

The next range of hills was bare of trees, as if a horde of sheep had clipped them clean—green grass rippled in the wind like a green sea, and the hills rolled away like a greater sea—from the height of their ridge, they could see twenty more ridges spread out like pleats in green wool.

Mag raised a hand. "Is that an eagle?" she asked.

Far to the north-east, a great bird rode the air over the hills.

The Keeper looked under his hand.

The captain looked too. The great creature was farther away than he had imagined, and he looked and looked until he appreciated what he was seeing, and then his heart beat in pure fear.

"Good Christ," said Mag.

"My God," said Gawin.

"That's the Wyrm of Erch," said the Keeper.

It was flying. It was larger than a castle, and it was flying over the hills to the north. Even as they watched, the titanic dragon turned—for a moment its immense and spiky tail was clearly silhouetted against the northern sky, and its huge wings swept out on either side.

"Good Christ," Mag said again.

It was faster too.

The captain couldn't take his eyes off it.

So, Harmodius said in his mind. *So.* The dead Magus sounded, if anything, more awestruck than the living captain.

The wind-storm of its wing beats began to echo across the hills. The only sound the captain could imagine like it was the beat of the great mills in Galle—he'd heard them in the low country.

Whoosh.

Whoosh.

It was as big as the hills.

His riding horse began to panic. Mag's threw her with a sudden twist and bolted, and all the horses went wild. The captain dismounted, hauled his horse's head down, and knelt by the seamstress.

"Nothing hurt but my pride," she snapped. "And nothing much there to bruise."

The Wyrm was coming right at them.

Its wings swept up, their tips almost touching, and then down, and the power of their passage left a swath of matted grass far below as the Wyrm passed over them. It was enormous. The captain was able to count to ten while the immense thing passed over him. His riding horse stood frozen in terror and the dragon's shadow covered the ground for a hundred paces in all directions—more. It covered the sun.

He blinked his eyes and looked again.

Look in the Aether, said Harmodius.

The captain raised his *sight and staggered in renewed awe. If Thorn had been a pillar of green, the Wyrm was—was the sun.*

The captain shook his head.

Gawin threw his head back and whooped.

Bad Tom laughed aloud.

"Now that, my friends," he said, "is a Power of the Wild, and no mistake."

They rode down into the next valley as the rain clouds came on, building to the north over the loch. A series of lochs fell away for leagues—larger and larger, until they merged into a sheet of water twenty leagues or more away. It was a superb view. In front of them, just short of the first loch, was a ford over a burn. They got cloaks off their saddles as they came to the stream. No one spoke much.

The rain came down like a curtain, sweeping from the north end of the valley, cutting off the view of the lochs.

Beyond was only rain, and black cloud.

"It's like the end of the world," Mag said.

The captain nodded. Ser Alcaeus crossed himself.

They crossed the stream quickly at a cairn. The captain rode off to the side, and then rejoined them. "Let's move," he said. "The water here rises very quickly and very high."

Gawin watched the water. "Salmon in that loch," he said wistfully.

On the far side was a narrow track that rose on the hillside. It was just wide enough for a horse, and they picked their way in single file, with the Keeper at the head and Bad Tom last.

It took them an hour to climb the ridge, and the rain caught them in the open again. It was cold, and they were soaked through despite heavy cloaks and hoods.

Up, and up they went.

At the top of the ridge was a seat of stone facing west.

The captain looked at it. So did Mag. It held the residue of power.

The Keeper didn't stop. He rode down the far side.

From the very top, just beyond the High Seat, the captain could see the ghostly impression of crags to the north—far away, and gleaming white. Almost everything else was lost in the rain, although they were above it for a few hundred paces, and then they rode back into it.

Down and down, and trusting his horse. His light saddle was soaked, and he worried for his clothes. For summer, this was *cold* rain.

His brain was running wild.

"We're going to *visit* that?" he asked, sounding more like Michael than he would have liked.

Ranald turned and looked back. "Aye."

It was afternoon by the time they came out of the bottom of the clouds and could see, through gaps in the rain curtain, another valley of lochs. It was oriented differently—in this one the lochs grew smaller as the valley rose to the east and north, into high crags.

The Keeper reached the first ford, marked again with a cairn of stones that leaped to the eye in the naked, empty landscape of green grass and rock and water.

"Water's high," he shouted.

The captain leaned out and watched it for a long minute. They could hear rocks being rolled under the water.

The stream rushed down a narrow gorge above them, gathered power between two enormous rocks, and shot into the loch on their right—a sheet of water perhaps three hundred paces long and very deep.

Bad Tom laughed. He roared, "Follow me," and turned his horse's head south. He seemed to ride straight out into the loch, yet his horse was virtually dry-shod as he rode a half circle a few paces out from the shoreline.

The captain followed, as did Ranald. Looking down into the water, he could see a bank of rocks and pebbles just under the water.

"In the spring run-off," Ranald said, "the force of water pushes all the rock out of the mouth of the stream. Makes a bank—like yon." He laughed. "Any hillman knows."

Tom looked back at the Keeper. "Aye. Any *true* hillman."

The Keeper shot him a look, but Tom was immune to looks.

They started up the valley, wet and feeling surly.

The trail followed the stream past a magnificent waterfall, and then they climbed the cliff—the trail was just wide enough for an experienced rider to stay mounted, and it cut back and back—nine switchbacks to climb a few hundred feet. Ser Alcaeus's war horse balked, and would not climb until Ser Alcaeus dismounted, walked back, and fetched him.

Mag dismounted at a switchback and looked at the captain.

He understood. She was not going to *ask* for help. He took her horse by the reins.

"Thanks," she said.

She began to walk up the track.

He led her horse.

At the top of the cliff there was another loch. It was smaller, deeper, trapped in narrow cleft and dammed off by the ridge of rock that made the cliff. Above the loch was a long, grassy ridge that rose and rose. Above it all towered a mighty crag, covered in snow—but the snow line was still as far above them as they had come in two days.

The trail ran along the banks of the loch, in deep grass.

There were sheep high on the hillsides.

The only sound was the muted roar of the waterfall coming off the loch behind them, and the distant babble of the stream off the glaciers running into the top of the loch.

There was a gravel beach at the top of the loch. The captain caught the Keeper and pointed to it. "Camp?" he said.

The Keeper shook his head. "He's telling us to go away. This weather's unnatural." He shrugged. "We're in for a bad night."

The captain was looking through the rain at the distant beach. "I see wood there."

Mag nodded. "I saw rowans up in the highest valleys," she said.

"Rowan, alder, and older things," agreed the Keeper. "We can't have a fire, this close to the Wyrm."

"Why not?" the captain asked.

"The Wyrm has rules." The Keeper shrugged.

The captain shook his head. "Taking living wood might incur the wrath of a Power," he said. "Dead wood on a beach, however—" He managed a smile and shrugged off the rain. "There's an overhang there. Gather all the horses against it to break the wind."

The Keeper shrugged. "On your head be it. If we turn back now, we can have better weather before sunset."

Gawin rubbed water out of his moustache. "Tell me why we didn't camp by a loch with fish?" he asked.

The captain looked out over the rain-swept sheet of water. "I'd bet a golden leopard to a copper there's salmon in this water," he said. "But I wouldn't be the man to catch one."

Gawin smiled. "You don't know much about salmon, brother, if you think they can climb a hundred foot of falls."

"My bet stands," the captain said. "But to catch one would be a deadly insult to our host, and as the Keeper has noted, he's not in love with us at the moment."

Mag cackled. "So worried about a bit of wet. I'm twice the age of most of you, and I can roll up in a wet cloak and sleep. My joints will cry in the morning, but what of it? I saw a dragon fly in the dawn." She looked at them. "I'm not turning back, gentles."

They constructed a shelter from spear poles and heavy wool blankets, pinned down with the biggest rocks on the beach. The wind tested it for a while, but didn't seem interested in a real contest.

The captain rode off with Ser Alcaeus, and together they roamed the long beach and picked up every stick on it—it made a respectable woodpile.

"And where'd it come from, I'd like to know?" asked the Keeper.

The captain shrugged. "Our host put it out for us to find, I expect."

Gawin, a practised hunter, took a fire kit from his pack and looked at his brother across the fire pit. "Like being boys again," he said.

"We never tried to light a fire in a storm like this," the captain said.

"We did, too," said Gawin. "I couldn't get it lit, you used power, and Pater cursed you."

"You're making this up," the captain said, shaking his head.

Gawin gave him the oddest look. "No," he said. He used his body and his soaking cloak to cover the fire pit, and the captain's quick hands laid a bed of twigs—damp, but dry as drift wood ever is. Gawin put a bed of dry tow from his fire kit inside a nest of birch bark.

"Bark from home," he said.

The captain shrugged.

Gawin laid charred linen deep in the tow, and then struck his fire steel against a small shard of flint until spark flew. The char-cloth lit, he dropped it into the nest in his hand, and blew. Smoke billowed out. He blew a second time, a long, slow breath, and more smoke came.

The captain leaned over and blew.

Before his breath was out, Gawin blew, and the whole nest burst into flame. Gawin dropped it onto the waiting twigs, and both men added more, and more—speed and accuracy embodied.

In two cracks of lightning, they had a fire.

Maggie laughed. "You could have just magicked it," she said. "Instead of showing off with your woodcraft."

Gawin frowned.

The captain smiled. "I avoided the use of power for many years." He shrugged. "Why waste it?"

She nodded, understanding.

They made tea from the water of the loch, ate cold meat, and curled up to sleep. The stones of the beach were cold and wet, but the wool tent and the warmth of the horses won out in the end.

They took watches in turns. The captain took the mid watch, and he sat high above the beach on a rock. The wind was gone, and with it the rain, and he watched a thousand thousand stars and the moon.

May we talk?

No.

You've closed your door and you aren't responding to Mag and she's confused. You are linked to her. The courtesy of mages requires you—

No. The captain looked out over the loch. *Go away. Not at home.*

His head hurt.

In the morning, they drank hot tea, ate fresh Johnny cake made in ashes on a flat rock by Mag, and rode on. The horses were tired and cold, but by a miracle none of them were lame or sick despite a cold night on a mountainside. They followed the trail up over the green ridge at the north end of the loch, down into a shallow, high valley of green turf with the stream ripping through, full of rain water. From there down a rocky course at the centre, and then they cut back twice, riding up another ridge. The green of the hills was deceiving—what looked like one endless ridge proved to be a succession of them, one merging to another in the grey light.

The Keeper shook his head. "It wasn't like this the last time," he said.

Ranald laughed. "Never the same twice, is it, Keeper?"

The Keeper shrugged. "This is only my second trip, Ranald."

Bad Tom grunted. "Never been, meself. But Hector said it was different every time."

Up and up.

They climbed the next ridge as the sun struggled through the curtain of cloud, and at the top of the next ridge, in a fold of the earth, sat a shepherd's cot with a curl of peat-smoke coming out of a low chimney.

Sheepfolds extended right out from the walls of the stone house, as if the whole place were built for sheep.

The trail led from their ridge to the door of the shepherd's cot, straight as a lance.

"Biggest sheep I've ever seen." Alcaeus was rubbing the water out of his hair.

They rode down the track. The stone wall by the cot had a gate with richly worked iron hinges and the captain leaned over and opened it.

On the far side, hidden by the crest of the hill, was a brick horse barn. It had eleven stalls.

The captain grinned. "I'll take this as a sign we're welcome," he said.

The brick horse barn looked very out of place.

"I know this barn," Gawin said. "This is Diccon Pyle's barn." He looked at Ranulf, who nodded.

"From Harndon," Ranulf said. "I was just thinking of it. Warm, snug—" He blew out a breath.

They took the horses into the barn. Their hooves rang on the brick floor, louder than the captain would have thought possible. There were oats in every manger, fresh straw on the floors, clean water in the buckets.

They unsaddled the horses, and took the gear off the pack animals. The captain curried his new destrier and put a blanket—ready to hand—over him. Gawin and Alcaeus did the same, as did the Keeper and Ranald. Bad Tom stood in the doorway, a sword in his hand.

"I don't like this. It's fey." Tom thumbed the edge of the blade.

"Not a problem you can solve with a sharp blade," said the captain. He got the tack off Tom's big gelding. "Relax."

Tom didn't leave the doorway. "I want to get this over," he said.

Ranald went and took his arm. "Not the way to go, Tom. Be *easy.*"

Mag smiled at Ser Alcaeus. "Would you be so kind as to have the saddle off my horse, ser knight? I'm a poor weak woman."

Ser Alcaeus grinned.

Mag gathered her cloak, pushed past Bad Tom, and walked to the door. She knocked politely.

The knock sounded as loud as the crack of a trebuchet in the silence.

The door opened.

Mag went in. The Keeper paused at his currying and dropped the brush. "Damn," he said. And ran for the door, but it was already closed. He knocked, and the door opened, and he was gone.

"I think the rest of us might as well go in together," the captain said. He wiped his hands on straw. He walked up to the door. "You, too, Tom."

Tom was breathing hard. "It's *all magick.*"

The captain nodded and spoke carefully, as he would to a skittish horse or a scared child. "It is, that. We're in his hands, Tom. But we knew that."

Tom stood straight. "You think I'm afraid."

Ranald made a motion of negation.

The captain nodded. "Yes, Tom. You are afraid. If you weren't, to be honest, you'd be some sort of madman."

"Which you may be, anyway," Ranald said.

Tom managed a smile. "I'm ready."

The captain rapped at the door.

And it opened.

The croft was low and close yet surprisingly spacious. The rooftrees were just above the captain's head height, too low for Tom, and the building had a roof-end hearth, not a proper fireplace at all. The fire in it was enormous, filling it like a furnace, so that individual logs couldn't be made out in the inferno—but just enough heat escaped to make the room pleasant on a cool summer evening.

Around the fireplace were heavy wooden chairs, covered in wool cloths. Some cloths were armorial, and one was an ancient tapestry, cut up and sewn to cover the chair.

The cot beams were black with age, but carving could still be seen on them.

Over the fireplace, a pair of swords were crossed and, on the main beam, a spear was carefully set on a long row of iron nails.

Mag sat with the Keeper, her legs crossed. And beyond her sat a small man smoking a long pipe.

He was so very ordinary that their eyes passed over him, at first. He wore a plain wool cote of coarse wool, and leggings of the same, and his weather-beaten face was neither handsome nor ugly, old or young. His eyes were black.

He opened them, and they were instantly arresting.

"Welcome," said the Wyrm.

The captain bowed. He looked around, and none of his companions was moving—except that the men behind him in the doorway were suddenly sitting in chairs, hands on their knees.

He hung his cloak with theirs, and went to a seat.

"Why is no one speaking?" he asked.

"You are all speaking," the Wyrm said. "It is easier for all of us if I deal with each in turn, in privacy."

"Ah," said the captain. "I'll wait my turn."

The Wyrm smiled. "I can talk to you all at once," he said. "It is you who needs the feeling that there is structure, not me." He took a pull on his pipe.

The captain nodded.

Of course time means nothing to them, Harmodius said.

"Are the two of you together?" the Wyrm asked.

"There's just one of me," the captain said. "I can't speak for Harmodius."

The Wyrm smiled again. "Very wise of you to see that. You know that if you do not rid yourself of him, he will, in time, demand control. He cannot help himself. I offer this information free of obligation."

The captain nodded. A cup of mulled wine appeared at his elbow. He picked it up and drank it gratefully.

"Why have you come?" asked the Wyrm. "You, at least, had to know what I was."

The captain nodded. "I guessed." He looked around. "Are there rules? Do I have three questions? Fifty?"

The Wyrm shrugged. "I don't want visitors. I try never to look into the future. All that is for my busy, busy kin. They plot, and strive. I live. I seek truth." He smiled. "Sometimes I grow lonely, and a lucky traveller is brought in for entertainment." His smile became a feral grin.

The captain drank more wine. "What of the Lachlans?"

The Wyrm pulled on his pipe, and smoke wound to the ceiling and up into the draught of the roaring fire. "That is your question?"

The captain shook his head. "No, but they are my sworn men and I need to know they are being well served."

The Wyrm smiled. "The concept of fealty comes so naturally to men and I am having a difficult time being bound by it. But I will deal fairly with Tom and Ranald. Ask your own."

The captain swirled his wine, and clamped down on a question about Amicia. "Can the conflict between Man and Wild be resolved?" he asked.

"Is that your question?" asked the Wyrm.

"Yes," said the captain.

The seated figure smoked. "How delightful." He walked to the mantelpiece and opened a stone jar, took out a handful of old leaves and tamped them into the bowl of his pipe. "Do you believe in free will, prince?"

The captain was growing hot, and he stood up and took off his cote and hung it by the mantel to dry with a muttered "beg your pardon" to his host. He sat again.

"Yes," he said.

"Why?" asked the Wyrm.

The captain shrugged. "Either I have free will, or there's no point in playing."

The Wyrm rocked its head back and forth. "What if I were to tell you that you only had free will in some things, and not in others?"

The captain found he was chewing one of his riding gloves. He stopped. "I'd suggest that my power to affect the universe is about the same whether I have free will in every action or only in one."

"Interesting," said the Wyrm. "Man and the Wild are merely concepts. Philosophical constructs. If they were created to represent—to symbolize—opposition, then could they ever be reconciled? Can alpha and omega switch places in the alphabet?"

"Next you will tell me there is no Wild. And there is no Man." The captain smiled.

The Wyrm laughed. "You've taken this class before, I take it."

"I sat at the feet of some philosophers in the East," the captain said. "I had no idea they were dragons, although, now that I think of it—"

The Wyrm laughed again. "You please me. So I will answer your question. Man and the Wild, while being two sides of a coin, can live together—just as the coin lives perfectly well in the purse."

"Separate?" the captain asked.

The Wyrm shrugged. "Nothing about a coin is separate, is it?" he asked.

The captain leaned back in his very comfortable chair.

"My brother died," Tom said. "He was your liege man, and he died. Tell us who killed him?"

The Wyrm shrugged. "He died outside my circle," he said. "I concede that I wasn't paying very much attention. I further concede that while my mind was taken with other affairs, some of the Wild peoples crossed my lands without my leave. But in truth, Tom, and Ranald, my circle is a creation for my own convenience. I scarcely trouble men, in or out of it, and you two are the first to demand some sort of action of me in a long enough amount of time to be meaningless."

"So you won't avenge him," Tom said. "Just tell me who killed him?" he asked.

"Are you telling me what I'm doing, or asking?" the Wyrm asked politely. "Is this your question?"

Ranald leaned forward. "Yes," he said. "It sounds odd but it isn't the Sossag I'm after, though they slayed Hector and me, too. It's Thorn. Thorn sent them—he summoned them. Drove them to war."

The Wyrm threw back his head and laughed. "Are you simple, Ranald Lachlan? The Wild Peoples do exactly as they please. They are not children. If they raided your brother, they did so apurpose."

"They'd never ha' been at the fords if it hadn't been for Thorn." Tom was insistent.

The Wyrm put his chin in his right hand. "How much of the truth would you like, hillman? Shall I tell you enough to spark an epic revenge? Or shall I tell you enough to render you incapable of action? Which would you prefer?"

Ranald chewed the end of his moustache. "What could you tell us that would make us unable to act?" he asked.

Tom glowered.

The Wyrm sat back and put his pipe down, put his hands behind his head. "The Sossag who killed Hector is called Ota Qwan. He is a worthy enemy for you, Tom—driven, passionate, highly skilled. Your riddle is that, in time, your captain will want him as an ally." The Wyrm smiled.

"And so you render Tom incapable of action?" Ranald asked. "You don't know Tom."

The Wyrm shook his head. "No. Because behind Ota Qwan was Skadai, who made the decision to risk my wrath and raid the hillmen and the drove. He's already dead, though. Behind Skadai is Thorn, who was pushed into war—" the Wyrm was smiling, "—by one of my kind, to whom you and your brother are less than ants, and who wishes to encompass not just the end of your brother, but the death of every man and woman in the entire circle of the world. I should offer you my thanks—I have just realised that I have slept through a cycle of drama. Things are moving out in the world. Damn the lot of you."

"His name?" Tom said.

"Tom Lachlan, you are a name of fear among men from East to West. Daemons and wyverns wet themselves in fear at the mere mention of your name." The Wyrm gazed at Tom with affection. "But my kind—nothing in your arsenal can harm us."

"His name?" asked Tom.

The Wyrm leaned forward. "I would like to deal with this myself."

Tom slapped his thigh. "Now you're talking, Wyrm. A good lord stands up for his man. But I'll help ye. Tell me his name, and together we'll put him down in the dust."

The Wyrm shook his head. "Are you to be drover, Tom?"

Tom shook his head. "I doubt I could. I'd kill every loon as bade me nay."

The Wyrm nodded. "Ranald?"

"I'd be proud to be drover. But I seek to be knighted by the king—to have a little treasure—so I may wed a lady." Ranald felt like a small boy confessing to stealing apples.

"None of these things is my concern," said the Wyrm. "Although the two of you are a pleasure to converse with."

"He's the man of reason," Tom said. "I'm the man of war. Two sides of a coin."

"Nothing about a coin is separate," the Wyrm said.

Mag sat with her hands folded in her lap.

"And how may I help you?" the Wyrm asked her.

"I'd like to defeat and destroy the sorcerer known as Thorn," she said.

"Revenge?" asked the Wyrm.

She shrugged. "A dog bit one of my children some years ago. He'd bitten other children. My husband went out with his crossbow and put the dog down." She met the Wyrm's eyes. "I'm sure that there was some revenge involved."

"But it was, in the main, it was about the other children?" asked the Wyrm.

She nodded.

"You are a very modest woman," said the Wyrm. "You allow men to speak their minds, and you keep yours to yourself."

She smiled and looked at her hands in her lap.

"But you, the Goodwife of Abbington, intend to encompass the destruction of Thorn, who has put himself on the path to be a Power." His black eyes sought hers.

She wouldn't let him in. "That's right," she said easily.

The Wyrm whistled soundlessly. "This war that you have all just experienced has enhanced your powers to a wonderful degree. Indeed, I was able to see you—really see you—as far away as Albinkirk."

Mag gave way to a satisfied chuckle. "I always knew I had the talent," she said. "But thanks to the old magister and the Abbess I know things, now." She looked up. "Terrifying things."

"Do you doubt God?" asked the Wyrm.

Mag turned her head away. "Who are you to ask that? Satan?"

The Wyrm laughed. "Not hardly, Mistress. Satan's idle young cousin, perhaps."

"Will you answer my question?" she asked.

"You haven't asked one," he said gently. "You've implied that you'd like my help in attacking Thorn, and you've implied that you'd like to know if there is a god."

She straightened her back. "I can find my way to God without you," she said.

"Good," said the Wyrm.

"I'd like your help with Thorn," she said.

"That's the other side of the same coin, surely," said the Wyrm. "If you can decide for yourself about God, you scarcely need me to tackle a mortal sorcerer."

"It would be easy for you," said Mag.

"No argument at all. In the end, that would be me putting down the dog. For *my* reasons." He put his chin in his hands.

She shook her head. "I understand, but I'd like you to separate the two sides of the coin."

"Nothing about a coin is separate," the Wyrm said.

"Nothing about a coin is separate," said the Wyrm.

The captain looked around to find all his companions also blinking like people coming out of sleep.

"It has been a great pleasure meeting you," he said. "The beds are warm, and the fire is real enough, and the food is, if I say so myself, exemplary. Please don't stint with the wine. I'd be affronted if you didn't try the harp on the wall." He smiled at them. "I have little interest in the affairs of the world, but I am choosing to help you, almost entirely to serve my own ends. Which, I will add, are infinitely less threatening to you and yours than any of the rest of my kin's might be. I seek only to be left alone—I have my own ambitions, and they have nothing to do with war, conquest, pain, or hate." He smiled, and just for a moment, they saw an enormous head with fangs the length of warships, slitted eyes as tall as church spires. "You will be my allies. You will go out in the world and serve my ends with your own plans and your free will." He smiled. "I doubt that we will succeed, but if we do we'll have the satisfaction of having been vastly the underdogs." He nodded, as if to himself. "Ah—the party-favours. I've made certain artefacts—or gathered them—for this. To each, her own. And in parting—" The Wyrm smiled at all of them. "May I leave you with some genuine wisdom, in place of all the humdrum claptrap? Do well. Act with honour and dignity. Not because there is some promised reward, but because it is the only way to live. And that is as true for my kind as for yours."

The captain was still pondering a smart remark when he realised that the Wyrm was no longer among them.

That was amazing, Harmodius said.

They lingered over breakfast.

"The marmalade is like—" Mag giggled, her mouth full of warm, crusty bread with rich new butter.

"Like God-made marmalade?" asked Ser Alcaeus.

"I feel like a thief," Ranald said. He'd taken one of the swords from over the fireplace.

Tom took down the other. He grinned. "God," he said, flicking his thumb over the blade. He gave a moan of pleasure as the blade he'd chosen swept through the air.

The Keeper shook his head. He had a box in his lap. "I'm afraid to open it."

Ser Alcaeus rose and took down the sword hanging behind the main roof beam—with a belt and scabbard. It matched his arms—a surprisingly short sword with a heavy wheel pommel. "These are things left for us. Indeed, unless I miss my guess, the whole cot is made for us."

"I'm not leaving until the marmalade is finished," Mag said, and laughed. She picked up her napkin to get the stickiness out of the corners of her mouth, and there was a chatelaine on the table beneath it—gold and silver and enamel, with sharp steel scissors, a needle case full of needles, and a dozen other objects suspended on chains—including a pair of keys.

"Oh," she said, and flushed, her hand to her bosom. "Oh, par dieu. It is magnificent."

Gawin tried some of the marmalade. "I had the most remarkable dream," he said. "I wore a green belt—" He stumbled to silence. There was a green belt around his hips, worked in green enamel with gold plaques, and from it hung a heavy dagger in green and gold.

The captain stood under the roof beam, looking up at the spear.

"Just take it, man!" said Tom.

The captain rubbed his chin. "I'm not sure I want it," he said.

Take it! Take it! Harmodius couldn't control himself.

Five feet of ancient blackthorn, knotty and yet straight as an arrow. And at the top, a long, heavy blade gleamed.

"Someone has taken the magister's staff, and fitted it like a glaive," the captain said.

Take it, you fool.

The captain rubbed his chin. "I'm going to see to the horses."

So much of my power. Please? He wouldn't have brought it here unless he trusted us to use it.

"I can't help but notice that his gifts either bind, are pointed, or are double edged," said the captain. "Belts and blades."

Don't be a fool.

Am I a fool to be slow to make use of tools I do not understand? asked the captain. *The stakes are very high. I will probably take it in the end. But not right now—*

He took his time currying the horses. They looked fat and happy. It had been a way of hiding from his father when he was young.

When they were all gleaming like the sun on the water of the high loch outside, he went back into the cot—so much bigger on the inside than the outside—and took the spear down from its nails.

It was a heavy blackthorn shaft, but the butt was spiked in bronze and inlaid in gold, and the head was magnificently worked—folded steel, carefully chiselled.

Oh. Empty. Harmodius lost all interest in it. *Not mine at all.*

The captain hefted it for a long time.

Then he frowned and tucked it under his arm.

One by one they filed out of the cot. Mag left last, and closed the door behind her.

She looked puzzled. "I thought it would…vanish," she said.

"He's not showy," the captain responded.

They all mounted, and rode over the ridges. In two ridges, the cot was gone, hidden in the folds of earth.

"If I ride back, will there be aught there?" Tom asked.

The captain shrugged. "Does it matter?"

"You know what?" Tom said. "He reminded me of you. Only—more so." He laughed.

The captain raised an eyebrow. "I think I'm flattered, Tom," he said.

Tom patted the sword at his side. "I have a magic sword," he said happily. "I want to go try it on something."

Ranald shook his head. "Tom, you *hate* magic."

Tom grinned. "Och. You can teach an old dog a new trick, if ye are patient."

Gawin shook his head. "Why us?"

The captain shook his head.

They rode on.

The woodsmen were gone. There was no pile of bodies, no line of graves, no rusting tools. Merely gone.

Over the Irkill a stone bridge stood on heavy pilings, as wide as two horsemen abreast or a single wagon, and on the other side sat a new keep—a square tower—with a small toll house.

It was solid, and smelled of new masonry. The Keeper sat in the road, looking at it.

"Open it," said the captain.

The Keeper looked at him.

"The box—open it." The captain crossed his arms.

There was an anticlimactic moment as the Keeper rooted in his malle and emerged with his box. He opened it.

The box held a circlet, an arm ring, and a key.

The key fitted the door of the keep.

The circlet fit on his brow. He tried it and then snatched it off.

"Damn," he said.

"He's telling you something," said Ranald.

"The arm ring is for the drover," said the Keeper. "I know it."

Ranald looked at it. "Leave it lie, then," he said. "I'll come back in spring, and we'll see."

They rode back to the inn.

Toby unpacked his master's portmanteau and appeared at his elbow. "M'lord?" he asked.

The captain was playing piquet with Maggie. He looked up.

"What do I do with these?" he asked. He held up two velvet bags. They all but glowed a deep, dark red.

"Not mine," the captain said.

"Begging your pardon, m'lord, but they was in your bag." Toby held them out again.

The captain looked in one, and laughed. "Why, Toby, I've just discovered our host was more thoughtful than I had imagined. Come here." He gestured to his new squire. "I assume these are for you." He handed the bag over.

In it was a pair of silver spurs. Rich squires wore such things.

Toby gasped.

The captain shook his head. "He knew we were coming, but we sent Toby back." He looked in the other bag. And frowned.

A small, and very beautiful ring, gleamed in the bottom of the bag. It said "IHS." "Ah," he said. "This is too much," he said quietly, and flung the bag across the room.

It bounced off the wall.

He went back to his cards.

In the morning, when he went to pay the Keeper, he found the ring among his coins.

Give it up said the magister. *He wants her, as well. You two are not done with each other, it seems.*

He embraced the Keeper. "Got anyone going west to Lissen Carak?" he asked.

The Keeper grinned. "In the autumn, maybe, and then only with twenty swords," he said.

The captain wrote a brief note on parchment. "Send this, then." He wrapped the ring in the parchment. It gave him the oddest feeling.

"Go well, Captain," said the Keeper. "Stop here when you come west for the tournament."

The captain raised his eyebrows.

"You are a famous knight," the Keeper said with his child-like delight in knowing news the others didn't know. "The Queen has ordained that there will be a great tournament at Lorica, at Pentecost in the New Year."

The captain rolled his eyes. "Not my kind of fight, Keeper."

The Keeper shrugged. "So you say."

They spent five days riding over the mountains to Morea. They came down the pass north of Eva and the captain took them south and then east over the hills to Delf. He didn't seem to be in a hurry. Gawin and Alcaeus were of the same mind, and Tom and Ranald saw the whole trip as an adventure, riding high on the hillsides, searching out caves...

"Looking for a fight," Mag said in disgust. "Can we get home?"

"Home to our company of hired killers?" said the captain.

Mag looked at him and shook her head. "Yes," she said. "If you must. Aren't you—excited? Hopeful? Interested?"

He was watching the two hillmen ranging high above them. Alcaeus had purchased a good goshawk from a peddler and was flying him at doves. Gawin was riding ahead, feet crossed over the pintle of his saddle, reading.

He shook his head. "Not really," he said. "I think I've just been enlisted by one mighty Power to fight another in a war not of my making, over things I don't understand." He rubbed his chin. "I swore off being a tool when I was a child."

"The Wyrm is good." Mag put a hand on his arm. "I can feel it."

The captain shook his head. "Mag, what do my thoughts of good and evil mean to the worms in the road? I can be the most honourable knight who ever lived, and my horse's iron-shod hooves will crush their soft bodies every step, after a rain." He smiled at her. "And I won't even know."

Down in the deep valley ahead of them, he could see rows of tents; a palisade; neat circles of heavy wagons, and over all, a banner, black, with lacs d'or worked in gold.

"Damn you," she said. "Why can't we just act? Why can't we simply win?"

The captain sighed. "Men love war because it is simple," he said. "Winning is never simple. I can win a fight—together, we can win a battle." He rubbed his beard. Down in the valley, men were pointing and messengers were mounting horses. "But turning victory in battle into something that lasts is like building a place to live. So much more complicated than building a fortress."

He pointed at the riders. "Luckily for me, those men are bringing me word of our contract. A nice little war." He forced a smile. "Something we can *win*."

Harndon City—Edward

Edward finished his first rondel dagger—a fine weapon with a precise triangular blade and an armour-piercing point—and handed it to Master Pyle with trepidation. The older man looked it over, balanced it on the back of his hand, and threw it at the floor, where it stuck with a satisfying *thunk*.

"Very nice," he said. "Hand it to Danny to be hilted. I'll have a project for you in a few days—until then, cover the shop."

Well—shop work was clean and dull, but Edward was courting his Anne in the long summer evenings, and shop work allowed him to dress well—fine hose, a good doublet, not shop-worn linen stained in nameless chemicals and burned with a thousand sparks.

Anne was a seamstress, and her hands were always clean.

Most evenings she would dance in the square by her house, and Edward would swagger his sword and buckler against other journeymen—he was becoming a good blade.

He was designing himself a fine buckler—sketching in a sure hand with charcoal—when the shop door opened and a small man came in. He was middling. And not very memorable.

He smiled at Edward. He had odd black eyes, and he tapped a gold coin on the heavy oak table where customers examined the wares. "Fetch me your master, young man," he said.

Edward nodded. He rang a bell for another shop boy and sent him to the yard, and Master Pyle appeared a few minutes later. The dark-eyed man had spent the time looking out the window. Edward couldn't tear his eyes away, because the man was so very *difficult* to look at.

He turned just a moment before the master appeared, and met him at the counter.

"Master Pyle," he said. "I sent you some letters."

Master Pyle looked puzzled. Then he brightened. "Master Smith?"

"The very same," said the odd man. "Did you try my powder?"

"I did. Scary stuff, and no mistake. Shot a hole in the roof of my shed." Master Pyle raised an eyebrow. "Not very consistent, though."

The man's dark eyes sparkled. "Mmm. Well, perhaps I didn't explain entirely. Try wetting it with urine after you've mixed it. Dry it in the sun—far from fire, of course. And then grind it back to coarse powder, very carefully."

"If I was an alchemist, all this might entertain me, Master Smith. But I'm a blade smith, and I have many orders."

Master Smith appeared confused. "You make weapons, though."

"All kinds." Master Pyle nodded.

"The very best in Alba, I've been told," Master Smith said.

Master Pyle smiled. "I hope so."

Master Smith rocked his head back and forth. "Is this a matter of more money?" he asked.

"I'm afraid not." Master Pyle shook his head. "It's just not my trade."

Smith let out a sigh. "Why not?"

Edward looked at Master Pyle very hard, willing him to turn his head.

"I have more orders than I can manage, and this is very untested." Master Pyle shrugged. "It would take months, perhaps years, to perfect."

Smith shrugged. "So?"

Edward was all but hopping up and down. Master Pyle turned his head and glared at him. But it wasn't his hard glare.

"This is my journeyman, Edward. He made both of the test devices. He's very competent, and perhaps he'd be willing to do the work for you." Master Pyle looked at Edward. "Want to try, Edward? Your own commission?"

Edward beamed.

The odd, dark-eyed man rocked his head again. "Excellent, then." He put two sheets of vellum down on the shop counter. "Have a look at these, and see what you think," he said. "Tube, stock, powder, and match. I want you to make them all."

"Just one?" Edward asked. "Delivered where?"

"Oh, as to that, I'll send you my directions. It is for some friends." He laughed. "Just one, and then you destroy all your notes. Or I will find you. Understand?"

Edward looked at the man. He didn't seem very dangerous. And yet, he did. And just for a moment, he seemed to have scales on the backs of his hands.

"How much?" Edward asked carefully. "Do I get paid?"

644

"Absolutely," the strange man said. "Fifty gold nobles in advance. Fifty more on completion."

Edward had to struggle to breathe.

Master Pyle shook his head. "I'll get a notary."

Harndon Palace—The King

Just above them, in the great fortress of Harndon, Master Pyle's friend the king lay with his wife. He had two new scars on his heavily muscled thighs. She had one on her back.

Neither found the other a whit less fascinating.

When the king had done his thorough worship of her, he licked her leg and bit her gently and rose. "Men will mock me," he said. "A king who loves only his wife."

She laughed. Stretched like a cat, fists clenched and turned inward to the best advantage of her breasts and back. "I," she purred, "beg leave to doubt your Majesty."

He laughed and threw himself back down by her like a much younger man. "I love you," he said.

She rolled atop him and kissed him. "And I you, my lord."

They lay for a while in companionable silence, until royal squires in the hall started to make noises that indicated that they had royal work to do.

"I have set the date for your tournament at Lorica," the king said. He knew how much she wanted it. "It will help—after the battle. After Pentecost next."

She took in a deep breath, also to her advantage, and clapped her hands together.

"And I ordered Master Pyle to build two of your military carts with the Wagoner's Guild," he said. "To test the concept. I'll show them at the tournament. Ask men with retinues to build to the pattern." He shrugged. "It will be a start."

"And the Red Knight?" she said.

He reacted as if he'd been stung.

She shook her head. "His company had standard wagons, built to the purpose in Galle." She dimpled. "So I didn't invent the idea, apparently."

He shook his head. "I hadn't noticed."

She shrugged, again to her advantage.

"If you don't get dressed, the new ambassador from the Emperor will find me a *most* tardy host." He reached for her.

"I've taken the liberty of inviting him to the tournament," the Queen said. She watched the king like a hawk.

He didn't flinch.

"Ah," he said.

The camp was snug on the late summer evening. And the return had been enough like a homecoming to make him cry. He smiled a great deal, and rode through the camp.

Gelfred was sitting on a wagon, feeding—

"Goodness gracious, Gelfred! Do we have Parcival?" The captain slid down from his riding horse and shocked his hunt master with an embrace.

The eagle bated and said *squaaack*.

Gelfred nodded. "Wonderful bird." He looked around. "Not quite right, of course. Neither you, nor, pardon me, the Abbess is a king. Or queen." He grimaced.

The captain gave him a quick nod. "We'll ask the Emperor for a special chrysobull, shall we?" he laughed. "Although, to be honest, I'm pretty sure the Abbess almost was the Queen."

Gelfred looked shocked.

Ser Alcaeus nodded. "I suspected the same."

Ser Gawin looked at the captain. "I'll be the slow brother. What are we talking about?"

In the captain's head, Harmodius laughed. A nasty, gossipy laugh. *So! You did see who she was.*

"The old king's mistress, Gelfred. That's what men called her. Sophia Rae. To whom Hawthor the Great offered marriage after the Battle of Chevin, and was refused." The captain smiled. "Imagine having been Hawthor's lover and Richard Plangere's *at the same time.*" He shook his head. "And then an Abbess for thirty years." He reached out and smoothed the bird's plumage. "Hawthor must have given her the bird. He must be quite ancient."

The bird's eyes were fathomless and gold, with a black centre.

"I've heard of them living fifty years," said Gelfred.

The bird's grumpy eyes locked with the captain's.

"I see," he said.

Mag sat with Johne the Bailli in the last of the light. He had camp stools—comfortable enough, but backless, and she wasn't getting any younger. He was watching the stars.

"I see a lot of unfamiliar faces," she said, watching two men-at-arms go by. They paused in the light of Johne's lanterns, gave her an appraising look, and bowed.

"We did some recruiting," he admitted. He ran a hand down her back. Turned his head, and smiled. "All right, they all but attacked us. As soon as we made camp—every younger son in the North Country. Some Moreans, too. By the Saviour I would expect we have a hundred lances."

She sighed. "So many," she said.

He sat back. "Won't he be pleased? The young captain?"

She leaned over and kissed him gently. "I'm a sinful old woman, and I don't need to be seduced, if that's what your hand is supposed to be doing."

He stiffened, but then grinned. "My lady, I am out of practice."

They didn't talk much, for a moment.

"Am I clumsy?" he murmured.

"No," she said. She was thinking of blowing out the lanterns and lying on the carpet shamelessly. "No," she said.

"What then?" he asked.

She made a dismissive gesture and went to blow out the candles.

"You can tell me," he said.

"I'm just thinking of the captain. Of him being pleased." She shrugged. "You all think he's fine, and he is *not*. He's like a horse that's taken a wound, and keeps going. He looks fine, right up until he falls stone dead." She found she was leaning back into him.

He held onto her. "When I was young, I wanted nothing so much as to be a knight," he said. "I wanted it, and I fought for it. And I did not get it. And after more time and some bad things, I met your husband, and we survived a bad time. And then I became a decent man in a small town. I had some dark days and some good days." He shrugged. "And now—par dieu, now it seems that I may get to be a knight. And I may have you, my lady." He held her tight. "Which is by way of saying—our little captain will take many hurts. If they break him?" he shrugged. "Then they do. That is the way of it."

She nodded. And slipped a little closer to the carpet of their tent.

The captain sat with Ser Alcaeus and his brother in the last light. The great eagle sat on a perch in the shaded end of the tent, head muffled, squawking softly. The captain went and petted the bird and calmed him, and while he was doing so, Toby poured him wine. Ser Jehannes knocked at the captain's tent poles.

"Come," said the captain.

Ser Jehannes had Ser Thomas and Ser Antigone, and Toby poured them all wine. In the distance, Oak Pew slammed a fist into Wilful Murder's head. The archer sat suddenly. The captain shook his head.

"It's good to be home," he said.

Jehannes held out a leather wallet. "I know this is supposed to be a night to revel," he said. "But the messengers who brought these have been like bluebottles on horse manure, m'lord. Dispatches and letters," he said. He grimaced. "Most for our well-born recruit here." He motioned at Alcaeus. "Your uncle seems determined to hear from you."

"Your pardon," Alcaeus said, and broke the seal on a scroll tube of dark wood.

While he did so, Jehannes handed an ivory tube to the captain. He glanced at the seal and smiled.

"The Queen, gentlemen."

They all drank. Even Sauce.

He broke the seal while Alcaeus was still reading.

Alcaeus looked up. "M'lord," he said formally. "The situation has worsened. I must ask, in the Emperor's name, that we ride with all dispatch."

The captain was still reading his own. "Relax, gentles," he said. "We aren't riding anywhere tonight."

Alcaeus looked at white as a sheet. "The Emperor has been—taken. Hostage. A week and more ago."

The captain looked up and fingered his beard. "All right. That *does* constitute a crisis. Tom?"

"Ready to ride at first light it is." Tom grinned. "Never a dull moment."

"We live in interesting times," the captain said. "Everyone get sleep. We will be moving fast. May I assume this is part of the same—er—trouble for which your uncle is hiring us?"

Alcaeus shook his head. "I don't know." He shuffled. "I don't even know if he is alive, or still Emperor."

The captain nodded. "Dawn, then," he said. "We'll pick up information as we go."

Jehannes looked at the other parchment. "And the Queen?"

The captain sighed. "An invitation to a Deed of Arms," he said. "In the spring." He smiled. He looked out into the darkness. He was smiling. "Someone has kidnapped the Emperor, and we are going to be called on to save him," he said quietly. "I think we'll have to miss the tournament."

He looked around the table. "Remember this night, friends. Breathe the air, and savour the wine. Because tonight, it's all in the balance. I can feel it."

"What is?" Sauce asked. She raised an eyebrow at Tom, as if to say *Is he drunk?*

"Everything," the captain said. He laughed aloud. "Everything."

Acknowledgements

This book is the culmination of thirty ears of study, chivalric martial arts, real life, and role-playing. To be fair to all my influences, I'd have to thank everyone I've ever known. There's a Somali man who worked for me in Kenya in this book; a woman I met once in Marseille; a chivalric fighter I sparred with at a tournament a few years back—it's like that.

But several groups of people deserve my special thanks.

First, the friends of my days in university. Joe and Regina Harley, Robert Sulentic, Robert Gallasch, Gail Morse, Celia Friedman, Steven Callahan, Jevon Garrett, and another dozen—who played in the original Alba campaign. I am an unashamed nerd. Without you people, there would be little life on these bones.

Second, the friends of my reenactment hobby—most especially those who attend our yearly historic trek, where we wander off into the Adirondacks with eighteenth century equipment—or fourteenth century equipment—to learn what it is like to live with the past. We pack it in on our backs and we go places that—in some instances—no person has been in fifty years. These experiences have helped me write this book and I owe you all a debt of thanks for putting up with me. And all the people with whom I spar, in and out of armour—here, and in Ottawa and in Finland and Greece.

Third, the craftsmen who recreate the items that make history and fantasy come alive. Leo Todeschini of www.todsstuff.co.uk deserves a visit online—his stuff is incredible. Magical, even. Ben Perkins at www.barebowarchery.co.uk makes long bows and war bows that look and behave like the originals, as far as we know. Mark Vickers at www.stgeorgearmouryshop.co.uk and Peter Fuller at www.medievalrepro.com reproduce armour that is as near exactly like originals as makes little difference. Comfortable, too. I wear it quite often. www.albion-swords.com make superb, non-nonsense swords. They are not "like" the real thing. They are the real thing. Visit my website and you can see a dozen more craftsmen every bit as good.

Fourth, the teachers who taught me about history, about life and philosophy, about weapons, and about chivalry; Dick Kaeuper of the University of Rochester; Father William O'Malley, SJ, who may or may not forgive my theology; Guy Windsor, possibly the world's finest swordsman (he runs a school!) and Ridgeley Davis who taught me to be a much better rider. And to use a spear on horseback.

Fifth, the many people who have helped me in the publishing world; my Agent, Shelley Power; my gallant publicist, Donna Nopper, and most of all on this book, Gillian Redfearn, who gets credit in every step from creation to actual editing.

And last, the other teachers—the hundreds, if not thousands, of writers who inspire me to write. Medieval fishing? Theology? Hermeticism? Memory palaces? Jousting? Singing Neanderthals? Neurology? Ancient Greek philosophy? I owe a debt to the authors of hundreds of books for filling in the gaps in experience, or just teaching me a dying or dead craft.

And, of course, there's fantasy itself. I adore—nay, worship—J. R. R. Tolkien. For my taste, it is not just *The Lord of the Rings* or *The Hobbit,* but *Sir Gawain and the Green Knight,* from which I have borrowed shamelessly. And C. S. Lewis and their lesser known contemporary, E. R. Eddison. I will not claim Eddison is the best of the lot, but I will confess that my idea of what fantasy ought to do owes a great deal to Eddison, and to William Morris. Does anyone still read William Morris? Have a go. *The Sundering Flood* is one of my favorite books, not least because I share Morris's love for the crafts and the material culture. More recently, I love Celia Friedman, Glen Cook, Katherine Kurtz and Steven Erikson. My hat is off to Erikson – I think he did the most magnificent job of plotting in our generation. And C. J. Cherryh and Lois McMaster Bujold. I don't think either has ever written a book that I didn't enjoy.

I could go on. But I have to work on book two—*The Fell Sword.* If you want to know more, visit my website at www.traitorson.com. And if you want to wear armour in the Wild . . .

Well, we'll see if we can accommodate you.

Miles Cameron
August, 2012

extras

orbit

meet the author

MILES CAMERON is a full-time writer who lives in Canada with his family. He also writes historical fiction under another name. THE RED KNIGHT is his fantasy debut.

introducing

If you enjoyed
THE RED KNIGHT,
look out for

PROMISE OF BLOOD

The Powder Mage Trilogy: Book One

by Brian McClellan

*Field Marshal Tamas's coup against his king sent corrupt
aristocrats to the guillotine and brought bread to the
starving. But it also provoked war with the Nine Nations,
internal attacks by royalist fanatics, and the greedy to
scramble for money and power by Tamas's supposed allies:
the Church, workers unions, and mercenary forces.
Stretched to his limit, Tamas is relying heavily on
his few remaining powder mages, including the
embittered Taniel, a brilliant marksman who also
happens to be his estranged son, and Adamat,
a retired police inspector whose loyalty is
being tested by blackmail.*

*Now, as attacks batter them from within and
without, the credulous are whispering about omens of death*

and destruction. Just old peasant legends about the
gods waking to walk the earth. No modern
educated man believes that sort of thing.
But they should…

Adamat wore his coat tight, top buttons fastened against a wet night air that seemed to want to drown him. He tugged at his sleeves, trying to coax more length, and picked at the front of the jacket where it was too close by far around the waist. It'd been half a decade since he'd even seen this jacket, but when summons came from the king at this hour, there was no time to get his good one from the tailor. Yet this summer coat provided no defense against the chill snaking through the carriage window.

The morning was not far off but dawn would have a hard time scattering the fog. Adamat could feel it. It was humid even for early spring in Adopest, and chillier than Novi's frozen toes. The soothsayers in Noman's Alley said it was a bad omen. Yet who listened to soothsayers these days? Adamat reasoned it would give him a cold and wondered why he had been summoned out on a pit-made night like this.

The carriage approached the front gate of Skyline and moved on without a stop. Adamat clutched at his pantlegs and peered out the window. The guards were not at their posts. Odder still, as they continued along the wide path amid the fountains, there were no lights. Skyline had so many lanterns, it could be seen all the way from the city even on the cloudiest night. Tonight the gardens were dark.

Adamat was fine with this. Manhouch used enough of their taxes for his personal amusement. Adamat stared out into the gardens at the black maws where the hedge mazes began and imagined shapes flitting back and forth in the lawn. What was...ah, just a sculpture. Adamat sat back, took a deep breath. He could hear his heart beating, thumping, frightened, his stomach tightening. Perhaps they *should* light the garden lanterns...

A little part of him, the part that had once been a police inspector, prowling nights such as these for the thieves and pickpockets in dark alleys, laughed out from inside. *Still your heart, old man,* he said to himself. *You were once the eyes staring back from the darkness.*

The carriage jerked to a stop. Adamat waited for the coachman to open the door. He might have waited all night. The driver rapped on the roof. "You're here," a gruff voice said.

Rude.

Adamat stepped from the coach, just having time to snatch his hat and cane before the driver flicked the reins and was off, clattering into the night. Adamat uttered a quiet curse after the man and turned around, looking up at Skyline.

The nobility called Skyline Palace "the Jewel of Adro." It rested on a high hill east of Adopest so that the sun rose above it every morning. One particularly bold newspaper had compared it to a starving pauper wearing a diamond ring. It was an apt comparison in these lean times. A king's pride doesn't fill the people's bellies.

He was at the main entrance. By day, it was a grand avenue of marbled walks and fountains, all leading to a pair of giant, silver-plated doors, themselves dwarfed by the sheer façade of the biggest single building in Adro. Adamat listened for the soft footfalls of patrolling Hielmen. It was said the king's personal guard were everywhere in these gardens, watching every secluded corner, muskets always loaded, bayonets fixed, their gray-and-white sashes somber among the green-and-gold splendor. But there were no footfalls, nor were the fountains running. He'd heard once that the fountains only stopped for the death of the king. Surely he'd not have been summoned here if Manhouch were dead. He smoothed the front of his jacket. Here, next to the building, a few of the lanterns were lit.

A figure emerged from the darkness. Adamat tightened his grip on his cane, ready to draw the hidden sword inside at a moment's notice.

It was a man in uniform, but little could be discerned in such ill light. He held a rifle or a musket, trained loosely on Adamat, and wore a flat-topped forage cap with a stiff visor. Only one thing could be certain...he was not a Hielman. Their tall, plumed hats were easy to recognize, and they never went without them.

"You're alone?" a voice asked.

"Yes," Adamat said. He held up both hands and turned around.

"All right. Come on."

The soldier edged forward and yanked on one of the mighty silver doors. It rolled outward slowly, ponderously, despite the man putting his weight into it. Adamat moved closer and examined the soldier's jacket. It was dark blue with silver braiding. Adran military. In theory, the military reported to the king. In practice, one man held their leash: Field Marshal Tamas.

"Step back, friend," the soldier said. There was a note of impatience in his voice, some unseen stress—but that could have been the weight of the door. Adamat did as he was told, only coming forward again to slip through the entrance when the soldier gestured.

"Go ahead," the soldier directed. "Take a right at the diadem and head through the Diamond Hall. Keep walking until you find yourself in the Answering Room." The door inched shut behind him and closed with a muffled thump.

extras

Adamat was alone in the palace vestibule. Adran military, he mused. Why would a soldier be here, on the grounds, without any sign of the Hielmen? The most frightening answer sprang to mind first. A power struggle. Had the military been called in to deal with a rebellion? There were a number of powerful factions within Adro: the Wings of Adom mercenaries, the royal cabal, the Mountainwatch, and the great noble families. Any one of them could have been giving Manhouch trouble. None of it made sense, though. If there had been a power struggle, the palace grounds would be a battlefield, or destroyed outright by the royal cabal.

Adamat passed the diadem—a giant facsimile of the Adran crown—and noted it was in as bad taste as rumor had it. He entered the Diamond Hall, where the walls and floor were of scarlet, accented in gold leaf, and thousands of tiny gems, which gave the room its name, glittered from the ceiling in the light of a single lit candelabra. The tiny flames of the candelabra flickered as if in the wind, and the room was cold.

Adamat's sense of unease deepened as he neared the far end of the gallery. Not a sign of life, and the only sound came from his own echoing footfalls on the marble floor. A window had been shattered, explaining the chill. The result of one of the king's famous temper tantrums? Or something else? He could hear his heart beating in his ears. There. Behind a curtain, a pair of boots? Adamat passed his hand before his eyes. A trick of the light. He stepped over to reassure himself and pulled back the curtain.

A body lay in the shadows. Adamat bent over it, touched the skin. It was warm, but the man was most certainly dead. He wore gray pants with a white stripe down the side and a matching jacket. A tall hat with a white plume lay on the floor some ways away. A Hielman. The shadows played on a young, clean-shaven face, peaceful except for a single hole in the side of his skull and the dark, wet stain on the floor.

He'd been right. A struggle of some kind. Had the Hielmen rebelled, and the military been brought in to deal with them? Again, it didn't make any sense. The Hielmen were fanatically loyal to the king, and any matters within Skyline Palace would have been dealt with by the royal cabal.

Adamat cursed silently. Every question compounded itself. He suspected he'd find some answers soon enough. Adamat left the body behind the curtain. He lifted his cane and twisted, bared a few inches of steel, and approached a tall doorway flanked by two hooded, scepter-wielding sculptures. He paused between the ancient statues and took a deep breath, letting his eyes wander over a set of arcane script scrawled into the portal. He entered.

The Answering Room made the Hall of Diamonds look small. A pair of staircases, one to either side of him and each as wide across as three coaches, led to a high gallery that ran the length of the room on both sides. Few outside the king and his cabal of Privileged sorcerers ever entered this room.

In the center of the room was a single chair, on a dais a handbreadth off the floor, facing a collection of knee pillows, where the cabal acknowledged their liege. The room was well lit, though from no discernible source of light.

A man sat on the stairs to Adamat's right. He was older than Adamat, just into his sixtieth year with silver hair and a neatly trimmed mustache that still retained a hint of black. He had a strong but not overly large jaw and his cheekbones were well defined. His skin was darkened by the sun, and there were deep lines at the corners of his mouth and eyes. He wore a dark-blue soldier's uniform with a silver representation of a powder keg pinned above the heart and nine gold service stripes sewn on the right breast, one for every five years in the Adran military. His uniform lacked an officer's epaulettes, but the weary experience in the man's brown eyes left no question that he'd led armies on the battlefield. There was a single pistol, hammer cocked, on the stair next to him. He leaned on a sheathed small sword and watched as a stream of blood slowly trickled down each step, a dark line on the yellow-and-white marble.

"Field Marshal Tamas," Adamat said. He sheathed his cane sword and twisted until it clicked shut.

The man looked up. "I don't believe we've ever met."

"We have," Adamat said. "Fourteen years ago. A charity ball thrown by Lord Aumen."

"I have a terrible time with faces," the field marshal said. "I apologize."

Adamat couldn't take his eyes off the rivulet of blood. "Sir. I was summoned here. I wasn't told by whom, or for what reason."

"Yes," Tamas said. "I summoned you. On the recommendation of one of my Marked. Cenka. He said you served together on the police force in the twelfth district."

Adamat pictured Cenka in his mind. He was a short man with an unruly beard and a penchant for wines and fine food. He'd seen him last seven years ago. "I didn't know he was a powder mage."

"We try to find anyone with an affinity for it as soon as possible," Tamas said, "but Cenka was a late bloomer. "In any case"—he waved a hand—"we've come upon a problem."

Adamat blinked. "You . . . want my help?"

The field marshal raised an eyebrow. "Is that such an unusual request? You were once a fine police investigator, a good servant of Adro, and Cenka tells me that you have a perfect memory."

"Still, sir."

"Eh?"

"I'm still an investigator. Not with the police, sir, but I still take jobs."

"Excellent. Then it's not so odd for me to seek your services?"

"Well, no," Adamat said, "but sir, this is Skyline Palace. There's a dead Hielman in the Diamond Hall and..." He pointed at the stream of blood on the stairs. "Where's the king?"

Tamas tilted his head to the side. "He's locked himself in the chapel."

"You've staged a coup." Adamat said. He caught a glimpse of movement with the corner of his eye, saw a soldier appear at the top of the stairs. The man was a Deliv, a dark-skinned northerner. He wore the same uniform as Tamas, with eight golden stripes on the right breast. The left breast of his uniform displayed a silver powder keg, the sign of a Marked. Another powder mage.

"We have a lot of bodies to move," the Deliv said.

Tamas gave his subordinate a glance. "I know, Sabon."

"Who's this?" Sabon asked.

"The inspector that Cenka requested."

"I don't like him being here," Sabon said. "It could compromise everything."

"Cenka trusted him."

"You've staged a coup," Adamat said again with certainty.

"I'll help with the bodies in a moment," Tamas said. "I'm old, I need some rest now and then." The Deliv gave a sharp nod and disappeared.

"Sir!" Adamat said. "What have you done?" He tightened his grip on his cane sword.

Tamas pursed his lips. "Some say the Adran royal cabal had the most powerful Privileged sorcerers in all the Nine Nations, second only to Kez," he said quietly. "Yet I've just slaughtered

662

every one of them. Do you think I'd have trouble with an old inspector and his cane sword?"

Adamat loosened his grip. He felt ill. "I suppose not."

"Cenka led me to believe that you were pragmatic. If that is the case, I would like to employ your services. If not, I'll kill you now and look for a solution elsewhere."

"You've staged a coup," Adamat said again.

Tamas sighed. "Must we keep coming back to that? Is it so shocking? Tell me, can you think of any fewer than a dozen factions within Adro with reason to dethrone the king?"

"I didn't think any of them had the skill," Adamat said. "Or the daring." His eyes returned to the blood on the stairs, before his mind traveled to his wife and children, asleep in their beds. He looked at the field marshal. His hair was tousled; there were drops of blood on his jacket—a lot, now that he thought to look. Tamas might as well have been sprayed with it. There were dark circles under his eyes and a weariness that spoke of more than just age.

"I will not agree to a job blindly," Adamat said. "Tell me what you want."

"We killed them in their sleep," Tamas said without preamble. "There's no easy way to kill a Privileged, but that's the best. A mistake was made and we had a fight on our hands." Tamas looked pained for a moment, and Adamat suspected that the fight had not gone as well as Tamas would have liked. "We prevailed. Yet upon the lips of the dying was one phrase."

Adamat waited.

" 'You can't break Kresimir's Promise,' " Tamas said. "That's what the dying sorcerers said to me. Does it mean anything to you?"

Adamat smoothed the front of his coat and sought to recall old memories. "No. 'Kresimir's Promise'... 'Break'... 'Broken'...

Wait—'Kresimir's Broken Promise.'" He looked up. "It was the name of a street gang. Twenty...twenty-two years ago. Cenka couldn't remember that?"

Tamas continued. "Cenka thought it sounded familiar. He was certain you'd remember it."

"I don't forget things," Adamat said. "Kresimir's Broken Promise was a street gang with forty-three members. They were all young, some of them no more than children, the oldest not yet twenty. We were trying to round up some of the leaders to put a stop to a string of thefts. They were an odd lot—they broke into churches and robbed priests."

"What happened to them?"

Adamat couldn't help but look at the blood on the stairs. "One day they disappeared, every one of them—including our informants. We found the whole lot a few days later, forty-three bodies jammed into a drain culvert like pickled pigs' feet. They'd been massacred by powerful sorceries, with excessive brutality. The marks of the king's royal cabal. The investigation ended there." Adamat suppressed a shiver. He'd not once seen a thing like that, not before or since. He'd witnessed executions and riots and murder scenes that filled him with less dread.

The Deliv soldier appeared again at the top of the stairs. "We need you," he said to Tamas.

"Find out why these mages would utter those words with their final breath," Tamas said. "It may be connected to your street gang. Maybe not. Either way, find me an answer. I don't like the riddles of the dead." He got to his feet quickly, moving like a man twenty years younger, and jogged up the stairs after the Deliv. His boot splashed in the blood, leaving behind red prints. "Also," he called over his shoulder, "Keep silent about what you have seen here until the execution. It will begin at noon."

"But..." Adamat said. "Where do I start? Can I speak with Cenka?"

Tamas paused near the top of the stairs and turned. "If you can speak with the dead, you're welcome to."

Adamat ground his teeth. "How did they say the words?" he said. "Was it a command, or a statement, or...?"

Tamas frowned. "An entreaty. As if the blood draining from their bodies was not their primary concern. I must go now."

"One more thing," Adamat said.

Tamas looked to be near the end of his patience.

"If I'm to help you, tell me why all of this?" he gestured to the blood on the stairs.

"I have things that require my attention," Tamas warned.

Adamat felt his jaw tighten. "Did you do this for power?"

"I did this for me," Tamas said. "And I did this for Adro. So that Manhouch wouldn't sign us all into slavery to the Kez with the Accords. I did it because those grumbling students of philosophy at the university only play at rebellion. The age of kings is dead, Adamat, and I have killed it."

Adamat examined Tamas's face. The Accords was a treaty to be signed with the king of Kez that would absolve all Adran debt but impose strict tax and regulation on Adro, making it little more than a Kez vassal. The field marshal had been outspoken about the Accords. But then, that was expected. The Kez had executed Tamas's late wife.

"It is," Adamat said.

"Then get me some bloody answers." The field marshal whirled and disappeared into the hallway above.

Adamat remembered the bodies of that street gang as they were being pulled from the drain in the wet and mud, remembered the horror etched upon their dead faces. *The answers may very well be bloody.*